## ALSO BY E. C. OSONDU

*Voice of America*

# THIS HOUSE IS NOT FOR SALE

## E. C. Osondu

GRANTA

Granta Publications, 12 Addison Avenue, London W11 4QR

First published in Great Britain by Granta Books, 2015
This paperback edition published by Granta Books, 2016
First published in the United States by HarperCollins Publishers,
New York, 2015

A CIP catalogue record for this book
is available from the British Library.

1 3 5 7 9 10 8 6 4 2

ISBN 978 1 84708 483 5 (paperback)
ISBN 978 1 84708 818 5 (ebook)

Offset by M Rules

Printed and bound by CPI Group (UK) Ltd, Croydon, CR0 4YY

www.grantabooks.com

*In loving memory of my dearly beloved sister,*
*Felicia Maria Ezediuno Nwanze*

# THIS HOUSE
# IS NOT
# FOR SALE

# HOW THE HOUSE CAME TO BE

When we asked Grandpa how the house we all called the Family House came into existence, this was the story he told us.

A long, long time ago, before anybody alive today was born, a brave ancestor of ours who was also a respected and feared juju man woke up one day and told his family, friends, and neighbors that he had a dream. In the dream he saw a crown being placed on his head. He interpreted this dream as signifying that he was going to be crowned a king soon.

As was the custom in those days, a new king had to be crowned by a reigning king who would also hand him a scepter of office. This should not have been a problem but for a minor incident that had occurred in the palace many,

many years ago, before even those who were telling this story were born. You see, our ancestors had a bit of history with the palace.

We were told that my people once lived under the hegemony of an oppressive king in the distant past. Because they spoke a different language, and had two diagonal scarifications on each cheek, not much respect was accorded them. Not much was expected from them, either, other than the occasional payment of tributes to the king. They lived on the fringes of the society. They were neither full citizens nor bondsmen.

When a hunter among these ancestors of the family killed a wild boar he was expected to send the choicest part of the kill to the king.

When a girl child was born to them and it was seen by all eyes that she was indeed fair on the eyes and pretty, everyone began to refer to her as the king's prospective wife. When she grew up she would be taken to the palace so that the king would peek at her through a peephole. If she caught his fancy and he liked what he saw, she became one of his wives. If he didn't like her, she could then be married to someone else. It was said that some women who were pregnant in those days would eat bitter leaves, chew bitter kola nuts, and drink bitter fluids, putting themselves through all kinds of painful and bitter ordeals in order to ensure that their female offspring were born ugly.

The king had also mandated that the menfolk of the family should take part in the building of a large moat that was conceived to go round the kingdom like the Great Wall of China. This was going to be the king's landmark achievement. It was in the nature of kings to build something that they would be remembered by. In later years court oral historians could then intone that during the reign of so and so king a great wall was erected around the kingdom to protect his subjects from invasion. To build a moat, mud was needed, and this mud had to be kneaded. This was a hard task. The digging out of the mud from a wide and deep hole and the fetching of water to knead it and the ferrying of the mud on baskets on the head. A rebellious ancestor complained about this humiliating task of mud kneading and moat building and had suggested they knead the mud with palm oil instead. This was done.

The next morning, the king's palace was overrun by soldier ants.

It was important that a king should be feared by his subjects as such, any form of or hint of rebellion must be punished and crushed. This king was no different, he knew this rule of kingship and decided to teach these ancestors a lesson that they will never forget.

The king was determined to kill my ancestors. They fled on foot and would have settled in a town close to where they eventually settled but they were repulsed by the sight of *pregnant men*. This mystery would be later explained. The men were not really pregnant. Their large protruding bellies were a result of consuming lots of palm wine.

It was to this palace that this ancestor wanted to return in order to be crowned king and to be handed a scepter of office.

When this ancestor was getting ready to go on the trip he invited some of his brothers and neighbors to come along with him, but they refused. They all knew that the unleashing of the soldier ants incident had not been forgiven or forgotten. Palaces tend to have a long memory. Yet this ancestor insisted that some people should come along with him. He knew that he needed to be crowned in the presence of witnesses. He eventually persuaded two of his friends to go with him after he had promised them official positions when he became king.

As expected, immediately they announced their presence, they were arrested and detained. The next morning one of them was brought out to the king's courtyard. In the words of the king it was important to teach those who thought they could question royal authority a lesson they would never forget. The king was incensed for two reasons. He could tell from the diagonal tribal scarifications on the faces of these men, one of whom wanted to be crowned king, that they were the same people who had refused to build the moat and had unleashed the soldier ants that overran the palace. And now they also wanted to be crowned king. Unless this was dealt with ruthlessly, who knew what other form of rebellion they could incite his loyal subjects into committing? All the men, women, and children in the kingdom were assembled to witness this interesting spectacle. The king gave an order for the two men to be tied up. The king ordered that the first man be beheaded. It was done.

The next day the second man also had his head cut off. It was now my ancestor's turn. He had spent the entire period of his detention red eyed and head bowed in sorrow over the loss of his friends. His own safety did not concern him that much. He was the one who had persuaded his late friends to come along with him on the journey. It was for this fact alone that he felt some regret.

As he was tied up and the sword unsheathed from the scabbard to chop off his head as the king had ordered, a millipede crawled out from his thick mane of hair and emerged from the center of his head. It was dark brown.

"Halt," the king ordered his executioner.

He was a king, he had seen many things, but he also knew and respected strong juju. This was no mere mortal. The millipede was a sign that this man was a strong juju man. The king's attitude changed.

"Untie the man," the king commanded.

"Prepare him good food. Dress him in the best clothes and bring him into my presence tomorrow."

It was done.

When the ancestor was brought to the king's presence the next day, the king sent all his courtiers away and sat alone with my ancestor. My ancestor looked the king in the eye and said to him, "I know what keeps you awake at night. You are worried that you will die young like your father and your great-grandfather and all your ancestors who have been kings before you."

The king looked at my ancestor and nodded humbly.

"I will make you an amulet that will make you live to a ripe old age. You must go into the forest yourself and gather me some wild vines," my ancestor said to the king.

"I have thousands of slaves and servants that can do it, I

will send one of them or even a dozen of them to pluck you this vine," the king said.

"Yes, I know, but you must pick the wild vine yourself. It is important that you do this yourself because only you can extend your own life. No other hand can extend your life for you."

So the king went into the forest and came back with the wild vine. My ancestor plucked the leaves off the vine and twisted the vine into a twine and hung it to dry on a rafter by the fireplace. Three days later he summoned the king and asked the king to bring down the now-dry twisted vine. The king did.

"Twist it and see if you can break it in two."

The king twisted it, and the vine broke in two without much effort on the king's part.

"You must go into the forest once again and bring me the same vine," he told the king. Once again, the king complained but went to the forest and got the vines. This time, my ancestor ordered that the vine was to be hung up in the rafters and the fires must be kept burning at low heat for seven days. After seven days the vine was given to the king to break in two, but no matter how much he tried he could not break it in two. My ancestor now pounded the dry creeping vine in a mortar and used it to prepare a longevity talisman for the king that was to be worn around the neck. He also told the king.

"From now going forward, decree that when you or any of your descendants dies, they be buried in an upright position while seated on their royal stool. Only commoners deserve to be buried on their backs, lying down. When you get to the world beyond, you'll discover there are also hierarchies as we have here on earth, there are levels in the next world, you know. Over there, you'll also be counted among the royalty and accorded the deference and respect you deserve." The king was delighted by this idea of reigning among the living and the dead and decreed that this would be the manner in which all kings, including him, would be buried from then on.

"How do I repay you?" the king asked.

"You should grant me my original request. Crown me king."

"There cannot be two kings in the land," the king said. "Here's what I'll do. I will give you a large parcel of land somewhere in the outskirts, and money and men to start life afresh. I will also build you a mansion where you will live. A mansion that befits a strong juju man like you."

And that was how we acquired the land on which the Family House was built. The king also built this ancestor a mansion, but it was built out of mud. Many years later the son of the king was sent to visit the king of Portugal. When he came back, he described the kind of houses he saw in Portugal. As a final gift the king, who had now lived to a ripe old age, decided to build the Family House in the Portuguese architectural style for my ancestor. What my ancestor did not know was that the king had built him the house in order to keep an eye on him. He had instructed his soldiers to kill my ancestor if for any reason the king did not live to a ripe old age. This was how the Family House came to be.

# NDOZO

We were all woken up one morning by shouts of thief! thief! We were summoned to the large sitting room, the parlor. One of the women who lived in the house was kneeling down on the floor and was crying. Her name was Ndozo. She was one among the many women that sold for Grandpa in the market. She also had a little son whose nose was always snotty and who wore three aluminum crucifixes tied on a string around his neck and a talisman around the waist. They said she had been stealing from the money made from sales. She was one of the trusted ones. She was one of those that counted the money at the end of each day. She was accused of helping herself to some of the money.

"How long have you been stealing from the sales money?" one of the older men living in the house asked her.

Her interrogator's name was Sibe-Sibe. He had lived in the house for so long that no one remembered what he was exactly. He occupied that unclear borderland between servant and freeborn. All the servants feared him. Grandpa respected and trusted him.

"Not for such a long time," she said.

"One month? One year? Three months? Just tell us how long?"

"I don't remember how long," she said. "It is the devil. I promise never to do it again."

"We will show how we deal with thieves in the Family House."

Someone grabbed a Tiger razor blade from its packet and began to scrape off her hair. There was no pretense or attempt at giving her a proper haircut, the shoddier the job, the better, this haircut was intended to humiliate, not beautify. Soon most of her hair was on the floor though there were still small tufts of hair on some parts of her scalp. Some parts of her scalp were bleeding where the blade had nicked her skin.

They stripped her of her clothes, leaving only her underskirt made of different-colored cotton fabric. They made a necklace out of snail shells and strung it around her neck. She was given two empty milk cans and told to start clapping them together like cymbals. We were told to follow her as she was forced to walk out of the house half-naked.

"I will never steal again. It was the devil. I don't know why I did. This is my family. I have no other family. Please, I promise not to steal again."

But Grandpa wanted to use her to set an example. He said that it was important that we saw how thieves were treated so that we would never be tempted to steal in our lives.

As she was led down the steps out into the streets the men told her to sing. One of the men was holding a long *koboko* horse whip and would mockingly act as if he were going to whip her, at which she'd jump and the snail shells would make a mild rattling sound. She clapped the empty milk cans together and began to walk down the street as we followed her. We were told to make booing noises and jeer at her as we walked behind her. As soon as we left the house because it was still early morning, we passed by people bringing out their wares and women frying *akara*. They would pause in their morning activity and turn to us and she would be made to stand before them as she clapped the empty milk tins together and sing and we ululated behind her.

"What did you do?" they'd ask, even though they already knew from seeing her shaved head and the snail shell mock necklace around her neck.

"I stole."

"And what did you steal?"

"I stole money from the sales box."

"And what did you do with the money?"

"It was the devil that made me do it."

"Will you ever steal again?" they'd ask her.

"No, I will never steal again," she would say.

"Now do your song and dance for us again. It is a good song, we like hearing it."

She would dance and clap her empty milk cans together as she sang:

*Thief, thief, jankoriko*
*Ajibole ole*

We moved from the Family House through different streets and warrens and side streets. At some point she said she was thirsty because the sun was out and burning but she was immediately told to shut her mouth. She said she wanted to urinate but she was told to pee on herself. She said her throat was hurting and that she was losing her voice, but they asked if she would have stopped stealing if she hadn't been caught.

"It was the devil that made me do it," she said.

We were getting tired too, but still we walked and walked a bit more and she stopped and sang and stopped and sang and people asked her what she had done.

When we got back home she was told to go and kneel in the same corner where she had been kneeling when we woke up. She was not allowed to touch her son.

"You see how thieves are treated in the Family House?" we were asked.

"That is exactly what will happen to anyone who steals in this house, including my own children and grandchildren."

12 · E. C. OSONDU

The next morning when we woke up, Ndozo had vanished, leaving her infant son behind.

There were lots of stories about her disappearance. Some said she had been so consumed by shame, she had gone and thrown herself into the lagoon. Others said she had run back to her parents. Nobody could recall who her parents were. She was one of those that had come to live in the house in exchange for some money owed Grandpa until the money was paid back, then she could return to her family. But it was said that whoever borrowed from Grandpa was never in a position to repay because he jinxed them and many of them remained in the house and had children who also became a part of the Family House, helping around the house until they became old enough to go and start selling in the store.

It was said that before Ndozo left the house she had placed a curse on the house, saying that just as she had been put to shame that the house and its inhabitants would eventually be humiliated and come to shame.

Someone said that Grandpa had whispered that she was not going to be missed and that she had done a good thing by leaving her son behind.


Years later, a car parked in front of the Family House and a plump woman stepped out. She was dressed expensively. She shielded her eyes as she looked at the house, as if she needed to reassure herself that this was indeed her destination. She walked through the gate and entered the compound. It was

Ndozo. She greeted and asked for Grandpa. She excused herself and went back to the car. The driver began to carry things into the house. Plastic containers and clothes. She said she had come to take her son back with her. She was now a big trader in plastics in the neighboring country. She said she had been blessed with everything, good fortune and riches; her business had prospered. She had started out as an apprentice, selling plastics to a big trader over there, and because she was good in business, knew how to attract customers, and sell at a profit, all of them skills she had acquired from living in the Family House, she had made the business of her boss grow. She said that all she was today she owed to her time selling for Grandpa. Her boss soon opened a shop of her own for her and the shop had really grown in size. She was now a big distributor of plastics. She even had people selling for her. She was sorry for that theft of a long time ago but she was also happy that something good had come out of it. Here she was today, prosperous and independent. She had people selling for her and she would be disappointed if they stole from her. She was here to make restitution. She had found love, she had met a man who loved her and they were married, but she had been unable to conceive. People said that a woman must choose between the kind of wealth that can be counted, such as money and landed property and cars, and the type that cannot be counted, for you can count the number of cattle that you have but you do not count your children. Where was her son? she asked. She wanted to see him and touch him with her hands. In all the years that had gone by there had not been a day that his face and thoughts of him had left her mind.

There was silence. They let her words sink in, then they came at her like angry wasps.

"And you want us to believe your story. Your story is too sweet to be true."

"You have been stealing from the money box in the store before you were caught."

"You must have been sending all the money to your partners in the neighboring country who must have invested it for you."

"You were selling plastics, indeed. Don't we have plastic sellers here, how many of them have become rich, if what you claim is true."

"And you think you can just come back here and take your son back. Suppose we tell you that he fell sick and died, what then?"

She began to cry, and all of a sudden she was the old Ndozo. Her expensive clothes began to look like a masquerade costume. She said she knew it in her soul that her son was still alive. She said they should compute all the money and interest of the money she took from the money box all those years ago and she would pay it back.

She said she was ready to give all she owned to the family if only she could be allowed to leave with her son.

"And all the salt, all the pepper, all the soap, all the medicines, and all the clothes the boy had worn these years, was she ready to pay for them too?"

She pleaded with them to tell her what it was going to cost her.

"Suppose we tell you that the boy is dead. That after you left for days the boy refused to eat or drink. He kept pointing at the road, asking for his mother. Asking when she would return to cuddle the way he was used to being cuddled at night. He was told that his mother would soon be back. He cried even more and as he cried his body became hot and he began running a fever and then fainted. He was rushed to the hospital but the doctor said it was too late, his heart was already broken; the doctor said he had never seen a heart that broken in one so young."

"I know in my heart, the way only a mother can know, that my son is still alive, I can hear his heart beating."

"How can you call yourself a mother when you abandoned him when he most needed a mother's warmth, the joy of hearing you call his name, telling him that the evening meal is ready and he leaves his playmates and comes running toward you, his nose in the air, drinking in the aroma of well-made soup."

"All the years I have been away, I have always thought about him and about this house. I know I did bad and that was why I left. I have always wanted to ask for forgiveness for what I did and show my gratitude. I always thought that this will be a day of joy and reunion and reconciliation."

"So what were you expecting? You were expecting us to roll out the drums for a common thief who stole from the money box and fled to set up her own trading business with money stolen from this house?"

"To worsen matters you also left your own son to die in our hands."

At every turn they countered her pleading. They turned on her. They twisted her words. Her voice turned hoarse from begging. Her knees went sore from kneeling on the hard ground. The tears on her face formed a crusty, salty dry rivulet.

Finally she stood up and left.

Here is what we heard. She took all the things she had brought with her to share with people in the Family House. She took them to the Beggars Lane. That night, the king of beggars told all the female beggars to follow her to the Family House. When it was midnight, they all bared their buttocks on the house and began to rain curses on the house. They cursed and prayed for evil to befall us and did not stop until dawn began to whisper gently into the ears of dusk and then they departed.

Ndozo left for her trading post along the border and never returned. Her son was still alive but he grew up never knowing who his mother was.

# IBE

My cousin Ibegbunemkaotitojialimchi, meaning "O save me from my enemies so I can live to the evening of my days on this good earth," or Ibe for short, was staying in the Family House that summer too. Unlike some of us who would be going back to our homes after the long summer holidays before school reopened at the end of the rainy season, Ibe and his mom didn't know when they would be returning to their home in the North. He and his mother left the North because his father had married a second wife. Ibe was the same age as me, but he appeared to know more about the ways of the world. He knew many secrets. He claimed he could perform magic tricks. He claimed he could speak many languages, including a smattering of Hindi, Chinese, and some Arabic.

Ibe said if one wanted to beat one's opponent's team in a soccer match then one must go and capture the biggest redheaded *agama* lizard that one could find. *Agama* lizards were abundant, always sunning themselves unconcernedly on cement blocks in the adjoining uncompleted building. Kill the *agama* lizard, Ibe said, and tie a little piece of red cloth around the lizard's neck, drive a pin through the lizard's head and bury it in a hole by your goalpost. According to Ibe, you have effectively *tied* your opponent and no matter how much they tried they could never get the ball past your goal mouth or score a goal against you.

Ibe said it was also possible to padlock an enemy's brain so the person would fail their exams. Here's how—buy a Yeti or Tokoz padlock, unlock the padlock, and simultaneously whisper your enemy's name and the incantation *read and forget, read and forget* seven times, as you lock the padlock and throw the keys away. When your enemy gets into the exam hall, he'll forget all he has read because you have effectively padlocked his brain.

Ibe said the best soccer coaches gave their players tea laced with an intoxicating pill capsule. This way, the players never got tired while playing and had relentless stamina. He said the reason why India never featured in the soccer World Cup was because they had strong magic. In their first and only appearance in the World Cup, according to Ibe, they had scored over a dozen goals against their opponent. Their opponent's goalkeeper later told the sporting press that each time an Indian player shot the ball in his direction, he saw over a dozen soccer balls hurtling toward him and became confused as to which to catch; he inevitably caught the wrong one. Ibe said this was the reason why Indians had moved on to cricket, where it was normal to score a century.

Ibe said if one loved a girl and did not want her to leave you for another boy, then one should mix one's blood with that of the girl in a blood covenant. A blood covenant was easy, he said. Make an incision on the girl's wrist and make an incision on yours with a sharp razor blade, allow a drop of blood from your wrist to drop into the incision on her wrist to mix your blood with hers; both of you should then dip your finger into the mixed blood and touch it to your tongue. After the blood covenant, if the girl attempts to leave you for another boy, she'll lose her mind and go insane. He knew a girl who wandered around the streets in the northern part of the country half-naked, picking up rubbish. Everyone knew it was because she had broken a blood covenant with her boyfriend.

Ibe said if you want to see your girl in your dreams, place her picture under your pillow and call her name seven times before you fall asleep, and she'll most certainly come to you in the dream.

Ibe said that if you wanted to know all life's secrets, all you needed to do was read a book called *The Sixth and Seventh Books of Moses*. The book contained all the secrets of the world, including the secret way to riches. But there was a catch, according to Ibe. The book must be read at midnight by the light of a lone red candle. The candle must not burn out before one finished reading the entire book. If the candle burns out and one has not finished reading the entire book, madness was sure to follow. Ibe claimed he owned the book and had a red candle too, but was waiting a few more years before reading the book and growing very rich.

Ibe said he knew how to make a potion out of leaves and feathers that could protect us from snakebites and scorpion stings, but he was not going to show it to me because, from past experience, each time he used the potion, snakes and scorpions would crawl out of their holes and would begin following him around almost as if they were taunting him to find out if his potion was effective or not.

Ibe said the market in the town where they had lived in the North was a place of wonder and spectacles. He said that magicians and entertainers came to the market and that he and his friends were allowed to go watch them. He said he had once watched as a magician brought out a sharp sword and attempted to run it through his own belly, but the sharp sword was unable to cut through the skin. The magician had then asked for a volunteer from the crowd. A few volunteers had come forward, including Ibe. They tried cutting the man with the sword but the sword would not cut through the skin. Ibe said when he attempted cutting the magician's belly with the sword, the skin felt like steel.

Ibe said that his father worked for the federal government. His father worked for the national telephone service as a telephone operator. His father could not leave his post because he was an important man. He could reach the head of the country through his little finger. He said his father had memorized the entire country's telephone numbers and area codes. He was an important man.

Ibe said that he did not like the girls in this city because they had flat noses. The girls in the northern part of the country were fair skinned and had pointed noses. They were shy but beautiful.

Ibe said he was going to order a talisman from India called *pocketneverdries*. He said if one had the talisman in one's pocket, one will never run out of money to spend, one will always have the correct amount of money down to the smallest change to make all one's purchases.

Ibe said our *suya* here tasted stringy and was completely juiceless because the meat was from old cows, whereas the *suya* in the North was juicy and succulent because it was made from young calves and rams.

Ibe's mom went to the post office every Friday to check if there was a letter from her husband. He was supposed to write and tell her when he was coming to beg Grandfather so she could return to his house. Whenever she returned from the post office empty-handed, as always she would lock herself in her room and would not talk with anyone for a few days.

Ibe said one could make money from hiring out one's services to a beggar as a stickboy. One simply led the beggar by his stick and went with him from door to door shouting *Bambi Allah*. He said he once had a part-time gig as a stickboy. But he also said the beggars over here were all con men: they only pretended to be blind but they were not really blind. He said they applied gum arabic to their eyes to appear blind and washed off the adhesive at night before they prayed.

Ibe said that this our city was a bad city because unlike in the North, where there was a sign saying WELCOME TO THE NORTH. COME AND LIVE IN PEACE, no sign welcomed anyone to this city except for the billboard proclaiming YOU ARE NOW IN THIS CITY. According to Ibe, nobody was welcome here and one was here at one's own risk.

Ibe said the strongest man in the whole world was not Mighty Igor, the wrestler we all watched on World Wide Wrestling every Thursday at 8:00 PM, but a man called Kill-We. Kill-We had a single bone, unlike us mere mortals, who had multiple bones. He could pull a stationary tractor trailer with one hand. As a result of his special powers the government had to build him a special house outside of town limits because when he snored in his old house, which was in the town center, the foundations of nearby houses shook and his neighbors couldn't sleep. Ibe said Kill-We toured all the schools in the North showing off his prowess—splitting logs of wood with his bare hands and breaking cement blocks with the edge of his palm.

Ibe said that down the street from the house where they lived in the North also lived two *men* who were not really men but women. They walked like women, they tied wrappers on their chests, they waved their hands about like women when they talked and their eyes were ringed with kohl and they painted their fingernails and toenails bright red with nail polish. According to Ibe, at night important and rich men in gleaming black Mercedes-Benz cars came to visit the men who were not really men but women and take them out to town. The men who were not really men but women would return in the early hours of the morning heavily loaded with gifts. They would go to the market and buy stuff to cook. They made such delicious chicken stew with lots of thyme, curry, *tomapep*, and pure groundnut oil; one could smell the aroma of their stew a mile away.

Ibe said that entertainers brought monkeys, hyenas, and baboons to perform in the market. Some of the monkeys were dressed up in ties and some dressed up as women. The monkeys performed dancing tricks. At the command of their owner they would lie down and jerk their waists around like common *karuwa*.

Ibe said it was fine to steal from idols because there was only one God. Idols were blind, they could not see, they were dumb and could not speak. We would wander away from the Family House to where three roads intersected to pick up shiny coins left there by idol worshippers for good luck. He would boldly pick up the pennies, three-penny and five-penny coins. He would kick aside and upturn little sacrificial earthenware pots that contained palm oil and little dead chicks. He would gather all the coins and we would use the money to rent chopper bicycles from the bicycle repairer. We would spend the remainder of the money to buy *suya* beef kebab. He would take a bite and complain, *kai northern suya is best I would not eat this suya for free in the North.*

Ibe said idols had no tongues and it was good to steal from

them though he did believe in magic. He said most drivers that plied the road in the northern part of the country had special magical powers that helped them vanish if they were involved in an accident. At the point at which their vehicle collided with another, their magical power made them vanish and then they would come walking toward the wrecked car from the opposite direction without a scratch. Ibe said he would get this amulet as soon as he was old enough to drive. He said he had tried to drive but was not tall enough to see through the windshield while seated.

Ibe said we were going on a big *mission*. We were going to be like Harrison Ford in *The Temple of Doom*. We both wore pretend helmets that he had made from foolscap sheets. Ibe was the leader of the expedition. We passed the area where three roads intersected. We left the major road. We headed toward the outskirts. Facing us was a small building. It was no bigger than a small shed. It was held up by solid timber pillars on four sides and roofed with corrugated iron sheets now turning rusty. Inside was a large mud sculpture of a matronly figure of a woman carrying newborn babies in both hands. Behind her were bottles of Mirinda, Crush, and Fanta. So many bottles. Some looked like they had been there for a long time; their crown corks were getting rusty. Fresh and cooked eggs lay around. There were lots of shiny coins everywhere; some half hidden in different crevices on the mud sculpture, and there were cowry shells too. On the ground and lying around were different colors and makes of plastic baby dolls and sweets and toffee. Ibe said that these were things left for the goddess by ignorant women who wanted babies. Ibe said that men and women made babies by sleeping together. Ibe said *let the mission begin.* Ibe put a couple of sweets in his mouth and told me to do the same. I put a Hacks in my mouth but spat it out when he wasn't looking. I did not like its peppery taste. Ibe began to scoop coins into his pockets. What are you waiting for? he asked. This is free money. I took a few coins and then we heard approaching footsteps and we fled.

Ibe said we should go to the cinema and watch an Indian movie starring Amitabh Bachchan or Dharmendra. Ibe said Indian actresses were the most beautiful women in the whole wide world. He said they were even more beautiful when they were dancing and that sometimes in the movies while they were dancing, it would start to rain and what luck this was because the rain would plaster their wet saris to their skin and one could catch a glimpse of their breasts.

Ibe paid for the movie with the money we got from the *mission.* Ibe bought *suya,* Ibe bought Fanta, Ibe bought Wall's ice cream, Ibe bought FanYogo, Ibe bought Fan ice orange slush, Ibe bought *guguru,* Ibe bought *epa.* Ibe said we should walk into the movie theater like Harrison Ford walking into the Temple of Doom, we should walk in with a swagger and we should be swaying from side to side because no one could stop us. We did.

Ibe's stomach is distended and swollen like that of Baba-Uwa the *otapiapia* seller who wears a false beard and pads up his stomach with old clothes and dances around the neighborhood of the Family House screaming *only one drop, only one drop* is all you need to kill the cockroach, the mosquito, the lice, the mice, the ant, and the bedbug bugging your life, only one drop of *otapiapia* is all you need.

Ibe said I should come close. I go closer to him. Ibe is sweating. Ibe is clutching his stomach like some pregnant woman holding her jiggling stomach as she rushes to catch a *danfo* bus. Ibe says we must keep our secrets secret. Ibe said the difference between men and women is that men can keep secrets. Ibe's breath is stinky, smelly and damp and green and fetid like the shrine of the goddess. Ibe said do not breathe a word of what happened to anybody. Ibe's breathing is coming out with some difficulty like that of an old transport lorry.

Ibe said put your right hand on the left part of your chest and swear that you'll keep our secret secret. I do as Ibe says.

I say to myself, *What if I do not reveal the secret and Ibe dies?*

Ibe's mom said the Aladura prophetess who wears a white soutane and walks by the family house every early morning chanting *Jehovah El morija yaba sha sha sha* and clanging away on her little silver bell told her Ibe was going to live but she needed to buy a white cow and go with her to the Atlantic Ocean to drown the cow in the center of the ocean. This way the cow's soul would be taken in exchange for Ibe's.

Ibe's mom said she knew who was responsible for Ibe's sickness. She said it was not an *ordinary* sickness. She said it was the evil *karuwa* that her husband had brought into their marriage bed to stain her marriage bed that wanted to kill her first and only son so that she would leave her marriage empty-handed.

She said when Ibe was born a prophet had told her that Ibe's star was so bright its brightness was blinding. She said star destroyers had seen how great her son was going to be and were planning to kill him to stop his star from shining.

Ibe's mom said she was going to consult Nurse Eliza. Nobody knew if Nurse Eliza ever attended a nursing school. People said when she was growing up someone had told her that she looked and walked like a nurse and she had taken those words to heart and had started out without any training by prescribing Panadol for every illness. Now she had graduated to administering injections.

Nurse Eliza said that Ibe's blood was poisoned. She said Ibe's blood required *flushing*. She said Ibe would need to drain all the blood in his body because it was contaminated and it needed to be flushed out and replaced with fresh blood. She said she would need to buy blood from healthy donors, not the hepatitis-contaminated blood sold by junkies and prostitutes who hung around the General Hospital. She asked for a large amount of money. She said blood was expensive because *blood is life*.

I am a married widow, Ibe's mother said. I have no money.

In that case I will just place the boy on a drip, Nurse Eliza said, and hooked Ibe up on a drip. The rusty metal pole of the drip set one's teeth on edge as it was dragged across the concrete floor of the Family House.

Grandfather said Ibe's mom was a stupid woman. He said she was playing with her son's life. He said it was her stupidity that had made her run away from her husband's house because her husband had a concubine. He said if Ibe died because of her carelessness then she had truly left the marriage empty-handed.

Grandfather said if Ibe's mom knew what was good for her, she should carry Ibe and start running to Faith Hospital.

Ibe's mom said that nobody goes to Faith Hospital anymore, that the owner belonged to a blood-sucking secret cult and that people went into his hospital alive and came back dead.

Grandfather said in that case call my friend Doctor Williams.

Doctor Williams said he was no longer practicing. He said his hands shook but that he would come and take a look at the boy.

Doctor Williams said Ibe had appendicitis and that it was liable to burst any moment from now if the boy was not rushed to the hospital to get that thing cut off. Doctor Williams said cutting off an appendix was as easy as cutting off the neck of a chicken, any doctor could do it.

Ibe said he was proud of the little pink scar under his belly. Ibe said appendicitis was caused by swallowing orange and guava seeds instead of spitting them out. If one didn't spit them out they accumulated and after some time one's appendix began to swell.

Ibe said he had told the doctor that he wanted to watch while they cut his stomach open to remove the appendix. Ibe said he told the doctor he was not afraid of pain and had refused to be sedated. He said first he had pretended to close his eyes, then he had opened both eyes and had watched the doctor open up his stomach and cut out the appendix with a surgical blade and tie up the loose ends. Ibe said the doctor had placed multicolored threads inside the different parts of his intestine as he cut. He said he had asked the doctor why he did this and the doctor had said so that I will not be confused by your internal organs and cut your big intestine instead of your appendix.

Ibe said that while he was lying in bed sick he had gone to heaven and had seen God face-to-face. Ibe said God had a long white beard that reached down to God's feet and swept the ground as God floated around in cream-colored bell-bottom pants.

Ibe said he now had the secret of death in his pocket. Ibe said he was never going to die because he had died once and that was the way it was because it was written that *you can only die once and after that eternal life.*

Ibe said before he died he saw people carrying his corpse inside a small coffin. Ibe said he was both inside the coffin and yet outside of the coffin. He said he could still remember snatches from the song the people carrying his corpse were singing:

*Ona, ona, nudo, nudo*
*Onabagonu ebe osi bia*
*Onwu, onwu, onwu.*

Ibe said God was really angry when he was brought to the throne of judgment. Ibe said God asked the people who had brought him why they had brought before his throne this young boy who still had a lot of work to do on God's good earth and was destined to live until the evening of his days. God told them to send Ibe back to the world because it wasn't yet Ibe's time to die. Ibe said when he opened his eyes he was in the hospital wearing a white gown.

Ibe said that everything in heaven was white with the exception of God's cream-colored trousers. The cloud through which God walked was white. God's long beard, which touched God's feet, was white, the angels were all white in color and the trumpets through which they blew the hymn *Hosanna in the Highest* also gleamed white.

I said to Ibe, I know what caused your sickness, what made your belly swell. It was the sweets and money we took from the shrine of the goddess when we went on the *mission*.

Ibe told me to shut my mouth. Ibe said God had sent him back from the dead because he was not afraid of idols. He believed in only one God. Do you think God would have allowed me to come back from the dead if God didn't like the work I was doing here on earth?

Ibe's mom had a new spring in her footsteps. She said the *foolish man* has written, referring to Ibe's dad. The foolish man is now begging. The foolish man has carried both oil and water and now knows which is heavier.

Grandfather said she should shut up and stop making a fool of herself and start packing her things so she could return quietly to her husband's house.

# GRAMOPHONE

Whenever the uncle we all called Gramophone, behind his back, walked into any room with a radio on or some music playing, it was immediately turned down or turned off. He would sometimes use two fingers to block both ears when loud music from the record store down the road wafted into the Family House. He was called Gramophone because he would clean and dust every part of the sitting room but would not go near or touch Grandfather's four-in-one Sanyo stereo. When this was pointed out to him once, he shrank back and said he could dust and clean everything in the sitting room but not *that Gramophone*, he said, pointing to the Sanyo stereo. We were warned not to whistle songs around him. Whistling was not encouraged in the Family House at any rate, whistling in the daytime was said to attract snakes while whistling at night attracted evil spirits.

He sought refuge in the Family House many years ago, having killed a man or, as we were told, he had not actually killed the man but the man had died from their encounter and he had had to flee from the village at night. He knew that there was only one place on this earth where no arm no matter how long could reach him, and that was the Family House.

Anytime someone sang any popular song around him, he would cover both ears with his hands like a little child that did not want to hear or listen to an instruction. On days that Grandpa was happy, he hung the loudspeaker of his Sanyo stereo on the outside wall of the house facing the street so that passersby could hear the music playing. Many would stand and listen to the music for a while. Grandpa usually did this when a new LP was released by any of the popular musicians. When a new LP was released, Grandpa bought the record and played it over and over again while a small crowd stood outside enjoying the music. Some in the crowd whispered that this was what it meant to be a rich man. They praised Grandpa for not being selfish. He actually spreads his wealth, so that even those who have no music system can stand in front of his house and enjoy the music, they said.

On such days Gramophone would go to his room and plug his ears with cotton wool and would not emerge until late at night, when the hubbub had died down and the music turned off. When he emerged his eyes would be red and would appear as if he had just finished crying. Those who knew in the Family House would shake their heads. They were the ones who told us his story in bits and pieces, but at the heart of the story was a gramophone record player.

He used to live in the village and was the first man to buy a gramophone record player. His nickname back then was Cash. He was also the owner of I Sold in Cash Provision Store.

In the evenings when people were back from the farms and had finished the day's business, they would sit outside their homes to take in the cool night breeze. Cash would tie his gramophone to the passenger seat of his bicycle and would pedal slowly through the village. As he pedaled past homes, people would call out Cash, Cash. If it was their lucky day, he would gently alight from his bicycle, untie his gramophone. A table would be produced and a piece of antimacassar spread on top of the table on which he would then gently place the gramophone like the special guest that it was. His hosts for the evening would request whatever record they wanted played. A favorite was a play featuring Mama Jigida and Papa Jigida, a bickering couple who quarreled all the time because Papa Jigida was always broke. Sometimes people requested some local musical star. Cash would search through his collection and say, *I don't have the record by that particular musician but I have this one and they both play their guitar in the same way. Listen to it, you'll like it.*

Cash was always a welcome guest and people would bring out their best drinks and kola nuts to entertain him. A few would even put some money by the record changer for him to buy batteries. For many, just having the gramophone sitting there was enough. For first-timers Cash would flip through his pack of LPs arranged in a carton and pick out something. He would bring out the LP, dust it with an orange cotton handkerchief, and gingerly place the record in the changer. First there was a little crackle as the pin scratched the record and then the voices would begin to sing or talk and would float into the surrounding inky darkness.

Whoever thought of putting people in that box must indeed be a wizard, one of the householders would remark.

That is what I keep telling our people, the white people have their own witchcraft but they don't kill their brothers and sisters with it, they invent things like the airplane and the car and this gramophone.

At this point a bottle of half-drunk aromatic schnapps still in its original carton would appear, and drinking would commence while the gramophone made music. Cash would occasionally bring out a record to play. He would begin by introducing the musician. Some of the artists were from the Congo and sang in Lingala. Even though Cash had never been to the Congo he would sometimes translate these songs, especially after a few shots of schnapps:

*I am but a poor orphan*
*My mother saved and scraped to buy me a guitar*
*I will never forget my mother's sacrifice*
*I will play this guitar until I die.*

Rotate Provision and Fancy Store was everything Cash Provision Store wasn't. Take the word *Fancy* that was a part of its name. People wondered what the word *Fancy* meant at first, but were not left to wonder for long. Not only did Rotate stock and sell provisions, but he also sold baby clothes, and women's hats and gowns and shoes—these were the fancy goods, according to him.

Cash prided himself on the fact that he sold in cash, hence his nickname, as opposed to credit. Rotate did not mind offering credit and would quickly write down the customer's name and how much was owed in a blue-ruled Olympic Exercise notebook. The only proviso was that customers had to pay a little against what they owed before he could offer more credit.

Rotate installed his own gramophone in his store and hung both loudspeakers from the door. His gramophone was always playing music. He played not only highlife, but also some Western music by KC and the Sunshine Band and Sonya Spence and Don Williams and Skeeter Davis and Bobby Bare.

A bottle of watered-down gin filled with anti-malaria herbs was placed on a table in the store. Customers who had no money could have a free shot of watered-down gin, listen to music, and chat. Some ended up buying an item even if it was just a cigarette.

While Cash closed his store as soon as darkness came, Rotate lived in his store and encouraged people to knock on his window at any time if they needed to buy something. Rotate also had a medicine box out of which he sold tablets. *Just tell him what ails you and he'll mix some tablets that'll cure you*, people said about Rotate.

People no longer talked in whispers about how Rotate got his name or made the money with which he opened his Provision and Fancy Store. They all knew he had made his money from a marijuana farm. When news of the farm reached the ears of the police, a detachment of policemen was sent to arrest him. According to people who were there, the police inspector who led the team had asked Rotate if he did not know that it was illegal to plant marijuana.

"No, sir, I did nothing wrong. I was only practicing crop rotation."

"What do you mean by crop rotation?"

"Well, sir, in school we were taught in agricultural science that it was not good for the soil to plant only one kind of crop from year to year so I decided to rotate the crops. Yam last year, marijuana this year, and corn next year," he shot back.

He was arrested and detained at the police headquarters, but he bribed the police and was released.


When Gramophone heard that another store had opened he went to congratulate the new owner and even sat down ready to share drinks. He knew Rotate's story. Unlike Rotate, he had made his own money by using his bicycle to ferry items to distant markets for female traders. But he believed in live and let live. Rotate did not offer Cash any drinks. According to Cash, the man had rejected his extended hand of fellowship.

Cash began to worry when he noticed that items on his shelf were beginning to expire without being sold. Biscuits, tea bags, tins of milk all sat on the shelves until they expired. He stopped moving around with his gramophone in the evenings to people's homes, preferring to stay in his store instead and play the records in the hope that customers would come in to buy. Rotate's store on the other hand was attracting the younger crowd, who had money to spend and spent it quickly, unlike the older people who counted every penny and loved to haggle.

Cash began to introduce new things. He now sold *chin-chin* and *puff-puff* and buns in a glass-sided display box glass, but Rotate had *beer-beef*—chunky pieces of beef spiced up and fried until they were really dry and filled the mouth—when chewed they were said to enhance the taste of beer on the tongue. Rotate sold sausage rolls, which had the advantage of never going bad. Rotate only bought and sold certain items during certain seasons. Schoolbooks and exercise books when school resumed in September, machetes and hoes at the start of the farming season, raincoats and boots at the start of the rainy season, and Robb, Mentholatum, and Vicks inhaler when the harmattan season set in. Whereas Cash used to pile up all the items in his store even when they were out of season and sometimes even sold brown and faded exercise books to pupils at the beginning of the school year, the stuff from Rotate's store always smelled fresh and new.

And then Rotate bought a Yamaha motorcycle, an Electric 125. It was electric blue in color and flew through the dusty village footpaths like a bird. It made Cash's Whitehorse Raleigh bicycle look shabby and prehistoric.

People began to talk about the fall of Cash and the rise of Rotate. Cash had a framed picture in his store that showed two men. In one half of the picture, the man who sold in cash was smiling and looking prosperous in a green jacket and a fine waistcoat with a gold watch dangling from a chain and gold coins all around him. The other man who sold on credit was dressed in rags and looked haggard. All around him were the signs of his poverty; a rat nibbled at a piece of dry cheese in a corner of the store. A wag suggested that Cash should change his name to Mr. Credit.

Someone came and whispered to Cash that the reason his former customers were running away from his store was that Rotate had been spreading terrible rumors about him. He said that Rotate told people that he opened the soft drinks he sold and mixed them with water in order to get more drinks, that he duplicated keys to padlocks before he sold them.

Cash was angry when he heard these stories and decided to confront Rotate. His plan was to tell Rotate that the sky was wide enough for every manner and specie of bird to fly without running into each other or knocking each other down with their wings. His plan was to tell Rotate that they could indeed practice *rotation* in their business by taking turns to sell certain items so that they didn't create a glut. But Cash's visit was unsuccessful. Rotate rebuffed him, telling Cash— *There is no paddy in the jungle, you mind your business, I mind my own. Every man for himself, God for us all.*

One day there was an early-morning police raid on Rotate. They knew exactly where to look and they found wraps of marijuana in empty giant tins of cocoa beverage. According to some people, the leader of the team had told Rotate to give out everything in his store because this time he was not coming back.

But Rotate did come back after three weeks and he promptly declared total war on Cash, claiming that Cash had ratted him out. Rotate returned from detention red-eyed. He said he was going to wipe out his enemies once and for all. *When you kill a snake, there is no need to leave the head lying around, you must sever the head and bury it in a deep pit*, he boasted. He told his customers to buy only from him; even if there was something they needed and he didn't have it, he would buy it for them the next time he went to the market.

According to Rotate, there were only two kinds of people in this world, those who were for Rotate and those who were against him. He said that there was no way the police would have known where he kept his marijuana cache if someone had not worked as an *informant*. He said if his enemies were jealous because he was the owner of an ordinary motorcycle, then what were they going to do when he bought the fully air-conditioned Peugeot 504 station wagon that he was going to buy soon. Though Rotate had dropped out of school early in form three in secondary school, he still threw around terms from the various subjects he had studied in school and justified his nefarious trade in marijuana by quoting the law of demand and supply. He said having only one store in the village was the equivalent of creating a monopoly. He said he believed in democracy, which was why he played his gramophone for all, unlike Cash, who only played for his favorites. He said he was planning on expanding his business and bringing democracy to the village. He planned to expand his business and open a full-fledged boutique selling ladies' and children's clothes and would also open a chemist shop that would sell medications. He said he was practicing what he had learned in his business methods class in school.

Cash did his best to reach out to Rotate. He sent a couple of individuals who were close to Rotate, the people who bought marijuana from him. Rotate said to them, "The police told me that the person who told them about me and my business told them to lock me up for good, that he did not want them to ever release me from detention. Think of what would have happened if I was never released. Who else could possibly tell them that?"

Soon after his release, Rotate bought an electric generator and a fridge and began to sell cold drinks. Cash had a gas lamp in his store and this was considered a major boost in a village where darkness descended without warning and was impenetrable and dense. But people also told Rotate that the two records Cash played over and over again were songs in which the musicians talked about enemies. One of the songs had the refrain:

> *My enemy, you are not my creator*
> *You are not the owner of my destiny*
> *Your hatred of me, and your anger against me will kill you.*

We had never seen Grandpa dance, but he always told us that the day when Gramophone got married he would dance and dance. When we asked Grandpa why he did not dance he would respond, *If you give me a reason to dance I will dance.* Win a scholarship to study in England and I will dance. If you people give me a good reason to dance I will dance. The only person that dances for no reason is the madman down the street, and even the madman has a reason, it is only that we don't know his reason. But the day your uncle gets married, I will dance for the whole world to see.

Cash would later tell people that when he walked into Rotate's store that evening, he had gone in to make peace. To talk to Rotate as one man to another. He had hoped that they could work things out and settle their differences once and for all over drinks. When Cash walked into Rotate's shop and greeted Rotate, Rotate did not respond to the greeting but said to Cash:

"You are not yet satisfied with informing on me and setting the police after me. You are not satisfied with spreading rumors about me. You are not satisfied with lowering your prices so that people will stop buying from me and buy from you, no you are not satisfied and now you have come to greet me with juju, or you think I don't know who your juju man is, you think the moment you open your mouth to greet me and I respond I will now become a zombie, and slavishly do all your bidding,"

As Rotate said this he came out of his shop and gave Cash a shove. Cash shoved Rotate back. Rotate slumped and fell to the ground. As he lay on the ground, his entire frame shook a couple of times, a little foamlike thing came out of the side of his mouth, his eyes rolled back into his head, and he stopped breathing.

That night a neighbor came to Cash's house and asked Cash whether he was waiting for the police to come and get him and send him to jail for the rest of his life.

—If you know what is good for you, you better start running to the house they call the Family House. You know the big man's house in the city. No one can touch you there—

That was how Cash came to live in the Family House. He was the one who knew where everything was. If an item was misplaced he knew where to find it. If a lightbulb needed to be fixed or the television antennae needed to be turned or there was a hard task that no one else could do in the Family House, he was the man for the job. He had a bunch of keys with him at all times.

The case did not go away. Rotate's people did not give up. They called the police and Cash was charged in absentia with murder. Grandpa tried persuading them to reduce the charge to manslaughter so Cash could serve a few years in prison and be released, but the family refused. After many years, Rotate's uncle, who was at the head of the family's pursuit of justice, died. His relations who were left were tired of the case and the cost of going

to court. Many big stores were now in the village and the story of
Cash and Rotate's rivalry seemed like an ancient folktale. Some
people from Rotate's family soon sent an emissary to Grandpa
that they wanted a settlement. Rotate had died single. The family
wanted money to be paid, enough money to cover the cost of him
marrying a wife and they wanted many white animals, a white
cow, a white goat, a white sheep, a white chicken, or the cash
equivalent. Grandpa called them for a meeting and it was nego-
tiated down. Eventually they accepted. They were paid. They in
turn paid off the police and told the police to close the case.

We were spending the holidays in the Family House the
day the man formerly known as Cash, now Gramophone, got
married. Grandpa had given him one of the girls who lived in
the house. Her father had owed Grandpa some money and she
had come to live in the Family House until the debt was owed.
We were told that by the time her father was ready to repay
the debt the girl said she did not want to return to her father's
house anymore or some other person said that her father had
died and nobody bothered to come for the girl after that.

On the day that Gramophone got married, there was a big
party in the Family House. The entire street was invited and
there was lots of music, but he did not block his ears when
he was led out to dance with the bride. Grandpa also danced
and danced. The kids from the poorer houses were so excited
to have bottles of soft drinks to themselves. They were urged
to drink as many as they wanted. Some of them had so many
drinks and poured some away and screamed to each other ex-
citedly about pouring a half-finished bottle of soft drink away.

I remember that at some point in the night the man in charge of the music had wanted to turn off the music, but Grandpa had instructed that the music be played until morning. As we rolled in our sleep toward morning we could still hear the music playing in front of the family house.

In time Gramophone/Cash had children and told Grandpa that he wanted to return to the village. This is your home now, Grandpa said to him. His children soon joined the many children who lived in the Family House and would grow up to work for Grandpa.

# UNCLE AYA

They came from every part of the city. Some came all the way from the surrounding villages and towns. Others had walked long distances and their sweaty feet had accumulated a fine coating of dust. A few had brought cooking utensils and some foodstuffs along with kerosene stoves. The poorer ones had brought along firewood and sawdust to light a fire and cook with.

Grandfather always said that in a great man's house you'll find at least one eccentric person. This was his usual response to the antics of Uncle Aya. Grandpa was of the view that each great household had both good and bad people. You'll find wise men, lawyers, doctors, and the occasional mad fellow or eccentric. He said Uncle Aya was the eccentric in our great household and urged members of the household to at least accommodate his eccentricities.

A few years back Uncle Aya had started corresponding with a certain Pastor Jonah from the West Indies who was also founder of End of the World Ministries. Uncle Aya would sometimes enlist us to help distribute their badly printed tracts, the black ink spilling from the words and the words aslant, some of the printed words smudged beyond recognition—inviting people to their crusades, healing crusades, everyday crusades, miracle crusades, Bible crusades. They usually used a large open space almost the size of a football field behind the Family House. This was where they showed *Photo-Drama of the First Day of Creation*. Not really a movie as such but moving photo slides. It showed how the earth was created from darkness. I recall some of the conversation around us as the images flashed.

—So someone was there with a film camera filming God as he made the earth?—

—Wonders will never end. So filmmaking was invented before man was created?—

—Or was God holding a camera as he was creating the earth?—

End of the World Ministries had many teachings that made it soon begin to attract a lot of members. They believed that it was justified to drink alcohol but not justified to get drunk because Paul had written to Timothy to drink a little wine for the sake of his stomach. They said that somewhere in the Bible God had said, *Wine makes the heart of mortal man to rejoice.*

They believed it was not a sin to have more than one wife if you had married both wives before coming into *knowledge*. That was the expression they used when talking about their past lives before they became members.

—I used to be a violent criminal before I came into *knowledge*, but I am now a changed person since I came into the knowledge—a new member would say during Testimony Time.

They said all members shared everything and one should be happy to give the shirt off one's back to another member of the church. They did not believe in elaborate funerals—a simple coffin, a few songs about waking up to behold the glory of the Father in heaven, and the burial. This was so loved by the poor because funeral expenses were usually high and those who could not bury their dead relations elaborately always faced one misfortune or another. But their greatest belief, the one that attracted more and more people to the group, was their belief that the world was coming to an end on a certain date.

They kept Sundays holy. There was to be no cooking, no lighted fire for cooking purposes, no raised voices, no eating or drinking till after the service, no work only rest, prayer, reading of the word, and groaning in the spirit and prophesying. If unfortunately a member died it was not to be announced on a Sunday. In fact it was kept a secret and no member's family ever said that a member had died on a Sunday. Nothing must taint the holiness of Sunday.

I remember that for their first miracle crusade, which was to be led by Pastor Jonah, Uncle Aya had printed a lot of flyers and

they had gone through the town with raised banners calling on
members of the public to come with all their illnesses to the crusade ground and be healed by the man who had raised the dead
in his home country, this was Pastor Jonah.

They had been attacked when they went to the Beggars
Lane, the place where the beggars lined up to receive alms,
to invite the blind and lame beggars to come to the healing
crusade in order to be healed. The king of the beggars had
told the beggars to attack Uncle Aya's group with sticks and
stones.

—Did we tell you we want to be healed? Why do you want
to deprive us of our means of livelihood?—

The members of the End of the World Ministries had returned from the event very excited. According to them, this
was *persecution*, they had been persecuted for their beliefs and
this was the final sign that would occur before the end of the
world.

But that particular crusade was never held because Pastor
Jonah took ill. He had caught malaria and lay on a narrow
iron bed in Uncle Aya's room sweating heavily and muttering in a strange language. His thick giant-typeface Bible
(the Amplified Version with Annotations and Comprehensive Concordance) lay closed beside him, lying side by side
with the immobile slides of *Photo-Drama of the First Day of
Creation*. When he burst out in a foreign tongue, Uncle Aya
would come closer to him, holding an open exercise book and
a pen poised to jot down his words which he declared were
words of prophecy.

"Don't let this your pastor die in my house, you better take him to the hospital," Grandfather told Uncle Aya.

"How can he die? Have you not heard that he raised the dead in his home country?"

"Well, if he dies here there'll be no one to raise him from the dead. Besides, why can't he help himself by healing himself of the malaria that is about to kill him."

"He is not suffering from malaria; he is in a trance receiving prophetic messages from God."

Eventually, Pastor Jonah recovered from the malaria attack and went back to the West Indies. Then he returned again, and they were preparing for the greatest event of all—the ending of the world. They said the world was going to end on a certain date at night. Probably on the first of September. They had already given out the date and they began encouraging their members to give out all of their material things, in fact all their earthly property, because they were all going up to heaven, and in heaven they would not need earthly things anymore. They were encouraged to sell what they could and bring the proceeds to Pastor Jonah. They were told to donate the things that they couldn't immediately sell. Gold and silver were always welcome as donations to the church.

The fame of the ministry soon spread and many people began to attend their prayer meetings.

—I was unemployed but now I don't have to worry about getting a job anymore because the world will end on the first of September. When I get to heaven I never have to work again because all we will do from morning to night and night to morning is sing Hosanna in the highest with Angel Michael and the rest of the heavenly hosts—

—I was always worrying about having a baby for my husband but I am not worried anymore because the world is coming to an end, I don't want a pregnancy to stand between me and heaven—

—I have sold my uncompleted building and given the money to the church, according to Pastor Jonah, there are many mansions in heaven and we will pick and choose the one we want—

—I just got a loan but I have given the money to the church because I am leaving for heaven and I will not need to repay the loan—

And so many were already disposing of anything that would stand as an encumbrance to heaven. I remember that Grandfather's response to all of this had been to quote from the prayer book of the Anglican Church, the part that said— *World without End Amen.* Grandfather had also remarked that if the heaven was going to fall and cover the earth it shouldn't be of concern to only one individual but should be the concern of all who lived here on earth under the sky.

When Pastor Jonah and Uncle Aya were asked how the world was going to end, was it by water like the flood of Noah or was it by fire because the Bible refers to God as a consuming fire, they both replied that they did not know. The only thing they said they knew was that God was going to take his people, the members of the church who had come to knowledge, up into heaven before unleashing his judgment on those who were left on earth.

Uncle Aya, we were told, had been a weird one since he was little. It was said that when he was younger and chickens were being killed to make stew for Christmas celebrations, he would gather the other children in the house around the slaughtered chicken and tell the kids to close their eyes while he prayed for the dead chickens. He told the other children that chickens had souls and that if he didn't pray for the chickens the chickens would lose both their bodies and their souls. He prayed for sick animals. He would lay hands on them and whisper things. He dreamed dreams and saw visions. While in elementary school, he predicted the death of a classmate from measles.

Grandpa sent him to a boarding school. One day on a school picnic beside a lake, one of his classmates had pushed him into the lake. It took a while before the teacher's attention was called and a senior student dived into the lake and rescued Uncle Aya. The story was that when they brought him out of the lake his stomach was swollen to three times its size. They had to give him mouth-to-mouth resuscitation and then someone suggested pressing his stomach. Water came out of his mouth. He sneezed and came to. When Grandpa heard about the incident, he went and brought him back from the school. They say Grandpa said it was a taboo for him to be the one who buried his children instead of the other way round. After the incident, Uncle Aya began telling stories of the things he had seen while he was underwater. A beautiful place with double-story buildings all constructed with solid gold. He said the buildings sparkled and glittered.

"What happened to the boy is bigger than what his mind can contain, it sure shook up his mind," Grandpa said.

First he was taken to the hospital to see a doctor but the doctor said there was nothing wrong with him, then he was taken to see a prophetess of a white garment church. He began living in the church and wore only flowing white soutanes. He began to see religion in mundane everyday activities. When smoke rose out of the Family House chimney he watched it to see if it went up in a straight line or dispersed. If it went up in a straight line he would say it is acceptable unto the lord, if it curved or dispersed he would say that there was something unholy being cooked. He would go days saying he was on a white fast and would eat only food that was white in color—white corn pap, white bread, white yams, egg whites, and avoid things cooked with oil.

At other times he would insist that before any chicken was slaughtered or any goat or sheep for that matter that he had to pray for its soul and make the sign of the cross across its heart. He would conduct funerals for dead birds and dead lizards and insist that they had souls and he wanted their souls to make heaven.

The story of how much he loved God was usually illustrated with an incident from his childhood. He had been given two coins. The coin with a higher denomination was for him to put in the offering box in church while the smaller coin was for him to buy a Popsicle for himself when he finished at church. As he jumped across an open drain on his way to church, the larger coin flew out of his pocket into the open drain.

Sorry, there goes my Popsicle money, God, he said, and looked up to heaven, your own money is still intact.

Another kid would have said, Sorry, God, but that was your money that just fell into the drain.

The End of the World Ministries wasn't Uncle Aya's first religious movement. Years back he had founded another religious movement that combined the teachings of Islam, Christianity, and Ancestor worship. The movement picked a few of the things that it liked in the different religions and its members were free to pray in any way they saw fit according to the ways of the three religions. They were free to marry more than one wife if they promised to love all the wives equally. They celebrated on Christmas day, fasted during the month of Ramadan, and worshiped ancestors on designated months.

Uncle Aya consulted oracles using divination beads made from the seeds of the African star apple. But he could also see the future when he wore a white soutane and fell into a trance and would claim to see angels who whispered the secrets of men and women into his ears. It was with the syncretic movement that he had first gotten into trouble and nearly got the Family House burned down. He claimed he could see the future. His fame had reached some young military boys who were planning a coup to overthrow the ruling military government. They had come in the dead of night to ask him if their coup was going to be successful. There had been a few attempts in the past to overthrow the military head of state, but he was said to have more than nine lives. Uncle Aya had told them to leave and come back in three days' time and allow him time to fast, do some ablution, and consult the ancestors. When they left, he had dressed up and gone to the director of Military Intelligence to tell him that some young soldiers were planning to overthrow the head of state. The young soldiers were apprehended, because merely thinking of a coup was a punishable offense. They were tried before a military tribunal and sentenced to long jail terms. Some of their fellow soldiers had heard of the ignoble role Uncle Aya had played in the whole affair and had attempted to burn the house down one night. They were in mufti but of course they were soldiers and knew how to move about at night without being heard. The fire was put out before much damage could be done to the house. The attempt had failed and Uncle Aya had to lie really low for a while. And then one day he had bought a little pamphlet by Pastor Jonah from a pavement vendor of used books. He said it was something about the title and the man with a raised fist on the cover that had caught his attention.

The night began with a lot of the members eating the meals they had cooked. There were to be no leftovers, since that would be such a waste because there would be no one to eat the food the next day. People invited others to come over and share their food. And then the eating was soon over and members were instructed to go and change into fresh clothes and to look neat and tidy.

"You dress up when going before a judge. Shouldn't you

dress even better as you go to meet your God?" This was Pastor Jonah encouraging people to go and put on their best clothes.

Soon Uncle Aya appeared wearing well-ironed black pants and a clean white shirt rolled up to his elbows. He ran and swerved through the crowd as he pointed in different directions. "Our savior e dey here?"

"Yes, e dey," the people screamed back while they too pointed in different directions. "Our savior e dey here?" "Yes, e dey." Is our savior here, yes he is here.

There had been yet another incident in Uncle Aya's past when he was nearly killed by soldiers if not for Grandpa's intervention. The government had declared a curfew. By this time Uncle Aya had joined another prophetic church and would routinely go to the church to pass the night. He said that 3:00 AM was when the spirit of God usually visited and that it was important to be in a holy place like the church so that the spirit wouldn't turn back because the place it was visiting was polluted.

On his way back from church he ran into soldiers who pointed their flashlights in his face and asked:

"Who goes there? What is your name? Why are you out at this time? Did you not hear of the curfew?"

"I am the man of God and I am coming back from the Lord's errand like Angel Gabriel."

"Kneel down there and start crawling on your knees."

"I kneel for no mortal. I only kneel for my maker," Uncle Aya replied.

"Then prepare to meet your maker," one of the soldiers said, and fired his gun.

Uncle Aya raised his hand into the air and screamed, "Oh my Lord and my God, receive the soul of your servant!"

But Uncle Aya was not dead. The soldier had shot into the air and was only having fun. The soldier was in fact drunk.

Uncle Aya had screamed, thinking he had been shot.

Grandfather heard the scream and assumed he had been shot and ran out, for this was happening close to the house.

"Who are you?" one of the soldiers asked.

"I am his father," Grandfather said, pointing at Uncle Aya, who was by now kneeling on the ground.

"You must be God then, because he told us his father is in heaven."

"Who is your commander?" Grandfather asked.

"Why do you want to know?" the drunk soldier said, and rushed at Grandfather and hit him on the head with his Mark 4 rifle.

"You will pay dearly for this," Grandfather said, holding his head, which was already bleeding.

And the soldiers looked at themselves, gathered their stuff, and fled.

This incident happened on the first of September. On September first the next year, Grandfather developed a blinding headache. It was a headache like no other. Black cloths had to be spread on all the windows so no drop of sunlight could penetrate into the house. The headaches were soon to be known as Grandfather's September headaches. They came every September without fail, marking the day he was hit on the head by soldiers with a gun because of Uncle Aya.

Lightning flashed across the sky. They paused in their chorus singing. Many raised their eyes to the sky. It was going to happen, finally.

But it didn't. There was a little drizzle that lasted no longer than three minutes. The type of drizzle known as kerosene rain because of the way it dried up quickly like kerosene.

As light began to erase the darkness and some of the crowd could now see each other clearly, screams began to emanate from the crowd. Uncle Aya announced that Pastor Jonah was going inside the house to seek the face of the Lord and to get answers.

There was a shout of my bicycle here. And over there a shout of my sewing machine. And yonder a shout of my fridge. And even farther down a louder scream of my TV.

—I have given out all my earthly property what am I going to do? How can I continue living? What am I going to tell my neighbors? The world will make me their laughingstock—

Slowly the crowd became angry. First it was sachets of plastic water that were hauled at the house, then someone picked up a piece of stone and hauled it at one of the louvers on the window upstairs. The louver shattered. Others seemed to take a cue and began to haul objects at the house. Uncle Aya fled inside. A voice in the crowd said someone should get petrol so they could burn both the house and the lying pastor down and send the pastor to heaven to go and seek God's face. Another stone scattered yet another windowpane.

And then a shot rang out. Grandfather was standing on the balcony. He was holding his double-barreled gun. He fired off yet another shot into the air, and the crowd fell silent.

"Did your pastor tell you that this was his house? Did he tell you that he built this house or that it belongs to him? Did I join you people in your madness? While you were waiting and praying for the world to end was I not in my bed sleeping? Why should you burn down my house?"

And so the crowd began to disperse. First one person and then another. Until there was nobody left.

# ABULE

Even those of us who were considered too young to know knew that Abule's wife was a loose woman who went with other men. It came as no surprise then when one morning her husband took out his double-barreled rifle and began going from house to house threatening to kill all the men who had been sleeping with his wife. She was from a different part of the country. One of the stories told about her people was that it was not uncommon for a husband to entertain a visiting overnight guest with one of his wives. It was considered a gesture of genuine hospitality. If the visitor did a good job the wife would put out a bucket of water in the bathroom for him to take his bath the next morning. If he didn't please the woman, he would have to get his own bathwater for himself the next morning.

The woman's name was Fanti, and she had a little shed where she sold rice and beans and stew and *dodo* and macaroni and pasta. People would stop over on their way to work to buy food and chat. Oftentimes by midafternoon all the food was sold. On days that she didn't sell all she would put the food in a cart and hawk up and down the street. She was jovial and always laughing. She let men touch her. Her husband was a retired daily paid laborer who had worked with the railways. He was a man who walked gingerly and gently, as if he was afraid to tread too hard on the earth. His house had a piazza and he would usually sit on his hammock and drink tea. He was retired and was a pensioner. He responded to the greetings of both old and young with just one phrase—*'Allo dear.*

It was not long before Fanti started selling beer in her shed. She would sell food in the morning and start beer sales in the afternoon. Soon her place became a gathering point for some of the young men who lived on the street. They said she had relationships with at least three or four of the men. What was said of her was that she was the type that could never be satisfied with one man.

It was a gray morning when the first shot rang out. Fanti's husband, Abule, had fired that warning shot in the air. He had his shiny double-barreled gun and was walking down the street with the gun slung over his shoulders. Later people who were close to him would say they heard him muttering the words, *Today is today, it will all end today.*

He stood in front of the house of one of his wife's supposed lovers and screamed his name.

"Come out if you call yourself a man, today is the day it will end." Abule shouted the words out aloud as he held the gleaming rifle and raised it and pointed it at the house.

Doors slammed shut as people went into hiding, women and children running under their beds to hide.

"Come out or I'll come and get you myself. You call yourself a man. Come out if you are a man," he shouted again.

When there was no response he walked to the door, pushed it open, and began to walk down the corridor. No one knows till today how he knew the exact door of the man who was said to be one of his wife's lovers. He was a bricklayer. Abule kicked the door open. The lover was attempting to push the window open to escape when Abule fired off the first round. The shot got the fleeing man in the shoulder. He screamed and fell over the window into the yard. Abule brought out another bullet from the pocket of his dark brown railway-issue overalls. It was shiny, its silver head encased in a red plastic shell. He was walking round to the back of the house to the window where the man he had shot earlier lay when he changed his mind and began striding down the street to another house down the road. The house belonged to another man who was always in the wife's store. He was an *agbero*, a motor park tout; he got a cut from every fare paid by travelers to the driver. He hung around the motor park calling passengers, helping them board, and collecting a commission. He was the one who had insisted that Fanti start selling beer even though she did not have the required license.

Abule walked into the man's house. The man was still in bed. He prodded him with the nozzle of the double barrel. The *agbero* man was not fully awake; he jumped up and rubbed his eyes. Abule cocked his gun and shot him in the head at close range. The man fell back on the bed. There was blood on the unpainted cement wall. Abule walked out.

Only the sound of gunshots broke the silence of the street. All the people on the street were in hiding. There were no screams. Abule was humming a railway work song as he walked back home. His walk was jaunty and springy. He even had a little smile on his face and he licked his thin lips over and over again.

"Come out, Fanti. I have finished your men. Now it is your turn," he said aloud for people to hear.

He went inside to where he kept his bullets and reloaded. He walked into Fanti's bedroom, but she had fled. He stepped out of the house and stepped into the road. He raised his gun and released a shot into the air.

Grandpa heard the shot and came out of the house and looked into the street from the open balcony.

Abule was still shouting and saying that anybody who considered himself man enough should come out. He said those who were sleeping with his wife who called themselves men should come out and show themselves as brave men. He went to the backyard of his house and came out with a half can of gasoline and a box of matches. He walked to the shed where

Fanti sold rice in the daytime and beer in the evenings. He half covered the mouth of the gasoline gallon with one finger as he began to spray the gasoline on the small wooden shed. When he was done spraying he struck a match and the small shed began to blaze. All the while his gun was hanging on his left shoulder. He watched the shed burn for a bit and walked back to his house in fast strides. He stood in his piazza holding his gun. Once more he shouted that anyone who considered himself a man should come outside. The doors remained locked and the street was silent. The street was still empty. Grandfather walked out of the Family House in small, slow steps. He did not walk like someone in a hurry.

Abule, Abule, Grandfather called the name twice. Abule turned; he raised his gun and positioned it, as if about to take a shot. He looked up and noticed it was Grandfather.

"Man of courage, the fearless lion, great warrior, the big wizard," Abule hailed Grandfather.

"Put down your gun and let's talk. Let's talk like two men. If there is any doubt that you are a man of courage I have never been among the doubters."

"It takes a man of courage to drive a train, that dragon that belches smoke from here to Kaura-Namoday."

Grandfather was only flattering Abule. Abule was not a locomotive train driver. He had joined the railways as a laborer and had retired as a lowly laborer but the inflated praise words brought a smile to Abule's parched face.

"Give me the gun," Grandfather said. "Hand it over."

Abule looked at Grandfather and shook his head from side

to side in refusal. He was suddenly transformed into a child refusing to hand over a favorite toy.

"Give me the gun. When you hand me the gun we can talk man to man. I cannot talk with you if you are holding a gun over my head," Grandfather said.

Abule handed over the gun. Grandfather held the gun sideways in the middle, and as if breaking it, cracked the gun open and the two bullets popped out. He put the bullets in his pocket.

Grandfather called out to someone in the Family House to bring over a kettle of tea. The tea was brought over and Grandfather made a cup for Abule. Abule blew into the cup and took a sip.

"You are the only good man in this neighborhood. Since I built my house here they have always troubled me. I suffered during my time in the railways. Carrying heavy items on my bare head in the sun. Pouring gravel on the tracks. Carrying wood for repair of the tracks. I saved every penny to build this house and to marry. I could not marry from my own people because I didn't want trouble, my people and their *wahala*. But they didn't let her rest. Now my life is ruined," Abule said, and began to cry.

"You should not allow a woman to ruin your life," Grandpa said. "You have killed one man. The other man is still alive, he survived. I will talk to the police. They will understand. I will help them understand. Go inside and take a bath and wear fresh clothes. I will contact the police. Don't say a word when they get here, let me handle everything," Grandfather said.

That day we heard a new phrase for the first time. It was our favorite expression for many weeks. Grandpa told the police that Abule had committed *a crime of passion*.

Abule was sent to jail but for only about eighteen months for manslaughter. The *agbero* man was not well liked in the first place. Grandpa put Abule's house up for rent while Abule was in prison, and when Abule came out Grandfather handed over the rent money collected in his absence to him.

"You are the only good man on this street. I have said that before and I say it again," Abule said.

He was thankful but he said he could no longer live on the street. He was old and tired. Being in prison had worsened things. Grandfather offered to buy the house at a ridiculously low price. Abule agreed. He handed the certificate of occupancy to Grandfather. Abule went to live in the village. Grandfather converted the house into shops facing the street and put the shops up for rent.

# TATA

By the time Tata lost her third baby at birth, other people in the Family House were calling her a soul stealer. Some people said she was the one stealing the souls of her dead babies. None of the children lived longer than the seventh day. First they stopped drinking breast milk. They began to run a fever, and a few days later they started hiccupping and then died. As the body of the third child was being taken away from the Family House to be buried, people whispered among themselves.

—Poor children, they didn't want to live in this world on the seventh day. Instead of being christened, they are being buried on the day their naming ceremony should have taken place—

—This is no ordinary death. All three children died before they are named—

—The worm eating the apple is inside the apple. I think the woman must be a witch. You know with the soul stealers they don't care once it's your turn you have to bring your own child's soul to be eaten because you have also partaken in the eating of other people's children, that's the law of the coven—

—But what I heard is different. They say you usually have to give them the child whom you love most to show how much loyalty you have to the coven—

—But if she really is a witch, how come she has to sacrifice all three of her children? Is she the only one in the coven?—

—They do it according to rank and seniority. The senior soul stealers don't have to sacrifice their own children. I hear it is also a power thing the more children you sacrifice the more power you have and the earlier you'll attain a higher position—

All the whisperings got to Tata's ears. She was one of the wives in the house. She stopped the men who were carrying the body of the dead baby to the cemetery for burial.

It hadn't been easy for her to conceive either. Most of the female herbalists she went to said she had a hot womb that was too *hot* for a baby to grow in and had given her herbal medications to *cool* the womb.

She carried the dead child to the shrine of the river goddess. She cried to the river goddess. The priestess of the river goddess told her to wait with the body in the shrine. She waited. Later that day the priestess told her to remove her clothes and change into white clothes. She did. She told her to wrap the dead child in a white sheet. She did. She told her to wait by the riverbank. When it was getting to late evening, the river goddess asked her to wade into the water with the dead child. When she got into the middle of the water she saw a figure rising out of the water toward her. She was very fair skinned, a little plump, her face glowed silvery like a fluorescent light, she told Tata to give her the dead baby. Tata handed the baby to her.

—In place of the baby I'll give you something that'll take you places and make you better known than even your husband and all the men. The only thing is that you must promise to venerate my name. Before you start anything you must give honor to my name. And from today you must dress only in white. Everything in your life has to be white. She was requested to drop the dead child into the river. She did. As the child sank, a medium-size mirror floated to the top of the water. Pick up the mirror—she was commanded.

She did.

—This mirror will help you catch soul stealers and wizards. It will help catch thieves. It will help identify any person who commits any crime and denies it. This mirror works better than any detective. All you need to do when people come to you is get a set of drummers to drum and sing my praises, let them sing the praises of the river goddess. As the singing and drumming heighten, bring out the mirror and begin to chant my praises. I will show you who has committed the crime. In fact the perpetrator of the crime will appear in the mirror and all eyes will see them. This mirror will give you wealth. It will make your name known all over the world—

"And will it give me children?" Tata asked.

—No, it will not give you children. Every woman comes to this world with a certain number of children in her womb. You were destined to have three. They are gone—

"What about one, just one child?"

—You will have no children of your own but the noise of children, and people will never depart from your compound—

That was how Tata Mirror got the name Tata Mirror. She returned to the family house and told Grandpa what she was told. Grandpa knew that this was a great business opportunity. He carved out a consultation room from one of the rooms facing the street downstairs. He donated two of the boys in the house to her as drummers. He made a signboard and put it in front of the house. The signboard said: WHATEVER YOU ARE SEARCHING FOR MY MIRROR WILL FIND IT. WITCHES AND WIZARDS, CHILDREN, LOST ITEMS, ETC.

We would later learn to beat those same drums ourselves.

Those who were there when it happened said the first case that was brought to Tata was the young man who died down the street. He was from a polygamous home. He always took the first position in school. He was both senior prefect and sanitation prefect in his secondary school. When he finished secondary school he wanted to go to the university to study medicine but was offered a place to study pharmacy, but medicine was his first love so he decided to wait for a year and then reapply. He got a job as a cashier with a bank. Because he was a levelheaded boy he still lived with his mother. On his way to the bus stop to take a bus to work in the morning people would marvel at the sparkling white shirt he wore.

—That boy's brain is faster than a calculator, I hear—

—Look at the white shirt dazzling like an angel—

—I hear he is going to the university next year to become a doctor—

—He will make a good doctor he is so kind and caring—

—With the kind of money he is earning from the bank some of his mates would go to rent their own apartments so they can drink, smoke, and bring girlfriends home. But just look at him he still lives at home, helping his mother—

—Other kids should learn from him. Nowadays as soon as they are in form two they stop greeting older people. They start flying the collar of their shirts—

One day at work the young man turned to the cashier sitting next to him and said, "I want to take off my tie. It is getting very hot in here."

"Are you sure you don't have a fever?" the other cashier replied. "The air-conditioning is on."

"I really, really, need to take this tie off."

"Go ahead, if you want to, you can, but if the supervisor sees you without a tie you'll be in trouble."

He removed the tie and dropped it on the floor.

"I am still feeling quite hot," he said after a few minutes.

"I think you should go to the first-aid box and take some paracetamol. Or do you want me to call the supervisor so he can excuse you to go and see a doctor?"

"I am not sick. I just feel hot," he said and took off his shirt.

When his colleague noticed that he had pulled off his shirt he rushed to the outer office to call the supervisor. When he came out of the outer office with the supervisor, the cashier was out of his cubicle. He was stark naked. He was fanning himself with his shirt. "I still feel very hot," he kept muttering. All the bank's customers fled the banking hall.

He turned out to be Tata's first major client. His family was called to the bank. He was bundled to the hospital, but the doctor took one look at him and diagnosed his condition as *home trouble*. He said it was not the kind of illness that should be brought to the hospital. The young man was still complaining of heat even though only a blue bedsheet covered him. Someone must have mentioned Tata, because the young man was soon brought to Tata's room in the Family House. His mother was there, so were his father and his father's second wife. The drummers began to pound their drums. We could only peep through the green mosquito netting into the room. In a small earthenware pot on the fire a mixture of water and white loam was boiling angrily.

Tata was clad in a white woven cloth, on her right hand she held a mirror and on the left a fan decorated with chicken feathers. She began to dance and hop about. First on one leg, then on the other one. She spread out both hands the way a bird would spread out its wings and moved around the room in speedy spurts, as if propelled by a force inside of her that eyes couldn't see. Finally she stopped in front of the two wives. The young man was sitting quietly now. He was rocking back and forth. His eyes were glazed, but he had at least stopped screaming about his body being on fire.

"You know yourself, you know who you are. Say what you did to him," Tata said, glaring angrily at both women. They were both sitting on carved wooden chairs.

"If the river goddess reveals you, you'll die. Reveal yourself now or the repercussion will be dire."

Both women shrank back. Tata began to dance once again as the drums picked up a beat and increased its tempo. The music of the drums was heady, it did something to the spirit, first it was mournful, then it turned stirring and hypnotic, even.

Tata began to peer into her mirror. She looked into the mirror and covered her eyes, as if frightened by what she saw. She looked into the mirror again. She laughed, but there was no joy in her laughter.

Two aluminum cups were dipped into the boiling pot of clay and given to the women to drink from. The younger wife drank first. As she drank she was urged on by Tata. Drink everything. Those who have nothing to hide find this to be a refreshing drink. Those who have something to hide think it poison. Drink and drain the cup. It was now the turn of the boy's mother. She was reluctant to drink.

"Why do I need to drink? I am not on trial. It is my own son they are trying to kill."

"Yes, which is the more reason for you to drink and show the whole world that you have clean hands."

"I have nothing to hide. I bore him. The world knows that I can never harm a child that came out of my own womb. I carried him for nine months."

"Are you afraid to drink?"

"No, I have nothing to be afraid of. I have not done anything."

"Then drink it."

"I don't want to drink on an empty stomach. I have not eaten since I heard of my son's troubles."

"It is like food. Consider this milk from the river goddess."

By this time the drums had become silent. Tata looked into her mirror and shook her head. The boy's mother drank. She was urged to drain the cup. She drank and drained the cup and then she began to talk.

"It was me who did it. I cooked my son. I boiled him. They said I had to do it. They said I had taken part in the killing of other people's children and that it was now my turn. They said I should bring them the son I loved most. I refused; I told them he was my life my future, my retirement hope. They said I would get a big title. They said I would be promoted. They told me I would be cruising around in a pleasure car in our world. I was reluctant to do it but I was persuaded."

"Can he be cured? Can he still return?" the father of the boy asked.

"He has been cooked and eaten. All that while he was screaming about being hot he was being boiled in a cauldron."

The boy's father spoke again, he was pleading.

"You must be able to do something. Beg the goddess for us, we will sacrifice whatever she wants to save my son."

"It is too late," Tata said. "Your son is gone. They have taken his spirit. This is a mere husk you are looking at."

Before his burial a mob gathered and said they wanted to lynch his mother. She was not lynched. One of her brothers, a pastor in a white garment church, would take her away for deliverance from the spirit of witchcraft. This same brother of hers would one day spit at the Family House while walking past it and refer to the house as a demonic and fetish house. Her husband would accuse Tata of putting strange liquids in a cup and forcing his wife to drink it.

Tata's fame as a witch catcher grew. Every day, there was drumming in the house. And soon enough a new group of people began living in the house. These were people who had confessed their witchcraft but were left behind out of shame by their families.

How can they follow us back home after the evil they have done? their families asked. Grandpa had not envisaged this fallout from Tata's new line of business, but he was happy about it. New hands meant more working hands, and more money. These men and women became his washermen. They washed, starched, and ironed neighborhood laundry for a pittance. Initially a few people on the street were reluctant to bring their laundry to the Family House but the price was too good and whites came back sparkling, smelling clean and well ironed. Yet people talked.

—It is even stated in the holy books that a witch should not live but die—

—These are not witches anymore. Once a witch has confessed, all her power is gone—

—How do you know? Have you been a witch before?—

—No, but one knows things. Witchcraft is like a secret society. Once you reveal their secrets, they expel you—

—Yes, they expel you but you still have their secrets with you—

—You can tell that these people who live in that house still have supernatural powers—

—Why do you say that?—

—They wash clothes and do all kinds of domestic work but they never get tired. And look at the clothes they launder for people, always clean and sparkling. They have sent the other washermen out of business—

—They act strange. They don't make eye contact, always staring at the ground. They never speak. They are always working—

—I think they are just grateful to have a place to stay. They are grateful to be alive—

—After all the lives they took and all the evil they have committed in their coven they should just let them die—

—Well, you know how they are in that house. Anything that'll make them money they are for it—

—Money, money, that is all they know—

Tata's business continued to boom. Communities would invite her to come and consult her mirror as to the reason why their sons and daughters were not getting ahead, why were they not growing like other communities. Sometimes she would ask them to cut down a large iroko tree in the center of the town and name the top of the tree the meeting place for soul stealers and wizards. Some would want to know why their market was not big or did not attract people like other markets. She would tell them that soul stealers bought and sold there at night and did not want people to trample on their space in the daytime. Her drummers would beat their drums, she would dance, she would prance around and then she would command one of her boys to start digging somewhere in the market. They would unearth a large pot covered with moss and cowrie shells. She would tell them that this pot was buried by soul stealers. And soon thereafter the market began to boom.

Tata would come back home with gifts of money and drinks. Once she came back with two cows. Grandpa said he didn't know anything about rearing cows and called a passing cattle herder from the cattle-rearing tribe to come and take the cows away. This honest cattle herder would return many years later with over a hundred cows for Grandpa.

Yet tongues wagged. People were angry at Tata's fame and Grandpa's growing wealth.

—She must be a witch herself, otherwise where does she get all her powers from?—

—She might be a witch; it is just that her witchcraft power is bigger than that of the people she was making to confess—

—Nothing lasts forever. Witchcraft has been existing since the beginning of time—

—Even the white man has his own witchcraft, only theirs is white witchcraft and they use it to invent great things like airplanes and ships—

—Our people use theirs to pull other people down, that is the problem—

As Tata's fame grew, so did the whispering and gossip. By this time the mirror looked worn and aged. One day a young woman came to the Family House with the dead body of her young child. The child must have been about two years old. She said she was on her way back from spending some time with her mother-in-law when she was stopped by an older woman whom she didn't know so well. She was carrying her baby on her back. The older woman told her to wait, that she needed to adjust the neck of her sleeping baby. The older woman helped her adjust the baby's neck and then touched the baby on the neck and remarked that the baby was one chubby child. She thanked the old woman and began to walk home. A few minutes later, the baby began to cry, he was sweating profusely. By the time she got home the baby was crying even harder and was gasping for breath. She gave the baby a cold bath and without toweling him dry brought him into her room and laid him under the fan. She stepped out of the room to get a little something to eat. When she stepped back in, the baby had stopped breathing. She picked the baby up and began to wail. Neighbors told her to bring the baby to Tata to find out who it was that killed the baby, because this was apparently not a natural death.

When Tata told her that it was the older woman who had touched her sleeping child that day, she took the dead baby home and told everyone she met on the way what had happened. A mob followed her to the house of the older woman. The older woman escaped, but the crowd set the house on fire. The older woman ran to the army barracks to alert her son, who had built her the house. Her son sent a detachment of soldiers to the family house. The soldiers came and took Tata away.

People began to talk on the street. Some of them were happy over the detention of Tata in the Army Cantonment by the soldiers.

—About time this came to an end. Witch this, witch that, everyone has become a witch since she brought her accursed mirror—

—The mirror has done more harm than good, brothers and sisters and family now view each other with suspicion. Even children view their parents with suspicion—

—When you give a child *akara* these days he'll tell you let me run home first and show it to my parents—

The soldiers who detained Tata said that at night they heard the sound of dashing waves pounding against the walls of her detention room, they said the place seemed to be floating. They eventually released her.

A few years later Tata became the founder of a church. Her followers wore white, flowing garments and each church had to be built near a flowing stream or river.

# JULIUS

The Family House was in a festive mood. Brother Julius was returning home after many years abroad. If you asked any of us the name of the country he was returning from, we would have said to you that he was returning from a place called Abroad. Till today we do not know for sure what country he had lived in abroad, whether the United States, U.K., or in Germany or even Russia.

His return was marked by his anecdotes from almost every country in the Western hemisphere. According to Brother Julius, in Russia everything belongs to everybody, everyone shares. What is mine is yours. There was no private ownership of property. You entered the unlocked Lada car parked down the street with keys in the ignition, you do your errands; you leave the car keys in the car, and the next man who needs it picks it up. Share and share alike, everyone is happy. Everybody, including their president who was not called President but Comrade, lived in the same-size flat with the same type furnishings, he told us.

According to another of his stories, while we are waking up, the Australians are going to bed. Australia is the end of the world and the end of the earth. If you walk too far out on the Australian desert you'll walk off the edge of the earth and fall into another planet.

The British love tea and will drink tea when they are happy and drink tea when they are sad. They'll drink tea when they are hungry and when they are full. They love their cats and their dogs and all their pets. They have a society for the protection of animals and none for the protection of their fellow humans. They'll hug a tree to prevent it from being cut down but their ancestors sent debtors and their children to prison and would go to watch a prisoner being hanged and sit down for a picnic of sandwiches after the execution.

What was remembered most about the day he returned was that there was so many free soft drinks that we used our half-drunk soda drinks to wash our hands, like we did when Gramophone got married. We also ate so much fried lamb meat that there was a long line in front of the toilet the next day. He was Grandpa's favorite son; even our parents whispered that it was Grandpa that had spoiled him.

He had been sent abroad to study in the first place because it was said that the course of study he wanted to pursue was so complicated that no university in the continent offered it.

People needed no invitation to come and eat. There was more than enough food for everyone. After eating, the people on the street gathered to pick their teeth, belch, and talk.

—Now that the son has returned from abroad he will bring some civilization into the house—

—He should at least send those scary souls living in the house away. They scare everyone. I couldn't even take the food offered by one of them earlier today—

—He will change things, even from the way he speaks. If you were in the next room you'd think it's a foreigner speaking—

—What can he do? What will he change? Was it not the money from the house that sent him and kept him abroad all these years?—

—He should have gone to stay elsewhere if he was different. Since he returned to the same house he is part of it—

—Exactly what did he study abroad? Is he a doctor, lawyer, or engineer?—

—What did he spend all these years studying?—

—I hear that what he studied is so specialized that no university in our continent offers it—

—We are still here. We are not going anywhere. We are watching. We shall see—

The expectation of both Grandpa and every other member of the family was that Brother Julius would get a job, marry, buy a car, and move into his own house, but this didn't happen. Brother Julius had a different plan. Brother Julius wanted the party to continue and it did for days and days after his arrival. There was talk of a job but Brother Julius had everyone, including Grandpa, confused about what exactly he had studied in school and what could be done with his qualification. Someone said he had mentioned international criminology, but when he was asked if that meant he could join the police force he said that was very far from what he studied.

All of these things would not have been a major cause for concern. After all, people said that there was enough money in that house to feed all the people on that street for all the years of their lives. Trouble started when Brother Julius began to entertain the hairdresser popularly known as Man-Woman, who lived two streets away. A man, he was known all over the neighborhood for his feminine ways. He painted his long nails pink. He had his hair in Jheri curls. He preferred tight white trousers. He swayed his waist from side to side when he walked. He tied his towel on his chest and not on his waist on his way to the bathroom. He stood and gossiped with women all the time. And when the women said something funny he laughed in a tinkling manner and covered his mouth coyly with his fingers.

He was known to be generous, and even those who didn't like him had no reason to be hostile toward him. The womenfolk liked him and confided in him. He had the secrets of the menfolk in his hands. Initially it did not surprise anyone that Man-Woman came to the Family House to greet Brother Julius. The man had just returned from abroad and well-wishers were free to walk in and have a drink or even just to see the face of the returnee. The strange thing about the visit was that they hugged like long-lost brothers and had eyes only for each other, such that without being told other guests who were sipping soft drinks and White Horse whiskey, had to slip out of the room. When they left they heard the door shut behind them and then there were soft girlish giggles from Man-Woman. In the days that followed, Man-Woman began to bring different guests to the house. They ate, drank, talked, ate some more, drank tea, and laughed loudly. The only time Brother Julius said anything to anyone was in response to Grandpa's accusation that he was having an everlasting party and that no party lasts forever, when he told Grandpa that this was not a party but that he was holding a *salon* with his new friends.

—And what is this we hear that he has turned that house into a hotel for all kinds of people—

—He claims it is not a hotel but that he is holding a *salon*—

—What is that? Did he go abroad to learn hairdressing?—

—Don't we have enough barbing and hairdressing saloons on this street already?—

—Even Kafa calls himself a London-trained barber and his London-Style Barbing Saloon has been there since that boy was a kid—

—He says it is not that kind of saloon. His is a *salon,* a place where they gather to talk about ideas for the betterment of society—

—So why do they shut the door when they discuss these ideas?—

—You are asking me as if I've been in there with them. I am not a member—

—So tell me why is it that it is only people like Man-Woman who attend the meetings?—

—What society do they want to make better, they want to destroy the world that they met with their strange ways?—

—I heard that all those men who enter that room *follow their fellow men*. They go with their fellow men—

—Shhhh, hush, don't say that. This world is live and let live—

—But how do they make money from this *salon*?—

—They say the *salon* is not meant to make money, it is for the discussion of ideas for the betterment of society—

—If it does not make money, how can it better society?—

—You are asking me?—

—Who do you want me to ask; did you hear that I am a member of their secret *salon*?—

—If it is a secret society, that one is good. The secret society members help themselves. Once you give each other the secret handshake, it is like you are both born of the same mother. You will give the other person the shirt on your back—

—But who pays for all the drinks and food and tea that they consume in their meetings—

—They have money in that house. Money is not their problem. First I thought it was the man from abroad funding the thing but I hear he did not return with a single brass farthing—

—He keeps telling everyone that his things are still on the high seas, that he could not carry much with him on the flight—

—Well, all I can say is that if they cannot make the world better, let them not ruin the world, they had better leave it the way they met it—

The parties continued. Now, there was no longer anything furtive about them. They were having parties. They were playing loud music. Some people who said someone saw men holding the waist of other men and they were dancing *hold-tight* in there.

Grandpa finally summoned Brother Julius for a man-to-man talk. He asked him when his stuff would be arriving from abroad. Brother Julius responded that the shipping company said the goods may have been missing on the high seas or that the ship lost its route due to high winds but would be arriving at the ports soon.

What about getting a job? he was asked.

He said by the nature of what he studied he was more comfortable setting up a consultancy firm.

And what exactly had he studied that had no name or that was only mentioned in vague terms?

He was an expert in the area of international criminology.

Had he considered joining the state secret police? Force CID at police headquarters?

He was not in the same field as the secret police.

And then Grandpa, having circled the subject as much as he could, asked Brother Julius about what was bothering him most. It wasn't the issue of getting a job, that wasn't a problem at all. There was enough money in the house to feed generations to come. As Grandpa used to tell us, the difference between him and others was that he had planted a money tree in the Family House, which will continue to bear fruit into the future if not in perpetuity.

"People have been whispering about the company you keep. That all kinds of people come to the house. *Such and such* people. People they do not quite know how to describe. People that are neither birds that fly in the air nor four-legged animals that walk on land."

Brother Julius responded that he was a grown man and that he would keep the company of whoever he wanted.

Grandpa said he didn't have a problem with that, but it would be better if Brother Julius did what other grown men did, such as getting a good job and getting a car and driver and moving into their own flat, and if they wished, they could live the highlife lifestyle to the fullest by throwing a party every weekend or every day for that matter.

One of the surprising members of the *salon* was a married man named Seleto. He was a happy fellow, always smiling and buying people drinks in neighborhood bars. People wondered what he was doing with the *salon* crowd.

—He is probably there for the free drinks. He loves to drink with people—

—He can afford to buy his own drinks. He always offers to buy for people—

—He probably doesn't know what is going on there—

—Maybe they have initiated him, you can never be sure—

—You mean converted him?—

—It is like a club, when you join, then you become a member—

—I hear there are benefits of being a member. They say they can recognize themselves anywhere—

—They say a lot of important people are members and that they reward each other with jobs and contracts—

—I think Seleto and Julius were in high school together. He is just keeping the company of an old schoolmate—

One morning Seleto's wife ran into the Family House, screaming. She was dragging her husband with her. She screamed. She wailed. She cried. She cursed.

"What have you people done with my husband's manhood?"

"What did you use his manhood for?"

"Why have you people stolen the thing that makes him a man?"

"I warned him when he started coming to this house. I told him the house is evil. I told him that only bad stories ever came out of the house. I told him to start following other women, to get a girlfriend, but he would not listen. Was it the drinks in this house? My husband can buy his own drink and everyone knows that."

She started screaming one more time.

"Come outside, you, and give him back his thing." She was calling on Brother Julius.

"All the evil that you people have been doing in darkness I know it would come to light. Now it has come to light. Come and repair the damage you have done."

People had come out of their houses by this time and were looking at the house and listening to Seleto's wife.

—What did she say happened to her husband?—

—She said they took his manhood—

—How did they take it? Has it disappeared completely?—

—I do not know. Nobody has seen it—

—You remember a few years back there was the case of disappearing manhood—

—Oh yes I remember. We were warned to stop shaking other people's hands. First we were warned to stop shaking the hands of strangers and then later we were told to stop shaking the hands of anybody because it wasn't just strangers that were doing it—

Brother Julius came out and so did Grandpa. They were asking Seleto's wife to calm down and to stop screaming. They said that whatever the problem was, it could never be solved by screaming. They asked Seleto to say what happened, but Seleto pointed back at his wife.

"Since he began to come to this house to party every evening he has not been living with me as a husband should. He always complains that he is too tired or too drunk to do it. So this morning I got angry and threatened to leave him unless he agreed to do it with me only to discover that what made him a man is no longer there."

"Disappeared, how? How has it disappeared? Show us."

They looked around and drove the children away and asked Seleto to pull up his flowing djellaba.

Nobody was quite sure what they were going to see when he pulled it up. Was the place going to be flat or sealed off completely? How would he pee?

According to those who saw it, they said Seleto's manhood was still there but it had shrunk and was looking like it wanted to run back into wherever it originally emerged from.

—We thought you said it is gone but it is still there—they said to Seleto's wife.

"You look at it with your two eyes—does it look alive to you?"

—If it is dead, then you go wake it up. After all, you are his wife—

"It wasn't dead until he started coming here. That was when he stopped looking at me like a woman."

—You better leave if you do not want us to lock you up—she was told.


As we later heard, Grandpa called Brother Julius aside and asked him to go back overseas and promise never to come back, that he would have all his expenses taken care of. He agreed. He departed with none of the fanfare with which he had returned. He departed like a thief in the night.

Those who asked after him were told that he had been offered a job abroad because there was no company in the country that could retain the services of a specialist in international criminology like Brother Julius.

# BABY

Baby lived in the Family House. Though she was older than us, we all called her Baby. Baby was not really a name as such. It was more of a placeholder. A baby born in the father's absence, perhaps the father was on a journey, was called Baby until the father returned from his trip, and then there would be a ceremony when the baby was properly christened with a proper name.

Baby was often described as behaving like someone who fell off a moving train. We sometimes saw overloaded trains with passengers hanging on the door and windows and some who were squatting on the roof hurtled down the rail tracks on its way to the terminal. To imagine someone falling off this train and surviving it was difficult to do, but anyone who did must have had their brains pretty shook up.

There were many stories about Baby. It was said that the reason she was banned from going to the major department store was because she was in the habit of quarreling with the mannequins.

"Am I not greeting you?" she was said to have said to one, and hissed.

"At least, if you do not have the courtesy to greet, you should have the courtesy to respond to people's greetings."

And when there was still no response from the mannequin she had called to a passerby and complained.

"See this lady, she would not greet me and when I greeted her, would not respond," she complained.

All outlandish deeds were attributed to her. She was said to have nearly killed a little baby in her care who was running a fever. She had tried to force the baby into Grandpa's Frigidaire. When she was accosted she had responded that it was not her fault. She had been told that items went into the freezer hot and emerged cold.

We played pranks on her. At night we would call her and ask her to blow out the flashlight the way you would blow out a flame. She would blow at the flashlight furiously and we would laugh at her.

One of Grandpa's favorite sayings is that no person is completely useless in this life. So he put Baby to use and made her try her hand at many things. She was first in the machete shop selling stuff, but she could not tell the difference between large and small bills. She would give customers change that was more than the amount paid. It was noticed that whenever she was the one in the store the place filled up quickly because those customers she had given change or undersold items to would tell others, who in turn would tell others that Baby was the one selling. After that experience she was soon sent to hawk iced water in cellophane packs. Each was sold for one naira so nobody could cheat her. She was told not to sell to anybody who did not have the exact amount.

Baby hawked sachets of cold water on a construction site to workers building an overhead bridge. The workers were mostly from neighboring foreign countries. They loved Baby because they could grope her as much as they wanted without any objections from her. She laughed at every action. She would sell two dozen sachets during lunch break and go back to the store and bring back more. They all paid her. No one tried to cheat her. As long as she was willing to be groped they were all happy. There was one guy who didn't grope her. He would talk with her and was satisfied even if all she did was grin. His name was Asare. He was also from one of the neighboring countries. He was a bricklayer but worked with the construction company as a laborer because it paid more. He talked to her about missing his country. He talked to her about how people here were always in a hurry, unlike in his own country. One day he told her to come back to the construction site when everyone had left. He took her behind a concrete mixer, lifted her dress, and entered her. He was quickly done. He gave her money and told her to dump all the unsold water sachets into the lagoon. She complied.

Three months later Baby wouldn't eat. She grew pale. Someone heard her retching in the toilet. She cried. Grandpa asked her who was responsible for the pregnancy. She said it was *Akwanumadede*. *Akwanumadede* was a popular highlife song from one of the neighboring countries, and most of the construction workers from there were nicknamed *Akwanumadede* by their counterparts. She was asked to take them to the worksite. By the time they got to the construction site, the bridge was already completed and the workers had dispersed.

There was a childless rich trader who owned lots of stores close to Grandpa's store. The rich trader's name was Janet. She was a big distributor of smoked catfish, which she bought cheaply from the North, where they had it in abundance, and sold at a profit. She had her own house, a two-story building with the legend LET THEM SAY written on the entrance. She loved gold and had gold rings on every finger and a massive gold chain and pendant on her neck. People greeted her politely but talked behind her back.

—With no child of her own when she's gone, who will she leave all her wealth to?—

—Her womb produces money, not children—

—In life some people choose before they are born between wealth and children—

—And why does one need to choose when it is possible to be blessed with both—

—Her relatives will share all her stuff when she is gone. They will even sell that castle of peace mansion—

Nobody knows whose idea it was, but between both of them it was agreed that Janet should marry Baby. She would also become the father of the child that was in Baby's womb when the child was born. Baby would live with her and would meet as many men as she wanted to, but any child she had in the process would be Janet's child.

There was some talk that money had changed hands. There was talk of the unborn baby having a price tag, but since no one was there when Janet and Grandpa met, these were mere rumors.

Though they were both women and this was said not to be a common practice, it was known to happen. Though we were not told this, a woman could marry another woman. Baby would live under Janet's roof and cook and wash and take care of Janet as a wife would. Baby was free to pick any man she wanted. The baby born out of such a relationship would belong to Janet. It was going to be a big event. Janet was the husband to be and was going to pay for food, music, and drinks.

On the street people whispered about the strange wedding of Baby to another woman.

—It has never happened before for a woman to marry another, some said. The world is coming to an end, strange things are happening—

—Surely, the world is coming to an end—

—Oh it has. It used to be quite commonplace but that was in the olden days—

—They are doing this to her because she behaves like someone that fell off the train. This is what they usually do with people like her—

—So much evil goes on in that house—

—I think they are helping her, otherwise who else is going to marry her—

Baby began to be treated with a lot of generosity and kindness. People in the house were warned to stop addressing her as Baby and start calling her by her new name, Patience. How the name was arrived at, nobody knew. It was not a baptismal name, but all agreed that patience was a virtue and that Baby had lots of it and would need tons of patience in her new role. She was given the choicest portions of food. She got some new nice clothes. She was encouraged to take a walk around the neighborhood to show off her new clothes and her new look. As she walked around on her stroll people congratulated her on her forthcoming wedding. Her response to every comment was a sheepish smile. Behind her back people whispered.

—If they had a chance in that house, they would turn human beings into goats just so they can sell them off for profit—

—That is the kind of house that sold people into slavery in days gone by—

—What do you mean in days gone by? How is what they are doing these days different from slavery?—

—She is even lucky. She may likely have an easier life with Janet than she has had in that evil house—

—So she is to have no choice; any man that comes she opens her legs—

—Not really. Some choose to settle for one man, have all their children through the one man so the children don't look too different from each other—

—That Baby that laughs at everything. She is never going to be able to choose. She'll accept whatever is thrown at her—

The event was planned to be grand. Baby was taken to the market to shop for new clothes. She was taken to have her hair braided in a beautiful style. She was encouraged to invite her friends, but alas poor Baby had no friends. It was the first time that the whole street was invited to a party in the Family House. Janet invited her fellow traders. It was assumed by some of them that a relative of hers was getting married.

It was during the dry season and everywhere was hot. Sheds were built. Big red-and-blue metal drums were filled with cold water, and drinks were packed into the water to keep them cool. Women were hired to fry beef and cook *jollof* rice and *moin-moin*.

—Not even for a proper marriage between man and woman have I seen such preparation—

—So much food being cooked, so many drinks being cooled—

—I heard they slaughtered two cows and countless chickens—

—I don't blame the woman, though. It is a terrible thing to come to this world and leave empty-handed with no one to answer your name when you are gone—

—But what about the poor girl? It is almost as if they are selling her off—

—It is not just her they are selling off, they are selling off the unborn baby as well—

—Well, as for me, I have never been known to reject free food—

—Me neither, not when they have free drinks thrown in as well—

—Be very careful what you eat in that house—

—Why, it is food cooked for the public? Don't tell me you think they'll poison everybody?—

—There are things worse than poison. And poison may be even better, because it kills you and that is the end—

—So what is worse than poison, eh, tell me?—

—What if after eating you turn to *mumu*, a doddering fool?—

—*Mumu* for what? For eating *jollof* and chicken?—

—Why do you think they are able to keep all the people who work for them acting like *mumu*?—

—Ah, one has to be careful, I tell you—

—Once it has gone into the mouth and the stomach, it is not coming out again and the damage is already done—

—I don't think they are that totally gone to try to turn all the invited guests to *mumu*—

—I think at worst you can call it appeasement. They are using the food as *sara*—

—Which wouldn't be a bad thing. They need forgiveness for all they have done—

There was not much to the ceremony. The only major thing done was that drink was poured into a glass cup. Baby was expected to look around at the invited guests and give the drink to her husband. She had been warned ahead of time not to embarrass the guests by giving the drink to Janet. She knelt down and gave the drink to a young man seated next to Janet who was also dressed in white. The young man took a sip and handed the glass back to her and she drank. A large box was handed to Grandpa's representatives. Some said it was filled with money, some said gifts. That was the end of the ceremony, now guests could go outside to eat and drink their fill. When Baby said she had a headache and was going inside to rest, people said it was not surprising. Her new hairstyle must have given her a headache. She should wash her face with cold water and rest for a while.

People ate and drank and some even took some food home in plastic bags. Many who attended invited those they met on the way.

—They are still serving food. No discrimination, everyone who shows up gets served—

The plan was that on the next day, Baby would be taken to her new husband's house. This would be done quietly and not with the usual fanfare that would accompany someone moving into a man's house. This would have required singing and dancing and another round of feasting.

Everyone on the street woke up to hear that Baby was gone. The bride had disappeared. She left. Who had seen her?

Apparently at some point that night Baby had disappeared from the Family House without taking anything with her. She had left no trace or clues behind. She had confided in no one. This was strange, that she had planned and executed her escape. Even though she was considered to be feeble-brained by all, it was a surprise. Coupled with the fact that the walls in the Family House were known by all to have cavernous ears.

—That boy from the neighboring country who owns the pregnancy must have come for her—

—And you won't believe this but she was all smiles yesterday, nobody knew what she was planning—

—Is there a time that she doesn't smile?—

—She must have decided not to exchange a harsh master for a harsh madam—

—Who knows? It may all be their plan. You know how they are in that house—

—So what is going to happen to all the money the woman spent on the ceremony?—

—What about the gifts and the box filled with money that she gave to them?—

—What about the things you can't see, like the shame she is going to suffer at the hands of her fellow traders?—

—Some people are destined not to have children. That is her destiny. She cannot wash it away no matter how much she tries—

—It is not an easy destiny to live with—

—Is this not the reason why it is called destiny? Good or bad, you have to accept it because destiny can never be changed—

—One thing I know was that the food was great and nobody is going to ask me to return what has already settled finely in my stomach—

—Mine has already been converted to proteins and vitamins in my body—

—As for me, all I can say is it serves them right. What kind of abomination is that? A woman being given in marriage to another woman—

It would be assumed that this would be the last we'd hear about Baby but it wasn't. Baby came back one day a few months later. Her skin scratched and with scabs in places. Her hair matted. Those who first saw her said she looked like a madwoman. Some said she looked like someone who had returned from the dead. And the story she told was that she had indeed come back from the dead.

Baby said that on the night of her wedding ceremony she had gone to the bathroom in order to wash her face to see if her headache would ease but discovered the bathroom was occupied, so she decided to take a bowl of water and go wash her face in the backyard. She said she scooped the water with her hands and was about to splash some on her face when she felt a hand tap her on the shoulder and a voice said *follow me*. This was the last thing she recalled. She said the next place she found herself was in a mud hut deep in the forest along with some other men and women. As she came to in the hut, a tall, dark giant handed her a piece of red cotton cloth and told her to undress and tie the cloth around her chest. The people around her were cowering, very scared, some were sweating, a few were muttering prayers or incantations, but she couldn't be sure. She heard someone say that they had been kidnapped and that they were going to be used for money rituals by having their heads cut off and their eyes gouged out and their breasts cut off. It was dark, they were all standing, at intervals the door of the hut would burst open and the giant with the lantern would come and grab someone and take them outside, never to return. And so Baby slept standing, waiting for them to come and grab her. Her headache was completely forgotten.

The next night the giant came for Baby. She had been given nothing to eat since her capture but she didn't feel hungry. They took her to another hut. There was a giant carved pot-bellied statue covered with blood. There was a juju priest with a fly whisk. He touched Baby's head with the whisk. Baby shuddered more out of the fact that the whisk felt ticklish. He touched her breasts; he touched her belly and jumped back.

"Why did you bring this one to me? Can't you see she is already with child? And besides she is incomplete. She is not a complete human being. Take her away from here and get me a complete human being."

Baby was taken away. When she got back to the hut, those who were standing in the hut touched her and asked her, What happened? How come you came back? Why did they bring you back? And they shrank back as they asked her these questions because none who left had ever returned.

She did not know how long she stayed in that hut. She couldn't quite recall if she ate or drank. All she remembered was that one day they released her. She was taken a ways from the hut by the giant and after walking some distance in the forest was given a shove on the head and told to move along and not to look back and never to come back.

She said she wandered in the forest for a long time. When asked how long she wandered in the forest she would say for a long time. Numbers had never been her strong suit. Eventually she ran into a hunter who asked her what she was searching for so deep in the forest and she responded that she was lost. When asked where she came from, she responded that she lived in the Family House. The hunter said he knew where the Family House was and brought her back home. She was asked where the hunter was so that he could be thanked for saving her life but she said the hunter had simply dropped her off and left.

—Have you heard the story the bride who scampered on her wedding night is telling?—

—She says she was captured and kidnapped by ritual killers but had managed to escape. She told another person that the ritual killers let her go because only people who had all their faculties intact could be used for rituals. She was rejected by the gods—

—She had to come up with a story that would be more fantastic than a woman marrying another woman—

—She sometimes acts as if she is not *complete, not all there*, she is not the type that would make up stories—

—Why, but she was smart enough to escape on the night of her marriage—

—Don't be fooled, I know her type. She at least knows where to put it when she is doing the thing with a man, or does she put it in her nose?—

—We have heard of some people putting it in places more peculiar than the ears. And in that house too—

When Baby was asked what happened to the baby in her womb she said she didn't know. At what point did she notice the pregnancy was no longer there? she was asked.

"One day the pregnancy was there and then the next day I looked at my belly and the pregnancy was no longer there."

Baby had gone back to being her old inarticulate self, who talked like someone who fell off the train.

There was talk of meeting with Janet and returning her gifts and money to her, but Janet sent word that they could keep it. She said she was happy that the marriage hadn't worked out and that she was sure Baby would have given birth to children that were not complete human beings, since she was not a complete human being herself.

# OLUKA

O f all the things that were said about the house, this was the one thing that was considered the factor that led to its fall—the death of a child. No one could say for sure that they saw it happen but it was like the smoke before the fire. As the saying goes—the owl cried last night and the child died in the morning, who can deny that the owl had a hand in the child's demise?

Quite a few people are of the view that this was the worst thing that had ever happened not only on the street or in the country, but the worst thing that had ever happened anywhere since the world was created, in fact in the history of mankind on this good earth.

Uncle Oluka was one of Grandpa's older sons. He was quite successful and had his hand in many businesses, including a block-making factory. He was married to a very beautiful lady we all called Miss because she was a school-teacher by profession. Miss did not have a child. When we were brought to the Family House over the long summer holidays, Uncle Oluka and Miss would come around too, but since they had no children of their own to leave behind in the Family House, a certain silence and quietness seemed to follow them around. Yet Miss was very generous and loved children. She always had a gift for all the kids in the house, a piece of candy here, a coloring book there, a stick of red chalk. What I remember most about her was that she left a faint trace of her cologne on everything she touched. Her cologne smelled like carnations.

Still there were those who did not want to see any good-ness in her kindness. They said spiteful things behind her back and even within her earshot.

—How can two men be living in the same house? A woman that cannot bear children is no better than a barren fruit tree. What do you do to a barren fruit tree? You cut it down with an ax and use its wood for firewood—

—Why is the man struggling to acquire all that wealth? Who is he going to leave it to when he dies? Why work so hard when you have no heir to inherit all the wealth you'll leave behind you when you die—

—You know what they do in my place to such women? They send them packing; they throw their stuff outside the house and sweep away their footprints with a broom so that they can take their aridness along with them—

—Don't forget she is someone's daughter? It is not her fault—

—Are we not saying the same thing? She is someone's daughter; that is the main reason we are asking that she in turn should be someone's mother. The same way her mother gave birth to her is the same way she should give birth to someone too—

—But that is not even the worst thing about this whole shameful story. The most shameful part of it is that she has never had a miscarriage, not even one, so we can say she tried but it is not her fault or that she is going to have another one—

—And the poor husband always makes his own clothes from the same fabric as his wife. Is it "and co" they call it, or is it "me and my wife," I have forgotten the name—

—Ah, you people, God will judge you people one day—

And then Miss became pregnant. For a long time she had not been to the Family House, and when she turned up, she was many months gone and her belly was protruding heavily.

Soon, the story was all over the street and the same tongues who had excoriated her could not say enough good things about her patience and how her pregnancy was a testimony to God's everlasting faithfulness and mercy and kindness.

—God is not sleeping—

—It would have been a grave injustice on the part of nature for them not to have children. Such a beautiful couple. They are made to produce beautiful children—

—She loves children too. She always distributes sweets and biscuits to all the children on the street. You know

God listens to the unspoken prayers of children because they are so innocent—

—Not only that, unborn children select kind couples to have as parents. Children oftentimes choose the homes they want to be born into—

—But you have to give it to the husband too. He is a real upright guy. All these years he withstood the pressure to marry a second wife, not once did he consider throwing her out of the house. People talked a lot and called her all sorts of names—

—It is the way of the world. No matter what you do, people must talk. Have lots of children, they'll say uncountable children, uncountable troubles. Have none, they'll say you are selfish. No matter what you do, people must talk; it is the way of the world—

And then Miss had the baby, a boy. At birth the baby would not cry. The midwife was confused for a moment, and then she lifted the child up high with one hand and spanked the newborn baby's pink bottom, which was still smeared with blood, three times in quick succession. It was only then the baby sputtered a weak cough and then whimpered feebly.

"All babies cry when they are born because they are leaving their more peaceful world into this our chaotic and wicked world of ours," the midwife said.

Miss was weak and tired and was happy that the baby had come out at last after a long and painful labor. She was not bothered by the baby's not crying. All she wanted was to rest and for people to hear that she had given birth to a child.

"Well, if you don't want to cry, you can at least laugh," the midwife said, and began to tickle the baby. The baby made no movement but shut his eyes even tighter.

Almost everything was hard for the baby to do. He found it difficult to suck, difficult to fasten his slack lips around the mother's nipple. Difficulty with stooling and even when he managed to stool, it came out in little pellets like goat shit. He would not drink water. He would not sleep at night. Initially it was speculated he was still living in womb time and had yet to adjust to earth time. He did not open his eyes, and when he eventually did, would look at neither his mother nor any person but had his eyes focused on the ceiling.

"Every child is different," the midwife said. "Some come into the world on their head, some enter with both feet, and some even want to arrive this world sideways, with their bodies aslant in their mothers' womb. Some cry a lot, some play a lot, some neither cry much nor play much and grow up to be thinkers. I suspect your son is going to be a thinker one day."

And then the child began to cry. As soon as he discovered the joy of crying he took to it like a champion. Not only did he cry, but he seemed to relish it and would stretch taut both feet and both hands as he cried. He cried when he was being given a bath, he cried when he was feeding, he cried when he was held, and cried when he was put in bed. Even when he slept, he slept fitfully and would sniffle and smother a cry even in his sleep.

Miss was unhappy and her eyes rimmed red from lack of sleep and worry, but her husband had never been happier.

"Remember what someone once said to me? You have been married now for many years and we have not even once heard the cry of a baby from your house. I am happy because the cry of a baby can now be heard from my house at all times," he said.

But soon he too began to worry. Eating was difficult for the baby and so was keeping down his food. When they tried to make the baby burp, he simply vomited up everything he had been fed.

The child was named Amaechi—who knows what the future holds.

And as it turned out, one never knew with Amaechi.

He could not sit, he could not stand, and he could not lie on his belly or lie on his back. He had no food preferences, he loved neither water nor breast milk or powdered milk. He slept in the daytime albeit fitfully and cried through the night.

Uncle Oluka began what would turn out to be an almost endless consultation with doctors to find out what was wrong with Amaechi. They did scans and X-rays and tested his urine, his poop, his saliva, and even his sweat but found nothing wrong with him.

They consulted a native doctor. The native doctor told them to bring a white ram and a black ram, a white cock and a black hen, they did.

The native doctor took the child from the mother and tickled him, the child did not smile or show any sign of being tickled, the native doctor turned the child over and spanked him lightly on the buttocks, the child did not scream but whimpered lightly.

"This one does not want to be here. This one is not meant for this earth. He was forced to come here and wants to return from where he came. His days here won't be long, you'll see."

They took Amaechi to a priest of a white garment church, Baba Aladura. The priest closed his eyes.

The priest hummed a tuneless song.

The priest spun around on both legs like a dervish,

The priest shook and shivered like one with a fever.

The priest began to sweat and wipe fat drops of sweat off his brow.

Finally, the priest spoke in a whistling singsong voice that sounded like a whisper.

"It is not good to force the hand of God. There is a difference between God's will and the perfect will of God. When a beggar asks you for alms and you are reluctant to give, you give the beggar your alms in the worst possible way. When you force the hand of God, he gives you, but not a perfect gift. We shall bathe this one for seven days and seven nights in the Atlantic Ocean."

It was done.

Nothing changed.

Amaechi was taken to the university hospital. They ran tests. They X-rayed his bones. They took urine samples. They took stool samples. They found nothing.

No one quite remembers who it was that said it to the couple or if the couple came to this decision themselves. The voice said to them—*Kill this child before this child kills you.* Amaechi was brought to the Family House and it was done.

How was the child killed?

Was a pillow placed on his face and used to suffocate him?

Was the child placed facedown in a basin of water and drowned?

Was the child physically strangled with bare hands?

No one knows for sure except the person who did it. The only thing the relieved parents were told was that the child died without putting up a struggle. He did not struggle one bit. He was happy to go.

People said that the couple should adopt a child after their ordeal with Amaechi, but others countered that an adopted child would never be considered a full member of the family. The couple did not listen to anyone. First their visits to the Family House became few and far between, then they finally stopped coming.

# GABRIEL

Gabriel was considered the unluckiest person on earth. After his string of misfortunes his relations told him to come and live in the Family House, perhaps his luck would change if he lived under a lucky roof. Gabriel started out as a farmer. He planted yams and a few other crops. He wanted to be a rich man. He said his ambition was to own a house with twenty-four rooms. He didn't prosper as a farmer of yams. His yam harvest was usually poor. One year his harvest was good and he built a barn for his yams. He was proud of his yams. He boasted he would sell them and start work on his twenty-four-room house. That year there was a mysterious fire. Gabriel's barn caught fire and most of the yams got burned. He invited people to come with palm oil stew to the farm and eat free roasted yam. How much roasted yam could people eat?

The next year Gabriel planted tomatoes. He had gone to a nearby village to learn how to grow tomatoes. He said he was going to buy a pickup truck from the proceeds of his first tomatoes when he sold his first harvest. He said he would supply a manufacturing company the fresh tomatoes they needed for the manufacturing of their tomato puree. After he had planted the tomatoes, just before they would start ripening, a strange worm attacked the tomatoes. They shrank, they changed color, and they rotted and began to stink. That was how Gabriel's tomato-planting adventure ended.

Gabriel decided to move in a totally new direction and went into the lumber business. Lots of people in the business were switching from handheld saws to motor saws. With the handheld saw, cutting down a tree was a lot of work. First the men had to dig a long trench into which the tree would hopefully fall, and then two men clad only in underwear would hold the saw from two ends and start sawing away. It took weeks for the tree to fall, though they lucked out sometimes when the tree was only half-cut and then there was a storm.

Now someone had invented a motor saw that could fell trees within minutes and actually cut them up into manageable flat small parts. The popular brand was Dolmar. Gabriel's plan was to get a loan from the cooperative society and buy one of the new machines and then hire a sawyer to operate the machine. He would transport the timber to the big city and sell it off there. He got the loan from the cooperative society and bought the motor saw. He called friends to celebrate the purchase of the motor saw. He boasted that he was soon going to become a millionaire. He said this motor saw was going to be the first of many more to come. That although this was his first, he would soon buy more. He also said he was going to buy a lorry with an iron body that would be transporting the logs to the big city for him and then he said that there was nothing stopping him from having his own timber shed in the big city. He said he could even start exporting his product to America, where he heard that even the rich built their houses with wood.

The man whom Gabriel hired to operate the new chain saw was nicknamed Sawyer; no one recalled what his real name was anymore. He was dark, a bit squat, and had really big muscular arms. He was adept at using the handsaw and would sing as he sawed, sweating heavily and ignoring the midges and tsetse flies that sucked away on his sweat and blood. He had not been trained to use a chain saw but said he would read the manual overnight. He did read the manual and used the saw to cut off a small tree to the admiration of onlookers. Some noticed that his hands shook and that the powerful machine seemed to want to jump off his hands but he gripped it firmly. He was a strong man.

That night Gabriel threw a party. He invited people to come and eat and drink. He bought the drinks with the remainder of the money that he had borrowed from the cooperative society. He was in a boastful mood. He said that this was just the beginning of great strides in business and once again drew a map of some of the things he planned to do and how he was going to expand his business and export timber to

America. People drank and danced, including Sawyer. A few whispered that they hoped Gabriel's luck would change, because behind his back Gabriel was nicknamed the man with the shit touch—everything he touched turned to shit.

Sawyer set out early for the forest with an assistant and the chain saw on his shoulders. The assistant carried a half gallon of gasoline. They first cleared around the tree with a machete, then Sawyer started the chain saw. It jumped into life and this startled Sawyer but he held the engine firmly in both hands and began to cut into the huge *iroko* tree. The trouble with the new machine was that it cut so far into the trunk quickly and he could not quite gauge the direction in which the tree was leaning. He cut and jumped back, and shielded his eyes from the sun's glare as he looked to see the direction in which the tree was tilting but he was not successful. Although it was only midday, Sawyer told his assistant that they should go home. He hoped that there could be an overnight storm that would help fell the tree.

When Sawyer came back so early, even without asking him, Gabriel was already boasting to people that the new saw could fell a dozen trees in a day. Sawyer explained to him that he decided to come back early so he could consult the manual but that he was sure the next day he would have mastered the saw.

Early the next day, Sawyer's assistant was screaming and panting as he ran into the community. He had apparently run all the way from the forest, where they were felling the timber.

"Sawyer, the tree fell on him. He is under the tree. Him and motor saw."

—Who is asking you about motor saw? Is his waist broken? Or his legs? Or his hands?—

"All of him is underneath the felled tree."

—Oh, no, was he screaming when you were coming?—

"I could not see him. He was under the fallen tree. I could not help."

The men gathered themselves together, including Gabriel. It took a lot of effort to roll the fallen tree aside. The Sawyer was dead and buried forcefully into the soft earth. The motor saw was smashed to smithereens, with pieces scattered all over. Even the rock-hard white end of the spark plug was ground up finely.

The sawyer's family came for their son's body. They also came with a long list of things Gabriel should buy before they could bury their son. A white cow, seven black chickens, seven white chickens, seven yards of Hollandaise Dutch wax cloth, kola nuts, six bottles of aromatic schnapps, a bag of rice, and the money to marry a bride for their dead son who had never married. If all of these were not purchased, their son would not be buried, but even if he was buried his spirit would not be at rest and would haunt Gabriel and pull him into the neither-living-nor-dead world, where the spirit was now wandering.

Gabriel borrowed more money, some of his relatives contributed, they pleaded with the sawyer's family to tamp down their demand. Finally, the family agreed. They reduced their demand. Instead of aromatic schnapps they accepted a bottle of local gin *ogogoro*. The sawyer was buried.

Gabriel did not rest, he was soon embarking on another business venture. He had met a man called Adamu who was a cocoa buyer. Adamu supplied dried cocoa to the manufacturers of cocoa drinks and chocolate makers. So he claimed. He appointed Gabriel his buyer. Gabriel's job was to buy from the local farmers on Adamu's behalf and Adamu would pay Gabriel a commission. Adamu drove a big Honda 175 motorcycle.

—Won't he give up? Is it not apparent to him that wealth is not in the stars for him?—

—Why does he keep struggling, you cannot change destiny—

—Some people never learn, if he had been left alone and no one came to his help the other time with the sawyer case, he probably would be dead by now—

—I don't blame him, life is a struggle. The day you give up struggling is the day you die—

—If I were him I'd stop and ask myself why I am the only one who never finds success—

—He boasts too much, that is his problem. He was already boasting of how he would build a three-story house even before the first tree was felled by the motor saw—

—It is not good to boast, sometimes one's boasting falls into the wrong ears—

Gabriel was given a bicycle by Adamu. It was not free. It was on loan, and the full cost was going to be deducted from Gabriel's commission. Gabriel was proud of his new bicycle and the smell of the woven bags with which he was to collect the cocoa. Even when he fell from the bicycle he boasted that it was better to fall from a bicycle than to fall while walking on foot. A younger cousin of Gabriel's had the job of driving away greedy goats from the cocoa spread out to dry properly while his friends played soccer.

Adamu soon came and picked up the bags of cocoa collected from different individuals by Gabriel. When Gabriel asked for payment, Adamu said to him not to worry. He would sell to the companies that buy the cocoa and then he would come back to pay. That was the last that was heard from Adamu. Even the bicycle, Gabriel soon discovered, had been bought on credit and was soon repossessed by the seller. Creditors flocked to Gabriel's house. They wanted their money back. Even those from the cooperative threatened to send him to prison.

—Why doesn't he go and try his luck somewhere else?—

—Can't he see that as long as he remains here he will never make any progress in life?—

—The forces holding him down are more than the eyes can see—

—He will just kill himself or be killed by those dragging him over money owed—

—His best bet would be to move to the house of his distant relation—

—You mean the man who owns the Family House?—

—Yes, his luck would definitely change there—

—If you live under the roof of a lucky man and his shadow falls over you, that may erase all the years of bad luck—

—To tell you how lucky the owner of the Family House is, everything that is planted around the house multiplies and bears so much fruit that the fruits weigh down the trees. Even the chickens and dogs and cats in that house multiply. Everything they sell, even water, sells out fast. It is a lucky house—

—The story I heard is different. They say he takes the luck of all those living under his roof—

—What I heard is that he uses their life to extend his own life—

—Gabriel is better off anywhere but here at any rate, his creditors will drag him to an early grave—

One morning Gabriel arrived at the Family House, presumably leaving his bad luck behind and hoping to start afresh.

He was soon going to the shop to help sell. He offloaded machetes from the truck. He helped wrap them in cement paper. He helped arrange them according to their different designs, sizes, and shapes. He was learning. He was happy. He was already thinking of how one day he would own his own store. He was thinking of how he would have a machete-loaning scheme for farmers who would then give him half of the harvest at the end of the year.

One day Gabriel was walking back to the Family House when he saw something a dull golden color on the ground. He picked it up. It was an empty bullet shell. He put it in his pocket and continued walking home. When he was lying down in his corner at night he brought it out of his pocket and began to polish it with a piece of soft cotton cloth. As he continued to polish it the color began to change, it was now glowing. This became his pastime every time he was in bed. He loved the way it felt in his hand. He loved the way it responded to the cotton cloth. He would put it in his pocket all day and would only bring it out when he was lying in bed.

Gabriel was on his way back to the Family House when he heard running footsteps approaching. People were shoving him out of the way. Some people fell, stood up, and continued to run. Some lost their balance but regained it and continued to run. Gabriel did not see any reason to run. He was as a matter of fact fascinated. There was always one spectacle or another in the city. This was going to give him something to reflect on and chuckle about when he lay down later that night, polishing his toy.

"Hey you, don't move. Don't move one inch," a voice commanded.

Gabriel could not imagine that these words were meant for him. He continued to watch people who were fleeing. They now seemed far away. They were no longer running. They looked like small objects in the distance, but he could see them looking back nervously.

Two strong arms gripped him. He was startled. He turned around. They were armed policemen. They were chasing a thief or a robber, it was not clear but they were after someone. Now they had him.

Gabriel did not return home. Nobody knew where he was. He was arrested and searched. The shiny empty bullet casing was found in his pocket. There was no need to ask him any further questions. He was taken straight to prison.

By the time he was eventually released he had lost a lot of weight. He was told to remain in the Family House and see a doctor but he refused. He preferred to return to the village.

People in the Family House said his case was like that of the man who was visited by death. Death showed him a list of names, your name is top of my list I must kill you today. Unknown to death, this man made the best-tasting yam pottage. Don't kill me until you have tasted my pottage, the man pleaded. Death agreed. After all, Death reasoned, I will still kill him today whether on an empty stomach or on a full belly and why not do it on a full belly. The man went and prepared the most delicious yam pottage for Death. Even the aroma made Death's mouth water. The man served Death the yam pottage in beautiful dinnerware. Death was taken aback by the man's act of hospitality, nowhere had he been this welcome or well received. Death enjoyed the food so much that after eating, Death decided to take a nap. As soon as Death began to snore, the man went to Death's list and moved his name from the top of the list to the bottom. Death soon woke up, stretched, and decided that he was going to do the man a favor and repay the kind host for the hospitality. Death decided that instead of starting from the top of the list, he would start at the bottom.

Until this day people still say that if living in the Family House could not cure Gabriel of his bad luck, nothing on earth could.

# CURRENCY

Uncle Currency, according to what we heard, had the best job in the world—his job was burning money. His job was to throw bundles of old, torn, discontinued currency notes into a huge furnace. He spent money the way others drank water. People said, how do you expect him to treat money with any respect, when he burned money every day? We heard that he entered his workplace wearing only his underwear and emerged wearing the same so that he would not have the opportunity of pocketing some of the money headed to the incinerator. But he was soon bringing bundles of currency into the Family House. How did he do it?

The bundles of currency were not new, in fact some did look tattered and torn, but money was money, and they could be Scotch-taped and repaired. Some looked moldy and even smelled, but it was the smell of money and you could always give them a bath. It was from him that we first saw money being given a bath. He would fill a large basin with clean water. Powdered detergent was poured into the water and the old currency was poured into the soapy water and stirred around gently. The water was poured away and then the currency was rinsed. The money was taken indoors and placed on an ironing board, and white paper placed between the board and the money and then the currency was ironed. It emerged crisp and ready to be spent.

Currency was said to be a model worker, or so we heard initially. He always had a stack of shiny coins on the table in his room. Things began to change when he started coming back to the Family House with a large bag that looked like a postman's carrier bag.

Initially he would go to work in the mornings and come back later in the evening, but soon we were told that he was now working what was referred to in quiet tones as *permanent night duty*.

We were expected to tiptoe around his room when we were passing by it because he was on permanent night. Either he had just come back from work and was tired and sleeping or he was sleeping before he left for work.

We would later hear that it was during night duty that Currency and his colleagues and the policemen and soldiers who were the security guards at the mint came together and held a meeting.

—How can we be burning money when it is what we work for?—

—We don't even have enough of it and we are burning it—

—But we must show that we are doing our work—

—We can burn something, it doesn't have to be money—

—We can burn newspapers and other forms of paper—

—How do we do this without anybody finding out?—

—We are all in this together and, come to think of it, we are not doing anything wrong, we are merely helping—

—I agree we are helping; it is like eating food that is going to be thrown away regardless—

Soon we heard in the Family House that there was an underground building being constructed outback. Everyone referred to it as underground until the bricklayer, a man nick-named Puei who always had a menthol cigarette burning on his dark lips, told us it wasn't an underground building but a basement. It was in this new basement that Currency was piling up the money he was bringing in from work. Initially he and his colleagues had been operating on the principle that if they stole too much the owner would notice, so they burned half of the money and kept half, but soon enough they were not even burning any at all. They were now burning ordinary paper and taking all the money for themselves.

Evidence of the money coming into the house was every-where. The house was repainted in white and there was even a suggestion that it should now be called the Whitehouse, but someone mentioned that another Whitehouse was already in existence in a far-off country. A new borehole was dug and a water pumping machine installed. New electrical fixtures were installed. New carpets were laid. Even the old wire mosquito nettings on the windows that had turned tobacco brown from dust exposure were replaced. And of course these changes did not go unnoticed.

—Have you heard the latest? The son is bringing money to the house in bags—

—Money in bags? That must be juju money. Only the banks have enough money to carry in bags—

—He works at the security mint where they print money—

—I know someone else who works there, it doesn't mean they can take the money as they please—

—He works in the incinerator. He works at the place where they burn the money—

—Ah, so it is money that should be burned that he is bringing home—

—That is a big one, but how does he do it?—

—He is not alone. They have people at the top—

—I don't blame them, though, why burn money. This money that is so scarce that we poor people never have enough—

—If you ask me, I think they should find a new way of disposing of the money. Why burn it? Why not just give it to the poor?—

Soon rumors began to circulate about money that should be burned finding its way back into circulation. Someone later attributed the leak to one of the people in the team who had bought a used car and had a sign boldly painted on the back windscreen that proclaimed: MONEY HAS NO MASTER. Others said it was because of the lavish lifestyle of some of those in the team. When confronted, a certain one among them had said that money was like smoke—it could not be hidden.

One night Uncle Currency and his colleagues were arrested while on night duty. They were caught red-handed stuffing bales of cement paper into the furnace while another member of their team stuffed old currency into a van. They were first taken to the office of head of security for questioning.

"Tell me everything and we'll make it easy for you," the head of security said to the men in the team, who were all wearing only white briefs, as they were all expected to not wear anything with pockets while working.

"Tell me, how long has this been going on?"

The men were silent. They had all agreed that if and when this day eventually came, they were all going to swallow their tongues and not utter a word.

"Keeping silent will not help you. We just need to be sure the money has not fallen into the wrong hands."

Still the men were silent.

"You know every piece of currency has a number. This means we can trace the money, and anybody caught spending it will be arrested. We do not number the money for nothing."

The men remained silent because deep down they knew the security manager was lying; they had spent some of the money and nobody had noticed any difference, the money had simply done what they were told money did best, which was to circulate—it had gone back into circulation.

The long and the short of it was that the case died. The men in the team were asked to resign. They were told never to say a word to anyone as to the reason why they lost their jobs. They were told to keep whatever it was they had stolen and to never step foot in the mint again, they should not even return to visit their former colleagues. Those who heard said that the men told the security supervisor that they would share their loot with him and he let them get off slightly. Others said that it was because the men in the team had enough money to consult the best native doctor and the best Aladura Prophets and this helped them to get away with their crime. Whatever it was, Uncle Currency was now without a job. He told those who would listen that he had amassed enough money to pay himself a pension even if he lived as long as Methuselah.

One morning we woke up and Uncle Currency's posters were on walls and electric poles and on trees and empty drums and on house gates and on corner shops and roadside stalls. He was contesting for elections as a councilor. The man who was the present councilor had been a councilor for so long that many assumed that his name was councilor. He had never faced a challenger, and when he heard that Uncle Currency was contesting against him he sent emissaries to him to ask that Uncle Currency withdraw from the race.

"Wait until I die, I am not greedy. I am not the type that will say I want my son to be a councilor because I am councilor. You are still young. Wait until I pass away in office and then you can take over."

People on the street wondered why Uncle Currency was going into politics to contest as an ordinary councilor.

—Why doesn't he want to stay home and start enjoying his money?—

—Why does he want to waste his stolen wealth on politics?—

—He should go and contest for something bigger and leave the old councilor to continue—

—He is not happy that he is not in prison for theft—

—Why are you complaining, this is the only chance we have to get our hands on that money. Let him contest. At least he'll spend that money and some of it will get into our hands—

—Do you want to vote him in, the council doesn't have enough money for him to steal—

The councilor soon sent a delegation to Grandpa to tell Uncle Currency to forget about his ambition for now and wait for the councilor to serve out his term.

"He is not a child, he is a grown man. I cannot tell him what to do."

"You can at least advise him to wait his turn. I waited my turn. That is the way we met it, it is the better way."

"I think he has his mind made up. There is nothing I can do."

"At least you can help me inform him that a young man may have more clothes than an old man but he cannot have as many rags."

It was assumed that no one would be attracted to Currency's campaign, but they were wrong. Early the next morning women brought out large iron pots, bags of rice, vegetable oil, and tomatoes, and a cow was slaughtered. As the aroma of *jollof* rice rose into the air and spread into nostrils, people began to gather in front of the Family House. It was free food.

You need not bring anything but yourself. The food was free, served in a plate and a spoon provided. It was like a party. After the feasting people were told to spread the word, the slogan was OUT WITH THE OLD AND IN WITH THE NEW.

When the old councilor heard the slogan they said he cursed aloud, saying those who are singing *out with the old*, may they never grow old, may they never taste old age, may they perish young.

Soon, though, the slogan was in people's mouths, and was being shouted from street to street. It began to crop up in regular conversation between people. If a man bought a new shirt and his friend observed that he had a new shirt on he would tell his friend that we now live in an age of out with the old and in with the new. If a man had a new girl-friend, he would say that he was following the new slogan to get rid of the old and bring in the new.

The cooking and sharing of food continued. It was a party every day. In the morning people gathered and sat on iron chairs while waiting for the food to be ready. As soon as the food was ready there was no need to line up to be served; the food was brought to them right where they were sitting.

Three days before the election Uncle Currency disappeared. Better put, he vanished. People saw him in the morning going from door to door, then they didn't see him again. Kidnapping was out of the question, no one kidnapped a grown man in broad daylight.

Tata Mirror was consulted. She said all that her mirror showed to her was that he was going to return. People were sent out to search for him. The next day his posters were mysteriously pulled down from trees and electric poles and walls and iron gates. People who came for their free food were sent away. They were told to join the search party.

A delegation was sent to the old councilor to find out if he had anything to do with Currency's disappearance. His response was to raise his palms outward and upward. Everyone knows that I have always played politics with clean hands. I know nothing about this and I will be vindicated.

By the day of the election, Currency's candidacy was already forgotten in keeping with the saying that you cannot give a man a haircut in his absence. People went in and voted. They came out smiling and saying to no one in particular that it wasn't their fault that the other candidate decided to abscond, if perhaps he was around they would have voted for him because they had not forgotten the free food he gave to them.

Just before the election the old councilor came up with a new slogan—New Is Good but Experienced Is Better. When asked if he knew anything about his missing opponent, he gave the same response, showed his hands, spread them out, raised them heavenward, and answered—my hands are clean.

—We all know how he made his money—

—You cannot start with evil and end up with good—

—Like the old councilor said, life is turn by turn, you wait your turn in life—

—Good things come to those who wait—

—In our generation the saying was that the patient dog gets the bone but for this generation they believe the patient dog starves to death—

—At least he shared his money by giving food to the masses—

—What is food, you eat it today and you shit it out the next day. The old councilor brought pipe-borne water to our neighborhood—

—Sad, though, no one deserves that fate, better to be dead and buried than to disappear and give false hope—

And then one morning a few days after the election, Currency wandered back into the Family House. He looked like he had not slept or had a bath for days. He could not say a word. He simply stared at everyone. He couldn't respond to any questions.

He was given a bath, his clothes changed. He was given a haircut. The next morning he took up a position that he would occupy for the rest of his life. He pulled a wooden chair and sat on the balcony overlooking the street and began to count from one to five thousand, after which he would start from one . . . He would occasionally dip a finger on his tongue, as if to moisten the finger, then commence counting all over again.

When he was called inside to eat he would go in and eat. He spoke no words to anyone. He gave the impression of someone who did not understand words. But when he started his counting there was a serene, satisfied look on his face and he actually articulated the words out aloud. Because of this it was at least known that he still had the ability to speak. But for the numbers, he said no other words and made no other sounds. He showed no interest in the people around him.

People did talk about the man who sat on the balcony of the Family House counting numbers. Children on their way to school would watch him as his lips moved, wondering if the numbers coming out of his mouth were the same as the ones their teachers wrote on the blackboard in school.

—But this world is bad simply because he wanted to be a councilor, an ordinary councilor, look at the high price he had to pay—

—He should have just continued to enjoy his money and leave politics for those who know how to play it—

—How do you know it was the old councilor that did it to him?—

—That is true, I never heard anybody accuse the old councilor of being that evil—

—You know he got a lot of money when he worked at the place where they print money. They even had to build an underground house for the money—

—So what are you suggesting? You think they did this to him because of his money?—

—I am not saying anything, don't ask me questions to which I have no answers—

—There is nothing they will not do in that house for money—

—You should rephrase that to say: there is nothing they have not done in that house because of money—

And so Currency sat from day to day on that wooden chair on the balcony of the Family House counting away one . . . two . . . three . . .

# SOJA

We all called him Soja, a corruption of the word *soldier*. We heard that when Soja was much younger and only a member of the Boy Scouts he was already using his Boy Scouts uniform to intimidate bus conductors and avoid paying his bus fare. It was no surprise when he absconded from school in form two and took the train to the army depot up north to train as a soldier.

Later when he returned from training wearing his well-starched army uniform and gleaming black boots, he regaled listeners with stories of his time at the training camp. He said one of the duties of fresh recruits was to sweep the nearby military cemetery where all recruits who died in training and the soldiers who died in local and foreign wars were buried.

He said the sergeant-major who was their training instructor would bark at them to sweep the graves thoroughly. He told the fresh recruits that they'd be buried there sooner or later. Sooner if they died during their training or later if they died on the battlefront. You have sold your body and soul to the army and we can do with it what we like. Among other things, the sergeant-major told them that the first soldiers were bandits.

He made them stand on their heads for any infraction. Soja had a bump at the center of his head when he returned and he proudly showed this off. He said the weaker recruits had a small square piece cut from their foam mattresses that they slipped under their head when they were asked to stand on their heads.

He said time and again the sergeant-major asked them to repeat and chant the motto of the training camp. They all shouted—*There Is No Going Back*. Yes, there is no going back for you. If you die here we bury you here. If you run away, better kill yourself because if we catch you, we'll kill you. They frog-jumped them, they belly-crawled them through razor-sharp barbed-wire fence; they made them do push-ups until they felt they were doing push-ups even in their sleep.

They took them into the bush and made them practice shooting at one another with live bullets. The sergeant-major boasted that one trainee soldier died during training for each of the twelve years that he had been training army recruits. He said this was the thirteenth year, and because thirteen was an unlucky number he was hoping that at least two or more recruits would die in training instead of one.

Soja later said that his time at the training camp was the best time in his life. He said that what the country needed was a sergeant-major to drill all citizens every morning and everyone would fall in line and the country would be shipshape.

Soja was discharged from the camp with the rank of *korofo*. Meaning that he had no rope but he was a soldier and had his uniform, his beret, and his boots. What he told people when he came back from training was that every soldier was given a shot annually. It was this shot that made soldiers superhuman. He said that every soldier was given an ampoule of liquid bravery. That was what the shot was; it was pale, like the color of blood. He said after the shot the soldier had a mild fever and then woke up feeling as strong as stone.

Soja's first job was with the Environmental Task Force. Their job was to ensure that everywhere was clean. Streets swept, gutters and drains cleared, ensure there was no street trading. They patrolled streets and markets and roads and looked along the rail tracks for those who broke the law by selling their goods there. The task force was made up of soldiers, a few naval personnel, and an air force corporal. They drove around in a dark blue Toyota Hilux truck.

Initially people commended them for the good job they were doing. They made tenants and landlords sweep clean their gutters, cleared drains, and swept streets. They made street traders leave the streets, which helped the flow of traffic. They ensured that everyone stayed home and cleaned their homes on special days designated for cleaning and sanitation. But all these soon got old.

It was not long before Soja started bringing home baskets of produce, used coats and pants and dresses. The task force now carried out raids. They would swoop in on unsuspecting street traders, brandish their guns, chase them away with a *koboko*, and throw their goods into the Toyota Hilux truck. They would sometimes throw the traders in with the seized goods, drive with them a little ways, dispossess them of the money in their pocket, and then throw them out of the truck, meanwhile not returning the seized goods to them. Every day Soja brought different types of goods to the Family House. The edible things like chicken, tomatoes, pepper, and other foodstuffs were consumed in the house. The other items like clothes and sometimes electronic equipment were sold off. The traders would sometimes be made to buy back their own products. The task force was actually supposed to charge repeat offenders to the Environmental Tribunal set up for this purpose, but they didn't.

—What they are doing is worse than armed robbery—

—They are stealing with authority backing, it is pure authority stealing—

—Does it mean no one can stop them?—

—I thought the work of soldiers was to go to war and fight; now they are waging war against hardworking traders—

—This is their time *jare*, let them enjoy it. After all, life is turn by turn; it may be your turn tomorrow—

—It will never be my turn to steal—

—It is always from that house that all things both good and bad emerge—

—Can you imagine the poor traders being forced to pay twice for their own goods? They have to buy back their seized stuff—

—This is why the price of goods continues to go up, and they always go up and never come down—

—I hear the task force members gather to share money and goods like robbers after a successful robbery operation gathering to share their loot—

—People are now lobbying to join the task force but initially people called them glorified sanitary inspectors, ordinary *wole wole*—

—They have the support of the authorities who are higher up—

—They make returns to the big *Oga*'s every day—

—Ah, in spite of all the money they have in that house, they are still collecting from the sweat of the poor—

—Is that not what they specialize in? One day is one day, the monkey will visit the market one more time and will not make it back—

—Is it monkey that they say in the proverb or the baboon?—

—Monkey or baboon, what does it matter? It will for sure not return from the market—

People complained that before the government could ban street trading or clear the street of roadside traders they should provide shops and build more market stalls. Soja and his colleagues in the task force were no longer interested in charging those they arrested to the tribunal. In some cases they were not even interested in letting the trader pay a bribe to get their goods back. They were not interested because they were opening their own stores and selling all kinds of dry goods. When they seized or confiscated enough DVDs they opened a DVD store; if they seized enough children's wear they opened a shop to sell these. The fear of the task force was the beginning of wisdom. Traders in the major markets supported members of the task force. They said roadside and street traders ruined their business because they had no overheads and could therefore sell their stuff at a cheaper rate.

And then one day Soja fell sick. He could not empty his bowels for seven days. He was given lots of oranges and grapes to eat to *soften* his belly. At intervals he'd be led to the specially made toilet in the backyard and asked to try and push.

—Try. Try harder. Push as if you are having a baby—

"I am pushing," he would respond through clenched teeth.

Nothing happened. His eyes became muddy colored. He said he had no strength. He walked like a man with a heavy weight attached to his waist.

—We said it that one day the chicken would come home to roost—

—Look at him now is he not the one suffering—

—What punishment can be worse than not being able to pass stool?—

—It is the spirit of all the poor people they deprived of their means of livelihood that is now haunting them—

—Think of all the curses that were rained down on them when they confiscated innocent traders' goods—

—What made it worse was that they even began selling off the goods and opening their own stores—

—They must have offended someone whom they shouldn't have offended—

—That is true. There are people who must not be offended—

And then Soja began to use the toilet and could not stop going. He went so many times and had the urge to go so much that he sat on a wooden bench by the door of the toilet.

It would be assumed that Tata Mirror would have been able to find a cure for Soja's illness, but Tata said that if a person did you no harm and you decided to harm them, then if the victim in their anger decides to place a curse on you, no god or goddess will come to your aid. She said that Soja had offended a very old woman whose only means of livelihood was going to the bush market to buy tomatoes directly from farmers, which she later sold at a profit. She said that she sold tomatoes along the railway tracks because she was too poor to rent a stall in the market. She said that on the day Soja and the members of his task force had seized her tomatoes, she had begged them but they had refused, that what stung her was the fact that she had called Soja her son—help me, my son, she had cried, but Soja had pushed her away and actually whipped her with his *koboko*. As the members of the task force drove away with her basket of tomatoes, she wept. According to what Tata said, the woman had woken up at midnight and had taken off all her clothes and had placed a curse on Soja and his task force colleagues.

All through these events Soja's wife had decided to take him to a white garment church for healing. The members of the white garment churches wore no shoes because they believed that all the earth was a holy ground. They wore only white garments as a proclamation of their holiness. They drummed and danced and fell into trances and saw visions. They proclaimed all kinds of fast—white fasting in which they ate only white things like pap, milk, white bread; dry fasting, in which they ate nothing at all; and sweet fasting, when they ate only honey. They had special feast days, too, on which they killed rams and sheep and cooked *jollof* rice and drank warm soda. Soja's wife had benefited from his being a member of the task force. She used to be a trader herself and had actually had her goods seized, which was how she had met Soja and moved in with him. She had opened a small store where she sold some of the stuff that was gotten from the raids on traders.

—Did we not say it?—

—Are they not the ones running from herbalist to native doctor to white garment church now?—

—We said it then that they were stealing from the poor, hardworking traders who were only struggling for their daily bread—

—Even the special injection they give to soldiers could not save him from this illness—

—They said that for seven days he could not pass stool—

—And seven days later he started passing stool and could not stop—

—They should go and beg all those poor market women and men that they stole from—

—Even the wife has closed down her store—

—No more confiscated goods; what is she going to sell in the store—

—Was she not confiscated herself? How did they meet? She was one of the traders helping her mom, whose goods were confiscated. She was thrown into the task force truck. That was how she met him. She followed him back and began living with him—

—Their eyes have not started to see *pepper*. Very soon they'll be consulting *Alaafa*—

Soja had lost a lot of weight, and with his shaven head and his emaciated body in the flowing white garment he took to wearing, he looked like the angel of death. He was told to wear the white flowing soutane at all times because it would make his body the temple of God and death should have no dominion over it.

Instead of Soja getting better, he developed boils and rashes all over his skin. There were tiny boils where his eyelashes used to be, one boil for each eyelash. He had rashes on his skin. The head of the prayer band at the white garment church where he was being looked after said he should be taken to the world headquarters of the church so that his spiritual leader could say the word and Soja would be healed.

It was hard to get ahold of the spiritual leader because there was usually a long line of people waiting to see him. They said all he did was utter a word or phrase and the supplicant's problem would be solved. To a woman crying because of her sick child he could say *cry no more your tears will become tears of joy*. This would mean that the child would be healed.

He would say to a spinster *you will no longer walk alone,* meaning she would soon get married. Cryptic phrases that were assiduously recorded by a bearded acolyte called the Scribe. He took down every word and utterance, coughs, and sighs of the spiritual leader.

Invoking esprit de corps with the policemen who served as guards for the spiritual leader, Soja and his wife were able to jump to the front of the line and see the spiritual leader, who said to Soja—*I release you to your destiny.* Even the Scribe could not interpret the expression. What was Soja's destiny? Was his destiny to live or to die? They left more confused than before. Soja's wife decided to take him to an Islamic sheikh who was reputed to heal by dipping his prayer beads into water and giving the water to the supplicant.

—Have you heard what I heard?—

—They say the spiritual leader of the white garment church could not heal him—

—I hear that man is powerful. If he could not help, there may be no hope—

—He sure is powerful. He eats no meat. Fasts for forty days and nights without touching any food—

—If the problem is one that he cannot solve, then the man should return home, put his affairs in order, and start waiting for death—

—His wife is still carrying him about from one healer to the other—

—I hear she has taken him to the powerful gray-bearded sheikh, the Islamic preacher and healer—

—I hear those ones are powerful too. They use words from their holy books—

—He has really suffered. Look at him, all bones—

The first thing that was demanded of Soja before he could see the sheikh was that he needed to convert, he should change his name and shave his hair.

He wanted to argue with them but they explained to him that it was all one God. He was only called by a different name. He agreed. His new name was Ahmed. He was happy. He covered his head with a *taj*, a cap worn by the Muslim faithful.

Finally he got to meet the sheikh. The sheikh shook his hands and touched his right hand to his heart in the Muslim fashion and said to Soja/Ahmed—*Inna lillahi Wa inna ilaihi Rajioon*. What the sheikh said to him was the Islamic prayer for the dead.

Grandpa said Soja's wife should stop carrying him from place to place. He said Soja knew what was wrong with him. He should say the truth.

After this people began to speculate about Soja's illness and the cause.

—You know when he was in the task force some of the female roadside traders bribed them—

—Of course everyone knows that they collected bribes—

—No, not that kind of bribe you are thinking about—

—The women who they took to their head office the task force head office you know—

—You mean they did things to the women?—

—Some of the women used what they had to bribe the task force people and get their goods back and free themselves—

—They got a lot of it, some members as time went on even preferred to be bribed that way. They say Soja was that way—

—Probably, that is what is killing him now?—

—Was it that he did it with another man's wife?—

—Not sure—

—If it was the one people got from doing it with another man's wife, the victim will fall off the woman, crow three times like a cock, and die—

—So if it wasn't that one what was it?—

—You won't hear it from my mouth. You know what it is that is killing him—

Soja finally died. They say he refused to go quietly. They said he died fighting. He struggled, he rolled from one side of the bed to the floor, he sweated, his labored breathing could be heard about three houses away. And then he stopped breathing. He was finally at rest.

Soja was buried in the military cemetery. Because of the speculation that whatever had made him sick was a result of his task force duties, his colleagues rallied, they contributed money for him and tried to get his gratuity and payment out very quickly. They were planning to give the money to the wife, but it turned out she was not the next of kin. Soja had never officially married her. Grandpa was the next of kin. He was the one who got all the money except for the contributions and the gratuity. Soja's woman cried, she begged, she threatened, she cajoled.

Grandpa asked only one question—she should receive the payment in her capacity as what?

Soja's woman did what she had heard the old woman did

to her husband. At midnight she stood in front of the house, bared her buttocks at the house, and cursed the house and those who lived in it.

She later repented and came back to beg Grandpa when she discovered that she was pregnant with the late Soja's child. Grandpa gave her a small space in front of the Family House where she could fry and sell bean cakes.

# FUEBI

Soja's wife, who now had a daughter named Fuebi, was using the small corner outside the Family House given to her by Grandpa to sell *akara* fried bean cakes. It was a good location to sell *akara* because of the many feet that passed by the house. Her mother fried the *akara* in hot oil while Fuebi wrapped the hot balls in newspapers for customers. Beside them on a tray were loaves of bread, which they also sold. Beside the loaves of bread lay a pile of old newspapers. One of Grandpa's acts of kindness was to allow them to make use of the space in front of the Family House to sell. Fuebi's mother may have been beautiful many years ago, but she was now the same ochre-white color as the smoke that emerged from the cheap firewood with which she fried her *akara*. Fuebi was beautiful. She sparkled. She had a gap on her upper incisor, which was considered a mark of beauty. She had dimples. Her skin glowed. She smiled a lot. This was despite the hard work she had to do every day. Frying *akara* was the final task in a very laborious process that began with soaking the black-eyed peas in water overnight and washing off the tough skin the next morning. Washing and rinsing and pouring the water into an open drain very far from the house because the smell from the bean water was awful. Then carrying the washed beans to the communal grinding machine store where she joined the line to have the beans blended, then returning home to go to school. Coming back from school to go buy firewood and going to broad Teacher's place to collect old copies of the *Daily Times*. It was a tough job, but Fuebi never complained. She was always smiling. During a pause in sales or on days when due to rainfall the sales and frying came to a halt, the woman would turn to Fuebi and point at herself.

"Fuebi, hmmm, you must not let your life be like mine. Look at me, stained and faded like an old piece of cloth. How much do we make from all this suffering? From morning till night, fetch water, grind beans, grind pepper, cut onions, haul wood, build a fire, blow the fire, sit by hot fire and hot oil, all for what? All for a profit of a half a penny, all for penny and half penny. Your life must not be like mine. You must not allow suffering to steal your beauty the way it stole mine. Any slightest opportunity you get you better start running far away from here, far away from all this suffering. Suffering and beauty are not friends, and never will be."

"You are too hard on yourself," Fuebi would say to her.

"What do you know? You are not a child anymore. You had better open your ears and listen very well to what I am telling you. The day you have the opportunity to run away to where suffering cannot reach you with her evil claws, run and run very far away."

"Things can only get better, don't worry."

"Before our own very eyes things are getting worse. Look at me, eh, just look at me. If not for the death of your father, I know this is not where I would be. Death has done its worst. The good die young."

And then, one evening the answer to her prayers. Fide, the patent medicine dealer, pulled up in his car and asked to be sold some *akara*. Fuebi remembered the song that wafted from the car's speakers—it was "You're My Best Friend" by Don Williams. She would learn later that this was the only kind of music that Fide played. Fide called it sentimental music.

"I don't play with my sentimental songs," he would say to her when they got to know each other better. Fuebi would never forget this song because it was also the song to which he would insist on fucking her without protection, insisting he wanted her skin to skin, which would eventually lead to her pregnancy. But all that was in the future. This night he wanted *akara*. Fuebi's mother wrapped a generous quantity of *akara* for him and told Fuebi to go give it to the man in the car. She could smell the air freshener in the car from where she sat. By the light of the car, Fide looked at the beautiful gap-toothed face handing him the *akara* and he smiled and switched off the engine of the car. He brought out his wallet, protuberant, bloated, and overloaded almost to spilling with cash. He searched for the largest denomination and gave it to her. She went to bring back his change.

"Keep the change," he said to her, and winked, and then he smiled at her and drove away slowly, trailed by the smell of his air freshener and the voice of Don Williams.

When Fuebi showed the change the man in the car had left for her to her mother, she stood up and danced wordlessly around the fire and the pot of boiling oil on the fire. After dancing she poured water to put out the fire and said they should go home.

"What about the customers who want to buy *akara*?" Fuebi asked.

"Give the *akara* in the basket to them but do not collect any money from them," she said.

"But why are we closing so early tonight?" Fuebi asked.

"We are closing early because what I saw while sitting on this chair that I sit on every day to fry *akara* is indeed very marvelous in my sight," she said, and broke into a Pentecostal church song.

"And what did you see?"

"You mean you did not see how that man was looking at you?"

"He was smiling and he told me to keep the change."

"I can tell you today that things are not going to be the

same for us again. Soon, you will see, I will no longer need to roast myself on the fire in the name of frying *akara*," she said, and began to pack her things. "Mark my words, you'll see, this is not the last time we will see him."

She was right. The next evening he was back. His car stereo was playing Don Williams. He shut off the engine of the car and asked for *akara*. Fuebi went to hand the *akara* to him. Again the fat wallet appeared. Again, he handed her the fat denomination. Again, he asked her to keep the change.

That night when they got home, Fuebi was given a lesson by her mother.

"It is true you are young but you were not born yester night. The ripe orange fruit that refuses to fall off the tree to be eaten by a good man soon becomes food for the birds. That man likes you. He has shown that he likes you. Now, it is your turn to reciprocate, show him that you like him before he turns away. Men do not have lots of patience and are not good at waiting."

The next evening Fuebi not only took the *akara* to Fide, but she also sat in the car with him and asked him how his day went.

"Fine, my day always goes well. Honor to Jesus, adoration to Mary," he said, fingering the rosary that dangled from the rearview mirror.

"What do you do?" she asked.

"I do buying and selling."

"What do you sell?"

"I sell medicines, capsules, tablets. You know, like Panadol."

"That is nice," she responded.

"Do you take medicines?"

"I never fall sick," Fuebi said.

"I will come and take you out tomorrow evening."

"I don't know. I'll have to ask my mother."

"Don't worry. She is a good woman. I am sure she will say yes. Give her this envelope. Tell her it is from me."

Fuebi felt the envelope. It was filled with money. As she made to alight from the car, Fide drew her closer.

"Please stop, people are watching us."

"That is true. I will take you to someplace with fewer eyes next time."

When Fuebi handed the envelope to her mother, she sang and danced and said that indeed there was a good God in heaven who answered the prayers of the poor and sent them kind people to save them.

The next day Fuebi dressed up in her best, which was not much, and waited for Fide near where her mother sold akara. He pulled up, looked around, and told her to get into the car quickly. His manner was abrupt and he did not smile until they pulled out of the street.

"Like you said, there are too many eyes watching. One has to be careful."

He turned to her and told her she looked beautiful. He asked her if she was hungry. She said she was not hungry. He soon pulled up to a hotel and parked his car. The people at the reception seemed to know him very well and he took her up to a room upstairs.

"This is a good place for us to relax, away from all those eyes," he said.

She sat on a chair beside the bed and began to open the pages of a green Gideon's Bible by the side of the bed.

"Come and relax with me here on the bed. I am not going to bite you."

She joined him on the bed, and he wasted no time undressing her. As he took off her clothes he emitted a deep gurgling sound that seemed to emerge from some deep part of his throat. All the while he kept saying to her, you are beautiful, I am not going to bite you. With some force he pushed her legs apart and entered her. She felt a sharp pain. One moment he was in her and the next moment he was out. He looked down at her legs.

"This is your first time." It was a statement; not a question.

She nodded.

"You are a good girl, you are a very good girl and I will reward you." Once again he brought out two fat envelopes and gave them to her. "One for you and one for your mother."

Fuebi felt a little dull pain and throbbing below.

"Don't worry, the pain will soon go. If you feel any more pain, take two tablets of paracetamol. You'll feel better."

He dropped her off by the road near where her mother fried *akara* and drove off.

When she got home she gave both envelopes to her mother. Her mother opened them and began to dance around their room.

She told her mother that she was feeling a little tired.

"Don't worry. I'll boil you some warm water so you can take your bath and go to bed."

She took her bath and went to bed and was soon deeply asleep.

Twice a week, Fide showed up and took her to the same hotel. He seemed to take less and less time, after which he fell into a short sleep and snored, then would jerk up suddenly awake and tell her to get dressed, that he had some urgent business to settle in his store.

When Fuebi began to look pale and vomit in the mornings, her mother said that this was another answered prayer.

"Your father's spirit is too strong. I know he has been itching to come back to this world that he left abruptly due to bad people. See, now he is going to come back through you. And you have found a good man too."

When Fuebi told Fide her good news, Fide was angry.

"What do you take me for? Do you think I am an irresponsible man?"

"But what do you want me to do?"

"I am not the person who will tell you what to do. You are not a child. You know what to do."

"I don't know what to do."

"In that case, ask your mother, she will know where to take you."

"She says I should tell you, that you'll be happy."

"And what about my wife? And what about my daughters, will they be happy? And what about my reverend father, will he be happy?"

It was the first time Fide had ever mentioned a wife and children.

The next time Fuebi went to the store to wait for Fide, she spent the better part of the day waiting. She was told he had gone to the port to see to the release of his imported goods. When he came in and saw her his face changed.

"Take this note," he said as he scribbled something on the back of his card.

"Take this," he said, giving her an envelope.

He then directed her to go and see a doctor who would take care of her.

When Fuebi showed the note to her mother, her mother took the card with the scribbled note from her and said she was going to keep it as evidence. As for the money in the envelope, she said it was going to be used for baby clothes.

Fuebi eventually gave birth to twins. Two boys. The boys screamed lustily into the world. They were ravenous and began to eat as if they had been starving for the nine months that they had been in the womb.

"Look at their mouths, look at those greedy lips, just like their father's," Fuebi's mother said.

Fuebi was tired and was lying weakly on the bed. She had not seen Fide since the last time he gave her the money to go see his friend to take care of the pregnancy.

Word soon got to Grandpa that Fuebi had delivered a set of twins and that their father had refused to show up. Grandpa summoned Fide.

"What is this I hear about you refusing to see your God-given children?"

"It is not me, it is my wife. She will kill me. She has two

girls for me, two girls *only*. She doesn't want to hear that another woman had children for me."

"Are you a man or are you a woman who pees from behind?"

"And the priest will not be happy about it too."

"Were you thinking of the priest when you were doing it with her?"

Fide shook his head from side to side and began making squiggles on the ground with his big toe.

"Tell your wife that children bring children. She will see, as soon as these twins are under your roof, she too will give birth to her own male children."

And that was how it was settled. Fuebi moved into Fide's house. Just as Grandpa had said, Fide's older wife gave birth to a boy exactly one year later.

# TRUDY

Uncle Zorro returned from his studies abroad with a white woman as his wife. This was great news and there was a big party to welcome him and the wife. But when the wife, Trudy that was her name, said they were not going to have children, that was when the trouble started. Trudy had started making enemies of most people in the house when she began complaining about the treatment of the cats and dogs. She was the one who had insisted that they live in the Family House and not in the posh expatriate quarters, where they could have gotten one of the more opulent houses.

The cats and dogs were working animals and were not considered ornamental or solely pets. They could be petted on occasion when they did a good job, but such occasions were few and far between. The job of the cats was to keep the house mice-free. There were many corners and dark crevices in the house. Tiny rooms, closets, and pantries where all kinds of odds and ends were stored were good breeding grounds for mice. We were told not to feed the cats with food or they would lose their hunting skills and become lazy.

All the dogs went by the name Simple. Simple was the original name of the mother dog. All her offspring were also called Simple. There was brown Simple and black Simple and black-and-white Simple. They all worked. They kept the house secure at night by barking and attacking any would-be intruder. They went hunting with Grandpa. They were also expected to play with the children.

Trudy complained that the animals were not well treated; she carried the cats around and would feed them by hand. Soon enough the cats lost interest in hunting mice.

And what was this about the need to plant flowers around the house? She said that it was a big shame that a house as big as the Family House did not have a garden, she said it was uncivilized and a disgrace.

There was a *dogonyaro* tree behind the house. Everyone knew that the boiled bitter leaf of the tree was a good cure for malaria fever. The limber stalk of the tree was a very good medicinal chewing stick and kept stomach troubles at bay. The tree provided shade under which we played when the sun became too hot. There was an orange tree and an avocado pear tree. There were no plantain trees because we all knew they were breeding places for mosquitoes. There were useful flowers like queen of the night, which kept witches and evil people away with its pungent, cloying smell. But Trudy wanted a real garden.

"And are you going to plant things in your garden that people can actually eat?"

"Beauty is the whole point. It must not be about food all the time. We must also feed our eyes, and our brains need to be fed sometimes."

She was given a space to start her garden.

"She is not from here. She must be treated with extra kindness," Grandpa said. "If she left her father and mother and family and crossed the vast ocean to follow you here, then you must do all that you can to make her comfortable."

Trudy soon turned her attention to the way the children in the house were treated. She felt they were sometimes treated in a cruel manner.

In the meantime her husband, Uncle Zorro, was already working in the general hospital as a doctor and was assuring us that she would soon drop her foreign ways and adjust to living life the way we all lived it in the Family House.

She said that the house was a breeding ground for germs and that she was surprised we had not all perished from all kinds of germ-borne diseases.

A few people who knew about such things said Trudy was not going to last.

—The ones who stay learn our language. They eat our food. They wear our traditional clothes. They genuflect when they greet their elders—

—They get pregnant and have many children, not carrying a cat around like a baby the way this one does—

And then the news began to filter into the house that Uncle Zorro had a concubine. Nobody used the word *girlfriend*, because this was too light a word to describe the relationship. A girlfriend was someone seen occasionally. The case here was different. Uncle Zorro would drive directly from work at the hospital to his concubine's house, where he would eat his dinner, read a newspaper, and take a nap before coming back home long past midnight. It was even worse than that, he actually went over during his lunch break or his concubine would send over one of her girls to deliver his lunch to him.

And it was not just lunch; he was blatant about the affair. His car was usually prominently parked in front of his concubine's house, where every passerby could see it. He was said to have taken over the payment of the fees of some of his concubine's children from a previous marriage.

They had been seen at parties dressed in "and co"—they had on identical clothes—and when they both stood up to dance the musician had referred to the concubine as the wife of the world-famous London-trained doctor who could tell what ailed you merely by looking at your face.

As usual, people talked about this. As usual, they blamed the white wife.

—Man shall not live by bread and tea alone. Even the holy book said so. What is tea for breakfast, tea for lunch, and tea for dinner? The tongue of a black person will always crave pepper. Or was it not a piece of spicy alligator pepper and salt that were dropped on his tongue when he was being given a name on the seventh day?—

—But if it is pepper that he craves, can't he get a native cook and steward like his other colleagues who are married to foreigners?—

—It is the fault of his wife. She is the mother of cats and dogs. Tell me what man wants to be known as the father of cats and dogs?—

—But couldn't he have gone about it more discreetly? How come he is carrying on like he is the first man to have a concubine? Men have been having concubines since the beginning of the world—

—It is the nature of man to easily get bored with the taste of one soup. Man wants to sample a different soup from time to time. So, even if the man was married to a woman, from her he will still stray—

—He had better be careful, though. I hear his wife's people do not hesitate to shoot men who cheat on them—

—Where is she going to get the gun from?—

—They always carry their own gun, not your long-mouthed double-barreled gun; their own gun is so small it can fit into their purse—

—He had better watch out, then—

—But what does he see in that *secondhand* woman who already has three children for someone else?—

—Who are you to question another man's taste?—

Trudy had at this point started going from house to house with an interpreter to talk to the women. She said she was talking to them about safety issues, teaching them to keep themselves and their surroundings clean. Teaching them about things that'll make them better wives. But this was not the report that was received.

—She wants to convert our wives to her white ways. She will not succeed—

—What does she know about keeping a man? If she knew anything about keeping her man, would he be keeping a concubine?—

—My own wife told me with her mouth that the woman told her that she was the owner of her own body and that as such I her husband could not touch her without her permission—

—It is possible that her own husband got tired of asking for her permission like a schoolboy and decided to go to a woman whom he doesn't need to ask for permission—

—I hear some of the foolish women are listening to her. Maybe by the time their husbands drive them away she will marry them herself—

—How will that shock us? Is there anything that they'll not do in that house?—

Nobody knew for sure if Grandpa had heard about Uncle Zorro and his concubine. Of course, even a newborn child knew that Grandpa knew and heard everything. A day came when Uncle Zorro came to talk to Grandpa about marrying his concubine. He wanted to bring her into the Family House. Not just her but also her three children from her previous marriage. Grandpa was furious.

"This your wife, Trudy, that followed you all the way from across the seas, I have a question for you concerning her. Where are her parents?"

"Her parents are in their country."

"And where are her brothers and sisters?"

"They are also in their country."

"So she has no family here except you."

"None."

"So did you bring her all the way here in order to abandon her and cast her away like a piece of rag?"

"But she is not adapting."

"You are the one who has refused to adapt," Grandpa said. "Look at you, you say you are the educated person, but you have not shown any sign that your so-called education has had any impact on you. You cannot even hide the fact that you have a concubine from the eyes of the world, or are you the first? I must not hear that nonsense about bringing some other woman into this house again."

Grandpa could still roar when he wanted to and his bite was even more dangerous. Uncle Zorro prostrated and promised to reorder his steps.

But Grandpa was not done with him yet.

"You must not step foot in that woman's house again. I forbid you to have any further contact with her. You must not meet with her, not even secretly. If anybody sees your car parked in front of her house again you'll see what will happen to you. Behave the way young men your age behave."

"But the woman I have at home has no child."

"And I thought you said you were a medical doctor. If she doesn't have a child, is that not your problem? Don't you treat women who have no children in the hospital where you work?"

"But she doesn't even want to hear about it."

"Am I the one that will teach you how to marry your wife? Were you born yesterday? Anyway, the most important thing is that your foolish concubine business is over."

How this conversation filtered down to the ears of those outside the house, no one knows, but they did hear. And as usual they had their views.

—I hear he stood up for the woman—

—He even warned his son to stay away from the infamous concubine—

—If only he acts like this all the time the house will not have such a bad reputation—

—He spoke up for her. Truly, she journeyed over seas and mountains and ocean to come over here with him. Why would he treat her that way?—

As if Trudy had also heard what happened she too began to change her ways. She changed her name from Trudy to Tunu. She began to wear only traditional cotton dresses and head ties. She also established what would later become famous as the Infants Home School. In the morning when the bigger kids had gone off to school she would go from house to house picking up the smaller preschoolers. She insisted that they be bathed and ready; she would go from house to house picking up the kids, who would be singing and marching behind her.

Oftentimes mispronouncing the words of the song but singing loftily all the same.

> *Today is bright and bright and gay oh happy day a day of joy*
> *Today is bright and bright and gay oh happy day of joy.*

They would march to the Family House and she would spend the day with them singing and dancing and playing games. She persuaded her husband to informally consult when he came back from work in the evenings. And within a short time she could speak our local language like a native.

# AKWETE

Akwete was his nickname. The nickname had eclipsed his real name so much that hardly anyone recalled what his real name had been. His nickname was derived from his signature call as he pedaled into a street with bundles of clothing fabrics piled on top of each other on his carrier and some more piled on the handlebars. He sold every type of fabric—George, English wax, Hollandaise, Abada, and even Jubilee women's head tie fabrics. Children loved him; women loved him; husbands not so much. He persuaded women to buy his clothes no matter how little money they had. The cloth becomes yours as soon as you make a penny down payment. I'll write your name on it and keep it for you. The day you make your last payment I hand it to you. With that he persuaded the most reluctant women to buy from him. Akwete, children would scream, imitating his signature call.

After he had done selling he would come to the Family House to chat with Grandpa. He grew from being a bicycle owner to the owner of a Honda motorcycle and eventually bought a Peugeot pickup truck. When he was not selling clothes, traveling up and down to buy clothes or collect money from his customers, he loved to hunt. He had a double-barreled hunting rifle. He enjoyed hunting and told interesting hunting stories.

He said that every animal had a peculiar smell. He said that as a good hunter what he always did was to bury his nose in the belly of every animal he killed, that way, the animal's peculiar smell became encoded in his memory. The next time he went hunting, he could tell if that type of animal was in that particular bush. The moment he entered a forest to hunt, he would immediately exclaim, I smell an antelope, I smell a deer, I smell a wild boar.

Some people had unflattering things to say about him. He was a man who was ever smiling, as if he had discovered the secret of happiness as soon as he was born.

—What kind of man sells women's clothes?—

—Why does he not sell men's clothes?—

—What manner of man is always comfortable sitting around with women, haggling with them, sharing their jokes and letting women touch him?—

Whenever Akwete came to Grandfather's house and these words got to his ears, he would laugh and utter a couple of aphorisms.

"Even the money made from packing poop smells as sweet, money has no gender, let them say what they like, nobody can please the world."

Even his hunting exploits gave them something to talk about. For he was also a good hunter and would sometimes kill a wild boar and sell it for lots of money.

—How did he even become a hunter?—

—I never heard that he learned to hunt from anybody. We know that every hunter's father and grandfather were also hunters. Where or who did he learn his own hunting from?—

—One morning, he went to the market and bought a double-barreled gun and went into the forest and shot his first deer and brought it home—

—Does that story sound right to you, he was not even afraid of going into the forest alone at night?—

—What I hear is that some people have a talisman that turns them invisible in the forest and that way they can hunt and kill all those animals without the animals smelling them or hearing them approach—

To these comments Akwete simply replied that those who were interested in knowing about his skills as a hunter should go with him into the forest at night or should transform themselves into a herd of wild boar and see if he would not gun all of them down to the last animal. All these negative comments did not stop him from always smiling and joking with women and persuading them to make a down payment on his cloth fabrics with only a penny, just a penny, he would say again and again for emphasis, all the while laughing.

Akwete went hunting with this friend of his, a school-teacher named Joachim. It was not the first time they were hunting together. It was a moonless night and they both wore miner's lamps on their heads. They turned the lamp on when they heard the sound of an animal; they would temporarily blind the animal with the dazzling light and then shoot.

Akwete and Joachim separated and said they'd meet under a designated tree later on. Everyone knew Akwete hunted alone, which was why he had all the stories swirling around him. When Akwete narrated the story later to many people, it did not make sense to his listeners. In his words, the first thing he saw was two shiny eyes. As he inched closer, for he was crawling on his belly, he saw vaguely the gray outline of an animal that looked like a very enormous wild boar. Without putting on his hunting lamp he shot and then shot again. There was a loud wail and then a scream—*I am dead*—the wailing voice was Joachim's.

But how could this be? Akwete wondered. When he pointed his gun what he saw was an animal, not a person. He hurriedly carried Joachim in both hands while throwing his gun aside. As he took a few steps out of the forest, Joachim drew his last breath.

Akwete was screaming as he carried his dead friend into town.

"I did not kill him.

"I did not shoot him.

"It was an animal that I shot, not Joachim.

"It was when I moved closer that I saw it was my friend that was bleeding. Please somebody help me."

He was still crying and wailing, his hunting clothes stained with blood, as he cried to the Family House.

Akwete was loved by many but he was also a man with enemies and now they began to talk.

—Was I born today? Who says a human being and an animal have the same shape?—

—He should come up with a more believable story to tell us. He probably killed the man for prosperity rituals—

—He should have thought of a more believable story—

—There has always been something a little not straightforward about that man—

—Instead of following an honest trade like other men, he spends the whole day with other people's wives, cracking jokes with them, smiling with them, touching them and being touched by them and persuading them to go into debt for his colorful fabrics—

But there were also a few people who were on Akwete's side. A few people who knew about hunting said that a hunter who goes into the forest at night to hunt would often encounter quite a few strange things. They talked about animals that lured a hunter deeper and deeper into the forest until the hunter lost his way and ended up being hunted down and devoured by wild animals. They said it was not unusual to encounter animals that were not really animals but people. Evil people transformed themselves into animals to scare hunters. They spoke of birds with melodious voices that sang beautifully in the forest, songs so sweet that hunters dropped their guns and began to listen and listen till they forgot that they were hunters and dozed off for days until they breathed their last and then the bird with the melodious voice descended and pecked out their eyes. They talked of wild boars that had skin so tough no bullet could penetrate them.

—A successful man like Akwete should have been more careful. He has far too many enemies. He is too prosperous for evil eyes not to look in his direction. He has his motorcycle and is said to be planning to build a mansion, why won't evil eyes look at him—

—Remember when every day they offloaded tipper-load after tipper-load of white sand in the place where he was planning to build a house? After which they began offloading cement blocks for days—

—What about the mountains of gravel that were dumped on the same construction site—

—People wondered what kind of mansion he was planning to build—

—You know what they say about a man who spends years and years getting ready to go mad, the preamble for the house construction was like that—

Joachim's family insisted that there was foul play and wanted the full force of the law brought down on Akwete. Akwete ran down to his friend Grandpa.

"See, they want to destroy me. My enemies have finally got me. If I go to jail my business will be all gone by the time I return, that is, if I ever come out of jail alive."

"Panicking will take you nowhere. A man without enemies is an unsuccessful man. The problem is here. The right thing to do is to find a solution to it. You say the family does not want to be paid off. It means they want to make trouble. Nothing can bring back a dead person. But if they want to be unreasonable, there is nothing you can do."

"So do I simply fold my hands and go to prison?"

"Nobody said anything about you going to prison."

"So what is it going to be?"

"Someone will go to prison on your behalf. It has been done before. Whatever sentence is passed on you, that person will serve the jail time. We will ensure that the sentence is short. This is a case of manslaughter, not murder, for indeed Joachim was your friend and you had no plans to kill him, neither have you profited in any way from his death."

"So who will agree to go to jail on my behalf?"

"There are so many people under this roof, we will find somebody. You will reward him highly for serving your time on your behalf. You will marry him a wife. You will build him a house. You will set him up in business when he is released."

"That is not a problem."

It was done.

Uwa was the one who was asked to go to jail on Akwete's behalf. Uwa was the one who was often called upon to carry out any duty that people found impossible to do in the house. He untightened fast screws, he found lost things, he crawled into and out of tight corners, he once jumped into the well to bring out a child that had accidentally fallen in.

Promises were made to him.

"Look, you are young. You still have your best years ahead of you."

"By the time you come out you will live like a rich man for the rest of your days."

"You have nothing to worry about; as I am building my own house I will also be completing one for you. You will move into your own mansion as soon as you are out."

"You will definitely not regret doing this."

"Wives, children, a house of your own, and even a textile business of yours is guaranteed. I will put you in touch with the suppliers, and here's the good thing, you'll not need to peddle and hawk your goods like me. You'll sit gently in your store and all your customers will come to you."

Uwa did not need any convincing. What was his life worth? He could have done it for free.

No one knows for sure how things like this were arranged, but everyone knew that Akwete went on trial and was sentenced but Uwa was the person who went into the prison vehicle and was driven off to jail.

But soon after Uwa's departure for prison, Akwete became a completely different person. He began to drink. Just as he went from place to place trying to sell his clothes in the old days, he now went from one drinking place to another. He was often too drunk to sell his clothes or even to ride his motorcycle home after his drinking bouts.

—It is the spirit of the man he shot. Some people have a really strong spirit that cannot be appeased—

—What is he trying to mask by drinking? There must be something he is hiding from—

—He committed two forms of evil. He killed his friend and should have served the punishment, but, no, he has connections and will not serve his punishment like other people, he hires someone to serve his punishment for him, but look who is being punished now—

—You can run from your atrocities but you surely cannot hide from your atrocities, this is a lesson for all who do evil—

Soon Akwete was owing money to the large textile distributors who had sold him the clothes on credit. He had abandoned the house he was supposed to be building. He began selling off those things that he could still sell off in order to have money to drink.

A few people called him to talk to him about his new lifestyle but he mocked them.

"Don't worry about me. Worry about yourselves. You think my wealth is gone? My wealth that is on the way is going to be one hundred times bigger than whatever I had before. Don't worry yourselves; the same lips laughing at me now will be the same lips that'll praise me in the not too distant time."

By the time Akwete died, which was not long after Uwa had gone to prison, there was nothing of his wealth left. He even owed those whom he had been buying drinks from.

It was a few people who remembered him, especially the women who put money together to give him some kind of burial, befitting or not.

And what about Uwa?

He did the time and came out. He was released far ahead of time for good behavior. Even while in prison, he still put to use his skill for doing what ordinary people found difficult to do.

He was expecting to move into a mansion and be set up in business and to live happily from then on. He heard of the death of Akwete and the burial of his promises.

He returned to the Family House. He was not broken even one bit. To those who asked him how he felt, he had only one response.

"I still have my life, yes, I still have my life," he said to them, moving on to attend to some errand.

# IBE

Ibe said I must give the house a befitting name. We all called it
the Family House, I said. By what other name should I call it?
You must give the house a name that evokes prestige, a name that
will make people respect the people who lived in the house and
the house itself. So what name do you suggest I call it? You can
call the house White Castle of Peace. But it was not white in color,
it was not a castle, and it was not that peaceful, I said. You can call
it the Grand House on the Hill. You can call it Eagle Terrace. You
can call it the Purity Villa. You can call it Peace Haven or Giant
Oaks Villa. Give the house a good name because a good name is
better than gold, and a man's house is his castle and every man is
king in his own abode.

And what about Grandpa and all the things that happened in
the house? I asked Ibe. Grandpa was an illustrious and generous

man. He fed the poor and the beggars, he clothed the naked and the orphans and widows, he was a man of legendary generosity. He was more generous than Rockefeller. He mounted loudspeakers outside so that people could listen to the music he listened to, he entertained himself and others. He invited the whole street to come and watch television in his house, those who could not find space to sit inside watched through the window screen while some stood by the door, Ibe said.

And what about the woman that was stripped naked and had her head shaved and was paraded around the town? Ibe said the woman was only enacting a ritual drama. A drama? Yes, she was taking part in a traditional ritual for cleansing the community of the sins of everyone. She bore the shame of everyone. What she did for the community was like what Christ did for the whole world.

Are you sure about this? Trust me, I remember everything. She was rewarded richly for her role in that traditional ritual. But she was cursed as she moved through the community, don't you remember? You are the one who does not remember. People beckoned to her to come closer so they could drop some money into the calabash she was carrying on her head.

Do you remember the uncle who told his followers to sell all they had because the world was going to end? Of course, I remember him. He was a true prophet. He heard the voice of God. God actually told him he was going to destroy the earth, but like a good prophet he interceded with God to show a little mercy and give the people a chance to repent. And the people that threatened to burn down the house? Nobody threatened to burn down the house. The people went away rejoicing that their lives had been spared and that the world did not end. They went away singing his praises and calling him a true prophet.

And what about the soldiers who came to . . . ? What soldiers? Oh the soldiers. Grandpa had friends, some of whom were soldiers, officers, engineers, lawyers, policemen. All kinds of professionals came to the house.

And what about Baby? Oh, Baby? No man was willing to marry her but Grandpa was always generous so he found her a husband. He even paid the man to marry her, I think.

And what about all those kids in the house? I told you already that Grandpa was generous and kind and did not allow orphans to suffer so he brought them all under his roof and fed them and sent them to school.

Do you remember any suffering in the house? No one suffered in the house. It was the sound of laughter and the sound of spoons on teeth and the sound of food on its way down to the gullet that people heard coming from the house.

And do you happen to remember that one time that you were sick? Me sick? I have never been sick in my life. I was not sick. I was in a trance. I was seeing the future. I was sitting with God in heaven and he was showing me the future of everybody, including you. You had appendicitis but we thought it was because of the money and other stuff we took from the shrine. You imagine a lot of things, not as they were, but as you want them to be. I was in a trance and I saw God, he was wearing cream-colored trousers that swept the ground and his beard was as white as snow.

# HOW THE HOUSE CAME
# TO BE NO MORE

There were soldiers carrying guns and *koboko* horse whips. There were civilian members of the Environmental Task Force in yellow overalls. There was an engineer in blue overalls and a white safety helmet. There was a policeman on an impatient horse that refused to stand still. There was a top civil servant in the Ministry of the Environment dressed in a four-piece suit and tie under the dull yellow glow of the sun and suffocating heat. There was the operator of the bulldozer and his assistant. There was the bulldozer, yellow in color with a large CATERPILLAR logotype on its side. There was a photographer with a camera.

There was a new governor who had just been sworn in. Who had sworn to make the city a modern city. He said the city was filthy. There were open drains clogged with filth. The once-in-a-month sanitation program was not enough. People simply dug up the filth and dirt in the drains and shoveled them into the street and after a few days heavy rains ensured the dirt ended up right where it had come from. He was going to demolish the houses that blocked the city sewage and drainage system. He was going to ensure street trading was abolished. He wanted houses to have a fresh coat of paint and he insisted on the planting of flowers and palms along the major roads.

The Ministry of the Environment sent a notice that the Family House was sitting on a place that should have a major drain way. He sent his men to put four large *X*s on the four walls of the house. There were whisperings as to whether the Family House would go down or not. Some said that all the juju that lay buried in the house would ensure it didn't fall. Others said that the evil committed in the house was enough to pull the house down.

The morning the bulldozers came, accompanied by members of the newly constituted task force on the environment, no one told them that a former occupant of the house had been a task force member, that he was called Soja and that whatever had killed him was not unconnected with his duties as a member of one other task force a long time ago. Down the street a song boomed from a loudspeaker. The lyrics of the song went this way—*vanity upon vanity, all is vanity*. About half an hour later the track being played would change to another song titled *Oh Merciful God* . . .

There were also the people on the street who had gathered to witness the demolition of this house that had long been abandoned but of which they had heard strange stories.

—But why all the soldiers and policemen and guns and horses? Is it not an ordinary house?—

—That house is no ordinary house. Ordinary house, indeed—

—But it is not as if the house is going to run away. The house has no legs with which to run—

—If you knew all the things that have happened in that house you'd know that it can do more than run—

—People say that at night you could hear voices and sometimes cries emanating from that house. Even though no one lives there anymore—

—It casts a dark shadow on our street. They should demolish it so that light will take over from darkness—

—All the things they said happened in that house before you were born will make your ears tingle—

—But how would you feel if they decide to demolish your own house that you built with your own sweat and blood because the new ruler wants to beautify the city by planting flowers and painting houses—

—That house was built with the sweat of innocent, hardworking people—

—Wait; hold on a minute. What is going on? See, what did I tell you? That is no ordinary house—

The bulldozer was about to sink its teeth into the house when it belched and coughed and sputtered to a stop. It gasped and then its motor stopped running. There was a brief silence and then the horse neighed and made as if it was about to bound off, but it was restrained by the police rider.

"What is wrong?" the leader of the task force, the big boss from the Ministry of the Environment, asked.

The bulldozer operator and his boy jumped down, looking confused. This had never happened before. The bulldozer was almost new and had never stalled.

"Let me check the plugs, maybe they overflowed," he said, and brought out a handkerchief, wiped his face, and began searching for the plugs.

—You see what I told you, they must have buried something in that house—

—You don't do this kind of work if you are not strong. To do this type of work with an *ordinary* hand and with no protection is to court death—

—That is true, though. Even the engineers that construct bridges, white engineers, Germans, Israelis, American engineers, they buy rams sometimes cows or chickens to make sacrifices to the river goddess before they start constructing bridges—

—These ones should know better, they have been doing this job for long. They know that you cannot just demolish a house built by someone just like that—

The bulldozer started working again. This time the driver and the bulldozer went at the house as if doubly determined

182 · E. C. Osondu

and soon there was rubble and dust. As a part of the house came down the members of the task force who were standing a little distance away began to clap and cheer. The song playing from the record store came to an end and a new song came on: "My Father's Mansion in the Sky," *In my father's house there are many mansions*, the musician sang as the dust rose like a sacrificial burnt offering from the crumbled Family House into the sky.

# ACKNOWLEDGMENTS

I could never have done this alone. Heartfelt thanks to my family: Evelyn, Aisha, Michael, ChuChu, Cheta, CJ.

My agents Jin Auh and Jackie Ko in New York, and Sarah Chalfant and Luke Ingram in the U.K.

My editors Tim Duggan, Emily Cunningham, Bella Lacey, and Michal Shavit.

Oscar Casares, the New Writers Project at the University of Texas–Austin, where I served as a visiting assistant professor in the spring semester of 2013, and where some parts of this book were written.

And to my colleague Eric Bennett, who read an early draft of this book, for his encouraging words.

*Also by E. C. Osondu and available from Granta Books*
*www.grantabooks.com*

# VOICE OF AMERICA

A brilliantly original, deft and darkly funny short story collection
set in Nigeria and America. *Voice of America* moves from boys and
girls in villages and refugee camps to the disillusionment and
confusion of young married couples living in America, and then
back to bustling Lagos. These are stories of two countries and of
the frayed bonds between them.

'Hope and humour along with hardship and heartbreak. It's easy
to see why Jonathan Franzen is a fan' *Daily Mail*

'Osondu charts the borderlands where different cultures meet
with great skill' *Sunday Times*

'Compelling ... powerful storytelling' *Scotsman*

'Inventive and humorous' *Guardian*

'Wonderful' *Observer*

'Outstanding' *Financial Times*

# LOOKING IN CLASSROOMS

## SECOND EDITION

## Thomas L. Good
University of Missouri-Columbia

## Jere E. Brophy
Michigan State University, East Lansing

HARPER & ROW, PUBLISHERS
New York, Hagerstown, San Francisco, London

Sponsoring Editor: Wayne E. Schotanus
Project Editor: Robert Ginsberg
Designer: Helen Iranyi
Production Supervisor: Kewal K. Sharma
Compositor: Kingsport Press
Printer and Binder: The Murray Printing Company
Art Studio: Danmark & Michaels, Inc.

Photograph on p. 297 by Yeomans, Woodfin Camp
Photographs on pp. 298 and 299 by Editorial Photocolor Archives.

*LOOKING IN CLASSROOMS, Second Edition*

Library of Congress Cataloging in Publication Data
Good, Thomas L   Date-
    Looking in classrooms.

    Bibliography: p.
    Includes index.
    1.  Teaching.   2.   Classroom management.   I.   Brophy,
Jere E., joint author.   II.   Title.
LB1025.2.G62      1978            371.1'02            77–17038
ISBN 0–06–042402–8

*To Our Parents*

# CONTENTS

# 3.
# SEEING IN CLASSROOMS 33

# 4.
# TEACHER EXPECTATIONS 65

# 5.
# MODELING 117

# 6.
# MANAGEMENT I:
# PREVENTING PROBLEMS 163

# 7.
# MANAGEMENT II:
# COPING WITH PROBLEMS
# EFFECTIVELY 196

# 8.
# INDIVIDUALIZATION
# AND OPEN EDUCATION   249

# 9.
# CLASSROOM GROUPING   279

# 10.
# INSTRUCTION   338

# PREFACE

We are pleased by the positive reaction that the first edition received from students and instructors; its success has allowed us to proceed with this second edition. In this new edition we have retained the basic theme and format of the original and about 70 percent of the material. However, the content that remains has been heavily edited and rewritten to include relevant new research and to improve its language and communication.

A major addition to the book is a chapter on individualization and openness (Chapter 8). This chapter provides the reader with a basic orientation to key aspects of individual and open education programs, and it helps to develop concrete observation skills that can be used to examine those programs. Another major change in the book is a substantial new look at classroom grouping (Chapter 9). Discussion focuses upon the fact that desegregation and mainstreaming activities will increasingly force schools and teachers to deal with a widening range of student ability. This chapter discusses how to teach mixed-ability classes successfully and how to rearrange student groups to achieve desired effects.

Throughout the book, we have attempted to add content that will increase the reader's ability to conceptualize, measure, and improve classroom behavior. For example, additional information about case study techniques (Chapter 3) is included in order to help readers to actually *use* the case study as a tool. We feel that this additional skill (along with the scales for coding classroom behavior and advice on how to use them that was a part of the first edition) will enhance the reader's ability to see and to describe any classroom setting. Similarly, the management chapters, strongly oriented toward preventing misbehavior, have been expanded to include behavior modification concepts and the group techniques recommended by Glasser (Chapters 6 and 7). These additions increase alternative ways to think about preventing misbehavior and/or creating systems that support positive behavior.

Since we wrote the first edition five years ago, a great deal of imaginative research has taken place in classrooms, and we have discussed much of this research here. We believe that it is important for teachers to know about the findings of recent classroom research. However, much of teaching is still an art and we contend that if teachers are to be successful, they must develop a way to see, comprehend, and respond to the complex, rapid flow of classroom behavior. Ultimately, teachers have to find, develop, and continue to refine their own teaching style if they are to be successful. We feel that this book will help the teacher to develop a classroom language—a way to see, describe, and understand classroom behavior—that is an important first step in developing a teaching style that is both effective and personally satisfying.

We want to express our appreciation to those individuals and institutions who have supported us and who have made this revision possible. Outstanding typing support was provided by Barbara Kitchen and Barta Stevenson through the Center for Research in Social Behavior, University of Missouri, Bruce J. Biddle, Director, and the Institute for Research on Teaching, Michigan State University, Judy Lanier and Lee Shulman, Co-Directors.

Special appreciation and thanks are extended to our wives, Suzi and Arlene, and to our children, Heather, Jeff, Cheri, and Joe, for their encouragement. Finally, as in the first edition, we dedicate this book to all who teach and who attempt to structure exciting environments for students, but especially to our first and most important teachers—our parents.

THOMAS L. GOOD
JERE E. BROPHY

# 1/ CLASSROOM LIFE

This book has two major purposes. The first is to help teachers and students of classroom behavior to develop ways of looking at and describing what goes on in classrooms. The second is to provide teachers with concrete suggestions about ways they can have a positive influence on the interests, learning, and social development of their students.

Teachers are often unaware of much of what they do, and this lack of perception sometimes results in unwise, self-defeating behavior. Our intent is to show that the development of skills for observing and describing classroom behavior is a prerequisite for improving classroom teaching.

To the extent that teachers can become aware of what happens in the classroom and can monitor accurately their personal behavior and that of their students, they can function as *decision makers*. To the extent that teachers cannot do this, they will be controlled by classroom events. When teachers fail to control classroom events, progress is often not optimal for some students (typically the low achievers).

The first two chapters will sensitize the reader to the fact that it is difficult to perceive what takes place in the classroom. Life in classrooms proceeds at such a complex and rapid pace that it is difficult for the teacher or observer to monitor teacher and student behavior accurately. To make valid suggestions about how to improve classroom behavior, however, one must be able to see and assess what is happening in classrooms.

The remainder of the book is designed to provide teachers, observers, and researchers with suggestions about what to look for in classrooms. Following the introductory chapters are several chapters that contain suggestions about how teachers can interact profitably with their students. Furthermore, there are detailed suggestions about how to organize and manage classrooms for effective learning. Observation forms for coding classroom behavior are included at the ends of these chapters. The reader can use the forms to measure some of the behaviors discussed in the chapters. Thus, the chapters on classroom content have a twin focus: (1) to describe key classroom behaviors and make suggestions about effective teaching and (2) to provide ways to measure the presence or absence of some of these behaviors.

Much teaching is of a hypothesis testing nature. For example, we might assume that a student who has been out of his or her seat creating behavioral problems needs more structure (shorter assignments, more explicit directions, self-checking devices) to work alone productively. However, other factors may be producing the misbehavior. If the student's problem is not corrected by following up on the first hypothesis, other strategies will have to be used. Good planning is essential, but teachers must also be willing to examine and alter their plans as they execute them. Those who have a rich fund of knowledge about how students learn and develop will be able to develop better hypotheses about how to correct student problems.

To help you learn to do this, we have included many extended examples of classroom behavior in the text and have added practice exercises to help you learn to describe and cope with classroom behavior. Consistent with this philosophy of active involvement, we will begin with simulated dialogue from a classroom.

## MRS. TURNER: AN EXAMPLE

Before turning to a discussion of the problems that teachers face, it will be useful to sample a few moments of life in an elementary classroom. As you read the example, try to pinpoint those teaching behaviors that you feel are effective and those that you feel are ineffective. Think about what you would have done differently if you had been the teacher. Jot down your ideas and reactions as you read the material and try to note as many teaching strengths and weaknesses as you can find. This will give you a chance to describe and react to classroom behavior and to find out how much you can see in the example.

Mrs. Turner is a fourth-grade teacher at Maplewood Elementary School in a large university town in the South. She has 30 students in her class. Students at Maplewood come primarily from lower middle-class and working-class homes. Most are white (78 percent), and the rest (22 percent) are black. Sally Turner has taught at Maplewood since graduating from the university three years ago. Her husband is in his last year of law school and they plan to leave the city when he finishes school.

The following classroom scene takes place in March. The students have been reading about Columbus, and Sally's lesson plan involves two goals: (1) to review the basic facts surrounding the voyages to the New World and (2) to have students compare the uncertainties, dangers, and fears that Columbus and his sailors faced to those that astronauts confront on their journeys to the moon. The classroom begins as Sally passes out mimeographed copies of a map showing the sea routes that Columbus followed on each trip.

BILLY: *(almost shouting)* I didn't get no map.

TEACHER: *(calmly and deliberately)* Billy, share Rosie's map. Tim, you can look with either Margaret or Larry.

TIM: Can I look with Jill?

TEACHER: *(slightly agitated)* Okay, but don't play around. You and Jill always get into trouble. *(Most of the students turn to look at Jill and Tim.)* I don't want you two fooling around today! *(smiling with warmth)* Okay, class, now does everybody have a map? I wanted to pass out these maps before we start. You can see that the route of each voyage is traced on the map. It might help you to understand that there were different trips and different routes. Pay special attention during the discussion because you'll need to know the information for tommorrow's quiz. If the discussion goes well, I have a special treat for you— two filmstrips.

CLASS: *(in a spontaneous, exuberant roar)* Yea!

TEACHER: Who can tell me something about Columbus' background?

KAY: *(calling out)* He was born in 1451 in Italy.

TEACHER: Good answer, Kay. I can tell you have been reading. Class, can anyone tell me who influenced Columbus' urge to explore unknown seas? *(She looks around and calls on Jerry, one of several students who have raised their hands.)*

JERRY: He had read about Marco Polo's voyage to Cathay and about the fantastic riches he found there.

TEACHER: Okay. Jan, when did Columbus first land in America?
JAN: 1492.

TEACHER: Terrific! I know you have been reading. Good girl! Where did Columbus stop for supplies?

JIM: *(laughingly)* But Mrs. Turner, the date was on the map you passed out.

TEACHER: *(with irritation)* Jim, don't call out without raising your hand!

BILL: *(calling out)* The Canary Islands.

TEACHER: Okay, Bill. Now, what were the names of the three ships? *(She looks around the room and calls on Biff, who has his hand up.)* Biff, you tell us. *(Biff's face turns red and he stares at the floor.)* Biff Taylor! Don't raise your hand unless you know the answer. Okay, class, who can tell me the names of the three ships? *(she calls on Andrew, who has his hand up.)*

ANDREW: *(hesitantly)* The Santa Maria, the Nina, and the . . .

TEACHER: *(supplying the answer)* Pinta. Nancy, how long did this first voyage to the New World take?

NANCY: *(shrugging her shoulders)* I don't know.

TEACHER: Think about it. It took a long time, Nancy. Was it less or more than 100 days? *(silence)* The answer was on the first page of the reading material. Class, can anyone tell me how long the voyage took? *(No hands are raised.)* Class, you better learn that because it will be on the exam! Now, who can tell me why Columbus came to the New World? *(Mary and two other students raise their hands.)* Mary?

MARY: *(firmly and loudly)* Because they wanted to discover new riches like explorers in the East.

TEACHER: *(She pauses and looks at Max and Helen, who are talking, and at Jim, who is headed for the pencil sharpener. Max and Helen immediately cease their conversation.)* Jim, sit down this minute. *(Jim heads for his seat.)* What are you doing on the floor?

JIM: *(smiling sheepishly)* Jan wanted me to sharpen her pencil.

JAN: *(red-faced and alarmed)* Mrs. Turner, that's not true! *(Class laughs.)*

TEACHER: Quiet, both of you. You don't need a sharp pencil. Sit down. *(resuming discussion)* Good answer, Mary. You were really alert. Why else, Mary? Can you think of any other reason?

NANCY: *(calling out)* Because they wanted to find a short cut to the Eastern treasures. The only other way was overland, and it was thousands of miles over deserts and mountains.

TEACHER: *(proudly)* Good, Nancy! Now, who are "they"? Who wanted the riches?

BILLY: *(calling out)* Queen Isabella and King Ferdinand. She paid for the trip because she thought Columbus would make her rich.

TEACHER: Okay, Billy, but remember to raise your hand before speaking. Why do you think Columbus was interested in making the trip? Just to find money?

CLASS: *(calling out)* No!

TEACHER: Well, what problems did the sailors have? *(She looks around and calls on Jim, who has his hand up.)*

JIM: Well, they were away from home and couldn't write. Sort of like when I go to summer camp. I don't write. I was lonely the first few days, but . . .

TEACHER: *(somewhat confused and irritated)* Well, that's not exactly what I had in mind. Did they get sick a lot? Class, does anyone know? *(She looks around the room and sees Claire with a raised hand.)*

CLAIRE: Well, I don't remember reading about sailors getting sick with Columbus, but I know that sailors then got sick with scurvy and they had to be careful.

*(Hank approaches the teacher with great embarrassment and asks in hushed tones if he can go to the bathroom. Permission is granted.)*

TEACHER: Yes, good answer, Claire. Claire, did they try to prevent scurvy?

CLAIRE: They carried lots of fruit. . . . You know, like lemons.

TEACHER: Okay, Claire, but what special kind of fruit was important to eat? *(Claire blushes and Mrs. Turner silently forms "c" sound with her mouth.)*

CLAIRE: Citrus.

TEACHER: Very good! What other problems did the sailors have? *(She calls on Matt, who has his hand up.)*

MATT: Well, they didn't have any maps and they didn't know much about the wind or anything, so they were afraid of the unknown and scared of sailing off the earth. *(laughter)*

TEACHER: *(Noticing that many students are gazing at the floor or looking out the window, she begins to speak louder and more quickly.)* No, educated men knew that the earth was round. Don't you read very carefully?

ALICE: *(calling out)* But even though educated men knew the earth was round, Columbus' sailors didn't believe it. They called the Atlantic Ocean the "Sea of Darkness," and Columbus had to keep two diaries. He showed the sailors the log with the least miles so they wouldn't get scared. But the men threatened mutiny anyway.

TEACHER: *(with elation)* Excellent answer, Alice. Yes, the men were afraid of the unknown; however, I think most of them knew that the earth was round. Okay, Matt, you made me drift away from my question: Why did Columbus want to go—what were the reasons for his trip other than money? James, what do you think: *(James shrugs his shoulders.)* Well, when you read your lesson, class, look for that answer. It's important and I might test you on it. *(with exasperation)* Tim! Jill! Stop pushing each other this instant! I told you two not to play around. Why didn't you listen to me?

TIM: *(with anger)* Jill threw the map in her desk. I wanted to use it so I could trace my own map.

JILL: But it's my map and . . .

TEACHER: *(firmly)* That's enough! I don't want to hear any more. Give me the map and the three of us will discuss it during recess.

PRINCIPAL: *(talking over the PA system)* Teachers, I'm sorry to break in on your classes, but I have an important announcement to make. The high school band will not be with us this afternoon. So 2:00 to 2:30 classes will not be cancelled. Since I have interrupted your class. I would also like to remind you that tonight is PTA. Teachers, be sure that the boys and girls remind . . . *(During the announcement, many pupils begin private conversations with their neighbors.)*

TEACHER: *(without much emotion or enthusiasm)* It's not recess time yet. Listen, we still have work to do. Tell you what we're going to do now. I've got two filmstrips: one describes the astronauts' first trip to the moon; the other describes Columbus' first trip to the New World. Watch closely when we show these films because after we see the filmstrips, I'm going to ask you to tell me the similarities between the two trips. Ralph, turn off the lights.

HANK: *(returning from his trip to the restroom)* Hey, Mrs. Turner, why are the lights out in here? It's spooky in here!

ALICE: *(impishly)* It's the Sea of Darkness! *(Class breaks out in a spontaneous roar.)*

TEACHER: Quiet down, class! It's time to see the filmstrips.

The example of this fourth-grade class illustrates many points, including the fact that teachers are busy and that teaching is very complex. The hurried pace of classroom life is well illustrated. Sally had a constant stream of student behavior to react to and she had to make a number of decisions instantaneously. Several decisions were quite complex, and on occasion you may have expressed some bewilderment—"If I were the teacher, how would I have responded?"

If you did not take notes as you read the material, you should quickly reread the above example and write out your reactions to the teaching incident. What were the teacher's weaknesses and strengths? If you were to discuss this observation with the teacher, what would you tell her? You may want to repeat this exercise when you finish reading the book, in order to assess the perspectives and information you have gained between now and then. Complete the exercise now, then read our reactions to this teaching incident, which follow.

## REACTIONS TO THE EXAMPLE

Sally Turner, like most teachers, has some strong qualities and some weak ones. Let us begin with some of the good things that she does or attempts to do. First, Sally's attempt to breathe life into Columbus and ancient history by linking it to something significant in the students' lives is notable. She has thought about the lesson and has gone to the trouble to order filmstrips both of Columbus' voyage (a simulated description) and of the astronauts' trip to the moon.

She does a fair job of giving feedback to students about the correctness or incorrectness of their responses. After most responses, she provided feedback to describe the adequacy of student answers. Although this may seem to be a small point, it is often highly significant. Frequently, teachers fail to provide students with this information. They do not respond to student answers, or they respond in such a way as to make it difficult for some students to know if their response is correct. An instance of such ambiguous teacher feedback is: "So, you think it's 1492?" Although many students know whether the response is right or wrong, many low-achievement students will not know unless the teacher specifically confirms or negates their response. If students are to learn basic facts and concepts, they must know if their answers are adequate or incomplete.

### Teacher Questions

Many discussions are parrotlike sessions, with teachers asking a question, receiving a student response, asking a question of a new student, and so forth. Such discussions typically are boring and accomplish little other than the assessment of students' factual knowledge. Assessment of factual knowledge is important, but if that is all that is done in discussion, students may come to perceive that the teacher is interested only in finding out who knows the answers. When this occurs, "discussion" becomes a fragmented ritual rather than a meaningful, enjoyable process.

There are two major ways in which teachers can influence student answers: (1) by the type of questions the teacher originally asks the student and (2) by follow-up questions the teacher may pose to students after they respond. Sally Turner's initial questions were primarily factual questions. The students might have been more interested if they had been involved more directly in the discussion. This could have been accomplished with more questions of value and opinion. The following questions are types of discussion questions that could have been raised: Would you like to be an astronaut? Why would you want to go the moon? Why is it important to go to the moon? How would you like to be isolated from your parents and friends for several days? How would you feel being in a 5-by-7-foot room and unable to leave it? Would you like to be a sailor on a ship and stay on that ship week after week, not knowing where you were going or what you would see? Would you volunteer for such a voyage? Why? What is mutiny? Is it justified? Would you have felt like mutiny if you had been a crew member on Columbus' voyage? Was it important to discover the New World? Why? How do you feel when you are afraid or apprehensive?

Some of these questions (e.g., "Was it important to discover the New World?") could be considered factual questions, since the book probably gives an "answer." How students react to such questions depends upon the teacher. Too often teachers' questions say implicitly "tell me what the book said." Students should be encouraged to assess facts rather than to simply accept the reasons listed in the text. Even when factual questions are used, they can be used to stimulate pupil thinking. For example, the teacher might ask, "The book states two reasons why Spaniards wanted to discover the New World. What were these two reasons, and what beliefs and values underlay their reasoning?" Or instead of asking "When did Columbus discover the new World?" the teacher might ask why the trip wasn't made before 1492. In the teaching example, Sally made excessive use of factual questions and used too few questions of value and opinion that might have stimulated student interest in the discussion.

In addition, her students were not encouraged to ask questions or to evaluate responses of classmates. For example, Sally might have encouraged students in this way: "Today I have several questions that I want to find answers for. You have been reading the material for a week now, and you probably have some questions that weren't answered in the reading material. Maybe the class and I can help you answer these questions. Any questions that we can't answer we'll look up in the *World Book* or in the school library. I wonder why Queen Isabella picked Columbus to head the voyage? Why not some other sailor? I think that's an interesting question! Now, let's have *your* questions. We'll list them on the board and see if we have answered them at the end of the discussion."

Although it is not necessary to solicit questions for every discussion period, it is a good instructional practice to do so frequently. Such teacher behavior tells pupils that the purpose of discussion is to satisfy their needs and interests as well as the teacher's. Furthermore, the teacher's behavior in asking for questions says:

1. I have important questions and I want your viewpoint.
2. You certainly must have some important questions.
3. We'll have an interesting discussion answering one another's questions.
4. If we need more information, we'll get it.

This discussion stance, if used consistently, will in time teach students that discussion is not a quiz but a profitable and enjoyable process of sharing information to satisfy personal curiosity.

It is especially important that the teacher communicate enthusiasm and respect for students who ask questions. Some teachers call for student questions but then react to those questions in such a way as to discourage students from asking about issues that really interest them. Such teacher comments as "Well, that is not directly related to our discussion" or "That was answered in the book" may convince a student that he or she is the only one in class who doesn't know the answer, or that the teacher doesn't want students to ask questions.

**Teacher Questions After Student Responses**
Sally seldom encouraged the students to evaluate their own thinking (e.g., "Well, that's one way; what are some other ways that Columbus could have boosted his crew's morale?" "That's an accurate statement of how the crew members felt, but what about Columbus? Do you think he was fearful?"). Nor did she ask questions to help them evaluate the thinking of their classmates (e.g., "Sam gave his opinion about sailing with Columbus. Bill, do you agree with him? How do you feel?" "What are some other reasons in addition to the good ones that Tim gave?"). Such opportunities to explore a particular question in depth help to make the discussion more enjoyable to students, make it less "right answer" centered, and help

teacher and students alike to see if they *really* understand the material.

To reiterate, Sally did a good job of giving students feedback about the correctness of answers, and on occasion she did *probe* for additional information. The word "probe" means that the teacher seeks an additional response from the student after the first response, for clarification. Probing questions will stimulate pupils to provide additional information or to demonstrate more awareness. Smith (1969) points out several ways in which teachers can probe student answers:

1. Teacher Seeks Further Clarification by the Pupil ("What do you mean?" "Can you explain more fully?")—asking the pupil for more information or meaning.
2. Teacher Seeks Increased Pupil Critical Awareness ("Why do you think that is so?"—asking the student to justify his or her response rationally.
3. Teacher Seeks to Focus the Pupil's Response ("How does this relate to . . . ?")—after a good response teachers may want to focus attention on a related issue.
4. Teacher Prompts Pupil (Teacher: "Ralph, give me the missing puzzle piece." Ralph: "I don't know which one it is." Teacher: "Well, is it a big one or a small one . . . ?")—the teacher gives the student a hint, making it easier to respond.

Unfortunately, the word "probe" often conjures up a negative image to teachers. They react to it as though the word meant "pick the student's answer apart." No such usage is intended here. The appropriate meaning is to help students to thoughtfully consider the implications of what they do and say—to think about the material. Probing techniques should be gentle ways to focus students' attention and to help them think. For example, an automatic response to "When did Columbus discover America?" is an unthinking "1492." However, the question "Why not 1400 or 1450?" forces a consideration of what the world was like in 1400. In the same way, the question "Why not 1965 for a moon walk?" focuses discussion on a variety of factors (national priorities, safety, etc.).

This is not to imply that factual questions are unimportant or that they should not be used in discussions. Factual questions are very important, but we feel that they should be used with other types of questions so that students also consider the implications of the facts or the circumstances that produce them. Probing questions are an especially useful way to help students think more fully about material. A useful exercise for the reader would be to review the sample dialogue in Mrs. Turner's classroom and to note where probing techniques could have been useful. *Write out the actual probes you would have used.*

### How Does the Teacher Control Classroom Interaction?

An especially interesting fact in Sally's teaching was that she seldom (there was but *one* instance) called on students who had not volunteered. If you reread the dialogue, you will see that either students call out the answer or Sally calls on students who have their hands up. Often it is useful to call on students who do not raise their hands:

1. Shy students seldom raise their hands, and they need opportunities to speak in public and develop their communicative skills and self-assertion.
2. Low-achieving students often learn that to answer incorrectly is to receive public ridicule. Students who avoid public response opportunities need to be called upon and given opportunities to learn that they can participate successfully.
3. When students learn that their teacher only calls on students who raise their hands, they may begin to tune out discussions. Calling on students who do not have their hands up may increase student attention. Some teachers fall into the equally bad habit of calling on a student before they ask a question (although Sally does not exhibit this problem): "Jeff, what do you think about . . . ?" "Heather, state Boyle's law." This procedure tells students that they do not have to listen unless they are named.

We do not know why Sally fails to call upon students who do not raise their hands, but if this is her typical teaching behavior, the non-hand-raiser is seldom called upon in her class. A clue to explain Sally's behavior is provided by one incident. Recall that in the exchange with Biff, she scolded him for having the audacity to raise his hand without knowing the answer. This suggests that Sally wants "right" answers; that she is more interested in establishing her point and moving on with her lesson than she is in the learning of individual students. If a teacher typically responds this way, students will learn that they are not to raise their hands unless they are absolutely sure that their answer is correct. Often, calling on students who know the right answer is an unconscious teacher strategy for providing "self-reinforcement." Teachers may delude themselves into believing that they are doing a good job because some students consistently respond with good answers. Naturally, there will always be some students who are bigger risk-takers than others (such as those in the example who called out answers). If teachers consistently show that they want to hear "right" answers, however, many students, especially the timid non-gamblers, will be afraid to participate in class discussions.

Admittedly, one example of Mrs. Turner's classroom behavior is not enough information upon which to base any but the most speculative conclusions; however, such behavior should encourage an observer to look for more information to confirm or negate the notion that she does not want students to respond unless they know the answer. Some teachers, especially young, beginning teachers, unwittingly fall into the trap of discouraging youngsters from responding unless they know the answer "cold." This is because silence or incorrect answers are difficult to respond to and are often embarrassing or threatening.

The incident with Biff illustrates two important points: (1) Teachers may encourage students not to listen by falling into ineffective but consistent questioning styles. (2) Often, we can get enough evidence from what we see in classrooms to be able to make decisions and give firm suggestions to teachers, but at other times (e.g., the exchange with Biff), we may only note clues about teacher behavior or teacher assumptions. These need to be checked out by talking with the teacher or making additional observations.

### Different Teacher Behavior for Male and Female Students?

Interestingly, Sally does not praise boys but frequently praises girls. Again, it is not possible to say firmly that she favors girls, but it is reasonable to say that in this instance, the teacher was more responsive and supportive to female students.

It is notable that no male student received teacher praise. Also, while Sally makes very little attempt to work with any of the students when they give inappropriate responses, she is more likely to work with girls than with boys. When boys give an inappropriate response, she accepts the performance and either provides the answer herself or calls upon another student to answer. However, on two different occasions, she stays with a girl who is having difficulty responding. For example, when Nancy fails to respond to the question, "How long did the voyage take?" Sally attempts to make it easier, first by providing a clue ("It took a long time") and then by reducing the complexity of the question from a memory question to a choice question ("Was it less or more than 100 days?"). Similarly, when Claire can not remember the word "citrus," Sally provides her with a nonverbal clue.

Although we would want to collect more information describing Sally Turner's behavior toward male and female students, she may be more likely to praise the performance of girls and to stay with them and work with them when they do not answer correctly. Even though the frequency of questions that Sally asks boys and girls is similar, the *quality* of her feedback to boys and girls differs. The term "quality" refers to the *way* in which a teacher interacts with pupils. Does the teacher ask hard or easy questions? How long does the teacher wait for responses? Does the teacher praise answers? Does the teacher probe for more information?

**CLASSROOM MANAGEMENT**
In the area of classroom management (creating a learning environment, maintaining student involvement, etc.), Sally appears to be an average teacher. Students are generally attentive to her and to the discussion. Although the students do not appear enthusiastically engaged, they do pay attention and there are few interruptions. However, there are several areas in which Sally Turner could improve.

To begin with, she does not have enough maps for all the students. Equipment and material shortages inevitably lead to trouble, especially when students get to keep the material. A more careful count of the materials might have prevented both the minor delay at the beginning of the discussion and the major disruption (students fighting over a map) that occurred later. Upon finding the shortage, and after hearing Tim's request to sit with Jill, Sally might have responded: "Okay, that's fine. Sit with Jill, because I know you and Jill can share cooperatively. Billy and Tim, I'm sorry you didn't get maps. I failed to make enough copies, but I'll draw each of you a *special* map this afternoon." This would have accomplished two important things: (1) It would have assured Billy and Tim that they would get maps and made it less likely that they would "take the law into their own hands." (As will be pointed out in Chapter 6 on management, what the teacher does to prevent misbehavior from happening is substantially more important than what is done after misbehavior occurs.) (2) This response would have encouraged a more appropriate student expectation, and perhaps better cooperation, in Jill and Tim. The teacher's original remarks ("You and Jill always get into trouble . . .") placed Jill and Tim in the spotlight. Such remarks may have caused them to develop an inappropriate attitude about misbehavior. By implying that it was expected, the teacher subtly condoned misbehavior and made it more likely. The implications of the teacher attributing negative rather than positive motives to student behavior will be discussed in Chapter 4.

### Credibility

Sally has developed the bad habit of not following up on what she says. In this class situation, we hear her say on several occasions: "Don't call out answers, raise your hand." However, she repeatedly accepts answers that are called out and responds to these answers on several occasions with acceptance. Recall this instance:

TEACHER: *(with irritation)* Jim, don't call out comments without raising your hand.
BILL: *(calling out)* The Canary Islands.
TEACHER: Okay, Bill . . .

There were several times when the teacher accepted such responses. As we will see in future chapters, these discrepant teacher behaviors tell students that the teacher does not mean what he or she says. Such discrepancies, if they are consistent, may lead to countless discipline problems.

Whether or not students call out answers is not the point here. In the authors' opinion, there are times when students' academically relevant responses (particularly those of older students or younger children who have limited academic skills) should be encouraged, and times when students should be allowed to respond directly to the teacher or to one another without permission. However, teachers should be consistent in their demands. If call-out responses are not wanted, teachers should consistently communicate this fact. For example, when a student calls out an answer, the teacher should either ignore the student's response and call on someone else, or acknowledge the response indirectly ("Raise your hand if you want to respond. We don't want call-out answers today.") and call on another student ( who may or may not have a raised hand).

We mentioned call-out responses as being particularly desirable when the teacher is trying to get students to respond to one another and trying to encourage students to evaluate the adequacy of responses on their own. You may be prompted to ask, then, why call-out answers are sometimes bad. The two undesirable aspects of call-outs are: (1) students who are verbally aggressive dominate the discussion and (2) low-achieving students who take more time to process information may not even think about questions because other students answer them too quickly. The purpose of discussion is not to yield quick, automatic responses but to allow students to think.

There is at least one other area in which Sally could improve her classroom management. In two different discipline situations, she made use of rhetorical questions that caused her needless difficulty. For example, Jim has already started to his seat (which is what the teacher wants) when she needlessly asks, "What are you doing on the floor?" This question then touches off a more serious disruption. Similarly, in the Jill and Tim exchange, the teacher queries pointlessly ("Why didn't you listen to me?"), and again the situation deteriorates and the whole class is distracted. The use of questions in discipline situations will be discussed fully in Chapters 6 and 7, but here we can say that such rhetorical, aggressive questions typically lead to clowning or aggressive student behavior. Consider how you feel when someone says to you: "Why don't you listen?" "Can't you do anything right?" "Why are you always the difficult one?" These questions make most people feel irritated or aggressive. When we are treated aggressively, we respond aggressively.

**Introducing the Lesson**

Previously, we mentioned the teacher's negative expectations about student behavior ("You and Jill always get into trouble"). Sally also communicates undesirable expectations in other ways. Perhaps the most striking is her tendency to emphasize that the discussion is important only because it will prepare students for test material. Her behavior does not suggest that learning is fun or that she enjoys learning. Note especially Sally's poor introduction to the lesson. She places great stress on the fact that students will be tested on the material, but she provides little additional rationale for why they are discussing Columbus' voyage. Similarly, teachers often use only the threat of poor grades to motivate students. Contrast Sally's introduction with the one that follows:

TEACHER: Today we are going to talk about the astronauts' trip to the moon. For years and years, prior to the first space flight the possibility of space flight was debated. Several years ago many people thought such a trip would be impossible, and there were fears that the men would be lost in space due to some unknown causes. In fact, the unknowns faced by the astronauts were very similar to the fears that Columbus and his men faced when they voyaged to the New World.

Yesterday I passed out a list of questions that we are going to discuss about Columbus' voyages. Take out your discussion guides now. I am interested in hearing your responses to the questions, and I'll enjoy listening to you identify and compare the problems that Columbus and the astronauts faced. After the discussion, we'll see two filmstrips that are interesting descriptions . . . *(Class sounds its approval in a spontaneous cheer.)*

Here, the introduction more clearly suggests to the pupils what will happen and why. It also conveys a belief that the activity is enjoyable and important. Furthermore, beginning the lesson with a more recent event (the astronauts rather than Columbus) may increase student interest in the discussion. Sally's introduction should have been more focused and less tied to the assertion that "you'll need to know the information for tomorrow's quiz." At other times in the discussion, she also makes reference to the fact that listening is important because of future testing. Such behavior does much to convince students that learning is arbitrary, an irrelevant exercise done only to please adults or to receive high grades. This point will be expanded in Chapter 4.

### Spontaneous Reaction to Student Comments

Sally also failed to pick up on themes that students initiated spontaneously, even when they were related to the purpose of the discussion. Part of Sally's plan was to get students to appreciate the sense of adventure and apprehension that explorers face. On two different occasions, students indirectly brought up their sense of fear, but Sally failed to respond. Jim, for instance, mentioned the loneliness of the first few days of summer camp. Here Sally could have asked a variety of questions: "Why are the first few days of summer camp strange? How did you feel on your first day at school? How do you think you will feel on your first day at junior high? Why are we uncomfortable when we do something for the first time?" After such discussion, the fact that the newness of the situation faced by the explorers was both stressful and exciting would be more clearly appreciated by the class. A similar opportunity appears again at the end of the discussion when Hank verbalizes the spookiness of the room and Alice cleverly labels it as the Sea of Darkness. Sally could have profitably paused and pointed out that Alice's remark was a good one and perhaps have added, in a very quiet voice: "Okay, now listen. For one minute, no one will make a noise. Let's pretend that we are on the Pinta. We have been at sea for two months. It is now completely dark and there is no sound on the ship. The only noise is the roar of the sea and the creaking of the boat as it is tossed from wave to wave. We are all scared because no one has ever sailed this sea! What will we run into in the darkness? What is our destination? What will it be like when we reach it? Will the residents there be hostile?"

If successfully used, such techniques may increase student awareness of the fears and other feelings of explorers and may involve the students more centrally in the discussion. Teachers often stimulate very profitable and enjoyable discussions when they capitalize upon spontaneous student examples.

## SUMMARY

We have presented some of our reactions to the teaching incident. We hope that the teaching episode and our comments have caused you to think about teaching behavior. Perhaps you noted strengths or weaknesses that were not touched on in our comments, or perhaps you take exception to some of the comments. If so, that's fine! The purpose of the chapter was to involve you directly in the process of looking at classroom behavior.

In Appendix A, you will find five additional classroom scenes that provide teacher-student dialogue in elementary and secondary classrooms. You may want to read these cases now, in order to raise more questions about teaching behavior. The greatest use of these materials will most likely come after you have completed reading the text, however, because the cases will allow you to practice the skills and put to use the information you glean from reading the book.

In conclusion, this chapter provided an opportunity to "visit" and react to a classroom that was neither inordinately bad nor good. Sally, like most teachers, had a number of strengths and weaknesses. Sally is probably unaware of many of her teaching weaknesses, and she will not improve her teaching behavior unless she becomes aware of her ineffective techniques.

Are most teachers unaware of certain aspects of their classroom behavior, and of its consequences? If so, why are they unaware? How can they become aware of what they do in the classroom and more knowledgeable about how their behavior affects students? We turn to these questions in the next two chapters.

### SUGGESTED ACTIVITIES AND QUESTIONS

1. Watch a videotape or film of classroom behavior with a group of fellow students or teachers. List the major strengths and weaknesses that you will see and compare your list with others.

2. If films are not available, select one of the case studies in Appendix A. As you read the class description, list the teaching strengths and weaknesses that you perceive. Compare your list with those of others. How similar or dissimilar is the reaction to the teaching behavior?

3. Watch four or five 5-minute teaching segments that are drawn from different teachers. View the teaching segments with at least three other observers. After watching the filmed teaching, rank order the teachers on the following criteria:

a. I would feel most comfortable in this class.

b. I would learn the most in this class.

c. This teacher would be least likely to criticize me.

See if the teachers in the film were given the same rank order by all observers. Try to identify the teaching characteristics that made you respond as you did. What, for example, led each of you to think that you would feel comfortable in a particular teacher's classroom? If individuals feel differently about teachers (and they may), try to identify the characteristics that attracted some observers but repelled other observers.

4. Think about the grade level that you teach (or plan to teach) and identify the ten most important skills, attitudes, and/or behaviors that a teacher must possess if he or she is to instruct students effectively at this grade level. Keep this list so that you can compare it with the list you make after you have read the entire book.

5. Reread the example of Mrs. Turner's fourth-grade class and identify four situations in which she could have probed for student responses. Write out the actual probes you would have used if you had been the teacher. Read some of the case studies presented in Appendix A and identify places where teachers could have asked probing questions.

6. The authors provided a critique of Mrs. Turner's teaching. What additional teaching behaviors (strengths or weaknesses) did you find that we did not mention? Explain why you feel these behaviors represent strengths or weaknesses.

7. Assume that you were an observer in Mrs. Turner's classroom. During recess she asks, "Well, you watched the explorer unit today. What are my two major teaching strengths and my two major weaknesses?" How would you respond? Why do you feel that the strengths and weaknesses you suggest are the most important or basic?

8. The authors rewrote Mrs. Turner's introduction to have a more desirable effect upon students. Improve upon the introduction by writing your own. In general, what steps should a good introduction include? Why?

9. Why is it that teachers have a difficult time being aware of everything that occurs in the classroom?

10. The authors suggested that before conducting class discussion, it is often a good idea to solicit questions from students. Why is this a good idea? Under what circumstances might this plan be a poor approach?

# 2/ TEACHER AWARENESS

Our brief glimpse into Sally Turner's classroom revealed that her classroom was exceedingly busy and that she was probably unaware of certain aspects of her behavior and its impact upon students. In this chapter, we will present data to support the assertion that classrooms are busy places, that the fast pace observed in Sally Turner's class is common, that teachers are sometimes unaware of their classroom behavior, and that sometimes teachers do behave in self-defeating ways. Furthermore, we will argue that teachers do not perceive many classroom events because (1) classroom interaction proceeds at a rapid pace, (2) teachers have not been trained to monitor and study their own behavior, and (3) teachers rarely receive systematic or useful feedback. Finally, we will emphasize that neither teachers nor observers are likely to make sense out of classroom behavior unless they have a definite list of important behaviors to look for.

## CLASSROOMS ARE BUSY PLACES

Teachers lead busy lives. It has been pointed out that in a single day a teacher may engage in more than one thousand interpersonal exchanges with students (Jackson, 1968). A study of four sixth-grade teachers found that they averaged 80 initiations with individual students each hour (Jackson and Lahaderne, 1967). In addition to initiating exchanges, these teachers were also responding to questions and moving from location to location. Teachers engaging in so many contacts will be hard pressed to keep track of the number and the substance of contacts that they share with each pupil. It may not be important for the teacher to remember all classroom contacts; however, recalling certain information (the ten students who didn't get a chance to present their class reports, that John had trouble with vowel sounds during reading, and so forth) may be very important.

Teachers must constantly respond to immediate needs. While teaching, they have little time to reflect upon what they are doing or planning to do, because they are busy reacting to the present situation. Unless teachers are looking for signs of student disinterest or difficulty, they may not see them. The teacher's world is literally consumed by immediate demands. Teachers are so absorbed in their present work that it is difficult for them to get a total perspective on what happens in their classrooms. Gloria Channon (1970), an elementary teacher in New York City, describes it this way:

> The teacher, like the doctor in the midst of an epidemic, is so busy with the daily doings that she finds it hard to get some distance between herself and her functions, to see what is happening. As a result she is vulnerable to each day's experience in a special transient way.

Philip Jackson's book *Life in Classrooms* (1968) shows that teachers are so completely involved in classroom activities that they are hard pressed to explain specifically what they do or what they plan to do. The self-report data provided by teachers suggest that the demands of teaching leave little time for self-observation and analysis. *If teachers cannot conceptualize classroom life before they enter the teaching profession, they will have little time to develop this ability later.*

The teacher's world is filled not only with teaching demands, but also with supervisory and administrative functions. Teachers perform such diverse duties as supervising students on playgrounds and in lunchrooms, talking with parents about the progress of their children, grading homework, duplicating assignment sheets, collecting money, and filling out forms. Channon (1970) specifies additional duties that many teachers must perform: "She works like a dog. She fills out reading cards and duplicates office records, book inventories, lunch lists, class photo lists, state census forms, report cards, reports by the hundreds . . . she writes lengthy anecdotal records and case history forms for the guidance counselors."

Thus, classrooms are busy places. The hectic pace of classroom life interferes with teachers' ability to see classroom behavior—their

own and that of the students. A number of books written by former
and current teachers have appeared in print during the past few
years. Although these books often emphasize the negative, they
do present excellent analyses of problems that exist in some classrooms. The authors often suggest that they were not trained to
see and respond to what was happening in the classroom; instead,
they were responding to stereotypes or acting the way they felt
they were supposed to act. In particular, Herbert Kohl's *36 Children*
(1967) and John Holt's *How Children Fail* (1964) dramatically show
that the first step in the authors' changing their teaching behavior
was becoming aware of what they were really doing. We shall return
to this point later in the chapter to show that researchers have
reached a similar conclusion.

## CLASSROOM AWARENESS

What proof do we have that teachers are unaware of or misinterpret
their behavior in classrooms? Some particularly revealing information is provided by the minicourse training experiences at the Far
West Educational Development Laboratory (Borg et al., 1970). That
laboratory has prepared a number of in-service courses designed
to help teachers develop specific teaching skills. For example, their
minicourse on independent work activity is designed to help teachers develop appropriate skills for (1) discussing with pupils the meaning of working alone, (2) discussing the assigned independent learning task, (3) eliciting potential problems and solutions, (4) establishing
standards for what to do when finished, (5) providing delayed response to completed student work, and (6) evaluating pupils' success
in working independently. These points are clearly specific, and
at first glance it would appear that teachers would know if they
had performed such behaviors in their teaching. Such was not the
case. Borg et al. (1970) wrote:

> The questionnaire data revealed that the majority of teachers thought
> they had used most of the skills presented in Minicourse 8 in the pre-
> course lesson. The observational data does not support this belief. The
> same phenomena have been observed in the evaluation of other mini-
> courses: teachers often believe that they use a particular set of skills prior
> to taking the course, but an objective analysis of the data shows that
> this is not usually true.

If teachers are unaware of their performance when teaching small
groups of students in minicourse laboratory sessions, it is unlikely
that they could accurately describe their behavior when teaching
an entire class. Evidence that classroom teachers misinterpret their

teaching behavior has been presented by Emmer (1967). He reports that teachers were unable to describe accurately even simple classroom behaviors, such as the percentage of time that they and their students talked. Most teachers grossly underestimated the amount of time they talked.

More information to show that teachers misperceive their behavior at times is provided by Ehman (1970). In this study, ratings of teacher behavior made by students and by classroom observers were highly similar. Ratings of the same behavior made by the teachers themselves, however, differed sharply from the other two sets of ratings. The teachers could not accurately describe what they did in the classroom.

Discrepancies between teacher and student perceptions concerning the number of opportunities that students have for decision making have been reported by Wolfson and Nash (1969). Teachers consistently perceived students to be making many more decisions than students saw themselves making.

The six studies reported here demonstrate that teachers sometimes behave in ways of which they are unaware. In the following section, we will present a few studies that describe how teachers behave in classrooms. We do not have proof that teachers are unaware of the behavior described in these studies. Nevertheless, given the goals that teachers verbally express and the current training philosophy at teacher education colleges, it seems likely that teachers are not behaving in accordance with their intentions.

### Teacher Domination

Researchers have noted that teachers monopolize communication in the classroom. Adams and Biddle (1970) concluded that teachers were the principal actors in 84 percent of classroom communication episodes. Hudgins and Ahlbrand (1969) reported figures very similar to those obtained by Adams and Biddle. This suggests that teachers monopolize classroom discussion, even though most teachers do not want to do this and are not aware that they do it. Perhaps teachers behave this way because they do not know how to solicit extended pupil talk.

Students are not as free to act as teachers believe them to be. Jackson and Wolfson (1968) vividly demonstrate the number of constraints that interfere with the wants and needs of nursery-school children. Not all the constraints they report are due to teacher behavior. Many resulted when one child interfered with the goal of another (e.g., they both wanted the same toy). Nevertheless, the numbers of constraints upon nursery-school children are amazing.

Jackson and Wolfson concluded that about 20 constraining episodes occurred each minute in the group of 97 children. Bown (in Burkhart, 1969) had this to say about data Jackson had collected in nursery schools:

> . . . he found that the kids were actually free to initiate and carry through an action only 5% of the time . . . 95% of the youngsters' actions were essentially dictated. Now this is astounding and kind of unbelievable. I don't think a teacher could believe that she was doing this. I'm sure it would not correspond with the intellectual intent.

Bown also reported data drawn from video tapes of experienced teachers. He found that the average student in the sample made an independent, self-initiated statement about once every three weeks!

The extent to which this sample of teaching is representative of teaching in general is unknown. Data indicate, however, that teachers emphasize short factual questions and that this pattern has not changed much over time. Stevens (1912) looked in high-school classes and found that two-thirds of the questions asked by teachers were factual recall. Haynes (1935) looked at sixth-grade history classes and reported that 77 percent of the questions were factual questions. Gallagher (1965) found that even teachers of gifted students asked many factual questions. More than 50 percent of their questions were cognitive memory questions. Davis and Tinsley (1967) studied student teachers teaching high-school social studies classes and reported that roughly 50 percent of the questions required factual answers. Guszak (1967) found that 14 percent of the teacher questions in reading groups merely asked students to locate information in the book, and another 57 percent were short-answer fact questions.

Borg et al. (1970) summarized this literature and suggested that the types of questions teachers ask pupils have not changed in more than half a century, despite an increased emphasis upon the need for a variety of questions (Groisser, 1964; Sanders, 1966). Factual questions are needed, especially to see if students have the basic information that is necessary before useful discussion can take place. However, teachers use many more fact questions than they probably realize.

The studies in this section were reviewed to suggest that teachers are probably more directive than they realize. In the following section, we will present data showing teachers' classroom behavior to be uneven, with different students receiving different teacher treatment. Such differential and often discriminatory teacher behavior occurs partly because teachers are not aware of their behavior, or because they do not realize its consequences.

### Other Teacher Behavior

The teacher is the principal actor in the classroom. When teachers do allow students to speak, however, which ones do they call upon? Jackson and Lahaderne (1967) indicated that child contact with the classroom teacher varies widely within the same classroom. Looking in four sixth-grade classrooms for roughly ten hours each, they found that teachers interacted with some students as few as 5 times and with others as often as 120 times. In addition, the sex of students affects the quantity and quality of the communication patterns they share with teachers. Boys have more interaction with teachers than girls. The magnitude of this ratio varies with the nature of the communication, being greatest for disciplinary exchanges and smallest for instructional messages. In both elementary and secondary classrooms, males are more salient to the teacher and receive much more criticism than females (Meyer and Thompson, 1956; Lippitt and Gold, 1959; Jackson and Lahaderne, 1967).

Apparently, students' achievement level, as well as their sex, figures heavily in whether or not they respond frequently. Good (1970) and Kranz et al. (1970) found that high-achieving elementary students received more questions and praise than low-achieving students. Mendoza, Good, and Brophy (1972), Jones (1971), and Horn (1914) reported high-achieving students in secondary schools received more response opportunities than low-achieving students. Good, Sikes, and Brophy (1972) reported that in comparison to other students, low-achieving males in junior-high classrooms received inferior treatment, while high-achieving males received more frequent and more favorable contact with the teachers.

In addition to differences in the frequency of teacher contacts with students, the quality of interaction varies with the achievement level of the student. Rowe (1969) found that teachers waited significantly longer for more capable students than for less apt students before giving the answer or calling on another student. Slower students had to respond more quickly to avoid losing their turn. Rowe also reported that these results surprised the teachers, who were not aware they were behaving in this fashion. One of the teachers, after being told of the results of the study, said, "I guess we just don't expect an answer, so we move on to someone else."

Brophy and Good (1970b) studied the classroom behavior of four first-grade teachers toward high- and low-achieving students. They

reported only minor differences in the *frequency* of teacher contact
with students of differing achievement levels, but found important
variations in the quality. Teachers were much more likely to praise
high-achieving students, even when differences among the students
in the correctness of their answers were taken into account.

When high-achieving students gave a right answer, they were
praised 12 percent of the time. Low-achieving students were praised
only 6 percent of the time following a right answer. Even though
they gave fewer right answers, low-achieving students received pro-
portionately less praise. Similarly, low-achieving students were more
likely to receive teacher criticism for a wrong answer. They were
criticized 18 percent of the time, and high achievers were criticized
6 percent of the time. Also, it was found that teachers were more
likely to stay with high-achieving students (repeat the question, provide a clue, ask a new question) when they made no response, said
"I don't know," or answered incorrectly. In contrast, they were
more likely to give up on low-achieving students (give the answer
or call on another student) under similar circumstances. The teachers
were twice as likely to stay with high-achieving students as they
were to stay with low-achieving students. These results, in combination with Rowe's data, suggest that some teachers will expect and
demand performance from high-achieving students but give up on
low-achieving students and accept only minimal performance.

In subsequent work by Good and Brophy (1974), with different
teachers drawn from several schools, the teachers were surprised
and shocked when told what they had been doing. Besides giving
up easily with low achievers, some teachers consistently gave up
on some high achievers more often than on others. Again, the teachers were not aware of this behavior and had no ideas as to why
they did it. It is difficult for teachers to monitor the quality of their
interactions with students (as opposed to the frequency or quantity
of interactions). By quality, we mean the way teachers interact with
students. (What type of questions do they ask, hard ones or simple
ones? How long do they wait for students to respond? Do they praise
the students when they respond? Do they probe for more information or give the answer?)

It is important to note that not all teachers behave in a different
fashion toward high- and low-achieving students. After reviewing
a number of our own studies and the work of others, it became
apparent that the extent to which teachers are influenced by expectations and treat low-achievement students inappropriately varies
widely from teacher to teacher. Many teachers develop appropriate

expectations for low-achievers and treat them fairly (Brophy and Good, 1974). Many others, especially those who are unaware of their behavior, have difficulty.

Sometimes, the way a teacher groups students influences the flow of communication. Adams and Biddle (1970) discovered the existence of an action zone in the classroom. This action zone included the students who sat in the middle-front-row seats and in seats extending directly up the middle aisle. These students received more opportunity to talk than the others, possibly because the teachers tended to stand in front, where their attention was focused on the students in immediate view. In any case, students seated in this section of the classroom received more teacher attention.

Other seating patterns can influence the flow of communication and affect peer relations. Teachers often group students by ability in order to reduce the range of individual differences within each group and to instruct more effectively. Sometimes, teachers completely segregate classroom seating patterns on the basis of student ability. The top readers sit at the same table, the next best group sit together, and so on. This can be carried to such rigid extremes that there is little contact between high-achievement and low-achievement students. This is likely to set up status differences among students and engender an attitude of inferiority in low achievers that will alienate them from the mainstream of classroom life.

Rist (1970) presents a distressing longitudinal case study of one group of children progressing from kindergarten through second grade. Teachers created a caste system within this group of students. The high-status children mirrored the behavior of their teachers and communicated disrespect for the low-status children. Students who needed the most teacher help, those who were shy and not very verbal, were seated in the rear of the room when they began kindergarten. This made it difficult for them to have contact with the teacher. The teacher was not aware that the placement of these children in the rear of the room would reduce their contacts with her and slow their classroom progress, but this is what happened. Such rigid grouping patterns also prevent low-achieving students from learning from their classmates. There is reason to believe that students will learn from their classmates when given the opportunity to do so (Coleman et al., 1966).

Many of the studies reviewed above suggest that teachers can improve their contact patterns with low-achievement students. If low achievers are relatively ignored and treated with second-class status, they will progressively fall further behind their peers the longer they stay in school. Physical separation of students into rigid groups increases the probability that the teacher will treat them differently, with low-achieving students being treated less appropriately. Much of this will be done unwittingly by teachers, but it will be done nevertheless.

Teaching is more likely to be effective if teachers' goals and classroom behavior are in agreement. We have suggested that often there is a gap between what teachers do and what they think they do or want to do. There is no such thing as *the* appropriate teaching style. The correctness of an indirect or direct teaching style depends upon the objectives of the learning exercise and to some extent the personality of the teacher and the characteristics of the students themselves. However, if goals and teaching behavior aren't in agreement, teaching will be ineffective.

## WHY ARE TEACHERS UNAWARE?

We have discussed certain things that teachers do without awareness, and we will present additional examples later in the book. We will now discuss why teachers do this. Certainly, they do not act this way intentionally. We know this because, when interviewed, teachers express unawareness of some of their classroom behavior and are upset by it. This is true even when good teachers are interviewed in order to find out how and why they behave as they do (Jackson, 1968).

The first and greatest factor that makes it difficult for teachers to assess classroom behavior is that so much happens so rapidly that they cannot be aware of everything they do in the classroom. This problem can be solved, in part, through training. Awareness of everything that occurs, or even everything that only the teacher does, is impossible, but teachers can become more aware of their classroom behavior with practice.

A second factor limiting teachers' awareness in classrooms is that teacher training programs seldom equip teachers with specific teaching techniques or provide them with specific skills for analyzing and labeling classroom behavior. Conceptual labels are powerful tools for helping us to be aware of what we do. For example, the Brophy and Good (1970b) study reported that teachers gave up on low-achieving students who had difficulty responding to questions. However, at the time they gave up on the students, the teachers did not think of this as giving up. They were embarrassed by the silence, they thought that the student was embarrassed, and/or they wanted to keep the discussion rolling. Similarly, teachers in the Rowe (1969) study were not aware that they were giving low-achieving students less time to respond and thereby making a response more difficult.

These findings suggest that teacher training institutions had not given the teachers ways of labeling what they were doing. This is not to say that teachers should never give up on students in recitation sequences, for there are times when it is appropriate to move on. However, teachers should be *aware* that they are giving up and should be aware of how often they do this with low-achieving students. Otherwise, they will teach such students that the easiest way of reacting to a teacher's question is to make no response.

Similarly, teachers should be aware of the alternatives they have when students make no response or respond incorrectly: providing clues, probing, asking a simpler question, repeating the question, and so forth. This awareness can be learned if teachers are trained to identify and label specific teaching goals and specific skills to be used in reaching those goals. Being able to label specific teaching skills helps one both to be more aware of what one does in the classroom and to know how to respond when students act in specified ways.

Teacher education programs traditionally have not trained teachers to recognize and use specific behaviors. Instead, they have given teachers global advice (e.g., treat the whole child, individualize instruction) without linking it to specific behaviors. Smith, in his book *Teachers for the Real World* (1969), says it this way: "It does little good for a teacher to understand that he should accept the child and build on what he is if the teacher does not know how to assess what the child brings and lacks the skills necessary to work with him." He further notes:

> Teachers often appear to have no interest in children or even to fear them, because they simply lack the conceptual equipment to understand them. No matter how idealistic the teacher may be, he will soon find his hopes crushed if he is unable to understand and cope with disturbing pupil behavior.

We share the belief that teachers must be provided with specific, concrete skills if they are to be successful in the classroom.

Although many teacher education programs have begun to stress the ability to conceptualize and talk about specific behaviors, many others still do not. Most in-service teachers do not have a high vocabulary for describing what goes on in classrooms. Thus, the lack of training for conceptualizing and performing specific teaching behaviors helps account for teachers' poor self-awareness.

The third obstacle is that there is no formal, useful system of providing teachers with information about what they do. Pamboo-kian (1975) and McNeil (1971) point out that teachers are most likely to change when provided with information that shows a discrepancy between what they want to do and what they are doing. Teachers are unlikely to get this information unless they meet with their supervisors several times during the year. However, teachers rarely see their supervisors. A survey by the National Education Association reveals that only 34 percent of secondary teachers in the United States are observed even once during the year for a period of five minutes or longer. The median number of observational visits in secondary schools is one and the median in elementary schools is two, and only half of these visits are followed by a conference (McNeil, 1971). Unless they have a rare principal, teachers seldom receive direct, useful feedback about their teaching.

Moreover, under the present supervisory structure, teachers may view feedback from supervisors with suspicion and hostility. Teachers usually know that supervisors' ratings are unreliable. Also, teachers' more frequent disagreements with supervisors are over goals (McNeil, 1971). Tuckman and Oliver (1968) found that teacher behavior was not substantially changed by feedback from supervisors. In fact, when supervisor feedback was the only information teachers received, they changed their behavior in the opposite direction to that suggested by the supervisor. Feedback from students, however, had a positive effect. Apparently, the *source* of advice and the *basis* on which it is given are of concern to teachers. If they feel that supervisors do not spend enough time in the classroom to assess their behavior adequately, or that supervisors employ vague or irrelevant criteria, teachers may reject their supervisors' advice.

Student teachers in university training programs also seldom receive direct, useful feedback. In the following account, Medley (Burkhart, 1969) describes one supervisor's technique for providing a student teacher with information. Although the example may be extreme, it does suggest what we suspect to be a frequent problem in training programs: candidates do not learn specific teaching skills or a conceptual language for describing classroom behavior.

. . . This particular woman said, "Well, I didn't say anything to the student teacher because this is a very sensitive area. But when she did something that was particularly bad, I looked at her, and she understood." . . . we also interviewed the students, and believe it or not, one of the students said, "Well, Mrs. So-and-so didn't talk much. We just looked at this film, and when there was something that I had done particularly well, she looked at me, and I knew."

Medley, in this same source, also reported findings about the class-room behavior of student teachers. His major conclusion was that supervision and television feedback, as implemented in his study, had no effect on student teachers' behavior. Students and supervisors did not talk about *specific* behavior of mutual interest. He concluded, "The most important substantive finding is that the seminal problem in improving teaching may be perceptual in nature; that the key to helping teachers change their behavior may lie in helping them see behavior—see what they themselves—and others as well, are doing." We share Medley's feelings. The next section discusses ways in which teachers can get feedback about their behavior.

## FEEDBACK TO TEACHERS ABOUT CLASSROOM BEHAVIOR

Typically, there are only three ways teachers can obtain systematic and reasonably reliable information about their classroom behavior:

1.  Certain information can be collected from students. This alternative is not very useful for primary-grade teachers, however, because young children are not capable of pro-viding complex feedback. Intermediate-level students in elementary schools and secondary students can provide useful feedback, and teachers should actively seek out their opinions.
2.  Fellow teachers can be asked to observe and code behav-ior during a free period. This source of feedback presup-poses, of course, that fellow teachers have a free period and have the necessary observation skills. A strategy for creating reciprocal visits and exchanging information is provided in the last chapter of this book.
3.  Teachers can develop a conceptual system for labeling their own behavior.

The ability to describe one's own behavior heightens awareness of behavior as it unfolds in the classroom. A conceptual system allows you to classify what you are doing as you do it, making it possible for you to be aware of what you do and to remember how you have behaved. Many school districts now have video equipment so that teachers can see themselves in action. At first glance, video-taping seemed like a real learning aid—what better way for teachers to improve than to see themselves as others do? However, studies report that after teachers have viewed tapes, the changes in their teaching behavior have not been very impressive.

Seeing a film of oneself teaching is like sitting in a classroom watching another teacher. The behavior on the film is still rapid and complex. If you don't know how to look, you don't see very much. Research has demonstrated that when teachers view tapes with a consultant *who can provide specific feedback* or with materials describing what to look for, positive change occurs. Videotapes, if used appropriately, can help teachers to analyze and improve their own behavior. Reviews of the literature on the use of video and audiotape in helping teachers to improve their classroom behavior conclude that such materials are effective only if specific teaching behaviors are highlighted and discussed (Fuller and Manning, 1973; Peck, 1971; Baker, 1970).

The terms *conceptual* and *observational tools* refer to a descriptive vocabulary. Every social organization, game, or system has a language of its own. Some are simple; others, like the language of the classroom, are complex. For example, bridge has a unique descriptive vocabulary, as does football. If you cannot respond to such terms as "three no-trump" or "first down," then you cannot really understand the games. Such terms effectively increase one's understanding of one's partner's hand or of what took place on an athletic field. We want to make you more familiar with the language of the classroom so that you will be able to describe and understand what you do there.

## SUMMARY

In this chapter, we have shown that teachers are not aware of everything that goes on in the classroom, and that this lack of awareness at times interferes with their effectiveness. This problem exists for at least three basic reasons:

1. Teacher training programs spend little time training teachers to perform specific behavior or to describe specific teaching behavior.
2. Classrooms are busy places, and teachers (and students as well) are so busy responding that they have little time to think about what they are doing.
3. Teachers are seldom observed on any systematic basis. Consequently, they seldom get valuable information about ways to increase their effectiveness.

We have posited that teachers need to develop skills for looking at classroom behavior. Preservice teachers also need insight into their own behavior when they do their practice observation and student teaching. A major goal of this book is to help teachers acquire a classroom language for describing behavior and develop new ways of structuring classroom learning experiences.

## SUGGESTED ACTIVITIES AND QUESTIONS

1. The chapter has stressed that sometimes teachers are not aware of all of their classroom behaviors. When you teach (whether micro, simulated, or real), attempt to monitor your teaching behavior (e.g., the ratio of fact to thought questions) and see how your mental record compares with the actual record taken by a coder or with what you hear when you play back your tape-recorded lesson. Practice monitoring your behavior, listening to what you say as you teach, and comparing your mental list with objectively recorded lists. Most of us find it difficult to monitor our teaching behavior initially (we are so busy thinking about what we will ask next that we do not hear completely what we say), but improvement comes with practice.

2. Give two examples to illustrate how a teacher's lack of awareness about what he or she does in the classroom might result in inefficient or self-defeating behavior.

3. How could teachers improve their ability to see behavior in classrooms?

4. When entering a classroom, why is it important that an observer have a conceptual system for describing behavior and for noticing significant occurrences?

5. Describe the potential ill effects of placing students in learning groups on the basis of achievement or intelligence test scores. What possible advantages can be gained by grouping students?

6. Teachers obviously want low-achieving students to do well, but some low-achieving students receive less teacher contact and help than high-achieving students. How could teachers improve their interaction patterns with low-achieving students without reducing their effectiveness with other students?

7. Why is the use of video equipment (allowing teachers to see themselves teach) relatively ineffective unless it is combined with specific directions concerning what to look for or specific descriptions of what took place?

8. After reading this chapter, do you have any questions about the ideas, facts, or concepts presented? Are there topics that you would like more information about? If so, write two or three of your own questions and turn them in to your instructor for feedback, or trade questions with fellow teachers or students.

# 3/
# SEEING IN
# CLASSROOMS

We have discussed problems that teachers have in perceiving classroom behavior, and the difficulty of monitoring classroom behavior
that is both rapid and complex. Research shows that teacher perception of classroom behavior differs, at least in certain respects, from
that of students and observers (Ehman, 1970; Wolfson and Nash,
1968). So far, we have not tried to explain this. Why should teacher
perception be at odds with the views of other observers? After all,
students and observers also have seldom been trained to rate specific
behaviors, and they must also observe rapidly occurring events. Why
should observers see one thing and teachers another?

Part of the answer is that teachers or observers may miss parts
of classroom life because events move so quickly. The purpose of
this chapter is to highlight another reason: teachers and observers
can and do *misinterpret* classroom behavior. That is, the problem
of seeing in classrooms is a bit more complex than we have described
so far. While it is true that a fast classroom pace and not knowing
what to look for reduce one's ability to perceive behavior in the
classroom, another problem is that on occasion what we think we
see is not congruent with reality. Our past experiences, biases, and
prejudices can lead us to interpret what we see incorrectly rather
than to objectively see, describe, and analyze what really happened.

Anyone who wishes to observe accurately will have to examine
and become aware of his or her perceptual blinders. For instance,

a classroom observer who has been irritated by aggressive, highly verbal teachers may see such teachers as punitive and rigid, while another observer may see them as well organized and articulate. Similarly, a classroom teacher may see two students perform the same physical behavior but yet perceive the behavior differently. Imagine the following situation. Mr. Fulton, who teaches tenth-grade American history, is talking when Bill Rink calls out, "Why are we talking about this?" Mr. Fulton, knowing Bill to be a troublemaker and class clown, assumes that Bill wants to waste time or provoke an argument. Therefore, he responds aggressively, "If you would pay attention, you'd know what we are doing. Pay attention!" However, compare the response Mr. Fulton made above with his response to a different student. Jim calls out the same words with the same tonal quality, "Why are we talking about this?" But Mr. Fulton, "knowing" Jim to be a good, dependable student, hears his words not as a threat but as a serious question. He reasons that if Jim does not understand the purpose of the discussion, nobody does. He responds, "Jim, I probably haven't made this clear. Last Friday we discussed . . ."

Teachers on occasion react not to what they physically hear but to their *interpretation* of what the student said. Teachers' past experiences with a student often influence their interpretation of what the student seems to be saying. This is not to suggest that teachers should not interpret student comments but to argue that they should be *aware* when they do so. Some teachers fall into the unconscious trap of expecting a student to behave a certain way and then systematically coloring their interpretations of the student's behavior so that he or she appears to fulfill the teacher's expectation. Often the distinction between observed behavior and the teacher's interpretation of that behavior has been lost.

This chapter argues that anyone who tries to observe behavior will have to guard against the tendency of letting personal biases color what is seen. An exercise to help readers to identify their classroom biases is provided at the end of the chapter. After you have become more aware of the various teacher and student behaviors that incite your interest or disinterest, you will be able to interpret classroom behavior more objectively. General suggestions are also presented to help observers gather classroom data without unduly influencing the behavior of teachers and students.

## SELECTIVE PERCEPTION: AN EXAMPLE

Teachers often perceive classroom behavior according to their own experience. The following illustration taken from the book *Problem*

*Situations in Teaching* (Greenwood, Good, and Siegel, 1971) shows how the process might operate. As you read the example, note how Mr. Smith's attitudes influence his interpretations.

. . . consider Mr. Smith, who has frequently observed two students, Jean and Shirley, in his senior civics class whispering together in the back of the room. He has always ignored this behavior, hoping it would disappear. The two girls are very physically attractive to Mr. Smith, and very popular among their classmates. He wanted to befriend them, but they seemed to make fun of him at times. Once when he tripped over a wastebasket, they seemed to laugh louder and longer at him than anyone else in the room. At other times, they would whisper together, look in his direction, and begin to giggle.

Mr. Smith was not very popular when he was a student in high school. He was shy around girls, dated very little, and did not participate in varsity athletics, although he wanted to be admired and popular. He became a teacher, although he wanted to be a medical doctor, primarily because he felt that the local teacher's college was the only place that he could financially afford to attend and feel reasonably sure of being able to do the academic work required of him.

On the day in question, another teacher had hurt his feelings by criticizing the tie that he had worn to school. The other teacher had said, "Man, you are never going to be a swinger as long as you wear square ties like that." During second period civics class, Jean and Shirley once again whispered together in the back of the room, looked in Mr. Smith's direction, and began to laugh. Mr. Smith inferred from their behavior that they were talking about him. He told them to go to the Dean of Girls' office.

The Dean of Girls later told Mr. Smith that the girls had been telling one another jokes. Mr. Smith didn't really believe this "story" of the girls and told them in no uncertain terms that he was going to move them away from one another and that the next time they talked he would cut their grades. Both girls had confused and bewildered expressions on their faces and Jean began to cry. Shirley said, "Why are you treating us this way, Mr. Smith? We really thought that you were the one teacher that we have who really understands us!"

You can probably think of a great number of things that you would like to find out about Jean, Shirley, Mr. Smith, and others, before you begin to diagnose this case. A good starting point is to consider Mr. Smith's objectivity. Was he objective in examining the data? From a measurement standpoint, objectivity of this kind refers to the amount of agreement between observers. If two other teachers had observed the same behavior as Mr. Smith observed, would they have made the same inferences from the behavior of Jean and Shirley?

If Mr. Smith could remove his perceptual blinders for a moment, what would he have actually observed about Jean and Shirley's behavior and what would he have inferred? He had definitely seen the two girls whispering together, glancing at him and laughing at him from time to time. He could probably even guess how many times they have engaged in this behavior, if it were important. He did hear and see them laugh loud when he tripped over the wastebasket. Further, the Dean of Girls said the girls explained that they were telling jokes on the day that he sent them out of the class. Finally, we know precisely what the girls said to Mr. Smith when he talked to them later because we have an exact quote. We can't see the girls' faces or hear the way in which Shirley said what she did to Mr. Smith. Our data have many limitations, but they do provide some clues and suggest the need to collect additional information.

What kinds of inferences did Mr. Smith make from the behavioral data? Are there other interpretations that could be made? First, he seemed to feel that the girls saw him as an inadequate male. Second, he inferred that they were whispering and giggling about him and his inadequacies. After the incident was reported, Mr. Smith later said he refused to accept Shirley's statement concerning his adequacy as an understanding teacher. Are other inferences concerning the girls' behavior possible? Did Mr. Smith respond to the behavior that he observed, or did he respond to inferences that he drew from this behavior? Imagine Mr. Smith at some future time with some other teachers in the lounge during their "planning period." Imagine another teacher saying, "I have Jean Sinders and Shirley Merrick in my class this semester. Boy, what lookers! Hey, George, didn't you have some trouble with them last semester?" Mr. Smith: "Did I ever! They were always disrupting the class. Every time I turned my back they were whispering and giggling and making all kinds of noise."*

### Teacher Anxiety: A Source of Bias

The example presented above illustrates how a teacher's anxiety can lead to a distorted view of classroom events. Teachers who are insecure and who possess a poor teaching self-concept are especially unlikely to seek information about themselves and likely to distort "threatening" information when they receive it. Insecure teachers often prefer to interpret problems in ways to suggest that factors other than personal competency are the source of instructional difficulties ("students don't like me," "I don't like to teach").

It is known that many teachers report considerable tension and anxiety while engaged in teaching activities (see, for example, Coates and Thoresen, 1976). It is less clear how teacher anxiety influences teacher behavior and the anxiety and classroom behavior of students.

---

* From Gordon E. Greenwood, Thomas L. Good, and Betty L. Siegel, *Problem Situations in Teaching*, pp. 8–10. Copyright © 1971 by Harper & Row, Publishers, Inc. By permission of the publisher.

Still, it would seem difficult for a teacher who is excessively concerned about self to actively monitor interactions in order to see how others are *affected* by classroom events.

Student teaching is often a stressful event because of poor communication between the student teacher and the cooperating teacher. However, if self-concerns are excessive, student teachers should seek advice and help from the college teaching staff. People who are uncomfortable in the teaching act will have a difficult time in accurately seeing and helping students to fulfill their needs. To be a successful teacher, one has to develop technical competence and the self-confidence to use those skills.

### Observe Behavior—Don't Interpret

The teaching incident presented above also illustrates that inferences should be made *after* we have collected and examined descriptive information. Our own background, particularly our experiences as a student and our personal definitions of a good teacher, can lead us to draw erroneous conclusions. If the teacher does something we especially like (e.g., asks questions before calling on students), we may rate him high in all areas. Similarly, if the teacher does something we particularly dislike (e.g., humiliates a student who provides a wrong answer), we may evaluate him low on all dimensions of classroom behavior even if other aspects are positive. Thus, when viewing teacher behavior, it is important not to evaluate behavior as positive or negative independent of its effects upon students. For example, the teacher we see as hypercritical may be seen by his students as a person who sets high standards because he cares about them. As a case in point, see Kleinfeld (1975).

It is exceedingly difficult for an observer to sit in a classroom and note the behavior that occurs without attempting to *interpret* what the behavior means. Observers should concentrate on observing and coding, however, because time spent speculating about the possible motivation behind a student's or teacher's behavior increases the chances that the observer will miss significant aspects of classroom interaction. It is preferable to hypothesize about the causes of classroom behavior *after* an objective description of that behavior, particularly as hypotheses made while we are still observing in the classroom lock us into a narrow viewpoint. When we are looking for something, we are likely to find it. Remember the example of Mr. Smith and recall how his perceptual blinders caused him to interpret behavior to make it conform to his view.

Looking for specific behaviors in the classroom is one way to minimize the degree to which our attitudes and biases will color what we see. For example, if we believe a teacher to be caustic and ineffectual, it is less likely that such an attitude will interfere with our description of classroom life when we pay attention to behavior (e.g., how often the teacher calls on low-achieving male students) than it will when we attempt to describe the teacher in global, inferential terms (how good-looking, warm, friendly, fair, etc., is the teacher).

However, a focus on behavior does not 'in itself guarantee that one will see accurately. Behavior will be seen accurately only if the observer wants to do so and is willing to practice and to compare his or her observations with those of others. Nevertheless, a focus on behavior is a useful starting point for trying to see and describe classroom life.

One useful way to improve observational skills is by doing case studies that focus on one student or a few students. Case studies that involve the reporting of observed behaviors are particularly helpful. Such assignments facilitate one's ability to observe and de-scribe behavior accurately, and these skills are necessary to the gen-eration of effective, concrete plans for dealing with students. Tradi-tional case studies are excellent analytical tools for expanding one's ability to see and to interpret student behavior.

Readers who are unfamiliar with case study techniques are encour-aged to examine other references. Useful descriptions of how to conduct case studies can be found in Perkins (1969) and Shaffer and Shoben (1956). Gordon (1966) and Almy (1969) describe a variety of techniques for looking at student behavior in the classroom, and these sources are useful for students who want to learn more about child study. Below we will present some of our ideas about conduct-ing case studies. First, we will discuss our rationale for conducting a specific type of case study, and then we will discuss some general principles that are important to follow when doing a case study.

## DISCOVERING BIAS

We have noted that observers and teachers often misinterpret be-havior because their own backgrounds and biases lead them to color classroom behavior and because they attempt to interpret behavior prematurely. The first step in changing this undesirable behavior is to become aware of its presence and consequences. Teachers need awareness of both *behavior* (e.g., the teacher criticizes some students almost every time they give a wrong answer) and its *consequences* (e.g., the student volunteers less, begins to avoid the teacher, and hands in fewer homework assignments).

When we become aware of our attitude, we can often control

our behavior more optimally. For example, the teacher who unhesitantly says, "I am a fair grader. I am never influenced by the student as a person, and I grade only the paper," is often an extremely unfair grader. The fact is that knowing who wrote the paper does influence most graders. With certain students, teachers tend to *read more into the answer* than is really there (especially with students with whom they have worked closely). We demand more proof from other students—although a student's first paragraph in an essay is excellent, the teacher suspects this student does not really know the material.

Similarly, other factors, such as the quality of handwriting, may influence the way we grade an essay exam (Chase, 1968). Once teachers realize that they do have *biases* that interfere with grading fairly, they can take steps to reduce the effects of those biases. For example, teachers can mask the identity of the student who wrote the paper before grading it, can grade all papers on the first question before going to the next question, and can score only content and not penmanship.

In the same way, one can improve other weak spots if one becomes aware of them. Self-study is difficult to conduct. The most pervasive problem is the difficulty of admitting certain feelings and reactions because we feel that they are unprofessional or inappropriate. For example, we tend not to accept the fact that we react differently to different students.

Greenberg (1969) describes some of the myths that frequently produce teacher problems, such as the myth of "liking all students equally," and notes that such magnanimous behavior is impossible. Teachers will treat students in equally fair and facilitating ways if and when they are aware of their feelings about the students. This does not mean identical teacher behavior, however, because some students need more teacher contact, others need more opportunity to work on their own, and so forth. As human beings, teachers experience the full range of human emotions: they will distrust some students, they will be proud of certain others, some will delight them, and others they will want to avoid. Similarly, observers will have different reactions toward different teachers. If we are not careful, these feelings will interfere with our ability to see accurately.

Once we identify our feelings, it is possible to monitor classroom behavior more objectively. For example, if we realize that a student makes us uneasy because of his physical ugliness, filth or smell, embarrassing questions, or shyness, we can take steps to make the student more attractive to us. However, if we only think "I love all students," we are unlikely to identify our differential behavior toward students whom we dislike. The assignment outlined below will help you to identify some of your attitudes and preferences toward students.

### Case Study: For Self-Study

The case study assignment that follows will provide you with a direct opportunity to study your personal values, preferences, and attitudes. This case study forces you to consider the types of students (or teachers) that you find fun and exciting to work with and to identify the types of students who annoy, bore, or disgust you.

From the following list, select two contrast groups for study— any two except pair 1 and 4. If you are not in an observation course, pick peers who are in your class or pick two different college instructors and analyze their differential behavior. Better yet, arrange to observe in a class similar to the one you teach or will be teaching.

1.  Select the two students with whom you most enjoy working; that is, if you were the classroom teacher, which two students in the class would you select first to be in your own room? (Positive feelings)
2.  Select the two students whom you dislike the most in the classroom. (Negative feelings)
3.  Select two students for whom you have no strong feeling whatsoever. Use the class roster here so that you will not forget about anyone. (Apathy, indifference, do not notice when they are absent)
4.  Select two students (one boy, one girl) who best represent the child you would want your son or daughter to be like at this age. (Identification)

After selecting the four students, begin to observe them more closely during class activities. If you are observing in public schools and you choose to take notes during class, be sure to obtain the teacher's permission and let him or her know that the notes are about students and not the teacher. Some of you will be busy teaching during the day, so your notes will have to be made after class ends. The notes are for your own use, and the form you utilize is completely open. Bear in mind that any information you record in classrooms is confidential; students should never be identified by name. Even notes that you take in class should include no *actual* student names (notes are often lost). For this case study, it is *not* necessary to collect data from the school files, which might influence the observation anyway. Normal classroom behavior is sufficient.

Analyze the similarities and differences among the four students.

This analysis among students should provide you with clues regarding the types of student behavior that are likely to touch off positive or negative responses in your own behavior. You will then be in a better position to understand why you behave as you do and be able to change your behavior in certain ways in order to interact more positively with students who irritate you. You will want to raise some of the following questions when you compare and contrast the students:

1. What are the students like physically? How do they look? Do they have nice clothes? Are they attractive? Clean? Are they large or small for their age? Are they male or female?
2. What are their favorite subjects? What lessons bore them? What are their strong and weak points as students? As persons?
3. What are their most prominent behavior characteristics? Do they smile a lot? Do they thank you for your attention? Do they seek you out in the classroom—more or less than the average student? Do they raise their hands to answer often? Can they be depended upon to do their own work? How mature are they? Are they awkward or clumsy?
4. What are their social characteristics and what socioeconomic level do they come from? What is their ethnic background?

The goal of this exercise is not to put you through an intensive self-analysis. It is to start you thinking about the possible linkages between your feelings about students and the way students treat you and you treat them in the classroom. A valuable parallel exercise would be to list the teacher behaviors that provoke your interest or boredom. The purpose of such activities is, of course, to make you more aware of what you like and dislike, so that these attitudes will not interfere with your classroom observation and teaching.

## CASE STUDIES: SOME GENERAL COMMENTS
If you are puzzled about particular students, or even just interested in learning more about them, concentrated and sustained observation usually will reveal new insights and suggest interpretations and explanations. Case studies help teachers to overcome the tendency to see students only within the student role. Attention is focused on students as unique individuals, and an attempt is made to empathize with them. This involves trying to see the classroom envi-

ronment as the students see it, and to develop an understanding of what they are trying to accomplish when they respond to it.

First, who are the students? What are their background characteristics (age, sex, birth order, family background)? What are their orientations toward school? Toward the teacher? Toward classmates? What are their hobbies and interests? Their strengths and weaknesses as individuals? As students? Thinking about such questions and jotting down tentative answers are helpful in developing an open mind toward students and learning to look at them in new ways. These steps may help you improve your knowledge of a particular student before you even spend any time observing that student. For example, if you cannot name several strengths *and* weaknesses, your view of the student is probably biased. In our desire for simplicity and consistency in our perceptions, we tend to overstress things that fit together and reinforce our biases and to slight things that do not.

No special preparation or equipment is required for observing a student systematically. An ordinary notebook and pen or pencil will do. You should be near enough to see and hear the student, but not so close as to be inhibiting. Ideally, the student should not know you are observing him or her systematically. If possible, make observations of the student outside of class as well, during recess, at lunch, and between classes, when the student's behavior is likely to be more characteristic than it is when constricted by the student role.

If the student presents a problem, try to formulate the problem as specifically as you can, using terms that translate into observable behavior. Include any relevant qualifiers relating to the contexts in which behavior occurs (subject matter, size of group, time of day, type of situation). Such patterns in the student's behavior may help you to increase your understanding. You also might notice important differences between situations in which the student is and is not a problem (degree of interest in the topic, degree of structure in the activity, active vs. quiet activity, type of antecedent experience, presence of peers or other distractors, etc.). Whatever the activity, focus on the student, including times when he or she is a passive spectator. There is a tendency to observe the teacher or whoever else is the center of attention at times like these, but when you are doing a case study, it is important to concentrate on the student of interest.

Keep a running log of the student's behavior during periods of observation. Observations should be dated and clearly separated from one another in the continuous log, and they should be subdivided into natural units according to what was going on at the time (class periods and breaks between periods, different activities and settings within classes, etc.). The log should contain narrative descriptions of behavior along with interpretations about its possible meanings. It is important to keep objective descriptions of behaviors separate from subjective interpretations concerning meaning, because interpretations may change as more information is collected. Probably the easiest way to do this is to use only the left half of the page for keeping the log of behavior. Interpretations can be written on the right half of the page later, when you review your notes and think about what you have observed.

When recording for a case study, the goal is to include as much pertinent and interpretable information as possible, but to stick with the facts and avoid unsupportable and perhaps incorrect interpretations. This is not difficult to do, but it may take some practice to learn to sort vague information from interpretable facts, and interpretable facts from interpretations themselves. For example, suppose an observer were watching Ron, a white student, at a time when he became involved in an incident with Ralph, a black student:

> Ralph taps Ron, points, and speaks. Ron replies, shaking head. Ralph gestures, speaks. Ron strikes Ralph and a fight starts.

This information is factual, but it is too vague and sketchy to be much good. Even if the words of the boys are not heard, their gestures and the general nature of their interaction can be described much more clearly. Let's look at another example:

> Ron is working quietly until bothered by Ralph. He listens, then refuses. Ralph becomes angry and abusive. Ron becomes aggressive, triggering a major racial incident.

Assuming that the observer could not hear what was said, this is not so much an observation as an interpretation. Ron may or may not have "refused' whatever Ralph wanted, Ralph may or may not have "provoked" Ron, and the incident may or may not be "racial." These are interpretations. They fit the facts and may or may not be true, but this also can be said of many other possible interpretations. A good observation would have recorded the facts as follows:

> Ralph taps Ron on shoulder, shows his assignment, points to something, speaks. Ron looks, shakes head no, says something. Ralph replies with disgusted look, downward gesture of arm. Turns away when finished speaking. Ron says something to Ralph from behind, then slaps Ralph's head. Ralph responds as if attacked, fight begins.

This is about as much useful information as could be recorded without becoming interpretive. About all that is missing is a description of Ron's facial expression and general manner when slapping Ralph. This information would be helpful in judging whether the head slap really was meant as an attack (if so, it would be an unusual behavior).

The interpretation of this information would raise questions about its meaning. Who actually started the trouble, and what started it? Is it accurate to call this a "racial incident," or is the fact that one boy is black and the other white irrelevant? What really happened?

Ordinarily, the observer would get answers to these and related questions, because interactions as intense as fights usually involve loud talk which is easy to hear. However, without more information, the interpretation of these facts would have to be confined to speculation. The first fact is that Ralph interrupted Ron by tapping his shoulder, pointing to the assignment, and saying something. The shoulder tap apparently did not bother Ron, because he did not show any reaction to it. In fact, he did not appear angry until later. The fact that Ralph showed the assignment and pointed to something suggests that he was seeking help or information about it or was expressing an opinion. However, it is possible that Ralph did these things just to give the appearance of discussing the assignment, and that what he had to say to Ron had nothing to do with the assignment. If so, he could have made a provocative statement, but not necessarily.

Ron responded by shaking his head no and saying something. This could have been a refusal to listen, a refusal of a request, or an answer to Ralph's question, among other things. If Ralph had expressed an opinion, this could have been a disagreement by Ron. In any case, it is clear that Ron responded negatively to whatever Ralph asked or said.

Ralph's gesture and facial expression in his reply suggest disgust and/or anger. However, it is not at all clear whether he provoked Ron in some way. He might have, but he might also have been expressing his own frustration with whatever Ron had said. He might even have been giving an opinion. For example, he might have originally pointed out what he considered to be a stupid question and asked Ron if he understood it. Ron might have said that he didn't understand it either, and Ralph might have responded with a gesture and look of disgust while saying something like "Why do they ask us stuff like this?"

Just as Ralph's behavior may or may not have involved provocation, Ron's behavior may or may not have involved aggression. It could have been an attack on Ralph, perhaps in retaliation for something Ralph said. However, it also could have been horseplay. Boys frequently poke or slap one another as a way of teasing (but not attacking), and that could be what is happening here.

With a little imagination, we can think of several other interpretations of what happened between Ron and Ralph, but the above is enough to indicate the difference between factual observations and interpretations. Ambiguous situations like this are common when classroom observations are collected in case studies, which is why it is important to physically separate factual observations from interpretations of these observations. The factual observation record will remain constant even when interpretations change in the light of new evidence. Even when you are not formally entering observations in a case study record, the distinction between fact and interpretation should be kept in mind. The ability to maintain and be aware of this distinction is an important part of learning to be accurate when looking in classrooms.

You may have to experiment a bit in order to find the right level of generality for behavioral description. You should not attempt to record literally everything that you see, partly because this would not be possible, and partly because you would be recording a great deal of trivial information about momentary behaviors and expressive mannerisms that have no interpretive importance. On the other hand, in the interest of objectivity, it is important that you record observable behaviors. Thus, it would be appropriate to note that the student smiled or even smiled at the teacher, but it would be an interpretation to say that the student showed friendly warmth (as opposed to happy self-satisfaction, for example). Similarly, it would be appropriate to state that the student spent time apparently absorbed in thinking and problem solving, but it would be an interpretation to say that the student *was* thinking and problem solving. Perhaps he or she has learned to give this appearance while daydreaming.

Naturally, in making notes, you will want to highlight information relevant to your concerns about the student. However, your record should keep everything in proper perspective, even if it differs in the degree of specificity included about various episodes. For example, if you are watching a student who gets into trouble with peers, it would be appropriate for you to have detailed descriptions of what happened on the two occasions that he or she became involved in arguments during the observation period. On the other hand, it should be clear from the record that the two instances of peer conflict involved only a few minutes, and the record should provide a running account of what the student was doing during the rest of the period. In fact, when observing problem children, it can be helpful to keep the question "What does the student do when not misbehaving?" in the back of your mind. This will help cue your attention to behavior representative of the positive self that you have to learn about, build on, and ultimately begin to think about when you think about this student. To develop this information, it is important to fight the tendency to let halo effects structure your perceptions. Just as outstanding students have weaknesses, problem students have strengths.

Behavioral records should be reviewed and checked for completeness and accuracy at the first opportunity. At this time, you can also fill in initial interpretations, add clarification, and generally edit your notes to make them as useful as possible in the future. You may or may not be able to interpret everything you see, but your notes should be complete and unambiguous concerning what actually happened. In addition to a description of what transpired, there should be information about the qualitative or process aspects of the behavior (Was it random or purposeful? Was there anything unusual or noteworthy about it?) and explanations about the behavior. (Why did the behavior occur? What stimulated it? What was its purpose? What was its function?).

In reviewing behavioral comments, look for correlations and contradictions. Try to identify repeated patterns. Are they well known, or do they suggest new insights? Look for places where a particular pattern might have been expected but did not occur. These could be keys to understanding the explanations for patterns or to developing ideas about how to get the student to change. If your notes suggest certain hypotheses but do not contain enough information to allow you to evaluate them, try to identify what information you need. You might be able to identify specific situations that you could observe in the near future. For example, suppose the student challenged the teacher on each of two occasions when asked to read aloud. This could be a defense mechanism used in an attempt to avoid reading, perhaps because the student cannot read. You can't tell from only two instances, but you could watch for this in the future whenever the class is involved in oral reading, and you could see the student individually and try to develop more information about his or her reading achievement level. Information gleaned from these supplementary activities then can be added into the log at appropriate places dealing with the interpretation of the behavior.

## SIMPLIFYING THE OBSERVATIONAL TASK

In this chapter, emphasis has been placed on the need to study observer and teacher biases to prevent them from interfering with assessment. However, another major obstacle hinders perception in classrooms: the sheer physical complexity of the classroom can, at times, prevent us from seeing certain events. While the teacher instructs a reading group, four students may be at the science table, three listening to tapes at the listening post, four reading at their desks, and three writing at the blackboard. No observer can monitor everything that takes place in the classroom. Even relatively simple tasks may be impossible to code simultaneously. For instance, if an observer wants to code the number of hands raised when a teacher asks a question and whether or not the student called on by the teacher has a hand up, the observer may still be counting hands when the teacher calls on the student and will thus be unable to determine whether or not the student has a hand up.

One useful way to break down the physical complexity of the classroom is to study the behavior of a few students. Such students can be studied intensively, and their behavior will mirror what is taking place in the entire classroom. For example, the observer can choose to focus on a few students (perhaps two high, two middle, and two low achievers—one female and one male at each achievement level) or on a particular group of students (low achievers). Then a record can be made of everything these students do. For example, it might be useful to look at these differences between high, middle, and low achievers:

1. How often do low, middle, and high achievers raise their hands?
2. Do all students approach the teacher to receive help, or do some students seldom approach the teacher?
3. How long does the reading group last for each group of achievers?
4. Are the students involved in their work? How long do they work independently at their desks?
5. How often are students in different groups praised?

These questions represent a few of the many you can examine. Here, our purpose is not to suggest what to look for (this will come later), but to examine ways and procedures that will facilitate looking. Studies of representative students are an excellent way of reducing the complexity of looking in classrooms. These studies allow one to focus attention upon the teacher and only a few students, rather than trying to code everything that takes place in a large classroom. This focus on a few students is especially useful when you first begin to observe in classrooms.

Another strategy for aiding ability to observe in classrooms is simply to *limit* the number of behaviors that you look for at one time. The student observer, or teachers participating in self-evaluation or in-service programs, will do well to restrict their attention to only five to ten behaviors at any one time. When one attempts to measure too many things, one becomes confused and cannot measure objectively. It would be better for an observer to concentrate on certain behaviors for a couple of days and then start to code a new set of behaviors.

### Reliability

In addition to realizing their own biases and limiting the number of students and behaviors observed, observers should learn to estimate their ability to code classroom behavior accurately by comparing their observations with those collected by other observers. Perhaps this is the easiest way to determine if you are observing what happens and not allowing your personal biases to interfere with your observing. (A fuller description of reliability is appended at the end of the chapter. The reader desiring more information on reliability is referred to this material.)

In general, the observation forms presented in this book can be used reliably with very little practice. After discussing observation scales for a short time period (5 to 20 minutes, depending upon the scale), students should be able to achieve general agreement (60 percent to 90 percent agreement) and thus be able to use the scale reliably to code classroom behavior. Let us discuss agreement further. If observers are watching a videotape and coding the number of academic questions that a teacher asks, we may find that one observer tallied 16 instances of academic questions while another observer tallied only 10. The agreement between two observers can be estimated using a simple formula suggested by Emmer and Millett (1970):

$$\text{agreement} = 1 - \frac{A - B}{A + B}$$

The formula tells us to subtract the difference between the two observers' counts and to divide them by the sum of the two observers' counts. The $A$ term is always the larger number. Thus the agreement in this example would be:

$$1 - \frac{16 - 10}{16 + 10} = 1 - \frac{6}{26} = 1 - 0.23 = 0.77\%$$

### General Plan for Looking in Classrooms

What you look at in a classroom will vary from situation to situation and from individual to individual. Some observers will be able to focus on six behaviors, others may be able to code ten. Some observers may be in the classroom eight hours a week, some only four. Some observers may see two or three different teachers, while others will remain in the same room. Despite such situational differences, there are some general principles to bear in mind when looking in classrooms.

First, observers often try to reduce the complexity of classroom coding by focusing their attention exclusively upon the behavior of the teacher. This is particularly true of teachers in training who are still trying to determine what teachers do in the classroom. This is misplaced emphasis. *The key to looking in classrooms is student response.* If students are actively engaged in and enjoying learning activities, it makes little difference if the teacher is lecturing, using discovery techniques, or using small group activities for independent study.

Earlier, mention was made of the fact that some observers may see a teacher as punitive and rigid, while others see the same teacher as well organized and articulate. A good way to reduce your own bias in viewing teacher behavior is to supplement your observations with attention to the effects of teacher behavior upon student behavior. When you code in the classroom, reduce the number of things you look at to a small, manageable set, but look at both teacher and student behaviors.

Classroom teachers who want to receive relevant feedback about their behavior and that of their pupils, and observers who want to see what life in a classroom is like, must be careful not to disturb the *natural* flow of behavior in the classroom. By "natural" we simply mean the behavior that would take place in the classroom if the observer were not present. Students, especially young ones, will adjust quickly to the presence of an observer if teachers prepare them properly and if observers follow through with appropriate behavior. The teacher should make a brief announcement to explain the observer's presence, so that the students will not have to wonder about the observer or try to question him or her to find out for themselves. For example, a second-grade class might be told: "Mr. Ramon will be with us today and the rest of the week. He is learning about being a teacher. Mr. Ramon will not disturb us because we have many things we want to finish, and he knows how busy we are. Please do not disturb him because he too is busy and has his own work to do."

The observer can help the teacher by avoiding eye contact with the students and by refusing to be drawn into long conversations with them or aiding them in their seatwork—unless, of course, the observer is also a participant in classroom life. (Some university courses call for students to serve as teacher aides before they do their student teaching.)

Observers should not initiate contact with students or do anything to draw special attention to themselves (e.g., frequently ripping pages out of a notebook). It is especially important when two observers are in the same room that they do not talk with each other, exchange notes, and so forth. Such behavior bothers both the teacher and the students, and causes attention to be focused on the observers so that natural behavior is disturbed.

When students approach you while you are observing a classroom, you should appear to be busy and avoid eye contact unless the student speaks to you. In most situations, you can politely but firmly remind the student that he or she should be sitting down and working, and you can tell the student that you are very busy with your own work. Requests for help should simply be referred to the teacher: "I'm sorry, I can't help you. Ask your teacher, Mrs. Brown."

If children bring pictures that they have drawn especially for you, react to such gifts pleasantly, but with minimal response, and then send the child back to his or her seat.

Occasionally, the student may ask a question that the observer cannot redirect to the teacher. For instance, if the student asks: "Are you writing about me?" you need only make a minimal response ("I'm very busy writing about everything in the room and I have to keep at my work") and then direct the student back to his or her seat.

In advance of coming into a classroom, observers should talk with teachers about where they will sit in the room, how they should be introduced to the students, and how they should respond when individual students approach them. Without such preparation, both teachers and observers frequently are paralyzed when students approach the observer. Teachers are embarrassed because students are out of their seats, and they are indecisive about what to do because they do not know whether the observer wants to inspect the students' work or would prefer not to be bothered. Observers are often unskilled at dealing with students. They are not sure how to act when approached, except that they don't want to be a rude guest. These difficult moments in coding will be reduced if observers meet with teachers before the coding begins to discuss what they want to do and how they should be introduced. Mutual agreement should be reached about how to deal with students who are bent upon making themselves known to the coder. At such meetings, observers can also obtain curriculum materials and information about the students (seating chart, achievement ranking). Such information is necessary if the observer plans to conduct an intensive study of only a few children at different achievement levels.

## SUMMARY

This chapter has stressed the fact that objective coding of behavior is the way to guard against our biases and gain the most benefit from classroom observations. In particular, stress has been placed upon reducing personal bias in observing by (1) becoming aware of our biases, (2) looking for specific behavior, to break down the physical complexity of the classroom, and (3) checking our observation data against the observations of others. Exercises have been suggested for helping you observe your own or another's behavior objectively. Procedures for minimizing the observer's effect on the classroom have been discussed, along with techniques for observing unobtrusively in the classroom. These considerations should be borne in mind when you use the observation schedules following Chapters 4 through 9 to observe in classrooms.

This chapter, in combination with the previous two chapters, has identified many of the factors that block our perception of classroom behavior. In these introductory chapters, we have also discussed ways in which we can reduce problems of bias and complexity, as well as ways in which we can observe more objectively in the classroom. In the following chapters, we will develop the theme of looking in classrooms by providing detailed comment about *what* to look for in classrooms. The following chapters provide a focus on what could and should be occurring in classrooms. Furthermore, at the end of each chapter, you will find forms for rating scales that can be used to code or look for the presence or absence of the teaching behaviors that are discussed in each chapter.

### SUGGESTED ACTIVITIES AND QUESTIONS

1. Visit a classroom or watch a videotape of a classroom discussion and try to tally the number of times that the teacher: (1) asks a question, (2) responds to a student's answer, and (3) praises a student. Compare your tallies with a fellow observer by calculating the percent of agreement between your observations.

2. Try some simple observation with one or two others and attempt to code behavior reliably. For example, attempt to keep track of three goldfish. After five minutes of observation can you agree on which is fish one, two, or three? Can you agree upon

which fish moves the most? Which is the fastest when it does move? Which fish is the most aggressive or most playful? Most observers will find this seemingly simple task to be quite complex when they first attempt it. Do a similar exercise for a group of five nursery school children or five older students. Which child is the most aggressive? Which child is busiest? (Add other questions of your own.)

3. Think back over all the teachers you have ever had and list the major characteristics of your favorite teacher. What was he or she like as a person? What were the chief elements of his or her teaching style?

4. Similarly, list the distinguishing factors of your least liked or least effective teacher. Why were you more comfortable, more stimulated in one class than the other? Was it because of the teacher, the subject matter, the students in the class, or a combination of factors?

5. Identify the ten student characteristics or behaviors that will delight you most when you are a teacher. What does this list tell you about your personal likes and your teaching personality?

6. List the ten student characteristics or behaviors that are most likely to irritate you or make you anxious. Why do these behaviors bother you? How can you deal fairly with students who exhibit behaviors that are bothersome to you?

7. Why should classroom observers attune to student behavior as well as to teacher behavior?

8. What can observers do to minimize their disruption of the natural flow of classroom events?

## APPENDIX

### A Coding Exercise

Subsequent chapters in this book are followed by appendices containing observation forms that you can use to observe and record classroom behavior objectively. Before you can do so profitably, however, you will need to acquire certain basic coding habits and skills and to learn to check your coding reliability. These skills are not difficult to learn, but they do require a little concentration and practice.

A good way for you to begin is to carefully study the following example. The example provides coding instructions and coding sheets adapted from the authors' dyadic interaction observation system (Brophy and Good, 1970a), and shows the coding of Arlene and Suzi, two observers who coded in the same classroom at the same time. By using the same system to code classroom interaction with one or more friends and by computing agreement percentages as shown for Arlene and Suzi in the example, you can practice using this typical coding scheme and can assess your reliability as a coder.

The coding system shown in Figure 3.1 is typical of those presented later in the book, in that it applies only to certain kinds of teacher-student interactions; it is not used continually. You may have seen or used a different type of coding system that involved continual coding—recording information every 30 seconds, for example, regardless of what was going on at that time. The coding approach taken in this book is different. Instead of presenting a general system to be used continually, we provide a variety of forms tailored for use in specific situations. Certain forms are used when teachers are lecturing, for example, while others are used when they are giving seatwork directions, and still others when they are dealing with management problems.

Thus, you do not code continually with these forms. You use a given observation form only when the appropriate behavior is present (i.e., when *codable instances* are observed). When no codable instances are present, you do not code anything, or else you use a different observation form appropriate to the specific situation.

*Coding Question-Answer-Feedback Sequences.* In this example, teacher and student behaviors are coded during question and answer interchanges. Whenever the teacher asks a question and calls on a student to respond, the observers code information about whether the student is male or female, about the quality of the student's response, and about the nature of the teacher's feedback reaction to the student. If you have not done so already, study the coding instructions in Figure 3.1 before continuing.

Coding sheets are prepared so that this information can be quickly recorded by entering check marks in appropriate places on the coding sheet. No writing or note taking is required. The coding sheet is organized to follow the time sequence involved in coder decision-making, so that in coding a given interchange, the coders move from left to right across the page (see Figures 3.2, 3.3, and 3.4). As soon as they recognize that a codable interchange is occurring (i.e., the teacher has asked a question and is calling on a student to respond), the coders begin recording the information. When the teacher selects a student to respond, coders record his or her sex by entering a check mark under M or F. Then, after noting the student's response and the teacher's reaction to it, they code the quality of the response by entering a check mark under +, ±, —, or 0. Finally, they code the teacher's feedback reaction by entering one or more check marks in the appropriate teacher reaction col-

**FIGURE 3.1.** Coding Categories for Question-Answer-Feedback Sequences

STUDENT SEX

| SYMBOL | LABEL | DEFINITION |
|---|---|---|
| M | Male | The student answering the question is male. |
| F | Female | The student answering the question is female. |

STUDENT RESPONSE

| | | |
|---|---|---|
| + | Right | The teacher accepts the student's response as correct or satisfactory. |
| ± | Part right | The teacher considers the student's response to be only partially correct or to be correct but incomplete. |
| − | Wrong | The teacher considers the student's response to be incorrect. |
| 0 | No answer | The student makes no response or says he or she doesn't know (code student's answer here if teacher gives a feedback reaction before he or she is able to respond). |

TEACHER FEEDBACK REACTION

| | | |
|---|---|---|
| ++ | Praise | Teacher praises student either in words ("fine," "good," "wonderful," "good thinking") or by expressing verbal affirmation in a notably warm, joyous, or excited manner. |
| + | Affirm | Teacher simply affirms that the student's response is correct (nods, repeats answer, says "Yes," "OK," etc.). |
| 0 | No reaction | Teacher makes no response whatever to student's response—he or she simply goes on to something else. |
| − | Negate | Teacher simply indicates that the student's response is incorrect (shakes head, says "No," "That's not right," "Hm-mm," etc.). |
| − | Criticize | Teacher criticizes student, either in words ("You should know better than that," "That doesn't make any sense—you better play close attention," etc.) or by expressing verbal negation in a frustrated, angry, or disgusted manner. |
| Gives Ans. | Teacher gives answer | Teacher provides the correct answer for the student. |
| Asks Other | Teacher asks another student | Teacher redirects the question, asking a different student to try to answer it. |
| Other Calls | Another student calls out answer | Another student calls out the correct answer, and the teacher acknowledges that it is correct. |
| Repeats | Repeats question | Teacher repeats the original question, either in its entirety or with a prompt ("Well?" "Do you know?" "What's the answer?"). |
| Clue | Rephrase or clue | Teacher makes original question easier for student to answer by rephrasing it or by giving a clue. |
| New Ques. | New question | Teacher asks a new question (i.e., a question that calls for a different answer than the original question called for). |

**FIGURE 3.2.** Arlene's Codes

| NO. | STUDENT SEX M | STUDENT SEX F | STUDENT RESPONSE + | STUDENT RESPONSE ± | STUDENT RESPONSE − | STUDENT RESPONSE 0 | TEACHER FEEDBACK REACTION ++ | + | 0 | − | − − | GIVES ANS. | ASKS OTHER | OTHER CALLS | RE-PEATS | CLUE | NEW QUES. |
|---|---|---|---|---|---|---|---|---|---|---|---|---|---|---|---|---|---|
| 1 |  | ✓ | ✓ |  |  |  |  | ✓ |  |  |  |  |  |  |  |  |  |
| 2 | ✓ |  | ✓ |  |  | ✓ |  | ✓ |  |  |  |  |  |  |  | ✓ |  |
| 3 | ✓ |  | ✓ |  |  |  | ✓ |  |  |  |  |  |  |  |  |  |  |
| 4 | ✓ |  | ✓ |  |  |  | ✓ | ✓ |  |  |  |  |  |  |  |  |  |
| 5 | ✓ |  | ✓ |  |  |  |  |  |  |  |  |  |  |  |  |  |  |
| 6 |  | ✓ |  |  | ✓ |  |  |  |  |  | ✓ |  |  |  |  |  | ✓ |
| 7 | ✓ |  | ✓ |  |  |  |  |  | ✓ |  |  |  |  |  |  |  |  |
| 8 | ✓ |  | ✓ |  |  | ✓ |  |  | ✓ |  | ✓ | ✓ |  |  |  |  |  |
| 9 | ✓ |  | ✓ |  |  |  |  |  |  |  |  |  |  |  |  |  |  |
| 10 | ✓ |  |  |  |  | ✓ |  |  |  |  |  |  |  |  |  |  |  |
| 11 |  |  |  |  |  |  |  |  |  |  |  |  |  |  |  |  |  |
| 12 |  |  |  |  |  |  |  |  |  |  |  |  |  |  |  |  |  |
| 13 |  |  |  |  |  |  |  |  |  |  |  |  |  |  |  |  |  |
| 14 |  |  |  |  |  |  |  |  |  |  |  |  |  |  |  |  |  |
| 15 |  |  |  |  |  |  |  |  |  |  |  |  |  |  |  |  |  |

**FIGURE 3.3.** Suzi's Codes

| NO. | STUDENT SEX | | STUDENT RESPONSE | | | | TEACHER FEEDBACK REACTION | | | | | | | | | | |
|---|---|---|---|---|---|---|---|---|---|---|---|---|---|---|---|---|---|
| | M | F | + | +/− | − | 0 | ++ | + | 0 | − | −− | GIVES ANS. | ASKS OTHER | OTHER CALLS | RE-PEATS | CLUE | NEW QUES. |
| 1 | | ✓ | ✓ | | | | ✓ | ✓ | | | | | | | | | |
| 2 | ✓ | | ✓ | | | ✓ | ✓ | | | | | | | | | ✓ | |
| 3 | ✓ | | | | | | ✓ | | | | | | | | | | |
| 4 | ✓ | | ✓ | | | | ✓ | | | | | | | | | | |
| 5 | ✓ | | ✓ | | | | | | | | | | | | | | ✓ |
| 6 | | ✓ | | | ✓ | | ✓ | | | | ✓ | | ✓ | | | | |
| 7 | | ✓ | | | ✓ | | | | ✓ | | | | | | | | |
| 8 | ✓ | | ✓ | | | | | | ✓ | | | ✓ | | | | | |
| 9 | ✓ | | ✓ | | | ✓ | | | | | ✓ | | | | | | |
| 10 | ✓ | | | | | | | | | | | | | | | | |
| 11 | | | | | | | | | | | | | | | | | |
| 12 | | | | | | | | | | | | | | | | | |
| 13 | | | | | | | | | | | | | | | | | |
| 14 | | | | | | | | | | | | | | | | | |
| 15 | | | | | | | | | | | | | | | | | |

**FIGURE 3.4.** Arlene's Codes Superimposed over Suzi's Codes

| NO. | STUDENT SEX | | STUDENT RESPONSE | | | | | | | | | TEACHER FEEDBACK REACTION | | | | | |
|---|---|---|---|---|---|---|---|---|---|---|---|---|---|---|---|---|---|
| | M | F | + | ± | – | 0 | ++ | + | 0 | – – | – | GIVES ANS. | ASKS OTHER | OTHER CALLS | RE-PEATS | CLUE | NEW QUES. |
| 1 | | ✓ | ✓✓ | | | | | ✓✓ | | | | | | | | | |
| 2 | ✓ | | ✓✓ | | | | ✓ | ✓ | | | | | | | | | |
| 3 | ✓ | | | | | ✓✓ | ✓✓ | | ✓✓ | | | | | | | ✓ | |
| 4 | ✓ | | ✓✓ | | | | ✓ | ✓ | | | | | | | | | |
| 5 | ✓ | | ✓✓ | | | | | | | | | | | | | | ✓ |
| 6 | ✓ | ✓ | | | ✓✓ | | ✓✓ | | | ✓✓ | | | ✓ | | | | |
| 7 | ✓ | ✓ | ✓✓ | | ✓ | | | | ✓✓ | | | | | | | | |
| 8 | ✓ | | ✓✓ | | | | | | ✓✓ | | | | | | | | |
| 9 | ✓ | | ✓✓ | | | ✓✓ | | | | ✓✓ | | ✓✓ | | | | | |
| 10 | ✓ | | | | | | | | | | | | | | | | |
| 11 | | | | | | | | | | | | | | | | | |
| 12 | | | | | | | | | | | | | | | | | |
| 13 | | | | | | | | | | | | | | | | | |
| 14 | | | | | | | | | | | | | | | | | |
| 15 | | | | | | | | | | | | | | | | | |

umns. For example, if the teacher simply affirmed that a correct response was correct, and then went on to another question and another student, coders would enter a check mark in the + column. However, if the teacher had praised the response and then asked the same student another question, coders would have entered check marks in both the ++ and the New Ques. columns.

To see if you understand, try to code the following sequence:

TEACHER: Which is heavier, a pound of lead or a pound of feathers? George?
GEORGE: Neither one—they're both a pound!
TEACHER: That's right—good thinking, George!

To code this sequence correctly, you would:

1. Enter a check under M —George is a male student.
2. Enter a check under + —he answered the question correctly.
3. Enter a check under + —the teacher affirmed the answer ("That's right").
4. Enter a check under ‡ —the teacher also praised the student ("Good thinking").

Once the teacher's response to the student's answer (or failure to answer) has been coded, the information for that particular question-answer-feedback sequence is complete, and coders drop down to the next row and move back to the left side of the coding sheet to be prepared for coding the next sequence. The next sequence may be with the same student (if the teacher has repeated the question, rephrased or given a clue, or asked a new question, thus giving the student a second opportunity to respond), or it may be with a new student.

Thus each row contains information about a single question-answer-feedback sequence, and this interaction can be reconstructed from the coding sheets. In the example, both Arlene's and Suzi's sheets (Figures 3.2 and 3.3, respectively) show that in the first observed codable interchange: (1) the teacher called on a female student to respond, (2) the student responded correctly, (3) the teacher affirmed that her response was correct. Inspection of the second row on each sheet shows that Arlene and Suzi agree that the teacher directed the second question to a male student and that he also answered correctly. However, the coders are in disagreement about the teacher's feedback reaction. Arlene felt that the teacher's reaction was simply affirmation of the correctness of the student's answer, but Suzi saw the teacher's reaction as more intense or positive, and so she coded it as praise. This is the first of several coding disagreements between Arlene and Suzi.

How serious are these disagreements? Can their coding be trusted? To answer such questions, objective methods of assessing coders' reliability are required. An objective analysis of Arlene's and Suzi's reliability is presented below.

*Establishing Reliability.* To establish reliability, you will need to code in the company of at least one other person. This will allow you to assess reliability by comparing your codes with theirs and will provide the basis for clearing up ambiguities and misunderstandings through discussion of disagreements. Once good reliability is established, you can code semi-independently. However, it is wise to continue to check reliability periodically, even after initial proficiency has been established. This will help guard against the tendency to gradually drift into undesirable observation and coding habits over time. Even the use of structured, standardized observation instruments cannot guarantee against coding inaccuracies. Thus, even the most experienced coders need to recheck their reliability occasionally if they want to be sure that their observations can be trusted. This is especially important, of course, in research situations.

Two or more coders can check their reliability either by visiting in a classroom together or by coding the same film or video tape of classroom interaction. When films or videotapes are available, it is often advisable to use them in the initial stages of learning to code. Any number of coders can all code the same films or videotapes, and they can be replayed to refresh everyone's memory when disagreements are discussed.

At first, the major source of disagreement between coders usually is speed. That is, if one or both coders fall behind while trying to make up their minds about a code or trying to find the correct place on the coding sheet to record it, they may fail to observe or record one or more instances of codable interaction that occurred while this was going on. Such problems disappear rapidly with practice, however, and coders soon learn to keep up with the pace of classroom interaction.

Once both coders can keep up, disagreement between coders usually will occur not because one coder coded an interaction that the other one missed, but because both coders coded an interaction but coded it differently. That is, the two coders disagree in their observation of the instance in question. By analyzing and discussing these instances of disagreement, coders can usually identify common or repeated causes. For example, one coder may always code "good" as praise, while another coder might not consider "good" to be praise. Thus, the first coder would code many more instances of praise in the classroom of a teacher who frequently said "good." By identifying and coming to agreement about how to resolve those repeated sources of disagreement, coders can eliminate most unreliability.

## Computing Coder Agreement Percentages

Arlene and Suzi show general agreement in the coding example, but there are several disagreements. To assess their agreement precisely, they would compute agreement percentages. The computations involved are shown below.

Assessment of coder agreement in using this type of observation scheme requires getting answers to two questions: (1) When a codable interchange appeared, did both coders code it? (2) When both coders did code an interchange, did their coding agree? The first question deals with coding speed, the ability of the coders to keep up with the pace of classroom interaction. The second deals with coder agreement on how particular interchanges should have been coded.

Coder speed can be assessed with the formula given in the chapter. This formula can be used whenever agreements on frequency, or number of codes, is being measured. In our example, Suzi coded 11 interchanges, while Arlene coded 10. Applying the formula, agreement would be:

$$1 - \frac{A - B}{A + B} = 1 - \frac{11 - 10}{11 + 10} = 1 - \frac{1}{21} = 1 - 0.05 = 95\%$$

Thus, Arlene and Suzi showed good, but not perfect, agreement. Arlene missed 1 of 11 codable interchanges, while Suzi coded all 11. It is possible that both coders missed one or more other codable interchanges, but we cannot tell from the data. If the coders knew that they both had missed additional coding, they would have to take this into account in interpreting their agreement data. In this case, the 95 percent figure would be deceptively high.

To assess coder agreement on how particular interchanges should be coded, we turn our attention to those interchanges that both Arlene and Suzi coded. Suzi's extra coding (the seventh row on her coding sheet) is not used in this analysis because we do not know how Arlene would have coded this interchange and, therefore, we have nothing to compare with Suzi's coding. To facilitate comparison, Figure 3.4 shows Arlene's codes superimposed on Suzi's coding sheet (skipping Suzi's seventh row, because Arlene does not have a parallel set of codes; Arlene's seventh row belongs with Suzi's eighth row, and so on).

Coder agreement is computed separately for the three separate decisions that each coder had to make concerning each interchange: (1) the sex of the student, (2) the quality of the student's response, and (3) the nature of the teacher's feedback reaction. The method to be used in computing agreement is (1) establish the number of *coding decisions* that were made and (2) compute the percentage of these decisions upon which the two coders agreed.

Since 10 interchanges were coded by both coders, the coders each had to note the student's sex 10 times. Agreement between Arlene and Suzi on these decisions about student sex was perfect (10/10 = 100 percent agreement).

There were also 10 student responses to be coded as right, part-right, wrong, or no response. Arlene and Suzi also agreed on all 10 of these coding decisions (100 percent agreement).

Disagreements appeared in the coding of the teacher's feedback reactions to students. Twice Arlene coded "affirm" while Suzi coded "praise"; otherwise, the two coders agreed in coding a total of 10 teacher feedback reactions. Thus, they agreed in 10 out of 12 (83 percent) of the instances in which they both coded an aspect of the teacher's feedback. (There are 12 codes here, rather than 10, because the teacher showed two different categories of feedback on each of two occasions.)

Overall, Arlene and Suzi's agreement is quite good. One clear pattern of disagreement does show up: Suzi tends to code "praise" at times when Arlene codes "affirm." This occurred twice out of the five times that this particular distinction had to be made (i.e., their agreement for the praise vs. affirm decision was only 60 percent). We cannot tell from the data which coder is correct, if either is. Arlene and Suzi would have to discuss these instances of disagreement to discover the reason for them.

### Interpreting Classroom Coding

The example is too short to allow firm conclusions, but we can make some tentative hypotheses about the teacher on the basis of it. First, note that the majority of questions are answered by boys. If this proves to be a reliable finding, it suggests that the teacher is not calling on girls as much as would be desirable. This could be brought to the teacher's attention for discussion and possible action.

The students' answers show an appropriate success rate. The difficulty level of teachers' questions should be such that most, but not all, are answered correctly. This way the difficulty level is adjusted to student ability. Students can follow the lesson and respond without great difficulty, but at the same time the questions are not so old or easy that they present no challenge.

When the students in this example did not respond correctly, they tended not to respond at all. If this happens often, it may mean that the teacher is not waiting long enough to allow students to formulate a response, or that he or she is overly critical in response to wrong answers, so that the students hesitate to answer unless they are sure they are right. In any case, it usually is better that students make some response rather than remain silent when stuck. If they remain silent, it is likely that inappropriate teacher behavior is the reason.

A tendency to criticize students when they do not respond correctly shows up in this teacher's codes and may be part of the explanation for the students' tendency to remain silent when stuck. *Criticism is almost never appropriate* in these instances. However, note that the teacher also tends to praise frequently. Taken together, these codes suggest that the teacher may be generally overreacting to student performance here. He or she might do better to be more problem centered and less personal in feedback reactions.

The pattern of praise and criticism suggests that the teacher may be playing favorites and/or may prefer boys to girls, although much more data would be needed to find out for sure.

### Appropriate Use of Frequency Data
Frequency data involve counting the number of behaviors in a category that occur during a lesson or a week of observation. Most of the scales and ratings sheets presented in this book involve much counting. Your thinking about what happens in classrooms will be stimulated by information gotten just from looking at count totals.

However, if you have a research purpose, or if comparisons are to be made between teachers or students, it may be more appropriate to use a common frame of reference for comparisons. *Rates* (the number of behaviors per hour) and *percentages* (the percent of all behaviors of a particular type that an individual or group receives) are two convenient ways to summarize data.

We often observe for unequal amounts of time in different classrooms. If we observe in Class A once for two hours and once for three hours, and in Class B on two occasions for one hour each, it will be misleading to compare Teacher A and Teacher B in terms of frequency. Teacher A may total more thought questions, discipline problems, and so on, simply because we spent more time in that classroom.

However, Classrooms A and B can be compared meaningfully in terms of events per hour (rate). Assume that students approached the teacher to seek feedback about their work 30 times in Classroom A and 20 times in Classroom B. Rate measures reveal that students in Classroom B approached the teacher more often in work related situations

$$\frac{20}{2} = \text{ten times per hour}$$

than students in Classroom A

$$\frac{30}{5} = \text{six times per hour}$$

Converting frequency data into percentages and rates will help you avoid misinterpreting. For example, some teachers may appear to have few private contacts with certain students, but only because they have few contacts with students generally. Some teachers may have 200 or more private contacts with students a day; others may have less than 25. When describing teacher differences, the 200–25 difference is important and should be noted in frequency terms (200 vs. 25). However, when talking about differential teacher treatment of students, it would help to use percentage data. (What percent of the 200 or the 25 contacts went to high or to low achievers?).

In some situations, frequencies will not provide the information desired. This is likely to occur when you are interested in the regularity with which one behavioral act precedes or follows another. For example, if we wanted to know if teachers praised high- and low-achievement students differentially, it would *not* be possible to use frequencies (high-achievement students may get more praise because they answer more questions correctly). To examine the question of differential behavior, it would be necessary to determine what percent of low-achievement students' correct answers are followed by teacher praise (when low-achievement students do answer correctly, are they praised?) compared to the percent of time that the correct answers of high-achieving students are followed by praise.

### Conclusion

The extended example presented in the appendix shows how you would establish coder agreement and use coded information to draw inferences about teaching. The principles involved are applicable to any coding in the classroom. To check agreement on frequency or number of codes, use the formula:

$$\text{agreement} = 1 - \frac{A - B}{A + B}$$

To check agreement on how interchanges should have been coded, compute a percentage by dividing the number agreed upon by itself plus the number not agreed upon (i.e., agreements divided by total decisions).

To interpret coded information, look for suggestive patterns that give clues about appropriate and inappropriate teacher behavior (this will be discussed at length in the following chapters). Remember, though, that interpretations based on one or just a few observations are tentative and suggestive. Do not make judgments on the basis of insufficient evidence. At times, more meaningful comparisons can be made when frequencies are converted to rates or percentages.

# 4/
# TEACHER
# EXPECTATIONS

In Chapter 2, we mentioned studies by Rowe (1969) and by Brophy and Good (1970b) in discussing how achievement patterns can affect the ways teachers deal with different students. Rowe found that teachers would wait longer for an answer from high-achieving students. Brophy and Good found that teachers were more likely to give highs a second chance to respond in failure situations, and that they praised highs more frequently for success and criticized them less frequently for failure. Both of these studies provide examples of how teachers treat high-achieving students in ways likely to insure continued success, while treating low achievers in ways likely to slow their progress even further. Let us look at some related examples.

Palardy (1969) studied the reading achievement produced by two groups of first-grade teachers. Using a questionnaire, he identified 10 first-grade teachers who thought that boys could learn to read just as successfully as girls, and another 14 teachers who thought that boys could not learn to read as successfully as girls. Five teachers from each group were selected for further study. All taught in middle-class schools, used the same basal reading series, and worked with three reading groups in heterogeneously grouped, self-contained classrooms.

The students were exactly comparable on the reading readiness scores taken in September, so that there was no initial group difference. However, differences were obtained in March. Boys whose teachers believed they could achieve as well as girls averaged 96.5 on these reading achievement tests, while those whose teachers did not believe that they could do as well as girls averaged only 89.2. The girls in these classes averaged 96.2 and 96.7, respectively. Thus, in the classes where teachers did not think boys could achieve as well as girls, the boys did, indeed, have a lower level of achievement.

Another study in this vein was conducted by Doyle, Hancock, and Kifer (1971). These investigators asked first-grade teachers to estimate the IQ's of their children, shortly before an IQ test was given. The teachers' IQ estimates were then compared to the IQ's obtained from the tests. The comparisons showed that the teachers tended to overestimate the IQ's of girls and to underestimate the IQ's of boys. These estimates were related to reading achievement. Even though there was no IQ difference between boys and girls, the girls showed higher reading achievement. Furthermore, *within both sexes*, the children whose IQ's had been overestimated by the teachers had higher reading achievement than those whom the teachers had underestimated.

These studies show that school achievement is not simply a matter of the child's native ability; teachers' expectations and behaviors are also involved. Several other studies have shown this same result with different types of students in different types of settings. Douglas (1964), in a massive study of the tracking system used in the British schools, found that children who were clean and well clothed and who came from better-kept homes tended to be placed in higher tracks than their measured ability would predict. Once in these tracks, they tended to stay there and to perform acceptably. Mackler (1969), studying a school in Harlem, also found that children tended to stay in the tracks in which they were placed, even though initial placement was affected by many factors other than measured ability. The findings of Douglas and of Mackler show that: (1) teachers' expectations about a student's achievement can be affected by factors having little or nothing to do with his or her ability, and yet (2) these expectations can determine level of achievement by confining learning opportunities to those available in one's track. A student placed needlessly in a low track is unlikely to reach his or her potential, because the teachers do not expect much and because self-concept and achievement motivation are likely to deteriorate over time.

Studies in three different settings showed that student learning was affected by the expectations induced in instructors. Beez (1968), working with adult tutors who were teaching Head Start children, Burnham (1968), working with swimming instructors teaching pre-adolescents how to swim, and Schrank (1968), working with Air Force mathematics instructors, all found the same results. In each study, the teachers' expectations were manipulated by the experimenter. Sometimes the teachers were led to believe that the children or classes they would work with had high learning potentials; some-times they were led to believe they had low learning potentials. There was no factual basis for these expectations, since the groups had been matched or randomly selected. Nevertheless, in each case, students of instructors who had been led to hold high expectations learned more than the students of instructors who had been led to expect little. Beez (1968) monitored the teaching behavior in his study and found that the achievement differences were a direct result of differences in the teaching to which the children were exposed. Tutors who had high expectations attempted to teach more than those with low expectations, and they succeeded in doing so.

In a study similar to that of Beez, Rubovits and Maehr (1973) asked 66 undergraduates (prospective elementary teachers) to teach a lesson to groups of four seventh- or eighth-grade students. Each group contained two black and two white students.

The teachers were found to treat black students less favorably than white students. They gave less attention to the blacks: called on them less frequently, encouraged them to continue with a state-ment less frequently, ignored a greater percentage of their state-ments, criticized them more, and praised them less. These findings are distressing even though they occurred in an experimental set-ting. They suggest that white teachers may have a tendency to treat black students inappropriately (probably because they underesti-mate their potential).

## TEACHERS' EXPECTATIONS AS SELF-FULFILLING PROPHECIES

Each study presented above illustrates how teachers' expectations can function as self-fulfilling prophecies. That is, teachers' expecta-tions affect the way they treat their students, and, over time, the way they treat students affects the amount that students learn. In this sense, then, expectations are self-fulfilling: teachers with high expectations attempt to teach more, and teachers with low expecta-tions tend to teach less. As a result, both groups of teachers tend to end up with what they expected, although not with what they might have achieved with different expectations in the first place.

Robert Rosenthal and Lenore Jacobson's *Pygmalion in the Class-room* (1968) created wide interest and controversy about this topic.

Their book described research in which they tried to manipulate teachers' expectations for student achievement to see if these expectations would be fulfilled. The study involved several classes in each of the first six grades of school. Teacher expectations were created by claiming that a test (actually a general achievement test) had been developed to identify late intellectual bloomers. The teachers were told that this test would select children who were about to bloom intellectually and, therefore, could be expected to show unusually large achievement gains during the coming school year. A few children in each classroom were identified to the teachers as late bloomers. They actually had been selected randomly, not on the basis of any test. Thus, there was no real reason to expect unusual gains from them. No factual basis existed for the expectations induced in the teachers.

However, achievement test data from the end of the school year offered evidence that these children did show better performance (although the effects were confined mostly to the first two grades). Rosenthal and Jacobson explained their results in terms of the self-fulfilling prophecy effects of teacher expectations. They reasoned that the expectations they created about these special children somehow caused the teachers to treat them differently, so that they really did do better by the end of the year.

Controversy has raged over this topic ever since. The findings of *Pygmalion in the Classroom* were widely publicized and discussed, and for a time were accepted enthusiastically. Later, however, after critics (Snow, 1969; Taylor, 1970) had attacked the Rosenthal and Jacobson study and after a replication failed to produce the same results (Claiborn, 1969), the idea that teacher expectations could function as self-fulfilling prophecies began to be rejected. For a recent critical analysis of teacher expectation research, see Dusek (1975).

We think the evidence now available supports the idea that teacher expectations are sometimes self-fulfilling (see Braun, 1976, and Brophy and Good, 1974). However, this statement requires some explanation, both about the research available and about the way the process is defined and described.

Regarding research, one must make a distinction between two types of studies in this area. The first type, which includes Rosenthal and Jacobson's work as well as the work of others who have tried to replicate that study, involves attempts to *manipulate* or induce teacher expectations. That is, the investigators tried to create expectations by identifying "late bloomers," using phony IQ scores, or providing some other fictitious information about the students' ability. The second type of study, exemplified by the first four studies discussed in this chapter, uses the teachers' own expectations as they exist naturally. No attempt is made to induce expectations. Instead, the teacher is simply asked to make predictions or to rank or group students according to achievement or ability.

Studies involving induced expectations have produced mixed, mostly negative results. In some of these studies, the seeming failure of teacher expectations to affect teaching behavior occurred because the teachers did not acquire the expectancy that the experimenter wanted them to have. The most obvious case is where teachers know that the expectancy is not true. This was shown by Schrank (1970) in an adaptation of his earlier study of Air Force mathematics courses. For this second study, Schrank merely simulated the manipulation of teacher expectations; the teachers actually knew that the students had been grouped randomly rather than by ability levels. Under these conditions, even with instructions to teach the groups as if they had been tracked by ability level, no expectation effects were observed. Similar results were found by Fleming and Anttonen (1971), who tried to falsify IQ information on children. They found that the teachers did not accept the phony IQs as real and, therefore, did not allow the scores to affect their treatment of students. When faced with too great a discrepancy between what they saw in their everyday contacts with students and what a test purported to reveal about them, the teachers rejected the test data.

These results suggest that attempts to induce expectations in teachers will fail if the expectations are too obviously and sharply discrepant from the students' observable characteristics. Credibility of the source is probably another important factor. Teachers are much more likely to accept the opinions of the principal or the teacher who worked with the students the previous year than the opinions of a researcher who comes in, administers a test, and leaves without acquiring any more personal knowledge of the students.

Thus, the negative results in studies using induced teacher expectations should not necessarily be taken as disproof of the self-fulfilling prophecy idea. The negative results are more likely due to failure to induce the desired expectations in the teachers than to failure of teacher expectations to affect teacher behavior. Naturalistic studies using teachers' real expectations about their students have often shown that high and low teacher expectations are related to differential teacher behavior (Cornbleth, Davis, and Button, 1972; Brophy and Good, 1974). These studies suggest that teachers' expectations may have self-fulfilling prophecy effects, causing the teachers to behave in ways that tend to make their expectations come true.

It is likely that many students in most classrooms are not reaching their potential because their teachers do not expect much from them and are satisfied with poor or mediocre performance when they could obtain something better (Brophy and Good, 1974). An example of the fact that teacher attitudes are associated with student achievement is the finding that one of the few attitudes that differentiated teachers who were getting good student gains in their classes from those who were not was the belief that students could and would learn (Brophy and Evertson, 1976).

Overenthusiastic popular accounts of *Pygmalion in the Classroom* have sometimes misled people about the self-fulfilling prophecy idea. Sometimes, they imply that the mere existence of an expectation will automatically guarantee its fulfillment or that a magical and mysterious process is involved (just make a prediction and it will come true). Most teachers rightfully reject this idea as utter nonsense. However, this is not what we mean when we say that teachers' expectations can act as self-fulfilling prophecies. We refer here to something resulting naturally from a chain of observable causes, not to something akin to magic or ESP.

### How the Process Works

The fact that teachers' expectations can be self-fulfilling is simply a special case of the principle that any expectations can be self-fulfilling. The process is not confined to classrooms. Although it is not true that "wishing can make it so," *our expectations do affect the way we behave in situations, and the way we behave affects how other people respond.* In some instances, our expectations about people cause us to treat them in a way that makes them respond just as we expected they would.

For example, look ahead to the time when you accept your first teaching job and receive notice about which school you are being assigned to (or look back on this experience if you have gone through it already). Unless they already have information, most teachers in this situation want to find out as much as possible about the school and the principal with whom they will be working. Often, information can be gathered from a friend already teaching at the school. Suppose the friend says, "Mr. Jackson is a wonderful man. You'll love working for him. He's very warm and pleasant, and he really takes an interest in you. Feel free to come to him with your problems; he's always glad to help." If you heard this about Mr. Jackson, how do you think you would respond to him when you met him? Think about this situation for a few moments. Now let's think about another situation. Suppose that your friend said, "Mr. Jackson? Well, uh, he's sort of hard to describe. I guess he's all right, but I don't feel comfortable around him; he makes me nervous. I don't know what it is exactly, it's just that I get the feeling that he doesn't want to talk to me, that I'm wasting his time or irritating him." How do you think you would act when meeting Mr. Jackson after you had heard this?

If you are like most people, your behavior would be quite different in these two contrasting situations. Given the first set of information about Mr. Jackson, you would probably look forward to meeting him and would approach him with confidence and a friendly smile. Among other things, you would probably tell him that you heard good things about him and that you are happy to be working with him and are looking forward to getting started. Given the other set of expectations, however, you would probably behave quite differently. You would be unlikely to look forward to the meeting in a positive sense, and you might well become nervous, inhibited, or overly concerned about making a good impression. You would probably approach him with hesitation, wearing a serious expression or a forced smile, and speak to him in rather reserved, formal tones. Even if you said the same words to him, the chances are that they would sound more like a prepared speech than a genuine personal reaction.

Now, put yourself in Mr. Jackson's place. Assume he knows nothing about you as a person. Take a few moments to think about how he might respond to these two, very different approaches.

Chances are that Mr. Jackson would respond quite differently. In the first instance, faced with warmth, friendliness, and genuine-sounding compliments, he is likely to respond in kind. Your behavior would put him at ease and cause him to see you as a likeable, attractive person. When he smiles and says he will be looking forward to working with you, too, he will really mean it.

But what if Mr. Jackson is faced with a new teacher who approaches him somewhat nervously and formally? Again, he is likely to respond in kind. Such behavior is likely to make him nervous and formal, if he is not already. He is likely to respond in an equally bland and formal manner. This is likely to be followed by an awkward silence that makes both you and Mr. Jackson increasingly nervous. As the authority figure and host, Mr. Jackson will probably feel compelled to make the next move. In view of your behavior, attempts at small talk would be risky, so he probably will get down to business and begin to speak in his capacity as principal, talking to you in your capacity as one of his teachers.

These examples show how expectations can influence behavior and how the behavior in turn can help produce the originally expected results. Teachers who expect Mr. Jackson to be friendly and who approach him in a warm manner make it easier for him to feel at ease and to be friendly. On the other hand, teachers who expect him to be cold and who approach him formally tend to make him nervous, so that he responds in a way that does appear cold.

The examples also show that it is not just the existence of an expectation that causes self-fulfillment; it is the behavior that this expectation produces. This behavior then affects the other person, making him or her more likely to act in the expected ways. In the classroom, the process works like this:

1. The teacher expects specific behavior and achievement from particular students.
2. Because of these different expectations, the teacher behaves differently toward different students.
3. This treatment tells the students what behavior and achievement the teacher expects from them and affects their self-concept, achievement motivation, and level of aspiration.
4. If this treatment is consistent over time, and if the students do not resist or change it in some way, it will shape their achievement and behavior. High-expectation students will be led to achieve at high levels, while the achievement of low-expectation students will decline.
5. With time, students' achievement and behavior will conform more and more closely to that originally expected of them.

The model clearly shows that teacher expectations are not automatically self-fulfilling. To become so, they must be translated into behavior that will communicate expectations to the students and will shape their behavior toward expected patterns. This does not always happen. The teacher may not have clear-cut expectations about every student, or those expectations may continually change. Even when the expectations remain consistent, the teacher may not necessarily communicate them to the student through consistent behavior. In this case, the expectation would not be self-fulfilling even if it turned out to be correct. Finally, the student alone might prevent expectations from becoming self-fulfilling by overcoming them or by resisting them in a way that makes the teacher change them. Thus, a teacher expectation requires more than its own mere existence in order to become self-fulfilling. It must lead to behavior that will communicate the expectation to the student, and this behavior must be effective in moving the student in the expected direction.

### Practice Examples

We have provided some practice examples you can use to sharpen your own understanding of the self-fulfilling prophecy concept. Read each example and see if you think a self-fulfilling prophecy was involved. If so, you should be able to identify: (1) the original expectation, (2) behaviors that consistently communicate this expectation in ways that make it more likely to be fulfilled, and (3) evidence that the original expectation has been confirmed. If the example does not contain all three elements, it does not illustrate a self-fulfilling prophecy.

1. Coach Winn knows that Thumper Brown is the son of a former All-American football star. Although he has never even seen Thumper carry the ball, he predicts, "That boy will help our team in his sophomore year." In practice sessions, Winn treats Thumper like all the other players. He carries the ball the same number of times in the drills as the other runners, and the coach praises him only when his performance deserves it. Thumper wins a starting position in his sophomore year, becoming an outstanding player and being named to the all-conference team.

2. Judy, a junior education major, tells her roommate, "I'll bet Ralph brings me flowers for our pinning anniversary." On their Monday night date, Judy remarks, "Ralph, the funniest thing happened. Ann knitted a sweater for her pin-mate for their pinning anniversary and it practically reached his knees." During another conversation the same evening, she says, "Yes, the initiation went perfectly. It was lovely, absolutely lovely. I love the sorority house at initiation time. The flowers are so nice, especially the roses. They are so special. They make me feel warm and happy." When Ralph arrives Saturday night for their anniversary date, he presents Judy with a lovely bouquet of roses.

3. Mrs. Explicit is giving directions to John Greene, a second grader who is frequently in trouble. Mrs. Explicit has no

confidence in John's responsibility, so she gives him detailed instructions: "John, take this note to Mrs. Turner, whose room is at the end of the hall, across from the room where our fire drill exit is. This is a big responsibility, and I want you to remember . . . you will not make noise in the hall . . . don't stop to look in any other classrooms . . . and above all, don't go outside." John responds, with an obviously pained look, "Mrs. Explicit, don't you trust me?"

4. Dean Helpful counsels a few students in addition to his normal administrative duties. He does so because he is very interested in current student problems, and he enjoys the opportunity to stay in tune with student life. In September, the dean begins to counsel Tom Bloom. The dean knows that Tom will probably flunk out of school at the end of the semester. His entrance scores are very low and his writing skills are particularly poor. He is also socially withdrawn and shy, making it unlikely that he will get to know his instructors very well or receive much special help from them. The dean tells Tom that he may encounter academic difficulty, and urges him to enroll in the reading clinic and to devote extra time on Saturdays to his studies. In addition, he has Tom report to his office once a week. Tom realizes that the dean expects him to have trouble unless he works hard. He begins to work as hard as he can and keeps it up for the whole semester. When the grade slips are mailed in January, Tom finds he has made a B average.

5. Mr. Graney knew that Beth Burton would be a problem. He had had her older sister the year before and she was uncontrollable. Trying to keep Beth out of trouble, Mr. Graney seats her at a table far away from the other third graders in the room. Before long, though, Beth begins to throw things at the other children to attract their attention.

6. Jill Flywood, a pilot, is taking her brother Randy on his first plane trip. Jill really wants to put a scare into Randy, hoping that he will stop his daily begging for rides. Jill puts the plane through a rapid series of tight loops and then ends with a vertical dive, leveling off only at the last moment. Jill was so successful that she even frightened herself when she momentarily lost control of the

plane. However, Randy loved the ride and wants to know when he can have another.

7. Mal Chauvin is a young physics professor teaching undergraduates for the first time. He is especially concerned about reaching the girls in his class, because he expects them to have a difficult time. He thinks that most of the girls at the college are there just to get a husband, and he does not think they have much interest or aptitude for physics. To avoid embarrassing them, he never calls on them to answer a mathematical question or to explain difficult concepts. He also shows his concern by looking at one of the girls after he introduces a new point and asking, "Do you understand?" However, the girls usually find this more embarrassing than helpful, and in general they do not do very well in his course.

8. Miss Ball is concerned about the peer-group adjustment of Dick Stewart, one of the boys in her second-grade class. Although Dick had participated all year long in the races and group games conducted during recess, he began to withdraw from the group in the spring when she started the children playing baseball. Although Dick was coordinated well enough, he had not played much baseball and had difficulty in both hitting and catching the ball. As a result, he was usually one of the last children chosen when teams were selected. After this happened a few times, Dick began to withdraw, claiming that he did not want to play because he had a headache, a stomachache, or a sore foot. This did not fool Miss Ball, who recognized that Dick's embarrassment was the real reason.

To help Dick compensate for his deficiencies and to see that he did not lose peer status, Miss Ball began allowing him to serve as umpire for ball games. This way he had an important and active role. She reinforced this by praising and calling the other children's attention to his umpire work. In private contacts, she reassured Dick that he should not feel badly because he was not playing and there could not be a ball game without an umpire.

In the last few days of school, Miss Ball decided to let Dick play again, now that his confidence was built up. She was gratified to see that he was picked earlier than usual by the team captain. However, his batting and catching were just as bad as they had been before. The next day, he was the last one chosen and he begged off, complaining of a headache.

### Answers

Let us see how well you were able to identify self-fulfilling prophecies. If we have been successful in describing the process, you should have correctly classified each example.

In case 1, Coach Winn's original expectancy about Thumper is fulfilled. However, there is no evidence that Winn behaved in some manner to influence Thumper's performance. Thus, it would not be correct to say that the coach's prediction acted as a self-fulfilling prophecy, even though his prediction was accurate.

Case 2 is an example of a self-fulfilling prophecy. Judy expected to receive flowers, and consciously or subconsciously communicated this expectation to Ralph. Ralph took the hint and fulfilled her original expectation.

In case 3, Mrs. Explicit's original expectancy is "If I don't give Johnny explicit instructions, he will take advantage of the situation and misbehave." She subconsciously communicates this expectation in her behavior toward Johnny. However, even though Johnny gets her "real message," there is no evidence that his behavior changes in the direction of her expectation. Therefore, this is not an example of a self-fulfilling prophecy. If Mrs. Explicit were to continue to treat Johnny this way, however, he might begin to behave as she expects. At this point, her expectations would have become self-fulfilling.

Case 4 is an especially interesting and instructive example. The dean fears that Tom will flunk out, and he communicates this expectation to Tom. Tom gets the message, but reacts by working as hard as he can to prove himself. He ends up doing very well, despite the dean's original expectation. Similar examples occur every day in doctors' offices. A doctor who fears that his patient is about to have a heart attack will quickly place him on a strict diet and exercise program. He also schedules the patient for regular appointments so that he can check his progress. In this way, a heart attack is avoided and the person's general health improves. Both the doctor and the dean communicate serious concern, but they follow this up with attempts to deal with the problem. If, instead, they communicated hopelessness and did nothing to change the situation, their expectations probably would have been fulfilled.

Case 5 is a classic illustration of a self-fulfilling teacher expectation. Mr. Graney expects the girl to be a problem and, therefore, begins to treat her like one. His treatment involves separating Beth from her peers and forcing her to misbehave to get peer attention, so that his expectations become fulfilled.

Case 6 is a tricky example. Jill fully expects to scare her brother by dangerously maneuvering her plane. Ordinarily, her behavior would have been effective, since Jill scared even herself by flirting with tragedy. However, Randy had not been in a plane before and assumed that his sister's behavior was routine. He did not perceive the clues, or did not interpret them correctly, so that her behavior did not communicate fright. In this case, Jill's expectation was not fulfilled, even though she consciously and deliberately tried to fulfill it. This can happen in the classroom if the student does not perceive the teacher's behavior as the teacher intends it. For example, a comment like, "That's not quite right," would be discouraging to high-achieving students who thought they had answered correctly but might be encouraging to low-achieving students who doubted that they were even partially correct.

Case 7 is another example of teacher expectations as self-fulfilling prophecies. Despite his good intentions, the teacher's treatment of the girls in his class tends to erode their confidence and reduce their opportunities to learn through participation in class discussions. The result is low motivation and low performance, just as the teacher expected.

Case 8 also illustrates how a teacher's expectation can be self-fulfilling, even though the expectation itself might be unformulated and unrecognized by the teacher. Miss Ball's conscious intention is to build Dick's confidence so that he will participate in ball games. However, her approach takes into account only his attitude and not his need for practice in hitting and catching the ball. Although she may never have thought about it this way, her approach follows from the basic expectation that Dick cannot hit or catch and, there-fore, needs some alternate role. This is very different from the idea that Dick cannot hit or catch and, therefore, needs to be taught to do so. Miss Ball's attempt to solve the problem involves many good things for Dick, but not the things he most needs: practice at hitting and catching the ball. As a result, by the end of the year, he is even further behind his classmates in these skills than he was earlier.

This last example is one of many that could have been given about how teachers will adopt inappropriate strategies if they define a problem improperly. This is often done by teachers who are con-cerned about their students' self-concepts. They sometimes confuse the relationship between self-concept and abilities, thinking that they have to improve self-concept before abilities will improve. Usually, the opposite is true. Low self-concept results from low abilities, and improvement in abilities will produce improvement in self-concept. When students show handicaps, inhibitions, or lack of skill, the appropriate teacher strategy is to provide remedial instruction and extra practice or opportunities to learn. Although well-meant, attempts to make students feel better by providing compensation in other areas rather than by dealing directly with their problems, are not what they need.

Low achievers who receive inappropriate or critical treatment will fall further and further behind other students. Cooper (1975) points out that the less supportive environment that teachers sometimes provide for low achievers may be an attempt (perhaps unconscious) to gain control over interactions with these students. Cooper (1977) notes that teachers perceive interactions with low-expectation students as time consuming and typically less successful than interactions with other students. Negative comments by teachers may reduce the willingness of low-expectation students to seek teachers out for help.

A negative, critical environment may also convince low-expectation students that *effort* on a task is not related to teacher assessment of their work (e.g., teachers are more likely to criticize them when they approach with questions than when they avoid contact and turn in incorrect or incomplete work). In time, they may learn to make less effort.

This argument illustrates the model presented earlier (Brophy and Good, 1970). If teachers consistently treat low achievers inappropriately, such behaviors eventually may convince students that the classroom game is fixed: for them, there is little, if any, relation between effort and reward. Cooper (1977) found that the removal of teacher criticism from interactions with low-expectation students resulted in an increase in the rate of initiation by students who had previously been most criticized.

In a separate study, Cooper (1976) examined the extent to which teachers' participation in a treatment program would change their expectations and behaviors and those of their students. He classified teachers into two groups: those with "alterable" and "unalterable" expectations. Unalterable teachers were those whose expectations were *most* predictable on the basis of student sex and IQ. Alterable teachers were those whose performance expectations were not tied as closely to student characteristics.

Cooper reasoned that low-expectation students in "alterable" teachers' classrooms would benefit more from the treatment program than similar students in "unalterable" teachers' classrooms. The six teachers who participated in the program were presented with information about research on teacher expectations, given feedback about their teaching behavior, informed of the personal control hypothesis (teachers may criticize low-achievement students to reduce contact), and asked to change their behavior toward specific students.

All six teachers taught young children (kindergarten through second grade), so their students probably did not have rigid expectations about the extent to which their personal efforts resulted in better performance or more teacher reward. At the beginning of the year, there were no differences between high- and low-expectation students in perceived effort-outcome relationships. However, by the end of the year, high-expectation students had higher effort-outcome scores than low-expectation students. Also, low-expectation students in unalterable classrooms tended to have lower scores than high-expectation students. There was no such trend in the classrooms of alterable teachers.

Students in "alterable" classrooms made higher achievement gains in reading than students in unalterable classes. However, the spread in achievement between high- and low-expectation students in alterable classes was *less* than in unalterable classes. Thus, not only did students assigned to alterable teachers achieve more than students assigned to unalterable teachers, the distance between high- and low-expectation students decreased in the classrooms of alterable teachers.

Some teachers' expectations and behaviors can be influenced by intervention, leading to changes in student perception and achievement. However, it may be difficult to change teachers who form their expectations on the basis of student characteristics such as IQ and sex (as opposed to classroom behavior).

We agree with Dusek (1975), who argues that we need to know more about the cues (and their appropriateness) that teachers use in forming expectations about students. Apparently, the alterable teachers in Cooper's study were using student cues other than sex and IQ, but unfortunately, we do not know what these cues were. Cooper's results are based upon a very small sample of teachers, so it will be important to replicate and extend the findings to other age levels. The study provides strong support, however, for the contention that teacher behavior can influence student expectations (effort-outcome) and that such expectations may control student behaviors.

## SELF-CONCEPT
Others too have argued that student expectations are critical forces in the learning process. Braun (1976) argues that low student expec-

tations help perpetuate the low expectations of teachers. When students expect good things to happen, they act in a way to bring those results about. If students expect negative things to happen, they act in a way to fulfill those expectations. Teachers who communicate appropriate and positive expectations will still have to deal with students who have low opinions of themselves. Let us examine how students' views of themselves develop and influence their perceptions of behavior.

For a while, Larry is surrounded on the playground by his third-grade classmates as he hands out small treats. The children briefly cheer and clamor around him, but they disappear as soon as the candy is gone. Larry is average in height and weight, and his physical characteristics are not particularly striking. However, he is painfully shy.

His academic performance is a bit below average but not enough to make him stand out. He always listens carefully and does everything exactly the way the teacher directs. Sometimes, his attention to detail is so great that it actually interferes with his work. Larry seldom talks in the classroom, rarely leaves his seat, and is seldom visited at his desk by his teacher or classmates. He would like more contact, but whenever he is with other children, he feels uncomfortable and threatened.

Larry goes through his school day *unnoticed*. His life at home is similar. Both parents love Larry, but implicitly they have given up on him. His father finds it difficult to react to Larry's unassuming, low-key approach to life. He finds it particularly irksome that Larry accepts his constant defeats and setbacks in life (disappointing grades, mediocre athletic performance, peer rejection) as if they were expected and unchangeable.

When Larry was a preschooler, he preferred to stay home because older children on the street picked on him. His mother (unaware of the problem) enjoyed having him at home. She actively encouraged him to stay home by playing games with him every afternoon. Now she has become concerned, however, because Larry is so withdrawn and socially inhibited. She wishes that he had friends and interests other than quiet play at home.

Although both parents have been concerned about Larry for a couple years, neither has ever mentioned it, and Larry's life (including the way his parents deal with him) continues to unfold in the same basic way. Larry's view of what he is and can be is based upon the *interactions* that he has had with his parents and others. Over time, these experiences have solidified, and he has developed a stable way of viewing his environment and himself.

Larry's behavior on the playground communicates at least two messages. First, he is unhappy (he has no friends and nothing to do in the afternoon). Second, he feels that he must buy friendship. Perhaps he feels that he is not attractive or interesting enough to have friends, or perhaps he does not know how to form friendships.

Larry's plight is of a lonely person searching for social attachment and camaraderie. Unfortunately, his poor self-concept and feelings of inadequacy may go undiagnosed and uncorrected at school. For example, his attempts to reach other children (via free candy) may be seen only as violations of playground rules by his teachers. His parents also may ignore or misinterpret signals in the home. Ultimately, Larry may accept loneliness as an unalterable part of his life.

### Different Third Graders: Different Self-Concepts

Terry, another third grader, is also an average student with physical characteristics and academic aptitudes similar to Larry's. However, his behavior at school is completely different. He volunteers to answer questions, and he interacts often with other children and is well liked by them. Although he can work well alone, he prefers not to and will actively seek opportunities to work with other students. After school, he always leaves with three or four classmates. Terry is happy and looks forward to school, to play, and to visits with friends after school. He also enjoys his family life.

John is another third grader of average ability, size, and appearance. He is basically confident and happy, but his day-to-day behavior differs from Terry's and Larry's. For example, John likes to work alone. He will occasionally join with others to work on class assignments, but he generally prefers individual work. On the playground, he participates in group games and he plays hard. After school, he rarely goes to the home of a friend or invites a friend over. He has a number of hobbies that he fully enjoys, however, and a couple of afternoons each week he will go to the "Y" for basketball. He seldom makes arrangements in advance. He simply goes and plays with whomever is there. The activity (not the people) is the important thing to him. He enjoys the physical activity involved in basketball because he is good at it and because he enjoys competition.

We have had quick glimpses of three third-grade boys. Two of the boys appear to be reasonably happy and well adjusted. However, we have also seen that different things make these two individuals happy. In part, self-acceptance is a function of an individual's perceptions or beliefs about his or her goals and the extent to which these goals are satisfied. Terry wants to be with people, but John is more individualistic. Although both can function in situations that demand individual or social functioning, each one has developed stable preferences and is beginning to structure his life around them.

Larry is unhappy and may be headed for an unfulfilled, empty life. Unlike John and Terry, he does not have stable, positive perceptions of himself around which to organize his life. He needs people, but at the same time he is afraid of them. Although he generally works alone, he derives only momentary pleasure from such activity. He doesn't know how to get what he wants, and he is beginning to stop trying.

### Emergent Views of Self

How did these three boys develop their unique patterns of behavior? All came from homes of parents who cared about them, and all had similar physical characteristics and mental aptitudes (none had harsh environmental experiences, such as regular beatings by parents or malnutrition). The three boys are the way they are largely because of their early experiences and the subtle but systematic opportunities and rewards they experienced. Let us consider a few hypothetical examples of what their early home life may have been like.

As an infant, Larry was encouraged to be at "mother's side," but was not rewarded for achievement in the games he played with her. In general, he was vaguely dependent upon her, but not in explicit ways which would have helped him to partially control their interactions or to understand them. Furthermore, children of his age were seldom invited to his home. When playmates did visit, his mother "hovered" over him to be sure that he did not offend the playmate or get into mischief. He was denied the opportunity to interact with other children regularly and to benefit from normal mistakes.

His father expected too much of him too soon. He had been an only child himself, and had limited experience with young children. His early attempts to play with Larry (e.g., trying to get Larry to throw a ball when Larry could hardly lift the ball) were not rewarded, and he assumed that Larry wasn't interested. Eventually, he avoided active, vigorous interaction with Larry. Larry enjoyed being with his dad, but somehow he always had the feeling that his dad did not like being with him.

Terry, on the other hand, enjoyed frequent contact with other children. His parents encouraged visits with neighborhood peers and reinforced his interest in reaching out to others by allowing him to phone friends regularly and ask them over occasionally. His mother exercised moderate supervision when friends visited, providing sufficient structure and management to guarantee that play time was generally rewarding, but allowed the children to solve minor quarrels on their own. Terry's father took him and a friend or two to sports events and movies regularly, so that Terry associated friends with "good times" at an early age. Both parents approved of Terry's friendships, and they communicated this approval directly and indirectly to Terry.

John's early opportunities for frequent social contact were limited because no children his age lived on his block. However, the contacts he did have were satisfying. He spent most of his time, though, in a variety of individual activities. He likes to compete and to achieve within the limits of his capability, but does not need others to really get involved in a project. He imitates his parents, who model strong and rewarding interests in individual activities and who enjoy competing and achieving.

These vignettes illustrate the contention that children learn who they are, their values, and their interests through their day-to-day contacts with others. Young children who are developing a sense of identity are especially vulnerable to the modeling and feedback of others. Parents are the main sources, but children also can estimate their attractiveness, potential, and other qualities, from contacts with other children (siblings, peers) and with important adults.

Children are not born with inadequate self-concepts. Self-worth is learned in interactions with others. Children who are continually discouraged from exploring the world (not allowed to climb the couch, restricted in social interactions, constantly reminded of bicycle safety, etc.) will learn to look to others to *initiate* behavior. Personality characteristics such as sociability, initiation of activity, fear of competition, achievement motivation, and locus of control are all *learned* in interactions with the environment.

### Self-Concept: A Definition

We have seen that children of generally similar physical and mental potential may behave quite differently, and have suggested that this is partly because of their past reinforcement history and experiences. Children who are rewarded (for example, by parent approval) for playing the piano are likely to continue to play. Eventually, the practice will help them to develop skill, and skillful playing may lead to the view: I am a good piano player. Such a view in itself controls much behavior. Given free time, such people will practice the paino for relaxation and satisfaction.

There are many different definitions of self-concept. Typically, the term refers to the total affective regard that one holds for him or herself. However, the "self" is made up of countless *parts* and *evaluations* (e.g., I need time to make decisions; that's good, it's important to think things out; that's wishy-washy, I wish I could make quicker decisions). Usually, it is more important to discuss *specific aspects* of self-concept than general self-concept.

McCandless and Evans (1973) divide the self into three interrelated components: self-concept, self-esteem, and identity. Self-concept is defined as "an individual's awareness of his own characteristics and attributes, and the ways in which he is both like and unlike others." They define self-esteem as the value people place on themselves and on their behavior (good, bad). Identity is an awareness of and willingness to accommodate group expectations and social responsibility (anticipated future development). Obviously, all three of these "images" influence behavior.

According to many developmental psychologists, the self-concept is theoretically important because it affects both *perception* and *action*. La Benne and Greene (1969) argue that individuals behave according to how they *perceive* the situation and themselves at the moment of action. Students' self-concepts stabilize relatively early (by age 10 or so), and after that point, most are unwilling to accept evidence that they are better or worse than the view of self-worth (see, for example, Aronson and Mills, 1959). Hence, once a negative view is formed, a person reacts to cues from the environment in terms of his or her self-view. This is why we feel that the data presented by Cooper are so important: they illustrate that students may learn from teachers whether or not to believe that there is a relationship between effort and progress. Those students who conclude that there isn't are likely to get stuck in a circle of low expectations.

We suggest that the development of a favorable self-concept is dependent upon two major factors: behavioral success (mastery of assigned school work) and the student's *perception* of his progress ("Sure I did it, but the assignment was the stuff they give fourth graders. It wasn't what the other seventh graders do."). Teachers must be positive but honest in their feedback with students; however, they also must attempt to alter destructive self-perceptions that students bring to learning situations. Low expectations are destructive because they reduce students' task motivation and the time and effort that they are willing to devote to activities.

As Braun (1976) notes, however, teacher action to boost a student's self-concept must be genuine and consistent. Students will persist in their way of looking at things unless a teacher can systematically convince them that they have potential and can achieve. In the following discussion, we will point out some of the ways in which we can communicate positive and appropriate expectations to students.

## APPROPRIATE TEACHER EXPECTATIONS

How can knowledge about the self-fulfilling prophecy effects of teacher expectations be applied by the classroom teacher? Several suggestions offered in an attempt to answer this question are presented in later sections of this chapter. Before getting to them, however, we wish to discuss two frequently made suggestions that we do *not* think are appropriate. Either suggestion would effectively eliminate undesirable self-fulfilling prophecies if teachers could follow it. The first is that teachers should have only positive expectations; the second is that they should have no expectations at all.

In a study of relatively effective and ineffective fourth-grade mathematics instructors, it was found that effective teachers were moving through the curriculum faster than were teachers who were getting less achievement from comparable students (Good, Grouws, and Beckerman, 1977). Teachers can go too fast as well as too slow (more on this in the chapter on individualization); however, we wanted to point out that when teachers underestimate potential, lower achievement follows.

Some authors have suggested that teachers try to avoid self-fulfilling prophecy effects by avoiding forming expectations altogether. This means refusing to discuss students with their previous teachers and avoiding or ignoring cumulative records or test information. This is not a good suggestion, however, for two reasons. First, expectations cannot be suppressed or avoided. Experiences tend to stay with us and make an impression on us. When events occur repeatedly, they gradually are seen as expected and normal, and expectations are reinforced every time repetition occurs. Thus, teachers build up expectations about their students simply from interacting with them, even if they try to avoid other sources of information. Second, the question of whether other sources of information are examined is not as important as the question of how information is used. Information about students will create expectations about them, but it will also be useful in planning individualized instruction to meet their specific needs. The teacher should try to get information and use it in this way, rather than to avoid obtaining information. Suggestions about how teachers can profitably use information in school records and test data are presented in Brubaker (1968).

The suggestion that teachers should have only positive expectations is appealing on the surface. Confidence and determination are important teacher qualities, and a "can do" attitude helps cut large problems down to workable size. However, this must not be carried to the point of distorting reality. Students show large individual differences in learning abilities and interests, and these cannot be eliminated through wishful thinking. Some students are capable of more than others, and teachers will only frustrate both themselves and their students if they set unrealistically high standards that some or all cannot reach.

Expectations should be appropriate rather than necessarily high, and they must be followed up with appropriate behavior. This means planned learning experiences that take students at the level they are now and move them along at a pace they can handle. The pace that will allow continued success and improvement is the correct pace and will vary with different students. Teachers should not feel guilty or feel that they are stigmatizing slower learners by moving them along at a slower pace. As long as students are working up to their potential and progressing at a steady rate, the teacher has reason to be satisfied. There will be cause for criticism only if the slower children are moved along at a slower pace than they can handle because the teacher's expectations for them are too low, are never tested out or reevaluated, and, consequently, are unalterable.

Expectations built up through repetition can be very compelling. If John has turned in completed homework every day this year, he probably will do so again tomorrow. If Susan has been among the bottom five in class on every math test this year, she probably will be on the next one too, unless her teacher provides extra math instruction and practice and takes additional special steps, such as giving shorter but more frequent tests to Susan and other students like her.

Regular repetition of student behavior will build up strong expectations in all teachers, including (and perhaps especially) teachers who try to deny or suppress them. Inevitably, some of these expectations will be pessimistic. However, teachers can avoid undesirable self-fulfilling prophecy effects if they remain alert to the formation of and changes in their own expectations, and if they monitor their own behavior to see that negative expectations are not communicated. To the extent that such expectations do exist, they should be of the helpful variety that encourage teachers to combine expressions of concern with behavior geared to remediate the difficulty. Saying that a student needs help is bad only if the teacher does not provide that help in a positive, supportive way.

### Forming and Changing Expectations

Teachers form some expectations about their students before they even see them. The individual cumulative record files provide IQ data, achievement scores, grades, and teacher comments that create expectations about achievement and conduct. Other expectations are picked up in chats with colleagues who taught the students in earlier grades. The reputation of the family, or the teacher's prior experience with an older brother or sister, may also condition what he or she expects from a particular student.

Some teachers deliberately try to avoid being influenced by the past. They do not look at records or seek information about their students until they have had a chance to see them and form their own impressions. This is not necessarily an improvement, however, since a lack of data from the files does not prevent most teachers from forming strong and general impressions very quickly. In one study, for example, first-grade teachers were able to rank their children in order of expected achievement after the very first week of school. Furthermore, these rankings, made without benefit of any test data, were highly correlated with achievement ranks from tests given at the end of the year (Willis, 1972). Thus, first impressions lead to specific and largely accurate expectations about students, even in teachers who are aware of the phenomenon. Rather than trying to eliminate expectations, teachers must remain aware of them and see that they do not lead to inappropriate treatment of certain students. If low expectations lead to inappropriate teacher behavior, they may well become self-fulfilling. For example, a first-grade teacher who expects a particular child to have great trouble in learning to read may begin to treat the child differently from the way she treats other children. To avoid pressuring or embarrassing the child, she may call on him infrequently and only to read easy passages. Over the year, this will mean that the child will receive fewer opportunities to practice, and whenever he has trouble reading, the teacher will give him the word and quickly move on to another student. So long as this keeps up, the child will gradually fall further and further behind his classmates in reading ability.

His reading ability will not improve even if the teacher attempts to compensate by allowing the child to be first in the lunch line, to sit near her, or to take notes to the office frequently. Like the efforts of Miss Ball in our example of the student inept at baseball, these are misdirected and inappropriate intervention strategies for the low-achieving reader. The child may enjoy these activities and may become more receptive to the teacher and her instruction efforts, but he will not improve in reading unless he gets the instruction and practice he needs.

A teacher who behaves this way is reacting to a label (low achiever, low potential, slow learner) instead of the student as he is. A subtle shift has taken place in which the teacher has lost focus on instructing the student, on taking him from where he is to some higher level of progress, and has become fixated on the status quo. This somehow makes the lack of progress acceptable and, at the same time, reinforces the teacher's low expectations.

To avoid falling into this rut, teachers need to keep their expectations open and to bear in mind their role as instructor. If expectations are allowed to become too strong or too settled, they can begin to distort perception and behavior. The teacher may begin to notice only those things that fit his expectations, and may start deviating from good teaching practice.

Once formed, expectations tend to be self-perpetuating. This is true for students as well as teachers because expectations guide both perceptions and behavior. When we expect to find something, we are much more likely to see it than when we are not looking for it. For example, most people do not notice counterfeit money or slight irregularities in clothing patterns. However, treasury department officials and inspectors for clothing manufacturers, who have been trained to look for such deviations, will notice them. Similarly, valuable rare coins and unusual abilities and aptitudes usually are not noticed except by those who are on the lookout for them. This is part of the reason why teachers often fail to notice good behavior in students who are frequent discipline problems in the classroom. They are used to misbehavior from these students and are on the lookout for it, so they tend to notice most of the misbehavior that occurs. With a set toward misbehavior, however, they miss a lot of the good behavior that someone else might have noticed and reinforced.

Expectations not only cause us to notice some things and fail to notice others, they also affect the way that we interpret what we do notice. The optimist, for example, notices that the glass is half full, while the pessimist observes that it is half empty. Mistaken beliefs and attitudes about other people are self-perpetuating and difficult to correct because of their tendency to influence how we interpret what we see. If we are convinced that a person has particular qualities, we often see these qualities in him when we observe him.

Consider the teacher who asks a complex, difficult question and then gives his students some time to think about the answer. After a while he calls on Johnny Bright, whom he sees as an intelligent and well-motivated student. Johnny remains silent, pursing his lips, knitting his brow, and scratching his head. The teacher knows that he is working out the problem, so he patiently gives him more time. He has an attentive and eager expression as Johnny begins to speak. Finally, Johnny responds with a question, "Would you repeat that last part again?" The teacher is happy to do so, because this indicates that Johnny has partially solved the problem and may be able to do it by himself with a little more time. He asks Johnny what part he wants repeated and then obliges. He then waits eagerly, but patiently, for Johnny to respond again. If someone interrupted the teacher at this point to ask him what he was doing, he might respond that he was "challenging the class to use creativity and logical thinking to solve problems."

Suppose, however, that the teacher had called on Sammy Slow instead of Johnny Bright. The teacher knows that Sammy is a low achiever, and he does not think Sammy is very well motivated, either. When called on, Sammy remains silent, although the teacher notes his pursed lips, his furrowed brow, and the fact that he is scratching his head. This probably means that Sammy is hopelessly lost, although it may mean that he is merely acting, trying to give the impression that he is thinking about the problem. After a few seconds, the teacher says, "Well, Sammy?" Now Sammy responds, but with a question instead of an answer, "Would you repeat that last part again?" This confirms the teacher's suspicions, making it clear that any more time spent with Sammy on this question would be wasted. After admonishing Sammy to listen more carefully, he calls on someone else. If interrupted at this point and asked what he was doing, the teacher might respond that he was "making it clear that the class is expected to pay close attention to the discussion, so that they can respond intelligently when questioned."

In this example, the teacher's expectations for these two students caused him to see much more than was objectively observable to a more neutral observer. The observable behavior of the two boys was the same, and they made the same responses to the initial question. Yet the teacher interpreted the behavior quite differently by reading additional meaning into it. His interpretations about the two boys may have been correct, but we (and he) cannot tell for sure because he did not check them out. Instead, he acted on them as if they were observable facts, so that his treatment of Sammy was grossly inappropriate.

Although the need to continually check out and adjust expectations may seem obvious, it can be difficult to do, in everyday life as well as in the classroom. (For example, the widely advertised brand is not always better than the unknown brand, the more expensive item is not necessarily better than the cheaper one, nor is the large economy size always a better bargain than the regular size. Yet every day most people automatically accept such things without checking them out.)

Similarly, the fact that a student could not do something yesterday does not mean that he cannot do it today, but the teacher will not find out unless the student is given a chance. Expectations stress the stable or unchanging aspects of the world. The teacher, however, is a change agent who is trying to make students something different from what they are today. Teachers, therefore, must keep their expectations in perspective. To the extent that they are negative, expectations represent problems to be solved, not definitions of reality to which a teacher must adapt.

### Basic Teacher Expectations

The following sections in this chapter will present certain basic attitudes and expectations teachers must have if they are to do their jobs successfully. Descriptions and examples of how these expectations are communicated to students through observable behavior are also provided. When these types of inappropriate behavior are observed in a teacher, the problems may be due, in part, to inappropriate expectations about teaching in general or about a particular student in the classroom.

*The Teacher Should Enjoy Teaching.* Teaching brings many rewards and satisfactions, but it is a demanding, exhausting, and sometimes frustrating job. It is hard to do well unless you enjoy doing it. Teachers who do enjoy their work will show this in their classroom behavior. They will come to class prepared for the day's lessons, and will present lessons in a way that suggests interest and excitement in promoting learning. They will appear eager for contact with students, will keep track of their individual needs and progress, and will take pride and satisfaction in helping them overcome learning difficulties. Difficulties and confusion in students will be perceived as challenges to be met with professional skills and not as irritations. When students do achieve success, the teacher shares in their joy. In general, teachers who enjoy their work see themselves as benevolent resource persons to their students and not as wardens or authority figures.

What about yourself? If you are a teacher, how do you feel in the classroom? Do you feel at home and enjoy yourself there, or would you really rather be somewhere else? If you are a student observer, how do you feel about the work of a teacher? Is this work that you would enjoy as a career?

If your personal response to these questions has been negative, some careful thought and reassessment is in order. If you think you cannot and will not really enjoy teaching, you should avoid going into it or should get out of it if you can. If you do not enjoy it but are open to change, do not give up. You may have been operating with inappropriate attitudes and expectations about teaching, which may have prevented you from enjoying the satisfactions that the job offers. Or you may have serious but remediable faults in teaching technique. In either case, after you have read this book and practiced systematic observation of your own and other teachers' classroom behavior, you may become aware of facts about yourself that you never realized before. Once awareness exists, change is possible, and you may be able to reorient your approach to the teaching role and to sharpen your specific teaching skills. This in turn can enable you to find the enjoyment that you can and should expect from work as a teacher.

*The Teacher's Main Responsibility Is to Teach.* The teacher's job involves many roles besides that of instructing students. At times, the teacher will serve as a parent surrogate, an entertainer, an authority figure, a psychotherapist, and a record keeper, among other things. All of these are necessary aspects of the teacher's role. However, they are subordinate to and in support of the major role of teaching. Important as they are, they must not be allowed to overshadow the teacher's basic instructional role.

It sometimes happens that teachers working with young children will become more concerned with mothering or entertaining the children than with teaching them. In these classes, much of the day is spent in reading stories, playing games, working on arts and crafts projects, singing and listening to records, show-and-tell, and enrichment activities. Often, the teachers basically do not like to spend time teaching the curriculum, and feel they must apologize to or bribe the children when lessons are conducted. This type of teacher is meeting his or her own needs, not those of the children. By the end of the year, the pupils will have acquired negative attitudes toward the school curriculum, and they will have failed to achieve near their potential.

Research by Thomas (1970) suggests that this problem is peculiar to adults. Thomas studied the tutoring behavior of college tutors and fifth- and sixth-grade tutors working with second-grade students in reading. Even though the college students were senior education majors enrolled in a reading methods course, the fifth- and sixth-grade tutors were just as effective for producing reading gains in the second graders. Thomas noted interesting differences, however, in the behavior of the two groups of tutors. The college students spent much time trying to coax the children into liking them, into enjoying the reading materials, and into practicing the reading skills. In contrast, the fifth and sixth graders were more direct and business-like. They accepted the fact that the second graders were having reading difficulties and that the tutoring sessions were for teaching them with the materials in front of them and not for discussing matters outside the lesson.

At the higher grades, failure to teach is sometimes seen in teachers who have low expectations about their own classroom management abilities or about the learning abilities of a particular class. Where homogeneous grouping is practiced in a junior high or high school, for example, teachers assigned to a period with a low-achieving class may sometimes abandon serious attempts to teach their subject. They may, perhaps, attempt to entertain the class, or else merely act as a sort of proctor who is interested only in seeing that the noise does not get out of hand. Such behavior indicates a serious lack of confidence in the teacher, either in his or her own ability to motivate and control the class or in the students' ability to learn or to become interested in the subject matter. It represents a total surrender to failure expectations, because emphasis has been switched from teaching the class to merely keeping the class happy.

*Teachers Must Understand That the Crucial Aspects of Teaching Are Task Presentation, Diagnosis, Remediation, and Enrichment.* Failure to be clear about crucial aspects of teaching characterizes teachers who favor high achievers over low achievers or who pay more attention to answers than to the thinking processes that a student goes through in reaching an answer. Such teachers sometimes act as if the students are expected to learn on their own with no help from them. If a student does not catch on immediately after one demonstration, or does not do his work correctly after hearing the instructions one time, they react with impatience and frustration.

Such behavior represents a fundamental failure to appreciate the teacher's basic role. The teacher is in the classroom to instruct. This involves more than just giving demonstrations or presenting learning experiences. Instruction also means giving additional help to those who are having difficulty, diagnosing the source of their problem, and providing remedial assistance to correct it. It means conducting evaluation with an eye toward identifying and correcting difficulties and not merely as a prelude to passing out praise or criticism. It means keeping track of students' individual progress, so that they can be instructed in terms of what they learned yesterday and what they should learn tomorrow. It means finding satisfaction in the progress of the slower students as well as the brighter ones.

There are many aspects of teacher behavior that help indicate whether or not the teacher clearly understands what he or she is supposed to be doing with the students. The handling of seatwork and homework assignments is one good indicator. The purpose of such assignments is to provide students with practice on the skills they are learning and to provide the teacher with information about their progress. Teachers should monitor the students' performance on seatwork and homework, noting the particular error patterns that occur. This will suggest the nature of individual students' learning problems and the nature of the remedial actions the teachers should take. However, some teachers fail to use seatwork and homework in this way. They simply pass out the work and then collect and score it, without following up the scoring with remedial teaching.

Teachers can create negative attitudes toward seatwork assignments if the assignments are inappropriate or if they are not adjusted to individual differences within the classroom. Seatwork assignments should be made with specific instructional objectives in mind. This may mean separate assignments for different groups of students in a class. Assignments that are too difficult or too easy for a given student will not fulfill their instructional purpose. In particular, overly simple and repetitive seatwork will rightly be regarded as annoying busywork by the students. Teachers sometimes create this attitude in otherwise well-motivated and bright students who tend to do the seatwork quickly and correctly. If the teacher's method of handling students who finish quickly is to assign them more of the same kind of exercises, the students will learn to slow down their pace or hide the fact that they have finished. Teachers would do much better to assign alternate activities of the students' choice, or to allow them to move on to more challenging problems of a similar type.

Another important indicator is the way the teacher responds to right and wrong answers. When teachers have the appropriate attitude, they accept either type of response for the information it gives about the student. They neither become overly elated about correct answers nor overly depressed about incorrect answers. They use questions as a way to stimulate and to acquire information about the student's progress.

Inappropriate expectations can even be communicated through praise. Although praise and encouragement are important, they should not interfere with basic teaching goals. If the teacher responds with overly dramatic praise every time a student answers a simple question, the class will likely be distracted from the content of the lesson. A contest in which the more confident and outgoing students compete for teacher recognition and approval will probably result. The better strategy is to follow a simple correct answer with simple feedback to acknowledge that it is correct. The teacher should then advance the discussion by asking another question or adding information to expand on the previous one. Praise can be saved for times when it can be given more effectively and meaningfully, especially during contacts with individual students. Criticism, of course, should be omitted entirely. In general, the teacher's behavior during question and answer sessions should say, "We're going to discuss and deepen our understanding of the material," and not, "We're going to find out who knows the material and who doesn't."

When praise is given to students, it should be specific praise that reinforces their feelings of progress in learning new knowledge and skills. Empty phrases like "how nice" or "that's good" should be avoided in favor of more specific statements. Praise should stress appreciation of the student's efforts and the progress he or she is making, and usually should be focused on more general progress rather than on single isolated successes. All of this helps to reinforce the teacher's role as a resource person who facilitates learning, as opposed to a judge who decides who has learned and who has not.

*Teachers Should Expect All Students to Meet at Least the Minimum Specified Objectives.* Although all students cannot reasonably be expected to do equally well, reasonable minimal objectives can be established for each teacher's class. Naturally, most students will be capable of going considerably beyond minimal objectives, and the teacher should try to stimulate this development as far as their interests and abilities allow. However, in doing so, teachers must not lose sight of basic priorities. Remedial work with students who have not yet met minimal objectives should not be delayed in favor of enrichment activities with those who have. Ways that teachers can use grouping, peer tutoring, and other techniques to make time for such remediation are discussed in Chapter 8.

Teachers with appropriate attitudes will spend extra time working with the students who are having difficulty. Their behavior when interacting with these students will be characterized by supportiveness, patience, and confidence. In contrast, teachers with inappropriate attitudes will often spend less time with the students who most need extra help. When they do work with these students, they will tend to do so in a half-hearted way that communicates disappointment and frustration. Such teachers are often overly dependent on achieving easy success and eliciting many right answers. They will need to change this attitude if they are to acquire the patience and confidence needed to do effective remedial teaching with slower learners.

*Teachers Should Expect Students to Enjoy Learning.* Teachers can and should expect students to enjoy learning activities, including practice exercises, and they should back these expectations with appropriate behavior. This is one of the most common areas where teacher expectations become self-fulfilling. When teachers do have the appropriate attitude toward schoolwork, they present it in ways that make their students see it as enjoyable and interesting. Tasks and assignments are presented without apology, as activities valuable in their own right. There is no attempt to build up artificial enthusiasm or interest; the interest is assumed to be already there. Comments about upcoming assignments stress the specific ways in which they extend or build upon present knowledge and skills. Comments about present work reinforce the students' sense of progress and mastery. The teacher does not try to give learning a "hard sell," or to picture it as "fun." He or she does not expect the students to enjoy it in the same way they enjoy a trip to the circus or a ride on a roller coaster. Instead, the teacher expects the quieter but consistent satisfactions and feelings of mastery that come with the accumulation of knowledge and skills.

Teachers with a negative attitude toward school learning behave very differently. They see learning activities as unpleasant but necessary drudgery. If they believe in a positive approach toward motivation, they will be apologetic and defensive about assignments and will frequently resort to bribery, attempting to generate enthusiasm artifically through overemphasis on contests, rewards, and other external incentives. If they are more authoritarian and punitive, they will present assignments as bitter pills that the students must swallow or else. In either case, the students will quickly acquire a distaste for school activities, thus providing reinforcement for the teacher's expectations.

Other evidence of inappropriate teacher attitudes toward school activities includes: a heavy stress on the separation between work and play, with work pictured as unpleasant activity one does in order to get to play; a tendency to introduce assignments as something the class *has* to do, rather than merely as something they are going to do; the use of extra assignments as punishments; and practices such as checking to make sure that everyone has signed out one or more books from the library. Teachers with negative attitudes also have a tendency to discuss academic subjects in a way that presents them as dull and devoid of content. For example, they tend to say, "We're going to have history," instead of, "We're going to discuss the voyage of Columbus," or "Read pages 17 to 22," instead of, "Read the author's critique of Twain's novel." All these behaviors tell the students that the teacher does not see school activities as very interesting or very pleasant.

*The Teacher Should Expect to Deal with Individuals, Not Groups or Stereotypes.* As a rule, teachers should think, talk, and act in terms of individual students. This does not mean that they should not practice grouping, or that terms such as "low achievers" should not be used. It does mean that teachers must keep a proper perspective about priorities. Grouping must be practiced as a means toward the goal of meeting the individual needs of each student. Similarly, labels and stereotypes are often helpful in thinking about ways to teach individuals better. Ultimately, however, the teacher is teaching John Smith and Mary Jones, not Group A or "low achievers." The way teachers talk about students in their classes is an indication of how they think about them. If there is continual mention of groups to the exclusion of individuals, the teacher may well have begun to lose sight of individual differences within groups, and to overemphasize the differences between groups. If this has happened, observers will probably note that the teacher has too many choral responses and not enough individual responses in group situations, that he or she has not changed the group membership in a long time, that groups are seated together and spend most of the day together, or that the teacher spends more time with the high group and less with the low group.

Similarly, observers should be alert to teachers' use of oversimplified, stereotyped labels in describing certain students (immature, discipline problem, slow learner, etc.). The teacher may be reacting more to these stereotypes than to the student's individual qualities, and may well fail to notice behavior that doesn't fit the stereotype. This will show up in behavior such as labeling or criticizing the student directly, describing problems without trying to do anything about them, or treating the student on the basis of untested assumptions rather than observed behavior. These behaviors suggest that the stereotyped label has begun to structure the teacher's perception of the student.

*The Teacher Should Assume Good Intentions and a Positive Self-Concept.* Teachers must communicate to all of their students the expectation that the students want to be, and are trying to be, fair, cooperative, reasonable, and responsible. This includes even those who consistently present the same behavior problems. The rationale here is that the teacher's basic faith in the student's ability to change is a necessary (but often not sufficient) condition for such change. If students see that the teacher does not have this faith in them, they will probably lose whatever motivation they have to keep trying. Thus, teachers should be very careful to avoid suggesting that students deliberately hurt others or enjoy doing so, that they cannot and probably will not ever be able to control their own behavior, or that they simply do not care and are making no effort to do so. Even in cases where this might actually be true, there is nothing to be gained and much to be lost by saying so to the student. Such statements will only establish or help reinforce a negative self-concept and will lead to even more destructive behavior ("If they think I'm bad now, wait until they get a load of this").

Serious failures on the teacher's part should be brought to his or her attention immediately by an observer, since the teacher still may be able to salvage the situation somewhat by convincing the student that what was said was spoken in anger and not really meant. However, if the student is convinced that the teacher did mean what was said, the teacher's chances of establishing a productive relationship with the student are seriously and perhaps permanently damaged.

*The Teacher Should Expect to Be Obeyed.* Some teachers have serious discipline problems of their own making. Usually, the cause is failure to observe one of the principles for establishing classroom rules that are discussed in Chapter 5. Obedience is usually obtained rather easily by teachers who establish fair and appropriate rules, who are consistent in what they say, who say only what they really mean, and who regularly follow up with appropriate action whenever this is necessary. This produces credibility and respect; the students are clear about what the teacher expects of them and know that they are accountable for meeting these expectations.

There are many observable teacher behaviors that damage or undermine teachers' credibility and, therefore, their ability to command obedience. Among these behaviors are: inconsistency about rules; playing favorites or picking on certain students; making threats or promises that are not kept; making vague threats or promises that clearly do not have any meaning or implications for the future; failure to explain general rules or principles, so that reactions appear to be arbitrary and inconsistent to the students; indecisiveness or hesitancy in giving instructions; failure to listen to the whole story or get all the facts, so that hasty and ill-conceived solutions have to be retracted and changed; failure to take any action in response to obvious and serious defiance that cannot be simply ignored. These behaviors will convince students that teachers do not know what they really want and do not mean what they say; that they do not really expect to be taken seriously and obeyed. This will tend to make students question any test instructions, rather than accept and obey them. This can be prevented if teachers can show the students that they are quite serious about what they say, well aware of what they are saying when they say it, and seriously intent upon seeing it carried out. These points will be developed more fully in the following chapters.

*The Teacher Should Expect Some Difficulties.* Despite what has been said in this chapter and in other parts of this book about confidence and positive expectations, there inevitably will be difficulties, and teachers must expect them and be prepared to deal with them. This may, at first, appear contradictory to what has been said previously, but a careful analysis will show that it is not. Granted, while positive expectations may go a long way toward solving and preventing problems, they will not prevent or solve all problems. Expectations are not automatically self-fulfilling. However, positive expectations are necessary and important. Without them, the situation would be considerably changed. To the extent that positive expectations initiate behavior that does lead to self-fulfilling prophecy effects, they help prevent and solve problems that otherwise would appear. The benefits of self-fulfilling prophecy effects related to these positive expectations simply would not be gained if these expectations were not there in the first place.

In addition, the self-fulfilling prophecy effects of negative expectations must be considered. Where no negative expectations exist, undesirable self-fulfilling prophecy effects cannot occur. Where negative expectations do exist, however, some are likely to result in behavior that will produce undesirable self-fulfilling prophecy effects, thus adding to the teacher's burden. In addition to problems that would have been there anyway, there are added problems caused by the teacher's own negative expectations.

An additional benefit of consistent positive expectations is that they cause teachers to examine their own behavior and to ask what they might do differently to help the situation. This is an important function, since teachers, like everyone else, are strongly tempted to take credit for success but to blame failure on things outside themselves. This was shown, for example, in a study by Good, Schmidt, Peck, and Williams (1969). They asked 14 fifth-grade teachers and 14 eighth-grade teachers to describe the students in their classrooms who presented the biggest problems to them and to explain why the students presented problems. In responding to these questions, teachers mentioned themselves as part of the problem in only 4 of 74 cases. The other 70 were seen as problems of limited student ability, poor student attitude, or a home life that did not support the school. Most of these cases were described as if they were permanent, unchangeable situations.

Similar results were found in a study by Quirk (1967). Without informing the teachers, who were actually the subjects in his experiment, Quirk arranged for some to think they had succeeded (that their students had learned) and for others to think they had failed (that their students had not learned). He then asked the teachers to assess their performance. He found a strong tendency for teachers who had experienced success to take credit for it by attributing it to their own presentation. In contrast, teachers who had been led to experience failure usually blamed it on the students or on factors other than their own teaching presentation.

Such rationalizing is not particularly malicious and not confined to teachers. We all want to see ourselves as likable, competent, and successful, and we all tend to repress or explain away the things that do not fit this self-image. Such defensiveness is not necessary in teachers who adopt positive, but appropriate, expectations for their students. Because the expectations are appropriate, the teacher does not need to feel guilty or dissatisfied if slower students do not do as well as better students. Success is defined as progress in terms of the students' capabilities. Since the expectations are also positive, they remind the teacher continually to think in terms of forward progress and to analyze problems and question his or her teaching approach when progress is not evident. This helps the teacher to stay on top of the situation and to adapt quickly to changes as they appear. The teacher will recognize and exploit breakthroughs as they occur and will respond to failure with a search for another way to do the job rather than for an excuse or explanation.

Even though appropriately positive attitudes and expectations are not automatically or totally effective by themselves, they are necessary and important teacher qualities. Teachers will not always succeed with them, but they will not get very far at all without them. Attitudes and expectations usually cannot be observed directly, of course, but teacher behavior can be observed and measured. Observation instruments for recording teacher behavior related to the basic teaching attitudes and expectations discussed are presented in the appendix for this chapter. By measuring such behavior in other teachers and by becoming conscious of it in your own teaching, you can learn to detect and eliminate the undesirable self-fulfilling prophecy effects that result when inappropriate attitudes and expectations are present.

## SUMMARY

In this chapter, we have shown how teachers' attitudes and expectations about different students can lead them to treat students differently, so that teachers' attitudes and expectations sometimes become self-fulfilling. A particular danger is that low expectations combined with an attitude of futility will be communicated to certain students, leading to erosion of their confidence and motivation for school learning. This will confirm or deepen the students' sense of hopelessness and cause them to fail even where they could have succeeded under different circumstances.

Expectations tend to be self-sustaining. They affect both perception, by causing teachers to be alert for what they expect and to be less likely to notice what they do not expect, and interpretation, by causing teachers to interpret (and perhaps distort) what they see so that it is consistent with their expectations. In this way, some expectations can persist even though they do not fit the facts (as seen by a more neutral observer).

Sometimes low expectations or defeatist attitudes exist because the teacher has given up on certain students and accepts failure in teaching rather than trying to do anything further with them. In these instances, inappropriate attitudes and expectations help the teacher to take his or her mind off the problem or to explain it away. Such an attitude or expectation explains ("Johnny's limited intelligence, poor attitude, and cumulative failure in school have left him unable to handle eighth-grade work; he belongs in a special education class") and, therefore, seems to justify the teacher's failure with this student. The attitude psychologically frees the teacher from continuing to worry about the student's progress and from seeking new and more successful ways to teach the student.

Once a teacher and student become locked into such a circle of futility, they tend to stay there. The teacher's behavior causes the student to fall even more behind than he or she might have otherwise, and this failure in turn deepens and reinforces the teacher's already low expectations.

Teachers can avoid such problems by adopting appropriate general expectations about teaching and by learning to recognize their specific attitudes and expectations about individual students and to monitor their treatment of individual students. In particular, it is essential that teachers remember that their primary responsibility is to teach, to help all students reach their potential as learners. It is natural that teachers form differential attitudes and expectations about different students, because each student is an individual. To the extent that these are accurate and appropriate, they are helpful for planning ways to meet each student's needs. However, they must constantly be monitored and evaluated, to insure that they change appropriately in response to changes in the student. When teachers fail to monitor and evaluate their attitudes, expectations, and behavior toward students, they can easily get caught in the vicious circle of failure and futility described above.

By keeping a general focus on instruction as their main task, and by training themselves to observe students systematically with an eye toward their present progress and needs, teachers can maintain a generally appropriate orientation to the classroom. They can reinforce this by learning to recognize and evaluate the attitudes and expectations that they form spontaneously in daily interactions with students. This will enable them to correct inaccuracies and to use accurate information in planning individualized treatment.

Remember, teaching attitudes and expectancies can be your allies and tools if properly maintained and used. However, if unquestioningly accepted and allowed to solidify, they can become defense mechanisms that lead you to ignore or explain away problems rather than solve them. Therefore, learn to control your attitudes and expectations—don't let them control you!

### SUGGESTED ACTIVITIES AND QUESTIONS

1. Which students in your preservice teacher education courses (or teachers at your school) are the brightest? What behavioral evidence and information have you used to form your opinions? How accurate do you think your estimates are?

2. When teachers form their expectations about how students will perform in their classes, do you think that teachers tend to underestimate or overestimate the following types of learners: loud, aggressive males; quiet, passive males; loud, aggressive females; quiet, passive females; students who are neat and who follow directions carefully; students with speech impediments; and students

who complain that schoolwork is dull and uninteresting? Why do you feel that teachers would tend to overestimate or underestimate the ability of these student types?

3. Analyze your own attitudes about classroom learning. As a student, did you see learning assignments as typically enjoyable? If you did, why was learning fun for you? Was it because you did well or because learning per se was fun or exciting? When learning was not fun, was it due to particular teachers or subjects?

4. What can you do as a teacher to make learning more enjoyable for your students?

5. Write an original example of a self-fulfilling prophecy. Illustrate an example that happened to you, a relative, or a classmate. Be sure that you include each of these three steps: an original expectation, behaviors that consistently communicate this expectation, and evidence that the original expectation has been confirmed.

6. Select scales that are designed to measure teacher expectations and use them to rate real teachers or videotaped teaching situations.

7. Role-play (you be the teacher and let classmates play pupils at a specific grade level) the beginnings and endings of lessons. Try to communicate appropriate expectations.

8. Read one or two of the case studies in Appendix A (p. 399) and list all instances when teachers communicate positive or negative expectations. Compare your lists with those made by others.

9. How can a teacher's overemphasis on praise and right answers interfere with student learning?

10. Should teachers hold expectations for student performance?

11. Why do the authors stress that expectations should be appropriate rather than necessarily positive, and that they must be followed up with appropriate behavior?

12. How do teachers form their expectations about students?

13. Explain in your own words why expectations, once formed, tend to be self-perpetuating.

14. Discuss ways in which inappropriate teacher expectations may lead to inappropriate teacher behavior.

15. In particular, how might a teacher's use of homework and seatwork assignments communicate undesirable expectations to students?

## APPENDIX

Observation forms for measuring teacher behavior related to the basic teacher attitudes and expectations discussed in the chapter are presented in this appendix. Each form has a numbered title, a definition of the classroom situations in which it should be used, and a description of its purpose. Although all the forms share these common properties, they differ from one another in several ways. Some are confined to strictly behavioral categories and require simple counting of observed events, while others require the coder to make inferences or judgments and score the teacher on more global rating scales. Also, some call for only a single coding for a single event, while others involve coding several items of information about series of events that occur in sequences.

Skilled coders can use many of the observation forms during a single observation, so long as they do not require themselves to code two things at the same time. At the beginning, however, it is best to start with one or two forms while you acquire basic observation and coding skills.

The observation forms define the applicable classroom situation and then list several alternative ways that the teacher could respond in the situation. The different teacher behaviors listed are most often mutually exclusive, but sometimes more than one could occur in a given situation. To use the observation forms correctly, you must be able to: (1) recognize when relevant situations are occurring that call for use of the form, (2) accurately observe the teacher's handling of the situation, and (3) accurately record this information on the form. If the teacher shows more than one codable behavior in the situation, simply number consecutively the different behaviors that the teacher shows. This will preserve not only the information about which different techniques were used but also the sequence in which they were used.

### Using Coding Sheets

An example of how the coding sheet would be used and how the information recorded on it can be recovered later is presented on p. 106. This example shows the coding sheet for teacher's behavior when introducing lessons or activities or making assignments (Form 4.1). This form is used to measure the teacher's motivation attempt (if any), as opposed to his or her specificity or completeness in presenting the assignment (the latter is covered on a different form). Form 4.1 is used whenever the teacher introduces a lesson or activity or makes an assignment to the class or to a group within the class.

On this form, the observer would note carefully what attempt the teacher made to build up interest or *motivate* the students to look forward to or to work carefully on the lesson or assignment; this information is numbered by categories and those numbers are used to record the behavior in the coding columns.

In the example, the coding sheet shows that three such instances were observed by the coder (the coding sheet has room for 50 instances). Note that the first code the coder has entered is a 4. This indicates that the teacher began a lesson or gave an assignment with no attempt at all to motivate or build up interest. Some directions may have been given to get the group started, but no attempt was made to build up to the activity—"Yesterday we finished page 53. Open your books to page 54. Mark, begin reading with the first paragraph." The teacher also did not promise rewards or threaten punishment for good or bad performance in the activity.

The teacher's behavior the second time he or she introduced a lesson or activity is coded in the next row. Here the coder has entered both a 1 and a 3. This indicates that the teacher began with a gushy buildup, but later also mentioned the information or skills that would be learned in the activity.

The third row also shows a 1 followed by a 3, indicating again that the teacher introduced a lesson or activity with an excessive buildup, followed by mention of the information or skills to be learned.

Although not enough instances are recorded to make interpretations with great confidence, a pattern is noticeable in the three instances coded. The teacher appears to be basically positive in his or her presentation of lessons and activities. No negative motivation attempts (apology, threat of test, or punishment) appear. However, in attempting to provide positive motivation, the teacher may be overdoing it, in that the observer coded two instances of overdramatic buildup.

If this did indeed develop as the teacher's stable pattern, some guidelines for additional questions and observations would emerge. What would be the effects of this overdramatizing on the class? Would it tend to amuse them or cause them to lose respect for the teacher? Would it train them to begin to complain or suspect unenjoyable activities if the teacher failed to give the coming activity a big buildup? If there were evidence that the teacher's overacting was having these kinds of effects on the class, he or she might be advised to try to tone down the motivation attempts. If there appeared to be no adverse effects on the class, it might be advisable for the teacher to continue the present style of motivating the class and instead work on changing problem behaviors that appear to have negative consequences.

The observation forms in this appendix, as well as all of the forms following subsequent chapters, will be partially filled in, to show how they look after being used in the classroom. However, we will no longer add our interpretations of the data shown on these sample coding sheets. Studying the partially filled in coding sheets will help you quickly grasp what is involved in using each observation form. In addition, it will provide a basis for practicing interpretation of coded data. If possible, arrange to compare your interpretations of these data with the interpretations of a friend or colleague. Discuss any disagreements in detail, to discover the reasons for them and to determine what additional information (if any) would be needed in order to resolve the matter with confidence. Your instructor or in-service leader can help you to resolve coding difficulties.

The observation forms are divided up so that each measures just one or only a small number of related teacher behaviors. Thus, each form is a self-contained observation instrument that can be used independently of the others. Once you have acquired some skill as a coder, however, you will want to observe several aspects of teacher behavior, using several different forms. To do this, you may find it convenient to combine several forms onto a single coding sheet. There are many ways to do this, and personal preferences and convenience are the primary criteria for deciding whether or not a given method is desirable. To show how this can be done, we have provided a sample coding sheet in Figure 4.1 that combines Forms 4.1, 4.2, 4.3, 4.4.

The four forms were compressed onto a single coding sheet by using only key terms rather than the full behavior category descriptions that appear on the originals. Use and purpose descriptions are omitted entirely, since it is assumed that the coder is already familiar with the four original forms. The result is a sheet with spaces to code up to 50 instances of each of the four teacher behaviors. A coder would use this sheet until all 50 spaces were used for one of the four behaviors; then he or she would switch to a new sheet.

Figure 4.1 shows only one of many ways that these four forms could have been combined onto a single coding sheet. For your own coding, feel free to create coding sheets that meet your preferences and needs. There is no single right coding sheet; the one that you like and that does the job is the one you should use.

Generally, all the information you need to code is on the sheet. For example, in Figure 4.1, column one, you can see that most of the ways a teacher can motivate students when introducing a lesson have been summarized into nine categories, and if the teacher's behavior cannot be described in one of these nine categories, use the tenth category. Occasionally, users will have to supply some information of their own. Notice scales representing Forms 4.3 and 4.4 (individual praise and individual criticism) in Figure 4.1. When individual students must be identified, as in these examples, users will have to supply their own identification codes. In the first in-

**FIGURE 4.1.** Sample Coding Sheet Combining Four Observation Forms

| MOTIVATION ATTEMPT, INTRODUCING ACTIVITIES | EVALUATIONS AFTER ACTIVITIES | INDIVIDUAL PRAISE | INDIVIDUAL CRITICISM |
|---|---|---|---|
| 1. Gushy build-up | 1. Praises specific progress | 1. Perseverance, effort | 1. Poor persistence, effort |
| 2. Enjoyment | 2. Criticizes specifically | 2. Progress | 2. Poor progress |
| 3. New information, skills | 3. Praises general progress | 3. Success | 3. Failure |
| 4. No motivation attempt | 4. Criticizes general performance | 4. Good thinking | 4. Faulty thinking, guessing |
| 5. Apologizes | 5. Ambiguous praise | 5. Imagination, originality | 5. Triteness |
| 6. Promises reward | 6. Ambiguous criticism | 6. Neatness, care | 6. Sloppiness, carelessness |
| 7. Warns of test | 7. Praises good behavior | 7. Obedience, attention | 7. Breaks rules, inattentive |
| 8. Threatens to punish | 8. Criticizes misbehavior | 8. Prosocial behavior | 8. Antisocial behavior |
| 9. Gives as punishment | 9. No group evaluation | 9. Other (specify) | 9. Other (specify) |
| 10. Other (specify) | 10. Other (specify) | | |

| CODES | | CODES | | STUDENT NUMBERS AND CODES | | STUDENT NUMBERS AND CODES | |
|---|---|---|---|---|---|---|---|
| _4_ 1. | __ 26. | _5_ 1. | __ 26. | _14_ 1. 3 | __ 26. | _16_ 1. 3 | __ 26. |
| _4,3_ 2. | __ 27. | _5_ 2. | __ 27. | _23_ 2. 3,4 | __ 27. | _21_ 2. 3 | __ 27. |
| _4,3_ 3. | __ 28. | _6_ 3. | __ 28. | _6_ 3. 3 | __ 28. | _5_ 3. 3,4 | __ 28. |
| __ 4. | __ 29. | _5_ 4. | __ 29. | _18_ 4. 3 | __ 29. | _12_ 4. 3 | __ 29. |
| __ 5. | __ 30. | _9_ 5. | __ 30. | __ 5. | __ 30. | __ 5. | __ 30. |
| __ 6. | __ 31. | _5_ 6. | __ 31. | __ 6. | __ 31. | __ 6. | __ 31. |
| __ 7. | __ 32. | _3_ 7. | __ 32. | __ 7. | __ 32. | __ 7. | __ 32. |
| __ 8. | __ 33. | _5_ 8. | __ 33. | __ 8. | __ 33. | __ 8. | __ 33. |
| __ 9. | __ 34. | _9_ 9. | __ 34. | __ 9. | __ 34. | __ 9. | __ 34. |
| __ 10. | __ 35. | __ 10. | __ 35. | __ 10. | __ 35. | __ 10. | __ 35. |
| __ 11. | __ 36. | __ 11. | __ 36. | __ 11. | __ 36. | __ 11. | __ 36. |
| __ 12. | __ 37. | __ 12. | __ 37. | __ 12. | __ 37. | __ 12. | __ 37. |
| __ 13. | __ 38. | __ 13. | __ 38. | __ 13. | __ 38. | __ 13. | __ 38. |
| __ 14. | __ 39. | __ 14. | __ 39. | __ 14. | __ 39. | __ 14. | __ 39. |
| __ 15. | __ 40. | __ 15. | __ 40. | __ 15. | __ 40. | __ 15. | __ 40. |
| __ 16. | __ 41. | __ 16. | __ 41. | __ 16. | __ 41. | __ 16. | __ 41. |
| __ 17. | __ 42. | __ 17. | __ 42. | __ 17. | __ 42. | __ 17. | __ 42. |
| __ 18. | __ 43. | __ 18. | __ 43. | __ 18. | __ 43. | __ 18. | __ 43. |
| __ 19. | __ 44. | __ 19. | __ 44. | __ 19. | __ 44. | __ 19. | __ 44. |
| __ 20. | __ 45. | __ 20. | __ 45. | __ 20. | __ 45. | __ 20. | __ 45. |
| __ 21. | __ 46. | __ 21. | __ 46. | __ 21. | __ 46. | __ 21. | __ 46. |
| __ 22. | __ 47. | __ 22. | __ 47. | __ 22. | __ 47. | __ 22. | __ 47. |
| __ 23. | __ 48. | __ 23. | __ 48. | __ 23. | __ 48. | __ 23. | __ 48. |
| __ 24. | __ 49. | __ 24. | __ 49. | __ 24. | __ 49. | __ 24. | __ 49. |
| __ 25. | __ 50. | __ 25. | __ 50. | __ 25. | __ 50. | __ 25. | __ 50. |

stance, under *individual praise*, we see that student 14 received teacher praise for successful accomplishment (category 3).

Thus, depending on their coding goals, users will have to supply appropriate code numbers. For example, if a coder is interested in how teachers praise male and female students, respectively, then he or she need only use a 1 when girls are praised and a 2 when boys are praised. Obviously, in Figure 4.1 the coder is coding the entire class, because, in the second instance of a teacher praising an individual student, the student's number is 23. If you are interested in coding the behavior of an entire class, simply assign each student a unique number and use this number whenever interactions involving that student are coded.

### Predictions, Expectations, and Untested Assumptions

The following list of predictions and interpretations illustrate decisions that teachers have made about students. In each case observed, the interpretation was simply assumed to be true—it was not tested out or verified. Even if verified, however, such interpretations should not be verbalized to the students, because of the undesirable incidental learning that may result. Read the list to help establish what is meant by an *untested assumption* about a student. As you observe additional examples in classrooms, add them to the list for future reference. The key is that the teacher behaves as if the assumption is true, without first testing it out.

1. The student is not ready for a particular book or problem.
2. The student can't be trusted or believed and, unless proven innocent, is guilty.
3. The student can't be allowed to use special equipment because it will only be broken.
4. The student must be isolated from others because he or she has no self-control.
5. The student will cheat unless you take precautions to prevent it.
6. The student can't talk quietly and, therefore, should not be allowed to talk at all.
7. The student won't like (or understand) the activity coming up next.
8. The student obviously knows the answer because he or she is smart (or obedient, or has a hand up).
9. The student will need help in finding the page (or other things the student can easily do him or herself).

10. The student will cause trouble unless seated next to the teacher.
11. The student will need a "crutch" to be able to do this exercise and, therefore, should be given one.
12. The student is daydreaming, not thinking about schoolwork.
13. If Johnny or Sally Bright doesn't know the answer, no one will.
14. The student will fail next week's test.
15. It's Friday afternoon, so the class will be rowdy.
16. The student just doesn't care about schoolwork.
17. All you can do for this student is see that he or she gets lots of sunlight, water, and air.

**FORM 4.1.** Introducing Lessons, Activities, and Assignments

*USE: When the teacher is introducing new activities or making assignments*
*PURPOSE: To see whether or not the teacher pictures school work as worthwhile or enjoyable*
*Observe teacher behavior when introducing activities and making assignments. For each codable instance observed, record the numbers (consecutively) of each category applicable to the teacher's behavior.*

BEHAVIOR CATEGORIES

1. Gushes, gives overdramatic build-up
2. Predicts that group will enjoy the activity
3. Mentions information or skills the group will learn
4. Makes no attempt to motivate; starts right into activity
5. Apologizes or expresses sympathy to group ("Sorry, but you have to . . .")
6. Bribes, promises external reward for good attention or work
7. Warns group, or reminds them, about test to be given later
8. Threatens punishment for poor attention or work
9. Presents the activity itself as a penalty or punishment
10. Other (specify)

NOTES:

CODES

| | |
|---|---|
| 1. _4_ | 26. ___ |
| 2. _1,3_ | 27. ___ |
| 3. _1,3_ | 28. ___ |
| 4. ___ | 29. ___ |
| 5. ___ | 30. ___ |
| 6. ___ | 31. ___ |
| 7. ___ | 32. ___ |
| 8. ___ | 33. ___ |
| 9. ___ | 34. ___ |
| 10. ___ | 35. ___ |
| 11. ___ | 36. ___ |
| 12. ___ | 37. ___ |
| 13. ___ | 38. ___ |
| 14. ___ | 39. ___ |
| 15. ___ | 40. ___ |
| 16. ___ | 41. ___ |
| 17. ___ | 42. ___ |
| 18. ___ | 43. ___ |
| 19. ___ | 44. ___ |
| 20. ___ | 45. ___ |
| 21. ___ | 46. ___ |
| 22. ___ | 47. ___ |
| 23. ___ | 48. ___ |
| 24. ___ | 49. ___ |
| 25. ___ | 50. ___ |

**FORM 4.2.** Evaluations After Lessons and Activities

*USE: When teacher ends a lesson or group activity*
*PURPOSE: To see whether the teacher stresses learning or compliance in*
*making evaluations*
*When the teacher ends a lesson or group activity, code any summary*
*evaluations he or she makes about the group's performance during the activity.*

BEHAVIOR CATEGORIES

1. Praises progress in specific terms; labels knowledge or skills learned
2. Criticizes performance or indicates weaknesses in specific terms
3. Praises generally good performance, for doing well or knowing answers
4. Criticizes generally poor performance (doesn't detail the specifics)
5. Ambiguous general praise ("You were very good today.")
6. Ambiguous general criticism ("You weren't very good today.")
7. Praises good attention or good behavior
8. Criticizes poor attention or misbehavior
9. No general evaluations of performance were made
10. Other (specify)

NOTES:

Teacher uses stock phrase (" You were really good today; I'm very pleased ").

#13 cut off by bell; might have praised him otherwise.

CODES

| | | | |
|---|---|---|---|
| 1. | 5 | 26. | |
| 2. | 5 | 27. | |
| 3. | 6 | 28. | |
| 4. | 5 | 29. | |
| 5. | 9 | 30. | |
| 6. | 5 | 31. | |
| 7. | 3 | 32. | |
| 8. | 5 | 33. | |
| 9. | 9 | 34. | |
| 10. | 5 | 35. | |
| 11. | 5 | 36. | |
| 12. | 5 | 37. | |
| 13. | | 38. | |
| 14. | | 39. | |
| 15. | | 40. | |
| 16. | | 41. | |
| 17. | | 42. | |
| 18. | | 43. | |
| 19. | | 44. | |
| 20. | | 45. | |
| 21. | | 46. | |
| 22. | | 47. | |
| 23. | | 48. | |
| 24. | | 49. | |
| 25. | | 50. | |

110

**FORM 4.3.** Individual Praise

*USE*: *Whenever the teacher praises an individual student*
*PURPOSE*: *To see what behaviors the teacher reinforces through praise, and*
*to see how the teacher's praise is distributed among the students*
*Whenever the teacher praises an individual student, code the student's*
*number and each category of teacher behavior that applies*
*(consecutively).*

| BEHAVIOR CATEGORIES | STUDENT NUMBER | CODES |
|---|---|---|
| 1. Perseverance or effort, worked long or hard | _14_ | 1. _3_ |
| | _23_ | 2. _3,4_ |
| 2. Progress (relative to the past) toward achievement | _6_ | 3. _3_ |
| | _18_ | 4. _3_ |
| 3. Success (right answer, high score), achievement | _8_ | 5. _1_ |
| 4. Good thinking, good suggestion, good guess or nice try | _8_ | 6. _1_ |
| | _8_ | 7. _1_ |
| 5. Imagination, creativity, originality | | 8. __ |
| 6. Neatness, careful work | | 9. __ |
| 7. Good or compliant behavior, follows rules, pays attention | | 10. __ |
| | | 11. __ |
| 8. Thoughtfulness, courtesy, offering to share; prosocial behavior | | 12. __ |
| | | 13. __ |
| 9. Other (specify) | | 14. __ |
| | | 15. __ |

NOTES:

*All answers occurred during social studies discussion.*

*Was particularly concerned about #8, a low-achieving male.*

| | |
|---|---|
| | 16. __ |
| | 17. __ |
| | 18. __ |
| | 19. __ |
| | 20. __ |
| | 21. __ |
| | 22. __ |
| | 23. __ |
| | 24. __ |
| | 25. __ |

**FORM 4.4.** Individual Criticism

*USE: Whenever the teacher criticizes an individual student*
*PURPOSE: To see what behaviors the teacher singles out for criticism, and to*
*see how the teacher's criticism is distributed among the students*
*Whenever the teacher criticizes an individual student, note the student's*
*name or number and code the behavior that is criticized.*

| BEHAVIOR CATEGORIES | STUDENT NUMBER | CODES |
|---|---|---|
| 1. Lack of effort or persistence, doesn't try, gives up easily | 16 | 1. 3 |
| | 21 | 2. 3 |
| 2. Poor progress (relative to expectations), could do better, falling behind | 5 | 3. 3,4 |
| | 12 | 4. 3 |
| 3. Failure (can't answer, low score), lack of achievement | 5 | 5. 1 |
| 4. Faulty thinking, wild guess, failure to think before responding | | 6. __ |
| | | 7. __ |
| 5. Trite, stereotyped responses, lack of originality or imagination | | 8. __ |
| | | 9. __ |
| 6. Sloppiness or carelessness | | 10. __ |
| 7. Misbehaves, breaks rules, inattentive | | 11. __ |
| 8. Selfish, discourteous, won't share; antisocial behavior | | 12. __ |
| | | 13. __ |
| 9. Other (specify) | | 14. __ |
| | | 15. __ |

NOTES:

*All answers during social studies discussion.*

*Teacher sharply critical of student #5; seems irritated with her generally.*

16. __
17. __
18. __
19. __
20. __
21. __
22. __
23. __
24. __
25. __

112

**FORM 4.5.** Teacher's Use of Tests

*USE: When the teacher gives a quiz or test*
*PURPOSE: To see if the teacher uses tests appropriately as diagnostic tools*
*and teaching aids, rather than merely as evaluation devices*
*Code items A, B, and C when the teacher gives the test. If possible,*
*code items D, E, and F after observing how test results are used.*

## BEHAVIOR CATEGORIES
A. Test content
1. Test mostly requires integration or application of knowledge or skills
2. Test is balanced between memory and integration or application
3. Test is mostly rote or factual memory; no thinking or application involved
B. How is test presented to students?
1. Test presented as a diagnostic aid to the teacher—assesses strengths and weaknesses
2. Test presented without explanation, rationale, or discussion of follow-up
3. Test presented as a threat or hurdle to the class—to find out who knows the answers and who doesn't
C. What expectations are communicated in the teacher's directions to students?
1. Teacher gives positive directions (eyes on your paper, guess if you're not sure)
2. Teacher gives negative directions (no cheating or else, no guesswork)
D. Is the test reviewed with the class?
1. Test is reviewed and discussed with class
2. Test scored by teacher, not reviewed with class
E. How does the teacher follow up with students who scored poorly?
1. Teacher arranges for remediation with those who do not meet minimal standards and retests to see that they reach those standards
2. Some remediation attempted, but teacher doesn't retest to ensure mastery
3. No evidence of remedial efforts with those who perform poorly
F. How does the teacher follow up if the whole class scores poorly? (code NA if Not Applicable)
1. Teacher reviews or reteaches material that was not mastered and retests to ensure mastery
2. Some remediation attempted, but teacher doesn't retest to ensure mastery
3. No evidence of remedial efforts when material was not mastered

## CODES

| TEST | | A | B | C | D | E | F |
|---|---|---|---|---|---|---|---|
| *Spelling* | 1. | 3 | 2 | 1 | 2 | 3 | NA |
| *History* | 2. | 2 | 3 | 1 | 1 | 2 | NA |
| | 3. | | | | | | |
| | 4. | | | | | | |
| | 5. | | | | | | |
| | 6. | | | | | | |
| | 7. | | | | | | |
| | 8. | | | | | | |
| | 9. | | | | | | |
| | 10. | | | | | | |

**FORM 4.6.** Teacher's Use of Ability Grouping

*USE: In classrooms in which the teacher has grouped the students for small-group instruction*
*PURPOSE: To see if the teacher is using grouping appropriately as a means of individualizing instruction*

GROUP COMPOSITION AND INSTRUCTION TIME

| GROUP NAME | NUMBER OF BOYS | NUMBER OF GIRLS | START OF LESSON (TIME) | END OF LESSON (TIME) | LENGTH OF LESSON |
|---|---|---|---|---|---|
| *Astronauts* | 3 | 5 | 8:31 | 9:00 | 29 |
| *Magicians* | 4 | 5 | 9:08 | 9:35 | 27 |
| *Champions* | 4 | 3 | 9:45 | 10:00 | 15 |
| | | | : | : | |

*Note any information relevant to the following questions:*
1. Is the class arranged so that each group is seated together as a group? *No*
2. How long have these particular groups been operating? *Since October 15*
3. Does the teacher plan to regroup? When? *Beginning of second semester*
4. Does the teacher teach the groups in the same order each day? *Yes*
5. If time for a group lesson runs short, does the teacher make it up later? *Usually not*
6. Do the groups have differential privileges regarding what they are allowed to do without special permission? *Astronauts have access to supplementary readers (considered too difficult for other two groups).*
7. If the teacher groups for more than one subject, are the groups the same or are they different? *Groups only for Reading*
8. Does the teacher show differential enthusiasm or emotion when working with the different groups? *Seemed more subdued, less involved when working with the Magicians.*

*Record any descriptive or evaluative statements the teacher makes about a group.*

| GROUP | TEACHER'S COMMENT |
|---|---|
| *Astronauts* | *I'm proud of your progress – Keep up the good work* |
| *Champions* | *We're almost to the end of the reader; keep up the good work and we'll finish it by Friday.* |
| *Champions* | *Let's stop reading and get ready for recess. It's time to have fun and relax.* |
| | |
| | |
| | |
| *Astronauts* | *This is the best reading group.* |
| *Magicians* | *This the middle-achievement group in reading.* |
| *Champions* | *This is the lowest reading group.* |

114

**FORM 4.7.** Teacher's Use of Time

*USE*: *Whenever activities are introduced or changed*
*PURPOSE*: *To see if the teacher spends time primarily on activities related to teaching and learning*
*Record starting time and elapsed time for the following teacher activities (when more than one activity is going on, record the one in which the teacher is involved). Totals for the day are entered in the blanks in the lower left corner of the page.*

BEHAVIOR CATEGORIES
1. Daily rituals (pledge, prayer, song, collection, roll, washroom, etc.)
2. Transitions between activities
3. Whole-class lessons or tests (academic curriculum)
4. Small-group lessons or tests (academic curriculum)
5. Going around the room checking seatwork or small-group assignments
6. Doing preparation or paperwork while class does something else
7. Arts and crafts, music
8. Exercises, physical and social games (nonacademic)
9. Intellectual games and contests
10. Nonacademic pastimes (reading to class, show-and-tell, puzzles and toys)
11. Unfocused small talk
12. Other (specify)

NOTES:

# 3, 5, 7 = *Reading Groups*

# 11, 13 = *Math lesson & seatwork*

# 9 = *outside recess ( free play )*

TOTAL TIME PER CATEGORY

| BEHAVIOR CODE | TOTAL MINUTES |
|---|---|
| 1. | 20 |
| 2. | 24 |
| 3. | 38 |
| 4. | 88 |
| 5. | 30 |
| 6. | |
| 7. | |
| 8. | 15 |
| 9. | |
| 10. | |
| 11. | |
| 12. | |

CODES FOR EACH NEW ACTIVITY

| | STARTING TIME | BEHAVIOR CODE | ELAPSED TIME |
|---|---|---|---|
| 1. | 8 : 15 | 1 | 15 |
| 2. | 8 : 30 | 2 | 3 |
| 3. | 8 : 33 | 4 | 27 |
| 4. | 9 : 00 | 2 | 5 |
| 5. | 9 : 05 | 4 | 25 |
| 6. | 9 : 30 | 2 | 4 |
| 7. | 9 : 34 | 4 | 36 |
| 8. | 10 : 10 | 2 | 5 |
| 9. | 10 : 15 | 8 | 15 |
| 10. | 10 : 30 | 2 | 2 |
| 11. | 10 : 32 | 3 | 38 |
| 12. | 11 : 10 | 2 | 5 |
| 13. | 11 : 15 | 5 | 30 |
| 14. | 11 : 45 | 1 | 5 |
| 15. | 11 : 50 | Lunch | |
| 16. | : | | |
| 17. | : | | |
| 18. | : | | |
| 19. | : | | |
| 20. | : | | |
| 21. | : | | |
| 22. | : | | |
| 23. | : | | |
| 24. | : | | |
| 25. | : | | |
| 26. | : | | |
| 27. | : | | |
| 28. | : | | |
| 29. | : | | |
| 30. | : | | |
| 31. | : | | |
| 32. | : | | |
| 33. | : | | |
| 34. | : | | |
| 35. | : | | |
| 36. | : | | |
| 37. | : | | |
| 38. | : | | |
| 39. | : | | |
| 40. | : | | |
| 41. | : | | |
| 42. | : | | |
| 43. | : | | |
| 44. | : | | |
| 45. | : | | |
| 36. | : | | |
| 47. | : | | |
| 48. | : | | |
| 49. | : | | |
| 50. | : | | |

**FORM 4.8.** Teacher's Predictions and Untested Assumptions about Students

*USE: Whenever the teacher makes a prediction about an individual or group*
*PURPOSE: To see what kinds of expectations the teacher communicates*
*directly*
*Record what the teacher says when making a prediction or directly*
*communicating an expectation about an individual or group, or when acting*
*upon an untested assumption. What does he or she predict (about whether*
*they can or cannot succeed, for example)? What untested assumption does*
*he or she act upon?*

GROUP OR        PREDICTION, EXPECTATION, OR UNTESTED
INDIVIDUAL      ASSUMPTION

_# 5_           Can't read astronaut's supplementary
                reader.

_# 14_          " Won't know this one " on Friday's test

# 5/ MODELING

Janice Taylor is an ambitious senior majoring in social studies at Compton College. She plans to teach after graduating and eventually to combine that career with marriage and a family. Presently, she is doing her student teaching at Oak Junior High School. The students at Oak come from middle-class homes, and this pleases Janice because as a student she attended a similar school and came from a middle-class home. At times, however, she feels quite apprehensive. She has not been in a junior high school for several years, and although she gained some useful information in her college classes, she has not taught. Will students obey her? Can she make them enjoy schoolwork? Doubts about her ability as a teacher become more prevalent as the time for her to assume teaching responsibility nears. She has been observing Mrs. Woodward's class for two weeks. One more week to observe, and then Janice is to become the teacher for the second-period (a slow class) and sixth-period (an average class) civics classes.

Janice watches Mrs. Woodward intensively because this is the first opportunity she has had to observe a junior high school teacher, and she wants to learn how to get the children to respond and to obey. Janice likes Mrs. Woodward and feels that she is a good teacher who treats the students fairly and is respected by them. However, Janice is basically a shy and soft-spoken person, and frequently becomes nervous when she is around loud, aggressive people. Conse-

118 LOOKING IN CLASSROOMS

quently, she is often upset by the forceful way in which Mrs. Woodward runs the class. She speaks in a loud, booming voice, and if students are misbehaving, she does not hesitate to give them a "tongue lashing" or to send them out of the room. Mrs. Woodward's favorite tactic when students are disruptive is to boom out, "I'm telling you once and for the last time (Alice and Ted, or whomever), listen to your classmates when they talk." Students typically stop after Mrs. Woodward pinpoints their misbehavior.

One week later, when Janice is teaching the class, she loudly addresses some misbehaving students in the same way, "I'm telling you once and for the last time, listen to your classmates. . . ." Think about these two questions:

1. Why did Janice imitate Mrs. Woodward's teaching style?
2. How might Janice have taught if she had taught with a different cooperating teacher?

In the previous example, the student teacher learned many things from observing a supervising teacher. (Indeed, this example is a rather common one. Several research studies have shown that the cooperating teacher greatly influences the teaching style of the student teacher.) Not all of the things Janice learned were directly connected with teaching, and relatively few of them were deliberately taught by Mrs. Woodward. Janice "picked up" beliefs, attitudes, and habits simply by observing them.

How does this happen? Research has shown that many things are learned without deliberate instruction by the teacher or deliberate practice by the learner. The learner only needs to see the behavior demonstrated by someone else to be able to imitate it for him or herself. A person who demonstrates the behavior is called the *model*, and this form of learning is often called *modeling* (Bandura, 1969).

When used purposefully, modeling can be a powerful teaching tool. Many things can be learned much more easily through observation and imitation than by trying to understand and respond to verbal explanations and instructions. This is especially true for younger students, whose abilities to follow complex verbal instructions are limited.

## AWARENESS OF MODELING

Most teachers recognize the power of prepared demonstrations as teaching tools. However, they are usually less aware of the more general modeling effects that occur in the classroom and less likely to take advantage of them through deliberate, planned modeling behavior. We all know how bad examples can lead to misbehavior, but we are less aware of the power of a good model's example to influence positive behavior. Children learn many things by imitating models rather than by being instructed in a systematic fashion. They learn to speak their native tongue this way, as well as most of their attitudes, values, problem-solving strategies, and social behavior; in fact, behavioral example is usually a more powerful influence than verbal instruction.

If there is discrepancy between our preaching and our practice, students will tend to do what we do, not what we say. This was shown in a recent experiment with childrens' altruism (Bryan and Walbek, 1970). Each child in the study played a game with an adult model. The game was designed so that each model and child could win money by succeeding at it. Unknown to the children, the experimenter controlled these winnings so that each model and each child won a specific amount. As part of the experiment, a box requesting donations for poor children was placed in the room where the game was conducted. Each adult model made mention of this donation box. Some of the adult models spoke in favor of donating, saying that it was a good thing to help the poor and that people should donate. With other children, the adult models complained about the donation box. They stated their winnings should be their own, and that nobody should ask them to donate part of their winnings to someone else. Half the time when the models preached in favor of donating, they followed up by donating part of their winnings. The other half of the time they did not donate, despite their words. Similarly, half the time the adult models who spoke against donating did not donate; the other half of the time, however, the adult models went ahead and donated some of their winnings even after speaking against it resentfully.

The results of the experiment showed clearly that the children's donating behavior was affected much more by what the adults *did* than by what they *said*. Children who observed the model donate part of his or her winnings tended to do the same themselves, regardless of whether the model spoke for or against donating. Similarly, children who saw that the adult did not donate tended not to donate themselves, even if the model had spoken in favor of donation. The children clearly took their cue from what they saw the models do, not from what they heard the models say.

The same thing happens in the classroom. If students perceive discrepancies between what the teacher says and what he or she practices, they will ignore what is said. Also, if they see discrepancies between what is demanded and what is actually allowed, they will guide their behavior according to what is allowed. For example, students will obey the teacher for the first few days if they are told to do their seatwork quietly and on their own. However, if it gradually becomes clear that the teacher does not intervene in any way when students do not work quietly or when they copy from one another, they will come to see that the teacher does not mean what he or she says.

This points up the need for teachers to be aware of their behavior in the classroom. Modeling effects can occur at any time, not just at those times when the teacher is deliberately trying to serve as a model. Remember, all that is required is that the students *see* the behavior modeled before them. The potential for modeling effects exists at all times; it is not something the teacher can turn on or off at will. What students learn from watching the teacher as a model may be either desirable or undesirable. Teachers are responsible for living up to their own ideals, and they must remain aware of their role as models in order to assure that most of what the students learn from observing them is positive and desirable.

### What Is Learned from Models

Exposure to a model can result in either or both of two responses by the learner: imitation and incidental learning. *Imitation* is the simplest: the learner observes the model's behavior and then imitates it to make it his or her own. Often this is used as a teaching technique, as when students observe their teacher perform a zoology dissection or a chemistry or physics experiment and then repeat the process on their own. However, unplanned and sometimes undesirable imitation also occurs. Students will often pick up distinctive expressions, speech patterns, or gestures that their teachers use, whether or not they are used consciously. They will also take their cue from the teacher in learning how to react in ambiguous situations. If the teacher responds to student embarrassment with tact and sympathy, the class will tend to follow suit. However, if he or she reacts with insensitive sarcasm or ridicule, they will probably laugh and call out taunts of their own.

Besides imitation, observation of a model produces *incidental learning*, sometimes called inferential learning. The learner observes the model's behavior and on the basis of these observations makes inferences about the model's beliefs, attitudes, values, and personality characteristics. Here, the learner is making inferences about why the model is behaving as he or she is or about what type of person would behave the way the model behaves. This is often called incidental learning because it involves acquisition of information in addition to or instead of what the model was trying to convey.

For example, suppose a teacher calls on a student to go to the blackboard and work out a mathematical equation. The teacher will serve as a model in the way he or she reacts to a mistake made by the student. One teacher might point out the mistake and ask the student to look the problem over again to try to find where he or she went wrong. Another teacher might inform the student of the mistake and then call on someone else to go to the board and do the problem correctly. Both teachers would be teaching the mathematical content, specifically, the question of how to solve the particular problem involved. However, the incidental learning acquired by the student called to the board and by the rest of the class in this situation would differ with the two teachers.

In the first case, the students learn: "The teacher is friendly and helpful. It is safe to make a mistake. You will have a chance to correct yourself if you can do so, or will get some help if you can't." In the second teacher's class, the students learn: "You had better be ready to perform when you get called to the board. The teacher wants to see the problem done correctly and has short patience for anybody who can't do it right. If you know the answer, raise your hand and try to get called on to go to the board. If you're not sure, try to escape the teacher's attention so that you don't get embarrassed."

Incidental learning of this type goes on whenever students observe their teachers reacting to errors. The teachers probably are not trying to teach the information that is learned incidentally; in fact, some of it is undesirable information that they would like to avoid if they knew about it. Nevertheless, the students will learn these things through observing them. How to do mathematics is only one of the things the students will learn in these situations.

By making inferences from teachers' behavior in other situations students will also learn about such things as teachers' moral, political, and social values, their likes and dislikes, and their feelings about their classes in general and individual students in particular.

**Factors Affecting What Is Learned from Observing a Model**
The potential for modeling effects exists whenever a model is being observed by learners. However, the amount and kind of learning that results from such observation depends on several other factors. These factors influence whether or not the learners are likely to imitate the model, and whether the information they learn incidentally is desirable or undesirable from the model's viewpoint. These

factors and their effects on modeling are summarized here. (For a more detailed treatment, see Bandura, 1969.)

One important factor is the situation. Modeling effects are more likely to occur in new situations or situations where the expected behavior of the learner is unclear. Like Janice Taylor in the example at the beginning of this chapter, when we enter a new situation and are unsure about what to do, we tend to "do as the Romans do," by observing and imitating models. In a sense, the behavior of the models we observe in such situations defines the situation for us. It tells us what is normal or expected. This was shown in a fascinating series of experiments on emotional reactions by Schachter (1964). He administered stimulating drugs to subjects in his experiments, but he did not tell the subjects what kinds of reactions they might expect from the drugs. He then put the subjects in rooms with models (confederates of the experimenter) to see how they would be affected by the models' behavior. Some models displayed anger and aggression, others showed a giggling euphoria. Most subjects assumed that the effect of the drug was to make them feel like the model that they saw appeared to feel, so that subjects exposed to aggressive models tended to become aggressive, while those exposed to euphoric models tended to become euphoric themselves.

Because modeling effects are strongest in ambiguous situations where people do not know what to expect and tend to observe models in order to find out, modeling effects in the classroom are likely to be especially strong at the beginning of the year. Based on early contacts with their new teachers, students will make inferences about the teachers and decide whether or not they like them, what kind of people they are, whether they invite or discourage questions and comments, whether or not they really mean what they say, whether they are interested in individual problems, whether they are patient and helpful or frustrated and discouraged in dealing with slow learners, whether they seem reasonable and open minded or opinionated and unapproachable, and many other things. Also, teachers' early behavior tends to set the tone for classroom climate variables, such as the degree of competitiveness in the classroom, the degree of pressure and tension felt by the students, the degree of organization and order, and the degree to which students are responsible for their own behavior.

It is vital that teachers model appropriate behavior from the first day of school. Opportunities to teach through modeling will be greater at this time because many things are still fluid or ambiguous. Later, when both the teacher and the class settle into predictable routines, it will be more difficult to effect change. Once patterns are established, they tend to persist, and firmly established expectations tend to lead to self-fulfilling prophecy effects such as those discussed in the previous chapter.

In addition to situational factors, modeling effects vary with the personality and behavior of the models themselves. A warm, enthusiastic teacher whom the students like will be imitated by them. The students are likely to adopt many of the teacher's attitudes and beliefs and to imitate his or her behavior. Students are less likely to imitate a teacher whom they dislike or do not respect, especially in the sense of adopting or conforming to his or her ideals. Much undesirable incidental learning will occur from observation of such teachers, but relatively few desirable modeling effects are likely.

The model's actual behavior and the consequences of that behavior are also important. Behavior that is seen as relevant or effective, or which has been rewarded, is likely to be imitated. Behavior that has been ineffective or has been punished is not likely to be imitated. Reward and punishment can be powerful factors and will sometimes lead students to imitate undesirable behavior even in teachers that they do not like or respect. Thus, hostile, sarcastic, or hypercritical teachers usually produce a destructive classroom climate. The students imitate such teachers, even though they dislike them, because the teacher not only models but rewards such behavior.

Teacher rewards and punishments will also influence student reactions to one another. When students observe the teacher praise or reward a classmate for a particular behavior, or when they discover through incidental learning that the teacher holds the classmate in high regard, they are likely to adopt the classmate as a model and imitate him or her. On the other hand, if they see their teacher reject or mistreat a classmate, they may imitate the teacher and begin to mistreat him or her themselves.

Other factors, such as the degree to which the student's attention is focused on the relevant behavior and the degree to which the student is given instructions and time to practice the relevant behavior, also affect the kind and amount of learning that takes place through modeling. These will be discussed in later sections of this chapter, which list several positive attitudes and behaviors that teachers can present through modeling. Some of these things are preached but not always practiced consistently by teachers. Others are things not often thought of as being taught in the classroom but which can be taught by teachers who are aware of their modeling role. Suggestions are made for how teachers can increase desirable outcomes through deliberate modeling. Also, behaviors are pointed out that should be avoided because they tend to produce undesirable incidental learning effects.

## TEACHING THROUGH MODELING

The most obvious use of modeling as a teaching device occurs in deliberate demonstrations that are given as parts of lessons. To teach many skills, especially to younger children, demonstration is the method of choice. Teachers differ in their skills as demonstrators, however, so that some demonstrations are more successful than others. Guidelines for effective demonstrations are presented in the following section.

In addition to formal demonstrations of skills, there are many other ways teachers can instruct or stimulate cognitive development through modeling. Especially important, for example, is teacher modeling of logical thinking and problem solving for students. Students cannot observe their teachers performing such operations unless the teachers share them by thinking out loud. Suggestions on how teachers can use modeling to stimulate development of these abilities in their students are given below, following the section on demonstrations.

### Effective Demonstrations

Some things can be demonstrated with little or no verbalization. Demonstrations are usually much more effective, though, if they are accompanied by verbal explanations. This is especially true for the kinds of things that are demonstrated by teachers. Usually, these demonstrations provide examples of more general principles or rules that the teacher wants the students to learn. Thus, the teacher should not focus simply on getting the student to be able to do the immediate problem; his or her focus should be on helping the student to learn the more general rule. Thus, a demonstration should not only show the student the physical movements involved in solving a problem, it should also include explanations of the thinking that lies behind the movements.

To say that demonstrations need explanations may seem obvious, but research shows that people usually leave out important pieces of information when explaining or demonstrating something to someone else (Flavell et al. 1968; Hess, Shipman, Brophy, and Bear, 1971). People tend to assume that the listener sees the situation the same way they do, so they often forget that certain things need to be explained. You have probably discovered this for yourself if you ever sought out a friend or relative for driving lessons, swimming lessons, or instructions about how to cook a complicated dish. Professional instructors can teach these skills to beginners with ease and efficiency. Most other people cannot do this, however, even though they may be able to drive, swim, or cook very well.

What's the trick? Expert instructors have broken the process down into step-by-step operations. They assume no knowledge in the learner. Instead, they define each term that they introduce and point to each part as they label it. They describe what they are going to do before each step and describe what they are doing as they do it. They have the learner master one step at a time, rather than trying to have him or her do the whole job at once. They take their time and give corrections in a very patient tone so the learner can concentrate on the task at hand and not worry about working quickly enough.

The things that teachers demonstrate in school are not usually so complex as the examples above, but the principles for effective demonstrations remain the same. Teachers will need to bear this in mind when demonstrating new skills (e.g., word attack, mathematics operations, art projects, and science experiments) and when giving instructions for seatwork or homework. Such strategies are especially important when doing remedial work with students who clearly do not understand how to perform the steps involved in solving problems. A good demonstration should proceed as follows:

1. Focus attention. Be sure that all are attentive before beginning, and see that their attention is focused in the right place. Hold up the object or point to the place you want them to look at.
2. Give a general orientation or overview. Explain what you are going to do, so that the students will have a general idea of what is going to happen. This will get them mentally set to observe the key steps as you go along.
3. If new objects or concepts are introduced, be sure to label them and have the students repeat the labels until you are sure they understand. A student cannot follow an explanation if he or she does not know what some of the words mean.
4. Go through the process step by step. Begin each new step with an explanation of what you are going to do next, and then follow through by describing your actions as you do them. Think out loud throughout the demonstration.
5. Perform each action slowly and with exaggerated motions to help insure that the students follow.

6. Have a student repeat the demonstration so you can observe him or her and give corrective feedback. If the demonstration is very short you can have the student do the whole thing and wait until the end to give feedback. If the demonstration is longer or more complex, break it into parts and have the student do one part at a time.

7. In correcting mistakes, do not dwell on the mistake and the reasons for it, but instead redemonstrate the correct steps and have the student try again.

These principles form guidelines for observing demonstrations. When a demonstration does not succeed, it is likely that one or more of these principles have not been followed.

Thinking out loud at each step is crucial, especially when the task is primarily cognitive and the physical motions involved are relatively minor or nonessential. If you only demonstrate procedures such as pouring into a test tube, placing a number on the board, or making an incision during a dissection, the student will not be able to follow you (unless he or she already knew what to do and therefore did not need a demonstration in the first place!). While the student watches you, he or she will need to hear you describe how you are filling the test tube exactly to the 10 ml. line, how you get the sum by carrying two 10 units and adding them to the rest of the numbers in the 10s column, or how you begin your incision at the breastbone and stop just short of the hip bones. Unless you verbalize the thinking processes going on in your mind as you work through a problem or demonstration, the processes will be hidden from the student. And, unless the student knows enough to figure out each step independently, watching your demonstration may give him or her no more information about what you are doing and how you are doing it than you would get from watching a magician perform a baffling trick.

### Modeling Logical Thinking and Problem-solving Behavior

Teachers should regularly think out loud when trying to solve problems, so that students can see them model the thought processes involved. Much of the school curriculum, especially in the first few years, is devoted to teaching simple facts and basic skills that are learned through rote memory and practice. Partly because of this, many children begin to assume that everything is learned this way— that you either know an answer or you don't. The possibility that they might arrive at an answer by thinking about the problem and working it out for themselves is not always recognized. This leads to a preoccupation with finding out what the right answer is at the expense of learning how to cope with particular types of problems. Instead of developing effective problem-solving strategies to use in these situations, some students develop strategies for covering up their ignorance. Many of these are discussed in John Holt's *How Children Fail* (1964). Teachers can help avoid these problems by modeling good problem-solving strategies themselves and by encouraging the development of them in their students.

The basic method of modeling for this purpose is to think out loud when problem solving. Often, this can be done in connection with lessons in the curriculum. In giving directions about how to do seatwork or homework, for example, and in doing remedial work with students who are having difficulty, teachers should verbalize each step in their thinking processes from beginning to end. Verbalizing will help students see the way the problem is approached and help them see that the answer is a logical conclusion following a chain of reasoning, rather than something that the teacher just knew and that the student must commit to memory.

Although this may seem obvious, we have observed many teachers who do not teach this way. Instead, they tend to ask, "Who knows the answer?" rather than, "How can we find the answer?" They fail to give enough stress to the thinking and problem-solving processes that the problem is supposed to teach. Among other things, such teachers spend more time with and are more rewarding toward students who are succeeding, and they are less accessible and less supportive toward those who most need their help. Other tell-tale behavior occurs in instances when students give answers that are acceptable but are not the ones the teacher was looking for. Instead of modeling respect for process by complimenting the student on the answer, "that's right, I hadn't thought of that," such teachers tend to reject these answers as if they were totally wrong. Unless the students are mature and secure enough to see this teacher behavior as unreasonable, it will tend to make them distrust their own problem-solving abilities, and they will begin to think in terms of guessing what the teacher has in mind rather than attempting to rationally work through a problem. It will also tend to depress student curiosity, creativity, and initiative.

Perhaps the best place to observe the degree to which a teacher models concern for process is in watching the way he or she handles errors in reading, seatwork, and homework exercises. Except for the relatively few things that are purely and simply matters of rote memory, errors in reading and in working out assigned problems are evidence that the student has not mastered the principles involved. The appropriate teacher response in such situations is to help the learner master these principles, not merely to give him the right answer to a particular problem. Yet many teachers typically respond to reading failures by simply giving the student the correct word (or calling on someone else), and they grade work assignments merely by marking answers correct or incorrect. Neither of these responses is usually of much help to the student.

Merely providing the correct answers to these single examples will not help the student to learn to cope with similar problems involving the same principles. He or she needs to know why the answer is correct, not merely to know what the answer is. The teacher needs to model the application of the principles by describing the process out loud, being sure to include each step in the problem-solving process.

Teachers can also model problem-solving processes in areas outside the regular curriculum. Opportunities to do so are presented whenever plans have to be changed, repairs or substitutions have to be made, or immediate problems have to be solved. These may include stuck drawers, equipment that will not function properly, science demonstrations that do not work, broken items that need fixing, and special events that require changes in plans or schedules. When things like this happen, teachers should share their thinking with the students. They should first define the problem, since it may not be obvious to the students. Then they should verbalize their thoughts about solutions, or better yet, solicit suggestions from the group if time permits. This will come as a genuine revelation to certain students who on their own would not think of fixing something that is broken or substituting for something that is missing.

Many students, especially those from disadvantaged backgrounds, fail to develop adequately what Rotter (1966) has called an "internal locus of control"—an appreciation of their own potential for affecting the world through goal-oriented thinking and problem solving. Such students tend to feel helpless in the face of frustrations and adversity, so that they often accept them passively instead of trying to cope with them more actively and effectively. They have learned to think in terms of accepting their fate rather than shaping it. Teachers can help combat this by modeling rational problem solving in their own behavior and by encouraging and rewarding it in their students.

Another way to model thinking and problem-solving strategies is through the use of games such as Password or 20 Questions. The following example shows how:

TEACHER: Today we are going to play a game called 20 Questions. John, you can help us get started. In a minute, I'm going to go over to the window and turn my back while you point to something in the room. When everybody has seen what you are pointing to, go back to your seat and call me. Then I'll come back and start asking you questions to see if I can figure out what you pointed to. I'll have to ask you questions that you can answer either "yes" or "no." If I'm smart enough to figure out what you pointed to in twenty questions or less, I win. Now, let's see if you can stump me. Remember, you can point to anything in the room that you want, as long as it is visible—something I can see. *(Teacher goes over to the window and looks out.)* Okay, I'm not looking now. Point to something you don't think I'll be able to figure out.

JOHN: Okay, we're ready.

TEACHER: All right, I'm going to turn around now. Don't give me any hints by looking at what John pointed to. *(Teacher turns around.)* Well, let's see. There's no point in guessing, because there are too many things it could be. I think I'd better try to narrow it down some. Now, what's a question that would narrow it down for me? I know—I'll find out where it is in the room. *(Teacher walks to center of room and points to the left side.)* I'm in the center of the room now. Is it somewhere on this side of where I'm standing?

JOHN: No, it isn't.

TEACHER: Good, now I know that it is somewhere on the right side of the room. I'll have to narrow it down some more. Let's see, Ralph is seated about halfway back there. Is it in front of where Ralph is sitting?

JOHN: No.

TEACHER: Okay, now I know that it is on the right side of the room somewhere in back of Ralph. Let's see, it could be something on the walls, it could be one of you, it could be something on a desk, it could be something that you're wearing . . . I'd better narrow it down some more. Is it a person or a part of the body?

JOHN: No.

TEACHER: Well, now I know it must be an object of some kind. Is it something that someone is wearing or that they have on their desk?

JOHN: Yes.

TEACHER: Good, that eliminates all those things along the wall. Well, let's find out if it's something somebody's wearing or if it's on a desk. Is it something on a desk?

JOHN: No.

TEACHER: Hummm, then it has to be something that one of these six students is wearing. Is it worn by a boy?

JOHN: No.

TEACHER: Well! Now we know that it is something that either Janice or Mary is wearing. Let's see . . . is it an article of clothing?

JOHN: No.

TEACHER: Good, that really narrows it down. It must be their jewelry or accessories. Let's see, is it worn on the head or the neck?

JOHN: No.

TEACHER: Ah! Now we're getting close. It looks like it has to be either Janice's ring or Mary's wristwatch. Now I'm ready to make a guess. Is it Mary's wristwatch?

JOHN: Yes.

TEACHER: Well! I win! I did it in only nine or ten questions. I thought I'd probably win, because I had it pretty well narrowed down after five or six questions.

By thinking out loud this way, the teacher models problem-solving strategies for the students. In addition, the teacher's reactions to "no" answers help reinforce the idea that such answers provided valuable information and were not a cause of disappointment. Overemphasis on getting answers and underemphasis on thinking processes have caused many students to become conditioned to think that they have failed or have asked a dumb question simply because the answer to a question is "No." Holt (1964) even noticed this tendency in children playing 20 Questions.

After modeling as in the above example, the teacher could follow through by having the students play the game themselves. Besides games such as 20 Questions and Password, riddles and brain teasers can be used to model and practice problem solving, as can exercises in which the problem and answer are given and the students are asked to show how the answer is reached. In all such activities, the teacher can model methods of approaching the problem efficiently and systematically and can acknowledge and reinforce these methods when they are used by the students.

### Modeling Curiosity and Interest in Learning for Its Own Sake

By the very nature of their jobs, teachers are, or should be, committed to learning. This commitment should come across in the teacher's classroom behavior. He or she should not only model interest in curriculum subject matter, but also commitment to learning and knowledge in general.

One important place teachers can model this is in responding to their students' questions, especially questions that are not covered in a textbook. Questions from the class are a sign of interest in the topic. They indicate that the students are participating actively in the discussion and thinking about problems rather than just passively listening. These are the teachable moments when the students are most receptive to new learning.

At these times, teachers should be sure to respond in a way that shows that questions are welcome and valued. First, the question itself should be acknowledged or praised: "That's a good question, John. It does seem strange that the Boston people would want to throw that tea in the water, doesn't it?" Then the teacher should attempt to answer the question, or refer it to the class for discussion: "How about it, class? Why would they throw the tea in the water instead of taking it home with them?"

If the question is one that neither the teacher nor the class is prepared to answer, some strategy should be adopted to find the answer. Relevant questions should not be simply dropped, or brushed aside as unwelcome intrusions. The teacher should promise to get the answer him or herself, or better yet, assign the student who asked it to go to the library (or other resource) to find the answer and then report on it to the class the following day. If necessary, the teacher should give the student guidance about how to get the desired information. This behavior helps to reinforce the idea that learning is important for its own interest value and worth pursuing for its own sake. It communicates the implicit assumption that students will want to know everything they can about American history, not just the particular facts in their textbooks. This helps place the book in context as a means to an end rather than an end unto itself.

Teachers do not have to wait until a student asks a question in order to model curiosity and interest in learning. This can be done in many different ways. Interest in reading can be modeled directly when the class goes to the library. Teachers can check books out at this time, too, and follow up later by giving their reactions to these books in class. During class discussions, teachers can model curiosity in the way they respond to questions for which they do not have ready answers. Here, they should not only respond warmly to the question itself, but also should follow up by sharing their thinking through verbalizing their thoughts about it: "I never thought about that before. Why didn't they just take the tea home with them? I doubt that they just didn't think about it. That tea was very valuable and they must have considered stealing it. So they must have decided not to steal it, but throw it in the water instead. How come?" The teacher could continue in this vein or else invite the class to make suggestions at this point.

Curiosity and interest in learning can also be modeled in the information the teacher gives the class about his or her private life. Although an interest in books, newspapers, magazines, and other educational resources can be stimulated through class assignments and projects, it can also be generated, perhaps more effectively, and with greater generalizability, through teacher modeling. When the teacher reads a book, magazine article, or newspaper item of interest, he or she should mention it to the class so they can read it themselves if they wish. Ideally, the teacher should have the item available to pass around so that students can note the reference or borrow the item if they wish to follow up on it. The teacher should also distribute announcements of coming television programs, museum exhibits, entertainment events, and other special events of educational or cultural value. Here again, a written announcement can help when passed around the class for individual reference.

It is important that references to out-of-school educational and cultural events be made in a way that leaves the decision about whether or not to respond completely up to the student. There should be no hint that the teacher is pressuring the students to take part or is planning to check up on them later to see if they did. (When assignments of the latter sort are made, they should be labeled as such, whether they are required of everyone or are voluntary projects for extra credit. Such assignments are valuable and useful, but they should not be confused with the kinds of totally voluntary suggestions advocated here.)

The teacher should make many of these totally voluntary suggestions, in addition to whatever projects or assignments are made. This is because it is important to model an interest in learning for its own sake (completely free of any connection with school tests or school credit) and to show that the teacher assumes that students, too, will have these interests. There will usually be a strong temptation after the announced event to check up on the students and see how many participated, but this temptation should be resisted. Comments volunteered by students should be acknowledged and encouraged, but there should be no head count to see who participated and who did not. The teacher can give personal impressions if he or she participated—specific statements about the most intriguing or interesting aspects, not general reports about how worth-while the whole experience was. If the teacher did not participate, he or she should say so if asked: "Unfortunately, I had to miss it, but I'd like to hear about it."

The teacher can also reinforce curiosity and interest in learning through the asides and comments made in passing during class conversations. Without belaboring the point unnecessarily, the teacher can get across to the class that he or she regularly reads the newspaper ("I read in the paper last night that . . ."), watches the news ("Last night on the six o'clock news they showed . . ."), and participates in other outside educational and cultural pursuits. The students should also be aware that their teacher thinks carefully about elections and participates in them, keeps abreast of major news developments, and otherwise shows evidence of an active and inquiring mind.

## SOCIALIZATION THROUGH MODELING

The previous sections described how teachers can use their role as a model to teach curriculum content and to stimulate thinking and curiosity. These uses of modeling are closely related to the teacher's role as an instructor to his or her students.

However, teachers also socialize their students through modeling. That is, they shape the values, attitudes, and behavioral standards that their students adopt. Students' ideas about appropriate and inappropriate behavior and about how they should look upon themselves and others are affected by what they see when they observe their teachers.

Research on moral development (reviewed in Hoffman, 1970) shows that children progress to successively higher levels of moral knowledge as they grow older. Young children tend to have a hedonistic or punishment-avoidance orientation. Their behavior responds more to their own desires and fears of punishment than to an intellectual moral system. By the time they reach elementary school, children have developed moral codes. However, these tend to be in the form of overgeneralized rules acquired from adults—a list of dos and don'ts without any real understanding. Some children never really develop much past this stage, so that even as adults their moral thinking is mostly confined to a set of overgeneralized rigid rules.

Where conditions for moral development have been more favorable, school children gradually develop a higher level of moral knowledge. Rules become less rigid as the child learns to take into account situational factors and to separate motives, intentions, and actions.

By adolescence, these rules usually are organized into a coherent, general moral system, so that the student not only can identify the most just or moral way of behaving in a given situation, but can also explain his or her choice by relating it to general principles of morality.

Although the situations producing good inner self-control and a highly developed moral sense are complex and not completely understood, at least two things appear to be important. The child must see ideal behavior patterns modeled by the adults around him, and he must come to see that rules are supported by rationales based on logic and consideration of the general welfare of people. Rules should not be seen as arbitrary demands to be followed only because they may be enforced by a powerful authority figure.

Teachers are in a good position to foster this development through the thinking and behavior they model in the classroom. They may be the primary influence in this area for many students, since many parents rarely use the child-rearing techniques that foster good moral development (Hess, 1970). Students who have been raised by arbitrary and punitive parents, who make and enforce but do not explain their demands, are likely to remain at an immature stage of moral development unless they are sufficiently exposed to other, more effective, adult models. When another adult does succeed in breaking the child away from a moral code featuring rigid rules and punishment avoidance, that adult is likely to be a teacher.

Some of the major ways teachers can use their positions as models to socialize their students are discussed in the following sections.

### Teachers' Credibility with Their Students

Credibility is vital in all human relationships. We tend to like and accept another person if we see that person as honest and reliable. Conversely, we are uncomfortable if we feel that the person does not know what he or she is talking about, does not tell the truth, or fails to keep promises. Only a few instances of this type can create mistrust, since most people believe that someone who has lied or otherwise proved to be unreliable in the past will repeat such behavior in the future.

The need for teachers to protect their credibility is even more important when working with young children than with older students or adults. Children tend to take things literally and to see things in a polarized, either-or fashion. They have difficulty making fine distinctions and taking into account extenuating circumstances. Thus, they will take teachers' threats and promises literally, even though these may contain exaggerations or figures of speech that the teacher does not literally mean. Promises or threats that are not followed through tend to be seen as lies or at least as evidence that the teacher does not mean what he or she says. Once children begin to perceive their teacher this way, they will tend not to believe threats or promises until they see them come true. They will also tend to test any teacher rule or control statement (this is discussed at greater length in the following chapter).

Problems in this area can be prevented if the teacher carefully monitors what he or she says to the class. Nothing should be promised or threatened that the teacher does not have every intention of carrying out. When unforeseen circumstances cause a change in plans, the reasons for the change should be fully explained to the class so that the teacher's credibility is maintained.

All teachers can expect problems in this area early in the year. Because of their experience with teachers during the previous year, or because of a history of unfortunate experiences with adults generally, some students automatically will doubt or even discount what a new teacher tells them. They will tend to be skeptical about threats and promises and may tend to interpret teacher behavior as being something other than what it is. Praise, for example, may be seen as an attempt by the teacher to "butter them up," or to "con" them out of some ulterior motive. A few may even believe that only a fool would trust a teacher or take what he or she says at face value.

With these students, teacher credibility must be established, not merely maintained. Teachers may not only have to model appropriately by practicing what they preach, they may have to call the students' attention to their own credibility. This may mean discussing the subject directly and pointing to the record: "George, you've got to understand that I mean what I say. I'm not playing games or talking just to hear myself talk. Think—have I misled you or made a promise I didn't keep? . . . Well, try to remember that. It's frustrating for me to know that you always think I'm trying to fool you or put something over on you. Maybe other people have let you down in the past, but I'm not them, and you've got to try to remember that. I try to give you and everybody else in the class a square deal, and in return I expect all of you to respect me and trust me. If I ever do anything to let you down, you let me know about it right away so that we can straighten it out."

It is sometimes helpful to use the local slang or street language in talking to students, especially adolescents. This should be done however, only if the teacher knows this language and feels comfortable using it. Students will understand more formal English, even though they might not use it themselves if they were trying to say the same thing. Furthermore, they will be aware that the teacher is struggling to communicate something very important in his or her own way of speaking. All of this helps reinforce the teacher's credibility. If the teacher were to affect the local slang or use it inappropriately, the students would probably pick this up and interpret it as more evidence that the teacher was trying to "con" them. Thus, the degree to which communication is honest and direct is much more important than the particular language in which it is phrased.

### Rational Control of Behavior
Another area to be stressed through modeling, especially by teachers working with younger students, is the importance of a rational approach to coping with the world and its problems. Piaget (1970), among others, has shown that young children often assume people's actions to be conscious and deliberate, and to think that they do things "because they want to." They have difficulty with concepts such as accidents and random events, tending to assume that someone deliberately made them happen for his or her own reasons. Because they are often treated authoritatively by the school and by their parents, however, they often do not see or understand the reasons behind rules and may ascribe them to the whims of the rule makers. This confusion often will persist through adolescence in students raised in authoritarian home backgrounds. Furthermore, almost all adolescents tend to resent and resist rules to some degree, as part of the process of becoming independent and self-regulating.

Thus, teachers at all levels should regularly spell out the rationales underlying their decisions and rules. There will be good reasons for a rule or decision if it is rational in the first place, and these reasons should be explained to the class. This sort of modeling has a double payoff. First, it stimulates the students intellectually, helping them to link causes to their consequences and to see rules as means of achieving larger goals rather than as goals in their own right. Second, it tends to motivate them, to make them more willing to accept the rule or decision. Like anyone else, students are more willing to accept and internalize rules they can understand.

Teachers cannot assume that students will figure out the rationales underlying rules by themselves. They need to be told. Without such explanation, many students will assume the teacher is acting arbitrarily, perhaps just to flaunt his or her authority or indulge a personal whim. By carefully explaining the rationales, teachers can help the class to see rules and decisions as carefully thought-out attempts to solve observable problems. Once the class learns to think this way, they will be capable of establishing their own rules on such matters as how limited resources can be shared fairly and how noise and disruptions can be minimized without undue restrictions on everyone.

For example, consider a third-grade teacher who has just acquired a View-Master for use in the classroom:

TEACHER: Now that you all know how to use the View-Master, I'm going to keep it here in the cabinet where you can get it and use it by yourselves. I think we need to talk about this, though, because there is only one View-Master and I know most of you will want to use it. We need to work out ways to see that everyone gets a chance.

JOHN: Why not let us sign up so we could take it home with us one day at a time?

TEACHER: No, we can't do that, because it has to stay at school. The principal feels there is too much danger of damage if we let people take it home with them. Also, I'd hoped to develop a plan so that many of you could use it on the same day. If only one of you had it each day, some would have to wait almost a month before getting a chance.

MARY: We could look at it together.

TEACHER: Well, I hadn't thought about that, but I guess you could if it didn't get too noisy. Remember, there will be a group lesson and seatwork going on while the View-Master is being used.

GEORGE: Well, it wouldn't be too noisy if just a few of us used it and if we went back in the corner.

TEACHER: Yes, I agree. I think that would work. But how will we decide who uses it at a given time?

SALLY: The first ones to finish their seatwork should use it.

TEACHER: I don't know about that, Sally. I wouldn't want you all to start racing through your work so you could be first to get at the View-Master. I want you to think about your work and do it carefully without being distracted or trying to work very quickly. Also, I want to make sure that everyone gets a chance.

JOHN: We could just make a list and take turns.

TEACHER: Well, maybe we could make three lists, John. One for each reading group. How about if we divide each reading group into three groups of three or four students each, and then have each group take turns with the View-Master? The first group could use it one day, the second group the next day, and the third group the third day. Then the first group would get its turn again.

MARY: Who decides what pictures to look at?

JOHN: Just take turns, naturally.

CHUCK: Yeah.

TEACHER: Yes, you and the other people in your group could decide on your order. When it's your turn, you would decide what pictures to look at. Does this plan sound good to you then? *(Class agrees.)* Okay, let's see if we've got this straight now. Each reading group will divide up into three groups, with three or four in each group. Every day, one of the three groups will use the View-Master during self-chosen activity time. The groups will meet at the small table back in the corner. One person at a time will decide what pictures to look at next. Is that it? *(Class agrees.)* Okay, remember to handle the View-Master carefully. Also, feel free to talk about the pictures, but keep the conversation quiet enough so that it doesn't disturb the rest of the class.

As a footnote to the above example, we might add one additional point: to model rationality successfully, teachers must apply the same standards to themselves as they do to the students. This means being ready to abandon a rule if a reason can be shown for it or if the reasons that led to its inception have since disappeared. In our example, it is likely that the rule about using the View-Master will be needed for only a few weeks. By this time, many of the students would no longer be interested in using the View-Master every time their turn came up. At this point, it would make sense to take into account this change in demand and modify the rule. The students should be allowed to work out the new rule themselves within whatever restrictions are needed to maintain classroom order.

### Respect for Others

Good teachers model respect for others by treating their students politely and pleasantly and by avoiding behavior that would cause anyone to suffer indignities or "lose face" before a group. Many well-intentioned attempts to help students learn politeness and good manners are undermined by teachers' failures to model the behavior they preach.

Respect for others must be presented effectively in the first place. Guidelines for social behavior should be presented as aspects of the Golden Rule ("Do unto others as you would have them do unto you"), not as rituals to be practiced for their own sake. Teachers should stress that in using politeness and good manners, one shows concern for the feelings of others and respect for their personal dignity. Students will find this more meaningful and will be more willing to cooperate than when they are asked to show good manners merely to please the teacher or to "be nice."

Teachers must then back up their verbal explanations and rationale with appropriate modeling. This often can be difficult, since teachers have responsibility for their classrooms and are continually exerting authority. Because of this, it is easy for them to slip into the habit of giving orders brusquely or of criticizing in nagging, strident tones. This is especially likely with younger students, who are sometimes treated by teachers and other adults as if they had no feelings or could not understand what was said to or about them. Usually, they do understand, of course, and they feel hurt or resentful when treated badly. This is why it is usually not only appropriate but desirable that teachers treat even the youngest students with the same respectful manner and tone of voice that they would use when dealing with another teacher. This holds also for interaction with hall guards, monitors, secretaries, janitors, bus drivers, and other school personnel.

As much as possible, directions should be given in the form of requests rather than orders. The words "please" and "thank you" should be used regularly. Tone and manner are also important. When directions are shouted or delivered in a nagging voice, the teacher's manner tends to distract from the verbal content and may cause anxiety or resentment.

What is said *about* students can be just as beneficial or destructive as what is said *to* them. Many teachers will regularly criticize a student in front of the class, or publicly comment about him or her to classroom visitors. For example, on our visits to classrooms, teachers have pointed at specific students while they explained the sordid details of a problem family background, listed the student's typical forms of misbehavior, or stated that they were having the student tested so he or she could be moved to a classroom for mentally retarded children. Sometimes such statements were made loudly in front of the entire class, while at other times the teacher spoke in more hushed tones intended only for our ears. Even in the latter cases, however, the student involved heard what was said and the rest of the class usually did, too. Naturally, all of the students were watching and listening carefully to what the teacher was telling us. Instead of modeling concern and respect for their students, these teachers were setting themselves up as "the enemy."

The potentially destructive effects of such behavior will be obvious to most readers. Yet, it is remarkably common, having occurred in about half of the classrooms we have visited. Others, notably Jonathan Kozol in *Death at an Early Age* (1967), have made similar observations. For whatever reason, adults will apparently make all sorts of statements when speaking to another adult about children and adolescents that they would never make to the student directly. In an extreme case known to the authors, a teacher who was leaving at midterm introduced her successor to the class by having each student stand in turn while she gave a lengthy description of his or her personal idiosyncrasies. Although such callous disregard for students' feelings is fortunately rare, instances like those mentioned above are commonplace. Apparently, the inhibiting factors that prevent us from treating people callously when we speak directly to them do not work as efficiently when we are speaking about them, even if they are clearly within earshot. In view of this, the safest policy probably is to avoid discussing individual students at all with visitors to the class. Visitors should be requested to save their questions until the students have gone home or at least are outside the classroom.

When the teacher does choose to speak to classroom visitors during class time, he or she should take advantage of the opportunity to model and reinforce desirable behavior. In describing class activities, for example, care can be taken to stress the skills that students are learning and the progress they are making. This should be done with reference to the class as a whole or to a subgroup within it rather than to an individual singled out for specific attention. The teacher could also take the opportunity to state publicly that he or she holds the class in high regard and is proud of them. Rather than describe to the visitors what individuals are doing, the teacher could invite the visitors to question the students themselves. This invitation will reinforce the idea that the teacher has pride and confidence in the students and will avoid putting them in the uncomfortable position of being talked about in a conversation between the teacher and the visitors. If a student is asked to do something or make some sort of presentation for the visitors, he or she should be asked politely rather than directed and should be thanked when finished. The student also should be introduced by name to the visitor.

Comments made about individuals should be restricted to their positive individual traits and their present activities or the goals they are presently working toward. ("Richard is a talented artist. He's making a poster for the class bulletin board right now.") Public comparisons with other students should be avoided. ("Jane is one of our brighter students.") These are some of the ways teachers can show their respect for the dignity and individuality of their students when visitors come to the classroom. Basically, this involves extending to the students the same degree of courtesy and respect that would be extended to fellow teachers if the visitor were being taken on a tour of the school instead of just one classroom. Courtesy and respect should be modeled at all times, of course, not just when visitors come.

### Fostering a Good Group Climate

Ideally, the group climate in the classroom is one of friendliness and cooperation. Some classes, however, are notable for jealousy, hostility, and unhealthy aggressive competition. When this occurs, the teacher is almost always contributing to the situation both through direct modeling and through teacher behaviors that indirectly foster ill will among the students.

Direct modeling includes sarcasm, vindictiveness, scapegoating, and other overreactions to misbehavior. If students see their teacher regularly react this way to frustrations or annoyances, they are likely to begin to do so themselves. The teacher's behavior will raise frustration levels in the students and, at the same time, will provide them with a model for dealing with it by taking it out on others.

Extreme forms of this classroom climate have been observed by Henry (1957), who speaks of "the witch hunt syndrome." Henry describes classrooms that are notable for destructive and hostile criticism of students by the teacher and by fellow students; for negative competitiveness, in which one student's loss is another's gain; for frequent accusations and attempts to elicit public confessions of wrongdoing; and for evidence of docility and powerlessness in the victims, who tend to accept such treatment rather than rebel against it.

Most of this negative classroom behavior was directly traceable to the behavior of the teachers. For example, they would initiate and maintain public witch hunts, in which students would be asked to publicly tattle on or criticize other students. The tattling would be followed by public criticism and punishment of the victim. Group hostility was further developed through practices such as emphasizing destructive criticism in the comments made about students' responses or work, and making it clear that similar comments were expected when students were asked to comment about one another's work. One teacher even organized a witch hunt formally by conducting a weekly hearing in which each student's behavior for the week was publicly reviewed and criticized.

There are other less extreme, but more common, teacher behav-

142    LOOKING IN CLASSROOMS

iors that also promote ill will in a group. Foremost among these
are playing favorites and rewarding activities, such as tattling, that
pit one student against another. Students should be praised and
rewarded for their good work, but not in ways that make one gain
at the expense of another (or even make it seem that way). At times,
praise of individual students or of parts of the group is useful and
appropriate as a means of motivating other students. These comments should be confined to praise, however ("Good job, Johnny—
that looks neat as could be"). There should be no blaming of others
and no invidious comparisons ("John's desk is nice and clean, but
look at the rest of yours. Why can't you be more like him?")

Behavior of this sort will only cause resentment, both against the
teacher and against the student being praised. Encouraging students
to tell on one another, or rewarding them for doing so, can have
the same effect. So can putting a particular student in charge while
the teacher leaves the room, telling him or her to write down the
names of anyone who misbehaves. So can passing out papers so
that students grade one another's and then call out the score of
the person they are grading (public reporting focuses too much attention on individuals' grades and invites problems such as ridicule and resentment). In general, anything that places a student in
the position of being against a classmate or of profiting from his or
her problems can cause harm to everyone involved. The class will
resent this teacher behavior, and the victim will probably resent
the behavior of the other students. "Teacher's pet" is in a bad
position also, since this probably will isolate the student from his
or her peers.

When a teacher inherits a class that is highly competitive and
hostile (usually because their previous teacher acted like the teacher
described above), he or she should do as much as possible to eliminate
this by fostering friendly, cooperative relations. Peer tutoring and
group project assignments can help, along with making very clear
how much individual integrity and success are valued and how little
interest there will be in assessing guilt or punishment. It will also
help to verbalize and model individualized standards ("Did I do
my best?") and recognition of individual differences coupled with
positive expectations ("Some people will take more time to learn
this than others, but you will all learn it if you keep at it").

### Showing Interest in the Students
The behavior of many teachers says "don't bother me" to their
class. Sometimes this is communicated directly, as when a teacher
greets a student who has come to him or her with a question by

saying, "Now what do you want?" This is especially common with younger children. Teachers often expect these children to have the same social sophistication as adults, including the ability to discriminate about when to approach the teacher and when to wait. Young children are less inhibited than older ones, and are less aware of how an adult might react when interrupted while talking or doing paper work. They are quite sensitive to hostility, however. Unless the teacher is very careful, a message intended to say, "Please don't bother me now, I'll be with you in a minute," can be perceived as, "Don't bother me—go away." Usually, only a few repetitions of this are required before the student follows the directions as he or she sees them.

To avoid this undesirable incidental learning, teachers must be emotionally prepared to deal with student questions and concerns as they arise. If there are times when the teacher does not want to be interrupted (such as when conducting small group lessons), this should be stated clearly and explained to the class. Whenever students do come to the teacher, the teacher should respond with concern and interest. Even if the student must be put off because something more pressing has to be handled immediately, this can be done in a way that reflects such concern. Tone and manner are more important here than the exact words used. The teacher should speak in a soft friendly tone, use the student's name, and include a positive statement about when this problem will be handled, "Not right now, Sally, come back when reading group is over." This short statement recognizes the student individually, shows concern for her problem, and states willingness to deal with it at a specific time. Compare this with, "Not now—we don't bother teacher during reading group." This reminds Sally of the rule, but does not show concern for her or reassure her that she is welcome to come back later.

A similar type of incidental learning often occurs when students come to the teacher to show their work or creations, or to tell something personal that they want the teacher to hear. Even if the student is not put off in a negative fashion, he or she often is dismissed quickly with an empty comment such as "Really?" or "How nice." Although these may be meant as positive responses, only the most dependent and attention-starved students will accept them as such. Show-and-tell and similar activities often produce this type of response in teachers who are not really listening to the students or watching what they do. Such teachers will occasionally give themselves away by saying something like, "That's nice," after a student has told a sad story. If a student is relating a story or showing and describing an object, the teacher should pay careful attention and ask relevant questions or make relevant comments.

Teachers can respond appropriately in these situations without getting into a long and detailed discussion with the student. A brief response will usually do just as well, provided it is a meaningful statement that is relevant to what the student has said or done. This means, of course, that the teacher must pay attention to what the student is saying or doing in order to respond appropriately. The response, then, should be meaningful and specific. When the student shows an artistic creation, for example, the teacher can ask the student to describe it (or can label it if it is clear what it is) or make some specific comments about it. When the student shows seatwork or homework, the teacher should point out any mistakes and review them with the student, or ask the student to try to correct them him or herself. If there are no mistakes, the teacher should compliment the student not merely for the paper itself but for the skill it represents, "That's good work, Jeff. You're really learning how to multiply."

Even deliberate, well-meant behavior by the teacher can sometimes cause unintended negative reactions. Inappropriate praise is probably the most frequent of these. Praise that is delivered in a straightforward, direct manner and is specific to the accomplishment being praised will be perceived as genuine by students and will be valued by them. Other sorts of praise, while well-intended, may have a different reception. One type is the vacuous or empty "That's good" or "How nice," especially when delivered with an insincere or disinterested manner. This is not truly praise, since the teacher has not really paid much attention to what the student has said or done. It is essentially a way of rushing him or her off, and it will be perceived this way by most students.

Overdramatized praise is equally undesirable. Students tend to be realistic about their accomplishments, since their peers are their severest critics. They monitor one another's schoolwork and creations, and they know roughly where they stand in each area. Therefore, when a teacher sucks in breath and gushes, "Isn't that wonderful!" they will react with healthy skepticism. The praise may be accepted as genuine, but perceived as overdone and perhaps embarrassing. Furthermore, consistent praise of this sort will usually cause the teacher one of two kinds of trouble. First, if a minority of the class tends to be favored with such praise, jealousy and hostility will be engendered among the others. A different sort of problem will arise if everyone is praised this way: a demand for it will be created. The students will see overdramatized praise as simply the way this teacher praises and will no longer be satisfied with ordinary praise. Credibility will be damaged because the students will begin to wonder if the teacher really means what he or she says when saying something without gushing. Respect will be undermined because even kindergarten children know that such behavior is appropriate only for infants, if at all. Thus, while they may view the teacher as warm and loving, they will also tend to see him or her as a comic figure to be laughed at or manipulated rather than respected. Suggestions on how to praise appropriately are given in the following chapter.

### Modeling Listening and Communication Habits

The phrase "teacher talk" conjures up in many people an image of long-winded, righteous nagging. The word "lecture" has a similar meaning for some people. These images usually are one result of experience with a teacher who talked *at* them rather than *to* them. Some teachers talk at their students regularly, and too many teachers do so more often than they realize.

Ideally, teachers should use a normal conversational tone in most situations. Their manner in giving explanations or asking questions in class should be the same as it would be if they were in the company of a group of friends. While a little acting is valuable at times, it should not replace teachers' natural style of behavior. They should not have one way of speaking with their students and a different way of speaking with adults, nor should they try to cultivate either a syrupy or a severe tone. These are phony and even very young children know it.

Questions should be genuine questions, requiring answers, and not merely rhetorical ones, seeking compliance or agreement. Most questions should require substantive answers, not merely "yes" or "no." Discussions should be true interchanges of knowledge and opinions and not merely monologues in which teachers ask and then answer their own questions. When questions are asked, teachers should wait for students to respond in their own words and not try to put words in their mouths for them. When students make responses or contribute to a discussion, teachers should model careful listening and hear them out, not cut them off as soon as they mention a key phrase the teacher wanted to hear.

In general, teachers must be good listeners and follow the same rules for polite discussion that they would follow in the company of other adults. If they do not, the students will quickly get the message and will begin to respond to their behavior by trying to figure out what they want and then giving it to them, instead of by listening to and thinking about their questions. The students may also imitate teachers' rudeness by butting in on one another or calling out answers when a classmate pauses to think.

### Modeling Emotional Control

One of the major problems facing growing children is achievement of an optimal relationship between emotions, feelings, and impulses on the one hand, and conscience, or feelings about correct and appropriate behavior, on the other. Infants start with little emotional control, but they acquire it gradually as they develop and learn about parental and societal expectations. When socialization is incomplete or unsuccessful, the result is an immature adult who lacks effective emotional control. Depending upon the prominent emotions displayed, he or she may appear happy but overly loud and socially inept, may be very dependent on someone else for reassurance or guidance, may respond to frustration or anxiety by withdrawing or turning to alcohol or drugs, or may act out anger and hostility by attacking other people. These are just a few of the behavior patterns observed in adults who have not learned to express their emotions in mature and socially acceptable ways.

A different type of adult emerges from a socialization pattern that has been too "successful," a pattern that has led the person to reject his or her emotions or to keep them under rigid control. Such people tend to be stern, sober, overcontrolled, and inhibited about their own emotions and feelings.

The optimum is somewhere between these two extremes of emotional immaturity and emotional overcontrol. To the extent that problems exist in a given individual, they are likely to be mostly in one direction or the other. Teachers, and educated people generally, are more likely to have problems with overcontrol of their emotions. Young children and many older students, especially those who come from disadvantaged areas, often have poor emotional control. This in itself can cause problems, especially if an overcontrolled teacher is teaching in a lower-class school.

To the extent that the teacher is comfortable and in control of his or her emotions, he or she can be a valuable model to students. This is especially true in regard to negative emotions, such as anger, hostility, fear, or frustration. By showing or reporting these emotions, the teacher helps communicate that they are normal and understandable. This will be reassuring to some students who may feel compelled to try to deny or repress their own similar emotions because they think they are dishonorable, sinful, or seriously abnormal. Because of the way they have been reared, these students have

difficulty distinguishing between the feeling or experience of emotion and the way it is expressed in behavior. For example, instead
of realizing that anger and aggression are normal emotions that
must be controlled and expressed in acceptable ways, they may
feel that they are never justified in becoming angry or that aggressive feelings must be repressed or denied. Fear is another emotion
that is often denied. Many boys especially would feel ashamed and
dishonored to admit that they were afraid in a situation, because
they see fear as something unacceptable rather than as a normal
reaction to be controlled and overcome.

Teachers can help break down tendencies to deny natural emotional reactions by freely discussing their own feelings and by taking
advantage of opportunities to point out that unpleasant emotions
are normal in some situations. Discussions in history and current
events, for example, provide many such opportunities. By discussing
the feelings of Columbus and his sailors or, better yet, by role-playing
these individuals, students can learn much about experiencing and
dealing with strong negative emotions. If these reactions do not
come out spontaneously, the teacher can point out that such emotions were natural and understandable under the circumstances.

This same thing can be done at a more direct level in discussions
about appropriate and inappropriate social behavior. This is especially valuable for junior high and high school students who tend
to develop inhibitions and fears about social acceptability with their
peers. Fear of ridicule before a group becomes very strong at these
ages, and students often inhibit impulses or actions or decline to
ask questions because they are afraid of being laughed at. They
will take pains to cover up inhibitions and areas of ignorance rather
than admit to them. This can lead to what Sullivan (1953) has called
"delusions of uniqueness," in which the students come to believe
that they may be the only one of their peers who has the fears,
doubts, or inhibitions that they have.

Teachers can be a big help here by discussing and role-playing
some of the situations their students deal with in the peer group
every day: reacting to half-serious jokes and jibes about personal
appearance or habits, dealing with conflicts between what the group
is urging and what conscience dictates, responding to flirtations from
the opposite sex, fears of losing face before the group, and so forth.
These activities will help place the fears and self-doubts in these
situations out in the open, and will help students see that they are
not alone in having such experiences.

To set up this kind of role-playing exercise, the teacher should
define each role in a hypothetical situation and briefly sketch the

interactions that are to take place. Then he or she should assign a student to each role, perhaps taking a role him or herself:

TEACHER: Janice and Matt, let's role-play a situation where one of the guys gives you a bad time. Pretend we're part of a big group at a pizza place. Matt, you're a guy who's interested in Janice and trying to make conversation with her to get to know her better. I'll be a friend of yours who keeps butting in with smart remarks. Janice, you pretend that we're two guys that you know well enough to say hello to, but that's all.

Role-play exercises like these will provide many opportunities for students to learn about emotional reactions. By leading discussions about how people feel in the situations that are role-played and about how the participants could or should react, teachers can help students develop insight into their emotions and confidence in their abilities to cope with stressful situations.

Teachers need to show that emotions are not only acceptable, but also controllable. This can be modeled directly, for example, in situations where the teacher has become angry him or herself: "Look, I've had about as much of this as I can take. I've tried to be patient and give you time to straighten yourself out, but you've kept bugging me for several days now and I'm starting to get angry. If you don't cut it out and begin to treat me with more respect, I'm going to be forced to resort to punishment. I don't want to do this, but you're not leaving me much choice." In this example, the teacher communicates anger, but in a nondestructive and controlled way.

Anger and misunderstandings between students can be dealt with by encouraging the students to verbalize their anger and the reasons for it, rather than to express it physically. The technique of role reversal (Johnson, 1970) is especially useful here. Each student involved can be asked to take the role of the other student as a means of helping him or her to see the other student's point of view, "Now if you were George, how would you feel after everybody laughed?" This promotes better understanding of the situation, and gives the students practice at verbalizing and controlling hostility instead of expressing it directly. Suggestions for handling disputes between students are given in greater detail in the following chapter.

Teachers must be comfortable with their own emotions if they are to discuss certain taboo subjects productively. Many students never ask the questions they would like to ask about sex or drugs, for example, because they know their teachers cannot tolerate objective discussions of these matters. Discussion is closed off because the teacher has made it clear that no decent person would even consider masturbation, fornication, or pornography, and that anybody who uses drugs is a dope fiend. Other teachers inhibit discussion by overreacting to what they consider to be obscene language. In these classes students can ask what they want to ask only if they are capable of using terms such as "penis," "vagina," or "copulation." If they know only the slang or street language substitutes for these words, and if they know that the teacher will not allow use of this terminology, they will not ask their questions.

Teachers should try to evaluate objectively their own emotional tolerance in taboo areas. If they can handle discussions in these areas without becoming flustered or upset, they can be a valuable resource to their students. If they cannot, it is probably better to avoid getting into such discussions, since it is not likely that flustered teachers would do much good, and they may well spread some of their inhibitions to their students.

If it is possible to do without penalty, teachers should also avoid situations in which they are trying to inculcate values or standards that they do not believe or accept themselves. Teachers are often put in this position when asked to implement a school's sex or drug "education" program, when the program is more propaganda than education. Generally, it is better for teachers to leave out those parts of the program that they cannot accept or to ask the principal to provide a substitute who can argue for them convincingly (if the principal or school board absolutely insists that these ideas be presented). If the teacher does try to present the ideas, the students will almost certainly detect that he or she does not believe them, and the teacher's credibility will be damaged.

Observers may notice teachers communicating negative emotions without realizing they are doing so. Noticeable anxiety may appear, for example, when the principal or some visitor enters the room or when a particular child acts up. Disgust may be registered by shrinking away from physical contact with a student or by a horrified expression following mention of a tabooed subject.

Observers can be of help to teachers by calling their attention to this evidence of negative emotion. This must be done with caution, however, because the teacher's behavior is an instinctive reaction that may be very difficult for him or her to change or even discuss. Fear or rejection of specific individuals can usually be dealt with effectively by calling the teacher's attention to it, discussing the problem, and suggesting some remedial steps. Changing the teacher's behavior in relation to taboo topics can sometimes be more difficult, however, since this behavior may be connected with a larger pattern of inhibition or neurosis. When this is true, the teacher may strongly resist getting into a discussion of his or her feelings on the subject. Even here, though, some discussion of how the teacher should behave in these situations in the future should be carried out. This is because certain students will be fascinated or amused by the teacher's negative reaction and may regularly do things calculated to produce it. At the same time, other students pick up the teacher's unhealthy negative emotions on the subject through imitation of the teacher as a model. Thus, some remedial plan of action is needed to prevent things from getting worse.

## SUMMARY

In this chapter, we have pointed out that students learn from their teacher simply by observing him or her as a model. Two types of observational learning that result from exposure to a teacher-model were described: imitation, in which the students copy what they see their teacher saying or doing; and incidental learning, in which they observe what the teacher says and does and then use this information to make inferences about his or her beliefs, attitudes, values, and personal qualities.

When students like and respect their teachers, they will begin to imitate them, as a way to be more like them and to earn their respect and affection. If the students do not like or do not respect their teachers, they are less likely to want to imitate them, although they will develop a picture (mostly negative) of their personalities by observing them.

Unfortunately, students may imitate rejecting and punitive teachers if they fear their wrath. This is not the positive kind of imitation that liked and respected teachers induce; it is a frantic attempt to "get on the teacher's good side" and escape or minimize punishment. The students, at least at first, imitate such teachers' behavior not because they think it is good or effective, but because they think the teachers will reward them if they do or will punish them if they do not. However, if bad habits originally learned this way become well established, they can persist long after the students escape the teachers who caused them in the first place.

Students may learn from observing their teacher model at any time, since all that is necessary for such learning to occur is the chance to observe the model. Teachers cannot choose to model at some times but not others; they cannot turn the process on or off at will. However, by learning to monitor their behavior more closely, and to consciously and systematically model when opportunities arise, teachers can use modeling as a teaching tool and can help insure that most of what their students learn from observing them is beneficial.

The most obvious use of deliberate modeling is in a lecture and demonstration. By learning to give clear and effective demonstrations, teachers can minimize their students' learning problems, as well as the time they themselves need to spend repeating and reteaching.

There are other ways, however, for teachers to educate through deliberate modeling. Thinking and problem solving skills can be taught this way if the teacher shares his or her thinking by verbalizing aloud each step involved in the process of solving a problem. This modeling should illustrate not only the logic and actions involved, but also the use of good scientific practices such as thinking about alternatives before responding and checking each step in a long process before going on to the next.

Intellectual curiosity and a value on learning can be modeled through comments and behavior showing that the teacher is interested in the subject generally and not just the textbook, that he or she values and will help find answers to students' questions, and that he or she reads, keeps abreast of current events, and shows other evidence of intellectual activities outside the school setting.

Teachers not only educate (in a more narrow sense) through modeling; they also socialize their students by infusing attitudes and values about behavior. A teacher who models rationality, emotional maturity, politeness and good manners, and personal respect in his or her classroom behavior will tend to induce these qualities in the students. In contrast, a hostile, sarcastic, or hypercritical teacher will produce a class atmosphere marked by these undesirable qualities.

In general, a teacher has little hope of inducing positive qualities in students if he or she does not model them personally. Students rightfully become cynical and resentful when they see a double standard of behavior (one for the teacher, another for them), or when they see clear discrepancy between what the teacher says and does. A basic factor determining where a teacher stands with students is the teacher's personal credibility, a quality that often is hard-won and easily lost.

Remember, if you want to command positive respect (not fear) from students, you'll have to model what you teach. Students looking for a model who embodies the qualities that you hold up as ideals should find that model in you.

## SUGGESTED ACTIVITIES AND QUESTIONS

1. Assume that you are a teacher beginning a new year with a group of students. Outline the points that you plan to make in order to convey your interest in the subject and in the students.

2. Define the situation you plan to teach in (subject content, type of student, grade level, etc.) and role-play activity 1 above with classmates or other teachers. Seek feedback from observers concerning how sincere they felt you were and how interested they were in what you had to say.

3. Use the rating scales at the end of the chapter to observe the modeling behavior of real teachers or apply them to videotapes. Identify positive and negative instances of teacher modeling and attempt to pinpoint any incidental learning that may be taking place. If films are not available, read the case studies in Appendix A (p. 399) and list positive and negative instances of modeling. Compare your list with those that others make.

4. Why does the cooperating teacher often exert a powerful influence upon the student teacher's classroom style?

5. In the example at the beginning of the chapter, Janice Taylor was student teaching in a school that was composed of students who came from homes that were similar (same socioeconomic level, etc.) to Janice's. To be a good model, should a teacher necessarily have the same socioeconomic origin or be of the same race as his or her pupils? What are possible advantages or disadvantages in matching teachers and students this way? Should students be exposed to teachers who have personalities similar to themselves, or will they learn more by being with teachers whose personalities differ markedly from theirs?

6. Why is it relatively useless to tell people to "Do as I say, not as I do"?

7. Why is it that the most powerful effects of modeling are likely to occur at the beginning of the year?

8. Describe in your own words the steps that are included in effective demonstrations.

9. How can a teacher model curiosity and interest in learning?

10. Explain the following statement: "What is said *about* students can be just as destructive as what is said *to* them."

11. Why do the authors suggest that when students make errors the teacher must do more than give them the correct answers?

12. In what ways can you as a teacher become more credible to your students? Be explicit.

13. Explain, in your own words, how you can help your students to learn that emotions are acceptable and controllable.

**FORM 5.1.** Getting Help from Students

*USE*: *When teacher requests a student to run an errand or perform a duty*
*PURPOSE*: *To see if teacher models politeness and respect for students*
*For each codable instance, code whether or not the teacher shows each of the four behaviors.*

BEHAVIOR CATEGORIES

1. Calls student by name
2. Asks rather than tells. Uses interrogative rather than imperative language form
3. Says "please"
4. Says "thank you"

NOTES:

*Doesn't say "please" but asks in polite manner.*

*Students appear eager to help her.*

| | CODES | | | | | | | |
|---|---|---|---|---|---|---|---|---|
| | **1** | | **2** | | **3** | | **4** | |
| | YES | NO | YES | NO | YES | NO | YES | NO |
| 1. | ✓ | — | ✓ | — | ✓ | — | ✓ | — |
| 2. | ✓ | — | ✓ | — | — | ✓ | ✓ | — |
| 3. | ✓ | — | ✓ | — | — | ✓ | — | ✓ |
| 4. | ✓ | — | ✓ | — | — | ✓ | ✓ | — |
| 5. | — | ✓ | ✓ | — | — | ✓ | — | ✓ |
| 6. | ✓ | — | ✓ | — | — | ✓ | ✓ | — |
| 7. | ✓ | — | ✓ | — | — | ✓ | ✓ | — |
| 8. | — | — | — | — | — | — | — | — |
| 9. | — | — | — | — | — | — | — | — |
| 10. | — | — | — | — | — | — | — | — |
| 11. | — | — | — | — | — | — | — | — |
| 12. | — | — | — | — | — | — | — | — |
| 13. | — | — | — | — | — | — | — | — |
| 14. | — | — | — | — | — | — | — | — |
| 15. | — | — | — | — | — | — | — | — |
| 16. | — | — | — | — | — | — | — | — |
| 17. | — | — | — | — | — | — | — | — |
| 18. | — | — | — | — | — | — | — | — |
| 19. | — | — | — | — | — | — | — | — |
| 20. | — | — | — | — | — | — | — | — |
| 21. | — | — | — | — | — | — | — | — |
| 22. | — | — | — | — | — | — | — | — |
| 23. | — | — | — | — | — | — | — | — |
| 24. | — | — | — | — | — | — | — | — |
| 25. | — | — | — | — | — | — | — | — |

**FORM 5.2.** Teacher's Response to Students' Questions

*USE: When a student asks the teacher a reasonable question during a discussion or question-answer period*
*PURPOSE: To see if teacher models commitment to learning and concern for students' interests*
*Code each category that applies to the teacher's response to a reasonable student question. Do not code if student wasn't really asking a question or if he or she was baiting the teacher.*

BEHAVIOR CATEGORIES

1. Compliments the question ("Good question")
2. Criticizes the question (unjustly) as irrelevant, dumb, out of place, etc.
3. Ignores the question, or brushes it aside quickly without answering it
4. Answers the question or redirects it to the class
5. If no one can answer, teacher arranges to get the answer himself or assigns a student to do so
6. If no one can answer, teacher leaves it unanswered and moves on
7. Other (specify)

NOTES:

#7 Explained that question would be covered in tomorrow's lesson.

CODES

| | | | |
|---|---|---|---|
| 1. | 4 | 26. | |
| 2. | 4 | 27. | |
| 3. | 1,4 | 28. | |
| 4. | 4 | 29. | |
| 5. | 4 | 30. | |
| 6. | 3 | 31. | |
| 7. | 4 | 32. | |
| 8. | 4 | 33. | |
| 9. | 7 | 34. | |
| 10. | 4 | 35. | |
| 11. | 4 | 36. | |
| 12. | | 37. | |
| 13. | | 38. | |
| 14. | | 39. | |
| 15. | | 40. | |
| 16. | | 41. | |
| 17. | | 42. | |
| 18. | | 43. | |
| 19. | | 44. | |
| 20. | | 45. | |
| 21. | | 46. | |
| 22. | | 47. | |
| 23. | | 48. | |
| 24. | | 49. | |
| 25. | | 50. | |

**FORM 5.3.** Teacher's Response to Unexpected Answers

*USE*: *When a student answers the teacher's question in a way that is reasonable but unexpected*
*PURPOSE*: *To see if teacher models respect for good thinking when a question doesn't lead to the expected response*
*For each codable instance, code each applicable behavior category shown by the teacher in reacting to a reasonable but unexpected answer.*

BEHAVIOR CATEGORIES

1. Compliments ("Why, that's right! I hadn't thought of that!")
2. Acknowledges that the answer is correct or partially correct
3. Gives vague or ambiguous feedback ("I guess you *could* say that...")
4. Responds as if the answer were simply incorrect
5. Criticizes the answer as irrelevant, dumb, out of place, etc.
6. Other (specify)

NOTES:

*Tends to respond minimally – looking ahead to the expected answer. Teacher actually reading Teacher's Manual a couple of times while children are responding.*

CODES

| | | | |
|---|---|---|---|
| 1. | 3 | 26. | __ |
| 2. | 4 | 27. | __ |
| 3. | 3 | 28. | __ |
| 4. | 3 | 29. | __ |
| 5. | 4 | 30. | __ |
| 6. | 3 | 31. | __ |
| 7. | 3 | 32. | __ |
| 8. | 3 | 33. | __ |
| 9. | 4 | 34. | __ |
| 10. | 3 | 35. | __ |
| 11. | 4 | 36. | __ |
| 12. | 4 | 37. | __ |
| 13. | 3 | 38. | __ |
| 14. | __ | 39. | __ |
| 15. | __ | 40. | __ |
| 16. | __ | 41. | __ |
| 17. | __ | 42. | __ |
| 18. | __ | 43. | __ |
| 19. | __ | 44. | __ |
| 20. | __ | 45. | __ |
| 21. | __ | 46. | __ |
| 22. | __ | 47. | __ |
| 23. | __ | 48. | __ |
| 24. | __ | 49. | __ |
| 25. | __ | 50. | __ |

155

**FORM 5.4.** Personal Relationships with Students

*USE*: *When teacher has been observed frequently enough so that reliable information is available*
*PURPOSE*: *To see if teacher models an interest in individual students*
*Note any information relevant to the following questions:*

1. Do students seek out this teacher for personal contact? Do they show things, make small talk, seek advice? *No. They usually come to him only when they need something (permission, help, supplies).*

2. Does the teacher actively seek out individual students for informal personal contacts or must they come to the teacher? *No informal contacts observed.*

3. Is the teacher accessible to students before, during, and after school hours? *Yes but see # 1*

4. When students tell the teacher things, does he or she listen carefully and ask questions, or respond minimally and cut short the conversation? *He often responds curtly or cuts short the conversation by giving a direction.*

5. When the teacher questions students in informal contacts, does he or she ask open-ended questions seeking their opinions, or leading or rhetorical questions that elicit only cliché responses or compliance? *No informal questions observed.*

6. How does the teacher react when students mention taboo topics? Does he or she tolerate discussion or quickly close it off? *Not observed.*

7. In general, does the teacher talk *to* students, or *at* them? Does he or she use a natural voice, or a special "teacher tone"?
   *Teacher is cold, standoffish. Students avoid him. He is "strictly business" in dealing with them. Much "teacher talk."*

156

**FORM 5.5.** Success Explanations

*USE: Whenever teacher makes a comment to explain a student's success*
*PURPOSE: To see if teacher models appropriate reactions to success, or if*
*he or she fosters undesirable incidental learning instead*
*For each codable instance, code each behavior category that applies.*
*How does the teacher explain good performance by students?*

BEHAVIOR CATEGORIES
1. Native intelligence or ability ("You're smart")
2. Effort or perseverance ("You worked hard, stuck to it")
3. Luck ("Looks like I picked the ones you knew")
4. Easy questions ("You should get those; everybody knows them")
5. Compliance ("You listened carefully, did as you were told")
6. Irrelevant attributes ("You're a big boy")
7. Cheating ("You copied" "Did someone tell you the answer?")
8. Other (specify)

NOTES:

#8: Sarcasm ("What - have you reformed?")

CODES

| | | | |
|---|---|---|---|
| 1. _5_ | 26. __ | | |
| 2. _4_ | 27. __ | | |
| 3. _1_ | 28. __ | | |
| 4. _5_ | 29. __ | | |
| 5. _1_ | 30. __ | | |
| 6. _1_ | 31. __ | | |
| 7. _5_ | 32. __ | | |
| 8. _8_ | 33. __ | | |
| 9. _5_ | 34. __ | | |
| 10. _5_ | 35. __ | | |
| 11. __ | 36. __ | | |
| 12. __ | 37. __ | | |
| 13. __ | 38. __ | | |
| 14. __ | 39. __ | | |
| 15. __ | 40. __ | | |
| 16. __ | 41. __ | | |
| 17. __ | 42. __ | | |
| 18. __ | 43. __ | | |
| 19. __ | 44. __ | | |
| 20. __ | 45. __ | | |
| 21. __ | 46. __ | | |
| 22. __ | 47. __ | | |
| 23. __ | 48. __ | | |
| 24. __ | 49. __ | | |
| 25. __ | 50. __ | | |

**FORM 5.6.** Failure Explanations

*USE*: *Whenever teacher makes a comment to explain a student's failure*
*PURPOSE*: *To see if teacher models appropriate reactions to failure, or*
*if he or she fosters undesirable incidental learning instead*
*For each codable instance, code each behavior category that applies.*
*How does the teacher "explain" students' failure?*

BEHAVIOR CATEGORIES
1. Low intelligence or ability ("You can't keep up")
2. Laziness or lack of perseverance ("You didn't work at it, gave up too easily")
3. Bad luck ("Looks like I picked the ones you didn't know")
4. Difficult questions ("That's a hard one, you're not ready for it yet")
5. Non-compliance ("You didn't listen, didn't do as you were told")
6. Irrelevant attributes
7. No cheating ("See, you can't do it by yourself" "I see no one gave you the answer this time")
8. Other (specify)

NOTES:

all "4's" were addressed to the low - level reading group.

#2 and #8: Errors here seemed to be because students were unable to do the work, not because they hadn't listened to directions or tried to follow them.

CODES

| | | | |
|---|---|---|---|
| 1. | 5 | 26. | |
| 2. | 5 | 27. | |
| 3. | 4 | 28. | |
| 4. | 5 | 29. | |
| 5. | 5 | 30. | |
| 6. | 4 | 31. | |
| 7. | 4 | 32. | |
| 8. | 5 | 33. | |
| 9. | 4 | 34. | |
| 10. | | 35. | |
| 11. | | 36. | |
| 12. | | 37. | |
| 13. | | 38. | |
| 14. | | 39. | |
| 15. | | 40. | |
| 16. | | 41. | |
| 17. | | 42. | |
| 18. | | 43. | |
| 19. | | 44. | |
| 20. | | 45. | |
| 21. | | 46. | |
| 22. | | 47. | |
| 23. | | 48. | |
| 24. | | 49. | |
| 25. | | 50. | |

**FORM 5.7.** Overemphasis on Misbehavior

*USE: When teacher has been observed frequently enough so that reliable information can be coded*
*PURPOSE: To see if teacher is fostering undesirable incidental learning about how he or she expects students to behave*
*Check any of the following observations that are evident in this teacher's class:*

1. Students not allowed to use resource or reference books because they might harm them.
2. Audiovisual self-teaching devices cannot be used without teacher supervision because students might harm the devices otherwise.
3. Students must spend at least a specified minimum time on seatwork, because they won't do neat work if allowed to do something else when they finish early.
  ✓ 4. Students never allowed to correct their own tests.
5. When teacher leaves room, a student is assigned to take down names of anyone who misbehaves.
  ✓ 6. Teacher dwells too much on cheating and takes elaborate precautions to prevent it.
7. Teacher spies on students, searches for forbidden objects, etc.

*Note any other observations concerning rigid rules and restrictions or other overemphasis on misbehavior.*

*Allows no talking during seatwork (because students might "cheat") During a short quiz, the teacher told students, "Move your desks apart so you won't be tempted to cheat."*

159

**FORM 5.8.** Group Climate

USE: *When teacher has been observed frequently enough so that reliable information can be coded*
PURPOSE: *To see if teacher models respect for individuals and avoids practices that foster destructive group climates*
        *Check any behavior categories that apply to this teacher's classroom behavior.*

### BEHAVIOR CATEGORIES

*POSITIVE*

_√_ 1. Makes a point of forbidding ridicule or hostile criticism; insists on respect for others

_____ 2. Uses peer tutoring, team learning, or other methods involving cooperation among students

_____ 3. Speaks well of class to visitors

_√_ 4. Publicly acknowledges and praises prosocial behavior (sharing, helping others, showing sympathy and good will)

_√_ 5. Other (specify) *Frequently uses subtle means of promoting good atmosphere (speaks of "sharing" answers and ideas, "helping" others solve problems, "working together" on projects, etc.)*

*NEGATIVE*

_____ 1. Encourages or rewards tattling

_____ 2. Publicly compares students or groups, causing embarrassment to one or both

_____ 3. Encourages or rewards destructive, hostile criticism of fellow students

_____ 4. Uses types of competitive practices that allow some students to gain at others' expense

_____ 5. Punishes boys by making them stay with girls (and vice versa)

_____ 6. Allows students to call out answers or insulting remarks when someone can't respond

_√_ 7. Has "pets" that get preferential treatment (rewards, privileges, helper roles, etc.)

_____ 8. Picks on certain students, or uses them as scapegoats

_____ 9. Other (specify) *While generally positive, tends to hold up students # 6 and #10 as examples to others.*

**FORM 5.9.** Positive Modeling

*USE: When teacher has been observed frequently enough so that reliable information can be coded*
*PURPOSE: To see if teacher takes advantage of opportunities to teach through deliberate modeling*
*Record any information relevant to the following questions:*

MODELING THINKING
When the teacher must solve a problem or think through a question, does he or she think out loud? Does the teacher allow students to hear the steps he or she goes through, or explain them after giving the answer?

*Does this well when reviewing seat work and homework, but often doesn't explain rationale when she answers students questions during discussion.*

Does the teacher include activities that allow students to practice thinking and problem solving (20 questions, brain teasers, solving hypothetical problems)?

*Uses drill-like games and contests but none that promotes thinking and problem solving*

MODELING COMMITMENT TO LEARNING
Does the teacher give evidence of a continuing active interest in learning (discuss newspaper or magazine articles, books, TV programs, special events, educational activities of teacher)? *Only in response to a question or comment from class.*

**FORM 5.10.** The Teacher's Credibility

*USE: When teacher has been observed frequently enough so that reliable information can be coded*
*PURPOSE: To see if teacher's behavior undermines his or her credibility with students*
*Below is a list of teacher behaviors that tend to undermine the teacher's credibility with students. Check those behaviors that are observable in this teacher.*

_____ 1. Teacher is gushy, overdramatic, unconvincingly "warm."

___✓___ 2. Teacher's praise is unconvincing because he or she continually uses a stock phrase or fails to specify what is being praised.

_____ 3. Teacher insists on "nice" or "acceptable" motives and thoughts, or tends to deny or explain away taboo problems rather than deal with them.

_____ 4. Teacher will resort to obviously false or exaggerated "reasons" in defending rules, decisions, or opinions, rather than admit mistakes.

_____ 5. Teacher promises when still uncertain whether he or she can deliver or fails to follow through on announced intentions.

_____ 6. When students express fears or suspicions, teacher responds with vague or unconvincing reassurances rather than investigations or detailed explanations.

_____ 7. Teacher cannot tolerate differences of opinion on matters of taste or values; tends to foist his or her own values on the students.

_____ 8. Teacher will not admit areas of ignorance or acknowledge mistakes.

_____ 9. Teacher tends to talk down to students, sermonize, or repeatedly harp on pet topics or gripes, to the extent that students are alienated or amused.

___✓___ 10. Teacher clearly favors or picks on certain students.

_____ 11. Students have learned that they can get teacher to change rules, decisions, or assignments by badgering him or complaining.

_____ 12. Teacher's assumptions about students' home backgrounds, values, interests, or life styles are grossly inaccurate.

_____ 13. Teacher brushes aside questions on complex or touchy issues by repeating platitudes or oversimplified "reasons" or "solutions."

___✓___ 14. Teacher sometiems appears not to believe what he or she is saying (specify).

_____ 15. Other (specify)

NOTES:

Overuses, "Very good, John."

162

# 6/ MANAGEMENT I: PREVENTING PROBLEMS

Classroom management is of major concern to almost everyone connected with education. (Under *classroom management,* we include the teacher functions variously described as discipline, control, keeping order, motivation, and establishing a positive attitude toward learning, among others.) New teachers often fear that they will not be able to control the class or that the class will not respect them. Even experienced teachers usually say that establishing good control is a major goal in the first few weeks of the year. Principals and other school administrators reinforce this concern, tending to give low ratings to teachers who cannot control their classes or who have discipline problems.

Approaches to classroom management depend upon teachers' attitudes toward learning and the sorts of relationships they establish with students. Four commonly observed types of classrooms are the following ones:

1. The class is in continual chaos and uproar. The teacher spends much of the day trying to establish or reestablish control but never succeeds for long. Directions and even threats are often ignored, and punishment does not seem to be effective for very long.
2. This class also is noisy, but the atmosphere is more positive. The teacher tries to make school fun for the students,

introducing many games and recreational activities, reading stories, and including lots of arts and crafts and enrichment activities. There are still problems, however. Many students pay little attention during lessons and group activities, and seatwork often is not completed or not done carefully. Lack of attention occurs even though the teacher holds these activities to a minimum and tries to make them as pleasant as possible.

3. This class is quiet and well disciplined. The teacher has established many rules to insure this and monitors the students' behavior closely to see that the rules are followed. Infractions are noted quickly and are cut short with a stern warning or with punishment when necessary. The teacher, who spends a fair amount of time attending to such misbehavior, appears to be a successful disciplinarian because the students are usually obedient. However, the atmosphere in class is uneasy. Trouble is always brewing just under the surface. Furthermore, whenever this teacher leaves the room, the class bursts into noise.

4. This class seems to run by itself. The teacher spends much time teaching and very little handling discipline problems. The students follow instructions and complete assigned tasks on their own, without close supervision. Students involved in seatwork or enrichment activities interact with one another, so noise may be coming from several sources at the same time. However, these are the controlled and harmonious sounds of students productively involved in activities, not the disruptive noises of boisterous play or disputes. When noise does become disruptive, a simple reminder from the teacher is usually enough to handle the problem. Observers in this class sense a certain warmth in the atmosphere, and go away positively impressed.

How are these four very different rooms to be explained? Maybe the students are different. Perhaps those in the first class are rebellious, while those in the fourth class are socialized and motivated. However, all four types of classes are found in every school, whatever its socioeconomic status, and many teachers have the same types of classroom atmospheres year after year. The differences cannot be attributed entirely to the types of schools or students involved.

Some teachers have chronic control problems. Others regularly gain respect and obedience with little apparent effort, even from students who were problems for other teachers the year before. The examples illustrate four familiar types of teachers. The first "can't cope," the second "bribes the students," the third "runs a tight ship," and the fourth "has few control problems."

Before reading on in this chapter, take some time to think about these four teachers. Assume that all four have roughly equivalent groups of students to work with at the beginning of the year. List three attitudes or behaviors for each teacher that might help explain why the classroom environment has evolved along the lines described. What expectations and assumptions might each one make about students and about the learning process? What might students learn from observing each teacher as a model?

## MANAGEMENT AS MOTIVATIONAL STIMULATION AND PROBLEM PREVENTION

The purpose of the previous examples and exercise was to help you focus on the teacher's role in shaping the learning environment or atmosphere in the classroom. There is no clear-cut atmosphere early in the year. It develops gradually in response to the expectations communicated by the teacher, the behavior he or she models, and the classroom management approach that is used. The same students will respond to different teachers differently. This is seen in junior high and high schools where the classes are taught by more than one teacher. The same class that is interested and attentive for one teacher can be rebellious and bored with another.

Generally, the most important determinant of classroom atmosphere is the teacher's method of classroom management, especially his or her techniques for keeping the class actively attentive to lessons and involved in productive independent activities. This is why the chapter title refers to management rather than to discipline or control. These latter terms have a connotation that we wish to avoid: the idea that motivating students is mostly a matter of dealing successfully with their misbehavior.

Although classroom management is often discussed in terms of dealing with misbehavior, research on classroom discipline (Kounin, 1970) and on behavior modification generally (Bandura, 1969) suggests that this approach puts the cart before the horse. Emphasis on behavior problems and on trying to get rid of them through punishment is ineffective, often making the situation worse. (The reasons for this will be explained later in the chapter.) Generally, it is much more effective to stress and reward desirable behavior and use management techniques that prevent problems from emerging than it is to deal with problems after they emerge. The key to classroom management success lies in the things the teacher does ahead of time to create a good learning environment and a low potential for trouble.

This was shown most clearly in a series of studies on classroom discipline by Kounin and his associates (Kounin, 1970). These investigators studied many different teachers, using interviews, on-the-spot note taking, and the coding of videotapes. They did not conduct an experiment or try to influence the teachers. Instead, they simply observed what went on in the classroom and developed ways to measure relevant teacher and student behavior. Their intent was to find relationships between teacher behavior and student behavior. The findings of several studies agreed: the teachers' methods of dealing with discipline problems were unrelated to the frequency and seriousness of such problems. Measures of discipline failed to differentiate teachers who minimized discipline problems from those who could not cope with them.

There *were* consistent differences between such teachers, however, and measures developed to capture them did correlate with measures of success in classroom management. None of these was a measure of "discipline," in the usual sense of this word. Instead, they were measures of classroom management techniques. These were teacher behaviors that increased the time students spent in profitable work activities and led to successful resolution of minor inattention problems before they developed into major disruptions. *This is why we will stress repeatedly that successful classroom management is primarily a matter of preventing problems before they occur, not the ability to deal with them after they emerge.*

This is not the whole story, of course. Problems emerge in all classrooms, and some students are disturbed enough to require special treatment. Suggestions for dealing with some of these special problems are made in the following chapter, after general techniques for classroom management are discussed.

## ESSENTIAL TEACHER ATTITUDES
Something as complex as classroom management cannot be reduced to simple cookbook recipes. There are general principles that apply to most situations, however, and these can be learned and practiced systematically. These principles will not eliminate or solve all problems, but they will handle most problems successfully. At the same time, they will leave the teacher in the best possible position for handling the problems that do require special solutions.

Before moving to specific suggestions, we wish to stress the importance of certain key teacher attitudes. We discuss these attitudes first because they must be present if the techniques suggested later are to be successful. *The attitudes and behaviors to be described complement and reinforce one another to form an internally consistent and systematic approach. Attempts to use isolated parts of this system as techniques or gimmicks will not succeed for long.* The success of this approach ultimately depends upon the teacher's ability to establish credibility with students and gain their respect. To do this, a teacher has to be perceived as an individual person, not an impersonal authority figure or "player of the teacher role." A teacher who tries to manipulate students by using gimmicks, without having established good personal relationships, will soon be resorting to threats and punishment.

Many teacher attitudes and other qualities basic to successful management have been discussed in previous chapters. They will be reviewed briefly here insofar as they relate to classroom management. In combination, these qualities make the teacher someone whom the students will respect and want to please, not merely obey.

To begin with, teachers must like the students and respect them as individuals. They need not be overdramatic or even particularly affectionate; if they enjoy the students and have genuine concern for their individual welfare, this will come through in tone of voice, facial expressions, and other everyday behavior. Even young children adjust quickly to a teacher's personality (Anderson and Brewer, 1945). There is no need for a quiet or undemonstrative teacher to emote in an attempt to impress the students with his or her concern.

It is important, however, to get close to students during private interactions. A teacher who is standoffish will be perceived as cold and will seem to be talking at rather than to the students, despite good intentions. Therefore, teachers should form the habit of bending close to students when speaking with them privately. In the early elementary grades, gestures such as patting the head or back, or resting the hand on the shoulder are often effective (unless resented by the student). These are among the ways that teachers can communicate concern or affection nonverbally when conferring with, praising, or encouraging students. Preschool and early elementary school teachers can use these techniques regularly.

Teachers working with older students ordinarily should not, however. These students will not want physical contact, and some might resent it or be embarrassed by it. Physical contact by an adult can be threatening for adolescents striving toward independence and autonomy. Secondary teachers should regularly bend close to students and deal with them at their level during private contacts, however, and should make an effort to get to know each individual. This will provide information about each student's individual interests and needs, knowledge that will be helpful in individualizing instruction. It will also provide a basis for showing concern and establishing warm relationships with students.

Teachers who get close to students and show concern for them are off to a good start. They must also establish and maintain credibility, however. Most students have been exposed to enough discrepancies between what adults preach and what they practice that they do not automatically believe what they are told by adults, including teachers. Some, especially those from economically depressed areas, may even automatically assume that the adult is trying to "con" them. They may find expressions of concern hard to accept as genuine, seeing such expressions as attempts to manipulate them out of ulterior motives. For these students, respect and credibility must be established, not merely maintained.

Credibility is established largely by making sure that words and actions coincide and by pointing this modeling out to the class when necessary. Once the teacher is established as a respectable and likeable person and as someone who can be believed, he or she will be in a position to practice the classroom management techniques to be described. When students like and respect teachers, they want to please them and will be more likely to imitate their behavior and adopt their attitudes. The students also will be more likely to sympathize with the teachers when they are challenged or defied, instead of allying with defiant students against them.

Credibility also provides the structure that the students want and need. If they can depend on what the teacher says, they will be less likely to test him or her constantly. Such testing often consumes a great deal of time, especially in classrooms in disadvantaged neighborhoods. Teachers who take time early in the year to listen to students and to explain the rationales underlying rules and assignments are making a wise investment. This will help establish credibility and reduce the students' tendencies to test the teacher throughout the year.

Teacher credibility also helps enable students to accept responsibility for their own behavior. When a teacher has established fair rules and enforced them consistently, rule breakers can get angry only at themselves. However, if the teacher lacks credibility because he or she makes empty threats or enforces rules inconsistently, rule breakers who are punished will likely be resentful or feel that they are being singled out unfairly ("Sally did it yesterday and you didn't do nothing").

Appropriate expectations are also involved in gaining respect and establishing credibility. Students tend to conform not so much to what the teacher says as to what the teacher actually expects. By interpreting the teacher's behavior, they will adjust to the teacher's habits and learn to identify discrepancies between what he or she says and means. If they learn that when the teacher looks up and says, "No talking over there," he or she really means "Keep the noise down to a tolerable level," they will respond to the second message, not the first. This would be all right, except that sometimes the teacher really means "Keep quiet." At these times, the students will react in the usual way, and misunderstanding and resentment may result.

To avoid this, teachers must carefully think through what they really expect from their students and then monitor their own behavior to see that it is consistent with their expectations. This monitoring will help eliminate empty, overgeneralized, or inconsistent statements. Observers can be very helpful here, since teachers are often unaware of inappropriate expectations. The teacher described as "bribing" the students in the example at the beginning of the chapter is a case in point. Even though liked and respected, this teacher had discipline problems when trying to organize the class for lessons.

Bribing students to learn reflects inappropriate attitudes toward learning. The teacher thinks of school-related tasks as unrewarding drudgery and assumes that students will not enjoy them. This attitude is picked up quickly by the class, who learn to wince, sigh, or protest whenever a play activity is stopped to begin a lesson. Their behavior will confirm and reinforce the teacher's expectations, and at the same time build up his or her guilt about making them learn. In turn, guilt will tend to make the teacher minimize the time spent in lessons and start to bribe students by promising them rewards if they will tolerate the lesson for awhile.

This type of teacher is not a positive influence on students, even though he or she may have their affection and, to a degree, their respect. Until there is a change in the teacher's attitudes and expectations about learning and about enjoyment of school activities, he or she will remain more of a buddy than an educator. The students will achieve poorly, and their next teacher will be faced with a rehabilitation job in motivating them for school.

To establish the groundwork for successful classroom management, teachers must: (1) have the respect and affection of the students; (2) be consistent and, therefore, credible and dependable;

(3) assume responsibility for the students' learning, seeing their own function as primarily one of teaching (as opposed to mothering, babysitting, entertaining, etc.); (4) value and enjoy learning and expect the students to do so, too; (5) communicate these basic attitudes and expectations to students and model them in behavior.

## GENERAL MANAGEMENT PRINCIPLES

If we assume a teacher has these personal qualities, what specific steps can he or she take to establish good classroom management? The rest of this chapter and the one that follows address this question, moving from general to specific situations, and from techniques that help prevent problems to techniques used in remediating problems after they have appeared.

The recommendations in this section all concern general principles of classroom organization. These principles are based on one or more of the following assumptions:

1. Students will be more likely to follow classroom rules when they understand and accept them.
2. Management should be approached with an eye toward maximizing the time students spend in productive work, rather than from a negative viewpoint stressing control of misbehavior.
3. The teacher's goal is to develop inner self-control in the students, not merely to control them.
4. Teachers will minimize discipline problems if their students are regularly engaged in meaningful work geared to their interests and aptitudes.

### Establish Clear Rules Where Rules Are Needed

Certain aspects of classroom management recur on a regular basis because they are part of the daily routine. These include storage of clothing and personal belongings, use of the toilets and drinking fountains, access to paper and other supplies, use of special equipment (supplementary readers, audiovisual aids, art supplies, etc.), and behavior during periods of independent work (e.g., what a student who finishes seatwork should do while the teacher is still busy with a lesson group).

In these or other situations where a rule is required, the rule should be explicit, and the rationale for it should be explained. Explanation is especially important at the beginning of the year. Students in kindergarten or first grade who are new to school will need demonstrations and lessons on the use and care of equipment. Many will never have used or even seen pencil sharpeners, audiovisual equipment, or certain arts and crafts equipment. A simple verbal explanation may not be enough. A demonstration followed by an opportunity to practice the behavior may be required before some students can do what the teacher wants them to do.

Demonstrations and practice will be less necessary with older students, but they will need thorough discussions of rules. Each new grade adds experiences that the students have not been through before. More importantly, teachers differ in their expectations and demands. Sometimes, last year's teacher will have demanded behavior that is contradictory to what this year's teacher wants, especially on the matter of what things the student must seek permission to do and what may be done without permission. Therefore, each teacher should specify rules clearly and demonstrate if necessary.

Rules should be kept to a minimum and should be clearly needed. If a rule does not have a convincing rationale, it should be discarded or revised. Rules should be means, not ends, and they should succeed in achieving their desired ends.

They should be presented to the class as means and not overgeneralized or presented as ends in themselves. For example, the rationales underlying rules about behavior during seatwork should stress that no one should disrupt a group lesson the teacher is conducting or disrupt other students who are still involved in seatwork.

There is a range of activities that a student who finishes seatwork can engage in without disturbing either the teacher or the other students still at work (read a supplementary reader, begin an art project, examine a science display, work on homework, talk quietly with another student who has also finished, etc.). This range will vary across teachers and students, but it still will be a range. An overgeneralized rule, such as "When you finish your seatwork you will stay quietly in your seats and not talk to anyone or leave your seats for any reason," would not be justifiable. This is much more restrictive than it should be and will cause more problems than it solves. Instead, the teacher should stress the basic goal of avoiding disturbances to students involved in lessons or seatwork, and follow this up by listing examples of acceptable and unacceptable behavior.

Ideally, rules should be elicited in guided discussion, not presented as laws. When teachers clearly define problems that need solution, students are capable of developing rules that will do the job. Participation in the establishment of rules helps students see the reasonableness of the rules and accept responsibility for keeping them. Also, helping to make the rules guides students in learning to plan their lives rationally and to see themselves as actively controlling their destinies rather than just responding to external pressures.

When rules are no longer needed or when they no longer do

the job they were meant to do, they should be modified or dropped. When presenting any such change, teachers should be sure to explain the reason for it, not just announce it. Better yet, they can open the problem to class discussion and invite students to develop their own solutions. Good classroom management involves establishing clear rules where rules are needed, avoiding unnecessary rules, reviewing rules periodically and changing or dropping them when appropriate, and involving the students as much as possible in establishing and changing them.

### Let the Students Assume Independent Responsibility

There is no reason for teachers to do things that students can do for themselves. With proper planning and instruction, even the youngest children can take out and replace equipment, sharpen pencils, open milk cartons, pass out supplies, carry chairs, and form orderly lines by themselves. Older students can also work independently or in small groups and can check their own work. Teachers sometimes insist on doing these things themselves or on controlling them through such rituals as calling names of the students one by one. This serves only to create delays, divert teachers from teaching tasks, and retard the development of independent responsibility in the students.

Teachers will sometimes say, "I tried to get them to do it themselves, but they couldn't." In this case, the students may need a demonstration lesson and an opportunity to practice the behavior involved, but they do not need the teacher to do it for them or to develop a ritual. Time spent in explanation early in the year and patience in tolerating slowness and mistakes while students learn to act on their own pay great dividends later.

Some teachers adopt overly rigid rules on the grounds that they are needed to prevent waste or vandalism: "If I let them sharpen their pencils, they'll sharpen them right down to the eraser." "If I put out supplementary readers, they'll steal them." "If I allow them to work in groups, they'll just copy from one another or waste time." This attitude represents an avoidance of the problem rather than an attempt to solve it. It also communicates negative expectations to the students. Prevention of this sort is appropriate for infants, but not for even the youngest school children. When students understand the rationales underlying rules, and when they know they are expected to follow rules, they will do so.

Needless rituals and delays can be avoided by letting students assume all of the classroom management functions that they can handle on their own. This procedure will help minimize the disruptions that often begin when students are idle during lulls in activities. It also will help students develop independence and responsibility.

## Minimize Disruptions and Delays

Management problems start and spread easier when students are idle or distracted by disruptions than when everyone is involved in productive activity. There are many things teachers can do to hold disruptions and distractions to a minimum.

Thorough daily planning is important here. Problems often begin when a teacher breaks the flow of a lesson or activity because he or she needs to prepare equipment that could have been prepared earlier or to look something up in the manual. Eliminate waiting time whenever possible. Unless there is no alternative, the entire class should never be lined up to do something one at a time. Instead, break the class into subgroups or appoint assistants to help.

For example, suppose the class is preparing to leave for lunch, and this preparation involves tidying up the room, getting lunch bags, and visiting the washroom. Thirty minutes or more can be spent on these activities by regimenting the entire class (holding up each lunch in turn and having the owner come and get it, having students come to the wastebasket one by one to throw away anything they have picked up around their desks, having the entire class form lines to go to the washroom all at the same time, etc.). This can be handled efficiently in a few minutes, however, through grouping. While part of the class get their lunches, others clean up their desks and throw away trash, and the rest can use the washroom. As groups finish one activity, they rotate into another. This way, the same goals are accomplished in less time and with much less regimentation by the teacher.

The time needed for distributing paper or other supplies can be cut down by having one student from each row or table pass things out. Distributing supplies is easier if items are stored where students can get them unaided. In the early elementary grades, supplies should be low, so that students can reach them, and stored neatly for easy identification and replacement. In general, items should be stored as close as possible to where they typically are used, to cut down traffic and reduce spilling and dropping.

Use of storage space should be determined by convenience. Store frequently used items where they can be taken out and returned most conveniently. Items that are used rarely or at a different time of the year can be stored in the harder to reach areas.

The room should be arranged to promote free and easy traffic flow. Heavily used traffic lanes (areas around the door, the drinking fountain, the coat rack, or lanes between the students' usual seats and special areas for group lessons) should not be obstructed. Traffic lanes should be wide enough for students to move freely without bumping into each other or into some of the furniture.

Delays and waiting time frequently result when there is high demand for something that is in short supply, as when the entire class must use paste from a single jar or get supplies from a single container. Much time can be saved here by storing small items (crayons, paste, pencils, etc.) in several containers instead of a single, large container.

Dead time in junior high and high school classes often can be prevented through advance preparation. Unless it is important for the teacher to model the motions involved, complicated diagrams, maps, or mathematical computations should be prepared on the chalk board before class begins or distributed on mimeographed sheets rather than constructed on the board during class. Similarly, many science experiments and other demonstrations can be partially prepared ahead of time when the preparations themselves do not need to be demonstrated to the class. Or, students can be usefully involved in these preparations activities, especially when they must be done during class time. The job will be speeded up and at the same time students will participate in the demonstration or experiment more actively.

Bear in mind that when students are asked to wait with nothing to do, four things can happen and three of them are bad: students may remain interested and attentive; they may become bored or fatigued, losing interest and ability to concentrate; they may become distracted or start daydreaming; or they may actively misbehave. Therefore, plan room arrangement, equipment storage, preparation of equipment or illustrations, and transitions between activities so that needless delays and confusion are avoided.

### Plan Independent Activities as Well as Organized Lessons

Usually, students spend a good part of their school day working at their seats on assigned seatwork or on activities they have selected for themselves. Disruptions often originate with students who are not working on their assigned work or who have finished it and have nothing else to do. Sometimes, teachers bring trouble on themselves by failing to provide worthwhile seatwork or by failing to have back-up plans prepared if seatwork is completed more quickly than anticipated. Kounin (1970) found that such teachers had more classroom management problems than their better prepared colleagues.

Seatwork is (or should be) a basic part of the curriculum, not merely a time filler. It should provide students with opportunities to practice the skills they are learning or to apply them in solving problems. If properly designed and used, the exercises also provide teachers with good information about how each student is progressing. Therefore, teachers should plan seatwork as carefully as they plan their lessons and should make its importance clear to students when assigning it. Students should know which skills or abilities they will develop in doing assignments.

The assignment should be specific. The teacher should assign particular exercises and not merely provide busy work without caring how many or which problems are done, and the work should be used for diagnosis and remediation (the teacher will check the work and follow up with students who do not understand). Checking seatwork will insure that students are held accountable for the assignment and will make it likely that the assignment will have its desired effects.

In addition to being specific about the seatwork assignments, the teacher should provide clear options for students who finish. At times, these options may mean additional specific assignments (e.g., reviewing the story they are going to study later in reading group). Where no specific assignment is appropriate, the teacher can make some suggestions. In any case, students should know clearly what options are available to them if they finish their seatwork early. They should not have to interrupt the teacher to ask if one thing or another is permissible. Nor should they be tied so closely to the teacher that he or she has to redirect their work every 15 or 20 minutes.

The teacher should also establish a clear-cut rule regarding getting help with seatwork. What are students to do if they are not sure how to do the work or if they have not understood the directions clearly? Different teachers will prefer different answers to this question (ask another student, come up to the teacher but wait quietly until the teacher can conveniently turn away from the group, ask a designated tutor or assistant, etc.). Regardless of what rule is adopted, however, it should be made very clear to the students.

Students must be provided with appropriate seatwork and other independent activities so that they will be profitably occupied when the teacher is busy with small group instruction. All students should know what their assignments are, what they should do if they cannot continue, and what they can or should do when they finish. These activities will provide a basis for responsible self-guidance and will minimize problems resulting from idleness or confusion about what to do.

### Encouraging Effort

Teachers should expect and desire students to seek help when they need it and should provide ways for them to get it. Confusion and uncertainty about how to do assignments are to be expected daily. Discovering and helping to clear up these problems are part of the essence of the teacher's role. After all, if students could learn new skills quickly and easily after seeing a single demonstration, they would not need specially trained teachers. Yet, some teachers regularly react with blame, frustration, or disgust when students indicate that they do not understand. Even when they follow up this initial reaction with remedial teaching, the damage is done.

Students in the classes of such teachers learn to cover up their inadequacies by giving the appearance that they understand the work. They will copy from a neighbor rather than leave an answer blank or seek out the teacher for help. Whether or not they really do understand, they will nod their heads reassuringly if the teacher asks, "Do you understand?" after a demonstration or a seatwork assignment. In general, they will develop the mechanisms that John Holt describes in *How Children Fail* (1964) by attempting to please the teacher at all costs and avoid any disclosure of confusion. Such defensiveness is almost certain to develop unless teachers view learning difficulties as legitimate and expected and see students' efforts to bring them to their attention as desirable.

Recognition of students' difficulties does not mean that teachers should drop whatever they are doing the minute a student expresses a problem or that they should do students' work for them. It does mean that teachers should plan to meet these needs and to set up ways to arrange for communication of problems and remediation through reteaching. If they do not want students coming to them while they are conducting group lessons, they should make this clear to them. At the same time, teachers should let the students know that they are welcome to come when the lesson is over or that the assignment will be reviewed and progress will be checked before beginning another lesson.

With students who appear convinced that they cannot do the work or who regularly try to get the teacher to do it for them, a fine line must be drawn between two extremes. First, the teacher should repeatedly encourage such students and express the belief that they will be able to succeed with continued efforts. Students' expressions of inability should not be accepted or even legitimized indirectly through such comments as "Well, at least try."

On the other hand, the teacher's availability and willingness to help must also be stressed. Students should know that they will learn the most by doing as much as they can for as long as they can and that they should not come to the teacher at the first sign of problems. If they have tried to solve a problem at length and have not been able to do so, then they should seek help. Consistent application of these principles, along with attention to progress, will help students to master skills and acquire confidence and healthier self-concepts.

Here is how the situation might be handled appropriately:

STUDENT: I can't do number 4.

TEACHER: What part don't you understand?

STUDENT: I just can't do it.

TEACHER: Well, I know you can do part of it, because you've done the first three problems correctly. The fourth problem is similar but just a little harder. You start out the same, but then you have to do one extra step. Review the first three problems, and then start number four again and see if you can figure it out. I'll come by your desk in a few minutes to see how you're doing.

Compare this with the following inappropriate treatment:

STUDENT: I can't do number 4.

TEACHER: You can't? Why not?

STUDENT: I just can't do it.

TEACHER: Don't say you can't do it—we never say we can't do it. Did you try hard?

STUDENT: Yes, but I can't do it.

TEACHER: Well, you did the first three problems. Maybe if you went back and worked a little longer you could do the fourth problem too. Why don't you work at it a little more and see what happens?

In the first example, the teacher communicated positive expectations and provided help in the form of a specific suggestion about how to proceed. Yet the teacher did not give the answer or do the work. In the second example, the teacher communicated half-hearted and somewhat contradictory expectations and did nothing to move the student out of the impasse he or she had reached.

Teachers must not only provide appropriate seatwork and clear-cut procedures for students to follow when they need help; they must also follow up by providing appropriate help when students request it. All of this support will insure that students will get the most out of their seatwork assignments and, at the same time, will minimize the potential for management problems that originate when students are idle or confused.

## CUEING AND REINFORCING APPROPRIATE BEHAVIOR
Previous sections have discussed how teachers can arrange the classroom to minimize management problems and can establish rules and procedures to ensure that students are clear about what is expected. However, rules will not handle all situations, and teachers need to know how to give on-the-spot instructions when they are needed. Also, regardless of whether a general rule or a specific instruction is involved, teachers should clearly specify and reward desirable behavior as a means of ensuring that students know what to do and are motivated to do it.

### Stress Positive, Desirable Behavior
Like everyone else, students find learning easier and more pleasant when someone is showing them what *to* do rather than what *not to* do. This is why most lessons begin with a demonstration for students to watch and imitate. Teachers would not think of teaching addition by naming all the sums that 2 + 2 do not equal. In general, learning a skill or concept directly is easier than learning it by trial and error.

Teachers usually are aware of the value of the positive approach when teaching school subjects, but they (and everyone else) often forget it when dealing with behavior. The result is a string of "don'ts," with emphasis on what students should not be doing. Such an attitude is not helpful to students, and it may create anxiety or resentment against the teacher. Therefore, teachers must train themselves to give behavioral prescriptions in positive terms, as in the following examples.

| POSITIVE LANGUAGE | NEGATIVE LANGUAGE |
| --- | --- |
| Close the door quietly. | Don't slam the door. |
| Try to work these out on your own without help. | Don't cheat by copying your neighbor. |
| Quiet down—you're getting too loud. | Don't make so much noise. |

| | |
|---|---|
| Sharpen your pencil like this (demonstrate). | That's not how you use a pencil sharpener. |
| Carry your chair like this (demonstrate). | Don't made so much noise with your chair. |
| Sit up straight. | Don't slouch in your chair. |
| Raise your hand if you think you know the answer. | Don't yell out the answer. |
| When you finish, put the scissors in the box and bits of paper in the wastebasket. | Don't leave a mess. |
| These crayons are for you to share—use one color at a time and then put it back so others can use it too. | Stop fighting over those crayons. |
| Use your own ideas. When you do borrow ideas from another author, be sure to acknowledge them. Even here, try to put them in your own words. | Don't plagiarize. |
| Speak naturally, as you would when talking to a friend. | Don't just read your report to us. |
| Note the caution statements in the instructions. Be sure you check the things mentioned there before proceeding to the next step. | Take time when doing this experiment, or you'll mess it up. |
| Be ready to explain your answer—why you think it is correct. | Don't just guess. |

Sometimes negative statements are appropriate, as when a student is doing something that must be stopped immediately (fighting, causing a major disruption). Even here, however, negative remarks should be followed with positive statements telling the student what he should be doing instead. Teachers should phrase instructions in positive, specific language that clearly indicates the desired behavior.

### Recognize and Reinforce Desired Behavior

Books and other sources of advice for teachers almost always stress praise and positive reinforcement. We will too, but only with several important qualifications. We think that praise can be valuable under certain circumstances, but if used indiscriminately or inappropriately, it will do more harm than good.

Given the almost universal stress on the importance and desirability of teacher praise, one might expect to find a great deal of support for it in the research literature. The literature suggests that praise is desirable only under some circumstances, however, and that it is not very important in any case. A theoretical basis for praise comes from the long and rich tradition of behavioristic psychology and its more modern form, behavior modification. Psychologists in this tradition have always stressed the importance of reinforcement as basic to providing both motivation and guidance to learners. Responses which are reinforced are more likely to be learned and repeated, and responses which are not reinforced are likely to be forgotten or extinguished. Praise is considered to be a form of reinforcement, so that it follows that teachers should praise students as a way to reinforce them when they act in desirable ways. All of this is quite sound in theory, but it does not hold up well in practice.

One problem is that humans are much more complex than lower animals, so that they do not always follow the "laws" of reinforcement as expected. For one thing, our thinking and speaking abilities enable us to learn through communication and modeling, so that we are not so dependent upon reinforcement. Also, we respond to a great many motives in addition to, and sometimes instead of, the desire to be reinforced (self-actualization, cognitive consistency, curiosity). Even when reinforcement is the primary motive, reinforcement from sources other than the teacher may be more important than anything the teacher does (acceptance by peers, for example). To the extent that other motives are operating, reinforcement from the teacher may be unnecessary or unimportant. In fact, some theorists have concluded that humans are sufficiently different from lower animals that reinforcement is actually inadvisable (Montessori, 1964; Moore and Anderson, 1969; Piaget, 1952). These writers suggest that teachers should capitalize and build upon intrinsic motivation for learning, without attempting to supplement it through extrinsic reinforcement, including praise.

Several studies conducted in a variety of settings in recent years have supported this point of view. It appears to be true that, for people of all ages and for a variety of settings and activities, if you begin to introduce extrinsic reinforcement for performing something that people are already doing, their intrinsic motivation to continue doing it will decrease (Deci, 1975; Lepper and Greene, 1975; Condry, 1975). Thus, praise not only is unnecessary; it seems to be self-defeating as a way to encourage students to continue with things they are already doing.

On the other hand, praise and reinforcement probably are important in establishing new behaviors. Reinforcement theory assumes that everything that people do is done for some kind of reinforcement, so that if they are not doing something, it must be because it is not being reinforced and possibly because something else is being reinforced instead (Bandura, 1969). Where this is the case, performing a functional analysis of the kind described in the next chapter and following up by changing the reinforcement contingencies so that the desired behavior is elicited and reinforced and competing behaviors are not reinforced is likely to produce good results. Thus, reinforcement, including praise, does have its uses. This difference between establishing a new behavior and maintaining an existing one is just part of a larger principle: there are individual differences in motivational systems, and the success of a given motivational effort will depend upon how well it fits the needs of an individual's system. One way to look at this is to hypothesize that, for a given person and a given situation, certain motives are relevant and others are not (Eden, 1975). In the case of the classroom, if the teacher is successful in linking performance of desired behavior to delivery of some *relevant* motivational consequence, the result is likely to be an *increase* in motivation to perform the desired behavior. On the other hand, if performance of the desired behavior results in some *irrelevant* motivational outcome, there is likely to be a small but real *decrease* in overall motivation to continue the behavior. If you think about this for a few moments, you should see why well-intended motivational efforts actually interfere rather than help if they are based on the assumption that students are responding to a particular motivational system when in fact they are not.

Besides reinforcement theory, stress on the importance of praise comes from writers interested in humanizing education. Typically, praise is contrasted with criticism. Within this argument (that is, considering only praise and criticism and not other alternatives that involve neither one), praise and an emphasis on the positive are preferable to criticism and an emphasis on the negative. The data on criticism are clear and consistent: teachers who often criticize misbehavior usually have greater difficulty in controlling their classrooms, as well as minimal success in fostering student learning (Brophy and Evertson, 1976; Dunkin and Biddle, 1974; Rosenshine,

1976). The story is different with praise. The frequency of teacher praise, especially praise for desirable behavior (as opposed to praise for good work), usually does not correlate at all with student outcome. When it does, it often correlates negatively. There are several probable reasons for this in addition to teachers' praise not fitting students' motivational systems. For one thing, teacher praise and criticism often function not so much as reinforcers but as indicators of teacher expectations and attitudes. Several studies have indicated that teachers inappropriately praise students for whom they have low expectations, or whom they dislike (Amato, 1975; Brophy and Good, 1974; Fernandez, Espinosa, and Dornbusch, 1975; Kleinfeld, 1975, Weinstein, 1976). When students have not performed well, praise (often inappropriate praise) might be a sort of consolation prize given by teachers who feel that they have to encourage their students even if (especially if?) they do not do well. In the case of behavioral praise, except for teachers who are systematically implementing behavior modification principles, such praise in practice may indicate that certain students are troublemakers and that the teacher feels uncomfortable in dealing with them.

The point here is that the kind of praise seen in a typical classroom usually does not function as reinforcement for desirable behavior. With some students, this may be because praise from the teacher is not a relevant or desirable outcome, so that teachers cannot use praise to reinforce such students no matter how successful they are in praising appropriately. With other students, the problem seems to be the nature of praise rather than its potential reinforcement value. That is, teachers' use of praise may not be systematic enough to allow it to function effectively as reinforcement.

Students will strive for attention and praise from teachers they respect. However, most teachers are quicker to criticize misbehavior than to praise desirable behavior. Also, much of the praise that is given is praise for isolated answers or relatively unimportant behavior ("Jack has his hands folded and is ready to line up."). Praise for extended effort and careful work is not nearly as frequent as it should be, and much praise is too general or vague. Student behavior can be shaped by teachers who make praise contingent upon showing desirable behavior, but only if they praise often enough and praise appropriately.

Failure to praise often enough will cause trouble with the students who most need approval and attention. When they are not getting enough of this from ordinary participation in activities, such students will develop other ways to get attention. For example, they may discover that they can get strong teacher responses by whistling, going to the pencil sharpener, tossing paper wads into the waste-basket, falling out of their seats, or using other attention-getting mechanisms. For these students, even the negative attention they get through such mechanisms is better than none at all. Also, their behavior often leads to rewards eventually. Teachers frequently follow up by coming to these students to talk with them privately about their behavior or to encourage them to get involved in work. This may lead to praise or expressions of warmth or concern. This may even be conscious on the part of teachers, if they recognize that such students need special attention. However, the effect is to reward such students for misbehaving. Instead of focusing on attention-getting behavior when it appears, teachers should ignore it. If it is too disruptive to be ignored, they should respond in ways that minimize attention to the behavior itself and instead lead the student back to the lesson or to productive work (see next chapter). Meanwhile, teachers can reduce the needs of such students to seek attention through misbehavior by paying closer attention to them when they are behaving desirably and praising this behavior in a positive way. Praise is especially important for discouraged or alienated students with poor self-concepts who may think that they are not capable of pleasing the teacher through desirable behavior.

In addition to praising frequently enough, teachers need to praise appropriately. Some guidelines for praising appropriately follow.

1. Praise should be simple and direct. It should be delivered in a natural voice, without gushing or overdramatizing. Even very young students will see theatrics as insincere and phony.
2. Praise is usually more effective if it is given in straightforward declarative sentences, "That's very good, I never thought of that before," instead of gushy exclamations, "Wow!" or rhetorical questions, "Isn't that wonderful!" The latter are condescending and more likely to embarrass than reward.
3. The particular behavior or accomplishment being praised should be specified. Any noteworthy effort, care, or perseverance should be recognized, "Good! You figured it out all by yourself. I like the way you stuck with it without giving up," instead of "Yes! That's right." Call attention to new skills, both to praise the student and to reinforce the value of the skill: "I notice you've learned to use different kinds of sentences in compositions. They're more interesting to read now. Keep up the good work."

4. Teachers should use a variety of phrases when praising students. Stock phrases that are overused soon become meaningless. They begin to sound insincere and give the impression that the teacher has not really paid much attention to the students.

5. Verbal praise should be backed with nonverbal communication of approval. "That's good" is not very rewarding when said with a deadpan expression, a flat tone of voice, and an air of distraction or apathy. The same phrase is much more effective when delivered with a smile, a tone communicating appreciation or warmth, or gestures such as a pat on the back. Statements like "You were really good today" are ambiguous. Students may take them as praise for compliance rather than for learning. Instead, teachers should praise in a way that specifically rewards learning effort: "I'm very pleased with the way you read this morning, especially the way you pronounced the initial consonants, and you read with so much expression. You made the conversation between Karen and Mr. Taylor sound very real. Keep up the good work."

6. Ordinarily, individual students should be praised privately. Public praise in front of the group or the whole class will embarrass some students and even cause problems with the peer group, so that it will function more as punishment than as reward. It is difficult to praise students publicly without sounding like you are holding them up as examples to the rest of the class. Delivering praise during private interactions avoids this problem and also helps show the student that the praise is genuine and not a gimmick used in an attempt to motivate other students.

7. It *is* a good idea to show appreciation for students' accomplishments and help in a public way, but without carrying through to the extent of praising them. Facial expressions and verbal comments that communicate genuine admiration for a student accomplishment or genuine appreciation for help given by a student are likely to be experienced as rewarding and also to reinforce desirable behavior through modeling. Such reactions of admiration or appreciation have more credibility than public praise, which often is perceived, with good reason, as an attempt by the teacher to manipulate the class.

When used systematically and appropriately, teacher attention and praise can help reinforce desired behavior in students. It helps students to know that their efforts and progress are seen and appreciated, especially if delivered in natural, genuine language that includes a description of the specific behavior being praised.

## GETTING AND HOLDING ATTENTION

So far, we have discussed general personal qualities and behavior of teachers that can help establish a good classroom atmosphere and maximize the time and effort students devote to learning. In this section, we will suggest techniques for dealing with everyday problems of minor inattention and disruption caused by boredom, fatigue, distractions, or other situational variables. Techniques for dealing with more serious and recurrent problems are discussed in the next chapter.

Kounin's (1970) research suggests that the most successful way to handle situational inattention and distraction is to prevent it from happening or, if it does occur, to check it before it spreads and becomes more serious. Several techniques for accomplishing this are discussed in this section. These techniques help focus student attention on lessons and, thereby, minimize the disruptions that begin as inattention or distractions. The basic principle involved is for the teacher to behave in ways that make students attend at all times, not merely when he or she is dealing with them individually.

### Focus Attention When Beginning Lessons

Teachers should establish that they expect each student's full attention to lessons at all times, including times when another student is reciting or answering a question. There are several techniques teachers can use for doing this.

First, the teacher should be sure to get students' attention *before* beginning a lesson. Some teachers fail to do this, or even deliberately start the lesson in a loud voice in an attempt to get students to pay attention. This is inconsistent with several ideas that teachers should be trying to promote. Briefly, it connotes rudeness, it places the teacher in the position of talking *at* rather than *to* the students, it reinforces the idea that one gains attention by talking loudly and breaking into conversations, and it causes the teacher to begin lessons without having the entire class set to listen and focus their attention properly.

For these reasons, teachers should never launch into lessons without first having gained full attention. The teacher should have a standard signal that tells the class, "We are now ready to begin the lesson formally." The particulars of this signal will vary according to teacher preferences and perhaps from lesson to lesson. One teacher might prefer, "All right, let's begin," while another might say, "Everyone turn to page 62." Whatever the method, teachers should develop a predictable, standard way of introducing each type of lesson. This will tell students that the transition between activities is over and a new activity is about to begin.

After giving the initial signal, teachers should pause briefly to allow it to take effect. Then, when they have the students' attention, they should begin briskly. Ideally, they should start by describing what is going to be done. This overview will help the class focus their attention and will provide motivation for learning. Teachers should then go right into the first part of the lesson proper.

Teachers should explain their expectations regarding responses to signals early in the school year. In the early grades, this might take the form of a structured lesson, in which the teacher models the signal, explains what students are to do when they hear it, and then has them practice it a few times. Signal responses can be introduced less formally with older students, but it should be clear that when the signal is given, everyone is expected to concentrate fully on the lesson.

The pause between giving the signal and beginning the lesson should be brief, just long enough for students to respond to the signal and to focus their attention. If the pause is too long, some students will begin to lose this sharp focus. The teacher should intervene quickly, therefore, if one or a few students do not respond. If the students are looking at the teacher, he or she should communicate through expression and gesture that they should now follow the instructions and pay attention. If they are not looking, the teacher should call their names. Usually, this will be enough by itself; if not, a brief focusing statement can be added, such as "Look here."

Once into the lesson, teachers should follow the guidelines for dealing with inattention presented later in the chapter. They should know how to keep attention as well as how to get it initially. Several teacher behaviors that help students maintain attention are discussed below.

### Keep Lessons Moving at a Good Pace

Teachers often begin with good attention but lose it by spending too much time on minor points or by causing everyone to wait while students respond individually, while equipment is passed out individually, and so forth. Attention will wander when students are waiting or when something they clearly understand is being re-hashed needlessly. Review lessons are abused in this way by some teachers. When students clearly know the material, the review should be cut short. There is no need to ask the next 35 questions simply because they are in the teacher's manual. If certain students in the group do need further review, it would be better to work with them individually or to form them into a special group rather than to make all the others go through the review too.

### Monitor Attention During Lessons

Throughout the lesson, teachers should regularly scan the class or group they are teaching. Students are much more likely to keep their attention focused on the lesson if they know that the teacher regularly watches everyone (both to see if they are paying attention and to note signs of confusion or difficulty). In contrast, teachers who bury their noses in their manuals, rivet their eyes on the board, or look only at the student who is now reciting or answering the question are asking for trouble.

### Maintaining Accountability

All students should be accountable for paying attention to lessons and for learning all of the material, not just the parts they recite or demonstrate. Several techniques are useful with students whose attention tends to wander. One is to develop variety and unpredicta-bility in asking questions. Students should know that they may be called on at any time, regardless of what has gone on before. Teach-ers should occasionally ask more than one question of a given student and occasionally question students again after they have answered an earlier question. They also should occasionally ask students to repeat answers just given by other students, to state whether or not the answer was correct, or to comment about it ("Paul, do you agree with Ted?").

In the early grades, accountability is not as important as careful monitoring. Until students are old enough to develop strategies for looking good when their turn comes along, while paying minimal attention in between turns, problems facing teachers are not so much accountability as anxiety, confusion, and short attention spans. In fact, Brophy and Evertson (1976) found that teachers who had students read in a particular predictable order (usually, moving sys-tematically around the reading group) got better results than those who called on students to read "randomly." It is not clear why this was so. Possible reasons include reduced anxiety (the predictable pattern provided structure that helped students to follow the lesson and minimized fears of being called on when they were not prepared) and elimination of competition for response opportunities (young students tend to wave their hands and call out in an attempt to get teachers to call on them, but there is no point in doing this when everyone takes a turn according to a preestablished pattern). In any case, it appears that the main problem facing teachers in the early grades is helping students to be *able* to follow lessons, not making sure that they *choose* to follow them. This is accomplished through such techniques as teaching the children in small groups, having them follow with their finger or a marker, monitoring them regularly to see that they have their place, and so on. Here, predictability is probably helpful.

When students develop to the point that they can keep track of the lesson without help from the teacher, and especially when they learn to anticipate by figuring out what they will be held accountable for and trying to practice it ahead of time, teachers will have to be deliberately less predictable. Here, going in order around the class or a subgroup would encourage undesirable habits, so that it becomes important to call on students in less predictable patterns. Notice that we do not say "random" patterns. This is because most investigations of the distribution of recitation opportunities by teachers indicate that presumably "random" patterns are not random at all. Because the brighter, better liked, and more competitive students are more likely to know more answers and also more likely to seek response opportunities, they tend to get called on more often, and some students rarely get called on at all. To make sure that this does not happen, teachers should keep track of who has responded and who has not. It is not necessary or even possible to see that all students get exactly the same number and kinds of response opportunities, but it is a good idea to see that response opportunities are not monopolized by a few students. This can be done by checking or tallying response opportunities in a log book. In fact, by using a simple coding system, teachers can keep track not only of degree of participation, but also of success and failure in handling questions of varying difficulty levels.

Accountability for paying attention and learning the material also can be fostered by putting questions to the class as a whole and allowing time for thinking before calling on a student to respond. Students are likely to think about the question and to try to form their own answers to it if they are given time to do so and if they know that they might be called on to answer it. On the other hand, if the teacher names a student to answer a question before asking it, the rest of the class will know that they are not going to be called on. This may cause some of them to turn their attention elsewhere.

Other potentially undesirable things that students, especially older ones, can learn from observing predictable patterns are: "The teacher only calls on students who raise their hands." "The teacher always begins with someone in the front row." "If I answer one question, I won't be called on again." "If I raise my hand and give the impression that I understand, the teacher won't check me out." "When we have practice examples on the board, the teacher always takes them in the same order that they are in the book."

Predictable teacher behavior of this sort probably will be picked up by students who are searching for ways to "beat the system." This means less attention and, in the long run, less learning.

### Stimulate Attention Periodically

When things become too predictable and repetitive, the mind tends to wander. There are several things teachers can do to help ensure continual attention as a lesson or activity progresses.

The teacher's own variability is one important factor. There is no need for theatrics, but lectures delivered in a dull monotone with a minimum of facial expressions and gestures soon produce yawns. Teachers should speak loudly enough for everyone to hear and should see that the students do too. More importantly, they should modulate their tone and volume to help provide stimulation and break monotony. It also helps to use a variety of techniques, so that the lesson does not settle into an overly repetitive or predictable pattern. Lectures should be mixed with demonstrations, group responses with individual responses, and reading or short factual questions with thought-provoking discussion questions.

Even extended presentations usually can be broken into several parts. By changing voice inflection or by using transitional signals ("All right," "Now," and others), teachers can help stimulate attention by cueing students that they are now moving into a new phase.

In addition to these more subtle techniques, attention can and should be stimulated directly at times. For example, teachers can arouse special attention to a question by challenging the class ("Now here's a really hard question—let's see who can figure it out") or by creating suspense ("Let's see, who will I call on next?"). When the type of question changes, this can be noted in a statement that will call students' attention to the change and at the same time stimulate interest: "All right, let's see if we understood the story."

"All right, you seem to know the theory, now let's see if you can apply it to a practical problem."

Teachers can model careful listening during discussions, and can stimulate it in students by sometimes asking them to show that they have listened to and understood what a classmate has just said before giving their own opinions. In using these techniques to ensure accountability, teachers must be careful to present them in ways that avoid threatening the students. These techniques are to be used for challenging the class, stimulating interest, and avoiding predictability, not for catching inattentive students in order to embarrass or punish them. If misused this way, they will only cause resentment and will not have the desired positive effects.

Techniques for stimulating attention should be used in ways that do not call attention to themselves. Emphasis on the techniques may cause anxiety or resentment, or at least distract attention from the content focus at hand. Usually, it would not be appropriate for a teacher to say, "Remember, I might call on you at any time to tell me what's happening, so pay attention." It would be better just to use this technique without calling attention to it, meanwhile stimulating interest in the topic and communicating expectations for attention in more positive ways as well.

Teachers can help ensure continual attention to lessons and discussions if they move at a brisk pace, monitor all the students, stimulate attention periodically through both subtle and direct techniques, and enforce accountability through variety and unpredictability in questioning patterns.

### Terminate Lessons That Have Gone on Too Long

This is especially important for younger students, whose attention span for even the best lesson is limited. When the group is having difficulty maintaining attention, it is better to end the lesson early than to doggedly continue. When lessons go on after the point where they should have been terminated, more and more of the teacher's time is spent compelling attention, and less of the students' time is spent thinking about and learning the material. Teachers are usually aware of this, but they sometimes pursue a lesson anyway because they do not want to get off schedule.

This attitude is self-defeating. Maintaining the schedule is no victory if it has been won at the cost of raising tensions in the teacher and the class. Also, the material will probably have to be retaught to some extent, since students do not learn efficiently under these conditions. The wise teacher tailors the schedule to the needs of the students.

Teachers sometimes prolong an activity needlessly because they want to give each student a chance to participate individually. This often happens in recitation lessons and in activities such as show-and-tell. While the teacher's purpose in wanting to give everyone a chance is laudable, it is not appropriate for this type of activity. When recitation becomes boringly repetitive or when show-and-tell becomes stilted and predictable, the teacher should move on to something else. Students who didn't get their chances to participate one day can (and should) do so later in the week.

Some teachers deliberately prolong repetitive activities in order to use them as a break or an opportunity to do paperwork. For this reason, show-and-tell sometimes goes on for an hour in certain early elementary classrooms. Similarly, older students are sometimes asked to read aloud from readers or to make repetitive recitations when these activities are not really needed or useful. As a result, the students become bored and restless, and their respect for the teacher can be damaged.

Students know that if activities are really important and teachers are really interested, the teachers will participate actively and pay careful attention to what is happening. If teachers only pay minimal attention while doing paperwork, even very young children will become bored. They know a disinterested baby-sitter when they see one.

### SUMMARY
In this chapter, we have pointed out that the key to successful classroom management is prevention—teachers do not have to deal with misbehavior that never occurs. The chapter goes on to suggest prevention techniques that teachers can use to hold management problems to a minimum.

Many problems originate when students are crowded together, forced to wait, or idle because they have nothing to do or do not know what to do. Crowding can be minimized in several ways. Classroom arrangement and equipment storage should be planned so that traffic is minimized and needed items are accessible. Problems that occur when everyone wants or needs the same item can be reduced by stocking several items rather than just one or by storing in several small containers rather than one large one.

Waiting can be minimized by allowing students to handle most management tasks on their own, by eliminating needless rituals and formalities, by simultaneously assigning different subgroups to do different jobs rather than having the whole class tackle only one job at a time, and by establishing rules where needed.

Confusion and idleness can be minimized by preparing appropriate independent work assignments in sufficient quantity and variety, and by seeing that students know what to do if they finish or if they get stuck and need help.

Good planning and preparation will minimize problems, but this must be complemented by appropriate everyday classroom teaching behavior. In particular, it is important to specify desired behavior in positive terms, to notice and call attention to positive behavior when it appears, and to specifically praise students for producing it.

Good planning and preparation and good motivating strategies provide a solid basis for preventive classroom management. It is then up to the teacher to follow through by using teaching strategies that maximize student attention to lessons and involvement in productive activities. Teachers should establish clear signals to gain students' attention and alert them to the fact that an activity is beginning. Upon gaining attention, they should provide a brief overview or advance organizer to tell students what is coming and help them prepare for it. Then they should keep the activity moving at a brisk pace, avoiding unnecessary delays. If an activity has gone on too long, it should be terminated.

To help hold students accountable for the material and to stimulate their continuing attention, teachers should vary their questioning patterns and avoid falling into repeated, predictable patterns that tempt certain students to try to "beat the system."

Teachers who learn and consistently apply the strategies presented in this chapter will maximize productive student activity and minimize the time students spend "in neutral," or misbehaving. Remember, though, that the classroom management approach presented here is an integrated system. Each aspect is important, and all aspects must occur in combination and mutually reinforce one another to be maximally effective. Attempts to use isolated parts as techniques are unlikely to succeed, especially over a long period.

## SUGGESTED ACTIVITIES AND QUESTIONS

1. Teachers should attend to *positive* student behavior. Why do you feel that many teachers spend too much time reacting to negative behavior, especially of a minor sort?

2. Teachers should make learning enjoyable rather than indirectly or subconsciously teach students that school assignments are done only to get a reward—adult approval, opportunity to play a game, a high grade, and so forth. Teachers sometimes do an excellent job in planning useful and enjoyable learning activities only

to undermine their efforts to foster intrinsic motivation by telling students such things as, "You've done so well today that I am going to give you a free hour after lunch so you can do the things you really want to do." What guidelines should a teacher follow when he or she summarizes learning activities? Apply your ideas by returning to the case study of Mrs. Turner that was presented in Chapter 1. What would be an effective way to end the lesson she presented? Write out your ending in a few sentences and compare it to the endings written by others.

3. Describe in your own words how teachers can praise appropriately. What type of student will be most difficult for *you* to praise? Why?

4. Why is it suggested that teachers show variety and unpredictability in asking questions? Watch a videotape of a teacher conducting a class discussion and determine whether the teacher's questioning style is unpredictable.

5. Think about the grade level you teach or plan to teach and specify the minimum set of rules that will be observed in your room. Be sure to state your rules in positive terms. Are your rules essential for establishing a good learning climate? Why?

6. Describe how you will establish rules in your classroom and what criteria you will use for adding or deleting them as the year progresses.

**FORM 6.1.** Transitions and Group Management

*USE: During organizational and transition periods before, between, and after lessons and organized activities*
*PURPOSE: To see if teacher manages these periods efficiently and avoids needless delays and regimentation*
*How does the teacher handle early morning routines, transitions between activities, and clean-up and preparation time?*

*Record any information relevant to the following questions:*

1. Does the teacher do things that students could do for themselves?

2. Are there delays caused because everyone must line up or wait his turn? Can these be reduced with a more efficient procedure?

3. Does the teacher give clear instructions about what to do next before breaking a group and entering a transition? *Students often aren't clear about assignment so they question her during transitions and while she is starting to teach next group.*

4. Does the teacher circulate during transitions, to handle individual needs? Does he take care of these before attempting to begin a new activity? *Mostly, problem is poor directions before transition, rather than failure to circulate here.*

5. Does the teacher signal the end of a transition and the beginning of a structured activity properly, and quickly gain everyone's attention? *Good signal but sometimes loses attention by failing to start briskly. Sometimes has 2 or 3 false starts.*

*Check if applicable:*

_____ 1. Transitions come too abruptly for students because teacher fails to give advance warning or finish up reminders when needed

_____ 2. The teacher insists on unnecessary rituals or formalisms that cause delays or disruptions (describe)

___✓___ 3. Teacher is often interrupted by individuals with the same problem or request; this could be handled by establishing a general rule or procedure (describe) *See # 3 above.*

___✓___ 4. Delays occur because frequently used materials are stored in hard to reach places *Pencil sharpener too close to reading group area, causing frequent distractions.*

_____ 5. Poor traffic patterns result in pushing, bumping, or needless noise

_____ 6. Poor seating patterns screen some students from teacher's view or cause students needless distraction

_____ 7. Delays occur while teacher prepares equipment or illustrations that should have been prepared earlier

**FORM 6.2.** Poor Attention to Lessons

*USE: When teacher is having difficulty keeping students attentive to a lesson*
*PURPOSE: To identify the probable cause of the poor attention*
*        When students are notably inattentive to a lesson or activity, what is*
*the apparent reason? (Check any that apply)*

_____ 1. Activity has gone on too long
_____ 2. Activity is below students' level or is needless review
_____ 3. Teacher is continually lecturing, not getting enough student
             participation
   ✓    4. Teacher fails to monitor attention—poor eye contact
   ✓    5. Teacher overdwells, needlessly repeating and rephrasing
_____ 6. Teacher calls on students in an easily predictable pattern
_____ 7. Teacher always names student before asking question
   ✓    8. Activity lacks continuity because teacher keeps interrupting
             (specify cause for interruption)
_____ 9. Activity lacks variety, has settled into an overly predictable or
             boring routine
_____ 10. Other (indicate)

Frequent delays while teacher finds place in manual.
This is also main reason for poor eye contact. #5 often
asks teacher for attention (and gets it) but then instead
of teaching the teacher elaborates for 30 - 40 seconds on
why the students should listen and when he ends the
sermon and begins the lesson several students have
"drifted" away.

# 7/
# MANAGEMENT II: COPING WITH PROBLEMS EFFECTIVELY

Consistent use of the techniques discussed in the previous chapter will hold inattention and misbehavior problems to a minimum, especially if discussions, seatwork, and other activities are enjoyable and appropriate to students' needs and interests. Some problems will still occur, however, and the teacher must be prepared to cope with them effectively. The present chapter contains suggestions on how teachers can train themselves to observe such problems when they occur, to diagnose their causes accurately, and to respond with appropriate action.

## DEALING WITH MINOR INATTENTION AND MISBEHAVIOR
This section explains how teachers can respond to minor inattention in ways that will check it before it becomes serious or begins to spread. (More serious misbehavior problems will be discussed later.) Techniques for dealing with minor inattention, distraction, or misbehavior all help the teacher achieve a single goal: *eliminate the problem as quickly as possible and with as little distraction of other students as possible.* The techniques should be used whenever this goal applies to the situation. In situations where this goal is not appropriate—for example, where misbehavior problems are serious or need some investigation and decision making—a different sort of response is required. These more difficult behavior problems will be discussed in subsequent sections. The suggestions in this section

apply to the following situation: one or more students are engaged in minor mischief, and the teacher wants to eliminate this behavior and return their attention to work as quickly as possible. The following teacher behavior will help to do this.

### Monitor the Entire Classroom Regularly

Kounin (1970) stressed monitoring as an important ability in successful classroom managers. He noted that these teachers showed "withitness"—their students knew that they always "knew what was going on" in their classrooms. When teachers regularly scan their classrooms to keep an eye on what's going on, they are able to nip potential problems in the bud. Also, they are in a better position to respond appropriately to problems. If they fail to notice what's going on, however, they are prone to make such errors as failing to intervene until a problem becomes disruptive or spreads to other students, attending to a minor problem while failing to notice a more serious one, or rebuking a student who was drawn into a dispute instead of the one who was responsible for starting it.

If teachers make such errors regularly, they will convince their students that they do not know what is happening. This will make the students more likely to misbehave and to test the teacher by talking back or trying to confuse him or her. Thus, it is important for teachers to scan their classrooms regularly, even while conducting small group lessons.

Seating patterns should be arranged so that this is possible. The teacher should always be able to see all of the students. For reading groups and other small group activities, the teacher should be facing the bulk of the class, who are involved in seatwork. The students in the small lesson group should be seated facing the teacher, with their backs to the rest of the class. This way, the teacher can monitor the whole class, and distractions to students in the group will be minimized.

When teachers are writing on the board or at their desks, or when they are talking with individual students, they should look up and scan the class frequently. Many conflicts between students begin when one student "starts something" while the teacher's back is turned.

It is not enough to simply communicate positive expectations about attention and work involvement and to provide meaningful activities; teachers must *show* students that they are alert and aware of what is going on in the room. To do this, teachers must monitor the classroom continually.

### Ignore Minor Misbehavior

It is not advisable for teachers to intervene every time they notice a problem. Often, the disruptive effect of the teacher's intervention will be greater than that of the problem being dealt with. When this is true, it is more appropriate for the teacher to delay action or to simply ignore the problem.

For example, a teacher may notice that a student has dropped a pencil or has neglected to replace some equipment that should have been put away. Such incidents will sometimes require action, but they rarely require *immediate* action. The teacher should wait until he or she can deal with them without disruption. Stopping a lesson or group activity to tell a student to pick up a pencil or put away a book will only cause more problems.

Much minor behavior can be ignored, especially when it is of the hit-and-run variety. For example, if the group is distracted because someone accidentally drops a book, or if two students briefly whisper to each other and then return their attention to the lesson, it is usually best to take no action at all. Intervention is not needed, because the students' attention is now back on the lesson. There is nothing to be gained by disrupting the lesson to call attention to minor misbehavior that is already completed. Even if the whispering were to resume, the teacher usually is still better off to avoid disruptive intervention. Instead, one of the techniques described in the following section would be preferable. The teacher's simplest and best response is to ignore minor management problems and fleeting instances of inattention that occur during activities.

### Stop Minor Misbehavior and Inattention Without Disrupting the Activity

When minor misbehavior is repeated or intensified, or when it threatens to spread or become disruptive, the teacher cannot simply ignore it; he or she will need to take action to stop it. Unless the misbehavior is serious enough to call for investigation (and it seldom is), it should be dealt with in a way that eliminates it as quickly and as nondisruptively as possible. There are several techniques teachers can use to quickly eliminate minor misbehavior. These techniques should be used in preference to more disruptive ones when the goal is simply to return inattentive students to work involvement and avoid distracting other students.

1. *Eye contact.* If eye contact can be established, it usually is enough by itself to return attention to the task at hand. To make sure the message is received, the teacher may

want to add a head nod or other gesture such as looking at the book the student is supposed to be reading.

Eye contact becomes doubly effective for stopping minor problems when the teacher regularly scans the room. Because students will know that he or she regularly scans the room, they will tend to look at the teacher when they are misbehaving (to see if they are being watched). This makes it easier for the teacher to intervene through eye contact. Teachers who do not scan the room properly will have difficulty using eye contact in these situations, because they usually will have to wait longer before students look at them.

2. *Touch and gesture.* When the students are close by, the teacher does not need to wait until eye contact can be established. Instead, he or she can use a simple touch or gesture to get their attention. This is especially effective in small group situations. A light tap, perhaps following with a gesture toward the book, will get the message across without any need for verbalization.

   Gestures and physical signals are also helpful in dealing with events going on in different parts of the room. If eye contact can be established, the teacher may be able to communicate messages by shaking the head, placing a finger to the lips, or pointing. These gestures should be used when possible, because they are less disruptive than leaving the group or speaking to students across the room. In general, touch and gesture are most useful in the early grades, where much teaching is done in small groups and where distraction is a frequent problem. Touching would be unwise with some adolescents who resent any attempt by a teacher to touch them.

3. *Physical closeness.* When the teacher is checking seatwork or moving about the room, he or she can often eliminate minor behavior problems simply by moving close to the students involved. If the students know what they are supposed to be doing, the physical presence of the teacher will motivate them to get busy. This technique is especially useful with older elementary students.

4. *Asking for responses.* During lessons or group activities, the simplest method of returning students' attention may be to ask them a question or call for a response. This request automatically compels attention, and it does so without mentioning the misbehavior.

This technique should be used with care, however, because it can backfire. If used too often, it may be perceived by students as an attempt to "catch" them. Also, the questions asked in these situations must be ones that students can answer or at least can make reasonable responses to. If students cannot meaningfully respond to the question because they were not paying attention to the previous one, the question should not be asked. This would only embarrass the students and force them to admit that they were not paying attention (thereby violating an important principle by focusing on the misbehavior instead of the lesson) or, if they dare, to respond with sarcastic or aggressive remarks.

Although it might be appropriate to ask a clearly inattentive student, "Joan, Tom says that the villain in the story was motivated by jealousy—what do you think?" It would not be appropriate to ask, "Joan, what did Tom just say?" Acceptable alternatives would be to move toward the student, to call the student's name and gesture, or to ask a question that the student can respond to even if he or she has not heard the previous one.

These are several techniques that enable teachers to eliminate minor problems without disrupting the activity or calling attention to the misbehavior. Eye contact, touch and gesture, and physical closeness require no verbalization and are especially effective with younger elementary students. Calling on the student to answer a question or make a response will be effective if not done too often and if the response required is reasonable.

## DEALING WITH PROLONGED OR DISRUPTIVE MISBEHAVIOR
So far, we have presented techniques for preventing inattention and dealing with minor misbehavior. Consistent application of these techniques will hold behavior problems to a minimum. However, what should teachers do when these techniques have not worked, or when the behavior is too serious to be dealt with without direct intervention? Suggestions for dealing with these more serious matters are presented in this section.

### Stopping Misbehavior Through Direct Intervention
When misbehavior is dangerous or seriously disruptive, the teacher will have to stop it directly by calling out the name of the student

involved and correcting him or her. Because such direct intervention is itself disruptive, it should be done only when necessary.

Like the techniques described in the previous section, *direct intervention should be used only when no information is needed.* Situations where no information is needed are those in which both the teacher and the students involved are very clear about what the students are supposed to be doing at the time. In addition, the particular misbehavior should be transparently obvious to the teacher. This would include such behavior as laughing and talking with a neighbor, shooting wads of paper or rubber bands, and copying a neighbor's work. In situations like these, where it is obvious that the student has become distracted from a well-defined task, the teacher does not need any special information to be able to act. He or she only needs to stop the misbehavior and return the student to the task.

In more ambiguous situations, where the student cannot reasonably be expected to know what he or she is supposed to be doing, or in situations where the teacher is not sure what is going on (e.g., if two students are talking, they may or may not be discussing the problem as directed), the teacher may need to get more information and make some decisions before intervening with direct instructions.

There are two basic ways for teachers to intervene directly. First, they can demand appropriate behavior. Intervention should be short, direct, and to the point. It should name the students and indicate what they should be doing. The teacher should speak firmly and loud enough to be heard but should not shout or nag. Commands such as "John! Get back to your seat and get to work" and "Mary and Laura! Stop talking and pay attention to me" are not appropriate when the students know that they are misbehaving; in those circumstances, it is not necessary to label the misbehavior or call attention to it. Instead, a brief direction telling them what to do will be sufficient: "John, finish your work" and "Mary and Laura, look here."

A second direct intervention technique is to remind students of rules and expectations. If clear-cut rules were established early in the year, after careful explanation or thorough discussion of the reasons for them, the teacher can then use brief reminders of these rules to prevent control problems or to stop them when they occur. Quick rule reminders can serve these purposes without causing teachers to sermonize excessively or to point out or embarrass individual students.

As with other forms of direct intervention, rule reminders should be brief and firm. In some ways, they are preferable to demanding appropriate behavior, because they help students internalize behavioral control. When students are clear about the rules and the reasons for them, rule reminders help the students see their own responsibility for misbehavior and help keep down conflict.

Rule reminders are often the best way to handle misbehavior, especially loudness and disruption, during independent work periods. When the class has become noisy, rather than attempt to name the offenders, it may be simplest for the teacher to say, "Class, you're getting too loud. Remember to speak softly and not disturb the reading group," or "Frank, if you have finished your assignment, you can work on vowel sounds at the listening post, but don't bother Kathy. Remember, we don't disturb people who are busy working."

Situations in which students know what to do but are not doing it because they are engaged in *disruptive* misbehavior call for intervention. Such intervention should be brief and direct, and it should stress appropriate behavior rather than misbehavior. Sometimes this can be done through a simple rule reminder; at other times, the teacher will have to indicate appropriate behavior in more specific detail.

### Inappropriate Intervention

We have presented suggestions for intervening directly to stop disruptive misbehavior that was easily interpretable. These suggestions concern what teachers *should* do. We will now consider what teachers *should not* do in these same situations.

First, the teacher should not ask questions in these situations. There is no need for questions; the situation is clear. The teacher's goal is simply to return the misbehaving students to productive work; there is no need to conduct an investigation. More importantly, the kinds of questions asked in such situations usually are not real questions but rhetorical questions. The essential meaninglessness of these questions, and the tone in which they are asked, show that they are not questions at all. Instead, they are attacks on the student: "What's the matter with you?" "Why haven't you finished the work?" "How many times do I have to tell you to get busy?" Such questions do no good and may cause embarrassment, fear, or resentment.

Teachers should also avoid threats and appeals to authority when stopping misbehavior through direct intervention. By simply stating how they want the student to behave, teachers communicate the expectation that they will be obeyed. If they add a threat ("Do it or else . . ."), however, they create conflict with the student and suggest indirectly that they are not sure the student is going to obey.

If a student should ask why the teacher is demanding a certain behavior, the teacher should give the reason. If the teacher should become defensive and appeal to authority ("You'll do it because I say so"), he or she will produce only anger and resentment. This constitutes a direct challenge to the student and may cause the student to lose face before peers, so that it may even result in an explosion against the teacher. Furthermore, if classmates feel that the teacher is treating the student unfairly, the teacher's relationships with other members of the class will suffer.

A third problem that teachers must avoid when stopping misbehavior through direct intervention is dwelling too much upon the misbehavior itself, commonly called nagging. In a direct intervention situation, there is no need or reason to describe misbehavior in detail or catalogue student misbehavior during the last week, month, or year.

Here again, this constitutes an attack on the student rather than a corrective measure. It places the teacher in conflict with the student, and it can endanger credibility and respect. If a teacher does this regularly, students may come to see it as funny. Some may even begin to disobey deliberately, just to see if they can trigger a new or more spectacular response from the teacher.

Difficulties with nagging often appear when teachers forget that they should stress the positive. These teachers get into ruts in which they regularly describe misbehavior instead of changing it. In effect, the teacher may be telling students that he or she has given up hope of change, "John, every day I have to speak to you for fooling around instead of doing your seatwork. It's the same story again today. How many times do I have to tell you? You never learn!" Given this teacher behavior, chances are that it will be the same story tomorrow and the day after. John probably will continue in this fashion unless the teacher realizes that his or her role is to change John's misbehavior and reinforce his appropriate behavior, not merely to describe his misbehavior and berate him for it.

Instead of merely nagging John, the teacher should try to isolate the cause of his misbehavior and to develop a solution. Perhaps the seatwork is too easy, too difficult, or otherwise inappropriate for John. Or John may have developed a "fooling around" relationship with a classmate, so that a conference, and possibly a new seating arrangement, is required. In any case, rather than let the situation continue, the teacher should discuss it with John, come to an agreement with him about the future, and follow through with appropriate treatment (these matters are discussed in detail in the following sections).

There are three kinds of behavior, then, that teachers should avoid when dealing with disruptive misbehavior that is easily interpretable: unnecessary and meaningless questioning, use of threats and arbitrary exertion of authority, and dwelling too much on the misbehavior (nagging). These reactions do no good, and they may cause needless anger, anxiety, or resentment.

## CONDUCTING INVESTIGATIONS

The previous section cautioned against questioning students when no information is needed. This section deals with those situations which are not clear enough for a teacher to act without getting additional information. Here, the teacher will need to question one or more students, and it is important that he or she do so appropriately. Unfortunately, many teachers (and other adults) question children and adolescents in ways that fail to get the information or produce negative side effects.

Questions should be genuine attempts to get information, not rhetorical questions of the type described in the preceding section. They should be direct and to the point and should concern matters of *fact* that students can answer. Questions about students' *intentions* should not be asked unless the teacher seriously needs this information: "Why did you leave the room?" "Why haven't you turned in your homework?" Some questions about intentions help establish what the student was doing and why. However, pseudoquestions about intentions should be avoided. Students should not be berated with rhetorical questions, "Did you think you could get away with it?" or confused with questions about intentions that they cannot answer, "Why didn't you remember to be more careful?"

When questioning students to establish the facts in a dispute, the best policy usually is to talk to each one privately and to confine the discussion to the students directly involved. This avoids putting individuals on the spot in front of the group, thereby minimizing needs to save face with lies or confrontations. If more than one student is in on the discussion, the teacher should question each one individually and insist that the others be quiet. If the teacher allowed others to jump in or addressed a question to the group, students would be likely to argue over who did what first to whom.

When discrepancies in stories appear or when one student appears to be lying, the teacher needs to guard against making snap judgments or accusations. He or she should point out the discrepancies, and perhaps indicate that certain statements are hard to believe. This must be done in a way that avoids rejecting anyone's statement out of hand and that leaves the door open for someone to change his or her story.

Teachers should make it clear that they want and expect students to tell the truth. Students will be motivated to do so if a teacher's words are backed with appropriate and credible actions that reveal the teacher as someone who wants the best for all concerned, not as an authority figure who is going to assess guilt. There must be no reward for lying and no punishment for telling the truth.

The facts need not always be established in clear detail. If the goal is to promote long-run development of integrity and self-control, not merely to "settle" an individual incident, it may be desirable to leave contradictions unresolved or to accept a lie or exaggeration without labeling it as such. This is especially true when the teacher is pretty certain that a student is not telling the truth but is unable to prove it.

Even if students are guilty, they will resent the teacher telling them they are lying. They will conclude that the teacher is picking on them or, perhaps, that the teacher has such a low opinion of them that they are expected to lie. In these situations, the teacher should remind students that he or she tries to treat them fairly and honestly and expects them to reciprocate; state that he or she "just doesn't know what to think," in view of the discrepancies and contradictions; state that there is no point in further discussion without new information; restate behavioral expectations and give them specific instructions. This will be most successful in achieving long-run goals. It avoids accusations and punishment, and it increases the probability that students who lied will recognize and regret their lies.

When a problem is serious and when the teacher is unclear about the facts, an investigation will be needed. This must be handled carefully because of the danger of putting students "on the spot" and setting off serious "face-saving" gestures. It is usually best to conduct investigations away from the rest of the class. The teacher should hear out all students involved but insist on questioning and getting information from only one at a time. Questions should elicit relevant facts and (sometimes) intentions and motivations. Students should not be browbeaten with rhetorical or confusing questions that express the teacher's frustration rather than seek information.

Sometimes, investigations will not yield a clear picture because someone has withheld or distorted information. It may be best to leave the matter unresolved rather than to expose the guilty party. This will add to the guilty student's shame and deny him or her the opportunity to feel picked on, so that the student will be more likely to change behavior.

Once the teacher has finished the investigation, he or she should resolve the issue. Usually, this will require only a rule reminder, although it may require some special action or new agreement. Resolution of the problem usually should *not* require punishment, although this will sometimes be necessary. The question of when to use punishment is taken up in the following section, along with suggestions about how to punish effectively.

## EFFECTIVE PUNISHMENT

Punishment can be useful to help a student control misbehavior, but only in some situations and only in combination with other techniques. Teachers who rely heavily on punishment (instead of using the management techniques described) cannot succeed, except in the most narrow and temporary sense. At best, they will be like the teacher described in the previous chapter who "runs a tight ship." They may achieve a grudging compliance, but only at the cost of high group tension and frustration and of being continually in conflict with their students. The class will obey them out of fear when they are present but will be out of control when they are not in the room.

Punishment can do more harm than good, especially if overused. Nevertheless, teachers should not hesitate to use it when circumstances call for it. To use it properly, however, teachers should know when to use it, what sorts of punishment to use, and how to apply it.

### When to Punish

As a general rule, punishment is appropriate only in dealing with *repeated* misbehavior. It is a treatment of last resort, to be used when students persist in the same kinds of misbehavior despite continued expressions of concern and explanations of the reasons for rules. It is a way of exerting control over students who are unable to control themselves.

Resorting to punishment is not a step that a teacher should take lightly. It signifies that neither the teacher nor the student can cope with the problem. It is an expression of lack of confidence in the student, telling the student that the teacher thinks that he or she is not trying to improve or, perhaps, that the misbehavior is deliberate. This can be damaging to the student's self-concept, as well as to the chances of solving the problem.

This is why punishment is inappropriate for dealing with isolated incidents, no matter how severe. In a single occurrence of misbehavior, there is no reason to believe that the student acted deliberately or, at least, that he or she will repeat it again in the future. Also, even with repeated misbehavior, punishment should be avoided when the student appears to be trying to improve. Here, teachers should give students the benefit of the doubt by assuming their good will in trying to improve and by expressing confidence in their ability to do so. Punishment should be used only as a last resort, when a student has repeatedly failed to respond to more positive treatment.

### What Punishment Does

The effects of punishment are limited and specific. Teachers need to know what it does and does not do, if they are to use it properly and avoid deluding themselves about its effectiveness. A great body of evidence (reviewed in Bandura, 1969) shows that punishment is useful only for controlling misbehavior, not for teaching desired behavior. Furthermore, punishment affects the expression of behavior but not the desire or need for that expression. *Punishment can reduce or control misbehavior, but by itself it will not teach desirable behavior or even reduce the desire to misbehave.* Thus, punishment is never a solution by itself; at best, it is only part of a solution. It will temporarily stop misbehavior, however, so it is appropriate when misbehavior is repeated and serious enough to require its use.

### Using Punishment for the Right Reasons

Punishment should be used consciously and deliberately, as part of the teacher's treatment of repeated misbehavior. Even though it is a last resort, it should not be used unthinkingly, as a way of getting even with a student, or as a way of "teaching the student a lesson." Students learn a great deal from hostile or vindictive punishment, but not the lesson that the teacher intends. When attacked personally, they respond, like everyone else, with anger, resentment, and a desire to strike back. Needless to say, this will not help solve the problem.

Even an uninvolved observer can tell when a teacher is using punishment to deal with his or her own frustrations or anger rather than as a deliberate control technique. This kind of punishment is usually accompanied by statements or thoughts like "We'll fix your wagon" or "We'll see who's boss." Statements like these do not indicate use of punishment as a technique; they are emotional outbursts indicating poor self-control and emotional immaturity.

### Types of Punishment

Different types of punishment are not all equally appropriate. Behavior restrictions, limitation of privileges, and exclusion from the group are recommended. Severe personal criticism, physical punishment, and assignment of extra work are not.

*Personal attacks on the student are never appropriate.* Severe personal criticism is not punishment and it cannot be justified on the grounds that the student needs it. It has no corrective or control function. It will only cause resentment, both in the victim and in the rest of the class.

Physical punishment can be useful and appropriate, especially for infants. We do not recommend its use in schools, however, for several reasons. First, it is difficult to administer objectively and unemotionally. By its very nature, it places the teacher in a position of attacking students, physically if not personally. This could cause physical injury, and in any case it will undermine the teacher's chances of dealing with the student effectively in the future. Second, physical punishment is usually over quickly, and it has an air of finality about it. Because of its intensity, attention is focused on the punishment itself rather than on the misbehavior that led to it. Third, because attention is shifted away from the misbehavior, physical punishment usually fails to induce guilt or personal responsibility for the misbehavior in the offender. He or she is much more likely to be sorry for having gotten caught than for having misbehaved. Fourth, physical punishment is only temporarily effective at best. Students who misbehave most insistently and defiantly usually come from homes where their parents beat them regularly as a form of discipline. Criminals convicted of assault and other violent crimes almost always show home backgrounds in which physical punishment was common. In general, physical punishment teaches people to attack others when angry. It does not teach them appropriate behavior, and change in behavior is what is desired in the long run.

Some teachers punish by assigning extra work. We do not recommend assigning extra school work as punishment because of what this may do to students' attitudes toward school work. Both teachers and students should see work assignments as opportunities for students to practice the skills they are learning. When work assignments are used as punishments, students are more likely to see school work as drudgery.

What about writing assignments that do not pertain to school work, such as copying behavioral rules or writing compositions about them? These assignments may or may not be effective punishment, depending on how they are handled. At first glance, writing out "I must not talk in class" a specified number of times might seem to be a good way to call a student's attention to the rule. However, this method calls attention more to the punishment than to the rule. Unless the student must write out the rule only a few times (five or ten), he or she is likely to resent this form of punishment or think it is funny.

In some circumstances, it may be effective to ask students to write compositions about how they should behave. This will force them to think about the rationales underlying rules, rather than to just copy the rules in rote fashion. If this form of punishment is used, the teacher should discuss the composition with the students. The punishment itself is only part of the treatment.

Personal criticism, physical punishment, and assignment of extra school work should not be used as punishment techniques. Compositions about classroom rules and the reasons for them may be appropriate. They should not be too long, however, and they should be followed up with a feedback conference. Methods of punishing effectively through withdrawal of privileges, behavioral restrictions, and exclusion from the group are discussed in the following sections.

### How to Punish Effectively

More important than the type of punishment is the way the teacher presents it to the student. It should be clear that punishment is being used as a last resort, and not because the teacher wants to get even or enjoys punishing. Students should see that their own behavior has brought the punishment on themselves because they have left the teacher no other choice.

Tone and manner are very important here. The teacher should avoid dramatizing the situation: "All right, that's the last straw!" "Now you've done it!" or making statements that turn the situation into a power struggle, "I guess we'll have to show you who's boss." Instead, the need for punishment should be stated in a quiet, almost sorrowful voice. The teacher's tone and manner should communicate a combination of deep concern, puzzlement, and regret over the student's behavior.

Whether or not it is fully stated in words, the implied message should be "You have continually misbehaved. I have tried to help with reminders and explanations, but your misbehavior has continued. I don't understand this, but I am worried about it and I still want to help. I cannot allow this misbehavior to continue, however. If it does, I will have to punish you. I don't want to do this, but I have to if you leave me no other choice." This approach will help make students see punishment as a thoroughly disagreeable experience that they will want to avoid. It will also make them more likely to see their predicament as their own fault and less likely to think the teacher is picking on them. If punishment becomes necessary, it should be related to the offense. If a student misuses materials, for example, it may be most appropriate to restrict or suspend his or her use of them for a while. If a student continually gets into fights during recess, he or she can lose recess privileges or be required to stay apart from classmates. If a student is continually disruptive, he or she can be excluded from the group.

Teachers should make clear the reasons students are being punished and what they must do to restore normal status. This involves making a clear distinction between the students' unacceptable behavior and their overall acceptance as people. Students should know that they are being punished solely because of their unacceptable behavior and that they can regain their status by changing their behavior.

Withdrawal of privileges and exclusion from the group should be tied closely to remedial behavior whenever possible. This means telling students not only why they are being punished, but what they may do to regain their privileges or rejoin the group. This explanation should stress that punishment is only temporary, and that they can redeem themselves by showing improved behavior: "When you can share with the others without fighting," "When you can pay attention to the lesson," "When you can use the crayons properly without breaking them." The students should have only themselves to blame for their punishment, but they should also be given a way to redeem themselves. This will focus their attention on positive behavior and provide an incentive for changing.

This is in contrast to the "prison-sentence" approach ("You have to stay here for ten minutes," "No recess for three days") and the "I am the boss" approach ("You stay here until I come and get you," "No more crayons unless I give you permission"). These techniques make no explicit improvement demands, and they make it easy for students to get angry or feel picked on.

Punishment that is closely related to the offense is more easily seen as fair. The students have no one but themselves to blame if they lose a privilege because they have abused it. On the other hand, if the teacher punishes by imposing restrictions in an entirely unrelated area, the students may feel that they are being picked on or attacked. An especially bad practice of this type is to lower students' grades as punishment for misbehavior. Except where the punishment is *directly related* and *proportional* to the offense, as when a student who cheats on a test is given a failing grade for that test (and only that test), students should *not* be punished by having their grades lowered. Lowering grades as punishment for misbehavior will cause bitter resentment and harm motivation for studying ("Why should I work if I can't get better than a C?").

Punishment should closely follow the offense. Again, students must see that their own behavior has brought on the punishment, that they have no one to blame but themselves. If punishment is too far removed from the offense or if it goes on for too long ("You'll stay in for a week!"), this connection will be lost. The misbehavior that led to the punishment will be all but forgotten, but the punishment itself will remain. So will a lot of anger and resentment.

Punishment should be flexible, so that students can redeem themselves and restore normal status by showing improvements. This gives the students some incentive to improve, and it helps drive home the point that teachers punish because they must, not because they want to. Teachers should avoid (or break) the habit of threatening inflexible punishments: "You'll stay after school for a week . . . get an 'F' in conduct . . . have to get special permission to leave your seat from now on." These threats are inappropriate overreactions that leave teachers stuck with either following them up or taking them back. Either way they lose. If they follow through and "execute the sentence," they will deepen the student's discouragement and resentment. If they back off, they will appear inconsistent or wishy-washy and will "lose face."

### Exclusion from the Group

Exclusion from the group does not always function as punishment. Teachers often misuse it in a way that actually makes it function as a reward. Ideally, the place designated for exclusion from the group should be located so that a student sent there will be excluded psychologically as well as physically. He or she should be placed behind the other students, where it is difficult to disrupt a lesson or distract attention. To help insure a feeling of exclusion, the student can be placed facing a corner or wall. In combination with the techniques for explaining punishment described above, this will make it likely that the exclusion will be experienced as punishment and will have the desired effects on behavior.

Exclusion should be terminated when the student indicates that he or she is ready to behave properly. If this is not said spontaneously, the teacher should go to the student when the opportunity arises and ask if he or she feels ready to participate in the lesson and behave. Stated intentions to behave should be accepted. The student should not be subjected to nagging about earlier behavior or to a "grilling" designed to elicit specific promises: "You'll stop calling out answers without raising your hand?" "You'll stop talking to your neighbor during the lesson?"

Also, when the student requests readmittance, the teacher should respond in a way that clearly accepts him or her back into the group. Vague phrases like "Well, we'll see" should be avoided. The student should be shown that the teacher has heard and accepted the student's intention to reform, and then instructed to rejoin the class: "Well, Susan, I'm glad to hear that. I hate to exclude you or anyone else. Go back to your seat and get ready for math."

Sometimes, an excluded student may come to the teacher with a half-hearted or tongue-in-check pledge to reform. Here, especially when there has been a previous history of failure to take exclusion seriously, the teacher may wish to reject the student's gesture and send him or her back to the place of exclusion. This should be done with caution, since it is better to give the student the benefit of the doubt than to risk undermining reform efforts. When a plea is rejected, the reasons must be made clear. The student must see that the teacher is acting on the basis of observed behavior: "I'm sorry, Johnny, but I can't accept that. Several times recently you promised to behave and then broke that promise as soon as you rejoined the group. I don't think you realize how serious this problem has become. Go back to the corner and stay there until I get a chance to come and talk to you about this some more."

### Punishment as a Last Resort

We cannot stress too strongly that punishment is a measure of last resort, to be used only when absolutely necessary. It is appropriate only when students persist in disruptive behavior despite continued attempts to explain and encourage desirable behavior. It is a way to curb misbehavior in students who know what to do but refuse to do it. It should not be used when the student's misbehavior is not disruptive or when the problem exists because he or she does not know what to do or how to do it.

First, punishment places attention and emphasis on undesirable behavior. Second, it tends to reduce work involvement and raise the level of tension in the room (Kounin, 1970). Using it to handle one control problem may contribute to causing several others. This is part of the reason why teachers who rely on punishment have more, not fewer, control problems. They try to treat problems with a stop-gap control measure instead of prevention and cure. Meanwhile, they undermine their chances for gaining the admiration and respect needed to treat problems successfully.

This does not mean that any non-disruptive behavior should be allowed to continue. Withdrawal, daydreaming, or sleepiness can be serious problems if they are characteristic and continuing. However, punishment is an unnecessary and inappropriate response to such behavior. This is also true for problems such as failure to answer questions or to do assigned work and for all situations in which the student needs instruction about what to do and how to do it. If students fail to turn in work, they should be made to complete it during free periods or after school.

## COPING WITH SERIOUS ADJUSTMENT PROBLEMS
Most classrooms have students with serious and continuing problems who require individualized treatment beyond that suggested so far. This section presents suggestions for dealing with them.

### General Considerations
Although different types of serious problems require different treatment, certain general considerations apply to all of them.

*1. Do Not Isolate the Student or Label Him or Her As a Unique Case.* Because expectations and labels can act as self-fulfilling prophecies, it is important that the problem student not be labeled or treated as special or different from the rest of the class. Interactions with the student concerning behavior should be as private as possible, not conducted in front of the class any more than necessary. The effect will be to cut down the need for face-saving behavior on the student's part and also to reduce the possibility that he or she can use misbehavior to gain attention.

*2. Stress Desired Behavior.* This method has been mentioned before, but it is doubly important for students who show continuing behavior problems. These are harder to eliminate once they become labeled as characteristic of the student. The label places undue attention on the student's particular form of misbehavior, and it tells the student that the teacher expects him or her to misbehave in this way. To avoid this, the teacher should regularly stress the desired behavior, not the misbehavior the student shows now. Stress on the positive must be more than verbal. The teacher must not only talk this way, but must think and act in a manner consistent with the intention of moving the student toward desired behavior.

A positive manner can be used even with things that appear to be almost completely negative, such as stealing or destruction of property. True, it would be awkward to reward a student for not stealing or not destroying property. However, these problems can be redefined in more positive ways.

If property destruction is due to impulsiveness or carelessness, the teacher can instruct the student about how to handle property carefully. If stealing results from real need (poverty), the teacher should plan with the student ways that he or she can borrow the items being stolen or earn the right to keep them. Meanwhile, the student can be praised for progress in "keeping the rules" or in "learning to respect the property rights of others." If the student has been stealing or destroying property to seek attention or to express anger, the teacher can work to help the student to recognize this and develop better ways to meet these needs. Here again, any positive progress the student shows should be labeled and praised.

By defining problems in a positive way, teachers give students a goal and suggestions about how to work toward it. This energizes both the teacher and the student, giving them the feeling that they are making progress. In contrast, when the problem is defined purely negatively ("You've got to stop . . ."), both teacher and student are left at an impasse. The student misbehaves and the teacher responds by criticizing and perhaps punishing. Both are left where they started, and the cycle is likely to repeat itself over and over again.

*3. Focus on the Student's School-Related Behavior.* When a student shows serious disturbed behavior in school, it is usually part of a larger pattern of disturbance. Many factors may contribute to the problem, including some that the teacher can do little or nothing about (broken home, inadequate or sadistic parent, poor living conditions). Some teachers give up hope when they hear about such things, feeling that the student will not change unless his or her home environment changes (Good et al., 1969). Other teachers become uninvited psychotherapists or social workers, trying to change the home as well as deal with the student in the classroom. This often does more harm than good.

Even though people show reliable individual differences and stable personality traits, most behavior is situational (Mischel, 1976). Teachers, for example, show certain behaviors during the school day that are associated with the teaching role. These behaviors are not included in teachers' behavior outside the school in their roles as husband or wife, parent, neighbor, and so forth.

This is also true of students, who learn to play the student role by showing the behavior that teachers expect and reinforce. It is this student role that teachers should stress. No matter what the student's home background, and no matter what personality disturbance the student shows, the teacher can and should expect him or her to behave acceptably as a student. Factors in the home or other out-of-school environments may need to be taken into account, but they should neither be used as excuses for failing to deal with the student nor allowed to become focal concerns that obscure treatment of school-related misbehavior.

Generally, then, teachers are advised to confine their treatment efforts to school behavior and to aspects of the home environment that are closely related to school behavior (such as asking parents to see that students get to bed early enough on nights before school and that they do their homework). These are appropriate and expected teacher concerns. They are also the areas in which teachers can be effective in dealing with the student. Going beyond these areas is risky, unless the teacher has the necessary expertise and a good relationship with both the student and his or her family.

*4. Build a Close Relationship with the Student, and Use It to Learn His or Her Point of View.* A student's failure to respond to a reasonable and patient teacher's normal behavior signals that some special problem is operating. Perhaps the student is unwilling to respond because of anger or other negative emotions or is unable to respond because of emotions or impulses he or she cannot control. Here, it is important for the teacher to build a close relationship with the student as an individual (as opposed to an impersonal student in the class), both to develop better understanding of his or her behavior and to earn the respect and affection that will make the student want to respond.

To do this, the teacher needs to take time to talk with the student individually, either after school or at conferences during school hours. The teacher should make clear his or her concern for the student's welfare (not merely about misbehavior) and his or her willingness to help the student improve. The teacher should encourage the student to talk about the problem in his or her own words, listening carefully and asking questions when confused. The best questions are simple and open-ended. They do not put words into the student's mouth or make guesses about what is going on in the student's mind.

The teacher should make it clear that he or she wants to hear what the student has to say, so that the student doesn't get the impression that the teacher is waiting to hear one thing in particular. The teacher might help by expressing puzzlement over the student's behavior and, perhaps also, by pointing out that the student is hurting him or herself in addition to causing problems for the teacher. This should not become a sermon, however, or get in the way of the main message that the teacher wants the student to tell his or her story in the student's own words.

Preferably, the discussion will produce something that suggests treatment procedures. If part of the problem has been the teacher's own behavior (if the teacher has been sarcastic or hostile, for example), he or she should admit this and promise to change. If the student makes a suggestion that is reasonable, it should be accepted. For example, a seventh grader may request that she not be asked to read aloud from her seventh-grade history book, since she reads at the second-grade level. This request could be granted, provided that a plan is devised to see that the student learns to read better. If the student's suggestion cannot be accepted, the reasons should be explained. The teacher may also wish to offer suggestions. These must be presented as suggestions, however, and not conclusions. The student should feel free to express an opinion about whether or not they will help. In any case, discussion should continue until suggested changes are agreed upon.

At times, these may be only partial solutions or steps toward solving the problem. Some problems are serious and deep-rooted enough that they are not going to be solved in one day or with one conference. It is sufficient as a first step if both parties communicate honestly during the conference and come away from it feeling that progress has been made.

Although serious behavioral disturbances require individualized treatment, there are some principles to use. Teachers should (1) avoid isolating the student or labeling the student as a unique case; (2) stress the student's progress rather than nag the student; (3) focus primarily on school-related behavior, even where severe out-of-school problems exist; (4) develop a close relationship, so that the student will strive to earn teacher affection and respect.

With any serious problem, the teacher should arrange a conference and question the student to discover how he or she sees the situation. Questions should seek to get the student to explain in his or her own words; they should not "put words into the student's mouth." This questioning phase should be followed by a discussion phase in which agreements about suggested solutions are worked out. Suggestions about individualized treatment of several behavior problems commonly faced by teachers are given in the following sections.

### Defiance

Most teachers find defiance threatening, even frightening. What is the teacher to do with a student who vehemently talks back or loudly refuses to do what he or she is asked to do?

To begin with, the teacher must remain calm so as not to get drawn into a power struggle. The natural tendency of most adults is to get angry and strike back with a show of force designed to put down the rebellion and show the student that he or she "can't get away with it." This may succeed in suppressing the immediate defiance, but it will probably be harmful in the long run, especially if it involves loss of temper by the teacher or public humiliation of the student.

If teachers can overcome the tendency to react with immediate anger, they will be in a good position to deal with defiance effectively. Acts of defiance tend to make everyone in the room fearful and uneasy, including the student who rebels. The other students know that the act is serious and may bring serious consequences, and they will be on edge waiting to see what those consequences are going to be. Teachers can gain two advantages by pausing a moment before responding to defiance: (1) they will gain time to control their temper and think about what to do before acting, and (2) the mood of the defiant student is likely to change from aggression and anger to fear and contrition during this time. It is helpful to ponder the situation for a few moments before responding, letting the class wait in silent anticipation.

When teachers do act, they must do so decisively, although with a calm and quiet manner. If possible, they should give a general assignment to the class and then remove the defiant student from the room for a conference. If this is not possible or if the defiant student refuses to leave for a conference, he or she should be told that the matter will be discussed after school. This should be done with a tone and manner that communicates serious concern, but no threats or promises should be made. The defiant student and the other students in the class should know that some action will be taken, but they should not be told exactly what it will be.

The following response would be appropriate: "Jane, I can see that something is seriously wrong here, and I think we better do something about it before it gets worse. Please step out into the hall and wait for me—I'll join you in a minute." An alternative would be: "Please sit down and think it over during the rest of the period—I'll discuss it with you later, after class."

It is important that defiance be handled in a private conference. The fact that defiance occurred at all is a signal that something is seriously wrong with the student and probably with the teacher-student relationship. This calls for discussion and resolution. Also, when the teacher's authority has been threatened by an angry outburst, both the teacher and the student will find it hard to handle the situation in front of the class. Both will be strongly motivated to save face, the teacher by demonstrating authority and the student by showing determination to stick with earlier defiant statements.

Teachers can minimize these problems by stating that the matter will be dealt with in a private conference. The statement tells the class that they will handle the situation and allows them to deal with the student in a way that does not humiliate or incite further defiance. They can even afford to let the student "get in the last word," because the matter will be taken up again later.

If the student wants to "have it out" publicly, teachers should flatly refuse. They should say that the matter is between the two of them, and that they do not want to cause embarrassment. They might also add that they are angry and want to wait until they calm down and think about the matter before taking action. If necessary, they should send the student out into the hall or to the principal's office.

Defiant acts usually culminate the build-up of anger and frustration in students. Difficulties at home or in relationships with peers may be part of the problem. However, the teacher is almost always part of the problem too. Students are unlikely to defy their teachers unless they resent them to some degree. Therefore, in discussing defiance with students, teachers must be prepared to hear them out. There must be discussion, not a lecture or argument. Students will likely accuse their teachers of treating them unfairly, and teachers must be prepared to entertain the possibility that this is true. If teachers have made mistakes, they should admit them and promise to change.

It is usually best to encourage students to say everything they have on their minds *before* responding to the points they raise. This helps teachers get the full picture and allows them some time to think about what they are hearing. If they try to respond to each separate point as the student raises it, the discussion may turn into a series of accusations and rebuttals. Such exchanges can leave students with the feeling that their specific objections have been "answered," but that they still are right in accusing the teacher of general unfairness. Regardless of the specific points raised, the teacher should express concern for the student and a desire to treat him or her fairly. This reassurance (backed, of course, by appropriate behavior) will be more important to the student than particular responses to particular accusations.

With some defiant students, it may be important to review the teacher's role. Students should understand that the teacher is primarily interested in teaching them, not ordering them around or playing policeman. They must see that the teacher's exertion of

authority is done for good reasons having to do with their own education and the education of their classmates.

Even serious cases of defiance can usually be handled with one
or two sessions like these, if teachers are honest in dealing with
the students and if they follow up the discussion with appropriate
behavior. Although unpleasant, incidents of defiance can be blessings
in disguise. They bring out into the open problems that have been
smoldering for a long time. The defiant act itself will usually have
a cathartic effect on the student, releasing much built-up tension
and leaving him or her more receptive to developing a more constructive relationship with the teacher. Much good can come from
this if the teacher takes advantage of it by remaining calm, showing
concern and willingness to listen, and following up with appropriate
behavior.

### The Show-off

Some students continually seek attention from teachers or peers
by trying to impress or entertain them. They can be very enjoyable
if they have talent for the role and confine their showing off to
appropriate times and places. Often, however, they are exasperating
or disruptive.

The teacher's basic method of dealing with show-offs should be
to give them the attention and approval they seek, but only for
appropriate behavior. Inappropriate behavior should be ignored.
When it is too disruptive to be ignored, the teacher should not do
or say anything that will call attention to it or make the student
feel rejected. Thus, a comment like "We're having our lesson now"
is better than "Stop acting silly." If students seek individual attention
at awkward times, they should be delayed rather than refused. They
should be told that the teacher will see them at a specified later
time.

When praising a show-off, praise only appropriate behaviors and
specify what is being praised. This will motivate the show-off to
repeat these behaviors to gain approval. In general, show-offs need
constant reassurance that they are liked and respected, and teachers
should try to fill this need. However, specific praise and rewards
should be reserved for appropriate behavior. Inappropriate behavior
should go unrewarded and, as much as possible, unacknowledged.

### Aggression

A basic principle of behavior modification is that desirable behavior
should be rewarded and undesirable behavior should be ignored.
The second part of this principle often cannot be applied to aggres-

sive students, however, because they may hurt classmates or damage equipment. When such harmful or destructive behavior appears, the teacher should demand an end to it immediately. If the student does not comply, the teacher should physically restrain him or her (if this is possible). If the student responds by straining to get away, making threats, or staging a temper tantrum, the student should be held until he or she regains self-control.

While restraining the student, the teacher should speak to the student firmly but quietly, telling him or her to calm down and get under control. The student should be reassured that the problem will be dealt with, but not until he or she calms down. If the student insists that the teacher let go, the teacher should say firmly that this will happen as soon as the student stops yelling and squirming. This verbal assurance can be nonverbally reinforced by gradually relaxing the grip on the student as his or her resistance gradually decreases. When ready to release the student completely, the teacher should do so quietly and informally. If this is done in a formal fashion, ("Are you ready to be quiet now?"), the student will likely feel the need to make face-saving gestures.

Restraint may be required if two students are fighting and do not respond to demands that they stop. The teacher should not try to stop a fight by getting between the participants and trying to deal with both at the same time. This will result in delay, confusion, or even in the teacher getting hit. Instead, the teacher should restrain one of the participants, preferably the more belligerent one.

The student should not only be restrained, but pulled back and away from his or her opponent, so that the student is not hit while being held. This will stop the fight, although it may be necessary to turn around and order the other participant to stay away. It is helpful if the teacher does a lot of talking at this point, getting the students to calm down and explaining that the matter will be dealt with shortly, when they comply. If the teacher does not talk and otherwise generally take over here, the students are likely to exchange threats and other face-saving actions.

Humor is helpful here, if the teacher has the presence of mind to use it. Threats and face-saving actions are effective and likely to be reinforced only when taken seriously. If the teacher responds with a smile or a little remark to show that he or she considers them more funny or ridiculous than serious ("All right, let's stop blowing off steam"), they are likely to stop quickly.

Once aggressive students have calmed down, the teacher should talk with them individually. If two students were fighting, it may be necessary to talk to both together. As usual, the teacher should begin by hearing the students out. It is important to help aggressive students see the distinction between feelings and behavior. Feelings should be accepted as legitimate, or at least as understandable. If students state that they hate the teacher or some other student or that they are angry because of unfair treatment, they should be asked to state their reasons for feeling this way. The feeling itself should not be denied ("That's not nice—you must never say that you hate someone") or attacked ("What do you mean? Who do you think you are?"). If the student has been treated unfairly, the teacher should express understanding and sympathy: "I can see why you got angry."

If angry feelings are not justified, the teacher should explain in a way that recognizes the reality of the feelings but does not legitimize them: "I know you want to be first, but the others do too. They have the same rights as you. So there's no point in getting angry because they went first. You'll have to learn to wait your turn. If you try to be first all the time, the others will think you are selfish and won't like you as much."

Although teachers can accept feelings and sometimes expressly legitimize them, they should not accept misbehavior. They should clearly state that the student will not be allowed to hit others, destroy property, or otherwise act out angry feelings in destructive ways. The student will be expected to exercise control and confine his or her responses to acceptable behavior.

Habitually aggressive students require resocialization to teach them new ways of dealing with their frustrations or anger. They must learn that frustration and anger do not justify aggressive behavior. They should be told to express feelings verbally rather than physically, and should be given specific suggestions or instructions about how to do this.

For example, students who "hit first and ask questions later" need instruction about handling frustrations and conflicts. They should be urged to inhibit tendencies to strike out and should be taught how to resolve conflict through discussion and more appropriate actions. They should be taught to ask classmates what they are doing or why they are doing it instead of assuming that their classmates are deliberately provoking them. They should be instructed to express their feelings verbally to whoever has caused them to become angry, because this person may not even realize that he or she made them angry or why.

If the students are old enough to participate meaningfully, role reversals in which each puts him or herself in the place of the other to reenact the situation are valuable. These should be followed with specific suggestions about how to handle situations that produce conflict. If they are already covered by rules, the students should be reminded of the rules. If not, rules should be suggested for the future.

In continuing conflicts over who goes first or who gets to use what equipment, a procedure ensuring that everyone has an equal turn would be appropriate. For short run or single events, a random method such as a coin toss might be better. Where the situation is complex and the students are old enough, some suggestions for give-and-take bargaining could be made. In a ball game, for example, a player who did not get to play the position he or she wanted to play could be allowed first choice in the batting order.

Students should be encouraged to settle disputes through discussion and bargaining by themselves as much as possible, but also cautioned to bring unresolved disputes to the teacher rather than allow them to escalate into fights.

Teachers should also try to help aggressive students see the consequences of their aggressive behavior, largely by appealing to the Golden Rule. Students can usually see that they dislike others who bully them, cheat them, or destroy their property. They will then be in a better position to understand why others dislike and avoid them for the same reasons. It is helpful to show by examples that they must learn to verbalize their feelings and seek solutions to problems with the others involved instead of striking out at them. They must see that others will know why they are angry only if they tell them and that hitting them will only make them angry too.

If aggression results mostly from students' failure to deal with certain situations (inability to share, inability to wait their turn, tendency to overreact to teasing or to accidental physical contact), the teacher should work specifically on these problems with them. Here, the teacher must stress that not only the students' behavior, but also their overreactive emotions are a part of the problem. To point out emotionality does not mean to instruct students to deny their feelings; their anger or resentment is real. It does mean that they will be expected to work on controlling their feelings in frustrating situations. They must see that certain frustrations are unavoidable and that by overreacting to them, they succeed only in making themselves unhappy and unpopular.

Cases in which a student attacks others for no apparent reason are more serious. Students who do this regularly may require professional treatment. Sometimes a child acquires a self-image as a "tough kid" and may actually want others to fear and dislike him or her. Even in these very serious cases, however, there are many things that teachers can do.

As with any other aggressive students, the teacher should attempt to talk with these students to understand them better and to explain behavioral expectations. Also, aggressive acting out will have to be dealt with directly as it occurs, as usual. There are other ways, however, for the teacher to cope with the problem indirectly. These techniques will help both the problem students themselves and the others in the class to see the problem students in a more positive light.

First, the teacher should avoid labeling them and avoid reinforcing any negative labels they may apply to themselves. The teacher should not refer to them as bullies or announce that they are being separated from their neighbors because they "can't keep their hands to themselves." Such actions imply that the students are different, that there is something permanently wrong with them, or that they cannot control themselves. These actions should be avoided in favor of ones that express confidence that the students can learn to behave acceptably.

The teacher can help aggressive students practice more positive roles by arranging for them to play such roles toward their classmates. It might be helpful for such a student to be used as a tutor, or to teach others useful skills that he or she knows (typing shoes, operating equipment, arts and crafts, music, or other talents). In reading and role-play situations, the student should be assigned parts that feature kindness, friendship, and helpfulness toward others. An ideal part would be that of an ogre whom everyone feared and disliked until they found out how good the ogre was underneath.

Cooperative and helpful behavior can be acknowledged and praised whenever it occurs. Also, potentially serious conflicts can be nipped in the bud if the teacher spots them early enough. He or she can turn a potential fight into a cooperative situation by making specific suggestions about how the students can handle it. For good measure, the teacher can express pleasure at seeing them cooperate together. Such behaviors help change negative self-concepts and make students see themselves as people whom others will like as friends.

So far, we have given suggestions about what teachers *should* do with aggressive students. Before leaving this topic, it is worth discussing one frequently advocated technique that we do *not* recommend. This is the practice of providing substitute methods for expressing aggression, such as telling the student to punch a punching bag instead of another student or to act out aggression against a doll while pretending that it is the teacher. Such practices have been recommended by psychoanalytically-oriented writers who believe that angry feelings must be acted out in behavior and who see substitution as a way of doing it harmlessly. The usual rationale is that acting out angry feelings has a cathartic effect that reduces or eliminates anger. Without such a release in behavior, the anger presumably will remain and grow, eventually to be released directly.

This suggestion has wide appeal because it has a certain face validity, especially the notion that expression of feelings has a cathartic effect. Most people do experience a catharsis if they "get it off their chests" or "have it out." This does not mean, however, that hostile impulses *must* be acted out behaviorally. Encouraging a student to act out anger against a substitute object will increase or prolong the problem, not reduce it. Instead of helping the student learn to respond more maturely to frustration, this method: (1) reinforces the idea that overreactiveness is expected, approved, and "normal"; (2) reinforces the expectation that whenever the student has angry feelings he or she will need to act these out behaviorally; (3) provides an inappropriate model for the rest of the class, increasing the likelihood that the problem will spread to them too.

The problem here is that the connection, "I need to act out angry feelings—I can release them through catharsis," is merely the end point of a chain of reactions. The connections "frustration—angry feelings" and "angry feelings—act out" precede the cathartic end point. Every time the end point of the chain is reinforced, the whole chain that led up to it is reinforced. The student is reinforced not only for expressing extreme anger harmlessly, but also for building up extreme anger in the first place and for believing that this emotion requires or justifies aggressive behavior.

Teachers are not doing any favors by encouraging students to act out hostility against substitute objects. They are merely prolonging and reinforcing immature emotional control. If kept up long enough, this will produce an adult who is prone to temper tantrums at the slightest frustration and who spends much time building up and then releasing hostile feelings. This sort of person is neither very happy nor very likeable and is immature.

The teacher should not try to get students to act out all emotions. Instead, he or she should work on helping them to distinguish between emotions and behavior and between appropriate and inappropriate emotions. Inappropriate emotions (unjustified anger or emotional overreactions) should be labeled as such, and the reasons they are inappropriate should be explained. Behavior that is simply unacceptable must not be tolerated, no matter how strong the student's emotions or impulses to act out. Acceptable (and more effective) alternatives should be explained and insisted upon. All aspects of the teacher's behavior should communicate the expectation that the students can and will achieve mature self-control. There should be no suggestion that they are helpless in the face of uncontrollable emotions or impulses.

### Unresponsiveness

Some students lack the self-confidence to participate normally in classroom activities. They do not raise their hands seeking to answer questions, and they will copy, guess, or leave an item blank rather than come and see the teacher about their seatwork. When they are called on and do not know an answer, they will stare at the floor silently or perhaps mumble incoherently. Sometimes, this "strategy" is successful because many teachers become uneasy and give the answer or call on someone else rather than keep such students "on the spot." Observers who see this should communicate it because teachers usually are not aware of it.

In general, fears and inhibitions about classroom participation should be treated indirectly. Attacking the problem directly by labeling it and urging students to overcome it can backfire by making them all the more self-conscious and inhibited (much research on stuttering, for example, shows this). The teacher should stress what the students should be doing, rather than what they are not doing. When they are called on, they should be questioned in a way that communicates that the teacher wants and expects an answer. Questions should be asked directly and should not be prefaced with stems like "Do you think you could . . ." or "Do you want to. . . ." Such phrases suggest uncertainty about a student and make it easy for him or her to remain silent. Also, questions should be asked in a conversational, informal tone. If asked too formally, the question may sound like a test item and may stir up anxiety.

Questions should be accompanied by appropriate gestures and expressions to communicate that the teacher is talking to the student and expects an answer. The teacher should look at the student expectantly after asking the question. If the student answers, the teacher should respond with praise or with relevant feedback. If the student answers too softly, he or she should be praised and then asked to say it again louder ("Good! Say it loud so everyone can hear"). If the student appears to be about to answer but is hesitating, the teacher can help with a nod of the head, a formation of the initial sound with the lips, or verbal encouragement ("Say it!").

If the student does not respond at all, the teacher can supply the answer, repeat the question, and then ask the student to repeat the answer. If the student mumbles or partially repeats, he or she should be asked to repeat it again and then praised when it is repeated. All of this is geared to make clear to students that they are expected to talk, to give them practice in doing so, and to reassure and reward them when they do.

Interactions with such students should be deliberately extended at times, both to give them practice at extended discussions and to combat the idea that they can keep interactions short and infrequent by laying low. If students answer an initial question correctly, the teacher should sometimes ask them another question or have them elaborate on the response. If they fail the initial question, the follow-up question should be a simpler one that they can handle. In general, questions that require them to explain something in detail will be the most difficult. Progressively simpler demands include factual questions requiring short answers, choice questions requiring them only to choose among presented alternatives, and questions that require only a yes or no response. If the students do not respond to any level of questioning, they can be asked to repeat things or to imitate actions. Once they begin to respond correctly, the teacher can move to more demanding levels as confidence grows.

Inhibited students need careful treatment when they are not responding. As long as they appear to be trying to answer the question, the teacher should wait them out. If they begin to look anxious, as if worrying about being in the spotlight instead of thinking about the question, the teacher should intervene by repeating the question or giving a clue. He or she should not call on another student or allow others to call out the answer.

The teacher should not allow a student to "practice" resistance or nonresponsiveness (Blank, 1973). Anxiety or resistance should be cut off before it gets a chance to build, and the teacher should be sure to get some kind of response before leaving the student. If the student does not respond to any of the questions requiring a verbal answer, he or she can be asked to make a nonverbal response such as shaking the head or pointing. Young children might be asked to imitate a physical action or even be manually guided until they begin to do it themselves. In any case, it is important to get some form of positive response before leaving the student.

Students at all levels should be instructed to say, "I don't know," rather than remain silent when they cannot respond. This will remove the stigma that some students attach to saying, "I don't know."

Many students will hesitate to say this because previous teachers have implanted the idea that it is shameful through such comments as "What do you mean you don't know?" By legitimizing "I don't know," the teacher makes it possible for nonresponsive students to answer verbally even when they do not know the answer.

These methods are difficult to apply in large group situations with extremely unresponsive students who often do not say anything at all. Here, the better course might be for the teacher to temporarily avoid calling on a student, working with him or her in individual and small group situations instead. This type of student needs to be brought along slowly. Time is required to get rid of strong inhibitions or fears, and much progress can be undone by trying to push too far too fast. With continued progress and regular success, confidence will grow and tolerance for being "on the spot" will increase. The teacher should continue to make sure to get a response of some kind from this student every time they have an interaction, and he or she should see that the student does not become regarded as someone who does not answer and who, therefore, is no longer asked to respond.

If this type of inhibition is widespread, the teacher may be causing or contributing to it. Observers should look for signs of overvaluing correct answers and showing impatience or disgust at failure. The teacher's handling of seatwork should also be observed to see if he or she is scaring students off by criticizing them instead of helping them when they come with questions.

### Failure to Complete Assignments

Certain students fail to complete seatwork and homework assignments. The method for dealing with this problem will depend on why assignments are not turned in. In some cases, students do not turn in work because they have not been able to figure out how to do it. This is not a motivational problem; it is a teaching problem. What is needed is remedial work to help them learn what they do not understand and to move them to the point where they can do it themselves.

Great patience and determination are needed in working with these students, because they need support and encouragement just to keep trying. If the teacher criticizes them, embarrasses them before the group, or shows impatience or frustration, they will likely begin to copy from neighbors rather than continue to try to do the work themselves.

The teacher should encourage these students by pointing out how far they have progressed from where they began, regardless of where they stand in relation to others in the class. The teacher will need to make time for remedial teaching with them or to plan some other remediation arrangement (see Chapter 9). In any case, slow learners need patience, more appropriate assignments, and remediation, not criticism or punishment for failing to do what they are unable to do.

For whatever reasons, there are some who could do the work but do not finish it or turn it in. The best way to deal with this problem is to stop it before it gets started, or at least before it grows. From the beginning of the year, teachers should be clear about instructions for seatwork and homework. Their purpose and importance should be explained, and this should be backed with appropriate behavior, such as collecting it, checking it, and giving feedback or remedial work when necessary.

Although the teacher may wish to make open-ended assignments (such as identifying extra problems to do for extra credit or "To see if you can figure them out"), each student should have a clear-cut minimum amount of work for which he or she is accountable. This amount may (and often should) vary from student to student for instructional reasons, but there should be a clear understanding about what each must turn in and when it is due.

Students involved in seatwork should be monitored closely to see that they are working productively. Teachers should make clear from the beginning of the year that students are expected to finish assignments before doing anything else during seatwork time. Clear procedures should be established for what students should do when they do not understand and cannot continue, as well as what they should do if they finish. The established policy must be enforced consistently, so that everyone forms the habit of doing seatwork.

Failure to turn in homework is a more difficult problem, because the teacher cannot monitor and intervene if the student is not working properly. He or she can keep a careful check of homework being turned in, so that students who did not complete it can be assigned to do so during free periods. If they do not complete the job during free periods, they should be kept after school. Here again, the policy must be established right from the beginning of the year that assignments are to be completed and turned in on time. If they are not, completion of the assignment will be the top priority item whenever the student is not involved in a lesson or other instructional activity.

Of course, this assumes that homework assignments are relevant in content and appropriate in difficulty level. If failure to turn in homework is common, the homework being assigned and the way it is monitored when it is turned in should be reviewed and adjusted. A few students may have a problem completing homework because of pressures from job demands or a poor home situation. Where this appears to be the case, the problem should be discussed at length with the student, and a mutually agreeable solution should be worked out. Schools should be flexible enough to make time and space available to students who realistically cannot do homework at home. Students in such situations need help, not more trouble.

In some cases, the teacher may wish to contact the student's parents regarding homework. This may or may not be helpful. The question of whether or not to bring the parents in on problems like this will be discussed in a later section.

## OTHER APPROACHES TO CLASSROOM MANAGEMENT

This approach to classroom management has been eclectic, stressing principles gathered from many theories. There are a few systematic approaches which stress principles developed within one theory or point of view. Two of the most prominent are the applied behavior analysis point of view known as behavior modification, and the classroom applications of reality therapy as presented by William Glasser. Readers seeking more information about classroom management are encouraged to investigate these approaches, which are described briefly here.

### Behavior Modification

Behavior modification approaches are based on the theories of Skinner (1953), who sees behavior as controlled by contingent reinforcements. Behavior that brings on or maintains reinforcement will be repeated, and behavior that is not reinforced will be extinguished (will disappear). This idea is simple in theory, but it becomes complex in practice because people sometimes respond unexpectedly to stimuli. Some are not motivated by stimuli that most people experience as rewards, and some respond positively to stimuli that most people view as punishments. Thus, it is not possible to develop a list of rewards and another list of punishments. The same stimulus can be rewarding, punishing, or irrelevant for different people or even for the same person in different situations.

To deal with this complexity, most behavior modifiers use the Premack principle (Premack, 1965) to define reinforcers. This principle states that reinforcement potential is based on the naturalistic frequency of behaviors. Behaviors that appear frequently under conditions of free response can be used as reinforcers to elicit and maintain behaviors that would not appear otherwise. Apparently, because the person experiences them as rewarding, high frequency behaviors can be used as reinforcers for less preferred behaviors by making the opportunity to engage in the preferred behaviors contingent upon performance of the less preferred behaviors. This definition of reinforcers is circular, because one cannot state that a particular behavior will act as a reinforcer for another behavior until after the fact, but it works well in practice. Further, it has the advantage of helping us recognize that many activities not usually thought of as rewards do in fact operate as reinforcements and can be used to help sustain other behaviors. In the classroom, this includes such things as access to enjoyable materials and assignments, opportunities to go to the library or to enrichment areas, and even opportunities to perform maintenance chores (for students who enjoy doing so).

The reinforcement that elicits and sustains behavior can be positive or negative. Positive reinforcements are what we usually call rewards. They can be used to motivate students to perform less desired behaviors by making the opportunity to enjoy them contingent upon performance of other behaviors. If students know that they will not be allowed to do some desired thing until they first complete their assignments satisfactorily, the opportunity to do what they want to do when they finish should serve as a positive reinforcer, helping motivate them to work on their assignments. Notice that access to the reinforcer is made *contingent* upon completion of the assignment. Reinforcement will occur only if the assignment is completed as specified.

Positive reinforcement involves *desirable* consequences for performance. Negative reinforcement involves contingency between performance and the opportunity to escape *undesirable* consequences. For ethical reasons, negative reinforcement must be used sparingly, but there are many important classroom applications, especially where students are presented with opportunities to escape undesirable consequences that otherwise would occur anyway. Students who are already being punished can have the punishment reduced or shortened by improving their behaviors to meet specified criteria.

Whereas behavior is elicited and maintained through positive and negative reinforcement, it is inhibited through extinction and punishment. Extinction is simply the removal of reinforcement. If you can discover what is reinforcing some undesirable behavior and can arrange to change contingencies so that the behavior no longer brings about this reinforcement, the behavior will stop. Extinction is most efficient when combined with positive reinforcement of desired behaviors. The most obvious example in school situations is when teachers begin to ignore attention-getting behavior by students that they were reinforcing unintentionally, and instead begin to reinforce these students systematically for performing desired behaviors.

Punishment is a more direct way to inhibit undesirable behavior. Theoretically, it should be used only when it is not possible to arrange contingencies so that undesirable behavior is not reinforced. Where this is the case, the only alternative might be to see that the undesirable behavior brings about negative consequences as well as reinforcement, and that the negative consequences are stronger than the reinforcers and sufficient to inhibit the undesirable behavior.

Note that behavior modification assumes that all behavior is under the control of reinforcements. This means that any behavior that appears spontaneously with regularity is assumed to be either reinforcing in its own right or instrumental in bringing about some desired reinforcement. Theoretically, any behavior that is within the person's repertoire can be produced by reinforcing it sufficiently, and even characteristic behaviors can be minimized through extinction or punishment. Extinction is the method of choice when it is possible to arrange contingencies so that undesirable behavior is not reinforced. Punishment is used only when this is not possible.

Behavior modification can be used to motivate attention and engagement in school work, in addition to motivating compliance with rules. Applying the Premack principle, teachers can provide reinforcement when students pay attention and do their work, and can withhold it when they do not. This can be done unilaterally by the teacher, although students can be given a more active role through *contingency contracting*. In contingency contracting systems, all students receive reinforcement contingent upon good behavior and/or successful completion of requirements, but requirements are individualized and formalized through contractual agreements between the teacher and each individual student. The form and content of contracts can vary considerably, depending upon the developmental levels of the students, their abilities, the kinds of rewards available for use as contingent reinforcers, and many other factors. Different kinds of contracts all have statements of contingency between the performance of specified behavior and the delivery of specified reinforcement.

For example, teachers can determine the level of performance (expressed as the number and types of assignments done to specified criteria, possibly along with earning at least a minimal score on a required test) that will be required for particular grades. A level of performance that will require sustained effort (for *this* particular student) can be required for a grade of "A," with lesser requirements for lower grades. Contracts then are prepared specifying the relationships between performance and grade. These can be formal records of the agreement, and they can even be signed by the students and the teachers.

Contracts for behavioral improvement can be developed using the same principles. A level of conduct that would represent the most that could reasonably be expected from *this* student at *this* time can be required for the maximum reinforcement available, and decreasing conduct levels can be required for lesser amounts of reinforcement. As behavior improves and students become able to control themselves more successfully, new contracts requiring better behavior can be introduced.

Contingency contracting as a primary and continuing approach to classroom motivation usually works best when students are presented with a variety of attractive reinforcements. These "reinforcement menus" might include opportunities to spend time in learning centers or other enrichment activities, permission to go to the library or some other place outside the classroom, permission to play games or engage in primarily recreational pastimes, and even time to just converse with friends. Specified good behavior and/or completion of assignments is rewarded with so many points, and these points can be "spent" on reinforcements.

The "prices" of different reinforcements vary, according to their attractiveness and the demand for them. The most attractive and popular ones are the most expensive. Occasional changes in the content of reinforcement menus and/or the prices for the items help provide variety and avoid satiation with the reinforcers (continued opportunities to enjoy a given reinforcer sometimes weaken its strength as a reinforcer because students come to value it less).

Theoretically, any behavior that is not a reinforcer itself is sustained by reinforcement, and it can be changed by changing the reinforcement contingencies. This is complex in practice because the potency of various reinforcements changes over time, and menus must be adjusted continually. Because of this, many believe that behavior modification is impractical as the primary method of classroom management. The fact that it focuses attention on reinforcements at the possible expense of learning, and that it is time-consuming and difficult to implement successfully, does make it impractical for most teachers. However, it does have strong points that all teachers should bear in mind. Perhaps most important is the continuous reminder that causes for, and solutions to, classroom management problems are to be found *in the classroom*. Clues about solutions can be developed by performing functional analyses of problem behaviors and identifying the stimuli that elicit and reinforce these behaviors. Problem behavior can be minimized by changing these reinforcement contingencies.

It is harder than it might seem to arrange contingencies so that desired behaviors are reinforced. Sometimes, behavior modification attempts fail because the proper contingencies are not established; at other times, the problem is in the presumed reward that is supposed to function as a reinforcer. Analyze the behavior modification attempts presented in the examples below. Are they likely to be successful? Why or why not?

1. Mrs. Bussey has set up a contingency contracting system. Students who turn in completed and correct work assignments get tokens that can be spent for desired reinforcers at a later time. However, the work must be complete and correct. If students come with incomplete or incorrect work, they must return to their desks and finish it correctly.

2. Mr. Cornucopia gives out a variety of goodies every Friday afternoon, as a way to motivate the students to apply themselves. He sees that everyone gets something, so that no one is left out, but he makes sure to give the more desirable items to students that he is sure have worked hard during the week. To make sure that the connection between the work and the reward is clear, he refers to this as "payday," and he says "Good work" to each student when passing out the goodies.

3. Mrs. Calvin announces that, from now on, the student who finishes the afternoon math assignment first will be allowed to dust the erasers.

4. Mr. Caries is frustrated because his students do not assume much responsibility for keeping their desks orderly and their general seating area clean. To call attention to this and encourage better habits, he occasionally (and unpredictably) announces that today the students who do a good job of cleaning up their desks and areas will get candy. After allowing enough time, he goes around to check desks and gives candy to those who have neat desks and clean areas.

Superficially, all four examples are similar—the teacher offers an extrinsic reward to increase or improve some performance. However, subtle differences among the examples make it likely that only Mrs. Bussey will succeed. She has arranged to have attractive reinforcers available, and students can get them only by turning in complete and correct work. Assuming that all the students can do the work that is assigned to them, the contingencies are such that opportunity for reward will function as a reinforcer for sustained and careful work on assignments.

Mr. Cornucopia will not succeed because there is no clear contingency between performance of the behaviors he is trying to reinforce and delivery of the reinforcements. All students got some kind of reward whether they applied themselves during the week or not, and differences in the attractiveness of rewards given to individual students depend less upon their effort during the week than upon his unsystematic perceptions and fallible memory. Some students will get rewarded even though they know that they do not deserve it, and others will get less than they deserve because Mr. Cornucopia does not realize how deserving they are. These two types of students will learn that there is no contingency between reward and performance. After a few weeks, it is unlikely that many or even any of the students will be motivated to work harder or more carefully by this gimmick, even though they will enjoy the goodies.

Mrs. Calvin's scheme is almost certain to fail for three reasons. It is ill-considered in the first place, because she should be trying to reward effort and accomplishment, not speed. Second, the possible chance to dust the erasers will operate as a reinforcer only for a minority of students in the class, those who are capable of working fast enough to finish first. Students who have little or no chance to finish first are not going to be affected favorably by this motivational attempt. Finally, it is unlikely that the intended reward would really function as a reinforcer. Few students are likely to be motivated by the opportunity to dust the erasers, and even those who are probably will tire of this activity before long. In other words, this is a relatively weak reinforcer that is susceptible to early satiation.

Mr. Caries also will fail. The reinforcements that he offers are contingent upon performance of the desired behavior when they are offered, but they only are offered occasionally and he always announces this beforehand. Thus, the contingency here is not "Students with neat desks and clean areas every day will get rewarded," but "Students with neat desks and clean areas on days that Mr. Caries promises rewards will get rewarded." By always announcing the availability of rewards ahead of time when they are available, Mr. Caries eliminates the possibility that these rewards will reinforce clean-up efforts when they are not available.

These few examples illustrate some of the many problems involved in using behavior modification in schools, and especially in using it as a basic motivation and control system for the class as a whole. The proper contingencies are hard to establish, and satiation with the available resources is a continuing problem. The method has been used successfully, however, especially when reinforcement menus are involved.

### Classroom Meetings
Glasser (1969) has developed an approach to classroom management that emphasizes self-control based on insight and group control based on social pressure rather than individually administered reinforcement. His ideas involve application of *reality therapy*, in which people who avoid or defend against seeing themselves and their actions as they really are learn to do so. This is accomplished by arranging for them to learn how others see them. When they find out that others react negatively to things they say and do, they usually are motivated to change. This is especially likely in the case of students confronted with classmates' negative reactions because classrooms are social systems that continue throughout the school year. Most students identify with their classrooms to some degree, and the desire to be accepted, combined with the knowledge that one must live with classmates for the rest of the year, constitutes powerful motivation.

Problems are discussed during classroom meetings in which the teacher and students sit in a circle and interact as a single group. The teacher presides but functions as a group leader rather than an instructor or authority figure. Classroom problems are brought up in the group meetings. They are presented as problems belonging to the class, not just the teacher. There is continuing stress on the notion that every student has responsibilities as a member of the class, including responsibilities to cooperate and help maintain a good learning environment. Students who fail to fulfill their responsibilities are faced with the fact that they will not be allowed to continue to behave this way. On the other hand, they find that they have not only the responsibility, but the power to solve their own problems. This is the purpose of the meeting (in the case of meetings devoted to discussion of problems).

In addition to discussing problems brought up by the teacher, the class discusses problems that students bring up in relation to themselves, other students, or the teacher. They are expected and encouraged to speak freely. The only limitations or rules are those necessary to keep the group functioning (one person talks at a time and others listen). The teacher may occasionally clarify or to try to keep the discussion on the topic until a solution is achieved, but no one is interrupted for faultfinding, criticism, or punishment. The continuing focus is the search for agreeable solutions, not fixing blame.

These meetings can be very effective for producing insight and changing behavior, but skill and good judgment are involved in leading them successfully. The teacher must be able to take the role of a group leader rather than an authority figure, and to cope with unanticipated and often serious emotional reactions. Teachers who cannot shed the authority figure role or tolerate the shifting of decision-making power from themselves to the group should not use this method. The same is true of teachers who are not prepared to deal with accusations, arguments, strong emotional reactions, and the like. These and other examples of strong emotional involvement happen in such groups regularly and provide excellent opportunities to build insight and foster psychological development, but the group leader must be able to deal with them constructively. Becoming upset or angry only makes things worse.

For teachers who are able to tolerate and respond effectively to strong emotional involvement, the group meeting approach might be effective or even ideal. Even for teachers who do not want to use the technique regularly, occasional class meetings of the kind that Glasser recommends can be useful (for example, in developing and revising classroom rules).

### ANALYZING STUDENT BEHAVIOR
Many forms of student behavior that sometimes cause problems for teachers have not been discussed in this chapter—for example, student habits that irritate or disgust the teacher, students who bait the teacher with provocative or embarrassing remarks, and various signs of mental or emotional disorder. These problems are hard to generalize about, because they usually require a specific diagnosis to determine why the student is behaving the way he or she is and to suggest possible treatment. Suggestions about how teachers can proceed in dealing with these problems are given below.

#### Should Anything Be Done at All?
As a first step, the teacher might ask whether or not it is wise to do anything about the problem. Certain behavior might be irritating to the teacher but yet be normal, or at least acceptable, in the

student's environment. Vulgar language and frequent references to sex, for example, are perfectly normal in a slum high school.

Also, some things the teacher may know about a student may have nothing to do with the classroom. For example, a teacher may discover that a boy who behaves acceptably in class has been drinking heavily or has fathered an illegitimate child. Unless the teacher has a close relationship with the boy, he or she might do more harm than good by becoming involved in the situation.

### Finding Out What the Behavior Means

To the extent that behavior problems occur in the classroom, the teacher should question and systematically observe the student. These observations will help the teacher gain a better understanding of the meaning of the student's behavior and the reasons behind his or her actions (if the student does not know the reasons or has not divulged them). When a student's behavior is particularly irritating, a teacher (or anyone) can easily become so concerned that he or she notices only the behavior and little else. It is important to *remember, then, that the student's behavior may be just a symptom of an underlying problem, and that this symptomatic behavior is not as important as the reasons that are producing it.*

If the behavior is just a habit, not part of a larger complex of problems, it can be handled straightforwardly. The teacher should insist that the student drop the irritating habit and learn more appropriate behavior. This explicit improvement demand should be supported by an appropriate rationale (appeal to school rules, to social convention, or to the Golden Rule).

Where students' habits are not fundamentally immoral, but are merely violations of school rules, social conventions, tact, good taste, or the teacher's personal preferences, this distinction should be made clear. Students should not be made to feel guilty, or to feel that their habits are a sign that something is seriously wrong with them. They should understand that the teacher objects to the timing of the act or the way it is carried out, but not to the act itself. Teachers are justified in forbidding habits that are disruptive or irritating enough to interfere with their teaching; however, such habits should not be described as worse than they really are.

If students' behavior seems to be more serious or complex than a simple habit and if they have not given an adequate explanation for it, careful observation is needed.

Observations should begin by trying to describe the behavior more precisely. Is it a ritual or focal behavior that is repeated pretty much the same way over and over (masturbation, spitting, nose picking), or is it a more general tendency (aggression, suspiciousness, sadistic sense of humor) that is manifested in many different ways? Perhaps the description can be narrowed down more specifically. Do the students show recognizable patterns? For example, do their suspicions center around a belief that others are talking about them behind their backs, or do they think they are being picked on or cheated? If they do think others are talking about them, what do they think the others are saying? If students laugh inappropriately, what makes them laugh? If this could be discovered, it might provide clues to what the behavior means.

### Arranging a Conference

Often, the simplest and best way to understand students' behavior is to talk to them about it individually. This can be done in conferences arranged during free periods or after school. The main purpose here, besides seeking information, is to show concern for the students. Teachers should note the observations they have made, state that they are concerned about the students' behavior, and ask the students to explain it. The main thing is to get the students talking and then to hear them out.

Students probably will not be able to state why they act as they do, and teachers should not expect them to. If the students had this much insight, they probably would not be behaving symptomatically in the first place. Instead, the hope is that clues or information will emerge from the discussion. If it does produce a breakthrough, fine. If not, something will still be accomplished if the student comes away with the knowledge that the teacher is concerned about him or her and wishes to help. In any case, the conference should be concluded in a way that gives the student a feeling of closure.

If the student's behavior has been disruptive, the teacher should clarify expectations and limits, as well as reach an agreement with the student about any special actions to be taken. If the problem requires no special action or if the teacher does not yet know what action to take, he or she can conclude by expressing pleasure at having had a chance to discuss the problem with the student and by offering to help in any way the student can suggest.

### BRINGING IN PARENTS AND OTHER ADULTS

Teachers should think twice before involving parents, principals, counselors, or other adults in a problem. This escalates the seriousness of the problem in the minds of all concerned and labels the student as a "problem student." The expected benefits of involving additional adults must be weighed against the possible damage that could result from such labeling.

Usually, the teacher should turn first to a counselor or school psychologist, if such a source is available. By discussing the situation with such a resource person, preferably after the person has observed in the teacher's classroom several times, the teacher might gain new insights or get specific suggestions. A knowledgeable principal, assistant principal, or fellow teacher might also provide this resource.

The resource person's title is less important than the quality of his or her observations and suggestions. If the person is usually helpful in providing insights or suggestions about dealing with problems, the teacher stands to benefit from talking with him or her.

Some resource people may deal with the student directly rather than through the teacher. Again, this resource may or may not be helpful. There is usually little point in having a student tested, for example, unless there is a physical problem suspected. Knowledge of the student's scores on an intelligence or personality test usually contributes nothing to the solution of his or her problem. Testing may make it worse, in fact, by labeling the student in a way that leads to unfortunate self-fulfilling prophecy effects. Thus, there is little point in bringing in other adults to deal with the student directly unless they can treat him or her effectively. Merely sending a student out of the room occasionally to talk to a counselor, vice-principal, or "disciplinarian" almost never does any good over the long run. If the student's behavior problem is in the classroom, it must be dealt with there.

Contacting the parents about a behavior problem can also be risky. After all, to the extent that a student has serious emotional or behavioral problems, his or her parents are probably the biggest single reason for them. Merely informing the parents will do no good. If the teacher gives parents the impression that they are expected to "do something," they will probably threaten or punish the student and let it go at that. Teachers should be careful not to give parents this impression unless they have specific suggestions to propose.

Sometimes, specific suggestions can be given, as when the teacher enlists the parents' help in seeing that the student gets enough sleep, does the homework, or eats breakfast. When making suggestions, teachers may also need to tell parents many of the things discussed in this book. The need to think of punishment as a last resort and the need to have confidence and positive expectations are two particular principles that many parents violate when their children have problems.

If the parents are called in mostly for information, this should be made clear to them. They should know that the teacher does not intend that they do something. The teacher should state his or her observations and concern about the student, and ask the parents if they can add anything that might help the teacher understand their child better or deal with him or her more effectively.

The teacher should question the parents to see how much they know about the problem, and what their explanation for it is, if they have one. If some plan of action emerges, it should be discussed and agreed upon with the parents. The teacher and parents should also agree on what the parents are going to tell the student about the conference. If no particular parental action is suggested, the conference should be brought to some form of closure by the teacher, "Well, I'm glad we have had a chance to talk about Judy today. I think you've given me a better understanding of her. I can't think of anything special or unusual that we should do with her. I'll keep working with her in the classroom, and let you know about her progress. Meanwhile, if something comes up that I ought to know, give me a call." The parents should emerge from the conference knowing what to tell their child about it and what, if anything, the teacher is requesting them to do.

## BEARING THE UNBEARABLE

Teachers are often in the uncomfortable position of being forced to try to cope with problems that really cannot be solved. If enough seriously disturbed students are in a single classroom, the teacher is not going to be able to deal with all of them successfully and teach the curriculum at the same time. When things get unbearable, something has to give; either the problem has to be whittled down some, or the teacher needs help from outside resources. Unfortunately, resources adequate to do the job usually are not available.

The resources that are available are often not successful. Parents and school disciplinarians are usually armed only with pep talks, threats, and punishment. Suspension from school merely deepens students' alienation and makes it harder for them to cope when they come back (if they come back). Placement in a class for the mentally retarded or emotionally disturbed, or in a reform school, although well meant and generally considered "treatment," often is the first step on a one-way ladder going down.

Genuinely therapeutic treatment is available, but unless the student's family is wealthy and willing to pay high professional fees, the student will likely have to go on a waiting list. If lucky, he or she may get treated a year or two later, but not now.

Thus, the only effective treatment that most disturbed students get will come from their classroom teachers (with the help of counselors, school psychologists, or other available resources). If the students are almost old enough to drop out of school or if they are in danger of being thrown out, this may be their last real chance to head off a pattern of lifelong failure and misery. It is for this reason that teachers must push themselves to their limits before giving up on any student. Even then, they should do so only for the sake of the rest of the class.

## SUMMARY

The key to successful classroom management lies in using the preventive techniques described in the previous chapter. Consistent use of these techniques will eliminate most classroom problems. Those that remain can be handled with the techniques described in the present chapter. Many major disruptions start as minor misbehavior, and teachers should know how to stop minor problems quickly and nondisruptively. To do this, they must form the habit of monitoring the classroom regularly so that they always know what is going on.

Much misbehavior can be ignored. When it is not disruptive and when the students quickly return attention to the lesson or assignment, it is best to let the matter go without interrupting the activity or calling attention to the misbehavior. If the misbehavior is prolonged or begins to become disruptive, direct intervention will be needed. When the students know what they are supposed to be doing and when the nature of their misbehavior is obvious, there is no need for the teacher to question them or conduct an investigation. The goal here is to return them to productive activity as quickly and nondisruptively as possible. Ideally, this should be done in a way that does not even call attention to the misbehavior. This can be done through eye contact, touch or gesture, moving closer to the students involved, or calling on them.

When it is not possible or advisable to use these nondisruptive techniques, the teacher should call the students' names and correct their behavior by telling them what they are supposed to be doing or reminding them of the rules. Intervention here should be brief and direct, and it should focus on desirable behavior. Questions, flaunting of authority through threats or harshness, and nagging should be avoided.

It will be necessary to question students when misbehavior has been serious or disruptive and when the teacher is unclear about the facts. Such investigations should be conducted privately, to minimize face-saving. The teacher should assure all students involved that they will be heard, but must insist that they wait their turn while he or she deals with one at a time. Questions should be confined to those seriously intended to elicit information.

The teacher should not make decisions or attempt to settle the issue until everyone has been heard out. After gathering as many facts as possible, he or she should take positive action aimed at both resolving the problem as it presently stands and preventing its return. This will mean clarification of expected behavior and perhaps a new rule or agreement. Ordinarily, there will be no need for punishment, which should be reserved as a measure of last resort to use with students who persist in the same kinds of misbehavior.

Because punishment is a stop-gap control measure rather than a solution, and because it involves many undesirable side effects on both the student being punished and on the rest of the class, it should be used only as a last resort. It should be clear to everyone that the student has brought punishment upon him or herself through repeated misbehavior, leaving the teacher with no other choice. Appropriate forms of punishment include withdrawal or restriction of privileges, exclusion from the group, and assignments that force students to reflect upon the behavioral norms they have violated and the rationale for them. Punishment should be related to the offense, should be as brief and mild as possible, and should be flexible enough so that the students can redeem themselves by correcting their behavior.

A few students with long-standing and severe disturbances require extraordinary corrective measures. Suggestions for dealing with several common types are given in the chapter. Such serious problems require careful observation and diagnosis, followed by individualized prescription and treatment. However, there are a few general principles. First, teachers should treat such students just as they treat other students as much as possible, so that they do not become "special cases." Second, teachers should continually stress the positive with such students, indicating the desirable behavior they expect and communicating the expectation that the student will improve. Third, teachers will usually have to form close individual relationships with such students, so that they will like and respect them enough to want to earn respect and affection in return. Fourth, teachers should concentrate on the in-school behavior of problem students; attempts to become the student's psychotherapist or the family's social caseworker often do more harm than good.

This chapter and the last have been eclectic, drawing ideas about classroom management from many sources. Readers wanting more information can consult sources that advise methods based on particular points of view, such as behavior modification and the reality therapy/classroom meeting approach of Glasser.

Although it is almost always useful to gather information and solicit advice, teachers should think carefully before involving anyone else in their relationship with a problem student. This step may escalate the problem in the minds of everyone, and could lead to undesirable self-fulfilling prophecy effects. Most relevant information can be gotten by observing and questioning students themselves, and most beneficial changes will come as a result of time spent establishing and using good relationships with them. Unless teachers are lucky enough to have access to an intervention expert with a generally successful record, they are likely to get more from observing and talking with problem students than from talking about them with parents or school personnel. Classroom problems must be solved in the classroom, regardless of what conditions may exist outside.

### SUGGESTED ACTIVITIES AND QUESTIONS

1. Reread the case presented in Chapter 1 and pinpoint the management errors that the teacher made. Then, using the content of this chapter and your own ideas, specify how the teacher should have behaved more profitably.

2. Ask your instructor or in-service leader to find films or videotapes of teaching behavior, and use the rating scales that accompany this chapter to rate the teacher's managerial ability. Try to identify as many good and poor techniques as you can. Whenever you spot an ineffective technique, try to suggest alternatives that the teacher could have used.

3. Summarize in five brief paragraphs the guidelines that a teacher can use to deal with the five classroom adjustment problems that were discussed in this chapter (defiance, show-off behavior, aggression, unresponsiveness, and failure to complete assignments). Practice your ability to deal with these problems in role-playing situations with a few other people. Specify a hypothetical problem, select someone to be a student and someone to be the teacher, and allow other participants to provide feedback. Did the teacher deal with the problem effectively? Did he or she seem sincere? What alternatives could have been used?

4. Review or construct your list of student behaviors or characteristics that are most likely to embarrass you or to make you anxious. Practice how you will deal with these situations in your classroom. For example, if students who threaten your authority are problems for you, list student behavior likely to touch you off and

practice how you would respond. Then role-play your responses with other participants. For example, how would you respond (or would you respond?) in this situation:

TEACHER: You're right, Frank, what I told you yesterday was incorrect. Thank you for looking this up and bringing it to my attention.

HERB: *(gleefully bellowing from the back of the room)* You're always wrong! We never know when to believe you!

5. Describe four techniques a teacher can use to eliminate minor misbehavior quickly and nondisruptively. (See also exercise 8 in Chapter 6, Suggested Activities and Questions.)

6. Why should teachers avoid threats and appeals to authority when stopping misbehavior through direct intervention?

7. Why do the authors not recommend the use of physical punishment in school settings?

8. In general, what steps can a teacher follow to make exclusion from the group an effective punishment (student misbehavior is markedly reduced or eliminated)? In particular, how does the teacher behave when excluding or readmitting students to group activities?

9. Why should teachers focus attention on students' school-related behavior rather than on their out-of-school behavior?

10. When is punishment necessary, and what is the most appropriate way to administer punishment?

11. A ninth-grade history teacher sees Jill Thomas grab (without apparent provocation) Bill Grant's comb and throw it on the floor. Jill and Bill begin to push each other. What should the teacher do? Be specific. Write out or role-play the actual words you would use. As a teacher, would you behave differently if you had not seen what preceded the pushing?

12. Ruth Burden, who teaches eleventh-grade English, has noticed that Ed James has slept through her class for a week. Should she arrange a conference with him? If not, what should she do? If so, what should she do and say at the conference? Assume that Ed relates that his parents fight nightly, and that after their arguments end, he is too upset to sleep. Should Miss Burden talk to the parents? If so, what should she say?

**FORM 7.1.** Teacher's Reaction to Inattention and Misbehavior

*USE: When the teacher is faced with problems of inattention or misbehavior*
*PURPOSE: To see if teacher handles these situations appropriately*
        *Code the following information concerning teacher's response to misbehavior or to inattentiveness. Code only when teacher seems to be aware of the problem; do not code minor problems that teacher doesn't even notice.*

BEHAVIOR CATEGORIES                                         CODES

A. *TYPE OF SITUATION*
    1. Total class, lesson or discussion
    2. Small group activity—problem in group
    3. Small group activity—problem out of group
    4. Seatwork checking or study period
    5. Other (specify)

| | A | B | C |
|---|---|---|---|
| 1. | 3 | 3 | 4 |
| 2. | 3 | 3 | 4,6 |
| 3. | 1 | 2 | 2 |
| 4. | 1 | 3 | 4 |
| 5. | 4 | 3 | 2 |
| 6. | | | |
| 7. | | | |
| 8. | | | |
| 9. | | | |
| 10. | | | |
| 11. | | | |
| 12. | | | |
| 13. | | | |
| 14. | | | |
| 15. | | | |
| 16. | | | |
| 17. | | | |
| 18. | | | |
| 19. | | | |
| 20. | | | |
| 21. | | | |
| 22. | | | |
| 23. | | | |
| 24. | | | |
| 25. | | | |

B. *TYPE OF MISBEHAVIOR*
    1. Brief, nondisruptive, should be ignored
    2. Minor, but extended or repeated. Should
       be stopped nondisruptively
    3. Disruptive, should be stopped quickly. No
       questions needed
    4. Disruptive, questions needed or advisable
    5. Other (specify)

C. *TEACHER'S RESPONSE(S)*
    1. Ignores (deliberately)
    2. Nonverbal; uses eye contact, gestures or
       touch, or moves near offender
    3. Praises someone else's good behavior
    4. Calls offender's name; calls for attention or
       work; gives rule reminder. No overdwelling
    5. Overdwells on misbehavior, nags
    6. Asks rhetorical or meaningless questions
    7. Asks appropriate questions—investigates publicly
    8. Investigates privately, now or later
    9. Threatens punishment if behavior is repeated
    10. Punishes (note type)
    11. Other (specify)

*CHECK IF APPLICABLE*
_____ 1. Teacher delays too long before acting, so problems escalate
_____ 2. Teacher identifies wrong student or fails to include all involved
_____ 3. Teacher fails to specify appropriate behavior (when this is not
           clear)
_____ 4. Teacher fails to specify rationale behind demands (when this is
           not clear)
_____ 5. Teacher attributes misbehavior to ill will, evil motives
_____ 6. Teacher describes misbehavior as a typical or unchangeable trait;
           labels student

NOTES:
    #1, 2, and 4 were all for student #12 ( he seems
to be the only consistent problem as far as
management goes).

**FORM 7.2.** Case Study

*USE: To do concentrated observations on one or a few students who are problems for the teacher*
*PURPOSE: To systematically gather information needed to understand the student's behavior and to make recommendations to the teacher*
*Use the codes on this page to record the student's behavior and link it to antecedent causes when possible.*

| A. STUDENT BEHAVIOR | TIME | | CODES | |
|---|---|---|---|---|
| | | | A | B |
| 1. Pays attention or actively works at assignment | | 1. | | |
| 2. Stares in space or closes eyes | 8 : 15 | 1. | 1 | |
| 3. Fidgets, taps, amuses self | 8 :23 | 2. | 6 | 1 |
| 4. Distracts others—entertains, jokes | 8 :24 | 3. | 1 | |
| 5. Distracts others—questions, seeks help, investigates | 8 :29 | 4. | 11 | 10 |
| | 8 : 30 | 5. | 1 | |
| 6. Distracts others—attacks or teases | 8 : 38 | 6. | 6 | 4 |
| 7. Leaves seat—goes to teacher | 8 :40 | 7. | 1 | |
| 8. Leaves seat—wanders, runs, plays | 8 :47 | 8. | 2 | 2 |
| 9. Leaves seat—does approved action (what?) | 8 :49 | 9. | 1 | 7 |
| 10. Leaves seat—does forbidden action (what?) | 8 :51 | 10. | 5 | 2 |
| 11. Calls out answer | 8 :53 | 11. | 1 | 6 |
| 12. Calls out irrelevant comment (what?) | 9 :00 | 12. | 9 | |
| 13. Calls out comment about teacher (what?) | 9 : 27 | 13. | 15 | 1 |
| 14. Calls out comment about classmate (what?) | 9 : 28 | 14. | 1 | 9 |
| 15. Deliberately causes disruption | 9 : 34 | 15. | 6 | 1 |
| 16. Destroys property (whose? what?) | 9 : 36 | 16. | 1 | 7 |
| 17. Leaves room without permission | 9 :45 | 17. | 9 | |
| 18. Other (specify) | : | 18. | | |
| | : | 19. | | |

B. APPARENT CAUSE
   What set off the behavior?
   1. No observable cause—suddenly began acting out
   2. Appeared stumped by work, gave up
   3. Finished work, had nothing to do
   4. Distracted by classmate (who?)
   5. Asked to respond or perform by teacher
   6. Teacher checks or asks about progress on assigned work
   7. Teacher calls for attention or return to work
   8. Teacher praise (for what?)
   9. Teacher criticism (for what?)
   10. Teacher praises or rewards another student
   11. Teacher criticizes or punishes another student
   12. Teacher refuses or delays permission request
   13. Other (specify)

NOTES:

   9:45  Recess.

| TIME | |
|---|---|
| : | 20. |
| : | 21. |
| : | 22. |
| : | 23. |
| : | 24. |
| : | 25. |
| : | 26. |
| : | 27. |
| : | 28. |
| : | 39. |
| : | 30. |
| : | 31. |
| : | 32. |
| : | 33. |
| : | 34. |
| : | 35. |
| : | 36. |
| : | 37. |
| : | 38. |
| : | 39. |
| : | 40. |

*Note any information relevant to the following points:*

*STUDENT'S EMOTIONAL RESPONSE*
1. Complaints (He is disliked, picked on, left out, not getting share, unjustly blamed, ridiculed, asked to do what he can't do or he's already done):


2. Posturing Behavior (threats, obscenities, challenging or denying teacher's authority):


3. Defense Mechanisms (silence, pouting, mocking politeness or agreement, appears ashamed or angry, talks back or laughs, says "I don't care," rationalizes, blames others, tries to cajole or change subject)

   *Grins while being "talked to", blames student #7 ("He hit me first").*

*Check if applicable:*

   ✓ 1. Teacher tends to overreact to student's misbehavior
   ___ 2. Student's misbehavior usually ultimately leads to affection or reward from the teacher
   ___ 3. Student usually acts out for no apparent reason
   ✓ 4. Student usually acts out when idle or unable to do assignments
   ___ 5. Student usually acts out when distracted by another child
   ___ 6. Student usually acts out in response to the teacher's behavior.

*POSITIVE BEHAVIOR*
1. Note the student's changes in behavior over time. When is he most attentive? What topics or situations seem to interest him?

   *Attentive throughout reading group.*
2. What questions does he raise his hand to answer?

   *Seeks to respond in all situations – whenever he thinks he can answer.*
3. What work assignments does he diligently try to do well?


4. What activities does he select if given a choice?

247

# 8/ INDIVIDUALIZATION AND OPEN EDUCATION

In this chapter, we will discuss two patterns of organization for school instruction that have become popular in recent years. Although the "traditional" self-contained instructional setting remains widely used, individualized and open classroom settings are becoming increasingly popular.

The goal of this chapter is to trace the evolution of these two organizational patterns, to describe the major characteristics of each, and to present research on the degree of effectiveness of these programs in terms of student achievement, reactions to school, and general development. Finally, the chapter calls for the integration of the best aspects of self-contained instruction, open education, and individualization, as the learning context dictates.

## INDIVIDUALIZATION: WHAT IS IT?

Unfortunately, the term individualization has no precise meaning. Quirk (1971) notes that sometimes it means that students are free to progress at their own rate, but that all students go through the same sequences of materials and are exposed to the same instructional methods. In some instances, it means that students are allowed to pursue some instructional objectives that fit their unique interests and abilities. In yet other cases, it is used in reference to situations where all students go through the same curriculum at their own pace, but are allowed to pursue goals and to demonstrate mastery in different ways (write a report, take an exam, pass an oral quiz, interview someone, etc.).

It should be clear that the term "individualization" is broad. To know that school X or teacher Y is using individualized methods is to know very little (it *probably* suggests that students have some freedom in how quickly they move through learning assignments). If we are to understand what "individualization" really means, we need to know the type of materials used, the type and range of assignments and instructional settings, and the form of evaluation.

In recent years, countless learning packages have been produced for individualizing mathematics, chemistry, etc. Teachers who want individualized materials will have no trouble finding them. The only difficulty will be in evaluating and differentiating useful from useless materials. What forces led to the development of materials for individualization?

### Pressure for Change

In the decades immediately preceding 1960, the self-contained age-graded classroom was the primary organizational plan in which public school students were instructed. Students received basic instruction from a single instructor (self-contained) in elementary schools. Even in junior high schools, students were likely to have a core teacher (language arts/social studies) for two or three periods a day. They were assigned to classes for instruction primarily on the basis of age. Third-grade students received the same basic instruction despite the fact that considerable individual differences in student ability existed. Although some teachers made modifications in the curriculum for the extremely bright or slow students, these often were minor (assigning more problems of the same type to the gifted). Essentially, students went through the curriculum at a similar pace. The only major exception to this pattern occurred in reading, where students received instruction in groups. Still, students' progress in reading was tied to the pace at which their groups moved.

In the 1960s, this basic organizational plan began to change dramatically in many schools. A variety of reasons, some positive, some negative, created the pressure for change. Many psychologists (e.g., J. McVicker Hunt, Jean Piaget) were beginning to characterize students as active learners capable of creating and fulfilling their own learning needs (as opposed to an earlier view of students as needing external structure, close supervision, and constant reinforcement). These new conceptualizations of the student were among the forces that led to the production of a variety of materials (filmstrips, programmed booklets) that allow teachers to individualize instruction without producing large amounts of the needed auxillary materials themselves. Hence, the emergence of curriculum materials written for students of differing ability levels (as opposed to materials written for the "standard eighth-grade student") made it comparatively easy for teachers to individualize aspects of their instructional program if they wanted to do so.

During the 1960s, negative reactions to the perceived quality of American schools also created pressure for changes in school organization. Schools came under close scrutiny because research data were being produced that led educators to question the traditional assumption that schools dramatically improved students' career chances. For example, the massive project conducted by Coleman et al. (1966) suggested that home variables, not what took place in schools, seemed to be the primary determinants of student educational attainments.*

In addition to such research, a number of books attacking public schools for a variety of alleged shortcomings were published during the 1960s. Glaring titles *(Death at an Early Age, Crisis in the Classroom)* suggested that major problems existed in American education. Books of this era commonly suggested that teachers and schools were insensitive to the needs of students. Schools were presented as boring and insipid institutions at best. Sometimes, they were characterized as maliciously cruel to students and as major impediments to the development of student potential. Some of the criticism was useful in stimulating thought and action and served as a powerful stimulus to examine what public schools were doing.

Unfortunately, the heavy criticism also led to sweeping changes in school programs, often without a careful analysis of the problems that a school was attempting to solve. Such "solutions," based upon fad movements, produced little positive change. Even the best of the school critics (e.g., Holt, 1964; Silberman, 1970) went too far by implying that the problems they discussed were common in all school settings and true of all teachers.

Interestingly, research that has asked students to describe their school experiences has consistently found that students do *not* describe their teachers or their experiences in school in negative

---

* Since this report, a great deal of data have been collected to show that many schools, and especially individual teachers, exert considerable influence upon student achievement. These results will be reviewed in Chapter 10.

terms (Jackson, 1968; Good and Grouws, 1975; Price, 1977). Most students in these studies have reported school to be an "okay" place.

The point here is not to argue that all schools are okay. We acknowledge that many school situations are boring, irritating, and unlikely to develop student interest and potential (especially inner-city secondary schools). But in general, most schools (especially elementary schools) are seen as acceptable by the vast majority of student consumers. Many students do register major dissatisfaction with their school experience, however, even though the majority of their classmates describe it as acceptable. Many of these students have real and legitimate problems to which schools should respond. In particular, the achievement and satisfaction of low-aptitude male students (especially black males) seem to suffer in self-contained classrooms. (See, for example, Bennett et al., 1976; Green and Farquahar, 1965.)

Differentiated awareness (Which students are unhappy? Which students are not achieving? Which students need to develop social interaction skills?) of school problems is important if meaningful change is to take place. Unfortunately, school reform often appears in an all or nothing fashion (instruction is all whole class or large groups, instruction is completely individualized, or the structure is "open" and all students are expected to generate learning goals). Programs that totally alter what is basically working for most students may have as many harmful as beneficial effects. In contrast, instructional changes that are based upon the specific needs of target students may reduce an existing problem without creating new ones (more on this later).

## INDIVIDUALIZATION: TIME FOR LEARNING

An examination of the amount of time necessary for individual students to learn a particular curriculum unit is one way to link classroom structure with the specific learning needs of students. Teachers have always been baffled concerning how fast to move through a unit. If the teacher is teaching the class as a whole and waits until every student has mastered the material, the time of high-achievement students is being wasted (listening to unnecessary examples and completing needless drill or review work). In contrast, when the teacher moves too quickly, slower students will have an inordinate degree of difficulty on the next unit because of their limited mastery of prerequisite skills or knowledge.

The central problem in grouping students for instruction on the basis of age (rather than ability or interest) and then teaching all students of the same age as a unit is that it tends to depress the learning gains of high- or low-achievement students. Which group is affected depends upon the pace at which the teacher sets the instruction. When teacher pacing is too slow or too fast, other problems can arise too (boredom for high achievers or frustration for low achievers).

Many individual teachers working in self-contained settings have been able to develop successful strategies to save time for face-to-face interaction with students and for individualizing parts of their programs. The new aspect of individualization that appeared in the 1960s was the willingness of some school districts to break up the age-graded curriculum, allowing students to work on material related to their ability and mastery levels (as opposed to standard material that was assigned to students because they were sixth- or tenth-grade students—material that often was too simple or too difficult). Perhaps the greatest utility of breaking up the rigid age-graded curriculum was that teachers were freed from the expectation of getting students "ready for" fifth grade or algebra II.

Competent teachers have always possessed the skill necessary for adapting to students' instructional needs. With the new availability of suitable materials and the money to purchase such materials, many teachers could individualize aspects of their instruction. What had prevented teachers from doing so was the expectation: "I must prepare the *class* for next year's grade level; teachers at that grade expect *all* students to have mastered grade level material and concepts." With the breakup of the age-graded curriculum, it was possible to think in terms of *individual* student needs rather than the needs of the *class*. Obviously, orientation toward class progress or the progress of individuals exerts a great deal of influence on the teacher (planning time, how they evaluate the success or failure of a lesson, etc.).

### Mastery Learning
Perhaps the most influential force calling for school reform and providing direction for change was the concept of mastery learning. It stressed that the achievement of slower students could be raised and that the use of time was one critical way in which teachers could deal with individual differences in learning ability.

When a teacher presents a unit of instruction to the class and then assesses student learning at a particular time, the amount of instructional time is essentially the same for all students. However, some students need more time to learn the same amount of material. John Carroll (1963) expressed the argument in the following way:

$$\text{Degree of Learning} = \frac{\text{(time actually spent)}}{(\quad\text{time needed}\quad)}$$

This formula suggests that an individual's degree of learning is a function of the time needed to learn a particular unit and the amount of time received. If the student needs eight hours to master the material but receives only four hours (e.g., two hours of teacher presentation and two hours of practice time), the student's level of mastery has to fall below 100 percent. Conversely, if a student needs only two hours to master the material and he or she receives four hours, then the student's time is being wasted.

Factors other than time are also involved. The two major considerations are the quality of instruction and student utilization of time. If teachers make poor presentations, choose inappropriate material, etc., the amount of time needed for mastery increases (at least for some students). Furthermore, if students do not utilize their time (don't listen to teacher presentations, spend large amounts of time daydreaming during seatwork), then the amount of time necessary for mastery increases.

For some time, it has been known that the single best predictor of student achievement is student aptitude. Brighter students achieve more than less capable students. At first glance, this seems reasonable: students who process information more quickly learn more than students with poorer aptitude for learning. However, the concern is not that some students learn more and more quickly, but that some students learn substantially less than they are capable of mastering. The argument of mastery learning proponents is that low-aptitude students are not given sufficient time to master basic skills, so that they are doomed to fail or to do relatively poorly on subsequent tasks. Furthermore, these failure experiences are apt to erode student motivation. Some students learn to "give up" in order to save face.

The works of John Carroll (1963) and Benjamin Bloom (1968) excited educators about the prospect of improving student learning by moving away from class pacing. Carroll and Bloom agreed that most students could learn if given sufficient time and if their willingness to persist could be aroused. Indeed, recent data suggest that the relationship between student aptitude and achievement can be altered (see Block, 1974; Bloom, 1976).

Bloom (1973a, 1973b) presents dramatic data to suggest that, under appropriate mastery conditions, most students can master learning material. He reports that 80 percent of students were found to master unit assignments that only 20 percent of students learned under nonmastery conditions. Furthermore, he found that the extra gain came at the expense of only 10–20 percent extra instructional time. Hence, additional study time for students may make a major difference in learning.

This mastery argument tends to focus attention on the fact that teachers go too *fast* for low-ability students. However, as pointed out previously, some teachers may go too *slow* for more capable students. In classrooms where this happens, the achievement rate of more capable students is less than it could be. Arlin and Westbury (1976) studied high school students' mastery of science material under class-pacing and self-pacing conditions. In their experiment, they found that the top one-third of the students in the self-paced group moved through the curriculum much more quickly than the teacher-paced group. Although the mastery argument is typically directed toward the needs of low-achievement students, it is equally applicable to all students: too much or too little learning time can depress achievement.

Successful programs of individualization need to accommodate both fast and slow students. This is comparatively easy to do in situations where students are generally motivated and prepared to learn. One plan that has been successfully applied in many situations (and has been especially popular in college settings) is the Keller Plan. We now turn to an examination of this program as an example of a mastery learning strategy.

### Keller Plan

One of the more popular formats of individualization to emerge has been the Keller Plan: the Personalized System of Instruction (PSI). The main features of the PSI are that it is self-paced (within administrative limits, the student can go as fast or as slow as he or she chooses), it is mastery-oriented (the student proceeds to a new unit only after the preceding unit is successfully mastered), and students control the examination schedule (the student takes the exam when ready and is not penalized by failure on a unit exam; he or she may repeat a unit exam as often as necessary). Furthermore, the material that the student is to master exists in written form. The student does not have to listen to a teacher in order to derive needed information and skills. Teacher lectures are held to a minimum (the purposes of lectures are to orient and stimulate students). In the Keller Plan, the teacher is available as a resource person to tutor the student as necessary. (For more details on procedural aspects of the program, see Keller, 1968.)

The PSI method has proved to be very popular. McKeachie and

Kulik (1975) point out its use in at least 850 college courses in psychology alone. PSI has also proved to be popular with students. McKeachie and Kulik (1975) found that students consistently report more favorable responses to the course than do students enrolled in conventional lecture courses. Students, when ranking the aspects of the PSI that they especially like, repeatedly list self-pacing and personalized interaction with instructors as the most desirable aspects of the plan. McKeachie and Kulik also found that student learning of course content in PSI classes was superior to that of students in conventional classes.

Robin (1976) has also favorably reviewed the Keller plan. In a review of 39 studies (in a variety of courses, different size classes, etc.), PSI classes regularly showed an 8–11 percent achievement gain over comparison classes. One important aspect emphasized in Robin's review is that a 100 percent mastery requirement produces better learning (retention) than a 50 percent mastery criterion. This is especially true for students with low grade point averages who started studying earlier and studied more often under the 100 percent mastery criterion than under the 50 percent criterion.

Perhaps the major reason that students do better in PSI classrooms is that they spend more time attempting to master criterion materials. Born, Davis, Whelan, and Jackson (1972) placed all course materials for an introductory psychology course in a single library and monitored students' study time. The difference between lecture students and PSI students was noticable. The average PSI student spent 45.5 hours in study time, whereas students in lecture classes spent but 30.2 hours. Such differences in *effort* may explain student *achievement* differences. Presumably, those students that need more time to learn can spend the extra time, if they choose to do so, when they know the precise concepts that are to be mastered.

The extra study time may be motivated by the belief that they *will* master the material if they spend sufficient time. In conventional lecture courses, students may not perceive a relationship between effort and successful outcomes. They may feel that mastery is dependent upon luck (e.g., which exam questions the instructor chooses to emphasize) or other factors.

Maasdorf (1976) presents data to show that an individualized instruction program was not only effective in increasing students' performance (in an introductory college course in German) but also effective in decreasing student anxiety. Although the effectiveness of individualization programs varies widely, there is reason to believe that when instructional goals are identifiable and materials are carefully prepared to reach those goals (as in the Maasdorf study), and when students are carefully monitored and motivated, individualization can work.

Despite the favorable findings of PSI techniques with college students, it is important to raise a few qualifications. First, one wonders what the results of PSI would be if all courses in the college curriculum were organized along PSI principles. Part of the motivation for the student may be its novelty, and hence increased student performance may be a function of participating in a new learning format. Furthermore, one wonders if students would or could spend additional study time if all courses used a self-paced format.

In elementary or secondary schools, some students do not have independent study skills. These skills have to be taught. Furthermore, students' maturation rates are such that the amount of time that can be devoted to individual work may have real limits. Finally, in the case of elementary and secondary schools (as opposed to college students), most work has to be done in the presence of other students who at times may make concentration difficult and delay or prevent contact with the teacher. Also, other students will demonstrate faster or slower rates of mastery. These factors are not present in PSI college instruction. They are major differences that the public school teacher has to accommodate.

These qualifications illustrate some of the difficulties that you will have to overcome in using PSI in a public school setting. For example, a high school course in biology ends in May, and it may be impossible to allow students to repeat all exams three or four times. However, to the extent that schools can solve such procedural problems, the mastery model has important application value. Indeed, a lot of mastery learning research (see Block, 1971; Bloom, 1968; 1976) has shown that a mastery learning model can be successfully applied to elementary and secondary schools for at least a part of the day (e.g., one subject) during a program of experimental research. What remains to be demonstrated is whether or not individualization can work in public schools without the presence and/or assistance of resource persons.

### Systems of Individualization

There have been some large-scale development efforts aimed at designing, testing, and developing useful sets of individualized materials and/or strategies for individualization. These programs are designed for widespread adoption in public schools. Three of these systematic efforts will be described briefly below.

Two widely used models are Individually Prescribed Instruction (IPI) and the Primary Education Project (PEP). Both of these systems were produced by the Learning Research and Development Center at the University of Pittsburgh. These systems identify a common set of minimum goals for students but allow for a variety of ways to reach those goals. Curriculum materials are presented in a sequential way and students are allowed to proceed at their own pace through the program.

Teachers in IPI programs guide the work of individual students, diagnose learning difficulty, and evaluate progress. They do not have to worry about curriculum development or selection. The PEP differs from IPI in that it provides for teaching the class as a whole at selected points (for more procedural information, see Wang, 1976).

Project PLAN is another packaged program of individualized materials. It was produced by the Westinghouse Learning Corporation, American Institutes for Research in the Behavioral Sciences, and several public school systems. Instructional units in the PLAN program identify the learning goal and the material that the student is to use in meeting it. The PLAN program also provides students with some opportunity to select goals and to devise plans for meeting these goals. (For more details, see Quirk, 1971.)

Individually Guided Education (IGE) is another effort to individualize education. Here, the emphasis is upon developing a system of education that helps students learn at their own pace in an instructional mode suited to their needs, as opposed to a set of instructional materials. Much of the development work on IGE was done by the Wisconsin Research and Development Center for Cognitive Learning, and the systematization of the concepts for school usage has been accomplished by the Institute for Development of Educational Activities, the educational affiliate of the Charles F. Kettering Foundation. The IGE model calls for both direct teacher instruction and student work on individual assignments (and individual goal setting and self-direction). The system calls for the specifications of basic learning goals (by the local teaching staff) and the use of criterion-referenced tests to determine if students are making satisfactory progress in the curriculum. (For more details, see Klausmeier et al., 1971a, 1971b; Schultz, 1974).

Even when teachers use a known program of individualization, it does not guarantee that the behavior of teachers and students will be alike in different settings. Teachers, teaching teams, and schools put their own faces on any curriculum or innovation. Indeed, there is considerable data to show that there is as much difference (often more) in the behavior of teachers using the *same* curriculum as among teachers using a *different* program. The name of a "program" does not provide a great deal of information about the aspects of day-to-day routines that students are asked to perform. Without observing or detailed questioning of the teaching staff, it is impossible to understand the degree of structure, performance expectation, and general level of individualization that is operating.

Unfortunately, available research has often ignored careful observations of how programs actually operated and has often failed to look for different effects on different types of students. However, available research does provide some support for the assertion that some programs of individualization are working.

## RESEARCH ON INDIVIDUALIZATION

Pavan (1973) and Martin and Pavan (1976) in a review of individual (nongraded instruction) education concluded that more individualized and small-group work was taking place in schools calling themselves nongraded or individualized than in control classes. Furthermore, they conclude that achievement is generally as good or somewhat better than achievement in comparison schools. It is important to realize that the magnitudes of differences found between individualized and comparison programs typically were not large. Furthermore, many individual studies of individualization have produced mixed results, showing that some aspects of individualization have desirable effects but more conventional classes have other advantages.

In a comparison of 12 PLAN and 12 control classrooms (drawn from grades one, two, three, and ten), Thompson (1973) reported that at least some of the surface aspects of individualization were occurring. PLAN students were found to spend most of their time working on individual projects whereas control students spent most of their time in whole-class work. Student time in group work was similar in both types of classrooms. Despite the change in work activity, however, positive changes in student self-esteem were not associated with involvement in project PLAN. Control students reported more favorable self-concepts than did PLAN students.

Students' perceptions of their work involvement provided some clues for their possible sense of frustration. To the question, "Do you think you are able to pick the work you want to do in school?" 40 percent of PLAN students responded *most of the time*, compared to 20 percent of control students. In responding to the question, "Are you able to finish your school work on time?" students indicated a possible reason for the lower self-concept scores. Seventy-one percent of the control students responded *most of the time* and none of them checked *hardly ever*. Forty-three percent of PLAN students reported *most of the time*, 40 percent *some of the time*, and 17 percent *hardly ever*. Hence, students may be perceiving themselves as failing to meet work standards (even though teachers may perceive their work rate and general progress as quite satisfactory). The stream of unending curriculum materials may project a sense of overwhelming demand in some students unless teachers work hard to produce more realistic expectations.

As we have pointed out elsewhere (Good, Biddle, and Brophy, 1975), students who are assigned a heavy dose of similar individual units may need built-in pauses at selected points to allow them to see that they have achieved new benchmarks in personal achievement and mastery. Ironically, a system dominated by *sameness* (day after day, another individual unit) may have equally depressing or boring effects as the teacher-controlled curriculum that individualization has attempted to replace.

In Thompson's study of PLAN classes, no comparison was made within the PLAN group. It is possible that *some* of these classes produced both a different pattern of teacher and student behavior and more favorable self-concept expressions. Program labels don't predict behavior in precise ways. (See, for example, Charters and Jones, 1973; Walker and Schaffarzick, 1974.)

Loucks (1976) studied the effects of IGE in an investigation of second- and fourth-grade student achievement in mathematics and reading and found no effects favorable to the IGE schools. When she reanalyzed the data on the basis of degree of individualization, however, she found differences between users and nonusers of individualized programs. Schools actually using individualized techniques outperformed comparison schools (on three of the four achievement comparisons).

Related findings have been produced by Price (1977). He also went beyond the label of IGE and attempted to find schools that were implementing the model. (Implementation was defined in terms of the 35 basic processes recommended by IGE; see Schultz, 1974.) He found that highly implemented schools had a favorable effect upon student achievement, especially in schools serving a relatively low-aptitude student population. Importantly, he found many schools that do not use the label IGE to be as successful, and in some cases more successful, in implementing IGE processes as some schools that called themselves IGE schools.

Unfortunately, most studies of individualization have not made careful attempts to define precisely the nature of the teaching occurring in the "individualized" program. Furthermore, most research has looked only at the overall effectiveness of individualization for all students. Individualization may have comparatively more effect (adverse or positive) on students of differing age, sex, race, socioeconomic status (SES), or aptitude.

Price presents data to show that girls in well-implemented IGE schools reported higher satisfaction than in all other schools. Furthermore, girls in well-implemented IGE schools had somewhat higher achievement than girls in comparison schools. His data also suggest that high-achievement students were doing a little better in well-implemented programs. However, other studies (see the review by Martin, 1973) have shown an advantage for boys and/or low-achievement students. Hence, again we see that the way a program is implemented is critical. Programs of individualization are apt to have a wide range of effects, including negative ones.

Price's results for higher-achieving students fit nicely with those of Shimron (1973), who studied student behavior within the IPI program. He argued that if the curriculum was matched appropriately to individual needs, students who move through it at comparatively slow and fast rates should not differ in the amounts of time they spend engaged on assigned tasks. (This assumption is based upon the view that tasks should be equally interesting for fast- and slow-moving students; differences in task completion should be because some students take more time to learn material, not because they waste more time.)

Findings reported in his small pilot study (only four fast and four slow second graders were observed) included the following: (1) faster students spent twice as much time working on assignments as slower ones, (2) much more work-related interaction with teachers occurred for faster than slower students, and (3) there were virtually no work-related contacts among students.

These data are consistent with Price's finding that high-achievement students appear to be making comparatively more progress than other students. These findings were also consistent with those of Arlin and Westbury (1976), reviewed earlier in the chapter. If teachers are not careful in monitoring their individualized programs, they may find that high achievers (who initiate more questions and feel more comfortable in approaching the teacher) may monopolize their time in subtle ways.

Shimron posits several possible explanations for understanding why slower students show less time on task behavior: (1) they need more gradual sequencing, (2) prerequisite tasks are not mastered, (3) units have little interest for them. To his list, we would add the possibility that these students need direct teaching. They need to see a live model or demonstration, to be asked questions, and to receive continuing feedback.

## IS TOO MUCH INDIVIDUALIZATION POSSIBLE?

We feel that tight adherence to an age-graded curriculum is an obstacle that overly controls student learning. However, we have also pointed out that individualization can occur in many forms, and that some forms are likely to be deficient. Programs that use poor material (time-filling as opposed to concept-building or skill development exercises) are inadequate by definition. An individualized program can be said to be effective when it helps to achieve optimal program goals. Implementation of an individualized program, like all teaching activities, involves the specification of intended effects (subject matter achievement, training in personal goal setting, ability to work cooperatively with fellow students). If the primary goal is subject matter achievement, and if students are mature and possess self-study skills, a high percentage of the day (but not the complete day) could be spent with students working individually on appropriate assignments. Even when achievement is the primary goal, however, too much individualization may get in the way. For example, secondary students have a great deal of interest in peer attitudes and support, so that at this level learning assignments that demand group work may have more motivational value for subject matter achievement than individual assignments.

When other goals are perceived as important, additional learning modes have to be built into the curriculum. For example, elementary students learn prosocial behaviors only if they have the opportunity to share and cooperate. To understand ways in which they differ from others and to respect differences in beliefs, preferences, and behavior, students of all ages need contact with students who differ from themselves. These goals at times will operate to reduce subject matter achievement. This is because grouping students on the basis of ability can sometimes help to promote achievement, but grouping students across ability levels may well detract from achievement goals. Grouping across ability lines will help to generate a necessary (but not in itself sufficient) condition for promoting greater respect for individual differences.

Furthermore, we would agree with Lipson (1974) that whole-class instruction has its own unique motivational value and, under certain circumstances, will facilitate student achievement. He argues that group lessons often give the learning activity more *perceived importance*. The public format and the chance for students to present their ideas to a group may sometimes seem more important than the completion of unit after unit in isolation. Also, whole-class instruction can save teachers and students a great deal of time. When the development work necessary for comprehending a concept can be presented to a large group of students at the same time, teachers will have time to provide individual students with more personalized feedback in private face-to-face contacts.

It is perhaps more appropriate to think of individualization as the attempt to accommodate the needs of individuals within a particular instructional group and to achieve a balance of instructional activity (individual work, small, group, large group) that is appropriate for that particular group and for the goals that the teaching staff has in mind (more on this in the next chapter). At this time, most of the research on individualization has been a comparison of the performance of students who receive relatively more individual assignments with the performance of students who basically receive group instruction. Patterns of instruction have not been studied in any detail.

Although allowing students to proceed at their own pace is appropriate, too much individualization *(when individualization is seen as the student working alone)* will have a negative influence upon achievement. The sameness of working alone on individual projects day after day will not motivate a number of students. Students, especially young students from low SES homes, need direct teaching if subject matter achievement is to occur.

Stallings and Kaskowitz (1974) report negative correlations between subject matter achievement and high occurrences of students working alone. Soar (1973) also found that too much individual work has a negative effect upon subject matter achievement. Both of these studies dealt with primary-age pupils who came from low SES homes. They suggest that concentration on individual study is not a good instructional strategy for such students. Unfortunately, many teachers associate independent work with quality education. This is not the case for some students.

Another common but erroneous argument is that individualization must take place within a team arrangement. Although some teaching teams work well, teaming is not essential and sometimes impedes learning by making it more difficult to monitor student needs and progress.

We have briefly examined the literature on individualized instruction. When the collective evidence is viewed as a whole, there is some reason to believe that student achievement can be affected in a positive way in well-implemented programs. Poorly implemented plans (insufficient or inappropriate learning assignments) and/or poorly managed programs (students have to spend large amounts of time waiting for teacher help) will reduce student achievement. There is also some reason to believe that individualization may have different effects for different types of students. Individualized programs that work well for most students may have subtle but consistently restraining effects on certain groups of students. Finally, we have argued that rigid adherence to a definition of individualization as students working alone is too narrow and limiting. It is more desirable to view individualization as the blending of individual, group, and whole-class assignments as needed by a particular group of students. Kepler and Randall (1977) argue that "Individualized instruction, with appropriate materials, should be recognized for what it is—an effective method for teaching some content areas, some skills, and some children—not a total educational program."

## OPEN CLASSROOMS

### Two Examples

Jane Stoverink team teaches with two other teachers, May Kline and Ted Smith, in an open classroom. They have two full-time aides to assist them in handling the 115 students that are under their direct supervision. The students are mostly "fifth-" and "sixth-" grade students although there are a few "fourth graders." The students come from middle-class homes and possess average or above average aptitudes. The teaching unit has been assigned one large open-space area for their instructional center. Most of the work goes on here. Each day, however, students in groups of 25 to 30 leave the central area and go with one teacher to a "regular" (enclosed-space) classroom for 30–40 minutes work in mathematics.

Students also receive regular work in reading. Each week, they are assigned a vocabulary to master and are encouraged to use the new words in a story they write. Furthermore, students are given reading quizzes frequently, so that the teaching staff can assess their progress in reading speed and comprehension. An hour is blocked out each day for free reading, and students select their own material (unless the student and teacher are working on an identified deficiency). Furthermore, students are expected to complete a one-page report when they finish a book. The rest of the day, students are allowed to pursue their other learning goals. In these activities, students are basically able to budget time in their own way to complete self-selected (but approved) project work. Each week students are requested to make out a tentative work plan (choosing from teacher suggestions, making their own plans). They are given the freedom to change the schedule from day to day; however, teachers stress the importance of completing schedules, and most students do.

Jerry Green, Mary Ellen Fischer, and Donna Jones teach in an open classroom setting. They too are responsible for about 100 fifth- and sixth-grade students (who come from middle-class homes) and are assisted by two aides. These students spend an hour or so each week in familylike activities with younger first- and second-grade students. Basically, the goal is to build school camaraderie and mutual trust by allowing older students to take responsibility for younger ones (read to them, help them work on projects).

The students spend another two hours each week in classroom discussion groups (30 or so students) with one teacher to talk about general problems in the learning area, to plan events that are of mutual concern, and so forth. Furthermore, each week, the students work one hour in a small group setting (three or four students) and exchange ideas about how to deal with social problems.

Hence, a great deal of time is spent in teacher-structured socialization experiences. During other parts of the school day, the students are generally allowed to pursue their own learning plans. Teachers try to reinforce student-initiated plans and to "motivate" students (suggesting possible ideas, etc.) if students have no plans. Students have general guidelines and suggested project lists, but teachers do not impose a structure (e.g., time deadlines) or have students place a structure on their work (logs, work schedule).

In general, students move through curriculum projects in a haphazard manner. Students who want to work often have a difficult time doing so because of the movement of other students around them and the high level of noise in the classroom. Students tend to pick assignments suggested by the teachers and to complete them in a leisurely manner. Assignments are often completed cooperatively by two or three friends.

Calling both of these two classrooms open masks as much information as it conveys. Certainly, both classrooms have students from more than one grade level, teaching teams, and large, well-equipped, open-space areas. But psychologically, the two atmospheres are quite different. In setting A, teachers communicate a belief in subject matter achievement and student work persistence, and they create an environment where these values can be fulfilled. In setting B, the teachers communicate an interest in socialization and affective development, and they create an environment in which these values can be fulfilled. If we looked at another "open" classroom, we might find students producing creative things (as opposed to socialization or subject matter achievement), but the point appears to be made in the two examples. Open education takes place in a variety of ways. To call a school or teaching unit "open" says very little about the form of instructional activities that take place. It is also possible to find major differences within open classrooms even when we find settings that at first glance seem highly similar. For example, we might find several classroom arrangements that look like setting A, but yet find that students in some of these classes performed much better than students in other classes. This is because individual teachers who implement a plan make a major difference in student growth. Teachers in one setting may stress problem solving in mathematics work. Teachers in another setting may stress skill practice. In yet another setting, equal emphasis may be placed on skill development and problem solving.

The two descriptions of "open" classrooms presented above illustrate how difficult it is to define open education. Katz (1973) has noted the difficulty of defining "open" education and has proposed several continuous dimensions to distinguish open-informal classes from traditional-formal ones. These dimensions appear in Table 8.1. As you look at this table, try to classify the two examples of open classrooms that you read about. (You may want to reread the two descriptions before examining Table 8.1.)

A critical question, of course, is how far on the continuum must a school be, and on how many dimensions (all, all but two, half?), to be classified as open. Unfortunately, when one reads research

TABLE 8.1.
COMPARISON OF OPEN AND TRADITIONAL CLASSROOMS

|  | OPEN-INFORMAL | TRADITIONAL-FORMAL |
| --- | --- | --- |
| Space | Flexible, Variable | Routinized, Fixed |
| Activities of Children | Wide Range | Narrow Range |
| Origin of Activity | Children's Spontaneous Interests | Teacher or School Prescribed |
| Content or Topics | Wide Range | Limited Range |
| Use of Time | Flexible, Variable | Routinized, Fixed |
| Initiation of Teacher-Child Interaction | Child | Teacher |
| Teaching Target | Individual Child | Large or Whole Group |
| Child-Child Interaction | Unrestricted | Restricted |

literature, it is usually not possible to know how a particular school fits into the framework proposed in Table 8.1. Hence, comparisons of "open" schools with other types of school settings may include schools that differ in major ways under the label "open." To further complicate the definitional issue, it should be noted that not all educators would accept the framework proposed by Katz. Many would add to or delete some of the defining aspects of openness that appear in Table 8.1.

**Research on Open Classrooms**
Space limitations make it impossible to review all studies that have examined open education. But we do want to discuss three studies that have attempted to look at the effects of open education in a reasonably comprehensive fashion. These studies seriously question the efficacy of open education for influencing achievement gains of students and even raise some questions about the effects of open programs on students' non-cognitive growth.

Wright (1975) published an interesting comparison of open and traditional instruction. Although his study involved only two schools, it is instructive and useful because of the variety of student outcomes that were examined and the close matching of students across the two school settings. The study was conducted in two suburban schools located two miles apart. Data were collected in fifth-grade classrooms.

Most students in the study had attended classes together in a traditional school through the second grade. The following fall, a new open-space school was built, and many youngsters transferred to the new school. Students chose to attend the new school on a voluntary basis. Wright identified 50 closely matched pairs of students in the two schools in order to test the effects of two and a half years of instruction in traditional and open settings. The students were matched on parents' educational level, their own achievement, their aptitude, and their attendance levels.

To measure school effects, nine achievement subtests of the Stanford Achievement Test (word meaning, paragraph meaning, spelling, language, arithmetic computation, arithmetic concepts, arithmetic applications, social studies, and science) were given. All comparisons favored the traditional school, and six of the nine differences were relatively large and statistically significant (the average difference was slightly more than half a year's difference in achievement).

Measures used to look for differences other than subject matter achievement included formal operational thought, locus of control, self-esteem, school anxiety, verbal creativity, and figural creativity. Overall analyses showed no difference between the two schools on these measures collectively. Individually, only one difference was significant: students reported higher levels of anxiety in open than in traditional schools.

These data show that students in the open school had a notable deficiency in academic skills in comparison to those in the traditional school. Furthermore, the data do not support the view that the open school was compensating in other areas: at least not in those measured in this study. (Very similar results have been reported by Grapko, 1973, who also compared an open-space and a traditional school: achievement was higher in the traditional school, especially for low IQ students.)

Neville Bennett and associates (1976) have reported a study of open education in England. The sample was focused upon the beliefs and practices of fourth-year teachers. Before collecting data, the investigators attempted to operationalize the terms "progressive" and "traditional" into concrete behaviors. Ultimately, they produced a list of 11 elements that, on the basis of literature reviews and interviews with teachers, appeared to capture the distinction between progressive and traditional classrooms (e.g., integrated vs. separate subject matter, active vs. passive student role, etc.).

They then used these 11 elements for constructing a detailed questionnaire asking 468 fourth-year teachers to describe their instructional practices, values, and beliefs. Ultimately, they grouped teachers on the basis of their questionnaire responses and selected for testing classrooms taught by teachers who appeared to represent different teaching philosophies and behavior. Three major types of classroom environments were sampled: informal (open), formal (traditional), and mixed.

The standardized achievement data were remarkably clear: in every comparison (English, mathematics, reading), formal methods produced better student performance than informal methods, and the differences were reasonably large (three to five months in achievement growth). Formal methods also produced higher mean gains than mixed methods, with the exception of reading, where the difference was not statistically significant.

Bennett and his associates also examined the achievement results to see if formal, informal, and mixed instructional modes had differential effects upon boys and girls or upon students of differing achievement levels. The only exception to the consistent pattern favoring *formal* methods was the finding that *low-achievement boys receiving formal instruction did worse* in all subject areas than boys in mixed or informal classes. Hence, these boys seemed to benefit more from less formal instruction.

Students' writing ability was also assessed by asking them to write stories on two different occasions. In one situation, students wrote a theme and were requested not to worry about grammar. In the other situation, the need for appropriate grammar and punctuation was stressed. The results of the two writing tests indicated that mixed and formal students were better at punctuation than students in informal classes. No differences in creative writing ability were noted. Non-cognitive student outcomes presented mixed findings. Students in informal classes reported better attitudes toward school and school assignments, but these students also reported more anxiety than students in formal or mixed classes. The level of self-concept reported by students was similar across all three settings.

Unlike the Wright study, these investigators included process measures of classroom behavior (although they were restricted to a very limited number of observations, a few classroom processes, and a few students). Observations were taken only in formal and informal classrooms. High-achievement students in formal rooms were observed to be engaged in significantly more task involvement than high-achievement students in informal classrooms. The involvement of high-achievement students in informal classes was no greater than the involvement of low-achievement students in formal classrooms. Middle achievers showed little difference across the two settings. Low achievers were observed to be considerably more involved in work in formal than in informal classes.

Unfortunately, observational data are not reported separately for low-achievement boys and girls. Given the finding that lower achievement boys did comparatively less well in formal classes, it would be reasonable to expect that their pattern of work involvement would differ from that of low-achievement girls across the two settings. If low-achievement boys are less involved in work in formal than in informal classes, then these data would strongly suggest that time on task (work involvement/opportunity to learn skills being measured on achievement tests) is directly related to achievement.

Within the limits of the data reported by Bennett et al., it appears that one probable cause of students' lower achievement in informal classes is that they work less. Perhaps the same argument can be made for low-achievement boys (they work less in *formal* classes), but these data are not reported. Unfortunately, other aspects of teaching and student behavior which might explain students' differential achievement and differential patterns of work involvement were not examined (degree of structure in learning assignments, instructional pace, type of feedback available). Hence, it is not possible to explain *how* higher levels of student task involvement were obtained in the formal setting.

Another examination of open education that merits attention is the collective work of several researchers who measured the effectiveness of openness on 8- and 11-year-old Canadian students (Traub, Weiss, Fisher, and Musella, 1973; Weiss, 1973; Corlis and Weiss, 1973). The team developed an instrument (DISC) to measure openness and designed a study to see if higher levels of openness were associated with more student achievement. Data also were analyzed with regard to the architectural forms of schools and the school populations being served (comparatively higher and lower socioeconomic levels). In the 18 higher SES schools, there was no consistent or important relationship between achievement and degree of openness or architectural type. However, in the 12 schools that served the lower SES population, *more open* programs were associated with *lower* achievement for both age groups of students. These data suggest that these students need more structure than they obtain in open classrooms.

The data in this study did show a relationship between positive student attitudes and openness in high SES schools, especially in the 11-year-old groups. However, higher verbal creativity scores were associated with less program openness. Furthermore, curiosity was not associated with openness in a direct way. Students who scored the *lowest* on curiosity measures were from closed architecture-low open programs and from open architecture-high open programs. Higher student curiosity levels were associated with a *moderate* degree of openness.

The findings on curiosity are in direct opposition to some of the basic assumptions of openness. Barth (1969) articulated three assumptions relevant to student curiosity and openness: (1) students will display curiosity behavior without adult stimulation, (2) exploratory behavior is self-maintaining, and (3) opportunity for active exploration in an environment that provides a wide assortment of manipulative materials will facilitate children's learning.

Subsequently, Corlis and Weiss (reacting to the data they had obtained) recommended a more structural hypothesis for educators who want to facilitate student curiosity. Specifically, they suggest the desirability of (1) providing *fewer* materials but selecting the materials carefully (the *teacher* is viewed as active planner) and (2) providing feedback to students as they explore new materials so that *goals* will emerge.

In general, the collective results of published articles on open education do not show a consistent, major impact on students' affective development (attitudes toward self, others, school, etc). (For examples of positive findings in open classrooms, including the citation of many unpublished studies, see Horwitz, 1976). Affective differences between open and comparison schools, when they do occur, tend to be very small. When *achievement* is considered, traditional schools consistently (though not universally) outperform open schools.

But remember that there are considerable differences within open and traditional schools. Some traditional classes (traditional in the sense of being self-contained) are more open in terms of classroom process than are some open classrooms (and vice versa). Kohler (1973) presents data relevant to this consideration. He found wide differences in students' self-concept scores within open and traditional schools. To understand the nature of these differences, he compared what was happening in the two schools (one traditional, one open) where students reported the highest self-concept with classroom processes in less effective schools.

The dimension that most notably separated the two effective schools from the other schools was their clearly defined and enforced rules for what should not be done (defined limits). Three other characteristics of the effective schools that the other schools seemed, at least in some degree, to lack were mutual respect, acceptance of students, and a demand for academic excellence. These dimensions are essentially the same factors that Coopersmith (1967) reported as characterizing the type of home environments that were associated with the development of children's self-concepts (structure, but freedom to improvise within the limits, and non-contingent acceptance of the child). Although authenticity and respect for students are present in most school programs that call themselves open, we suspect that academic and behavioral structure and high performance expectations are missing from many. Students need structure and limits if they are to evaluate their performance and to "see" increased levels of responsibility being given to them as a direct result of their ability to handle self-supervision demands that result from increased autonomy.

It seems clear that some degree of teacher structure must be present in the learning environment if achievement gains are to take place and if effective growth is to occur. The degree of structure will vary with the nature of instructional goals being pursued (subject matter achievement, for example, would demand comparatively more structure than most goals) and with the ages and general backgrounds of the students. Most open programs that operate at various educational levels seem to be the sorts of programs that make the most sense in secondary schools serving middle-class students. That is, many open programs that operate in elementary schools appear to have too little focus, too little teacher-imposed direction, and feedback and evaluation that are too vague and infrequent (especially in those programs that serve a large number of students who come from lower-class backgrounds).

## CONCLUSION

In reporting research on individualization and open education, we have discussed only a few studies. However, the review we presented is representative of the published findings presently available in the literature.

We think the data provide some support for individualized instruction. In those programs that are carefully conceived, well implemented, and frequently evaluated, achievement gains tend to occur. However, it should be noted that achievement gains typically are not large, suggesting that some students do not learn well in an individual mode. Some of these are dependent students who are anxious about teacher expectations and who find it difficult to get enough teacher attention to satisfy their affective or cognitive needs. Many students who have the cognitive ability and work skills necessary for working independently do not enjoy it, and as a result, achievement may suffer. Students who are socially motivated and stimulated by others benefit more from opportunities for public performance than from extended periods of private work (especially when that private work is not a prelude to public performance).

Still, if achievement for the class as a whole is the goal, a well-designed program of individual assignments is the single best way to achieve the goal. For young children and students with poor study skills, however, individual assignments need to be well planned, brief, and confined to only a small portion of the day. Such students need teacher assistance if subject matter achievement is to occur. Enthusiasm for the basically good idea of individualization must be heavily qualified when it is applied to the real classroom. As Glennon (1976) suggests, most students will benefit from sequential, systematic, and *structured* teaching.

Open education, at least in the extreme form that places a premium on a student-generated curriculum and unique learning goals, has not received support from research, as far as student achievement is concerned. The heart of the problem is the assumption that openness is good for all students. Friedlander (1975) describes the problem this way:

It is a gross oversight of available knowledge in psychology to assume that looser structure in the environment of the classroom is of some benefit for all children, just because it is a great benefit for some children (p. 467).

Good and Power (1976) argue that schools and/or teachers who present a constant environment day after day will tend to benefit and to penalize the same groups of students daily. Teachers need to balance instructional activities in terms of their goals and the learning needs of their students. In an inner-city elementary school, teachers will have to spend more time in direct teaching activity if students are to make progress in basic skill areas. In a suburban high school with a predominantly college-bound population, it makes more sense to stress self-directed and self-generated learning activities. But some students in the inner-city elementary school would benefit from self-directed learning, and some students in the suburban high school would benefit from direct instruction. Furthermore, we suspect that all students in both settings would benefit from a degree of appropriately planned variety. Elementary students would benefit from occasional work in small groups—where they pick their assignments, give reports to the whole class, complete their own projects in private, interview fellow students, publish class newspapers, prepare a budget for the class trip to the city zoo—even though the primary mode of instruction should be pleasant but persistent and academically demanding teacher-centered instruction.

Too often, organizational reforms that are designed to reduce identifiable problems simply produce new ones. This is because the change is too global. For example, in some cases, the *inappropriate pace* in self-contained classrooms is replaced by a boring *sameness* of individual units in individualized classes. The effect of overusing individual study is a decline in student motivation, which in time may make pacing at least as slow as that in self-contained classes but less fun and less interesting!

In summary, we reiterate the basic argument of this chapter: school organization (whole class, self-contained, individualized, multi-graded, open, etc.) does not make a school good or bad. Friedlander expresses the view this way:

I have been in some open classrooms that seemed like the blessed ideal of what schools should be like in terms of superior, humane teaching and learning; and I have been in open classrooms that could be compared only to the back wards of an unreformed mental hospital. (1975, p. 466–467.)

## SUGGESTED ACTIVITIES AND QUESTIONS

1. Visit a local school that purports to be "open". Describe the ways in which the school differs from the one you attended. How do students react? Do they seem involved? If there are two open schools in your area, visit them both and describe the ways in which they differ and the ways in which they are alike.

2. Observe in an open or individualized setting on at least five different days. Note the number and kinds of choices provided, student reaction to the choices provided, and the extent to which the students can handle the assignments without *undue* dependence on the teacher. Do the assignments seem more appropriate or interesting to certain students? Which students? Why?

3. From your own reading and experience with the concept of openness, react to the dimensions presented in Table 8.1. Which of these are critical? Why? What dimensions could or should be added from your point of view?

4. Would you prefer to teach in an individualized, open, or self-contained classroom? Why? In what ways does the teacher's role change across these settings?

5. Consider your own expectations now as a college student. How much structure do you want, and how much freedom do you want, in picking your own course goals? Talk to your friends in the class to see how different your needs are, and then attempt to design a classroom system (for your college course) that would satisfy all students' needs. Is it possible to do so?

6. Often, pressure on schools to change comes from public sources (e.g., information that achievement scores are declining) and from parents. Seldom do changes stem from a careful analysis of student opinion. Should students, as consumers, be given more of a say about day-to-day school procedures and routines?

7. Think back on your own school experience in high school. What was wrong with it? What changes could and should be made from your perspective? What was valuable and enjoyable? Will the changes that you suggest affect aspects of schooling that you found worthwhile or that someone else found worthwhile?

**FORM 8.1.** Student Independence in Individual Work

*USE: When students interact with teacher during periods of individual work assignment and/or in open settings.*
*PURPOSE: To see if individual students or students generally, over time, are becoming more autonomous learners.*
*Below is a list of student behaviors that could occur during seatwork assignments. Check each behavior as it happens.*

Frequency\*                                    Type Contact

_____    1. After beginning task, student seeks additional instructions about what to do.
_____    2. Student seeks confirmation about being on the right track ("Is this okay?").
_____    3. Student seeks substantive advice from teacher ("Is there another source that could be consulted?").
_____    4. Student seeks evaluative feedback ("What do you think about this conclusion?").
_____    5. Student tells teacher what was done and why (showing, justifying).
_____    6. Student asks teacher what to do next after completing the initial assignment (seeks direction).

\*In this particular example, the scale will yield information describing the frequency of different types of contact that occur with the teacher during a given amount of time. However, codes could be entered for individual students or for types of students by assigning them a number (high achievers = 1, middle achievers = 2, and so forth).

**FORM 8.2.** Student Involvement in Assigned Work

*USE: When some or all students are assigned individual seatwork*
*PURPOSE: Every two minutes, record the involvement levels of all students*
   *to assess degree of student involvement in assigned work*
*Number of students assigned to individual work:* _____
*Is teacher available to supervise assignment work?* _____
*Is aide(s) present to help?* _____

BEHAVIOR CATEGORIES

1. Clearly involved in assigned work.
2. Can't tell—may be thinking (code this rather than 1 or 3 if there is any doubt)
3. Definitely not doing assigned or chosen work.
4. Misbehaving.

| *Time* | *Student* * | *Number of Students in Each Involvement Category* | | | | | | | |
|---|---|---|---|---|---|---|---|---|---|
| 2:00 | _____ | 20 | 1 | 5 | 2 | 0 | 3 | 0 | 4 |
| 2:02 | _____ | 18 | 1 | 5 | 2 | 2 | 3 | 0 | 4 |
| 2:04 | _____ | 15 | 1 | 5 | 2 | 5 | 3 | 0 | 4 |
| 2:06 | _____ | 15 | 1 | 4 | 2 | 5 | 3 | 1 | 4 |
| _____ | _____ | _____ | 1 | _____ | 2 | _____ | 3 | _____ | 4 |
| _____ | _____ | _____ | 1 | _____ | 2 | _____ | 3 | _____ | 4 |
| _____ | _____ | _____ | 1 | _____ | 2 | _____ | 3 | _____ | 4 |
| _____ | _____ | _____ | 1 | _____ | 2 | _____ | 3 | _____ | 4 |
| _____ | _____ | _____ | 1 | _____ | 2 | _____ | 3 | _____ | 4 |
| _____ | _____ | _____ | 1 | _____ | 2 | _____ | 3 | _____ | 4 |
| _____ | _____ | _____ | 1 | _____ | 2 | _____ | 3 | _____ | 4 |
| _____ | _____ | _____ | 1 | _____ | 2 | _____ | 3 | _____ | 4 |

*It is possible to make a rating for *all* students or for some subdivision of the class:  H = high achievers; M = middle achievers; L = low achievers; G = girls; B = boys.

If several students are not involved, attempt to explain the lack of task engagement (students have finished, have given up, are waiting for the teacher, are distracted by others, no apparent reason).

**FORM 8.3.** Student Individual Work

*USE: Whenever students are working individually in the classroom*
*PURPOSE: To see how individual students use their time during independent work assignments*
*The observer should pick four to eight students and monitor every interaction as it takes place*
*Number of students in unit or class: _____*
*Number of students working as individuals: _____*

| Teacher Contact | | | | Peer Contact | | | | Leaves Seat | | |
|---|---|---|---|---|---|---|---|---|---|---|
| Created | | Afforded | | Created | | Afforded | | Material | | Misbehavior |
| Work | Procedure | Work | Procedure | Brief | Sustained | Brief | Sustained | Brief | Sustained | Brief | Sustained |
| | | | | | | | | | | | |

**FORM 8.3.** Student Individual Work (cont'd)

A target student is coded for a created contact with the teacher when the student approaches the teacher or signals the teacher to come to his or her desk. Afforded contacts are initiated by the teacher. If the interaction deals with the assignment directly, it is coded as work; if it deals with procedural aspects (permission to sharpen pencil, etc.), it is coded as procedural. Similarly, peer-created contact is coded when the target student creates contact with another student. If another student approaches the target student, it would be coded in the peer, afforded column. If contacts with other students are less than 15 seconds, they are coded as brief; if longer than 15 seconds, such as contacts are coded as sustained. Also, code target students when they leave their seats. The material column is coded if the student leaves to get the next assignment, check work, or engage in procedural activity (sharpen pencil, etc.). Misbehavior is coded when the student actively disrupts other students or is passively disengaged (stares out window).

The scale will be useful in identifying those students who show consistently high frequencies of behavior that merit additional study. (Why do some students avoid contact with teachers? Have they no need? Are they fearful? Disinterested? Why do teachers avoid contact with certain types of students?)

# 9/ CLASSROOM GROUPING

In the previous chapter, we noted that students learn at different rates due to differing aptitudes and persistence. Certain types of students learn better under some patterns of instruction than under others. In this chapter, we will continue the discussion of grouping students for instruction, suggesting more specifically how grouping patterns can facilitate or hinder the accomplishment of certain instructional goals. In particular, we will suggest that teachers can use different grouping patterns simultaneously.

Prior to this analysis, however, we will discuss the ways in which students are assigned to teachers for instruction. Obviously, the ability range of the students sets limits upon what a teacher can do in terms of instructional grouping and instructional goals. In the past several decades, schools have had the choice of assigning students to instructional units on the basis of "matched" or "mixed" ability levels.

Recent court rulings and legislative action have made it increasingly likely that schools will have more diverse student populations. There will be less separation of students along ability lines for the entire instructional day. To be successful, teachers will have to develop flexible grouping strategies that allow for either more or less ability grouping, as learning goals dictate.

In this chapter, we will present a review of the research on "mixed" and "matched" ability assignments. Then, we will describe two forces that make the teaching of mixed-ability student groups a more probable event in public schools. Finally, we will detail ways that teachers can deal with student diversity and achieve optimal classroom grouping plans.

## ABILITY GROUPING

The notion of ability grouping is a very appealing one; logic would seem to dictate that teachers could do a better job if differences in student ability were not so great. The teacher often goes too slow for the high achiever and too fast for the low achiever. Ability grouping is an attempt to reduce the range of student ability so the teacher can instruct more effectively. However, several authoritative reviews of ability grouping suggest that ability grouping per se is unlikely to have a positive effect on student achievement. Furthermore, such grouping is often found to reduce the achievement of low-achieving students and to fail in preparing students effectively for life in a pluralistic society (Borg, 1966; Findley and Bryan, 1971; Goodlad, 1960; Heathers, 1969; Johnson, 1970; Tuckman, 1971). In fact, most recent studies suggest that, when ability grouping does affect student achievement, the effect is usually negative: students placed into the lower ability levels, relative to other students, suffer an educational decline (Findley and Bryan, 1971).

These studies did not refer to ability assignments within classrooms, but to grouping by assigning students to *separate* classrooms. In such ability groupings, high- and low-achievement students are completely separated from one another and have no chance to interact. Such groups are often called *homogeneous groupings* because an attempt is made to substantially reduce the range in IQ or achievement among students in the same class. The students then are similar in aptitude or ability, hence the term "homogeneous."

In contrast, when children are assigned at random (e.g., all fifth-grade students' names are on a sheet in alphabetical order and the principal assigns every third name to classroom A), there is more mixture. Random selection results in a greater range of student ability or aptitude, and thus, the term "heterogeneous" is often applied.

Why has ability grouping (homogeneous grouping) failed? Johnson (1970) suggests that few attempts have been made to change teachers' behavior to enable them to take advantage of new situations. Teachers in schools that practiced ability grouping were not provided with new skills or curriculum materials aimed specifically for different levels of students. Goldberg et al. (1966) suggest that teachers did not adjust their content to meet the special needs of students at different achievement levels. They note that some teachers of the low-ability groups taught less content to low-level pupils and set lower achievement goals for them.

Available literature suggests that teachers do not change their behavior substantially to take advantage of being able to work with special levels of students, and that when they do change their behavior, the likely result is that *low-ability sections will receive a poorer quality of instruction.* Poorer instruction in these circumstances can probably be explained as follows: First, teachers underestimate the ability of students in low groups because the label "low ability" creates a rigid stereotype of student incompetence in the teachers' minds (Tillman and Hull, 1964). Second, the quality of instruction in the low-ability sections sometimes suffers because teachers do not enjoy teaching low-ability students. Teachers regularly report that they do not enjoy teaching the low group when students are ability grouped (Findley and Bryan, 1971).

*Group Placement Tends to Be Permanent*   Mackler (1969) concluded, from data collected in a longitudinal study of more than one thousand children in a Harlem ghetto school, that placement into a low-ability group has permanent effects upon the student. If a capable student is assigned to a bottom section, the road to the top is a very steep, demanding journey. Bottom first-grade classes are filled with immature students who cannot learn as quickly as students in top classes, and much teacher time is spent in dealing with student needs and problems rather than with instruction. Students will find it difficult to succeed under such circumstances, but if they do, they might make the next-to-the-top group in the second grade. If they do especially well, they may make the top group by the third grade. Mackler's data show that no student made it to the top group after the third grade. /

*Students Are Often Misclassified and Suffer Because of Low Placement*   Mackler's data would be less disheartening if there were but few mistakes made when students are placed into high, middle, and low groups. Students can be misplaced (every time students are assigned to ability groups with even the best instruments, at least ten percent will be misclassified), and when they are misplaced downward, they are penalized. What happens when students are placed into higher or lower groups than their scores justify? Douglas (1964) reports a study in which a group of high-ability and low-ability students were assigned, at age eight, to groups higher than their ability suggested and to groups lower than suggested by their ability. Three years later, the same results were observed for both high- and low-ability students: those students who were placed into higher sections improved; those students who were placed into lower groups deteriorated. These results are striking: students benefit from high placement and are penalized by low placement.

Tuckman and Bierman (1971) also report a gain for students who were misplaced upward. On standardized achievement tests given at the end of the year, high school students who had been placed in higher groups outperformed others who remained in their original groups. This did not hold for all students, but it did occur with enough regularity to demonstrate that placement of students in higher ability groups raises the performance of many students.

*Why Does Higher Placement Help Students?* It can be argued that improvement by these students is caused by (1) exposure to teachers who treat them differently because the teachers expect good performance, (2) opportunity to mix with brighter peers who model better skills and attitudes, and (3) better self-concepts and motivation resulting from placement in a higher group.

Data relevant to the first explanation have been produced by Schrank (1968, 1970). First, he studied the effects of group labeling on 100 enlisted airmen who were studying at the United States Air Force Academy Preparatory School. This school normally grouped its students for instructional purposes on the basis of demonstrated ability.

Schrank decided *not* to group students by ability, according to the typical practice, but instead to assign students to sections randomly. The sections still had ability labels, but neither the students nor the instructors knew that these ability labels had no validity. After seven months of instruction in mathematics and English, the class performances (midterms and final exams, etc.) of the airmen were analyzed. The findings were strikingly clear. Each section performed up to its ability label, achieving a higher mean grade than the next lower section.

However, in a second study, conducted at the United States Air Force Academy with 420 cadets, Schrank found that the ability-group label did *not* influence student performance as it had in the first study. The only difference in the second experiment was that the instructor *knew* that the groupings were random.

In combination, these two studies suggest that the effect of the ability label is, in part, dependent upon the teachers' belief in the ability groupings. That is, the ability label influences student behavior because it influences teacher attitudes and behavior. In any case, all four studies (Douglas, 1964; Tuckman and Bierman, 1971; Schrank, 1968, 1970) strongly suggest that low-ability students can achieve in classes where the work load and teacher demand for academic success are high.

*Rigid Within-Classroom Groups May Create Unhealthy Learning Environments* Ability grouping that places high and low achievers in separate classrooms causes teachers to treat students as a group and to ignore important differences in student needs. Also, working with the low group is often perceived as an unpleasant teaching task, one that teachers often begin with low expectations. However, caste systems that clearly differentiate and humiliate students can be created psychologically *within* classrooms where students are assigned heterogeneously. Indeed, low achievers in some of these classrooms may experience even greater problems of invidious comparison than they would as members of a low class, particularly if teachers help give the impression that slower students are inferior. Obviously, no respectable teacher would do such a thing consciously, but some teachers inadvertently behave in such a way as to engender or perpetuate classroom feelings of elitism.

Rist (1970) provides a gripping example of how powerful an effect teachers can exert on students. He followed a group of students from kindergarten through the second grade and showed how dramatic the influence of the first grouping was on their educational lives. After a few days in class, the kindergarten teacher began to call consistently on the same students to lead the class to the bathroom, to be in charge of playground equipment, to take attendance and carry messages to the office, and so on. On the eighth day of class, this teacher made permanent seating assignments.

At table 1, the table physically closest to the teacher's desk, the teacher placed those children who were highly verbal—the same ones who tended to approach the teacher without apprehension, who were free of body odor, and who came from relatively higher socioeconomic backgrounds. Interviews with the teacher suggested that these groupings were based on expectations of students' success or failure. On the eighth day of class, the teacher spontaneously verbalized low expectations for the performance of children at tables 2 and 3. Interestingly, children who were shy and had trouble communicating with the teacher were placed farthest away from the teacher, adding another barrier to their achieving contact with the teacher.

Rist followed 18 of these 30 children when they were placed into the same first-grade classroom, and he noted that all children who had been placed at table 1 in kindergarten were placed at table A (the best group) in the first-grade classroom. No student who had been placed at table 2 or 3 in kindergarten was placed at table A. Those students who had been at tables 2 and 3 were placed at table B, with the exception of one placed at table C. The students at table C, the low group, were primarily children who were repeating the first grade from the previous year.

Subsequent follow-up data in the second grade revealed the same pattern. There, the teacher termed the best group the Tigers, the middle group the Cardinals, and, unbelievably, the low group the Clowns. No student who had not been at table A in the first grade moved up to the Tigers. Students from tables B and C formed the Cardinals, and students repeating second grade from the previous year were the Clowns. Rist suggests that this teacher, instead of forming groups on the basis of expected child performance, formed groups according to how children had performed in school previously. Rist saw the slow learner locked into a self-defeating system at this point. No matter how well a child in the low group read, he or she was *now* destined to remain in the low group. Other studies all suggest the same conclusion: rigid ability grouping does more harm than good.

### Ability Grouping Research: A Qualification

In the past few years, school desegregation laws have been enforced much more vigorously than was the case previously. Such enforcement has resulted in a greater mixing of students from low and high socioeconomic levels. Hence, the range of ability levels within many schools is larger than it was. Much of the research on ability grouping was conducted prior to major integration efforts. Furthermore, this research was also collected prior to mainstreaming (the return of mildly retarded learners to the classroom). It is possible that, at some point, the spread of achievement level may become so great that a form of ability grouping will have to be invoked. (A plan that separates students of vastly different levels, but still allows students who differ in ability to have meaningful contact, will be discussed later in the chapter.)

Although we feel that the conclusion "rigid ability grouping does more harm than good" remains true under classroom conditions that presently operate, it is important to realize that many teachers face a wider ability range than was the case when much of the ability-grouping research was conducted. If anything, these differences are likely to increase, because of current social attitudes and judicial rulings. We now turn to a discussion of two issues that influence the range of ability in student populations: mainstreaming and desegregation.

## MAINSTREAMING

Sometime ago, many learners were removed from regular school programs and placed in special classes. It was felt that their needs could not be satisfied in regular classrooms, or that their presence interfered with the learning of other students. Special institutions were built, and special teachers were trained, to deal with their problems. Recently, many of these students have been returned to regular classrooms. This practice of removing students (who presumably suffer from some learning handicap) from special, segregated learning environments and returning them to regular classrooms is commonly known as "mainstreaming."

Historically, the courts supported the view that educators could deny school enrollment to students who might interfere with classroom procedure because of their physical or mental deficiencies. Flowers and Bolmeier (1964) review a number of court cases illustrating how courts supported the right of public schools to deny schooling to students for a variety of reasons: mental and physical deficiencies, health, flagrant misbehavior, pregnancy, and even unconventional clothes and personal appearance. These court decisions supported the viewpoint that school is a privilege for those who fulfill specific criteria, not a guaranteed right. Although some actions to separate students from school were appropriate (e.g., students with extreme mental or physical handicaps), many times schools exercised this power in a negative or capricious fashion (e.g., denying students education because of pregnancy or dress).

Recent court rulings have progressively moved toward a new interpretation of student rights. Enrollment in normal public school programs is becoming a right for more students (Cohen and DeYoung, 1973; Collings, 1973; Vaughn, 1973), and it is clear that courts have taken a new view toward the rights of the handicapped student. Gilhool (1973) argues that handicapped citizens no longer have to rely on the goodwill of others for access to public education; they are now legally entitled to it.

Legislative action has also influenced the rights of handicapped students. MacMillan, Jones, and Meyers (1976) point out that court action combined with new legislation led to the return of 11,000 to 18,000 EMR (educable mentally retarded) students from special to regular classrooms between 1969 and 1972 in California.

The federal government's support for handicapped students has become more explicit. For example, in December 1975, a bill was signed into law that greatly extended federal support for educating students who are mentally retarded, emotionally disturbed, or have specific learning disabilities. Historically, the major cost of educating handicapped students has been left to parents (who had to find private schools) and to state and local educational agencies. The new law specifies that, when the nature or severity of a handicap prevents a pupil's inclusion in a regular program, the state, with the aid of federal government, must provide special services at no cost to parents.

Progressively, court rulings, state laws, and federal laws are supporting the view that handicapped students have a right to free public education and should be enrolled in normal school programs whenever possible. Social attitudes, court rulings, and legislative acts collectively will guarantee that many special students who formerly would not have had access to public schooling will be in public schools for at least part of their instructional day. Despite these strong societal pressures, professional educators view mainstreaming with mixed expectations.

Chaffin (1974) states four reasons why mildly retarded youth are being returned to the classrooms:

1. Court litigation
2. Realization among special educators that "labeling" a child as a special learner has debilitating effects that are worse than the advantages special treatment provides
3. The equivocal results of research dealing with the effectiveness of special classes for the mildly retarded
4. Recognition that diagnostic instruments for identifying retarded children are imprecise, so that many students are improperly classified as "special learners"

These factors are important and cannot be ignored. However, MacMillan, Jones, and Meyers (1976) observe that students who are being returned failed in regular classrooms prior to being identified as EMR and that, after suffering the effects of a label, they are not likely to make substantial gains when they return to regular classrooms. Given that many teachers did not want and/or learn how to work with these students in the first place, it is likely that some will receive less attention and help than they were receiving in their special education classrooms. Under these conditions, mildly retarded students may even lose ground when they return to public classrooms, particularly if they are subjected to cruel treatment by peers. These authors point out that it is easy to put students back into the classroom but difficult to assure satisfactory social and academic growth. Although a strong proponent of mainstreaming, Dunn (1973) suggests that specific techniques for working with EMR students in regular classrooms do not exist.

As we have pointed out elsewhere (Good and Brophy, 1977), the mainstreaming concept will fail in some schools. In other schools, because of hard work by the school staff, it will work for many learners. Teacher expectations are critical. Unreasonably high or low expectations will lead to poor programs. Teachers who develop reasonable performance expectations and who demand appropriate resources (administrative support, resource teachers, special material including manipulative devices) will be able to help students to adjust to and cope more fully with the complexities of modern life.

Such students will present acute problems for teachers. They will take much more teacher time, because they need unique individual assignments, detailed feedback, and constant supervision. A few of these students will take much time because of behavioral disturbances. Teachers who are charged with the responsibility of integrating these students into their classrooms should be given *smaller classes* to help them have the time they will need.

## DESEGREGATION

Prior to the 1954 *Brown* decision, neighborhood schools served *relatively* homogenous student populations. Students who came from affluent homes lived in affluent neighborhoods and attended schools (especially elementary schools) with students from similar home backgrounds. Students who came from poor homes went to schools attended largely by students from other poor homes. In cities of any size, schools were segregated by neighborhood lines, and by social lines in some communities. Even though a minority student lived in the neighborhood, he or she often was denied access to the school because of social prejudice.

The *Brown* decision made the provision of separate school facilities for minority students illegal. Throughout the mid-1960s and the 1970s, the number of substantially all-black and all-white public schools was reduced by desegregation.

In small and moderately large cities (e.g., 200,000 or so), busing and general desegregation plans often had the effect of integrating schools more fully across social, socioeconomic, and ability lines. However, desegregation plans have had difficulty in large metropolitan areas because of the physical distance that separates poor from affluent neighborhoods (busing is both time-consuming and costly) and the decreasing availability of youngsters from affluent homes who remain enrolled in public schools (many affluent black and white middle-class parents have left the inner city to live in suburbs, and many others enroll their children in private schools).

Where desegregation activities have brought about more diverse student populations, teachers will have to accommodate new problems and opportunities. However, many inner-city school populations are largely homogenous, populated mostly by low achievers. As we know from the research on ability grouping, this is not conducive to student learning. Low expectations get in the way, as does the absence of better students that low achievers can use as models.

Some educators contend that mandated desegregation inevitably leads to lower achievement. However, there is growing evidence to suggest that teachers and schools can accommodate the learning needs of diverse student populations. For example, Wegmann (1977) notes that in White Plains, New York, white students were found to be doing as well or better academically after busing than before. Furthermore, black students also were doing better, and white families were not leaving the city. However, less favorable results have been obtained in other locations.

In an interesting case study, Eash and Rasher (1977) report the effects of mandated desegregration upon student achievement in Forrestville, a "bedroom" suburb of a large metropolitan area. The social mix of the community was 80 percent white and 20 percent black. In 1972, 90 percent of the black population was enrolled in one elementary school. Subsequently, under state mandate, a busing desegregation plan was put into effect. Two years after the plan was started, it was found that achievement for black and white children had improved. Significantly, black students were doing very *well* in a few schools but *poorly* in other schools. Some schools did a better job of meeting their needs.

After these achievement data were collected, subsequent in-service efforts were planned to improve instruction further, and student achievement in 1975–1976 was found to have increased over 1974–1975 levels. Also, attitudinal data suggested that both black and white students perceived the learning environment favorably. Hence, the in-service program appears to have paid off. Interestingly, then, this desegregation plan worked for most students although initially black students were considerably better off in some schools than others. In-service activities focused on improvement of instruction (helping teachers to use individualized and small-group procedures to instruct a broader range of students and help in selecting and using effectively a greater variety of instructional material) were helpful in raising achievement throughout the district. Eash and Rasher point out that the administrative office of the school district found it necessary to improve the supervisory and observational skills of principals in order to conduct appropriate in-service training. This probably encouraged principals to spend more time supervising instruction and helping teachers to adapt their instruction to student needs. Systematic feedback about one's teaching behavior can be a powerful force in improving instruction (more on this in Chapter 11).

Desegregation plans do not always work. Sometimes, forced busing is followed by lowered student achievement and by hostile attitudes among students and/or parents. There appears to be more difficulty in maintaining achievement levels when the minority population exceeds about 30 percent of the school population (Wegmann, 1977). However, achievement does not necessarily decline, and in many instances, achievement and attitudes have increased for both black and white students following desegregation. Those schools that make it work are staffed by teachers who focus upon the success of individual students and who adapt their instruction and materials to student needs.

Eash and Rasher (1977) conclude that the problems associated with desegregation are not unique, but instead are common instructional problems found in all schools: (1) how to teach students in the same classroom when there is a wide range of abilities, (2) how to organize a classroom which uses a wide variety of instructional materials, and (3) how to set up a classroom community that obtains the cooperation of students in maintaining behavior that permits learning.

In the remainder of this chapter, we will share ideas about how you can accomplish these three tasks. We now turn to another look at ability grouping.

## GROUPING: A STRATEGY FOR DEALING WITH HETEROGENEOUS LEARNERS

Not all teachers will work with EMR students who are being mainstreamed. However, most teachers will have to contend with students of limited IQ while also dealing with students who are very talented academically. Furthermore, most teachers will work with students of diverse backgrounds because of the increased belief that students with diverse backgrounds should have contact in public schools. There are still some inner-city schools and some suburban schools with relatively homogeneous populations, but most teachers will have to teach students representing a wide range of ability.

Earlier in the chapter, we argued that homogeneous (ability) grouping often is not a good instructional strategy in practice, especially for low-achievement students. It does not make sense to take EMR learners out of special facilities and then group them only with low achievers; both groups of students would suffer. Slower students can benefit from the stimulation of brighter students only if they have contact with them.

### Stratified Ability Grouping

However, it is possible that the spread in some school populations is so wide as to make a mild form of ability grouping profitable. Findley and Bryan (1971) describe a plan developed in Baltimore that successfully reduces the range of student ability in a class (making it easier to teach), but leaves a moderate range, so that the advantages of diversification can occur. Their description follows:

> The plan may be called stratified heterogeneous grouping. Under this plan, if three classes of 30 are to be formed from 90 children ready to start fifth grade, the children would be ranked in order of excellence on some composite—say, a standardized test battery—and then be subdivided into nine groups of ten each. Teacher A would be given a class consisting of the highest or first ten, the fourth ten, and the seventh ten; Teacher B would have the second, fifth, and eighth tens; Teacher C would then be given the third, the sixth, and the ninth (lowest tens) as shown below.

| TEACHER A | TEACHER B | TEACHER C |
|---|---|---|
| Group 1 (1–10) | Group 2 (11–20) | Group 3 (21–30) |
| Group 4 (31–40) | Group 5 (41–50) | Group 6 (51–60) |
| Group 7 (61–70) | Group 8 (71–80) | Group 9 (81–90) |

Note the several merits of this scheme. First, there is no top or bottom section; the sections overlap, so invidious comparisons between groups are minimized. Second, each class has a narrower range than the full 90 have: Teacher A has the top ten, but none of the bottom 20; Teacher B has neither the top nor the bottom ten; Teacher C has the bottom ten but none of the top 20. Third, teachers can give special attention where it is needed without feeling unable to meet the needs of the opposite extreme: Teacher A can give a little special attention to the top ten because the bottom 20 are not in the class; Teacher C can concentrate on the bottom ten, without fear of "losing" the top 20. Fourth, each class has leaders of appropriate capability to stimulate each other in a fair, competitive way while giving leadership to lower groups; note particularly that in Teacher C's class, the top group is the third ten, a group that has probably always had to play second fiddle to some in the first or second ten. Finally, no teacher has to teach the bottom group of a homogeneous plan, that mixture of disruptive, leaderless children who lack motivation and capability and make teachers like homogeneous grouping, but dislike to teach the slow groups.

Such a method of grouping is not offered as a complete answer by itself, but as a constructive step in the right direction. It is, moreover, compatible with other special teaching arrangements, like team teaching, peer tutoring, and early education.

The plan described above is one way to achieve a wider mix of students at different achievement levels in the same room without forcing a teacher to prepare instructional material for the full range of student learning needs. We feel that the plan is an interesting, workable strategy. However, three important points should be considered:

1. The groups do overlap, but they are different. Group A, for example, is still the highest group since it has the highest students from each third. Group C, in a relative sense, is the lowest group. Although Group C has many extremely capable students, in the minds of the teacher (and the students or parents), this group may become the "difficult" group to teach. Obviously, the strength of this grouping plan is that it minimizes group differences; however, sometimes, slight differences in ability become exaggerated in daily practice. When this plan is implemented, it would be important to see if any tendency exists for Group C to become a "low" group.

2. It is also important that teachers expect good performance from their low-achievement students. While we do not deny the fact that some teachers do not enjoy teaching low-ability students, we do insist that these students are capable of good performance when they receive enthusiastic instruction that is appropriately matched to their aptitudes and interests. Also, it should be realized that there are teachers who do enjoy teaching low-ability students and who find their teaching efforts to be important and very rewarding. If the primary motivation for grouping students is to avoid working with large numbers of low-achievement students, the plan will probably not work. Again we suggest that, if teachers do not feel that low-ability students can learn, and if teachers are unwilling to engage in remedial activities with these students, no grouping pattern will be successful.

3. A real strength of the plan is that it allows for students of differing ability to mix without leaving the teacher

with the time-consuming task of preparing instructional activities for every achievement level. Thus, the plan reduces the range of ability that a given teacher will instruct, but the range of ability in all classes is sufficiently wide to require teachers to treat students as individual learners and not as group members.

### Grouping Within Classrooms

Regardless of whether or not schools separate students into classes by ability, many teachers will group students within their classes by ability levels. Here again, this grouping should be considered carefully. For example, teachers can profit from grouping students who read at the same level into reading groups. However, this selection opens the door for teaching the students as a group rather than as individual learners.

Previously, we noted that even high-ability students who are appropriately placed into high-ability groups sometimes do not outperform high-ability students who remain in heterogeneously grouped classrooms. This probably occurs for two interrelated reasons: (1) teachers do not develop materials or methods suited to the unique demands of the student ability level they work with, and (2) teachers tend to view students within an ability group as similar and to treat them alike without attending to their differential needs. Consequently, some students are more likely to receive individualized instruction in rooms that are heterogeneously grouped.

Remember that heterogeneous assignment places students from varying achievement levels in the same room, so it is possible for low- and high-ability students to be grouped together or separated when it is advantageous to do so. Unfortunately, some teachers who group for one instructional purpose (e.g., reading) may make assignments throughout the day that keep the same students working together all the time. When this happens, students are ability grouped psychologically.

Despite the need to use instructional groups to save time, teaching still needs to be individualized within groups. If some students continue to have trouble even though most have mastered the material, the teacher must deal with those who continue to have difficulty. There is no reason to continue with the entire group; students who have mastered the material should be allowed to go on. But those who have not mastered the material need to learn it. Sometimes, this simply means repeating or reteaching the material. However, reteaching may mean presenting the concept in a different way with new examples. If the students did not learn it the first time, they are unlikely to learn it the second time unless the teacher presents it in a new way.

Teachers too often are tied to time limits and groupings. If a group is scheduled to meet for 30 minutes, they meet for 30 minutes, regardless of their performance. This rigidity often is wasteful. One way the teacher can meet individual needs within groups is to break the group down into even smaller units when the need or opportunity arises, releasing students who have learned and concentrating on those who need more work. Obviously, this will require a well-developed set of individualized tasks for students to work on when they leave the group.

### Grouping Should Be Flexible

Classroom grouping assignments should be reviewed regularly and routinely with an eye toward forming new groups. A group should exist because it facilitates teaching and learning by placing together students who have similar learning needs. When a student masters phonics, he or she no longer needs to be in a group that spends half its time on phonics drills. Groups are such convenient devices that they can keep teachers from thinking and dealing effectively with problems. Teachers place children into high, middle, or low groups and then do not think about them again; but if they are to be effective, they have to think about them. Grouping can be a powerful tool if teachers use it effectively to organize students for learning specific skills, and if they disband groups once their usefulness ceases and form new groups as new needs become apparent. One way to enhance the degree of flexibility that teachers have in grouping students is to share students with other teachers.

### Sharing Students with Other Teachers

When teachers share students, it is possible to combine the advantages of stratified grouping and the flexibility of increasing or decreasing the range of student ability.

Teachers may group in ways other than just within each classroom. For example, three first-grade teachers known to the authors devised their own grouping plan. Originally, students had been randomly assigned to each class. Each teacher taught and carefully observed the students in her class for a period of six weeks. Then the teachers divided the students in their classrooms into high, middle, and low groups for mathematics and for reading (the groups were not the same in each subject area), and one teacher took the high readers, another the middle readers, and the third the low readers. However, in mathematics, the teacher who had taken the low readers took the high mathematics students and the teacher who had taken the high readers took the low mathematics students.

Separate teacher assignments were undertaken so that students did not come to view one classroom as the dummy room, another as the brain trust room, and so forth. This plan also widened the students' experiences by enabling them to come into contact with different teachers and learn to cope with different classroom tempos. The students remained with their regular teacher for all other activities (science, social studies, art, music, lunch, and recess).

These students were ability grouped for instruction in reading and mathematics, but were in mixed-ability groupings for all other instruction. Many were working with three different teachers but yet spent most of the day with a single teacher: a condition that we think facilitates the affective growth of young children. An extra advantage to this plan was that, when students experienced academic difficulty, all three teachers frequently had pertinent knowledge of them and could help analyze their mutual teaching behavior and collectively answer the question, "What can we do differently to help them?"

These teachers were careful not to treat students as a group, even though they had been assigned together because of similar aptitudes. The teachers were using groups not as a convenient way to forget about individual students, but as a way to organize students for meeting specific learning needs. Some weeks, there were four mathematic groups. Other weeks, there were only two, depending upon progress during the previous week. In addition, the teachers made ample use of peer tutoring, allowing students to assist one another so that the teacher could spend more time with those who needed remedial or enrichment work.

In addition to changing the number of groups, the three teachers, who met weekly also frequently changed the composition of groups. At those meetings, the teachers compared students and exchanged suggestions on how to facilitate the growth of those who were not making satisfactory progress. The teachers, all outstanding, were notable in their capacity for blaming themselves, not students, when learning progress was not satisfactory.

It is possible for teachers in the same grades (or across grade levels) to work out arrangements so that in some subjects students are working closely with peers of similar ability and in other subjects with peers who are both faster and slower than they are, thus exposing them to a wide variety of learning experiences, both social and academic.

At times, teachers will group in order to teach a more homogeneous group of students, but most teachers will teach mixed-ability groups. We now turn to this topic.

## TEACHING MIXED-ABILITY CLASSES

Teachers' planning for a group of students who range in IQ from 85 to 140 is vastly different from the type of planning necessary for a group of students who range from 110 to 140. In the latter case, the teacher has to address individual differences in interest and work style, but the general academic demand can be similar for all students. However, when a teacher decides or is assigned to teach mixed-ability students in the same class, major adjustments in planning have to take place.

As the range of student ability in a class increases, the role of whole-class teaching (teacher presentation of information to students at the same time) decreases and the role of individual and small-group work increases. This is not to suggest that whole-class teaching disappears in mixed-ability classes: it continues to play an important role, but the frequency and duration of whole-class teaching is less in mixed-ability than in homogeneous-ability classes.

Students in mixed-ability classes will benefit from exchanging ideas in a large group setting (speaking before a group, etc.). Furthermore, managerial issues, unit introductions and reviews, use of equipment, demonstration of experiments, and certain other types of information exchange will lend themselves to whole-class presentations in mixed-ability classes. However, to reiterate, teachers' use of individual assignments and small-group work will need to increase in mixed-ability classes. The discussion here focuses upon ways in which teachers can develop individual and group assignments that allow students of varying abilities to work on *similar projects.*

One of the biggest problems that a teacher faces when making assignments in mixed-ability classrooms is reading ability. Some students can read well and will do so enthusiastically; others have limited skills and interest in reading. If teachers are to allow students of mixed ability to work on similar projects, they must solve the reading problem. One strategy for doing this is to gather a wide assortment of materials written at varying levels of difficulty on a *few* core topics (it is unrealistic to try to acquire and store several books on every curriculum topic).

Although they read books that differ in detail or vocabulary, students can still share a common focus on historical events (the Civil War) or famous persons (Booker T. Washington, Marie Curie, Babe Ruth). Furthermore, many stories of literary significance are written with a low vocabulary demand (e.g., Tom Sawyer). Students reading at different grade levels could benefit from reading these books, even though the teacher may later ask them to respond to the books in different ways.

Some tasks do not demand a great deal of reading per se; however, even activity assignments of an individual nature must be carefully prepared with the low achiever in mind. If slow students are to comprehend written instructions and to function independently, directions must be stated in very simple and explicit terms. Otherwise, teachers will spend inordinate amounts of time with individual students, clarifying directions and responding to managerial problems that stem from lack of task involvement (e.g., the students didn't know what to do). Teachers who provide directions simple enough for the least capable reader who will use that particular activity sheet will be providing a support system that allows students to gain confidence in their self-supervision skills. Also, such teachers will have more free time to interact with other students. Tasks need to become progressively more complex, however, as these students mature.

Cooke (1976) suggests a variety of ways for developing individual work cards for students of varying ability who are working on similar historical topics. Included in his suggestions are the following:

1. Develop a core card for each topic and subtopic, and require all students to complete activities at their individual paces.
2. Develop a number of option cards which provide guidelines for more intensive subject work, special activities, etc., and allow students to choose from the option cards.
3. Rather than develop option cards for a variety of students (because of practical restraints involved in producing a large number of individual cards), teachers might produce separate option (and/or core) cards for three or four ability levels.

Figures 9.1, 9.2, and 9.3 illustrate work cards that have been prepared for three different ability levels. The figures show how the same historical topic could be pursued in different ways by three groups of students. Figure 9.1 shows the assignment for slow 12-year-old students. Notice that the assignment focuses upon concrete details, helping the student to comprehend parts of a passage in order to find material to make comparatively simple judgments.

Figures 9.2 and 9.3 illustrate assignments for middle- and high-level students. Progressively, directions are written in less specific terms, students are encouraged to search different books, and page

**FIGURE 9.1.** Example of Work Card

Roman Britain  Work card 1

## HADRIAN'S WALL

    This is a picture of a part of Hadrian's Wall as it is now. You can also see the ruins of the Roman fort at Housesteads.
    Have a copy of *A Soldier on Hadrian's Wall* by D. Taylor on your table.

*Things To Do*

1. Write down these sentences and fill in the missing words. Pages 14 and 16 of *A Soldier on Hadrian's Wall* will help you.

    a. Hadrian's Wall was built from . . . . . . . . in the east to . . . . . . . . in the west. It is . . . . . . . . miles long.

    b. It was made of . . . . . . . .

    c. It measures . . . . . . . . feet high and . . . . . . . . feet thick.

    d. In front of the wall was a . . . . . . . . and behind it was a . . . . . . . . .

2. Imagine that you are the Roman officer in charge of building the wall. Write a letter to a friend in Rome telling him or her what the various buildings on the wall are and what they are used for. You can find out about these buildings in your book, pp. 16–20.

3. Draw a diagram of one of the buildings in your letter. Label all the parts and sizes of it. If you prefer, make a model of it to scale.

4. Draw and color a picture showing a scene from Hadrian's Wall, perhaps an enemy attack or soldiers marching along it. From the picture on this card, imagine what it must have been like on the wall.

**FIGURE 9.2.** Example of Work Card

Roman Britain                                                        Work card 2
                          HADRIAN'S WALL

This is a picture of Hadrian's Wall today.

*Read*

   *A Soldier on Hadrian's Wall* by D. Taylor

   *Roman Britain* by R. Mitchell

   *Roman Britain* by J. Liversidge, pp. 16–33

   *The Romans in Scotland* by O. Thomson, Chapter 3

*Things To Do*

1. Answer these questions as fully as you can:

   a. Why did Hadrian build a wall across Britain?

   b. If you were an enemy of the Romans trying to break through the wall
      from the north, where do you think its weakest points would be? You
      will need to find information about the various forts and defenses
      along the wall.

   c. Another wall was built 20 years later by the Romans in Scotland.
      Which Emperor built it? Why was it built? How different was it from
      Hadrian's Wall?

2. Imagine that you are the Roman officer in charge of building Hadrian's
   Wall. Write a report to the Emperor telling him why you have decided to
   change the wall from turf to stone and to alter the size.

3. Draw a diagram of a cross-section of the wall, or of a fort, and label it carefully. If you prefer, make a scale model of it.

4. *Either,* as the Roman officer, write an entry for your diary describing an
   incident on the wall.
   *Or,* draw and color a picture of the incident.
   Do both of these if you wish.

**FIGURE 9.3.** Example of Work Card

Roman Britain                                                    Work card 3
                              HADRIAN'S WALL

Consult the books in the class history library on Roman Britain, in particular
*The Roman Frontiers of Britain* by D. R. Wilson; *The Roman Imperial Army
of the First and Second Centuries* by G. Webster; *The Romans in Scotland* by
O. Thomson; *Handbook to the Roman Wall* by I. A. Richmond.

1. Why did Hadrian build a wall across Britain between the Solway and the
   Tyne? Why were no other routes suitable?

2. Find a picture of a British hill fort (e.g., Maiden Castle or Hod Hill) and
   compare it with Housesteads as a fortification. Illustrate your answer.

3. If you were an enemy of the Romans trying to break through the wall
   from the north, where do you think its weakest points would be? Why?

4. The Emperor Antoninus Pius decided to build a wall in Scotland in about
   A.D. 142. Imagine and write a conversation between Antoninus and his
   senior advisor about building the wall in Scotland in which they discuss
   why Hadian's Wall is no longer suitable, and in what ways the new wall
   should be different.

5. *Either,* make a scale model *or* draw a picture of part of Hadrian's Wall. Do
   both if you wish.

number references are omitted in favor of references to general sources or indexes. More deduction is demanded of students, and the use of supporting evidence for ideas is encouraged. For the most capable students, more initiative is demanded and more problem-solving questions are raised (dealing with conflicting accounts of history, etc.).

We believe students of all levels can benefit from problem-solving activities, as well as searching for facts and performing simple verification activities. The work cards in Figures 9.1, 9.2, and 9.3 are presented to illustrate the relative emphasis that students of varying achievement levels need in seatwork assignments. To the extent that students who need "structure" receive appropriate learning assignments as depicted in Figure 9.1, they will eventually need more type 9.2 and 9.3 assignments.

Teachers will have to decide when it is necessary to keep students of mixed ability working on the same topic. Perhaps the best strategy in a subject like history is to identify a core set of topics that all students can share and a separate set of topics that more capable students can pursue at a more complex and challenging level. For example, all students might be exposed to the major battles of the Civil War, but only the more capable students would be assigned to do research related to minor battles.

Teachers who teach mixed-ability students can make differential assignments that relate to the same topic in order to allow students to engage in brief class discussions and sharing activities. However, students can still be allowed to spend most of their time working as individuals on tasks that are appropriately challenging for their ability levels. Ideas for teaching mixed-ability students in a variety of subject areas are presented in a recent book by Wragg (1976).

Where students are not pursuing the same general theme at the same time, teachers can profitably spend a portion of their time on ability-grouped work and individual activity. Decisions that teachers make in terms of how much emphasis to place on mixed- and similar-ability teaching in various areas depend upon their teaching goals. Teachers also have to make decisions about how to structure the classroom. We will now discuss the relationship between classroom goals and classroom structures.

## GOAL STRUCTURES
The way a teacher structures learning tasks will have a major effect upon how students behave. The same task (e.g., apply a geometry theory to a given set of facts) will bring about different behaviors

when it is structured as an individual ("work alone"), cooperative ("do it with two other students"), or competitive ("let's see who can provide the quickest proof") task. The goal structure determines the degree of interdependence among students. Johnson and Johnson (1975) point out that there are three major forms of group structure: cooperative, competitive, and individualistic.

Following Deutsch (1949), Johnson and Johnson suggest that a cooperative goal structure exists when students perceive that they can obtain their own goals if, and only if, the other students with whom they work can obtain their goals. A competitive goal structure exists when students feel that they can obtain their own goals only if other students fail to obtain their goals. Individualistic goal structures occur when a student's achievement goals are unrelated to the achievement goals of other students.

When a teacher sets a goal structure, many aspects of the classroom are affected. For example, in a cooperative goal setting, there will be more interaction among students, more use of fellow students as resources, and a greater division of labor (e.g., one student does the historical research, another draws the time line, etc.). Johnson and Johnson (1975) argue that when the learning task is relatively complex (e.g., problem solving) or where a division of labor is useful, a cooperative learning setting will tend to facilitate achievement. Furthermore, the development of prosocial skills demands that students spend time in cooperative learning activities.

There are disadvantages to any goal structure. Perhaps the biggest disadvantage to cooperative goal structures is the large amount of time initially needed to set them up. Young children will not automatically cooperate when they are put together. Indeed, at times, children can be brutal in assessing (and communicating) the contributions that others are making (or failing to make) to the group effort. In secondary settings, small-group work will also have to be supervised regularly; however, the teacher is freed from the major responsibility of having to teach students how to share, how to listen, how to integrate the ideas of group members, how to handle disagreements, and so on (although some time will have to be spent with secondary students in these areas).

Teachers who would not think of assigning students learning tasks that were too complex (e.g., beyond their reading level) often place students in socially complex learning situations in which disagreement, frustration, and negative attitudes are likely to thrive. We learn to cooperate and to share as we learn any concept. Early in the teaching process (grades one and two), children should be given group assignments that are enjoyable, short, highly structured, and unlikely to lead to conflict. As students' cognitive and interpersonal skills develop, they can be given tasks that gradually become longer, more difficult, and less structured.

Obviously, group work takes time. When tasks are relatively straightforward (e.g., multiplication tables, writing sentences, balancing a checkbook), students' achievement will be higher under other goal structures. The group setting is best for tasks that are facilitated by diversity of opinion and a division of labor.

However, if affective goals are to be fulfilled (e.g., increased respect for individual differences), the division of labor that takes place in the group has to demand interdependence among group members. Aronson et al. (1975) found that when students needed the contributions of other students, their attitudes toward specific individuals changed. Students gained increased respect for others who differed from themselves in terms of race, but they did not change their attitudes toward all members of the opposite race. These data are important, because research in social psychology consistently has shown that simply placing people who differ in salient ways together does *not* change attitudes. Research has shown (often in summer-camp settings) that, when interdependence needs can be created, attitude shift is possible. Positive shift occurs if those mutual dependencies are fulfilled responsibly.

Creating a situation where one really needs someone else is much more difficult to do in a classroom than in a summer camp. If one student fails to live up to his or her responsibilities in a group, the other three or four group members can assume his or her work load, and the group goal can be accomplished (often with the nonworker receiving the same reward as the others). Aronson and his colleagues prevented this by having teams of students write a biography collectively, giving each student critically important pieces of information. Students had to listen to each group member if all aspects of the individual's life were to be integrated into the biography. Initially, some students would criticize weaker ones, so that they had to be reminded that they needed all contributions if the task was to be completed. Progressively, students came to understand the learning problems of other students and to appreciate their work efforts. In related research, it has been demonstrated that interdependent assignments can be used to increase the academic performance of minority students (see, for example Lucker, Rosenfield, Sikes, and Aronson, 1976).

If classroom teachers want to change attitudes, they will have to construct learning assignments that create real needs for cooperation. However, if a teacher does create real needs (the work of each individual is important) and then the students do not fulfill those needs, group hostility and *negative* attitude change will occur. (Note that Aronson et al. gave students critical information to guarantee that they could perform.) Teachers who want to produce *positive* attitude change must: (1) involve students in a task that interests them, (2) link students' responsibilities so that each has a critical role that cannot be fulfilled by any other student, and (3) carefully monitor and assist weaker members to be sure that they can fulfill their roles.

Many teachers do not define their role as one of socialization and are not directly concerned about changing student attitudes. Teachers who are concerned about general prosocial skills (sharing, listening) and cognitive growth do not have to concern themselves with the delicate task of creating an interdependent climate. Virtually all teachers will want students to contribute and share, but these goals do not demand that teachers develop group tasks where individuals have to contribute or the group will fail. Such tasks are difficult to construct.

### Student Teams

The use of student teams is another format for creating a shared dependency among students. Much research related to the teaching of mixed-ability groups and the use of competition has been summarized by DeVries and Slavin (1976). Their research and that of their colleagues has centered upon the use of teams in games and tournament competition (TGT). Competition is used to enhance student interest; however, efforts are made to keep the competition *manageable*.

High-, middle-, and low-achievement students are assigned to mixed ability teams. Students on each team are assigned to compete against students of similar ability in order to win points for their teams. For example, in mathematics, two students may try to see who can solve the most problem equations in fifteen minutes (fifteen pairs of students can be competing at the same time on math tasks of varying difficulty. Similarly, in language arts two students (or several students from each team) could be assigned a crossword puzzle to complete in a specified time period. Individual students or groups of students at each table who win the competition earn points for their team. Teams that accumulate the most points in a specified time period win the tournament.

The competition in team games is real and fun if structured in a manageable way (all students are paired in such a way that they have a real chance to win). However, the reward structure used in the TGT program is a cooperative reward structure. DeVries and Slavin stress four features:

1. Each group member must be individually accountable to the group for his or her behavior.
2. The participation of all members must be essential.
3. All members of the group must be rewarded at the group level for a group performance.
4. The group must be rewarded as a group frequently.

The team competition concept fulfills these four conditions reasonably well. First, the face-to-face competition assures the accountability and participation of all students; and, if teachers only reward group performance and provide for manageable competition (grouping students in such a way that all teams will win from time to time), the last two conditions will also be fulfilled.

The usefulness of TGT is based upon the assumption that team competition will produce conditions that facilitate learning. For example, some students will want to do well for their team and will study harder. Other students will want their teammates to do well and will spend extra time teaching them the basic material. Indeed, the research results on TGT suggest that increased peer tutoring is an important variable that helps to make the TGT concept effective.

In general, available data suggest that TGT techniques are associated with increases in subject matter achievement. Furthermore, there are data to suggest that TGT techniques are sometimes associated with increased cross-racial helping and friendship. Apparently, the close working interdependence among students inherent in a TGT arrangement can help set the stage for enhancing students' mutual respect and liking across racial lines.

However, if overused or used inappropriately (some groups don't have a chance to win), the TGT concept or educational games in general are likely to cause more problems than they solve. Furthermore, as DeVries and Slavin (1976) note, TGT techniques are most suited to those subjects which have goals that are easy to quantify— simple, concrete skills. Especially useful for a game format are short tasks which have only one correct answer and which test knowledge or skills that can be tutored by other children. Furthermore, as we have noted elsewhere, there are no data to suggest that abstract, cognitive material can be taught in game settings. Also, it is clear that many higher-ability students do not need the heavy structure of team competition to learn (Good and Brophy, 1977).

Typically, competition and cooperation are not mixed (as they are in TGT). We have discussed cooperative goal structures. Let's now examine individual and competitive structures.

### Individualistic and Competitive Goal Structures

Less emphasis will be placed on discussion of individual and competitive goal structures because most readers are quite familiar with them—they are the dominant goal structures in schools. Ideally, when an individual goal structure is created, the achievement of any one student is unrelated to the achievement of that same goal by other students. Mastery learning (see definitions and discussion in the preceding chapter) represents this concept in the ideal form. Students are expected to master a set of concepts and are allowed to move at their own pace until they do. If certain students master the material in three days and others master it in three weeks, they all obtain the same goal: credit for successful completion of the unit.

In practice, students apply their own "success criteria." If they regularly take longer to complete a unit than others do, they may impose the label of slow, inadequate, or dumb on themselves. Even though they are not in formal competition with other students, they create competition for themselves by observing the discrepancy between their speed in mastering units and that of their peers.

Teachers who consistently communicate to students the legitimacy of individual differences and who emphasize individual improvement (comparing what the student can do now to what he or she could do a month ago) will help to reduce the frequency of invidious comparisons with other students. No matter what the teacher does, students will compare their performance with peers, but such comparisons are less likely to reduce student motivation and/or produce self-defeating labels if they are made with the understanding that differences in individual progress are expected, and if the student can see his or her own progress.

Competition is especially useful when drill is needed. Games and competition can provide an interesting format for drilling vocabulary, number concepts, and so on. This is apt to be most successful when students are matched so that each has a realistic chance to win. Team games can add interest and spark learning if the competition can be controlled (the student competes against a student of equal abilities to try to earn points for his team). If overused, games and uncontrolled competition are likely to detract from learning rather than to enhance it.

The advantage to the individual learning assignment is that it allows students to focus on individual goals and to proceed at their own pace. If overused, boredom and managerial problems often result.

## DIFFERENT LEARNING TASKS FOR DIFFERENT STUDENTS

In the preceding discussion, we have emphasized the desirability of building different assignments around common themes in order to build a climate for communication across ability lines. However, students are not simply fast, medium, or slow processors of information. They have varying levels of energy, assertiveness, sociability, and patience. As teachers become proficient at recognizing and designing curriculum tasks that mesh with achievement needs (and building the volume of material necessary for teaching the curriculum in different ways), they can profitably turn their attention to students' personalities, learning styles, and preferences.

The number of student characteristics that could be listed for teacher consideration is endless, and little value would be served by presenting an exhaustive list. However, it seems reasonable to present a few student types with which teachers can expect to deal and to suggest ways to meet the learning needs of such students.

The five types of students discussed here are drawn from two attempts to describe the major types of students that teachers encounter. The first involved interviewing classroom teachers to characterize students on the basis of teachers' affective reactions to them (Jackson, Silberman, and Wolfson, 1969; Silberman, 1969). A small number of elementary teachers consistently described students in a way that suggested four types, each type reflecting a different teacher attitude: attachment, indifference, concern, and rejection.

Power (1974) collected data from 150 grade-eight science students in two high schools in Brisbane, Australia. He observed the classroom behavior of the students and collected detailed information about pupil ability, divergent thinking, personality variables (anxiety, achievement motivation, expectation of success), science achievement level, peer ratings, teacher ratings, and self-ratings. Power's study of cognitive, instructional, behavioral, and personality variables produced four types of students (success, social, dependent, and alienated). Here, the types reflect student adjustment to the demands of schooling.

Good and Power (1976) intergrated the two sets of students into the following five:

1. Success Students: These students are task-oriented and academically capable. They are cooperative in class and tend to be well liked by both teachers and peers.
2. Social Students: These students are more person- than

task-oriented. They have ability but value friendship more than achievement. While popular and possessing many friends, some social students are not well liked by their teachers because of their numerous "buzz/saw" social interactions.

3. Dependent Students: These students consistently look for teacher direction, support, and encouragement. They tend to achieve at a low level. Teachers generally express concern for dependent students (and some subtly reinforce their dependency). Peers tend to reject them.

4. Alienated Students: These are the reluctant learners. At the extreme, they reject school completely (some with open hostility; others by total withdrawal). Some become aggressive and create serious behavior problems. Others sit at the fringes of the classroom and refuse to participate. Teachers tend to reject those students who express alienation openly and to be indifferent toward those who express alienation passively.

5. Phantom Students: In most cases, these students are seldom seen or heard in the classroom. Some are the shy, mousy type fearful of contact with teachers and peers, but others are quiet, independent workers of average ability who desire and need little social interaction. These students seldom volunteer or create problems. Teachers have trouble remembering who they are, and express attitudes of indifference toward them (as do peers).

These descriptions are broad, and they represent only general outlines of student needs. Sometimes there are two types of students within one broad typology (alienated, phantom), so that teachers will need somewhat different strategies with these students. We stress this because it is important to realize that there are many ways to classify students (see, for example Hunt, 1975). This classification is only one way to look at students and stimulate thought about how their achievement might be faciliated. We think it is a useful way to look at student needs because the typologies (success, social, dependent, alienated, phantom) were developed from teacher reports and appear to be meaningful to teachers.

In Table 9.1, definitions of a few classroom variables are provided.* These variables are decisions that teachers must make when assign-

---

* The term "variable" implies that the teacher can manipulate processes (such as reading difficulty or amount of reading) and provide more or less work, depending upon the student.

TABLE 9.1.
## CLASSROOM VARIABLES

I. INFORMATION PROPERTIES
   a. Information source:
      Teacher or pupil, person or material, continuous vs. intermittent.
      (Teacher lecturing, films, many or single sources.)
   b. Information content—substantive, procedural, socioemotional (humor)
II. TASK PROPERTIES
   a. Readability: reading level of materials used
   b. Task difficulty:
      Number of errors made by pupils on task questions, or percent of pupils
      that complete the task, time taken to complete the task.
   c. Level of abstractness:
      Concrete, physical manipulation, specific reference (a diagrammed sen-
      tence, map, what happened on playground yesterday) or concrete prop,
      verbalizing, operationalizing with abstract symbols (freedom-equality dis-
      cussion, math symbols).
   d. Cognitive level:
      Facts, concepts, principles, problem solving, synthesis.
   e. Structure:
      Many small and clear steps, explicit directions, much feedback vs. few steps;
      directions; open; little feedback prior to completion of task. (Oral—lot of
      internal summaries, advance organized, post presented summary.)
   f. Task activity press "active learning":
      Time directly interacting with teacher, material, pupils vs. vicarious observ-
      ing, listening—silent reading.
   g. Choice: availability of options
   h. Interest, relevance of task
   i. Task variety:
      Variance of demand and mode and activity.
III. RESPONSE PROPERTIES
   a. Written, oral, physical
   b. Individual—group
   c. Public vs. private
   d. Competitive—cooperative
IV. FEEDBACK PROPERTIES
   a. Source: teacher, materials, peers
   b. Target: individual, group, class
   c. Wait time (availability of teacher for monitoring, etc.)
   d. Informativeness: no feedback, correctness of answer (right—wrong), redirect,
      (probing) diagnose, correct and explain
   e. Length: restricted vs. overdwelling
   f. Person or task
   g. Sign: +, 0, −
V. STRUCTURAL PROPERTIES
   a. Group size
   b. Location: nearness to teacher, materials
   c. Mobility of students
   d. Physical environment
   e. Population density—crowdedness
VI. TEMPORAL PROPERTIES
   a. Wait time
   b. Stage of learning: development, practice, review
   c. Length: duration of activity setting (time on each session of group work,
      peer tutoring, etc.)

*Adapted from* Good, T., and Power, C. "Designing successful environments for different types of students." *Journal of Curriculum Studies,* 8 (1976), 45–60.

ing work to students and when providing them with feedback about their work. In Table 9.2, these same variables are used to illustrate how the teacher could take student learning orientations into consideration when planning and assigning *individual* work. If the teacher has students working in groups or a whole-class setting, or if the teacher is stressing other goals (social learning, etc.), these variables would need to be manipulated in different ways.

Examination of Table 9.2 will illustrate that the needs of success, social, dependent, alienated, and phantom students are quite different. If the teacher is to give optimal treatment to all student groups, he or she must respond to these different needs.

Some student needs can be accommodated simultaneously (students are given assignments that vary in reading difficulty), but other needs conflict (it is difficult for the teacher to solve them at the same time). As has been pointed out elsewhere (Good and Power, 1976), successful students benefit from relatively long assignments

TABLE 9.2.
**INDIVIDUAL MODE ACHIEVEMENT: SOURCES OF CONFLICT**

| VARIABLES | SUCCESS | SOCIAL | DEPENDENT | ALIENATED | PHANTOM |
|---|---|---|---|---|---|
| **Task Material** | | | | | |
| difficulty | 6 | 5 | 2 | 1 | 3 |
| abstractness | 5 | 4 | 1 | 1 | 3 |
| cog. level | 5 | 4 | 1 | 1 | 3 |
| structure | 1 | 2 | 6 | 5 | 3 |
| public response | 0 | 5 | 3 | 1 | 1 |
| i. response mode | 0 | 5 | 6 | 6 | 4 |
| evaluation (comp) | 6 | 6 | 1 | 1 | 4 |
| activity press | 1 | 4 | 6 | 6 | 4 |
| variety | 5 | 5 | 1 | 3 | 2 |
| length | 6 | 2 | 2 | 3 | 6 |
| **Information Feedback** | | | | | |
| source—teacher | 2 | 2 | 6 | 6 | 2 |
| source—materials | 4 | 4 | 6 | 6 | 6 |
| target—individual | 6 | 1 | 6 | 6 | 2 |
| target—group | 1 | 6 | 6 | 1 | 3 |
| audience | 0 | 5 | 2 | 1 | 3 |
| wait time | 3 | 3 | 1 | 1 | 3 |
| informativeness | 6 | 3 | 2 | 2 | 3 |
| length | 5 | 3 | 1 | 2 | 2 |
| person + | 0 | 0 | 3 | 4 | 3 |
| — | 0 | 0 | 1 | 1 | 2 |
| task + | 1 | 3 | 5 | 6 | 3 |
| — | 4 | 2 | 1 | 1 | 2 |

*Code:* 0 = unimportant, irrelevant; 1 = low; 3 = moderate; 6 = high.

*Adapted from* Good, T. and Power, C. "Designing successful environments for different types of students." *Journal of Curriculum Studies,* 8 (1976), 45–60.

on difficult, challenging work. But individual assignments long enough to help successful students may be too long for other types. Social students do not respond well to lengthy individual assignments, especially if the work is not used in a subsequent public performance (a debate, class report, etc.). Because part of their achievement is based upon learning and performing in the company of others, long independent work assignments do not satisfy their immediate needs.

Some students need more contact with the teacher during seatwork than others. For example, dependent students (until they are taught minimal self-supervision skills and the confidence necessary for exercising these skills) will need much teacher feedback. During the first few minutes of a seatwork assignment, however, it is good teaching strategy to be sure that alienated students get involved in the work.

To compound the problem, successful students also need, periodically, time for sustained interaction. Although they are capable of productively maintaining themselves in work for long time periods, they need teacher feedback as they attempt to develop sophisticated skills for self-evaluation.

Different types of students have different needs, and it is hard to accommodate all needs at the same time. One suggestion for dealing with this problem is to change the nature of individual work and the focus of teacher feedback so that the format allows different types of students to "win." A second strategy is *not* to engage all students in independent work at the same time. Most conflicts develop because a teacher cannot meet the feedback needs of 30 students. By controlling the number of students involved in individual work at the same time, the teacher can better blend time demands.

For example, an elementary school teacher might make individual assignments to dependent, alienated, and social students during the early morning when these students are not involved in reading-group work. The relatively brief time (e.g., two 20-minute periods) for individual work could be used profitably by these students (who tend to react negatively to long individual seatwork assignments), especially if the teacher supplies answer sheets or self-checking devices that they can use to monitor their own work. Success students and phantom students might engage in brief small-group work projects during that same period. Then, after recess, the students might all be engaged in whole-class work in mathematics. In the afternoon, successful students and phantom students could be assigned to spend large amounts of time in individual work, while the teacher actively supervised the small-group work of other students.

The types of students described here are general constructs designed to stimulate your thinking about student needs and the desirability of providing some variety in classroom teaching. To include appropriate variety takes a great deal of time and commitment. We agree with McKeachie (1976) who contends that we need smaller classes and smaller schools in order to meet student needs. He further suggests that more teachers, more teacher aides, and more students teaching other students are needed.

Unfortunately, with declining budgets, it may be difficult to lower the student-teacher ratio. However, the use of students as teachers is a viable option if not overdone. Often, the high achiever is asked to do much of this at the expense of not having the chance to do more challenging or interesting work. We now turn to the topic of peer tutoring.

## PEER TUTORING

The reasons for using students to teach other students need to be clear if the program is have its intended effects. For example, the program might be to help students to develop social relationships through peer-tutoring contacts. The peer tutoring might be designed primarily to aid the development of the students who *do* the tutoring (as opposed to the students who are tutored)!

For example, Paolitto (1976) describes a program designed by Greenspan (1972) to facilitate the development of adolescent tutors by allowing them to work with young children. Greenspan found that the program did help tutors to increase the complexity of their understanding of development, although it had no substantial influence upon the adolescents' personal ego development.

Most teachers probably will want to design tutoring experiences to improve the subject matter mastery of the students being tutored, so most of the suggestions below are written with this in mind (although other goals will be mentioned from time to time). Readers interested in review and intensive discussion of available research can consult two excellent review papers: Paolitto (1976) and Devin-Sheehan, Feldman, and Allen (1976). They contain many examples showing that peer tutoring can have desirable effects upon students.

In a variety of situations, teachers and schools are allowing students to assist and guide the academic growth of their fellow students. In some situations, students within the same classroom tutor one another, while in other situations, fifth- and sixth-grade students tutor second and third graders. In still other settings, adults and college students tutor pupils from all age levels.

The increased interest in the use of students as tutors has stemmed in part from the realization that, for many students, school life guarantees their failure. Deutsch (1964) writes that when students fall behind other students (or when they enter school already behind), they do not catch up, and, in fact, the difference in school performance between these students and the rest of the class becomes wider each year. The wide differences in ability and interest among those who do perform well in school also create the need for teachers to personalize instruction if students are to progress optimally. Teachers in self-contained classrooms with thirty or more pupils seldom have enough time to individualize their instruction as fully as they would prefer.

### Some Advantages

One advantage to using student tutors is that the teacher is free to work with fewer students in face-to-face situations and has more time to work with students having very difficult learning problems. There are, of course, other potential advantages in allowing older students to assume partial responsibility for managing the academic progress of younger students. Young children who are aided by older students might learn to trust and to seek information from older students and other authority figures (such as teachers) instead of avoiding them or feigning competency. That is, in direct tutorial situations, students may learn that much may be gained by seeking information when they are confused or need facts. If the descriptive analysis of Holt (1964) is accurate, students, when confronted with the "unknown" in classroom activities, normally, evoke self-defeating strategies that allow them to "look good" but which interfere with their learning.

Certain gains might also occur for the older student who tutors younger ones. For example, he or she may develop interpersonal skills for relating to other persons more fully, and may also learn to care more deeply and honestly about the progress of others. Students helping others in reading or math, for example, may develop more interest in improving their own competency in the subject matter, and they may develop more empathy for the plight of their own classroom teacher.

Some students may learn more from one another than they learn from a teacher. Thomas (1970) makes this point when he writes, "Intuitively, many teachers know or suspect that they cannot communicate with some of their students." Consequently, another potential reason for using students as tutors is that the teacher may be unable to reach some pupils. For teaching some children, tutors may be more effective (perhaps because tutors use simple, direct language and examples that are more easily understood than those of the classroom teacher or because they have gone through the same learning problems fairly recently). Peer tutoring, then, has been advocated as a tool for helping both tutors and tutees to make progress in mastering subject matter as well as to increase interpersonal communication skills.

Let us consider some of the questions about the utility of peer tutoring. Does peer tutoring really work? If so, under what circumstances? Is the best strategy to let students in the same room tutor one another, or is it more efficient to let fifth- and sixth-grade students tutor younger students? Can all students be tutors? The number of adequate studies related to these questions does not justify firm conclusions at present; however, most of the data that do exist suggest that peer tutoring has some positive learning influence on both tutor and tutee and, at the same time, frees the teacher to work with students who need special help.

Cloward (1967) reports an experiment in which tenth- and eleventh-grade students who were at least two years below their age norm in reading were paid $1.35 per hour to tutor fourth and fifth graders who were having reading difficulties. Before the actual tutoring program began, the tutors were paid for attending planning sessions, and they were paid also for attending two hours of in-service training each week during the experiment. The students then tutored the younger children four hours a week for 26 weeks. Tests given five months apart showed that on the average the tutees gained six months, while the control children (children who were not tutored) gained three and one-half months. Experimental students who did the tutoring gained 3.4 grades, while control students gained 1.7. Students who did the tutoring gained 1.7 grades more than comparable senior high students who did not tutor. Thus, students who had experienced much failure and frustration themselves were able to sympathetically aid others and gain new confidence or new interest in their own reading ability in the process.

Such spectacular results have not always been replicated, and some research has shown very little change in tutee performance. However, in general, the literature is promising. Among the most important comprehensive sources available on peer-tutoring research are two dissertations completed at the University of Texas (Thomas, 1970; and Snapp, 1970). Students interested in a complete review of the literature are referred to these two sources.

Thomas' (1970) study is particularly interesting. He examined the relative effectiveness of fifth- and sixth-grade tutors and college tutors for tutoring second-grade students in reading. He found, in general, that the elementary school tutors were just as effective in tutoring second graders as were college students. Interestingly, the college students were seniors enrolled in a reading methods course who had almost completed their undergraduate teacher education.

Thomas describes some notable differences in the tutoring behavior of the college and elementary school tutors. Although the college and elementary tutors were equally successful in producing gains, they interacted differently with the younger students. Thomas (1970) stated it this way:

> In analyzing the different groups of tutors, one is struck by the differences in their approach to the tutees. The college age tutors seemed to be attempting to coax the tutees into liking them, into enjoying the reading materials, and into practicing the reading skills. The elementary age tutors, for the most part, were more direct and businesslike. They seemed to accept the fact that the tutees had problems in their school work, and seemed to feel that the tutoring sessions were for teaching those materials in front of them, not for going off in tangents and discussing matters outside the lesson.

Snapp (1970) reports that Ellson et al. (1965) have examined the tutoring behaviors of various age groups (college students, trained teachers, potential adult dropouts, etc.). Ellson concludes that programmed (clearly specified format) tutoring can be carried out effectively by fifth and sixth graders, and he notes that tutors gain at least as much as tutees. Perhaps the most striking conclusion Ellson advances is that college graduates and professional teachers are relatively unsuccessful as programmed tutors.

Thus, in different ways, Thomas' and Ellson's observations suggest that college students or professional teachers are not necessarily good tutors. Their lack of effectiveness may be due to a number of factors, such as (1) successful tutoring may demand direct instruction, whereas adults tend to be indirect, (2) the vocabulary and examples of an adult may be too complex for younger children, and (3) tutors who are close in age to the tutee may remember their own difficulty and frustration with the material and tend to keep a lesson-focus orientation longer than adults. The preceding statements are, of course, only hypotheses. However, although many adults are effective tutors, there is some reason to believe that the behaviors involved in effective individual tutoring may be different from teacher behaviors that are effective for working with groups of students.

There is also reason to believe that students *may be* more effective tutors if they are trained for their tutorial role. Niedermeyer (1970) presents data showing that fifth-grade students who were trained to tutor did, in fact, tutor differently from untrained tutors. Unfortunately, Niedermeyer did not determine whether trained tutors obtained more achievement from tutees than the untrained tutors. Thus, we know that college students tutor differently than do elementary school students, and that trained and untrained fifth-grade tutors behave differently in tutoring situations; however, no data indicate the specific behaviors of effective tutors. Although Thomas (personal communication) has related that training may be desirable in certain situations, his own experience has convinced him that even first-grade students can effectively work with classmates without elaborate training.

### Some Practical Suggestions

Thus, peer tutoring has been tried in a variety of settings, and it frequently results in increased achievement by students who do the tutoring, as well as by students who are tutored. Although some reports suggest that peer tutoring has not increased achievement, there are no reports indicating that students were harmed by the process. Also, even where no achievement gains result, teachers have more time to work with students who need individual help. However, it should be noted that the largely favorable results of peer tutoring experiments may be due, in part, to the fact that they have been conducted mostly by innovative school districts or teachers who have been careful to create a positive set or attitude toward tutoring for both the students being tutored and those doing the tutoring. That is, peer tutoring, like ability grouping, can be effective or not, depending upon how it is implemented. The following guidelines can be used to create peer-tutoring opportunities.

1. To begin with, the teacher should create the mental set that *we all learn from one another.* This is more readily believed by students when the teacher consistently models and points out to students how he or she learns from them. Again, the teacher can help reduce unnecessary competition in the classroom by stressing that the goal for all students is to learn as much as they can about essential school topics and about topics that are meaningful to them as individuals. Such behaviors help students to learn that the yardstick of success is how we compare to our past performance and not how much smarter or faster we are than someone else.

2. The second essential step in implementing peer-tutoring programs is to work out the procedural details. There are several essential procedural matters that should be noted. We suggest that the students be requested to help plan the program from the beginning. In general, these procedural matters need to be agreed upon:

a. Definite times of the day should be set up for tutoring, so that students quickly learn that there are specific class times for helping one another (to avoid continuous disruption in class).

b. Specific assignments need to be outlined. The teacher should mimeograph the directions each tutor is to follow each week. For example, "Johnny, this week from 8:00–9:00 you will work with Kay and Terry. On Monday, you will use the flash cards and review with them seven, eight, and nine multiplication tables. Repeat the tables twice for each of them and then get individual responses from each of them. The last time, write down the mistakes that each makes and return the sheet to me. On Tuesday, you will find audio-tape number 16. Play it for Kay and Terry and listen with them to the rhyming words. Then go to the word box and find the rhyming words sheet. Read the material sentence by sentence, and get Kay and Terry to identify the rhyming words."

c. Allow a tutor to work with one or two tutees for a week or two weeks so that you can make sequential assignments and so that learning exercises are not constantly starting anew. However, tutors in the same room should not work with any student or group for longer than a couple of weeks. This will prevent "I'm your teacher" attitudes from developing. Of course, these attitudes are much less likely to occur if older students or students from other classes at the same grade level are used as tutors. But since this is often impossible, the guidelines suggested here are presented for the teacher who is using student tutors within his or her own classroom.

d. Tutors should not be asked to administer real tests to tutees. One purpose of peer tutoring is to develop a cooperative sharing between students. Asking tutors to quiz their tutees often defeats this purpose.

e. All students in the room should, at times, be tutors, and all children in the room should be tutees. Slower students can help faster ones in the lower grades by listening to their spelling words or by checking their drill recitations in math. Teachers should see that students have the appropriate answer keys to perform this role adequately. In this way, students learn that they all need help and can benefit from one another.

f. Teachers need not keep to the tutor model (one child

flashes cards, the other responds) but can expand, when appropriate, to small work-team assignments (from two to eight students on a team). Shy students can be assigned to work with friendly, nonaggressive extroverts. Students with art talents can be paired with bright but artistically barren students to gather facts and then graphically represent them (e.g., to chart the major battles of the Civil War). These combinations allow students to work together and gain interpersonal skills as well as to master selected content. While the students are so paired, the teacher is free to meet with a reading group for a second time on the same day to give them needed extra oral practice; hold an enrichment discussion, bringing in new content with a fast group; move from team to team, listening to their ideas and conversing with children informally; and work with individual students who require special attention.

g. Both learning teams and peer tutoring will take a substantial amount of teacher time to get off to a good start, especially where students have not participated in these activities before. However, these are important techniques to free the teacher for other instructional tasks and to allow students to assume responsibility for helping others and constructively exchanging ideas in the classroom. Take your time, at first, and be sure that all students understand what they are to do.

The first week you ask students to tutor, you should model the behaviors you want. For example, pass out the mimeographed instructions and have all the students read them. Then select and sit with an individual student in the middle of the room while you tutor him or her in accordance with the directions. Do not just describe what to do. Actually do it, modeling the appropriate behaviors.

After this demonstration, you might select another two students, and have them model the next set of directions. Then you might wish to break everyone into pairs and go around listening and answering questions. After a couple of practice sessions like this, most students will be able to assist others, at least in repetitive drill-like activities.

The first week you implement a peer-tutoring program you may have a loud, somewhat disorganized room, as students argue over where to go and so forth. Remember that learning does not necessar-

ily require passive, quiet students and that any teacher trying a
new exercise will have minor adjustment problems as students learn
new roles.

    h. Pairing of best friends is often unwise for several reasons:
friends tend to drift away from the learning exercises;
the number of classmates that a given student interacts
with in the classroom is reduced; and friends, in a moment
of anger, are more likely to "play teacher" by becoming
excessively critical or indulging in ridicule. Although
many friends can work well together, many cannot, and
the teacher should use caution in such groupings.

    i. Communicate to parents that all students will be tutored
by classmates and will in turn tutor classmates during the
year. This is especially important in high socioeconomic
status areas where some parents may be upset upon learning that their daughter is being tutored by their neighbors'
son and may immediately begin to fear that their neighbors will feel they are inadequate parents. Needless concern can be eliminated if you communicate to parents
the purpose of the tutor program in a letter or visit and
point out that this occurs for one or two hours during
the day. List these times and invite them to visit whenever
they want to do so.

    3. The third essential skill needed to establish peer tutoring, in
addition to creating a positive set and establishing clear operating
procedures for the students, is creative organization. Although peer
tutoring will give you more time in the classroom, it takes a great
deal of planning time outside the classroom. Organization is the
key. Tutors need clear directions, but they also need variety. You
cannot program a spelling drill week after week. You have to plan
so that the tutors and tutees receive an interesting mix of topics
(e.g., one week drill review, the next week mutual library research,
the next week writing stories, and the next spending money in a
simulated grocery store or calculating batting averages).

    In addition to tutoring assignments, students should be given time
to work as learning teams. Sometimes students of similar aptitude
should work on a problem-solving task. At other times, combine
students whose weaknesses and strengths complement one another
in useful ways.

## INDEPENDENT WORK AND LEARNING CENTERS
Teachers can save much time for working with specific students
by carefully structuring time for students to engage in interesting,

creative tasks of their own choosing. Teachers often find that some students, particularly bright high achievers, finish their work sooner than others. These students are too often punished indirectly (given more of the same work to do, etc.) for rapid work. If anything, students in these circumstances should be rewarded. Biehler (1971) suggests a particularly good idea for older elementary students: an open-ended, personal yearbook in which the student is allowed to write stories and illustrate or embellish them, whenever he or she finishes assigned work. What each student puts in the book is completely left up to the student.

Other age-worn but, nevertheless, acceptable ideas include allowing students to work on book reviews on some aspect of a curriculum topic (e.g., American Indians) or to act as a resource specialist or to tutor other students. However, book reports, if overly structured, may do little to encourage reading for enjoyment and interest. Often it is useful for the teacher and the student to discuss the book not only for plot but also in terms of why the student liked or disliked the book. Occasionally, teachers should carefully structure long periods of independent work for all students (not just those who finish quickly) and thereby systematically save time for remedial, enrichment, and informal conversations with individuals.

To facilitate independent study, the classroom can be arranged in more optimal ways. Figure 9.4 shows how one teacher arranged her first-grade classroom. This diagram of the classroom was made as the teacher instructed a reading group. By looking at Figure 9.4, you can see how the teacher's room arrangement allows for both group work and independent student activities. Six students are in the reading group with the teacher and two students are reading at the independent reading table. The reading center, separated by bookcases from the rest of the room, provides students with a place where they can read their favorite books in comfortable privacy. Thus, as students finish their work properly, the teacher can allow some of them to go to the reading center and read a book of special interest in a quiet, relaxed way. The teacher may, at times, choose to use the reading center for independent but structured learning activity. For example, the student may be asked to write a book report on a book he or she chooses or one that is assigned.

We can see that eight children are working at the listening center, which is a portable tape recorder with eight earphones that can be wheeled from table to table. One student has passed out pencils and accompanying exercise sheets, while another student is in charge of turning on the tape recorder and turning it off when the taped exercise is completed. All students in the class have been

FIGURE 9.4. Physical Arrangement of a First-Grade Classroom   ⊗ Places occupied by students   ○ Empty seat

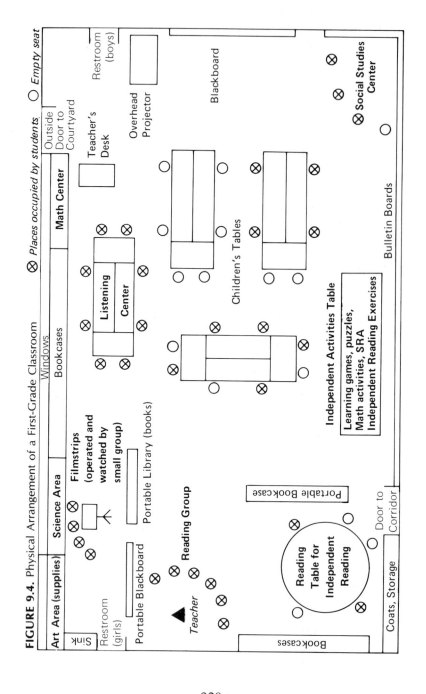

320

taught how to operate the recorder, and student helpers are assigned and rotated on a regular basis by the teacher. Similarly, four students are viewing filmstrips without direct teacher supervision. Again, all students have been taught how to operate the machine. The teacher allows "today's teacher" to run the machine and to call on students, in turn, to read the story which accompanies the pictures. When the students finish watching the filmstrip and complete the written exercises, they move to another activity at their seats.

When the arrangement shown in Figure 9.4 was made, nine children were working independently at their seats and three children were working at the social studies center. The observer noted that two of the students were "buddy reading" stories printed by their fellow classmates about the social studies unit, while the other student was busily painting a picture of a recent social studies field trip for the class mural. When he finished his painting, he crossed off his name on the social studies blackboard and another student began painting his picture. When the teacher terminates the reading group, all students will rotate to a new activity and, as we have pointed out previously, with careful teacher planning these shifts can be made quickly and effortlessly.

There are countless ways in which a teacher's classroom can be organized. Dollar (1972) suggests a room arrangement similar to the one depicted in Figure 9.5. As can be seen in this diagram, the traditional rectangular seating arrangement has been done away with, allowing the room to be filled with a number of potentially exciting learning centers. A teacher, if he or she so desired, could program most of a student's day around learning-center activities. Below is one student's schedule for an entire day. Although there would be a few others with the same schedule, there would be many different schedules within the room. For example, another student might begin the day reading with the teacher in a reading group and end it at the listening post.

JOHNNY'S SCHEDULE

| | |
|---|---|
| 8:30–9:15 | Math corner |
| 9:15–9:30 | Math with his group |
| 9:30–10:00 | Reading with his group |
| 10:00–10:15 | Morning recess |
| 10:15–10:30 | Social studies with entire class |
| 10:30–11:15 | Social studies in small project group |
| 11:15–11:45 | Lunch |
| 11:45–12:15 | Story center |
| 12:15–1:00 | Free selection |

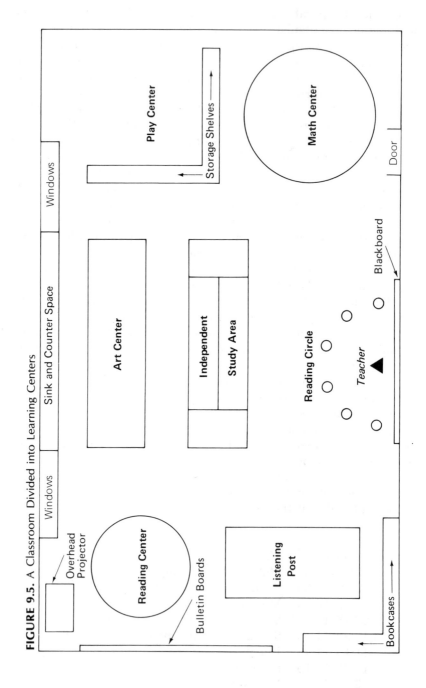

**FIGURE 9.5.** A Classroom Divided into Learning Centers

322

1:00–1:30    Math instruction with entire class
1:30–2:00    Art center
2:00–2:15    Recess
2:15–2:30    Listening post
2:30–3:00    Reading instruction—independent work at
the study area

The teacher, through careful scheduling, would allow students to be at different learning centers or working in different project groups; the teacher would then have time free for instructional work with a small group or for remedial work. Although many teachers may prefer not to use center arrangements this heavily, such arrangements provide excellent independent study areas, and most teachers who set them up will find that they add greatly to classroom flexibility by providing a wider repertory of assignments.

Teachers in some classrooms may not be able to set up five or six different learning centers at a given time. Physical limitations (e.g., chairs that are bolted to the floor) may allow room for only two learning centers. In such cases, teachers may provide variety by setting up a science and an explorer center for two weeks, and then setting up for another two weeks a creative writing and mystery reading center, and then music and historical centers. The list of possible centers is limited only by the teacher's imagination. The reader should have realized by now that learning centers are exciting educational alternatives, but if they are to be run successfully, teachers must spend a great deal of time organizing them properly. For example, the reader may properly ask, "Where does the teacher find time to make out all those schedules in addition to the time required to prepare for each student's individual instruction?" It is true that much advanced teacher planning is needed. However, teachers typically can plan a student's schedule for one-to two-week time periods, so that planning of new schedules is not necessary for each student each day.

In addition, many school districts now provide teachers time to plan instructional activities with other teachers at the same grade level. Although teachers will have to make schedules for their own individual pupils, good use of planning time can be made by sharing ideas about the content of learning centers and by preparing different activities for different learning centers, thus reducing the amount of planning time necessary for any one teacher. (More will be said about this sharing of planning time later in the chapter.)

Students need to know how to use learning centers. Like all classroom assignments, tasks at learning centers need to be clearly specified if students are expected to work on their own with a minimum of teacher guidance. Rules for using the equipment and handing in assignments must be clearly established. Rules and the activities that take place in learning centers, of course, vary with the age and aptitude of students. However, the following material from Dollar (1972) illustrates the general need for establishing rules and guidelines for academic assignments.

SOCIAL STUDIES
1. Choose a card and find the book to go with it.
2. Read the book or pages listed on the card and then answer the questions on your own paper.
3. Put your papers in the yellow basket and write your name on the back of the card.
4. You may answer the questions at your own desk or in the social studies corner.

READING CENTER
1. Pick a book from the shelf with a card in it.
2. Read the book.
3. Answer the questions on the card at your desk.
4. On a piece of paper put the title of the book and the number of the card. Number the questions as you answer them on your paper.
5. When you have finished, put your name on the back of the card and check your name on the chart.

PLAY CENTER
1. Only one person at a time may hammer or saw.
2. You may only use the hammer or saw between 8:00 and 8:30.
3. Leave the erector set, hammer, saw, nails, or boards in the center.
4. Clean up when you have finished.

MATH CORNER
1. There should be only three people playing math games at one time.
2. You may:
   a. play a game quietly
   b. work problems on the blackboard
   c. use the flannel board
   d. pick out what you like and return to your desk to work on it
3. To use the math cards in the box you must:
   a. pick out any card you want
   b. work the problems on your own paper at your desk
   c. when you finish put your paper in the basket, and sign the card on the back

LISTENING POST
1. Sit down at the table—no more than seven people at a time.
2. Pick a record to listen to. Only one person should work the record player.

3. Put on the headphones.
4. Turn on the record player and listen to a story.*

It may be useful to have "operational" rules such as those Dollar lists posted at each learning center. Such procedural guidelines allow students to function quasi-independently of the teacher. Teachers can use learning centers to expose students to a variety of interesting educational tasks. Young students, for example, might be asked to do independent work by listening to a story and then responding to questions about it. The questions can be simple, "Were there three bears in the story?" or complex, "Listen to the story for four minutes. Can you write your own ending?" The point here is that in creating learning centers, you are free to use your own imagination and to create your own material. Although companies do make filmstrips, tapes, and other materials that can be used for independent classroom work, some of the best assignments will come from spontaneous events that occur in the classroom.

For example, one day during a seventh-grade English class, the principal makes one of her frequent PA announcements. At the end of it, Joe Jordan says, loudly enough to be heard by half the class, including the teacher, "What in the world would it be like if one day she kept her mouth shut!" After the class snickering dies down, Mr. Thornton's appeal to logic, "But what would happen if she made no announcements?" leads the class to the general conclusion that nothing significant would be lost if the principal never spoke over the PA again, because teachers could make the announcements. He then decides to give the following assignment for independent work. "Assume there was no television, radio, or newspaper communication for two weeks. Write a theme on one of the following topics: (1) how would your life be affected, (2) how would attendance at a national sports event be affected, (3) how would someone wanting to buy a house be affected, (4) how could supermarkets advertise their 'Thursday-thru-Saturday' specials, or (5) think of your own topic and have me approve it."

If the class is interested in a topic and wants to pursue it, success is guaranteed. Although many commercially produced units are good, not all students will respond favorably to them. In working with older students, the best approach is to allow the students to choose among alternatives if their interest is to be captured. Let

---

* From Barry Dollar, *Humanizing Classroom Discipline* (New York: Harper & Row, 1972) Copyright © 1972 by Barry Dollar. By permission of the publishers.

us look at a few assignments that teachers can and have used in the classroom.

## Some Examples

The listening post is a popular learning place in the first- and second-grade classrooms. At a table in a corner of the room are several earphones that plug into a tape recorder. A group of six to eight students work at the table at a time. The tapes are stories (taken from supplementary information in teachers' editions of the textbooks; Science Research Associates' commercially produced products; *Weekly Reader;* or stories especially recorded by the teacher, based on special interests or incidents that have emerged in the classroom). Eight to ten Yes or No questions about the story come after it, followed by answers to the questions so that students can evaluate their own work. At the listening post are a stack of ditto sheets with ten spaces where the student can circle either Yes or No, a can of pencils, six to eight earphones, and the tape recorder.

To avoid confusion, one student can be designated as leader. The others quietly sit down and put on the earphones. The leader starts the tape recorder, stops it at the signal given on the tape, passes out paper and pencils for the questions, starts the tape recorder again, stops it at the end, collects the papers and pencils, and sees that the table is ready to be used by the next group. To enhance the learning activity by making it more autonomous, teachers can also put the correct answers at the end of the tape and thereby provide students with immediate and direct feedback. After a few drills on procedure, the group at the listening post will be able to function quite independently. The teacher merely rewinds the tape and signals the next group. Thus, even first graders can independently engage in carefully structured learning tasks.

In addition to tapes and filmstrips, learning centers can be filled with hundreds of mimeographed learning sheets. The complexity of the tasks, of course, varies with the age and aptitude of the learners. For example, in the math corner on April Fool's Day, the second-grade teacher might give students the sheet in Figure 9.6 and ask them to find the mistakes by circling all errors that appear on the calendar. (Students could be asked to make their own calendars and see if their classmates can find the errors they purposefully make.)

Many teachers have found special-feature learning centers to be useful. For example, the teacher may write an introduction to a mystery story (3 to 15 pages, the length varying with the age and aptitude of the readers). Younger students are requested to tape-

**FIGURE 9.6.** An Independent Work Sheet

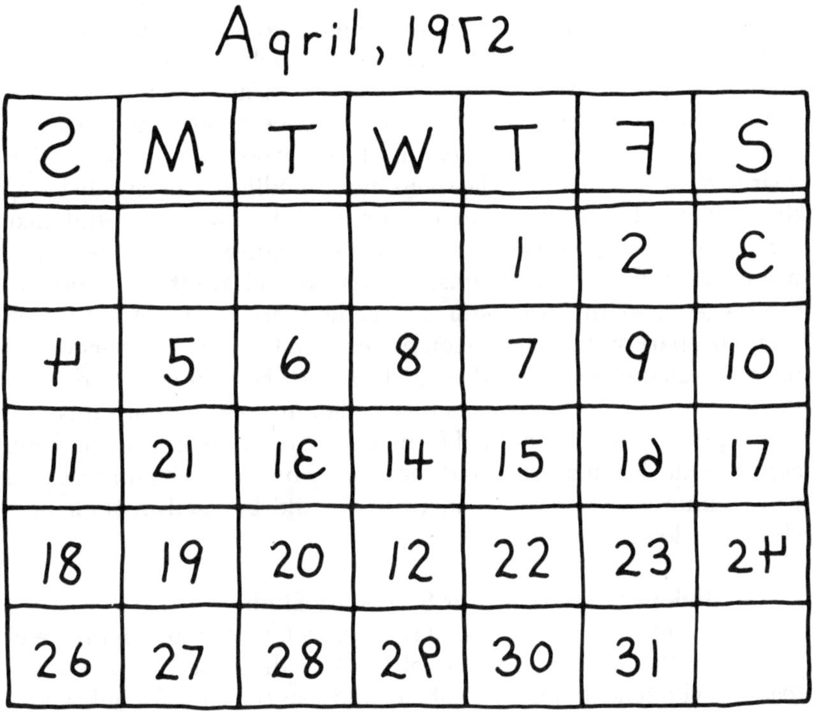

# Aqril, 19Γ2

| Ƨ | M | T | W | T | ꓭ | S |
|---|---|---|---|---|---|---|
|   |   |   |   | 1 | 2 | Ɛ |
| Ʉ | 5 | 6 | 8 | 7 | 9 | 10 |
| 11 | 21 | 1Ɛ | 14 | 15 | 1ə | 17 |
| 18 | 19 | 20 | 12 | 22 | 23 | 2Ʉ |
| 26 | 27 | 28 | 2ꟼ | 30 | 31 |   |

record their own endings to the story, while older ones may be requested to write their own endings and compare them to those of others. At other times in the special-feature corner, the teacher may simply have students respond to interesting questions: "On one page, tell how would you spend a million dollars. Think! Tell *why*, as well as *what* you would buy." "Relate in 200 words or less how you would feel if you (dropped, caught) the winning pass in a championship football game." "Assume that when you woke up today, it was the year 2025. Describe what you will actually be doing in the year 2025. How old will you be then? What job do you expect to hold? Will there still be jobs in the year 2025?" The ideas presented here are only a few of the many activities that teachers can create in the classroom.

However, the really good things will probably be the exercises you prepare especially for a class or a smaller group of learners, based upon a special interest that you have observed. A good idea would be for teachers at the same grade level to share ideas for independent learning centers at in-service meetings. In fact, one teacher could put together several weeks of math work while another makes multiple copies of listening tapes and assignment sheets and a third works on language arts units. Such sharing reduces the amount of preparation time for each teacher and enables teachers to produce high-quality units. Naturally, once created, the learning centers are valuable resources that the teacher can use year after year with only minor modifications (most modifications simply being the addition of new units to match spontaneous interests of students).

Similarly, a good project for preservice teachers in a college course would be to form work teams, dividing the class into four project groups (e.g., math, social studies, reading, and science) with each group preparing from five to ten projects. In this way teachers would have the chance to swap ideas and to learn how to implement the learning-center concept by actually planning sequential units and writing them into operational form. In addition, students could keep copies of all class materials and thus would be able to begin teaching with a number of concrete ideas that could be used in their own classroom learning centers.

### Independent Work for Secondary Students

The learning-center notion as discussed so far has much more relevance for the elementary school teacher than for the secondary teacher who teaches but one subject and sees students for only about one hour each day. However, certain subjects at the secondary level are well suited to independent study or independent group projects.

In addition to allowing students to learn from one another, the independent group project method allows the secondary teacher time to meet many students as individuals and works in a way similar to that already described for elementary schools. While students work in project teams, the secondary teacher is free to pass from group to group, sharing ideas and talking informally. The guidelines here are similar to those suggested for younger students working in project teams, except that students in secondary classrooms are able to work for longer periods of time without direct teacher assistance. Students may be assigned to one- or even two-week projects. Again, the assignments should be interesting, enjoyable activities that allow students to think about topics of interest and to cooperatively share ideas as they attempt to solve a problem.

Topics can be traditional assignments, such as all groups first do basic research on four political candidates who are seeking the presidential nomination, summarizing the basic stance of each candidate on selected issues; separate groups decide how their candidate would respond to a list of questions asked at a press conference in the South, North, East, and West; and then role-playing these press conferences.

The key points to note in such assignments are (1) students begin by having a common reading assignment, so that they share at least a minimum amount of information and have clear, specific knowledge that they can use to solve problems, (2) students are then placed into a position where they can summarize their information and apply it to a particular situation and, typically, are given a choice regarding which specialty group they want to work in, and (3) they are given an opportunity to share information with other groups by presenting the views of their candidate in a general classroom discussion, where (4) they have the opportunity to receive evaluative feedback (correcting factual errors or conflicts in their position) from the teacher and fellow students.

Most students enjoy the opportunity to work independently to gather facts on a concrete problem and use the information in simulated situations. Again, organization is the key. Teachers need to provide some structure to the learning task, identify pertinent resources, and let the students know how they will be held accountable. Of course, teachers need not structure all assignments. After students have been through the process once, the teacher can solicit and use student ideas in creating learning tasks. The most important elements of group work are that the assignment has a clear focus (whether teacher defined or group defined), that each student is held accountable for at least a part of the discussion, and that group tasks are enjoyable.

Topics need not always be traditional, content-centered assignments. Attitudes and awareness may be stimulated by combining factual knowledge with student impressions and values. For example, the above exercise would largely involve students describing and reciting what political journalists had written. Other assignments may begin with content and end with expressions of feelings. For example, tenth-grade males in a world history class might be divided into four independent groups. Each group would be presented with summary descriptions of the desirable physical and personality characteristics of women in four different countries in the 1850s, and they would then be asked to speculate about the cultural factors that led to and perpetuated the characteristics of the ideal woman in each of these countries. Female students in the class could be divided into four groups and asked to respond to such questions as: "What were the roles of women in each of these countries and to what extent were women satisfied with their respective roles?"

330 LOOKING IN CLASSROOMS

Later, group discussion could center on the frustrations that led to the women's rights vote in the United States and on why some countries and cultural milieus allowed women to assume more responsibility earlier than did others. When and under what circumstances did women become activists? How did men respond to the emerging independence of women? What is male chauvinism? Can a woman become president? What is the woman's role in contemporary American life?

Teachers who prefer not to use large amounts of class time for independent group work can still make efficient use of brief group assignments in the classroom. Teachers who lecture daily or who involve the entire class in daily discussion will be surprised at how effectively group assignments can enhance group discussion. Although the process can work in countless ways, the most basic procedure is as follows:

1. The previous night, the entire class is assigned certain pages to read in their texts.
2. At the beginning of the period, the teacher breaks the class into five small groups and gives each group two or three different questions to answer.
3. Each group is allowed 10 to 15 minutes to discuss their answers, look up information in textbooks, and so forth.
4. The class is brought back together and the teacher *randomly* calls on a particular group member to answer a question. He or she then encourages students from *other groups* to react to the adequacy of the answer and allows students who were in the original group to embellish the answer, defend it with logical argument, and so on.

If the teacher regularly assigns students to different groups, several good things occur. First, students are regularly interacting with many other members of the class, and in discussing interesting questions about course material, students have the chance to learn from one another. Students in small groups also have a greater chance to talk than they do in large groups, and the shy student, in particular, feels more comfortable in expressing ideas in safer surroundings (when these students learn that they can express themselves and that others are interested in what they have to say, it will be possible for them to speak more freely in front of the whole class). Students are task-oriented in these sessions because they know that any one of them may be called on to answer one of the group's questions, and they know that the teacher or a student in another group may ask them for a clearer answer or more information. Perhaps most importantly, this procedure mobilizes the students' attention, forces them to focus their thoughts on relevant questions, and helps to provoke learning. Finally, students, after listening and practicing their own responses, are interested in sharing their ideas and getting feedback from others. If the teacher conducts such sessions with interest in the students' answers and responds to their comments constructively, the students will learn that the teacher is genuinely interested in their learning, not just quizzing them about the reading assignment.

Of course, this approach, like any activity, can be overdone. Too much of even a good thing can become boring and trite. What we have tried to do in this chapter is to present a variety of ways in which the teacher can group for instruction. No one way is preferred. The particular learning goals and the idiosyncratic nature of a given class or pupil, as well as the particular teacher, dictate the most appropriate instructional patterns. Clearly, there are many times when teacher lecturing with little or no student comment is desirable (e.g., when a new unit is beginning and the students have read little related material). There are also times when oral student reports, peer tutoring, learning-center work, individual work, and project groups are appropriate. In fact, the effective teacher will probably engage in all of these activities at one time or another during the year, presenting the students with a variety of stimulating learning experiences.

### SUMMARY
We have suggested in this chapter that grouping students on the basis of their achievement level is often an undesirable instructional decision. Too often students lose their individual identities when they are placed in an ability group. That is, teachers sometimes treat students on the basis of their group placement. Students who learn more quickly or more slowly than other group members receive *group* assignments rather than individual assignments that are geared to the specific errors that the student made on his or her last work assignment. A group assignment is not likely to be geared to the student's unique special interests.

In addition to teachers' tendencies to treat students as group members rather than as individual learners, there are other disadvantages to ability grouping. For example, too often, under rigid grouping plans, students tend to stay in the same group year after year regardless of their progress. Also, rigid grouping plans make it likely that students will seldom receive sustained contact with high-achievement students. There is reason to believe that both high- and low-achievement students *can* learn from one another when they are placed together in learning situations.

Stress has been placed on organizing the classroom so that the teacher will have time to conduct remedial or enrichment work with individual students. Chapter 4 made the point that teachers too often act as referees, telling students what they do incorrectly but frequently failing to provide them with information or skills for correcting their *error set*, the predisposition to repeat the same mistake.

We suspect that teachers often act this way because they feel that they do not have time to perform remedial work and/or because the time to do this would take away too much time from other students. To help with this problem, a plan was advanced in this chapter for allowing students to pursue independent work in the classroom. Such techniques, when tailored to the specific demands of a particular classroom and teacher, will provide teachers with the necessary time for remedial work, while allowing students to develop increased capacity for organizing, directing, and evaluating their own learning.

Finally, the concept of peer tutoring has been discussed. The use of students to teach other students is certainly a strategy that teachers should consider and perhaps experiment with. However, like any other teaching technique, peer tutoring will be more useful to some teachers than others. Also, it should be noted that a teacher is not necessarily a good teacher if he or she uses peer-tutoring strategies or a bad one if he or she decides not to use them. Like any other classroom behavior, the usefulness of peer tutoring depends upon the effect it has upon students. If the technique helps students to learn more efficiently and involves them more directly in classroom life, it should be continued.

### SUGGESTED ACTIVITIES AND QUESTIONS

1. As a classroom teacher, if you use or plan to use ability grouping as an instructional pattern, state the criteria that you will use to assign students to groups and to rotate students from group to group.

2. Describe two or three types of learning centers (that were not discussed) and indicate the types of materials and activities that would be utilized at the centers.

3. With a group of teachers or fellow students who share a similar interest in teaching the same subject, prepare actual instructional material that could be used in a learning center.

4. Outline a plan (please use your own ideas as well as those presented in the book) that will allow students to spend a major

portion of their day at learning centers. Design the room arrangement for your classroom, specify the learning centers that are created, and make schedules for individual students.

5. When and under what circumstances might it be effective to group students for instruction?

6. Why has ability grouping been relatively ineffective?

7. In general, what types of students do teachers prefer to teach and why?

8. Why might placing students in a higher group than their achievement levels suggest have a positive effect on their subsequent achievement?

9. Why do students usually remain in low groups once they are placed there?

10. Why do teachers need to reevaluate their grouping patterns and frequently rotate students from one group to another?

11. What are some of the possible advantages that might occur when peer tutoring and individualized learning programs are utilized?

12. What proactive behaviors can teachers engage in to make peer-tutoring programs effective?

**FORM 9.1.** Student-Managed Learning Experiences

*USE: When teacher has been observed frequently enough so that reliable information can be coded*
*PURPOSE: To see if teacher is providing opportunities for students to make choices and manage their own learning experience*
*Record any information relevant to the following points:*

PROVIDING CHOICES
Does the teacher include time periods or types of activities in which students can select from a variety of choices in deciding what to do or how to do it?
*Only when (if) they finish seatwork. They can color or use supplementary readers.*

Can you see places where provision for choice could easily be included?
*Several learning centers could be created with available equipment, including some with audio-visual self-teaching equipment.*

COOPERATIVE LEARNING
Does the teacher encourage students to work cooperatively in groups at times? *Top reading group (only) reads on their own at times.*

Can you see places where provision for cooperative learning could easily be included? *Other reading groups could read alone, too, or at least do flashcard drills. Teacher often has children color a picture or do some other small activity related to topics studied that day. She could plan larger, cooperative projects just as easily.*

PEER TUTORING
Does the teacher ever ask students to tutor or otherwise assist their peers?
*Occasionally, if a child has been absent for a few days.*

Can you see ways the teacher could arrange to do this (if he or she does not)?
*Flashcard drills in both language arts and math.*

334

**FORM 9.2.** Small-Group Interaction

*USE: Whenever a small group of students is working and the teacher is not a formal part of the group.*
*PURPOSE: To determine how the group spends its time*
*Make a code every 15 seconds to describe what the group is doing at that moment.*

Frequency                                    Type Contact

_____      1. Reading (finding information etc.)
_____      2. Manipulating equipment
_____      3. Task discussion: general participation
_____      4. Task discussion: one or two person dominated
_____      5. Procedural discussion
_____      6. Observing
_____      7. Nontask discussion
_____      8. Procedural dispute
_____      9. Substantive (task relevant) dispute
_____     10. Silence or confusion

335

**FORM 9.3.** Individual Participation in Small-Group Work

*USE: When a small group is operating and the teacher is not part of the group*
*PURPOSE: To assess the involvement and participation of individual students*
*during small-group work*
*Observe the target student for 15 seconds and make a code. Repeat the*
cycle for the duration of the small-group activity. *

| | |
|---|---|
| _____ | 1. Reading (finding information) |
| _____ | 2. Manipulating equipment (filmstrip, slide rule) |
| _____ | 3. Participating in general discussion (telling and listening to others) |
| _____ | 4. Listening to general discussion |
| _____ | 5. Presents idea to group (others are listening to the target student) |
| _____ | 6. Talking to individual (an aside: the conversation is not part of the group discussion) |
| _____ | 7. Listening to individual (an aside: the conversation is not part of the group discussion) |
| _____ | 8. Passive (can't tell if student is involved) |
| _____ | 9. Misbehaving |
| _____ | 10. Leaves group |

*Note that it would be possible to use the form to code different individual students in the group (code one student for a minute, then switch to another student). Furthermore, the scale could be altered to provide information about the group. For example, the percent of the group that falls into each category could be noted.

**FORM 9.4.** Cooperative vs. Negative Behavior During Group Discussion

*USE: Whenever small group working without the teacher*
*PURPOSE: To see if cooperative or negative behaviors are being practiced*
*Below is a list of student behaviors that may occur during small group*
work. *Note each behavior as it occurs.*

Frequency                                    Type Contact

_____   1. Student criticizes another student (the person, not the idea).
_____   2. Student verbally states refusal to listen to another student.
_____   3. Student interrupts another student.
_____   4. Student ignores another student's request for information
      or clarification.
_____   5. Student defines problems as personal conflict.
_____   6. Student describes feelings.
_____   7. Student asks for feedback to his or her ideas or feelings and
      obtains useful feedback.
_____   8. Student asks another student to clarify and gets a
      clarification.
_____   9. Student defines problems as concerns to be resolved.

Describe the group behavior. Is the group on task? Operating smoothly vs.
confused? Cooperative vs. conflictive? Is the discussion cumulative (students
listen and build on previous statements vs. ignore previous comments)?

337

# 10 / INSTRUCTION

Previous chapters have stressed four major aspects of teaching: expectations, modeling, management, and grouping. Now we will consider a variety of topics related to instruction. These distinctions are artificial, of course. Aspects of teaching that we can separate for purposes for analysis are interrelated in behavior. When teachers make managerial moves, they also model prosocial behavior. Thus, some of the material discussed in this chapter has been touched upon previously. However, we now will take a sharply focused look at instruction.

In addition to the process of instruction, we will consider problems of planning instruction to meet student needs and monitoring the effects of instruction to ensure that intended results occur. The material in the chapter is drawn partly from the traditional body of theory and data on instruction and partly from recent research on teaching.

There are many different approaches to instruction. Some are mutually exclusive, but most are merely different. For example, Joyce and Weil (1972) identify and describe sixteen different approaches to teaching, classified into four groups or orientations (information processing, social interaction, focus upon the individual person, and behavior modification). Information-processing approaches organize instruction so that material is presented in ways that learners can process and retain most easily, and there is an attempt to foster information-processing skills in addition to presenting information to be processed. Social interaction approaches stress the group-living aspects of schooling. Instruction is arranged so that students interact with and learn from one another as well as the teacher, and there is a concern about fostering group relations as well as instruction. Personal approaches stress individual psychology and emotional development (self-actualization, mental health, creativity). Finally, the behavior modification approach stresses the sequencing of activity to promote efficient learning and the shaping and control of behavior through reinforcement.

Each model stresses certain things at the expense of others. For example, the advance organizer model, based on the work of Ausubel (1963), is an information-processing approach that stresses the organization and sequencing of instruction and especially the provision of advance organizers to facilitate learning and memory. Advance organizers are abstract generalizations about material to be learned. They aid learning by providing general concepts that can subsume a great many specifics and help learners remember them and see the relationships among them. This model concentrates almost completely on aspects of instruction that facilitate information processing, ignoring personal development.

In contrast, the non-directive teaching model (Rogers, 1969) takes a very different approach. It stresses building personal capacity for independent learning, attending to the development of self-concept as well as concepts about academic subjects. The organization of instruction is not stressed because this model assumes that instruction must be individualized to the learner's internal frame of reference. We do not teach people directly. Instead, we facilitate their learning by showing students how material is relevant to their own purposes and helping them to understand it.

Both of these approaches have merit. It would be a mistake for teachers to adopt either approach totally or ignore either approach completely. Knowledge about and consideration of the learner's frame of reference probably is helpful in teaching, and learning by discovery appears to be a valuable way to learn. However, some things are learned much more easily when sequenced in an optimal way and taught with advance organizers. It is true that instruction must be adapted to the needs of learners, but it also is true that many of the principles stressed by information-processing approaches are important for performing these adaptations. Until much more, and more prescriptive, research on teaching is available, we will have to continue to depend on models of teaching to provide guidance.

For a long time, there was not much research on teaching to

link teacher behavior to student outcomes, and much of what existed was confusing or contradictory. In fact, for a time it was commonly stated that particular methods and even particular teachers did not make a measurable difference in affecting student learning (relative to other methods or teachers). However, research conducted in the last ten years or so has shown that some methods and some teachers do consistently get better results than others (Good, Biddle, and Brophy, 1975). This may seem obvious to you, but it is difficult to document the effects of particular methods or teachers because so many other things affect students at the same time.

Researchers have had to develop experimental and statistical methods to eliminate or control the effects of some of these other factors, so that they could concentrate on the factors of interest and increase the chances that their effects would show up in analyses. This has been done with some success, but even now, when results are beginning to reinforce one another in a way that they never did before, the advantage favoring the more successful methods or teachers usually is small. Also, there is little evidence of one generic method best for all types of students and situations. Instead, what constitutes effective teaching varies according to the developmental levels and other characteristics of students and according to group size, subject matter, and other situational or context factors (Dunkin and Biddle, 1974; Good, Biddle, and Brophy, 1975; Good and Power, 1976; Rosenshine, 1976). Consequently, even though the principles that determine effective teaching are becoming more and more clear, you have to analyze particular situations to see which principles apply and whether or not they are being implemented properly. In other words, you have to look in the classroom if you want to talk about particular situations.

Therefore, let us stress at the outset that there is no simple definition of effective teaching or good teachers. For one thing, the personal attributes of teachers will interact with their general competence and teaching styles to determine outcomes. Teachers who are introverted and mostly interested in student achievement will be more successful with some types of students than others. Achievement-oriented students will do well in their classes, but those with less achievement orientation will not. In particular, more extroverted students who are oriented toward social relationships rather than learning will find it difficult to relate to these teachers as individuals or as instructors. Such students might also be difficult for introverted and achievement-oriented teachers to handle, although teachers who were extroverted and oriented toward social relationships themselves might enjoy working with these students and handle them successfully. Student characteristics will also make a difference. Some teachers are quite successful with advantaged students but might be much less successful with disadvantaged students, and vice versa.

Even where particular aspects of teaching appear to be generally effective, teachers use different approaches to accomplish the same effects. For example, there are many ways that teachers can show respect for their students. One teacher might make it a point to visit with each student each day. Another might visit students' homes and invite parents to visit the classroom. Another might devote classroom time to efforts to deal with student problems (e.g., a dispute over ownership of a pencil) rather than arbitrarily avoiding such problems through convenient rules (e.g., pencils with two owners are the teacher's property). Similarly, the teacher's role as a model in the classroom is important, but there is no single correct way to model such things as problem solving. Some teachers demonstrate for the entire class; others work with small groups; others have students model for their classmates.

Although it is not possible to specify how teachers should behave with complete detail, it is possible to note things that should occur regularly, and we can look for the presence or absence of these things. For example, we can observe the degree to which the teacher uses modeling when it is appropriate, even though we cannot say that a particular kind of modeling is best. This applies to the variables described in this chapter. We can say that certain things should take place, but the frequency of their occurrence and the ways they are performed depend in part upon teacher style and situational variables. These are just a few aspects of teaching that require teachers to act as *decision makers,* determining how general principles apply to their particular classrooms.

## THE MATCH

One of the most basic decision-making tasks is solving what Hunt (1961) has called "the problem of the match." This refers to the problem of matching the difficulty level and interest value of materials and assignments to the present skills and interests of the students. Typically, schooling is a compromise between ideal but prohibitively expensive tutoring and the need to hold costs down. The lock step curriculum, with standardized materials at each grade, and the familiar formula of 20–30 students per teacher, are the result. This works reasonably well for most students, despite obvious weaknesses, but the burden of individualization is on the teacher. The variations in readiness, ability, and interests that exist in any classroom make this a problem for all teachers. It becomes a more serious problem to the extent that students differ from the "average" students for whom the curriculum is intended. Teachers may have to supplement or even substitute for the curriculum in order to succeed (Brophy and Evertson, 1976). They will also have to devise ways to monitor student progress in order to see and respond to difficulties and ensure that materials are being used profitably.

### Difficulty Level of Material

If students are to work persistently, they must be able to perform the tasks they are asked to do. Few of us work very long if we do not enjoy success in the process. Persistence is determined largely by previous success on similar tasks (Sears, 1940). Students' abilities to do school assignments determine the degree to which they believe they can learn independently. One important thing to look for in classrooms is the degree to which there is a match between what teachers ask students to do and what the students are capable of doing.

A major factor determining how students learn is the relationship between the demands of lessons and what students already know (Ausubel, 1963). Hunt (1961) has argued that the teacher's task is to provide students with progressively more difficult work, but none so difficult as to frustrate them or erode their confidence. Ideal tasks present new challenges but can be solved independently by students. In practice, this means moving along in small steps and making sure that each step is mastered. New work phases in new challenges, but these are easy for students to handle successfully. The result should be continuous work on the assignment (because students understand what they are supposed to do and do it without becoming confused and unable to continue) and generally successful performance (confirming that they did in fact work on the assignment and were able to handle it successfully).

To determine the match between students and tasks, you may have to observe a classroom for several visits or monitor the work of several students. However, a quick assessment can be made by observing the variety of different books and materials being used. Even students grouped homogeneously will have different interests and academic abilities. If the entire class, or even all members of a subgroup, are treated the same, as if they were identical individuals, it is unlikely that the problem of the match is being solved.

For example, suppose that the day's assignments for the Bluebird reading group appear on the board as follows: reading, 8:30–9:00; write the ten sentences on the board, 9:00–9:30; math workbook pages 61–64, 9:30–10:00. . . . In some respects, this is a good sign: the teacher is well organized and obviously has done specific planning. Also, leaving the assignment copied on the board is helpful for students who forget what they are supposed to do. They can consult the board without having to interrupt the teacher or their classmates. However, if all of the Bluebirds have the same assignment every day, there may be problems. Consider Robin Miller, a particular Bluebird. Suppose that Robin does poorly on today's math work. Tomorrow, she should not work on pages 65–70 with the Bluebirds. Instead, she needs to correct the errors in her work on pages 61–64 and, in particular, to overcome the confusion that caused those errors. Every student cannot have individualized pacing for everything, but teachers should recognize individual strengths and weaknesses and try to provide assignments accordingly. Evidence of such differentiated assignments will appear in good teachers' classrooms.

A very instructive way to determine if teachers are matching tasks to student ability is to observe slow students. In many classrooms, these students never finish their assignments, and often their failure to finish prevents them from doing other things. For example, some early elementary teachers hold show-and-tell right before lunch, and participation in show-and-tell depends on being finished with work. In fact, the work itself may be involved in the show-and-tell. If students have been working on pictures related to a story in the reader, it may involve showing the pictures and describing them to the class. If low achievers have difficulty finishing their independent reading, many will not have pictures to share during show-and-tell. Furthermore, it is likely that these same students will be the last to finish every day, not just today.

More generally, it is important for students, especially slow ones, to form the habit of completing their work rather than giving up. The teacher may have to reduce the amount or difficulty of work for a while, monitor work closely and give feedback, and help slow students understand that they can finish with a positive feeling and without a sense of being overwhelmed. The latter is important because some students are convinced that they cannot succeed. This conviction leaves them ready to give up before they even start.

It is unrealistic to expect all students to progress at the same rate, but teachers can expect all students to show steady, continuous progress if they ensure that all of them have work that is appropriate in amount and difficulty level.

### Adapting Material to Student Interest

Work should be matched to interest as well as ability. Everyone's daily behavior confirms this fact. If we try to play bridge and enjoy it, we soon master the complicated set of rules that must be memorized in order to play the game well. On the other hand, we often fail to memorize telephone numbers that we dial frequently. More generally, we do not take an interest in tasks and learn to do them well when we do not enjoy them. Our interest, our drive to learn, helps us to focus attention and persist in learning even complex material *if we want to do so.*

Teachers usually can create interest, at least initially. The degree to which this interest is sustained will depend upon the match between the task and the students. For example, fourth graders may develop interest in using library books to collect information after listening to an enthusiastic introduction by the teacher. However, their interest might be dampened quickly by a few tranquilizing assignments: name the state bird for each state, find the birthdays of each vice-president, list the date for each state's admission to the union, and collect all the information you can about a famous explorer. True, some children will enjoy looking up the vice-presidents' birthdays. Just as importantly, others will find this exercise boring and pointless. If continually asked to use the library for such assignments, these students will learn that the library is a boring place where they find answers to someone else's questions.

If the goal is to teach students that collecting accurate information systematically in the library is an important, exciting activity, the teacher will fail with most students. Instead of giving every student the same assignment, choices could be listed. For example:

1. In which World Series in the last ten years were the most home runs hit?
2. How are sites for World Fairs selected?
3. Name the state bird for each state.
4. What are the causes of pollution?
5. Write your own question, get it approved, and then find the answer.

This set of questions will appeal to a much wider range of students. (Bear in mind that student interest determines the value of such questions in the first place.) If students are really interested in finding answers, the questions will help them develop appropriate attitudes toward resource books and skills for using them. Students' interests vary widely, so that few topics will appeal to everyone. Teachers will increase the chances that students will find tasks interesting if they allow for student selection of study topics whenever it is consistent with instructional objectives.

Obviously, there are some questions that students should work on independently of their interests, but not many. When possible, they should have alternative ways to fulfill requirements, so they will be more likely to enjoy their learning. As noted in Chapter 8, students can be given different assignments even when the whole class has read the same material. Little effort is required to make problems more meaningful. In addition to problems that require students to compute the latitude of London or the air time from Denver to Chicago, the same mathematics can be built into problems requiring the computation of batting averages or the costs of records. Presenting computational tasks within problems that are familiar and interesting to students not only increases the interest value of the problems, it may even make the problems easier for certain students (Stein, Pohly, and Mueller, 1971).

Students also are likely to respond better when lessons are related to one another rather than presented as isolated and perhaps meaningless activities. For example, in assignments involving written expression, students can use the week's list of new spelling words. This way, they will use the new words in meaningful contexts in addition to learning how to spell them correctly. Schools should not only provide information but teach students to use it, process it, and make decisions.

Teachers should consider why, and in what ways, the questions they raise are important to students. Most curriculum content can be related to student interests, and by pointing out these relationships, teachers can help students to answer their own questions while fulfilling curriculum requirements at the same time. Whenever possible, teachers should tell students why they are answering questions and why they should seek information, and should give choices in assignments and information about the relationships between the curriculum and everyday life. There is no reason for teachers or students to view school work as tedious or for teachers to feel guilty when students enjoy learning. *Learning should be fun.*

### Monitoring Work Involvement

It is important for teachers to ensure that materials and assignments result in the intended learning experience. This begins with thoroughness in presenting assignments. Students should know not only what they are supposed to do, but how to do it. Unfamiliar aspects should be demonstrated, and then the students should be given opportunities to practice sample problems for themselves. It is im-

portant for teachers to monitor the students' work on sample problems and to notice and correct errors. If many students are making
the same mistake, additional teaching or review is needed. This
should continue until the point is cleared up—as established by student success in working additional sets of problems, not just *apparent*
understanding of the explanation.

If students are confused about what to do or unable to do it,
they probably will give up serious attempts to work on assignments
(although they may put down answers). Worse yet, they may think
they know what to do when they do not, and end up practicing
errors. This "practice" will actually harm learning progress rather
than help it. A way to make sure that this doesn't happen is to
have all students work sample problems and check them before
releasing them to independent work (Brophy and Evertson, 1976).
This way, teachers can observe any confusion that might exist and
clear it up. Teachers who regularly get students to respond, rather
than assume that they understand explanations without checking,
can expect both more persistence in working on tasks and better
achievement.

Observers can watch teachers present assignments and can monitor the effects of presentations by observing students when they
are supposed to be working. Persistent engagement in seatwork
tasks (vs. giving up or doing something else) is associated both with
better performance on the task and better general learning over
the course of the school year (Bennett, 1976; Cobb, 1972; McKinney,
Mason, Perkerson, and Clifford, 1975).

It may be impractical for teachers to check all students when
presenting assignments, so that they may rely on observation of a
sample of students. Few teachers do this randomly. Instead, most
use a *steering group,* that is, a few students who are monitored
regularly and whose understanding is used as the criterion for either
continuing with a presentation or moving on to something else
(Lundgren, 1972). This can be quite effective for the same reasons
that "key precincts" can be used to predict the outcomes of elections.
However, the right students must be used as the steering group.
In the case of presentation of assignments prior to releasing students
to independent work, the steering group should be drawn mostly
from the weakest students in the classroom, because making sure
that *all* students understand the assignment is essential. Therefore,
observers have an additional criterion to use in assessing the effectiveness of assignment presentations: successful teachers systematically check the work of low achievers. Less successful teachers do
not do this as much and may fool themselves into believing that

everyone understands the assignment just because the better students do. The result is low task engagement when students are released to work independently, high rates of error, and frequent failure to complete assignments.

### Remedial Teaching

Remedial teaching is closely related to "the match." In both cases, teachers must recognize that problems exist and intervention is needed. If they are too concerned about moving along as quickly as possible, they may neglect, often without awareness, students who cannot keep up. Teachers often feel quilty about time spent with low achievers, because during that time they are not challenging the brighter students. However, as shown in Chapter 9, there are ways to increase time spent with low achievers, while at the same time helping faster students to progress with the use of relatively autonomous, self-guided methods.

There is too little remedial teaching in schools. Students who enter third grade without a good phonics background seldom learn phonics. More typically, they are given the same reading materials that other students receive, and they struggle to finish perhaps 70 pages while their classmates complete the book and move on to others. This will not do, especially with disadvantaged students. Brophy and Evertson (1976) found that a "can do" attitude, a determination to teach, was fundamental to teaching effectiveness with low SES students. Teachers who achieved success with them concentrated on teaching a limited amount of material *thoroughly* rather than "covering" a greater amount of material only superficially. They did not hesitate to supplement or even replace curriculum materials if they proved inadequate to the job, which they often did because most curricula are designed for middle-class children. Teachers in middle-class schools less often had to rely on their own resources, but even here, the successful ones had the same determination to keep at it until they found a way to succeed.

Teacher commitment to the belief that every student can and will learn is basic to remedial teaching. Bereiter et al. (1969) described what this attitude looks like in the classroom:

> The good teacher apparently intended to overteach. She hesitated to move on to another task until all the children in her group were performing adequately. The teacher who was not as good did not get as much feedback from the children. She did not seem to have the burning desire to teach every child. She let the children get by with performances that would not be acceptable to the good teacher. In one sense, the good teachers reminded one of Helen Keller's teacher as she was por-

trayed in *The Miracle Worker.* They felt that the children could perform and should perform if the teacher knew how to teach them. The teacher who was not so good seemed to have a mechanical view of the teaching process. It did not seem to bother her if the children did not perform well.

When looking in classrooms, note the relative concern and time devoted to remedial teaching. Is there evidence of it? Does the teacher meet with students who are experiencing difficulties? Too often, the "method" of remedial teaching is to assign the same reading to everyone but ask certain students only half of the questions. Sixth graders who read at the second-grade level should get books written at the lower level which cover the same material that other students are reading about. Books about famous people and history, for example, are written with different vocabularies for different reading levels. It is valuable for the slower students if some of these alternate sources can be kept available in the classroom.

Remedial teaching means adjusting the curriculum to the student, not vice versa. If students only read at the second-grade level, they should not be expected to read a fifth- or sixth-grade text and continually fail. As best they can, teachers should start with students where they are and advance them to more complex tasks as rapidly as possible. If they are not sure about deviating from the curriculum or obtaining other resources, they should consult with the principal, with reading specialists, or with remedial teachers.

Many investigators (Husen, 1967; Rosenshine, 1968, 1976; Shutes, 1969) have found that the opportunity to learn is an important determinant of what is actually learned. When learning is difficult, students require not merely exposure, but also opportunities to deal actively and at length with material and to practice responding to it or using it. It is this kind of active involvement that remedial teaching produces with slow learners. They may be exposed to fewer brief (and insufficient) learning opportunities, but they get more high quality opportunities that result in significant learning. Remedial teaching causes slower students to deal with more content in an active way, and thus to genuinely learn more.

As we saw in Chapter 8, Carroll (1963) has developed a model of the learning process that translates individual differences in learning rates into differences in time required for instruction and practice. Slow learners can learn most of what faster learners achieve, but they may take as much as five times longer to do so. Applications of this idea, especially in the mastery learning approach (Block, 1974; Bloom, 1976), have provided support for it. In general, when instruction is paced so that individuals can master what they are ready to learn at the rates they are able to learn it, students of all ability levels learn more efficiently, and general rates of achievement increase.

Remedial teaching probably brings about improvement in attitudes as well. For example, many low achievers do not think about or attack problems in a goal-oriented, problem-solving manner. Instead, they jot down the first thing that occurs to them and hand in their papers as quickly as possible. They are afraid to look back over their work (Holt, 1964). Students who keep this up long enough eventually learn that the classroom is not a place for serious, exciting learning. Instead, it is a place where confusing things happen for mysterious reasons.

Teachers can enhance slower students' sense of control and belief in their own ability to think by helping them see the relationships between teacher questions and specific strategies for finding answers. This means that if students cannot respond, the teacher will show them how they could have found the answer. By giving directions to the appropriate page or explaining the process involved, teachers help students learn that answering questions is a rational process involving systematic problem solving.

Students who are afraid to look back usually cope with assignments by "guess and look" techniques. They do not adopt active learner roles because they do not have control over the learning situation. Remedial teaching, coupled with an appropriate match of material to student needs, is the first step in helping students become active self-evaluators.

Remedial teaching is essential if the cumulative effects of failure are to be avoided. Low achievers fall farther behind each year that they remain in school. Disadvantaged students in particular require systematic remedial teaching. They often lack important skills assumed by the curriculum, and they will fall even farther behind unless these skills are developed or they are taught in ways that more realistically take into account where they are now. This problem arises regularly, and teachers who want to solve it will have to reteach lessons that were not learned the first time. Most of these lessons will have to be changed, not merely retaught. Repetition alone probably will not be enough. Lessons will have to be revised, by breaking them down into small steps and adding new examples and exercises.

Gagné (1970) has noted that the design of instruction (i.e., sequencing subtasks leading to the concept, principle, or other training goal) is more important in advancing learning than some of the better-known psychological principles such as reinforcement. Revision of lessons is a vital teaching task, as is the ability to generate student enthusiasm for "something old," a review topic. If you observe a class over several days, you should see signs of review work being pursued enthusiastically by teacher and students alike. There is no reason to apologize for remedial work, and every reason to engage in it.

The needs of faster students also are important. To achieve the appropriate match for all students, teachers will have to engage regularly in specialized activities for both fast and slow learners. Perhaps 20–50 percent of the day should be spent on recycled work with low achievers and enrichment work with high achievers. These figures will increase as the age of the students and their capacities for independent work increase (assuming that the students are in mixed-ability, self-contained classrooms).

### Providing for Self-Evaluation

Students should be taught to evaluate their own work. This habit and skill will be needed if they are to become independent, autonomous learners. We live in the midst of an information explosion and in an age when computers help us solve problems, but people still must identify the problems and evaluate the information they gather. If anything, the need to evaluate one's own work, assess one's own inadequacies, and determine what is needed to correct the situation (i.e., to define problems) is greater than ever. Yet schools still are oriented primarily toward presenting information (Covington and Beery, 1976)

Classrooms tend to be places for action, not reflection, unless teachers actively involve students in reflection and decision making. A few ways that this might be manifested are:

1. Students are occasionally asked to explain their thinking, even when their answers are correct. Asking students to explain themselves only when they have responded incorrectly implies that the teacher is interested only in the answer, not the thinking process behind it or other things related to it.

2. Students are asked to evaluate their own or others' work occasionally. This can be done in a variety of ways. When a student answers a question, the teacher can ask other students to react instead of reacting immediately. The teacher can hand students their papers and ask them to pick out the strongest parts of their work and explain why they are particularly good, or to pick out the weakest parts and explain why they are weak and how they can be improved. Students can exchange papers and try to determine how

to make classmates' papers better by adding ideas or arguments not considered by the authors.

Of course, allowing students to react to the papers of classmates must be handled carefully. Students should not critique one another until they have had practice in critiqueing themselves. Even here, it is advisable to restrict the scope of evaluation to something simple, such as "List two ideas that might make the paper better." This will eliminate the problems that occur when students are overwhelmed by too many "helpful" comments, will reduce pressures on those who have difficulty thinking up improvements, and will require those who can think of many improvements to concentrate on quality rather than quantity. Furthermore, when student feedback is anticipated, teachers can have students use numbers rather than names for identification purposes.

Such assignments are useful for teaching students the fun of sharing information and for demonstrating that there is no right way to prepare a paper. They also help students learn to look at and think about their work rather than turn in assignment after assignment without doing this. Repeated over time, this also helps students to see their progress. For example, an effective technique for early elementary grade students is to let them see and compare handwriting exercises done early in the year with others done later.

3. Students are allowed to make decisions. These can be relatively simple decisions about assignments or larger decisions involved in planning. In any case, there should be genuine opportunities for decision making by students.

For those who have not been trained in self-evaluation, teachers may have to ask simple questions, accept students the way they are, and help them develop skills as rapidly as possible. The ability to criticize oneself openly and without defensiveness is learned. Teachers can help foster it by creating opportunities for students to make decisions and by acting as reality therapists to help them evaluate decisions that are proposed or tried out.

4. The teacher responds when students ask questions about the topic at hand. Such questions signal student interest in and desire to learn about the topic. Teachers can influence learning significantly by taking time to deal with questions in depth, giving students information or providing them with resources and ways to pursue questions on their own.

5. Teachers allow students to question their behavior and the content of the curriculum. Students should not learn the curriculum blindly, without questioning any interpretations made in the book

or by the teacher. They should learn that a statement is not necessarily true just because it appears in a book, and should know that much of what appears in a book is the author's hypothesis, his best guess at present. Interpretations may be based upon extended study, but they still are conjecture. Students should realize this and be encouraged to make interpretations of their own.

Teachers should model this attitude, along with the notion that students can "play with" the curriculum by considering it from different points of view. They should occasionally ask students to question certain points and should express their own disagreements with the text when they have them. Also, teachers should take care to separate their own opinions and interpretations from established fact, thus encouraging students to take issue with them, as well. Finally, when students do give their opinions, teachers can help them to evaluate their thinking by asking them to explain their reasons and perhaps by questioning them or debating with them. All of these actions help maintain the attitude that complex issues may not have any single correct interpretation, and that the validity of interpretations depends on the logic and evidence that can be brought to bear in their support, not upon the authority or aggressiveness of the people who support them.

## GROUP INSTRUCTION

Presentation of information to the class assembled as a group is an important part of teaching. Several aspects of this task consistently affect student learning (Rosenshine and Furst, 1973). These include clarity and enthusiasm of teacher presentations, the use of a variety of teaching methods, and the maintenance of student attention.

### Clarity

Clarity in the teacher's presentations is essential if the students are to understand concepts and work assignments. Does the teacher communicate the objectives of lessons clearly? How long does it take for objectives to become clear? Do lectures begin without introductions or end without summaries, lack organization to provide structure and highlight main points, or otherwise lack sufficient clarity to enable students to follow them without confusion?

Ausubel (1963) has discussed the importance of "advance organizers" that describe what students are to learn before the instruction proper begins. For example, before describing 20 penalties that can occur during hockey games, a physical education instructor could provide a way to organize the information: "Today we are going to discuss penalties that might be called during hockey games. We will discuss the difference between minor and major penalties and describe 15 minor penalties and five major penalties. At the end of the period, I will show you 20 slides and ask you to name the penalty illustrated and state whether it is major or minor."

Advance organizers like these give students mental maps to use when listening to the teacher or reading. They can expand this structure as they identify relevant concepts and information. Without such advance organizers, listening and thinking may be disorganized and ineffective. A clear explanation of the nature of the assignment helps students to focus on the main ideas and order their thoughts effectively. This is because we are more likely to find something if we know what we are looking for. Therefore, before lecturing, teachers should tell the students what they will be expected to learn from the lecture and why it is important for them to know this information. After lectures, they should summarize the main points in a few simple sentences. Providing a clear introduction and a strong summary takes little planning and presentation time, but it can make a big difference in learning, especially in the degree to which students remember essential facts and concepts.

In addition to these organizational factors, presentations (or questions) can lack clarity because of vague or difficult language. Teachers who use clear and appropriate language that all students understand obtain high achievement from the students (Rosenshine and Furst, 1973; Good and Grouws, 1975). The dimensions of clarity have not been fully determined, but the following criteria indicate the general meaning of the concept: (1) the points that the teacher makes are clear and easy to understand, (2) the teacher spends little time answering questions about what he or she means (presumably because he or she is clear and does not need to be asked), and (3) the teacher uses few vague expressions such as "a little" or "many." Ratings of clarity involve inferences by observers, but they can usually be made with high reliability (see the scale at the end of the chapter).

### Enthusiasm

When teachers are enthusiastic about the subject matter they teach, students are more likely to be motivated to pay attention and to develop enthusiasm of their own. Ultimately, they are also more likely to achieve at higher levels (Rosenshine and Furst, 1973). There's a bit of Tom Sawyer in all of us. In particular, young people are likely to develop interests through modeling others, including teachers. If teachers appear to enjoy knowledge in general and specific subject matter in particular, students are likely to develop similar interests. If the teacher shows no enthusiasm, students probably will not either (if the teacher does not like to paint fences, why should the students?). Teacher enthusiasm is important even to college students, who frequently stress it in explaining why they like certain instructors and do not like others (Costin, Greenough, and Menges, 1971).

Like clarity, enthusiasm is a general teacher characteristic that is difficult to describe in specific terms. However, qualities such as alertness, vigor, interest, movement, and voice inflection are important. Enthusiastic teachers are alive in the room; they move around and come into close contact with more students; they show surprise, suspense, joy, and other feelings in their voices; and they make material interesting to students by relating it to their experiences and showing that they themselves are interested in it.

Because of television, teachers must have the dramatic qualities of actors, especially today. Teachers' efforts to prepare for today's students often are met with a chorus of "We've done that before" or "We've seen that before." Studies of children watching *Sesame Street* have revealed that they do not attend to an adult voice with a picture of an adult face on the screen for long. However, they do pay attention to an adult voice when it is accompanied by an animated figure, such as a bouncing chart or some puppets. Apparently, some children learn to tune out adults who stand relatively motionless while giving information, even before they enter school (Lesser, 1974).

Tom Sawyer-like characteristics have always been important for teaching, and if TV and kindergarten experiences have reduced the interest value of school, these factors are more important now than ever. In particular, teachers should be enthusiastic when stressing review or having students repeat or try to improve upon things done in the past. Many teachers do this regularly and well. Bereiter et al. (1969) provide this account:

When a good teacher pointed to a picture, and said, "What's this?" she expected all children to respond. If they didn't respond, she would perhaps smile and say, "I didn't hear you. What's this?" By now all of the children were responding. She would smile, cock her head and say, "I didn't hear you." Now the children would let out with a veritable roar. The teacher would acknowledge, "Now I hear you." and proceed with the next task. It was quite noticeable that the children performed well on the next task, with virtually 100% of them responding. Basically her approach was to stop and introduce some kind of gimmick if the children—all of them—were not responding or paying attention. She did not bludgeon the children, she "conned" them. It seemed obvious that they understood her rules; she would not go on until they performed.

It seemed that they liked performing, because when they performed well she acted pleased.

Apparently, there are at least two major aspects of enthusiasm. The first is the ability to convey sincere interest in the subject. This involves modeling, and even shy teachers should be able to demonstrate it. The other aspect is vigor or dynamics. Teachers who have difficulty doing this through voice and manner can use other techniques. For example, three days in advance, the teacher can tell students that "On Thursday we will role-play the Scopes Trial." This can be followed with information that will build interest and suspense. During the intervening days, this will help provide motivation for activities planned as preparation for the "big event." The teacher could ask students to imagine themselves in the places of historical persons: "Put yourself in the place of William Jennings Bryan and analyze the feelings, values, and attitudes of the people in that small Tennessee town. What arguments would you advance? What types of witnesses (Pastors? Medical experts? Who?) would you want to use?" Seatwork and homework assignments could also be related to the project: "Tomorrow we will select jurors for the trial. Before doing this, we need to find out the basis on which the prosecutor and defense attorney can reject witnesses . . ."

Of course, teachers must be enthusiastic about everyday topics and lessons as well, not just those related to special events. This is done by continually modeling enthusiasm in the very process of teaching, in the way that material is presented: calling attention to new information or skills, presenting tasks as positive challenges rather than unwelcome chores, challenging students to test themselves when they try to solve problems or apply new skills, and personalizing information by showing how it relates to students' everyday lives and interests.

### Using a Variety of Teaching Methods

The use of a variety of instructional methods was stressed in Chapter 9 as a logical consequence of the attempts to individualize. In addition, research on teaching reveals that variety appears (along with clarity and enthusiasm) as important for maintaining student interest and attention, and ultimately for producing higher achievement (Rosenshine and Furst, 1973). Systematic use of a variety of techniques produces better results than heavy reliance upon any one technique, even a good one. Variety makes it easier for students to sustain attention over long periods of time. Lectures mixed with small-group work, panel discussions, debates, and other devices add spice to classroom life. For years, writers have debated the relative merits of teacher lectures vs. discovery approaches that minimize teacher structure and rely upon independent learning by the student. Despite much evidence, neither approach is established clearly as better than the other, and neither is likely to be.

The lecture approach has been criticized as follows:

1. Lectures deny students the opportunity to practice social skills.
2. Lectures make the implicit assumption that all learners need the same information, and this usually is incorrect.
3. Lectures often are longer than the attention span of the students, so that they begin to "tune out."
4. Lectures only convey information; they do not affect attitudes or promote skill development.
5. Students can read facts on their own—why waste their time with lectures?

Most of us have known teachers whose lectures were dull, ineffective, vague, or simply too frequent and too long. However, the lecture method has much to recommend it, assuming that lectures are well organized, up to date, and presented appropriately. Ausubel (1963), among others, has pointed out that effective lectures provide students with information that it would take hours for them to collect. He and others would ask, "Why force students to search for information for hours when a lecture will allow them to get it quickly and then move on to application or problem solving?" Obviously, this point has merit. The important question is not "Should we lecture?" but "When should we lecture?"

Hoover (1968) outlines situations in which lectures seem especially appropriate:

1. When needed background information is not readily accessible to students.
2. When facts conflict.
3. When unique experiences enable a teacher, student, or resource person to give a lecture that contributes substantially to the clarification of issues.
4. When time is of the essence and data sources are scattered.
5. When a change of pace or variety is needed (oral reports and demonstrations fall into this category).
6. When the presentation of data is likely to result in greater understanding than would be possible otherwise.

These points seem well taken. Good lectures and presentations at these times seem not merely acceptable but preferable to available alternatives. Furthermore, some of the other criticisms of lecture methods can be met without abandoning the methods entirely. For example, consider the criticisms that lecture methods do not allow for student involvement in the learning activity or for students to develop social skills. Teachers could adjust to these needs while retaining the advantages of lectures by giving short lectures (perhaps 15 minutes) to structure problems and provide students with necessary information and then by breaking the class into small problem-solving groups. Teachers who can lecture in an interesting, enthusiastic way that crystallizes issues and helps students to raise questions that they can eventually answer themselves are providing valuable learning experiences. Lectures should be viewed not merely as convenient devices for presenting information, but also as ways to stimulate interest and raise questions that students will want to address later in groups or independent activities.

Teachers who lecture in a boring or irritating way should try to help themselves in the ways suggested in the next chapter because for *them* lecturing probably is a waste of time. One advantage of team teaching is that teachers with good lecturing styles can do most of the lecturing while other teachers can conduct small-group activities, supervise independent work, and plan special events.

Classroom discussions and small-group activities not only provide variety, but help students develop skills in expressing themselves orally and in working with other students on joint projects. Trump (1966) summarized the need for such activities this way:

Students need to learn how to orally express ideas effectively, to listen to the ideas of others, and to identify areas of disagreement and consensus and to respect each other in the process. These skills have to be taught and they have to be practiced. I am sorry to say . . . that these skills are not practiced in today's classrooms. What is called classroom discussion is little more than an oral quiz conducted by the teacher.

Each week, students can be assigned to work in small groups (5–15 students) to practice communication skills and solve problems. Small groups allow students to participate in problem-centered discussion, and many students are more comfortable in expressing themselves in small groups than in whole-class activities. Also, many more students are able to practice communication skills than would be possible in a single large group.

Motivation and interest often are affected positively when teachers involve students in small-group activities, provide them with interesting projects, and supply them with clear procedural guide-lines for accomplishing goals. Small-group work, if *well planned,* complements whole-class activities nicely by allowing students to learn in more social and active ways. Recently, materials and meth-ods have been developed exclusively for use with small groups (DeV-ries and Edwards, 1974). The materials include learning games, which allow students to learn and practice skills while playing enjoy-able games. A successful small-group method is the use of student teams. This involves dividing the class into small groups which coop-erate with one another in playing games or working on projects in competition with other teams.

### Student Attention

Clarity, enthusiasm, and variety in instructional techniques promote achievement primarily by helping teachers elicit and maintain atten-tion. This is basic because students must attend to and think about most learning tasks if they are to master them. A useful focal point for looking in classrooms is to assess student attention to learning tasks. Given all we know about attention span, it is not reasonable to expect students to be attentive at all times. Pencils have to be sharpened, resource books have to be returned, and many other factors are present that reduce student attentiveness (hunger, need to go to the bathroom, distractions from outside the room). The question we try to answer about student attention is, "What percent-age of the students are actively paying attention or involved in their work?" Teachers should be able to create learning environ-ments in which 80–90 percent of the students are attending at any given time.

Students need not be sitting quietly at their desks. They can be reading books on the floor, drawing at an easel in an art corner, or talking with other students about a group project. The only impor-tant consideration is whether or not they are actively involved in productive work.

Older students might be listening attentively or thinking about a problem even though they appear to be gazing out the window or staring blankly at the floor. Younger ones are more likely to be doing what they appear to be doing. A useful way to look in class-rooms, then, especially in early grades, is to determine the percent-age of students who appear to be actively involved in learning tasks, using indexes like the following:

1. When the teacher gives directions, how many students watch?

2. When the teacher finishes, how many students begin work?
3. When students are supposed to be working at their desks, how many are writing or reading?
4. When the teacher works with a reading group or subgroup, what percentage of the rest of the class remains actively working?

Interpretations of classroom attention data have to be made with care. First graders can be paying attention even though they may be squirming. Reflective students may spend time organizing and thinking about their work before beginning to write. However, if large numbers of students do not begin work promptly, something is wrong (unclear directions, lack of interest, etc.).

The authors have been in classrooms where 70–80 percent of the students were in neutral (sitting, doing nothing productive, wasting time). Situations like this occur most often when teachers who are strict disciplinarians conduct small-group lessons. If seatwork assignments are inadequate because faster students finish and sit with nothing to do and/or slower ones give up, many students will be in neutral. If the teacher has used strict disciplinary tactics to teach them not to make noise or get out of their seats, they have nothing to do but sit there. Teachers who control less rigidly but also fail to plan appropriate seatwork assignments typically have 20–30 percent of the class misbehaving (talking to other students who are trying to work, walking around the room aimlessly, pinching neighbors) and a high percentage of the rest in neutral.

In general, good teachers will have a high percentage of their students "tuned in" to learning tasks most of the time. Teachers who do not should examine their behavior and seek ways to improve. Perhaps they are accepting inattention. They may describe and label it but do nothing to change it. For example, when explaining an assignment, the teacher may say, "I notice that several of you are not paying attention. When we start our seatwork, you will be at my desk, asking for directions." The teacher may then continue to explain the seatwork. After the explanation, it is likely that several students will in fact come up to the desk to ask questions.

Teachers must intervene when students are inattentive. A good way to look at how teachers demand attention is to observe what happens when students continually call out answers without really listening to the questions, perhaps even before the teacher finishes asking them. It is also instructive to see how often students answer a different question than the one asked by the teacher or have their hands up before the teacher asks a question. In these situations, does the teacher recognize and deal with the problem or remain oblivious to it? Does he or she remind the class of the appropriate rule (i.e., listen to the question)? If not, what does the teacher do, and what are the effects?

It also is useful to observe how much time students spend in neutral. Teachers often are unaware of the extent of this problem, but they need to be alerted to it if they are to be expected to reduce it. Students should not be sitting in their seats, bored, with nothing to do. The appearance of attention may not guarantee that students are engaged in a *purposeful activity*, but it suggests that at least minimal conditions for learning are met and that it is possible for learning to take place. Attention is measurable, and it is associated with achievement (Lahaderne, 1968; Cobb, 1972; Samuels and Turnure, 1974).

## QUESTIONING

Teacher questioning has been one of the more popular topics in classroom research partly because aspects of it are among the easiest teacher behaviors to observe and code reliably. There are a great many classification schemes that categorize questions into types (and usually order them in some kind of hierarchy) and a great many studies that involved coding teacher questions into types and relating this information to achievement. Despite this, and despite well-publicized and accepted claims that divergent questions are better than convergent questions, that high-level or complex questions are better than low-level or simple questions, and that thought questions are better than fact questions, reviews consistently conclude that measures of type or level of question do not necessarily correlate with learning gains (Dunkin and Biddle, 1974; Rosenshine and Furst, 1973). Furthermore, recent studies that have yielded consistent findings in other areas report either more inconclusive results (Brophy and Evertson, 1976; Good and Grouws, 1975) or unexpected findings suggesting that low-level factual questions were preferable to more complex or abstract questions (Stallings and Kaskowitz, 1974; Soar, 1973). The latter findings come from studies of instruction of disadvantaged students in the early elementary grades, where schooling concentrates on mastery of the fundamentals of language arts and arithmetic. At these grades, and with these students, complex or abstract questions probably are not helpful.

In contrast to the confusing and unpromising data for type or level of questions, several studies agree in showing that the frequency of questions is related to learning (Brophy and Evertson,

1976; Stallings and Kaskowitz; 1974, Soar, 1973). There probably are at least two reasons for this. One is that teachers who have high rates of academic questions usually have well-organized and managed classes that spend most of their time on academic activities, compared to other classes where the teachers either lack control, and therefore spend less time in academic activities, or spend time pursuing nonacademic goals. Thus, a high frequency of questions means, among other things, that the class spends most of its time in learning related activities. It also means that the teachers are supplementing lectures, demonstrations, reading, and practice activities with opportunities for students to express themselves orally. This appears to be important both because it adds variety and because it is a valuable exercise in its own right.

Much advice about questioning techniques is available. It is based not on research but on logical analyses of the strengths and weaknesses of different questions with reference to instructional goals. The appropriateness of questions depends upon the purpose of the exercise and the characteristics of the students. For example, a teacher may ask questions to see if students are ready for an impending discussion, to determine if they have achieved learning objectives, to arouse their interest, or to stimulate critical thinking. A good question for arousing interest may not be a good question for assessing learning.

Although the complete definition of a good question depends upon context, certain guidelines can be applied to most questions. Groisser (1964) indicates that good questions are (1) clear, (2) purposeful, (3) brief, (4) natural and adapted to the level of class, and (5) thought provoking. Elaboration of these descriptions follows.

1. *Clear* questions precisely describe the specific points to which students are to respond. Vague questions can be responded to in many ways, and their ambiguous nature confuses students. For example, Groisser (1964) writes: "If a teacher of Spanish wished to call attention to the tense of a verb in a sentence on the board and asked, 'What do you see here?' the student would not know exactly what was being called for. Better to ask, 'What tense is used in this clause?' " Vague questions often result in wasted time as students ask the teacher to repeat or rephrase them. They fail to identify the specific attack point ("What's wrong with football?" vs. "Why do so many college players never receive a degree?" or "What about beer?" vs. "What ingredients are used to make beer?" or "Should 16-year-olds be allowed to buy beer?").

Questions can also be unclear if they are asked as part of an uninterrupted series. Groisser writes of a teacher who,

discussing the War of 1812 asks, in one continuous statement,
did we go to War? As a merchant how would you feel? How was
trade hurt by the Napoleonic War?' The teacher is trying to clarify
first question and to focus thinking upon an economic cause of the
ar. In his attempt, he actually confuses.

This teacher would have been more effective asking a clear,
straightforward question to begin with ("What was the cause of the
War of 1812?"), waiting for students to respond, and then probing
for economic causes if students failed to mention this area. Teachers
often ask two or three questions in one or rephrase their original
questions a number of times. When faced with such a series of questions, students do not know what the teacher is asking. Even if
the questions are answered as the teacher hoped, many students
will not profit from hearing the answer because they are confused
or distracted by the questions.

The usefulness of clear and specific (highly focused) questions has
been shown in some experimental situations (Wright and Nuthall,
1970; Rosenshine, 1968). Questions should *clearly cue students to
respond along specific lines.* This does not mean that the teacher
cues the answer; it means that the teacher communicates the specific
question to which the student is asked to respond.

2. Most of us agree that questions need to be *purposeful;* that
is, they should lead toward clear achievement of the lesson's intent.
Question series that are not planned in advance are seldom purposeful. (This is why it is useful to write out questions that will be asked
later during class discussion.) Teachers who ask most of their questions "off the cuff" will ask many irrelevant and confusing questions
that work against achievement of their own goals.

Questions should be asked in carefully planned sequences, with
teachers getting answers to each one before moving on to the next.
If questions are asked in integrated sequence, the activity is more
likely to be a learning experience than just a check to see if students
have mastered the material. Early questions should lead students
to identify or review essential facts. These can be followed with
questions to refine understanding of the information and eventually
to apply the knowledge to real or hypothetical problems ("Now
that we have identified the properties of these six pieces of wood,
which would you use to build a canoe . . . a huge sailboat?"). Planning will help ensure an orderly progression through the sequence
of objectives. Of course, prepared question sequences should not
hold teachers to rigid courses. Worthwhile side roads may be opened
up by pupil questions, and these should be pursued when they look
promising.

3. Questions should be *brief.* Long questions are often unclear. The longer the question is, the more difficult it is to understand.

4. Questions should be phrased in *natural, simple language* (as opposed to pedantic, textbook language) and should be *adapted to the level of the class.* This will help prevent the language of the question from interfering with the course of the discussion. Do teachers use words that the students understand? Can all of the students understand the teacher or only the brighter ones? If students do not understand, they cannot do what the teacher wants.

This does not mean that teachers should avoid big words. Students benefit from teachers who introduce new, big, unfamiliar words with precision. When it is clear, teacher modeling of sophisticated verbal communication abilities is valuable in helping students to develop these same abilities. However, teachers will need to remain aware of student vocabulary levels so that, when they do introduce new words, they can immediately clarify them and help students to make the words their own.

5. Good questions are *thought provoking.* Especially in discussion, questions should arouse strong, thoughtful responses from students, such as "I never thought of that before" or "I want to find the answer to that question." Questions or discussion sessions should force students to think about the facts they possess and to integrate and apply them. In Chapter 1, stress was placed on the use of probing questions to help students clarify their ideas, and on the importance of conducting discussions that center on topics important to students so that they are motivated to share ideas and seek additional information. In addition, questions should require students to analyze or synthesize facts, not merely list them.

Fact questions often are needed to see if students possess information basic to the discussion or to bring out relevant facts before posing more abstract questions. Other questions then should make students use the information, rather than just recite, and motivate them to want to respond. This is especially true as students move into the late elementary and secondary grades.

### Questions to Avoid
Groisser (1964) has also discussed certain question-asking habits that often lead to unproductive student responses. He describes four types as being particularly misused: (1) yes-no questions, (2) tugging questions, (3) guessing questions, and (4) leading questions.

1. Groisser advises against excessive use of yes-no questions because they typically are asked only as warm-ups for other questions. For example, the teacher asks, "Was Hannibal a clever soldier?"

After a student answers, the teacher says, "Why?" or "Explain your reason." Teachers hoping to get responses from other students often will ask yes-no questions like, "Do you agree with Jane's answer?" These yes-no questions confuse the lesson focus and waste time. It is better to ask the real question, "Why do you agree or disagree with Jane's answer?" without including the artificial yes-no question.

We see two additional dangers in yes-no questions or other questions that involve a simple choice between a few alternatives ("Was it Hamilton or Jackson?"). First, such questions encourage guessing because students will be right 50 percent of the time, even when they have no idea as to the correct answer. Holt (1964) describes vividly how students read teachers like traffic lights in such situations and how quickly they change their answers at the slightest teacher frown. With these questions, students are more apt to develop devious strategies for getting the teacher to cue the answer than they are to concentrate on the question itself.

The other disadvantage to yes-no and simple choice questions is that they have *low diagnostic power.* One valuable aspect of student responses, whether correct or incorrect, is that they cue teachers as to the most appropriate way to proceed. Unfortunately, because of the guesswork factor, responses to simple choice questions do not provide much of a basis for deciding whether or not students know the material. *Choice and yes-no questions should seldom be asked.* Choice questions sometimes are useful for low-achieving and/ or sensitive students who have a difficult time responding. They are relatively simple to answer, and this type of warm-up often helps these students respond better to more substantive questions that follow. For most instructional purposes, however, these questions should be avoided.

2. Tugging questions or statements often follow a partial or incomplete student response: "Well, come on," "Yes . . .?" Tugging questions essentially say to the student, "Tell me more." However, these questions are often *vague* and ineffective. When students are stuck for a response, they need a cue or some other kind of help. These questions provide no help, and they are perceived as nagging by the teacher. Brophy and Evertson (1976) found that it was best for teachers to give students the answer when they were unable to respond and unwise to try to elicit it by pumping them. Such pumping was pointless because the students would have given the answer if they knew it. When teachers did stay with the original student, it was better if they provided some kind of help than if they continued to demand the answer to the original question without giving any help at all. This study was conducted in second and

third grade, where most of the questions are factual ones and the students either do or do not know the answers. At higher grade levels, where questions become more complex and varying degrees of completeness and specificity are possible in developing answers, hints or clues are more likely to pay off in improved student response.

When students have responded to the initial question, teachers will be more likely to get additional information if they ask new, more specific questions than if they continue to ask, "What else?" "What's another reason?" and so forth. For example, a teacher might ask, "Why did the Pilgrims live in a fort?" A student might respond, "They built a fort to protect themselves from the Indians and from animals." If the teacher wants the student to focus upon the advantages of community living, the next question should cue the student to this aspect of Pilgrim life: "What advantages did the Pilgrims have living in a group?"

3. Guessing questions require students to *guess or reason* about a question either because they do not have the facts ("How far is it from New York to Denver?" "How many business firms have offices on Wall Street?") or because the question has no correct answer ("In the song 'Houston,' why do you think Dean Martin wanted to go there?" "How many games does a National Football League team have to win in order to make the playoffs?"). Guessing questions can be useful for capturing students' imagination and involving them actively in discussions. However, if they are overused or used inappropriately, they encourage students to guess and respond thoughtlessly rather than think.

The value of guessing questions depends upon how they are used. If the teacher just wants a guess, the question probably is pointless. However, if the teacher wants students to formulate hypotheses and make realistic estimates based on limited information, such questions can be valuable. The game 20 Questions is an excellent case in point, especially for young elementary students. If the teacher allows aimless guessing, the game will have little value. However, if the teacher models the game, demonstrating problem solving strategies, it can be a valuable learning experience.

Similarly, secondary mathematics students may learn to enjoy working with abstract formulas when they are introduced with questions like, "How many games will the Cardinals have to win if they are to win the pennant? Let's see, in the last ten years, the range has been . . ." or "How could we figure the formula? They have a six game lead with 22 games remaining to be played."

*Guessing questions are useful if they are tied to teacher strategies that help students think rationally and systematically and if they are designed to arrive ultimately at a thoughtful response.* Guessing questions used to encourage impulsive or irrational thought are self-defeating. The momentary enthusiasm such questions may generate is not worth the risk of teaching students inappropriate attitudes or habits.

4. Leading questions (such as "Don't you agree?") and other rhetorical questions should be avoided. They reinforce student dependency upon the teacher. *Questions should be asked only if the teacher really wants a response.* Questions such as the following should be avoided: "Kathy, you want to read about the Pilgrims, don't you?" Avoidance of such rhetorical and meaningless questions helps students develop the expectation that, when the teacher asks a question, something important and interesting is about to happen.

### Good Questioning Procedure

Techniques for asking questions effectively are discussed below, adapted largely from Loughlin (1961) and Groisser (1964). Common sense, logical analyses, and some empirical data suggest that these guidelines are reasonable. Before reading them, you may wish to pause and consider your strategies for asking questions. What criteria have you used (or will you use) to guide your behavior in asking questions of students?

Groisser suggests that questions should be planned, should be logical and sequential, should be addressed to the class, should allow students time to think, should be balanced between fact and thought, should be distributed widely, should be asked conversationally, should not be repeated, and should sometimes ask students to respond to classmates' answers.

The first two points have already been discussed. Both are logical and appeal to common sense. However, the usefulness of addressing most questions to the entire class may need some explanation. Teachers should get better attention if they do not call on a student until after they ask the question. The suggested pattern is: ask the question, delay and allow students time to think, and then call on someone. This way, everyone in the class is responsible for the answer. If the teacher names a student to respond before asking the question or calls on a student as soon as he or she finishes asking the question, only that student will be held responsible for the answer. Other students will be less likely to try to answer it in their own minds.

There are exceptions to most general rules of thumb, and Groisser has noted at least three situations where it makes sense to call on the student before asking a question: (1) the teacher notices an inattentive student and wants to draw him or her back into the lesson,

(2) the teacher wants to ask a follow-up question of a student who has just responded, or (3) the teacher is calling on a shy student who may be "shocked" if called upon without warning.

It seems clear that students need time to think, but how much time is optimal? Groisser's implicit hypothesis is that more students will think about the question and become involved in the discussion if teachers delay before calling on anyone. There is no definitive research to show that students actually use this time to think. However, Rowe (1969) found that teachers who prolonged their waiting time for five seconds got longer student responses. Perhaps if teachers delayed too long, pupil attention might wander. However, not waiting long enough seems a much greater danger than waiting too long. Five seconds might not seem like a long time, but teachers seldom wait even that long before calling on someone (Rowe, 1969).

It seems reasonable to expect that a short pause will heighten interest and increase readiness to answer. In addition, we think that teachers should wait for students' responses *after* calling on them. Rowe (1969) found that teachers were more likely to wait longer for responses from their more capable students than from their slower ones. The slower students, then, had to answer more rapidly than the brighter ones. This is one of many ways that low expectations may cause teachers to give up prematurely on certain students if they fail to answer immediately.

In general, teachers should never answer their own questions. If they question a low-achieving student, they should wait until the student makes some kind of response. It may be useful to rephrase, repeat, or give clues. However, students should learn that, when teachers ask questions, they expect answers, even if that answer is "I don't know" or "I'm not sure."

It probably is self-evident that questions should be balanced between fact and thought questions. However, this notion occasionally is lost when advocates play up the importance of complex or abstract questions and criticize fact questions. *Fact questions are important, especially for young students, who learn best if material is highly structured. Many of the questions asked in elementary school classrooms should be fact questions.* Some research has suggested that young children from disadvantaged backgrounds may learn more effectively when fact questions are stressed (Soar, 1973; Stallings and Kaskowitz, 1974). Students of all levels are likely to learn more when fact and thought questions are organized in sequences to emphasize key points and lead to goals.

Groisser and Loughlin both suggest that teachers should distribute questions widely rather than allow the same few students to answer most of them. The idea here is that students will learn more if they are actively involved in discussions than if they sit passively day after day without participating. We all know reticent students who rarely participate in discussions but still get excellent grades, but most students benefit from opportunities to practice oral communication skills, and distributing response opportunities helps keep students attentive and accountable. Also, teachers who restrict their questions primarily to a small group of active (and usually high-achieving) students are likely to communicate undesirable expectations (Brophy and Good, 1974) and to be generally less aware and less effective (Good and Brophy, 1977).

Another point noted by Groisser and Loughlin is that questions normally should not be repeated immediately. Of course, this assumes that the original questions were audible and clearly expressed. Teachers who continually repeat and rephrase their questions teach students that they need not pay attention, because they always will repeat the question if they should call on the student. This also is a sign of poor preparation or disorganized thinking.

Similarly, many teachers get into the annoying habit of regularly repeating student responses, "John has told us that in his opinion there were three fundamental reasons that accounted for the Civil War. First, he suggested . . ." This wastes time and teaches students that they need not pay attention to what classmates say, because the teacher will always repeat it. It lessens the value of pupil responses, and fails to hold students responsible for what others say.

Again, there are exceptions. Occasionally, it is advisable to repeat answers when working with young students in drill recitations. Statements like "Yes, two plus two equals four," "The tallest block is the red one," "Yes, we call this a circle," acknowledge that the student is correct while at the same time modeling speaking in complete sentences. This way of restating important points can also be useful when it is likely that some students have forgotten them (if there was a long delay between the question and the answer, for example). In general, repetition of answers is often appropriate when teachers are working with young children, when the questions deal with rote memory of factual material, or when the answers are short.

Another exception is the situation in which the teacher repeats the answer but rephrases it somewhat in order to summarize and pull together important material. This should not be done too frequently, though, to avoid indirectly teaching students that "The teacher always says it better than we can." Also, although teacher summaries are important, teachers should encourage students to summarize discussions and describe how classmates' comments fit with one another.

Students should receive information about the correctness or incorrectness of their responses. This is especially important for low achievers, who may have no idea about the correctness of their responses. In general, feedback is important both for motivating interest and for producing learning. Feedback lets the students know how they are doing or how much progress has been made. This probably seems obvious, but teachers sometimes fail to give feedback, especially to certain types of students (Brophy and Good, 1974).

Teachers should give some sort of response every time students answer questions. Feedback need not be long or elaborate, although sometimes it will have to be. Often, short comments like "right" or "okay" are all that is needed to tell students that they are on the right track. Unfortunately, the students who are most likely to receive no feedback after responses are low achievers (Brophy and Good, 1974), despite the fact that these students are least likely to know if the answers they give are correct or not. Without teacher feedback, they may never find out. Teachers do not have to provide feedback personally at all times. They can give students answer sheets so that the students can assess their own work, and they can allow students to help with this function by providing feedback to one another.

Some types of questions suggest to students that the teacher is more interested in quizzing them than in sharing or discussing information. A teacher can present the questions as challenges or as threats. Teachers who question students in harsh terms are likely to threaten them and make it difficult for them to share their thinking. Usually, questions should stress the exchange of information. The teacher is trying to assess knowledge. The student's answer, whether correct or not, conveys information. It allows the teacher to make decisions: Does the student understand? Can he or she go on to the next exercise? Does he or she need review? Questions that are interesting challenges and friendly exchanges of information are likely to generate maximum motivation and produce the most rewarding answers. They should be honest questions, asked because the teacher wants to see if a student understands the material, not aggressive questions asked in the spirit of "Say something and then I will tell you why you are wrong."

That is what Groisser means when he suggests that questions should be asked conversationally. He also suggests that allowing students to respond to one another is helpful for demonstrating teacher interest in obtaining student discussion. Groisser writes:

Many teachers seize upon the first answer given and react to it at once with a comment or with another question. . . . It is more desirable, where possible, to ask a question, accept two or three answers, and then proceed. This pattern tends to produce sustaining responses, variety, and enrichment. It encourages volunteering, contributes to group cooperation, and approaches a more realistic social situation.

Such techniques model teacher interest in the exchange of information about the topic area (as opposed to pushing for the right answer) and indicate that there is not always one right answer. Students are likely to listen more carefully to one another if they are called on occasionally to respond to one another's answers. Wright and Nuthall (1970) found that teachers who redirected questions to other students during science lessons got better achievement than those who did not. Having pupils react to one another's responses apparently is valuable in some situations, especially in the higher elementary grades and secondary grades. With young students (preschool—second grade), this may be too tedious and time-consuming to be worth the trouble.

Most of these aspects of questioning strategy can be observed easily in classrooms, and observers can give teachers useful feedback. A few aspects, such as the degree to which questions are woven into logical sequences designed to lead systematically toward goals, require a running record of the actual questions asked. This aspect of questioning can be determined more directly, of course, by checking to see if teachers have taken the time to plan sequences of questions. If they have, they should be using written guides in asking their questions rather than making them up on the spot. Forms for use in coding many of the other aspects of questioning techniques are presented following the chapter.

### SUGGESTED ACTIVITIES AND QUESTIONS

1. Several different aspects of teaching were discussed in this chapter; however, no summary synthesizing this information was provided. Show your mastery of the important aspects of the chapter by writing *your own* summary in a couple of typewritten pages. Compare your summary with the summaries made by classmates or fellow teachers.

2. What are some of the advantages and disadvantages involved when students are asked to summarize material on their own?

3. Plan a brief (15-minute) discussion. Write out the sequence of questions you will use to advance the discussion fruitfully, applying the criteria suggested in this chapter for asking effective oral questions. Role-play your discussion if you have the opportunity to do so.

4. The criteria for questions presented in this chapter were designed to aid teachers in asking *oral* questions effectively. In general, these criteria apply to written questions as well, but there are some exceptions. For example, why might a *series* of written questions that are all related to the same issues be an effective procedure? For example, "What were the major causes of the war? Were economic factors or diplomatic breakdowns more important?" Try to identify other guidelines or criteria that are applicable only to written questions.

5. As a teacher, how can you adapt lesson content to student interest? Be realistic and specific when you respond.

6. Review and revise (as necessary) the statements that you made after reading Chapter 1, when you attempted to identify teaching behaviors and characteristics that are signs of effective teaching. How much has your view of effective teaching changed?

7. You have now completed reading the substantive chapters of this book that describe effective teaching. What important aspects of teacher and student behavior have been neglected in this book? Why do you feel that these behaviors are important? Compare your list with ones made by others.

8. Role-play the process of introducing and ending lessons enthusiastically. Define the situation (age of students, etc.) so that others may provide you with appropriate feedback.

9. Why do some teachers feel uncomfortable when students perceive learning as fun?

10. Why should students be allowed to talk freely about opinions that differ from the teacher's or the book's?

11. Select some of the forms at the end of the chapter and use them in observing real or simulated teaching.

12. Discuss (with classmates or fellow teachers) specific ways in which you as a teacher can increase opportunities for your students to engage in self-evaluation.

13. Why is it important that students assume responsibility for evaluating their own learning?

14. What does the term "match" refer to?

15. Give concrete instances when lecturing might be desirable.

16. Why is it impossible to give a precise definition of the *effective teacher*?

**FORM 10.1.** Variety of Teaching Methods

*USE: Whenever the class is involved in curriculum-related activities*
*PURPOSE: To see if teacher uses a variety of methods in teaching the cur-*
*riculum*
*Each time the teacher changes activities, code the time and the type of*
*activity.*

| BEHAVIOR CATEGORIES | | START TIME | ·CODES A | B | ELAPSED TIME |
|---|---|---|---|---|---|
| **A. OBJECTIVES** | | | | | |
| What is teacher doing? | | | | | |
| 1. Introduce new material | 1. | 8 :30 | 2 | 5 | 10 |
| 2. Review old material | 2. | 8 :40 | 1 | 1 | 10 |
| 3. Give or review test | 3. | 8 :50 | 4 | 1,3 | 5 |
| 4. Preview or directions for next | 4. | 8 :55 | transition | | 5 |
| assignment | 5. | 9 :00 | 2 | 5 | 8 |
| 5. Checking seatwork in progress | 6. | 9 :08 | 1 | 1 | 11 |
| 6. Other (specify) | 7. | 9 :19 | 4 | 1,3 | 5 |
| | 8. | 9 :24 | transition | | 6 |
| **B. METHODS** | 9. | 9 :30 | 2 | 5 | 10 |
| What methods are used to | 10. | 9 :50 | 1 | 1 | 12 |
| accomplish objectives | 11. | 10:02 | 4 | 1,3 | 8 |
| 1. Demonstration or diagram at | 12. | 10:10 | transition | | 5 |
| blackboard | 13. | 10:15 | Recess | | 15 |
| 2. Lecture | 14. | 10:30 | transition | | 3 |
| 3. Prepared handouts (diagrams or | 15. | 10:33 | 1 | 7 | 27 |
| teaching aids) | 16. | 11:00 | 2 | 10,14 | 25 |
| 4. Media (filmstrip, slides, tape, | 17. | 11:25 | transition | | 5 |
| record, etc.) | 18. | 11:30 | Lunch | | |
| 5. Questioning students to check | 19. | : | | | |
| understanding | 20. | : | | | |
| 6. Inviting and responding to | 21. | : | | | |
| student questions | 22. | : | | | |
| 7. Focused discussion (prepared, | 23. | : | | | |
| sequenced questions) | 24. | : | | | |
| 8. Unfocused discussion (rambling, | 25. | : | | | |
| no specific objective) | 26. | : | | | |
| 9. Students take turns reading or | 27. | : | | | |
| reciting | 28. | : | | | |
| 10. Drill (flashcards, math tables, | 29. | : | | | |
| chorus questions) | 30. | : | | | |
| 11. Practical exercise or experiment | 31. | : | | | |
| 12. Seatwork or homework assign- | 32. | : | | | |
| ment | 33. | : | | | |
| 13. Field trip, visit | 34. | : | | | |
| 14. Game, contest | 35. | : | | | |
| 15. Other (specify) | 36. | : | | | |
| | 37. | : | | | |
| NOTES: | 38. | : | | | |
| | 39. | : | | | |
| | 40. | : | | | |

*1–11: Reading groups*
*15: Social studies*
*16: Spelling (Went around*
*room twice, then had*
*spelling bee)*

**FORM 10.2.** Seatwork

*USE: Whenever part or all of the class is doing assigned seatwork*
*PURPOSE: To see if seatwork appears appropriate to students' needs and interests*

WORK INVOLVEMENT
At fixed intervals (every 3 minutes, for example), scan the group and note the number of students working productively, in neutral, or misbehaving.

| | WORKING | NEUTRAL | DISRUPTIVE | | | | |
|---|---|---|---|---|---|---|---|
| 1. | 13 | 2 | 1 | 21. | | | |
| 2. | 14 | 2 | 0 | 22. | | | |
| 3. | 13 | 1 | 2 | 23. | | | |
| 4. | 9 | 7 | 0 | 24. | | | |
| 5. | 7 | 9 | 0 | 25. | | | |
| 6. | 6 | 10 | 0 | 26. | | | |
| 7. | 7 | 9 | 0 | 27. | | | |
| 8. | 8 | 4 | 4 | 28. | | | |
| 9. | 8 | 0 | 8 | 29. | | | |
| 10. | 7 | 1 | 8 | 30. | | | |
| 11. | | | | 31. | | | |
| 12. | | | | 32. | | | |
| 13. | | | | 33. | | | |
| 14. | | | | 34. | | | |
| 15. | | | | 35. | | | |
| 16. | | | | 36. | | | |
| 17. | | | | 37. | | | |
| 18. | | | | 38. | | | |
| 19. | | | | 39. | | | |
| 20. | | | | 40. | | | |

*During this 30-minute period the teacher was working with one reading group. The work-involvement coding refers to the other 16 students who were working independently.*

APPROPRIATENESS OF ASSIGNMENTS
What seems to be the problem with students who are not productively involved? (Check statements that apply.)
_____ 1. Assignment is too short or too easy—students finish quickly and do not have other work to do.
_____ 2. Assignment is boring, repetitive, monotonous.
__✓__ 3. Assignment is too hard—students can't get started or continually need help.
_____ 4. All of the above—assignments are not differentiated to match student needs.
*The Stars seemed too confused to get started.*

DISTRACTIONS
What distracts students from seatwork? What do they attend to or do when not working?
*Disruptions, especially by #12*

STUDENT ATTITUDES
What clues to student attitudes are observable during seatwork periods? When students can't get an answer do they concentrate or seek help, or do they merely copy from a neighbor? How do they act when the teacher's back is turned? Do they notice? Do they make noises and gestures? Do they seem to be amused by the teacher? Fear him? Respect him?

*#12 "passes licks" when he thinks he can get away with it. Problems occur when others strike back and disruption spreads. Other kids mostly concentrate on work.*

373

**FORM 10.3.** Feedback to Correct Answers

*USE: In discussion and recitation situations when students are answering
questions*
*PURPOSE: To see if teacher is giving appropriate feedback to students
about the adequacy of their responses*
*When a student answers correctly, code as many categories as apply to
the teacher's feedback response.*

BEHAVIOR CATEGORIES

1. Praises
2. Nods, repeats answer, says "Yes," "That's right,"
   "Okay," etc.
3. No feedback—goes on to something else
4. Ambiguous—doesn't indicate whether or not answer is
   acceptable
5. Asks a student or the class whether answer is correct
6. Asks someone else to answer the same question
7. New question—asks same student another question
8. Other (specify)

NOTES:

*Both praised answers were called out
by # 19, a high-achieving student.*

CODES

| | | | |
|---|---|---|---|
| 1. | 2 | 26. | ___ |
| 2. | 2 | 27. | ___ |
| 3. | 2 | 28. | ___ |
| 4. | 2 | 29. | ___ |
| 5. | 3 | 30. | ___ |
| 6. | 2 | 31. | ___ |
| 7. | 7 | 32. | ___ |
| 8. | 2 | 33. | ___ |
| 9. | 2 | 34. | ___ |
| 10. | 3 | 35. | ___ |
| 11. | 2 | 36. | ___ |
| 12. | 2 | 37. | ___ |
| 13. | 1 | 38. | ___ |
| 14. | 2 | 39. | ___ |
| 15. | 2 | 40. | ___ |
| 16. | 1 | 41. | ___ |
| 17. | 2 | 42. | ___ |
| 18. | 2 | 43. | ___ |
| 19. | 2 | 44. | ___ |
| 20. | ___ | 45. | ___ |
| 21. | ___ | 46. | ___ |
| 22. | ___ | 47. | ___ |
| 23. | ___ | 48. | ___ |
| 24. | ___ | 49. | ___ |
| 25. | ___ | 50. | ___ |

**FORM 10.4.** Feedback When Student Fails to Answer Correctly

*USE: In discussion and recitation situations when students are answering questions*
*PURPOSE: To see if teacher is giving appropriate feedback to students about the adequacy of their responses*
*When a student is unable to answer a question, or answers it incorrectly, code as many categories as apply to the teacher's feedback response.*

BEHAVIOR CATEGORIES
1. Criticizes
2. Says "No," "That's not right," etc.
3. No feedback—goes on to something else
4. Ambiguous—doesn't indicate whether or not answer is acceptable
5. Asks a student or the class whether answer is correct
6. Asks someone else to answer the question
7. Repeats question to same student, prompts (Well?" "Do you know?" etc.)
8. Gives a clue or rephrases question to make it easier
9. Asks same student an entirely new question
10. Answers question for the student
11. Answers question and also gives explanation or rationale for answer
12. Gives explanation or rationale for why student's answer was not correct
13. Praises student for good attempt or guess
14. Other (specify)

CODES

| | | | |
|---|---|---|---|
| 1. | 2 | 26. | |
| 2. | 2,6 | 27. | |
| 3. | 2,8 | 28. | |
| 4. | 2,10 | 29. | |
| 5. | 2,10 | 30. | |
| 6. | 2,12 | 31. | |
| 7. | | 32. | |
| 8. | | 33. | |
| 9. | | 34. | |
| 10. | | 35. | |
| 11. | | 36. | |
| 12. | | 37. | |
| 13. | | 38. | |
| 14. | | 39. | |
| 15. | | 40. | |
| 16. | | 41. | |
| 17. | | 42. | |
| 18. | | 43. | |
| 19. | | 44. | |
| 20. | | 45. | |
| 21. | | 46. | |
| 22. | | 47. | |
| 23. | | 48. | |
| 24. | | 49. | |
| 25. | | 50. | |

**FORM 10.5.** Assigning Seatwork and Homework

*USE:  When teacher presents a seatwork or homework assignment*
*PURPOSE:  To see if teacher's instructions are clear and complete*
*Each time teacher presents seatwork or homework, code as many behavior categories as apply.*

BEHAVIOR CATEGORIES

A. *DEMONSTRATIONS AND EXAMPLE PROBLEMS*
1. No demonstration was needed or given
2. No demonstration was given, although one was needed
3. Teacher demonstrated or called on students to do so. Activity was demonstrated in proper sequence, with no steps left out
4. Demonstration was poorly sequenced, or steps were left out
5. Each step was verbally described while being demonstrated
6. More verbal description should have accompanied the demonstration
7. Demonstration too long or complex; should have been broken into parts

B. *CHECKING FOR UNDERSTANDING*
1. The teacher never asked whether directions were understood
2. The teacher asked if the students understood, and no one said he or she didn't
3. The teacher called on one or more volunteers to demonstrate understanding
4. The teacher called on one or more non-volunteers to demonstrate understanding
5. The teacher failed to call on any low achievers (bottom 1/3 of group) to see if they understood

C. *DEALING WITH CONFUSION*
How did the teacher respond if one or more students was confused?
1. No one was confused
2. The teacher repeated directions and demonstrations, made sure everyone understood
3. The teacher repeated directions and demonstrations, but didn't make sure everyone understood
4. The teacher promised individual help to those who needed it before starting work
5. The teacher delayed giving help ("Try to do it yourself first")
6. The teacher told students to get help from other students
7. The teacher failed to deal with the problem directly, student remained confused, teacher never specifically told him what to do about it

D. *CLARITY ABOUT SPECIFICS OF ASSIGNMENT*
1. Students were not clear about which problem or pages were assigned
2. Students were not clear about what was required or optional
3. Students were not clear about what to do if they needed help
4. Students were not clear about what was allowed if they finished

CODES

| | A | B | C | D |
|---|---|---|---|---|
| 1. | 3,5 | 2 | 1 | |
| 2. | 3,5 | 2 | 1 | |
| 3. | 3,5 | 2 | 1 | |
| 4. | | | | |
| 5. | | | | |
| 6. | | | | |
| 7. | | | | |
| 8. | | | | |
| 9. | | | | |
| 10. | | | | |
| 11. | | | | |
| 12. | | | | |
| 13. | | | | |
| 14. | | | | |
| 15. | | | | |
| 16. | | | | |
| 17. | | | | |
| 18. | | | | |
| 19. | | | | |
| 20. | | | | |
| 21. | | | | |
| 22. | | | | |
| 23. | | | | |
| 24. | | | | |
| 25. | | | | |
| 26. | | | | |
| 27. | | | | |
| 28. | | | | |
| 29. | | | | |
| 30. | | | | |
| 31. | | | | |
| 32. | | | | |
| 33. | | | | |
| 34. | | | | |
| 35. | | | | |
| 36. | | | | |
| 37. | | | | |
| 38. | | | | |
| 39. | | | | |
| 40. | | | | |

**FORM 10.6.** Questioning Techniques

USE: *When teacher is asking class or group questions*
PURPOSE: *To see if teacher is following principles for good questioning practices*
*For each question, code the following categories:*

BEHAVIOR CATEGORIES

*A. TYPE OF QUESTION ASKED*
1. Academic: Factual. Seeks specific correct response
2. Academic: Opinion. Seeks opinion on a complex issue where there is no clear-cut response
3. Nonacademic: Question deals with personal, procedural, or disciplinary matters rather than curriculum

*B. TYPE OF RESPONSE REQUIRED*
1. Thought question. Student must reason through to a conclusion or explain something at length
2. Fact question. Student must provide fact(s) from memory
3. Choice question. Requires only a yes-no or either-or response

*C. SELECTION OF RESPONDENT*
1. Names child before asking question
2. Calls on volunteer (after asking question)
3. Calls on nonvolunteer (after asking question)

*D. PAUSE (AFTER ASKING QUESTION)*
1. Paused a few seconds before calling on student
2. Failed to pause before calling on student
3. Not applicable; teacher named student before asking question

*E. TONE AND MANNER IN PRESENTING QUESTION*
1. Question presented as challenge or stimulation
2. Question presented matter-of-factly
3. Question presented as threat or test

*Record any information relevant to the following:*
Multiple Questions. Tally the number of times the teacher:
1. Repeats or rephrases question before calling on anyone __II__
2. Asks two or more questions at the same time __0__

Sequence. Were questions integrated into an orderly sequence, or did they seem to be random or unrelated?
*Teacher seemed to be following sequence given in manual (led up to next history unit).*
Did students themselves pose questions? *No*

Was there student-student interaction? How much? *None*

When appropriate, did the teacher redirect questions to several students, or ask students to evaluate their own or others' responses? *No*

CODES

| | A | B | C | D | E |
|---|---|---|---|---|---|
| 1. | 1 | 2 | 2 | 1 | 2 |
| 2. | 1 | 2 | 2 | 1 | 2 |
| 3. | 1 | 3 | 2 | 1 | 2 |
| 4. | 1 | 2 | 2 | 1 | 2 |
| 5. | 1 | 2 | 2 | 1 | 2 |
| 6. | 1 | 3 | 2 | 1 | 2 |
| 7. | 1 | 2 | 2 | 1 | 2 |
| 8. | 2 | 1 | 2 | 1 | 1 |
| 9. | 1 | 2 | 2 | 1 | 2 |
| 10. | 1 | 2 | 2 | 1 | 2 |
| 11. | 1 | 2 | 2 | 1 | 2 |
| 12. | 1 | 2 | 2 | 1 | 2 |
| 13. | — | — | — | — | — |
| 14. | — | — | — | — | — |
| 15. | — | — | — | — | — |
| 16. | — | — | — | — | — |
| 17. | — | — | — | — | — |
| 18. | — | — | — | — | — |
| 19. | — | — | — | — | — |
| 20. | — | — | — | — | — |
| 21. | — | — | — | — | — |
| 22. | — | — | — | — | — |
| 23. | — | — | — | — | — |
| 24. | — | — | — | — | — |
| 25. | — | — | — | — | — |
| 26. | — | — | — | — | — |
| 27. | — | — | — | — | — |
| 28. | — | — | — | — | — |
| 29. | — | — | — | — | — |
| 30. | — | — | — | — | — |
| 31. | — | — | — | — | — |
| 32. | — | — | — | — | — |
| 33. | — | — | — | — | — |
| 34. | — | — | — | — | — |
| 35. | — | — | — | — | — |
| 36. | — | — | — | — | — |
| 37. | — | — | — | — | — |
| 38. | — | — | — | — | — |
| 39. | — | — | — | — | — |
| 40. | — | — | — | — | — |

# 11 / IMPROVING CLASSROOM TEACHING

We have described a variety of behaviors that should appear in the classroom and provided ways of measuring their presence or absence. We hope that teachers have been stimulated to look at their behavior and make plans for improving. In this chapter, we will present some guidelines for in-service training and self-improvement.

Remember, the perfect teacher does not exist. All of us can refine existing skills, discard ineffective ones, and develop new tactics. Some teachers are excellent lecturers and classroom managers but only average in stimulating independent student work and leading class discussion. None of us will ever be perfect teachers, few will even be excellent in all aspects of teaching, but all of us can become better teachers than we presently are. This, the continual process of improving our teaching skills, is the essence of professional teaching.

Teachers, like everyone else, are sometimes unwilling to engage in self-evaluation. Is this because they are not committed to their profession or are unwilling to do the extra work necessary to improve their existing skills? Is it because they feel they already function at optimal effectiveness? We doubt it. We think teachers will seek opportunities to evaluate and improve their teaching, if acceptable and useful methods are available. The fact that we have written this book attests to our belief in teachers' willingness to participate in self-evaluation and benefit from it. However, certain obstacles minimize self-improvement in some teachers. These must be removed if continuous development is to take place.

## THE SOCIALIZATION PROCESS

Teachers are hindered in their efforts to improve their teaching skills for several basic reasons. Perhaps the most fundamental problem is the socialization process we have gone through. Most of us have seldom engaged in self-criticism or self-evaluation designed not only to uncover weaknesses but also to eliminate such weaknesses. Most of us have occasionally engaged in destructive self-criticism; however, we seldom link criticism with constructive plans designed to improve our skills.

In part, we act this way because our past socialization (especially our experiences in schools) has not helped us to develop the needed skills. For example, has a teacher ever returned an "A" paper to you with these instructions: "Basically, your paper is very sound; however, I have identified a few flaws, and I am sure you will find additional ways to improve the paper when you reread it. Eliminate the weaknesses that I have indicated and build upon the paper in new ways that you discover by *thinking* about it again." Certainly, most of us have had to rewrite papers, but seldom "A" papers, and seldom have we been asked to rethink a paper and incorporate new ideas of our own into it.

Typically, we redo assignments because they are "inferior," and we repeat them only to incorporate someone else's criticism. Indeed, for most of us, school seldom allowed us time to *think* about what we were doing. We were too busy finishing assignments to think about them. John Holt's (1964) observation that students hurry to finish assignments so that they do not have to think, to worry, was true at certain times in most of our lives. Remember the feeling of relief when major tasks or final exams were completed? No matter how well or poorly we think we have performed, we feel relieved when we hand in the paper because we are finished. We no longer have control over the paper, and we do not have to think about it anymore.

Socialization in schools tends to emphasize: do not look back, keep moving forward. Although the advice to move forward is sound, only by examining our past and present performance can we monitor progress and determine if we are moving forward or merely traveling in circles. Relatively little of this is done in most schools.

A second difficulty is that school experience has often emphasized analytical thinking, not synthesis. The following behavior in a tenth-grade social studies classroom represents analytical thinking:

TEACHER: John, what's wrong with electing members of Congress every two years?

JOHN: *(hesitatingly and in a soft tone)* Well, ah, I think that they spend too much time trying to be reelected. *(John notices the teacher beaming and nodding, so he begins to speak more confidently and loudly.)* Since they face reelection every two years, they always have to seek money for reelection. Since they build their campaign chest primarily with funds from the people who financed their original candidacy, they owe these people a double debt. It is hard for them to be their own person.

TEACHER: Good answer, John. Carol, what does John imply when he says, "be their own person"?

CAROL: Well, that the candidates' debts to the people who have given money and their continual dependency upon them, ah, since they have to be elected every two years, puts them in such a position that they may cater to these people's needs. But even if members of Congress are strong, the two-year election procedure is bad because they continue to run, make speeches, raise money, and have little time to do their real jobs.

Although such discussions are important, they seldom go beyond an analysis stage that criticizes or defines the problem. For example, the teacher might continue this discussion by pointing out the desirability of controlling campaign spending and making the source of contributions public knowledge and then challenging students to go beyond common solutions that *others* have suggested. Seldom do classes attempt to develop their own unique solutions to problems. Yet this is the meaning of synthesis: taking the facts and readdressing the problem in a different fashion.

For example, the teacher might "playfully" suggest that senators, even though they are elected for six-year terms, spend much time running for reelection and that most of their decisions are made on the basis of "how does it affect my reelection chances?" He or she might suggest that politicians might still spend more time running for office than running the office even if their term was for ten years. The teacher could also call for students to suggest ways in which elected federal representatives could be held accountable to their local and national constituencies: "Should daily logs of their time expenditures be kept? What are the pros and cons? Should they hold regular office hours for the public? Should they spend a designated number of days in the district or state they represent? How can a broader set of candidates (non-lawyers) be encouraged?"

Demands are seldom made on students for original, practical suggestions. There are some teachers who stimulate this type of thinking from their students, but most teaching emphasizes analyses per se. Fortunately, in recent years, there has been increased emphasis upon process approaches and problem-solving activity, but most teachers were socialized in schools that demanded and rewarded analytical thinking. This heavy emphasis on criticizing gave most of us plenty of practice in pinpointing weaknesses but comparatively little practice in developing constructive alternatives.

Evaluation that we experienced in schools was external and non-constructive.. The way it was handled told us "where we stood," not "how we could improve." Thus, we tended to avoid evaluation. (For example, in Spanish class, if we had time to thoroughly translate the first two pages, we waved our hands vigorously to volunteer at the beginning of a lesson. However, we slumped in our chairs and hid behind our neighbor's head late in the period unless we knew the material thoroughly.) Since evaluation was so strongly associated with negative consequences, it often evoked the attitude of "I'm going to be exposed," not "I'm going to receive new information." Evaluation made us anxious. Our past socialization provided little training or inclination for self-evaluation.

### EXPERIMENTING AND GROWING
Teachers are unique individuals with different strengths and weaknesses. You have to develop a style that allows you to express yourself and stimulate students in your own way.

To achieve your own style, you may have to search and experiment with different teaching methods before you reach a style that is comfortable and right for you. We have stressed the desirability of using a variety of teaching methods because students have different learning needs and are often stimulated by different learning techniques. However, teaching techniques are justified if, and only if, they work in the classroom. They work when you feel comfortable using them and when students respond by learning and enjoying classroom assignments. If you systematically try an approach for a reasonable amount of time and it does not work for you in your classroom, *then discard the approach and develop techniques that work for you.* There is no need to teach the way your cooperating teacher did (he or she may have been a poor model) or the way you think you "should" teach, without regard to your own feelings or to the responses of your students.

If you are to improve your teaching, you must be willing to critically examine your classroom behavior and that of your students and be willing to try new ways of teaching when the present ones are not working. After identifying a basically satisfying style, successful teachers continue to experiment with new behaviors. Good teachers continually try to find new ways to relate to students.

### Teaching Is Difficult

Few teachers will be excellent in all aspects of teaching. Too often, teachers enter the classroom with unrealistically high expectations (I will capture the interest of every student at every moment, and every lesson I teach will be completely successful), so that when success does not match expectations, they become depressed and disappointed. When this occurs, there is a tendency to blame students for one's own inability to spark a response. If difficulty continues, teachers may withdraw and begin to justify and rationalize present behavior rather than to search for new styles of teaching. This occurs in part because teachers do not realize that other teachers also have difficulties. Every teacher will teach lessons that go sour, will say the wrong thing to students, and so forth. Teaching is difficult! We must not become complacent about mistakes but we must accept them and try to eliminate them.

Like everyone else, teachers tend to talk about successes, not failures. Thus, some teachers, especially young teachers, may become anxious and discouraged when they have trouble because they hear nothing but the good or interesting things that other teachers are doing. Some beginners fully expect to be accomplished teachers by October of their first year! These teachers experience feelings of disappointment and ineptness when they do not achieve easy success. They are reluctant to approach veteran teachers because they feel it would be an admission of failure.

If you have thoughts like this, dismiss them because they are nonsense. Teaching is difficult, challenging, and exciting work, but it takes time to develop and refine teaching skills. Most experienced teachers are sympathetic to the problems of beginning teachers and will be glad to try to help. However, few of us like to be approached by someone who says, "Tell me what to do." It is much better to approach other teachers by telling them that you have a teaching problem and would like to exchange ideas with them and benefit from their experience. Remember that all teachers, even veteran teachers, have classroom problems from time to time, and that the appropriate strategy is not to hide mistakes (as we learned to do as students), but to seek help and to solve the problems.

### How Do I Identify Good Behaviors?

Teachers must decide what is "good" practice by observing the effects of their behavior on students. (Do tests reveal appropriate learning? Do lectures lead students to raise their own questions? Do students appear to enjoy activities? Do anonymously administered questionnaires show student satisfaction?) There is no concrete formula for specifying good teaching because research examining teacher behavior has not yielded a definite set of teaching behaviors that are always clearly related to student growth (Dunkin and Biddle, 1974; Rosenshine and Furst, 1971; Rosenshine, 1976). The advice given in this book has been suggested by available research, but we have often gone beyond these data in order to supply prescriptive suggestions. These statements (about what should be occurring) will help to provide you with a map, a way of looking at classroom life.

There are many materials that teachers can use effectively for in-service programs that attempt to improve instruction. It is impossible to list all books that discuss the concerns of teachers, but we can mention a few. We have presented advice suggested by research and by the practice of good teachers. Other authors have also prepared books that suggest specific behaviors or skills that teachers might practice in their efforts to become better teachers: Borg et al., 1970; Dollar, 1972; Emmer and Millett, 1970; Mager, 1962; McNeil, 1971; Popham and Baker, 1970a, 1970b, 1970c; Johnson and Johnson, 1975; Coop and White, 1974; and Vargas, 1972.

Others have also provided realistic descriptions of classroom problems and teacher-student dialogue (Greenwood, Good, and Siegel, 1971; Amidon and Hunter, 1966). These materials may be useful in obtaining teacher participation in the early stages of in-service training programs. Teachers may initially be more comfortable talking about classroom problems per se than about personal problems. However, such materials should be used as a bridge to subsequent discussions about personal teaching problems and not used to *avoid* such discussion. Eventually, discussions should move from "How can that teacher deal with that problem?" to "How can we deal with our problems?"

In addition to reading about teaching behavior, teachers may also benefit from reading about other teachers' feelings about students and about being evaluated. Books by Greenberg (1969) and by Jersild (1955) are especially useful in dispelling such myths as "I will love all students at all times." In this same vein, teachers may benefit from knowledge about how other teachers react to the teaching task. For example, how do teachers know when they are doing a good job? Revealing interviews with experienced teachers are found in Jackson (1968). Also, there are books that provide useful information about how teachers and students perceive their classroom roles (see, for example, Nash, 1973; Lortie, 1975; and Rist, 1975).

There are a number of critical books that attack the present educational system and/or teacher training institutions as ineffective or self-defeating. In stimulating thinking, especially the search for alternative modes of instruction, these books are quite effective (Holt, 1964; Kohl, 1967; Smith, 1969; Silberman, 1970).

Reviews of research on teaching are extremely valuable because they critically question what is known about teaching and call for more research on explicit questions. These reviews show that very few teaching behaviors are invariably related to student achievement (Dunkin and Biddle, 1974; Rosenshine and Furst, 1971; Rosenshine, 1976; McDonald, 1976; Brophy, 1976; Berliner and Tikunoff, 1976; Good and Grouws, 1975). These materials are especially useful to teachers who want to engage in self-study programs, because they underline the fact that while empirical data provide some direction, teachers have to assume the responsibility for evaluating the effectiveness of their own classroom behavior.

Teachers can use these sources to stimulate thinking about classroom behavior and to develop plans for experimenting. However, we are perhaps putting the cart before the horse. Before changing, the teacher needs to assess present behavior.

### How to Start Self-Evaluation

The starting point is to find out where you are now and to make definite plans (changing certain behaviors, trying new instructional styles) for the future. Go back through the text of this book and list, on three separate pages: (1) behaviors that you think you perform capably at present, (2) those that you need to work on or that you have not tried, and (3) those which you are not sure how capably you perform. Take the first list and store it in your desk. This list represents progress that you have made as a teacher.

For example, you may note on this list that you already ask a variety of factual and higher order questions and that you ask questions before calling on students. On your list for Needs Work, you may note a tendency not to follow through on warnings and inconsistency as a classroom manager. After a few hours of thinking about strengths and weaknesses, you will have a rough map of your ability as a teacher. Now you are ready to begin work on the list of needed improvements and plan remediation so that you can move one or more items from the Needs Work list to the Okay list in the near future.

Some of the areas mentioned in this book may be blurred to you, in the sense that you do not know how well you behave in these categories. Perhaps you are not sure if you emphasize the intrinsic interest that lessons hold for the student rather than threatening "Pay attention or you'll fail the exam." Monitor your behavior as best you can, and begin to assign these areas to the Okay or Needs Work sheets as soon as you can.

Take time to assess yourself carefully, then, and draw a map of your strengths and weaknesses. Naturally, your map will differ somewhat from the map that your students would draw of you or one that an observer would draw after spending two weeks in your class. Which one of these maps is the most objective is a question that has no simple answer. In some situations, the students' map might be a truer picture. However, even where you can use only your own map, it can be a useful guide for making decisions if you can look at yourself openly.

### Make Explicit Plans

Teachers who attempt to improve their classroom teaching must be able to decide what they want to do and how and to determine if their plans are working. Too often, our half-hearted New Year's resolutions are never acted upon because they are vague. Resolutions such as "I want to be a better driver," "I want to help the community more," or "I want to be a more enthusiastic teacher," are seldom accomplished simply because they are not concrete suggestions that guide behavior.

The following resolutions are much more likely to result in behavioral change because they specify the desired change: "On long trips, I plan to stop and relax for ten minutes every two hours," "I want to keep my speed under 55 at all times," "I plan to devote ten hours a week from September through November to working on the community chest drive," "I want to tell students why a lesson is important before it begins," and "I want to model my sincere interest in the lesson."

These statements indicate how the individual is to behave in order to reach his or her goal. If the person stops for ten minutes after driving for two hours, the goal has been met; thus, self-evaluation is easy. Self-evaluation is relatively simple in many teaching situations. However, certain aspects of teacher behavior are more difficult to evaluate. For instance, teachers frequently set goals for students as well as for themselves. The teacher may say, "I want to tell students why a lesson is important before the lesson begins, and I want to model my sincere interest in the lesson so more students will pay attention and not engage in long private conversations with their neighbors." In this case, teachers need to evaluate both their own behavior and the behavior of their students.

In judging the behavior of students, teachers can see if students appear to pay attention and if they refrain from extended private conversations during the lesson. However, if teachers' goals become more complex and the evaluation more demanding, they will need to watch videotapes or seek the assistance of observers to help them assess their progress. These topics will be discussed later in the chapter.

The message here is simple. If you do not know where you are going, you are unlikely to get there. Teachers need to state goals in explicit language. Careful statement of the goal accomplishes two objectives: (1) the teacher knows exactly what behavior he or she is trying to effect and (2) the teacher can easily assess progress by examining his or her actual behavior in comparison with the behavioral goal. The key is to state goals in terms of explicit, observable behaviors.

### Action

After taking a look at yourself and stating explicit behavioral goals, the next step is to choose two or three behaviors that you want to change or new ones you want to try. Be careful in your zeal not to attempt to change too many things at once. Changing behavior, even our own, takes careful work, and it is easy to become overwhelmed and discouraged when we attempt to change too much too rapidly. Therefore, take a few things at a time and carefully monitor your progress.

For example, if you attempt to call on students randomly, you may have to write out the names of students in advance on flash cards so you can shuffle through the stack. Always calling on students who have their hands up is a difficult habit to break. Again, most people make more progress in the long run by changing only one or a few behaviors at a time, moving to new ones only when the newly acquired behaviors become firmly established habits.

After you decide upon concrete goals and after implementing the change for a couple of days, start to monitor the class for feedback about its effectiveness. For example, after you introduce lessons in ways that make it explicitly clear to the students why the lesson is important to them, try to assess whether more students follow the directions or seem interested. Similarly, if you start to call on students to react to fellow students' responses, note whether students seem to pay greater attention to the discussion topic.

Remember, the strategies listed in this book are not always appropriate; their effectiveness depends upon stimulating desirable student responses. Strategies that you invent yourself should be evaluated in the same way: what effect do they have on student behavior and attitudes?

### You Are Not Alone

Teachers may wish to begin their evaluation and, for a while, operate independently of feedback from others. However, all teachers will benefit from interacting with others and sharing ideas about classroom teaching and should begin to do this when they are ready to receive feedback.

Many school districts now have videotape equipment. If you are fortunate enough to have access to such equipment, arrange to have one or two of your typical lessons videotaped. Do not attempt to construct special units or to review old material. Teach your regularly scheduled lessons in your normal fashion. Then, when you start your assessment program, you do not have to depend on memory but can view yourself on tape and assess your weak and strong points. After a couple of weeks, make arrangements to retape your behavior in similar lessons so you can watch for signs of progress in your behavior and in the responses of students.

If your school does not have video equipment, check with your principal and see if the central office has the equipment. In many school districts, equipment is available for loan but often goes unused. Central school officials are usually delighted to loan video equipment. (If a school makes repeated requests, it is sometimes possible for equipment to be assigned to it permanently.) If it is impossible to secure video equipment, cassette audio recorders are readily available and can be used to collect useful information about the verbal behavior of teachers and students.

Teachers can use other sources to get relevant feedback. For example, many elementary school teachers work in team teaching or nongraded situations where it is easy to arrange for another teacher to watch them for a half hour or so. Similarly, teachers can use student teachers, student observers, and parents, on occasion. Secondary teachers can make arrangements to trade weekly visits during free periods with other teachers.

In arrangements that are not a part of a regular in-service training program, it is usually best to tell the observer what to look for specifically. Prepare an observation form for him or her to use (or use some of those included in this book). There is so much to see in the classroom that an observer may not notice the things that the teacher would like to receive feedback about. The teacher is a decision maker and, in planning his or her professional development, should be deciding upon which weaknesses to work on first; therefore, teachers should request rather specific feedback when they invite an observer into their rooms. The observer, of course, can always volunteer additional information to that requested.

Curriculum supervisors can also provide teachers with relevant feedback. Most supervisors are delighted when teachers make explicit observation requests. Often, supervisory visits are as frustrating for the supervisor as for the teacher. Since the supervisor may not know the goals of a particular lesson or how it fits into a unit, it is difficult for him or her to provide helpful feedback. However, armed with a specific request, supervisors can provide relevant feedback about areas of interest to the teacher.

Students are another source that teachers can tap for relevant information. Informal conversations and anonymously administered questionnaires will provide teachers with useful feedback. Teachers who have never solicited student comment may be dismayed at first when they see the variety of comment. Students have unique perspectives, and different students may label the same behavior as a weakness or a strength. However, if you look over their responses carefully, you can usually identify some items that most students label as good or bad. Then you can take action on these points of agreement.

We have found that student feedback is most useful if it is given anonymously. Also, rather than ask for global comments or ratings, it is usually better to ask for specific reactions. One method is to request three or more positive statements about strengths and three or more criticisms of weaknesses from each student. This forces students to be specific and to provide a more balanced critique than do global, free-response methods.

### In-service Education
Teachers can often use regularly scheduled in-service time for work in self-improvement groups. This is especially useful when in-service meeting time is devoted to small-group work with teachers who share common problems. In elementary schools, for instance, teachers at each grade level can meet in separate small groups. In secondary schools, teachers can be subdivided into smaller groups according to the subject taught (social studies, mathematics, English, etc.) so

that they may discuss common problems. Small groups provide an excellent place for teachers to receive feedback and suggestions from peers.

Self-improvement teams may wish to regularly view and provide feedback about one another's tapes. In particular, teachers can get peers to provide information about those aspects of teaching behavior of special interest to the teachers. This procedure is in marked contrast to the typical in-service program or consultation activity that provides teachers with training, information, or evaluative feedback that the consultant wishes to talk about. Teachers are not always interested in these topics. Teachers meeting in small study groups can structure in-service programs to have personal meaning and value.

Most principals will be delighted to allow teachers to spend in-service time functioning as self-study teams. Usually, teachers who want such a program need only to contact the principal and communicate the seriousness of their intent and their willingness to work out a strong in-service training experience.

In general, participation in self-study groups should be voluntary. The desirability of a voluntary program is probably self-evident. Nothing hurts a program (that involves the sharing of information) more than someone who participates solely because he or she has to do so. Consideration should be given, however, to those teachers who want to join a study group at some point but who are not ready to do so at the beginning of the year. It is perfectly reasonable and understandable for teachers to want to assess their own behavior and develop their own goals before joining a self-improvement group. Teachers should have a chance to join self-study groups when they are ready to do so.

Three rules should be kept in mind when in-service groups begin to function. The first one we have mentioned previously—group structure and feedback exist to provide teachers with information that augments their personal self-development. The group provides a unique set of eyes and resources to give a teacher information regarding behaviors about which he or she wants to receive feedback. Thus, *the teacher functions as a decision maker, planning his or her own developmental goals.* The group functions as a barometer, telling the teacher how he or she looks to them and suggesting alternative ways to reach the goals that the teacher has set. Teachers in the group will, of course, have their own viewpoints and each will react in terms of his or her own strengths, weaknesses, and preferences.

The teacher tells the group what his or her current goals are and outlines what behaviors and techniques they should examine when they view the teacher's videotape or come into the classroom to observe. Also, as previously mentioned, when a teacher or a group of teachers begins to engage in self-development activities, there is a tendency to do too much at once. Initially, the individual teacher should limit improvement areas to a few, so that full attention can be directed toward work on these new skills. Correspondingly, the group should help the teacher by restricting their comments to these designated behaviors. After the group has functioned as a group for a few weeks, then the teacher being viewed that week may begin to ask the group to focus on all dimensions of teaching that were exhibited in the film. When the teacher is ready for such feedback, the group can help the teacher to learn more about how others react to his or her teaching.

The second rule to follow, then, especially in the group's formative weeks, is not to overwhelm the teacher with information. Restricting discussion to a few areas will help, and it may be useful to limit the number of comments that each group member makes. We can profit from only so much information at a given time, particularly negative feedback. No matter how competent and resilient a teacher may be, receiving notice of fifty mistakes will tend to make the teacher give up (at least psychologically). Negative comments do not tell the individual how to improve and tend to immobilize behavior.

In-service groups may benefit from such an artificial rule as: each participant writes out a reaction to the two or three major strengths and the two or three major weaknesses of the presentation. This guideline limits the amount of information that a teacher receives initially, but it does focus the teacher's attention on a small, manageable list of "points to consider." The guideline also allows the teacher to have in writing (for future review) the basic reactions of each participant to the lesson.

Useful feedback should not only provide the teacher with a rough assessment of his or her strengths and weaknesses, but also should focus on specific ways to improve teaching. Ensuing discussions should focus on alternative procedures that the teacher might use to produce more desirable student responses. Effective in-service sessions allow the teacher to receive both a realistic reaction (positive and negative) to his or her performance on the behaviors in question and direct assistance in the form of information about alternative behaviors to use in the future. In-service self-study groups should not only evaluate present teaching, but also provide direction for subsequent teaching.

A third rule to bear in mind is to be honest. Self-study groups lose their effectiveness when individuals engage in either of two participatory styles: Pollyanna and Get-the-Guest. Too many teachers are unwilling to say what they feel about another teacher's behavior, perhaps because they are afraid that openness and frankness will lead other teachers to respond in kind when they are being evaluated, or because they feel that the teacher will be hurt by an honest reaction. Such masking of reactions is self-defeating. Teachers can grow only if they get honest, objective feedback about their behavior. Criticism followed by new ideas or approaches that may improve upon present practice is the best way the group can assist a teacher in self-development efforts. To be sure, we should reinforce the good things that a teacher does. We all like to know when we have done well, and it is especially important that we receive praise and encouragement when we improve. If a teacher has been working on a technique for a few weeks and shows improvement, let the teacher know about the improvement he or she has made as well as ways to continue improvement. But it is still important to note major weaknesses. If there is no critical comment, there is no impetus or direction for growth.

The other undesirable participant role is that of the carping critic, who criticizes excessively and thoughtlessly. Perhaps such behavior is motivated by the need for self-protection (if everybody looks bad, I'll be okay). Perhaps such teachers are just insensitive to the needs of others. At any rate, their behavior rarely does any good, and participants who cannot deliver criticism tactfully and who cannot link criticism with positive suggestions should be encouraged and helped by other group members to develop these skills. When participants are not willing to temper excessive criticism, they should not continue in the group, for their presence generally generates a great deal of hostility and prevents the development of an atmosphere that is marked by the sharing of information and positive planning to improve classroom instruction.

### The Principal as Facilitator

The school principal and other auxiliary school personnel (e.g., the school psychologist) can rotate from group to group and serve as other participants willing to share ideas with teachers. Of course, the principal can play a valuable role in the in-service development of teachers by soliciting funds to buy appropriate video equipment and by scheduling videotaping so that optimum use can be made of it. For example, it may be necessary for first- and second-grade teachers to have different in-service training days from the third-, fourth-, fifth-, and sixth-grade groups, so that all groups will have video equipment available to replay their tapes or the tapes of other teachers.

In general, the principal can create the conditions needed for suitable self-improvement groups. When video equipment is not available in the short run, the principal can help teachers arrange to visit and to observe other teachers. As we pointed out earlier, a major obstacle to improvement in the classroom is that many teachers teach in self-contained classrooms and do not receive systematic feedback from responsible sources about their teaching. Principals are valuable instructional leaders when they create opportunities for teachers to improve their skills by observing them and providing systematic feedback.

Films of teaching behavior that lend themselves to critical analysis are available. Principals may obtain these films and show them in small groups and allow teachers to code film behavior and to suggest alternative teaching methods. Although this procedure will help teachers to develop skills for objectively examining behavior, the principal should not force teachers to stay at this level for very long. If he or she cannot obtain video equipment, it is important to arrange for teaching pairs to visit one another for at least a half hour each week. The sooner teachers receive feedback, the sooner they can begin to plan improvement strategies.

Typically, when teachers find in-service training programs boring and a waste of time, the programs were unrelated to their needs as teachers. Much time and effort is currently being placed on developing curricula that are inherently more interesting for students and that allow students more opportunity for pursuing topics independently. Perhaps corresponding emphasis should be placed on developing ways for teachers to become more active in the development of in-service training programs that meet their needs and interests rather than subjecting them to a passive role. We feel that allowing teachers to use in-service time to engage in independent self-improvement activities, either as individuals or in groups, would be valuable.

After teachers begin to work on self-improvement, they will be in a position to advise the principal as to the type of university consultant that would facilitate their program. Teachers given the freedom and responsibility for planning their own in-service training typically view the task quite seriously and work earnestly to develop useful programs. As a resource specialist and general facilitator, the principal can aid immeasurably by supplying teachers with copies of the books mentioned earlier in this chapter and other books that the teachers request or that the principal feels are useful for stimulating teacher thought and experimentation. The best way a principal can influence and encourage the development of teachers is to have a genuine interest in their self-development and to model his or her own search and experimentation with ways of becoming a better principal.

### Teaching Centers

Teaching centers are becoming increasingly popular and provide yet another way of enriching the training of pre and in-service teachers. However, as Schmieder and Yarger (1974) note, a teaching center is difficult to define because of the many ways in which they operate. They offer the following general definition: "A place *in situ* or in changing locations, which develops programs for the training and improvement of educational personnel (in-service teachers, preservice teachers, administrators, paraprofessionals, college teachers, etc.) in which the participating personnel have an opportunity to share successes, to utilize a wide range of educational resources, and to receive training specifically related to their most pressing teaching problems." Centers have been created for a variety of reasons (legislative mandate, voluntary program in a school district, formal working agreements between universities and school districts, etc.).

Teaching centers could be used to provide the type of peer-feedback, in-service training that we described above. Clark (1974) points out that a critical problem facing teaching centers is the acquisition of materials that can be used to stimulate thinking about teaching and to help teachers to acquire new skills. Among the sources that Clark mentions are the *Resources for Performance-Based Education* edited by Houston (1973) and the *CEDAR Catalog of Selected Educational Research and Development Programs and Products* (1972).

The teaching center movement will provide both human and material resources that can be used to improve teaching. Teachers will have to be sure that programs fulfill their individual needs and respond to their questions rather than subtly pressure them to conform to a "popular style."

Feiman (1977) presents a very interesting account of the historical forces that led to the development of teacher centers and some of the major differences that exist among teacher centers as they function today. Teachers interested in the formation of a teacher center would benefit from reflecting upon the distinctions that Feiman makes, as such distinctions may help teachers to focus upon what they hope to achieve. The three major types of teacher centers identified by Feiman are: behavioral centers, humanistic centers, and developmental centers.

In brief, the behavioral centers focus on specific teaching behaviors and basically are concerned with helping teachers to improve classroom performance. Teachers are provided with a chance to view training films, etc., in order to develop technical skills. In the humanistic centers, it is assumed that teacher development will occur naturally as long as teachers get the feedback they want in a supportive environment. Development centers share many concerns of the humanistic centers (e.g., teachers must learn at their own pace, teachers must begin at their own starting point). In the development centers (as compared to the humanistic centers) less time is used for trading practical advice and more time is used to encourage initiative (i.e., fewer short term spontaneous encounters and less emphasis upon responding to immediate needs and more on creating awareness of fundamental needs and problems). Detailed distinctions among the three types of centers, as well as specific examples and locations of each center type, can be found in Feiman (1977).

## OPPORTUNITIES TO OBSERVE AND GET FEEDBACK CAN IMPROVE INSTRUCTION

Eash and Rasher (1977) reported that a school district's in-service program to help teachers individualize instruction was aided by classroom observation. Such training was useful for helping teachers to cope with the greater diversity of students brought about by desegregation activities and for improving student achievement in the district. Supervisory personnel needed additional training for their new roles because observation does not automatically improve instruction. It is useful only when conducted by competent persons who have a systematic way of looking at classroom behavior.

Feedback from students also can be useful in changing teacher behavior, but again, good results are not automatic. Several studies have reported that teachers do not change their behavior simply because they receive information. They need information about teaching behavior or goals that are important to them if the information is to be useful in changing their behavior. Too often, evaluation forms completed by high school and college students do not reflect teachers' goals. Or they ask questions that are so global or inadequate (e.g., the student doesn't have the information necessary for responding) that teachers reject the feedback as meaningless.

When teachers are given specific and accurate information, especially when teacher participation is voluntary, they can use it to improve instruction. For example, Pambookian (1976) reports that a discrepancy between teachers' perceptions of teaching and feedback from students can motivate teachers to alter instructional behavior. Pambookian argues that, if the discrepancy is large, there will be motivation for the teacher to change behavior. (We also suspect that the discrepancy should involve a goal that is important to the teacher.)

Pambookian (1976) found that, when a group of college teachers were informed about such discrepancies, they changed their teaching behavior. Instructors with student ratings lower than their own ratings improved their teaching the most. If student feedback is to have optimal value, teachers must be involved in the construction of the evaluative instruments to see that questions of personal importance are included, and instruments need to be *changed* occasionally to present teachers with information about different aspects of their behavior. Teachers also can use feedback from classroom observation to modify their behavior. Much inappropriate teaching occurs because teachers are unaware of their behavior.

In interviews with teachers, Good and Brophy (1974) found that many aspects of differential teacher behavior toward high and low achievers were unknown to teachers. This was especially the case with qualitative variables (e.g., What percent of the time did teachers "stay with" or "give up" on students generally? For high- and low-achievement students?).

When teachers were presented with specific information about their behavior that both intrigued and bothered them, they wanted to change their behavior. Subsequent observation illustrated that teachers did change their behavior, and there were signs that students were beginning to change their behavior as a result of changed teacher behavior.

An especially good illustration of the use of observation to improve teaching quality comes from a program directed by Martin (1973). The project "Equal Opportunity in the Classroom" was a major attempt to help teachers become aware of self-defeating treatment of low-achieving students and learn new ways to interact with these students. First, teachers were presented with detailed information about teacher expectation research. Then they discussed how subtle, unproductive differences might be taking place in their own classrooms. They were then trained in skills that were easy to use and observe.

Many of these skills were based on the Brophy—Good Dyadic Observation System (Brophy and Good, 1970b), but several others were added by the project team. The key was that teachers not only were trained to treat low-achieving students in specific ways, but also were trained to observe and code these behaviors. In addition to the training, teachers had the opportunity to observe and be observed by fellow teachers.

Teacher reports about the project were enthusiastic. In particular, they found it stimulating to be observed by other teachers (and get feedback from them) and to have a chance to observe other teachers themselves. Watching other teachers is a valuable way to *see* new techniques.

Observational data illustrated that teachers in the project treated low achievers much differently than control teachers (i.e., teachers who did not participate in the project). The attitudes of low-achieving students in the classrooms of trained teachers were better than those of low-achieving students in control classrooms. Furthermore, the *reading achievement* of both high- and low-achieving students was better in the project classrooms.

Additional support for our contention that teachers will change if their attention is called to the need for change is provided by Moore and Schaut (1975). One of their experiments involved observing teacher and student behaviors on the variables of interest before and after treatment. Thirty-six teachers were divided into experimental and control groups. During the study, teachers were given feedback about their behavior with ten randomly selected students. The observers focused upon students' lack of attention and teachers' responses to it. Experimental teachers gave more attention to inattentive students than did control teachers. After the experiment, the student inattention rate was only 5 percent for the experimental group but 23 percent for the control group. Furthermore, experimental teachers interacted with inattentive students more than one and a half times more than the control students. Such data strongly suggest that feedback to teachers can change their behavior and that of their students. However, again we want to emphasize that feedback does not change teacher behavior automatically.

Kepler (1977) also has stressed that teacher awareness of classroom behavior does not necessarily lead to corrective or more appropriate behavior on the part of the teacher. Although it is clear that descriptive feedback to teachers is an important first step in understanding classroom behavior, it is not an answer, *per se*. Much more information is needed about the ways in which feedback can be presented to teachers to optimize its value. Furthermore, more information is needed about the personal characteristics of teachers that make them more or less likely to benefit from feedback.

## DO LOOK BACK

The intent of this chapter is to encourage teachers to look at their classroom behavior and to plan ways to make classrooms more meaningful and exciting. Stress has been placed upon the fact that objective, improvement-oriented self-evaluation is difficult for many of us to engage in because we have not been trained to do it. Any significant new experience is always a challenge, and self-evaluation is no exception. Your first efforts to look at your own behavior openly will be difficult and perhaps frustrating. However, such analysis, if it is tackled one step at a time and linked to prescriptive strategies for improving behavior, will lead to self-growth and the satisfaction that accompanies becoming more effective.

This book was written to encourage you to look at your behavior and to assume responsibility for your development as a teacher. Certain scales and materials are included in the book to help you assess your behavior and plan new instructional strategies, but ultimately you and only you can evaluate the effects of your teaching. Do not avoid your responsibility by uncritically accepting someone else's advice or teaching philosophy.

Remember, a teaching strategy is good when two basic conditions are satisfied: (1) students learn the material that they are supposed to master and (2) students are interested and find the learning process enjoyable so that they initiate learning efforts of their own and can progressively assume more responsibility for planning and evaluating their own work.

It is up to you to identify teaching behaviors that meet these criteria and to weave them into a teaching style with which you feel comfortable so that you look forward to class and to teaching generally. You are the teacher, and *you* must assume responsibility for establishing a learning atmosphere that is stimulating and exciting for yourself as well as for the students. If you do not enjoy class, your students probably will not either!

### SUGGESTED ACTIVITIES AND QUESTIONS

1. Make a list of all books and ideas that you want to explore in the near future. Please do not limit your selection to materials listed in this text. Rank the three things you most want to learn. This will serve as your in-service map. Compare your notes with other teachers, and if you have similar interests, share material and collectively urge the principal to design in-service programs that will satisfy these needs.

2. Make a list of your teaching strengths and weaknesses. Make specific plans for improving your two weakest areas.

3. Read the cases in Appendix A and see if you can pinpoint

the teaching strengths and weaknesses that appear there. Compare your ratings with those made by others.

4. What are the possible advantages and disadvantages of using parents or retired but capable adults as observation sources to supply teachers with feedback about their behavior?

5. Why is it difficult for most of us to engage in self-evaluation?

6. Why do teachers benefit more from critical but prescriptive feedback than they do from vague positive feedback?

7. How can the school principal help to facilitate the development of effective in-service programs?

8. How can teachers initiate self-improvement programs?

9. Should young teachers seek advice from veteran teachers? If so, under what circumstances and in what manner?

10. As a teacher, how can you help your students to develop the skills and attitudes for examining their own work non-defensively?

11. We have stressed the need for you to seek evaluative comment and to analyze your behavior if you are to grow and to improve. We seek your evaluative comment. We would like to know how useful the book is from your perspective, and we would like to know about any deficiencies so that future editions of this book can be improved. We encourage you to write us with your feedback and suggestions. (What was your general reaction to the book? Is it relevant to teachers and future teachers? What topics were omitted that you feel should be in future editions? What advice or suggestions in this book did you disagree with and why? Did we communicate negative expectations or provide contradictory advice, and if so, where and how? Were there sections of the book that you found especially helpful, and why?) We will be delighted to receive your suggestions and criticisms, and your comments will be given serious consideration when a new edition of this book is written.

# APPENDIX A
# PRACTICE EXAMPLES

This appendix includes five brief examples of classroom life in elementary school and junior and senior high schools. These case materials will give you an opportunity to apply the material you have mastered in this book. Try to identify the teaching strengths and weaknesses that appear in the case teaching episodes that follow and to suggest alternative ways in which the teacher could have behaved differently to improve the classroom discussion. Then compare your insights with those of your classmates.

## CASE 1

Charles Kerr had done his student teaching on the secondary level with majors in social studies and PE. Since there was a surplus of teachers seeking positions in his field at the high schools in his area, he accepted a position as a sixth-grade teacher temporarily while waiting for an opening on the coaching staff of one of the athletic programs in the high schools. He teaches in an all-white middle-class school and he has good social rapport with his students.

TEACHER: Class, today we are going to talk about the upcoming presidential elections. The actual election is not for a whole

---

*Note:* We acknowledge the capable assistance of Kathey Paredes in preparing the first draft version of some of the examples.

year, but some men, senators mainly, have already announced themselves as candidates. Tom, tell me why men like the senators from Maine and Ohio have said they are going to run for President this soon.

TOM: Because they don't want the president to stay in office anymore.

TEACHER: A lot of people don't want that, but they aren't running; there's a good reason you haven't thought of yet; try again.

TOM: I don't know; I don't care much about the election.

TEACHER: Well, you should care; it won't be too long before you can vote and you need to be aware. Susanne, what reason can you come up with?

SUSANNE: Maybe people don't know them very well.

TEACHER: That's right. They need the advance publicity. Brian, what kind of elections are held in each individual state before the general election?

BRIAN: Preliminary?

TEACHER: The word's primary—but that was close enough. Craig, who can run in the primary?

CRAIG: Republicans and Democrats.

TEACHER: And that's it? Suppose I wanted to run and I'm neither one of those mentioned, then what?

BRIAN: You couldn't do it.

TEACHER: (impatiently) Jane, stop shuffling your feet that way— do you think I could run for president if I wanted?

JANE: I suppose so.

TEACHER: You don't sound very definite in your opinion; be decisive and tell me yes or no.

JANE: Yes!

TEACHER: All right—don't be wishy-washy in your opinions. Now, Tony, who would you like to see run for President?

TONY: The mayor of New York.

TEACHER: How about you, Janette?

JANETTE: The honorable senator from Texas.

TEACHER: Why?

JANETTE: Because he's attractive and colorful.

TEACHER: (sarcastically) Girls don't think logically sometimes. Bobby, could you give me a more intelligent reason than Janette?

BOBBY: Because he has had lots of experience.

TEACHER: In my opinion, I don't think that counts for much, but at least you are thinking along the right lines. Danny, what will be a major issue in this campaign?

DANNY: Crime.

TEACHER: *(with a loud, urgent voice)* Crime is always an issue; there's something else you should concern yourself about as an issue; I'll give you another chance.

BARBARA: *(calling out)* Won't the economy be an issue?

TEACHER: I'll ask the questions, Barbara, and you be thinking of some good answers! Danny, have you thought of it yet?

DANNY: Probably the economy and foreign policy.

TEACHER: Certainly. Rob, since you have been doing so much commenting to everyone around you back there, tell me, should we fight other people's wars? What should our foreign policy be with respect to small wars?

ROB: If they need the help and can't defend themselves.

TEACHER: Does that really sound sensible to you? Do you want to go to some distant part of the world and get killed?

ROB: No, but I don't think we should let other powers move in and take what they want either.

TEACHER: Of course not, but I don't think we should get involved in foreign affairs to the point of war and you shouldn't listen to anybody who tells you we should. Back to the issues; we decided war should be over and that we should get out no matter what the costs; there are a few more issues you might hear a lot about. Yes, Margaret?

MARGARET: Don't you think the war is just about over now and will be by the election?

TEACHER: No, I don't; if I did think so, I wouldn't have brought it up here; pay attention! We only have eight minutes more before the bell rings and then you can do what you want to do. Pay attention to the discussion and quit moving around. Now let's get back to my question. Tim?

TIM: There aren't enough jobs for everyone.

TEACHER: No, there aren't. I wanted to teach high school, but there are already too many of those teachers; so don't decide to be a high-school teacher because there may not be a job for you.

CONNIE: You mean I shouldn't become a teacher?

TEACHER: I would consider something else where there might be more job openings. What I would like you to do is find some resource material that will tell you more about the elections and what we can expect in the way of candidates and issues. John, when we go to the library what might you look for to find this information?

JOHN: Magazines.

TEACHER: Yes, which ones?

JOHN: *Time, Newsweek.*

TEACHER: Good, Where else, Leslie?
LESLIE: Newspapers.
TEACHER: Which ones?
LESLIE: Local newspapers.
TEACHER: You had better go further than that. Why should you look at more than one newspaper, Mike?
MIKE: Our paper might not have anything in it about elections.
TEACHER: No. The reason is that different papers have different views of the candidates. I want you to have two different viewpoints in your papers. Now, I want you to write a good paper on what we have discussed today using reliable resources. If you have forgotten the style you are to use, get out the instruction sheet I gave you a few weeks ago and follow it point by point. Tomorrow you are going to defend your positions to the class. The class will attempt to tear apart your papers. So write them carefully or else your poor logic will embarrass you.

## CASE 2

Linda Law is teaching for her second year at Thornton Junior High School. The students at Thornton come from upper middle-class homes and Linda teaches social studies to the brightest ability group of ninth-grade students. Today she is deviating from her normal lesson plans in order to discuss the Tasadays tribe that resides in the Philippine Rain Forest.

TEACHER: Class, yesterday I told you that we would postpone our scheduled small group work so that we could discuss the Tasadays. Two or three days ago Charles mentioned the Tasadays as an example of persons who were alienated from society. Most of you had never heard of the Tasadays but were anxious to have more information, so yesterday I gave you a basic fact sheet and a few review questions to think about. I'm interested in discussing this material with you and discussing the questions that you want to raise. It's amazing! Just think, a stone age tribe in today's world. What an exciting opportunity to learn about the way man used to live! Joan, I want you to start the discussion by sharing with the class what you thought was the most intriguing fact uncovered.
JOAN: *(in a shy, shaky voice)* Oh, that they had never fought with other tribes or among themselves. Here we are, modern man, and we fight continuously and often for silly reasons.
SID: *(breaking in)* Yeah, I agree with Joannie, that is remarkable. You know, we have talked about man's aggressive nature, and this finding suggests that perhaps it isn't so.

SALLY: *(calling out)* You know, Sid, that is an interesting point!

TEACHER: Why is that an interesting point, Sally?

SALLY: *(looks at the floor and remains silent)*

TEACHER: Why do you think these people don't fight, Sally?

SALLY: *(remains silent)*

TEACHER: Sally, do they have any reason to fight?

SALLY: No, I guess not. All their needs . . . you know, food and clothing, can be found in the forest and they can make their own tools.

TEACHER: Yes, Sally, I think those are good reasons. Class, does anyone else want to add anything on this particular point? *(She calls on Ron who has his hand up.)*

RON: You know what I think it is that makes the difference, well, my dad says it is money. He says that if these Tasadays find out about money, there will be greed, corruption, and war all in short order.

TEACHER: Ron, can you explain in more detail why money would lead to deterioration in life there?

RON: *(with enthusiasm)* Well, because now there's no direct competition of man against man. It's man and man against nature and what one man does is no loss to another man.

TONY: *(calling out)* Not if food or something is in short supply!

TEACHER: Tony, that's a good point, but please wait until Ron finishes his remarks. Go ahead, Ron.

RON: Well, money might lead to specialization and some men would build huts and others would hunt and exchange their wares for money and eventually men would want more money to buy more things and competition would lead to aggressive behavior.

TEACHER: Thank you, Ron, that's an interesting answer. Now, Tony, do you want to add anything else?

TONY: No, nothing except that Ron's making a lot of generalizations that aren't supported. You know, the Tasadays might have specialized labor forces. Now there's nothing in the article I read about this.

TEACHER: That's good thinking, Tony. Class, how could we find out if the Tasadays have a specialized labor force?

MARY: *(called on by the teacher)* Well, we could write a letter to Dr. Fox, the chief anthropologist at the National Museum, and ask him.

TEACHER: Excellent, Mary, would you write a letter tonight and tomorrow read it to the class and then we'll send it.

MARY: Okay.

*(The teacher notices Bill and Sandra whispering in the back corner*

*of the room and as she asks the next question, she walks half-way down the aisle. They stop talking.)*

TEACHER: What dangers do the Tasadays face now that they have been discovered by modern man?

TOM: *(calling out)* I think the biggest problem they face will be the threat of loggers who are clearing the forest and the less primitive tribes who have been driven farther into the forest by the loggers.

TEACHER: Why is this a problem, Tom?

TOM: Well, they might destroy. You know, these less primitive tribes might attack or enslave the Tasadays.

TEACHER: Okay, Tom. Let's see if there are other opinions. Sam, what do you think about Tom's answer?

SAM: Well, I do think that those other natives and loggers are a threat, but personally I feel that the Tasadays' real danger is sickness. Remember how, I think it was on Easter Island, natives were wiped out by diseases that they had no immunity to. I think they might be wiped out in an epidemic.

TEACHER: What kind of an epidemic, Sam?

SAM: Well, it could be anything, TB, you know, anything.

TEACHER: Class, what do you think? If an epidemic occurred, what disease would be most likely involved?

CLASS: *(no response)*

TEACHER: Okay, class, let's write this question down in our notebooks and find an answer tomorrow. I'm stumped, too, so I'll look for the answer tonight as part of my homework. I'm going to allow ten minutes more for this discussion, and then we'll have to stop for lunch. I wish we had more time to discuss this topic; perhaps we can spend more time tomorrow. In the last ten minutes, I'd like to discuss your questions. What are they? Call them out and I'll write them on the board.

ARLENE: I was surprised that the oldest of these people were in their middle forties and the average height was only five feet. It looks like living an active outdoor life, they would be healthy and big. What's wrong with their diet?

MARY JANE: I'm interested in a lot of their superstitious behavior. For example, why do they feel that to have white teeth is to be like an animal? . . .

## CASE 3

Mrs. Jackson taught school for two years in the 1950s then retired to raise a family. Now that her children are grown, she has decided to return to the classroom and has received a teaching position in a large city school. Her third-grade class is composed of equal numbers of black, Oriental, Mexican-American, and Anglo children whose parents work but are still very involved in the school's activities. Previously, Mrs. Jackson had taught in an upper middle-class school, and although she had adapted her lesson plans to the changes in curriculum, she had not expected to have to change her approach to teaching since children, their behavior, and their needs remain pretty much the same over the years. Today, she is reviewing multiplication tables with the class, working with everyone the first 20 minutes and then dividing the children into four groups to complete their assigned independent work. The teacher sits with one group and helps them with their lesson.

TEACHER: Today, children, let's review our 8 and 9 times tables; whichever group can give me all the answers perfectly will be able to use the math games during independent work instead of having to do the exercises in the book. John, what is $8 \times 9$?

JOHN: 72.

TEACHER: Tim, $8 \times 0$.

TIM: 8.

TEACHER: Wrong, tell me what $8 \times 1$ is?

TIM: 8.

TEACHER: Yes, now you should know what $8 \times 0$ is.

TIM: *(no response)*

TEACHER: Tim lost the contest for group 3.

JAN: *(calls out)* Why didn't you ask me, I know the answer!

TEACHER: I'm glad that you do, so you can teach Tim and your group will win next time. I'm going to ask Terri what $8 \times 2$ is.

TERRI: 16.

TEACHER: Mark, what is $8 \times 4$?

MARK: 32.

TEACHER: Lynn, $8 \times 6$?

LYNN: 48.

TEACHER: Judy, $8 \times 10$?

JUDY: 56, no. Wait a minute. *(Teacher pauses and gives her time to come up with another answer.)* It's 80, isn't it?

TEACHER: Yes, it is. Jeff, give me the correct answer to this one, and your group will have a perfect score; what is $8 \times 11$?

JEFF: *(Thinks a minute and Carrie, from another group, calls out.)*

CARRIE: 88!

TEACHER: Carrie, it was not your turn and now I'm not going to give your group a chance to win. I'm sure Jeff knew the answer and so his group has done the best so far. Now, Linda, let's see how well your group will do; what is 9 X 3?

LINDA: 28; no! 27.

TEACHER: Are you sure?

LINDA: I think so.

TEACHER: You must be positive; either it is 27 or it isn't. Class?

CLASS: Yes!

TEACHER: All right, Chuck, you don't seem to be listening so I will ask you the next one. What is 9 X 6?

CHUCK: *(counting on his fingers silently)*

TEACHER: We haven't got time to wait for you to get the answer that way and that's not the way I taught you to do multiplication. Let's see if your friend Bobby can do better.

BOBBY: *(looks at Marilyn without giving any response)*

TEACHER: Marilyn is not going to give you the answer; this was something you were supposed to learn for homework last night. Did you do it?

BOBBY: Yes.

TEACHER: Well, since you did the work you should be able to answer my question. Again, what is 9 X 6?

BOBBY: I can't remember.

TEACHER: Marilyn, do you know?

MARILYN: 56?

TEACHER: *(exasperated)* For as many times as we have done these tables, I don't know why you can't learn them. I think this group will have to go back and do some work in the second-grade math book until they are ready to learn what everybody else is doing. *(Class laughs.)* Now, let's look at our chart here and everyone together will recite the tables twice. *(Class reads down the chart.)*

TEACHER: I have written the pages and directions for each group on the board. Terri, your group may get the games out because you know your tables. Matthew, read me what your group is to do.

MATTHEW: "Find the products *(Matt falters on word, teacher gives it to him)* and factors" *(doesn't know word)*.

TEACHER: How can you expect to do the work if you can't read the directions? I guess I had better read it. Now does everyone understand? *(No comment from group.)* All right, go to work and I don't want any interruptions while I'm working with Tim's group. Chuck, you get out the second-grade books and start on the pages that I have written up here. I'm sure you understand what all of you have to do.

TEACHER: Will the monitors pass out paper? John, if you don't think you can do the job without chatting with your friends, you had better give the papers to someone else. Elaine and Mike, I like the way you are sitting—ready to go to work! Let's see how quietly we can all do our work today.

*(with group 3)*

TEACHER: Carrie, you're a good thinker, do this problem on the board for me.

*(Carrie does it correctly.)*

TEACHER: That's good. Darryl, you try this one—$(2 \times 3) \times 6$.

*(Darryl works it out.)*

TEACHER: There's another way; could you do that, too?

*(Darryl starts, but can't finish.)*

TEACHER: I'll finish it for you and then tell me what I did to get the answer. *(Writes $(2 \times 6) \times 3$.)*

DARRYL: You just changed the brackets.

TEACHER: Will I get the same answer? *(Chorus: yes!)* Paula, you make up a problem of your own and Ted will figure it out. *(She does.)*

TED: What is $7 \times 4$?

TEACHER: Ted, we just went all through this; now do the best you can.

*(Ted does and gets the wrong answer.)*

TEACHER: I guess Paula will have to do it herself. Tonight I'm going to give you extra homework so that you will know this type of problem perfectly.

## CASE 4

Matt Davidson teaches American literature at an all-white middle-class high school. The seniors in his class at Windsor Hills have been doing some concentrated study of Mark Twain's writings. They are of above average intelligence and have previously read two other novels by Twain.

TEACHER: Class, I know I didn't give you as much time to read *The Adventures of Huckleberry Finn* as we might ordinarily take; however, since you are familiar with Twain's style, his settings and characters, I knew you would be able to grasp the content and motives in the story without much trouble. *Huckleberry Finn* is considered to be a classic today, a real artistic work of fiction. Stylistically, why is this book considered to be a masterpiece, John?

JOHN: He used a setting in Missouri and adapted the narrative to the dialects common to that place and time.

TEACHER: Good. Was there one dialect only?

JOHN: No, I think maybe there were two.

TEACHER: Actually, there were several—Huck's and Tom's, Jim's, Aunt Sally's and others. Dialect here was a necessary ingredient to the fiction of the time. What sets the mood, what gives the structure to the story?

TERRI: *(calling out)* The time.

TEACHER: Could be to a small extent, but not what I had in mind, Terri. Where is the setting?

TERRI: St. Petersburg, Mo.

*(Teacher notices Matt drawing on a piece of paper and looks at him as Terri responds. When Matt looks up the teacher catches his eye and Matt puts away his paper.)*

TEACHER: All right. Could Twain have taken Huck to Phoenix, Arizona and related the story exactly the same? How about that, Tim?

TIM: I guess not, there's no Mississippi River in Phoenix.

TEACHER: Exactly. Develop that thought further, Tim—keep in mind the author himself.

TIM: Twain gew up in Hannibal and he probably saw much of what he wrote about.

TEACHER: You're right there. Did you want to add something, Melissa?

MELISSA: The story is probably semiautobiographical, then, with a few names and places changed.

TEACHER: Yes, I think so too.

MARK: *(calling out)* There probably weren't any slaves in Phoenix, either, so Jim might have not been in the story.

LARRY: *(calling out)* There might have been.

TEACHER: I think Mark is pretty close to the truth in what he said, Larry, but that's something for you to look into. So, locale is important. Now, what is the book about—is it just about a boy going down the river? Lynne?

LYNNE: It's an adventure story.

TEACHER: Could you lend a little more depth of thought to your answer? Is it just a comedy?

LYNNE: A thoughtful one.

ED: *(calling out)* It has a more serious element—satire.

TEACHER: I don't think we've discussed satire and I'm glad you brought it up. What is your definition of satire?

ED: Well, for instance, Aunt Sally and Aunt Polly always pretended to be so virtuous and Christian-like, but they were willing to sell Jim back into slavery. Huck wanted to get away from all the hypocrisy and fraud.

TEACHER: Very good! But, Huck had a hard time coping with this. What one particular quality or emotion did Huck have, as opposed to say, Tom, Linda?

LINDA: *(reading her book)* He was smarter?

TEACHER: That's not so much a quality—this is something he feels.

DUANE: *(calling out)* Sad, about the way people treat each other.

TEACHER: That's more what I was looking for, Linda. He was sensitive. Whom was he most sensitive about, Carol?

CAROL: Tom, I guess.

TEACHER: Oh no. He accepted Tom for what he was—a foolish little kid. The story revolves around Huck and one other person. Who, Bobby?

BOBBY: It was Jim. Huck knew slavery was wrong and was disturbed by it. Mr. Davidson, was slavery over yet?

TEACHER: No, this takes place in 1850 and slaves were not emancipated until the end of the Civil War in 1865. Your answer is correct. The way Tom treated Jim—always hurt his feelings; that hurt Huck, too. Chris, did Jim reciprocate this treatment toward the boys by being cruel in some manner?

CHRIS: I think he did.

TEACHER: Give me an instance when.

CHRIS: *(no response)*

TEACHER: Can you remember anything Jim did on the raft?

CHRIS: *(no response)*

TEACHER: Did you read the book?

CHRIS: No.

TEACHER: I think it's important you read it and I'm sure you will find it very captivating. Susann, who is the most admirable character?

SUSANN: Jim, because he was always loyal and dedicated to Huck no matter what.

GERRY: *(calling out)* No, I think it was Huck because he was always wrestling with his conscience and knew things were wrong.

TEACHER: Both answers are correct and show good reasoning. There is never one necessarily right answer when discussing literature—it's a matter of your interpretation as you read it and see it. Who are the villains? Kevin?

KEVIN: The most obvious are the Duke and the Dauphin.

TEACHER: Why, Leslie?

LESLIE: *(rustling through the pages)*

TEACHER: You don't need to look it up; just give me your impression of their characters.

LESLIE: They pretended to be royalty and Shakespearean actors,

but they really lied and cheated people out of their money.
TEACHER: Right, Huck's father was something of a villain, and the Grangerfords and Shepherdsons were certainly not the most upstanding citizens. Turn to page 254 and read this short passage with me. I think this pretty well summarizes Huck's feelings:
"But I reckon I got to light out for the territory ahead of the rest, because Aunt Sally she's going to adopt me and civilize me, and I can't stand it. I been there before."
TEACHER: A very important concept is contained here. Who can discover what it is? Yes, Marilyn?
MARILYN: He doesn't want to have any part of fancy clothing, going to school or church, or eating off a plate.
TEACHER: Yes, he wants his freedom. Let's do a little deeper analysis of Huck's character. I'm going to put some questions on the board and you tell me as best you can what Huck really thought about the Grangerfords, about slavery, about the Duke and Dauphin, and so forth. How did he confront and deal with these people?

## CASE 5

Joan Maxwell has been teaching the first grade for seven years in a small rural community school. Her students are children of primarily farm and ranch workers of lower middle-class background. Joan and her husband both received their degrees from a large university and now operate a lucrative business in the area. Joan is introducing a science lesson today; it's late fall and the children have been asked to bring in some leaves to show changes in leaf colors from season to season. The class has previously discussed seasonal changes and what weather patterns occur during these times.

TEACHER: Boys and girls, let's first review what we talked about last week when we were writing our stories about different seasons.
SHARI: (calling out) Do we have to do this? Why can't we do something fun instead of doing something we don't like?
TEACHER: We can't always do things we enjoy. Carol, do you remember how many seasons we have in a year?
CAROL: Three.
TEACHER: No, we wrote more stories than just three—think for a minute.
CAROL: Four!

TEACHER: All right, now can you name them for me?

CAROL: Fall, winter, summer . . .

TEACHER: Didn't you write four stories?

CAROL: I don't remember.

TEACHER: *(forcefully, but with some irritation)* You may have to go back and write them again. Who knows the fourth season? Can somebody in my special Cardinal group respond? John, you answer.

JOHN: Fall, winter, spring, and summer.

TEACHER: Good thinking! It helps us to remember seasons sometimes if we think about important holidays that come then. Tim, in what season does Christmas come?

TIM: *(no response)*

TEACHER: You weren't listening. I want you to put those leaves in your desk and not touch them again till it's time. Cory, when does Christmas come?

CORY: In the winter.

TEACHER: How do you know it's winter, Mark?

MARK: Because of the snow and ice and rain . . .

TEACHER: Does it snow here?

MARK: No.

TEACHER: How do you know it's winter, then?

MARK: *(no response)*

MARY: *(calling out)* It snows at Christmas where I used to live.

TEACHER: Mary, if you have something to say, will you please raise your hand? *(She does.)* Now, what did you say?

MARY: Where I used to live it did snow, but not anymore.

TEACHER: Right! In some places it does snow and not others. Clarence, why wouldn't it snow here?

CLARENCE: Because it's too warm?

TEACHER: It's not warm here! I told you this before a couple of times. *(turns to Tim)* I asked you once before to put those away and you can't seem to keep your hands on the desk, so I'm going to take them away from you and when we do our project you will have to sit and watch! Don't anyone else do what Tim does. Now, let's talk more about the fall season and get some good ideas for our story. What is another word for the fall season? Lynne?

LYNNE: Halloween.

TEACHER: I didn't ask you to give me a holiday, a word.

LYNNE: I can't think of it.

TEACHER: I'm going to write it on the board and see if Bobby can pronounce it for me.

BOBBY: *(no response)*
TEACHER: This is a big word, Bobby. I'll help you.
JUDY: *(calling out)* Autumn!
TEACHER: *(turns to Judy)* Is your name Bobby?
JUDY: No.
TEACHER: Then don't take other children's turns. Now, Bobby, say the word. *(He does.)* I think this is a good word to write in your dictionaries. Get them out and let's do it now.
JANE: I don't have a pencil.
TEACHER: That is something you are supposed to take care of yourself. Borrow one or stay in at recess and write it then. Let's look at these pictures of leaves as they look in the fall and spring. Mary Kay, can you tell me one thing that is different about these two pictures?
MARY KAY: The leaves are different colors.
TEACHER: Good. Tell me some of the colors.
MARY KAY: In spring, they are a bright green.
TEACHER: Right. Joe, how about the other ones?
JOE: They are brown and orange and purple.
TEACHER: I don't see any purple—you've got your colors mixed up. Tony?
TONY: It's more red.
TEACHER: Yes. Steve, we are finished writing in our dictionaries; put it away. You can finish at recess with Jane. Some people in our class are very slow writers. Take out your leaves now. Mark, how does that leaf feel in your hand?
MARK: If feels dry and rough like old bread. *(Class laughs.)*
TEACHER: Don't be silly! How did it get so dry? Marilyn?
MARILYN: If fell off the tree.
TEACHER: Yes, a leaf needs the tree to stay alive, is that right, Dave?
DAVE: You could put it in water and it would stay alive.
TEACHER: Not for long. Martha, what else can you tell me about these leaves.
MARTHA: I don't have one.
TEACHER: I don't know what to do about children who can't remember their homework assignments. You will never be good students if you don't think about these things. Mike, what do you see in the leaves?
MIKE: Lines running through.
TEACHER: We call those lines veins. Are all leaves the same shape?
MIKE: No, my leaf came from a sycamore tree and it has soft corners, not sharp ones.
TEACHER: That's good. I think you will be able to write an interesting

story. Two holidays come during the fall; who can name one? Terri?

TERRI: Halloween.

TEACHER: That's one; Jeff do you know another?

JEFF: *(no response)*

TEACHER: It comes in November and we have a school holiday.

JEFF: Easter?

TEACHER: No, that is in the spring; we have turkey for dinner this day.

CHORUS: Thanksgiving.

TEACHER: Now do you remember, Jeff? I would like you to write about Thanksgiving in your story, then you won't forget again. Now we are ready to put our vocabulary words on the board that we will use for our story and pictures.

*(Teacher notices Shari, Jim, and Rick exchanging their books but she ignores their misbehavior.)*

TEACHER: Ed, you come up here and Sally come up here and help me print our vocabulary words on the board. Ed, you print these four words *(hands him a list)* and Sally, you print these four.

TEACHER: What are you kids doing in that corner? Shari, Rick, Jim, Terri, Kim, stop fighting over those books. *(All the children in the class turn to look at them.)*

RICK: Mrs. Maxwell, it's all Kim's fault.

KIM: It is not. I wasn't doing anything. Shari, Rick, and Jim have been fooling around but I've been trying to listen.

TEACHER: Quiet down, all of you. You all stay in for recess and we'll discuss it then.

KIM: Not me!

TEACHER: Yes, all of you.

KIM: *(mutters to her friend)* It's not fair.

TEACHER: Kim, what did you say?

KIM: Nothing.

TEACHER: That's more like it.

TEACHER: Okay, Ed, put your words up.

ED: I've lost the list . . . *(Class roars with laughter.)*

# GENERAL
# REFERENCES

Adams, R., and Biddle, B., *Realities of Teaching: Explorations with Video Tape.* New York: Holt, Rinehart and Winston, 1970.

Almy, M., *Ways of Studying Children.* New York: Teachers College Press, 1969.

Amato, J., "Effect of pupil's social class upon teachers' expectations and behavior." Paper presented at the annual meeting of the American Psychological Association, 1975.

Amidon, E., and Hunter, E., *Improving Teaching: The Analysis of Classroom Verbal Interaction.* New York: Holt, Rinehart and Winston, 1966.

Anderson, H. H., and Brewer, H. M., "Studies of teachers' classroom personalities I: Dominative and socially integrative behavior of kindergarten teachers." *Applied Psychology Monographs,* 1945.

Arlin, M., and Westbury, I., "The leveling effect of teacher pacing on science content mastery." *Journal of Research in Science Teaching,* 13 (1976), 213–219.

Aronson, E., Blaney, N., Sikes, J., Stephan, C., and Snapp, M., "Busing and racial tension: The jigsaw route to learning and liking." *Psychology Today,* 8 (1975), 43–50.

Aronson, E., and Mills, J. "The effect of severity of initiation on liking for a group." *Journal of Abnormal and Social Psychology,* 59 (1959), 177–181.

Ausubel, D., *The Psychology of Meaningful Verbal Learning: An Introduction to School Learning.* New York: Grune & Stratton, 1963.

Baker, H., *Film and Videotape Feedback: A Review of the Literature.* Report Series No. 53, Research and Development Center for Teacher Education. University of Texas, 1970.

Bandura, A., *Principles of Behavior Modification.* New York: Holt, Rinehart and Winston, 1969.

Barth, R., *Open Education: Assumptions and Rationale.* Unpublished qualifying paper, Harvard University, 1969.

Beez, W., "Influence of biased psychological reports on teacher behavior and pupil performance." *Proceedings of the 76th Annual Convention of the American Psychological Association,* 1968, 605–606.

Bennett, N., *Teaching Style and Pupil Progress.* London: Open Books Publishing, Ltd., 1976.

Bereiter, C., Washington, E., Englemann, S., and Osborn, J., *Research and Development Programs on Preschool Disadvantaged Children.* Final Report, OE Contract 6–10–235, Project #5–1181. Washington, D.C.: U.S. Department of Health, Education, and Welfare, Office of Education, Bureau of Research, 1969.

Berliner, D., and Tikunoff, W., "The California beginning teacher evaluation study: Overview of the ethnographic study." *Journal of Teacher Education,* 27 (1976), 31–34.

Biehler, R., *Psychology Applied to Teaching.* Boston: Houghton Mifflin, 1971.

Blank, M., *Teaching Learning in the Preschool: A Dialogue Approach.* Columbus, Ohio: Merrill, 1973.

Block, J., ed., *Mastery Learning: Theory and Practice.* New York: Holt, Rinehart and Winston, 1971.

_____ ed., *Schools, Society, and Mastery Learning.* New York: Holt, Rinehart and Winston, 1974.

Bloom, B., "Learning for Mastery." *Evaluation Comment,* Center for the Study of Evaluation, University of California, Vol. 1, No. 2 (1968), 578–579, 594.

_____ "An introduction to mastery learning theory." Paper presented at the annual meeting of the American Educational Research Association, 1973 (a).

_____ "Mastery learning in varied cultural settings." Paper presented at the annual meeting of the American Educational Research Association, 1973 (b).

_____ *Human Characteristic and School Learning.* New York: McGraw-Hill, 1976.

Borg, W., *Ability Grouping in the Public Schools: A Field Study,* 2d ed. Madison, Wisconsin: Dumbar Educational Research Services, 1966.

Borg, W., Kelley, M., Langer, P., and Gall, M., *The Mini-Course: A Microteaching Approach to Teacher Education.* Beverly Hills, Calif.: Macmillan Educational Services, 1970.

Born, D., Davis, M., Whelan, D., and Jackson, D., "College student study behavior in a personalized instruction course and a lecture course." Paper presented at the Kansas Conference on Behavior Analysis in Education, Lawrence, May 1972.

Braun, C., "Teacher Expectation: Socio-psychological dynamics." *Review of Educational Research,* 46 (1976), 185–213.

Brophy, J. E., "Reflections on research in elementary schools." *Journal of Teacher Education*, 27 (1976), 31–34.

Brophy, J., and Evertson, C., *Learning from Teaching: A Developmental Perspective.* Boston: Allyn & Bacon, 1976.

Brophy, J. and Good, T., "Brophy-Good system (teacher-child dyadic interaction)," in A. Simon and E. Boyer, eds., *Mirrors for Behavior: An Anthology of Observation Instruments Continued.* Philadelphia: Research for Better Schools, Inc., 1970 (a).

—— "Teachers' communications of differential expectations for children's classroom performance: Some behavioral data." *Journal of Educational Psychology*, 61 (1970b), 356–374.

—— *Teacher-Student Relationships: Causes and Consequences.* New York: Holt, Rinehart and Winston, 1974.

Brubaker, H., "Are you making the best use of cumulative records?" *Grade Teacher*, 86 (1968), 96–97, 222.

Bryan, J., and Walbek, N., "Preaching and practicing generosity: Children's actions and reactions." *Child Development*, 41 (1970), 329–353.

Burkhart, R., ed., *The Assessment Revolution: New Viewpoints for Teacher Evaluation.* National symposium on evaluation in education. New York State Education Department and Buffalo State University College, 1969.

Burnham, J., *Effects of Experimenters' Expectancies on Children's Ability to Learn to Swim.* Unpublished master's thesis, Purdue University, 1968.

Carroll, J., "A model of school learning." *Teachers College Record*, 64 (1963), 722–733.

—— "School learning over the long haul," in J. Krumboltz, ed., *Learning and the Educational Process.* Skokie, Ill.: Rand McNally, 1965.

CEDaR Catalog of Selected Educational Research and Development Programs and Products, Vols. 1–2 (3rd Ed.). Denver, Colorado: CEDaR Information Office, 1972.

Chaffin, J., "Will the real 'mainstreaming' program please stand up! (or . . . should Dunn have done it?)." *Focus on Exceptional Children*, 6 (1974), 1–18.

Channon, G., *Homework.* New York: Outerbridge and Dienstfrey, 1970.

Charters, W. W., and Jones, J. E., *On Neglect of the Independent Variable in Program Evaluation.* Project MITT occasional paper. Eugene, Oregon: Center for Educational Policy and Management, 1973.

Chase, C., "The impact of some obvious variables on essay test scores." *Journal of Educational Measurement*, 5 (1968), 315–318.

Claiborn, W., "Expectancy effects in the classroom: A failure to replicate. *Journal of Educational Psychology*, 60 (1969), 377–383.

Clark, C., "Now that you have a teacher center, what are you going to put into it?" *Journal of Teacher Education*, 25 (1974), 46–48.

Cloward, R., "Studies in tutoring." *Journal of Experimental Education*, 36 (1967), 14–25.

Coates, T., and Thoresen, C., "Teacher anxiety: A review with recommendations." *Review of Educational Research*, 46 (1976), 159–184.

Cobb, J., "Relationship of discrete classroom behavior to fourth-grade academic achievement." *Journal of Educational Psychology*, 63 (1972), 74–80.

Cohen, J., and DeYoung, H., "The role of litigation in the improvement of programming for the handicapped," in L. Mann and D. Sabatino, eds., *A First Review of Special Education*, Vol. 2. Philadelphia: J.S.E. Press with Buttonwood Farms, 1973.

Coleman, J., Campbell, E., Hobson, C., McPartland, J., Mood, A., Weinfield, F., and York, R., *Equality of Educational Opportunity*. Washington, D.C.: U.S. Office of Health, Education, and Welfare, 1966.

Collings, G. "Case Review: Rights of the retarded." *Journal of Special Education*, 7 (1973), 27–37.

Condry, J., "The role of initial interest and task performance on intrinsic motivation." Paper presented at the annual meeting of the American Psychology Association, 1975.

Cooke, B., "Teaching History in Mixed-Ability Groups," in E. Wragg, ed., *Teaching Mixed Ability Groups*. London: David and Charles Limited, 1976.

Coop, R., and White, K., *Psychological Concepts in the Classroom*. New York: Harper & Row, 1974.

Cooper, H., "Controlling personal reward: professional teachers' differential use of feedback and the effect of feedback on students' motivation to perform." *Journal of Educational Psychology*, 69 (1977), 419–427.

_____ "The determinants of teachers' dispensation of academic praise and criticism." Unpublished doctoral dissertation, University of Connecticut, 1975.

_____ *Intervening and Expectation Communication: A Follow-up Study to the "Personal Control" Study*. Hamilton, New York: Colgate University, 1976.

Coopersmith, S., *The Antecedents of Self-Esteem*. San Francisco: Freeman, 1967.

Corlis, C. and Weiss, J. "Curiosity and openness: Empirical testing of a basic assumption." Paper presented at the annual meeting of the American Educational Research Association, 1973.

Cornbleth, C., Davis, O., and Button, C. "Teacher-pupil interaction and teacher expectations for pupil achievement in secondary social studies classes." Paper presented at the annual meeting of the American Educational Research Association, 1972.

Costin, F., Greenough, W., and Menges, R., "Student ratings of college teaching: Reliability, validity, and usefulness." *Review of Educational Research*, 41 (1971), 511–535.

Covington, M. and Beery, R., *Self-Worth and School Learning*. New York: Holt, Rinehart and Winston, 1976.

Davis, O., Jr., and Tinsley, D., "Cognitive objectives revealed by classroom questions asked of social studies student teachers." *Peabody Journal of Education*, 45 (1967), 21–26.

Deci, E., *Intrinsic Motivation.* New York: Plenum, 1975.

Deutsch, M. "Early social environment: Its influence on school adaptation," in D. Schreibner, ed., *The School Dropout.* Washington, D.C.: National Education Association, 1964.

―――― "A Theory of Cooperation and Competition." *Human Relations* 2 (1949), 129–52.

Devin-Sheehan, L., Feldman, R., and Allen, V. "Research on children tutoring children: a critical review." *Review of Educational Research,* 46 (1976), 355–385.

DeVries, D., and Edwards, K., "Student teams and learning games: Their effects on cross-race and cross-sex interaction." *Journal of Educational Psychology,* 66 (1974), 741–749.

DeVries, D., and Slavin, R., *Teams—Games— Tournaments: A Final Report on the Research.* Report No. 217, Center for Social Organization of Schools. Baltimore: John Hopkins University, 1976.

Dollar, B., *Humanizing Classroom Discipline: A Behavioral Approach.* New York: Harper & Row, 1972.

Douglas, J., *The Home and the School: A Study of Ability and Attainment in the Primary School.* London: MacGibbon and Kee, 1964.

Doyle, W., Hancock, G., and Kifer, E., "Teachers' perceptions: Do they make a difference?" Paper presented at the annual meeting of the American Educational Research Association, 1971.

Dunkin, M., and Biddle, B., *The Study of Teaching.* New York: Holt, Rinehart and Winston, 1974

Dunn. L., *Exceptional Children in the Schools: Special Education in Transition.* New York: Holt, Rinehart and Winston, 1973

Dusek, J., "Do teachers bias children's learning?" *Review of Educational Research,* 45 (1975), 661–684.

Eash, M., and Rasher, S., "Mandated Desegregation and Improved Achievement: A Longitudinal Study." *Phi Delta Kappan* 58 (1977), 394–397.

Eden, D. "Intrinsic and extrinsic rewards and motives: Replication and extension with Kibbutz workers. *Journal of Applied Social Psychology* 5 (1975), 348–361.

Ehman, L. "A comparison of three sources of classroom data: Teachers, students, and systematic observation." Paper presented as the annual meeting of the American Educational Research Association, 1970.

Ellson, D., Barber, L., Engle, T., and Kampwerth, L., "Programmed tutoring: a teaching aid and a research tool." *Reading Research Quarterly,* 1 (1965), 77–127.

Emmer, E., *The Effect of Teacher Use of Student Ideas on Student Verbal Initiation.* Unpublished doctoral dissertation, University of Michigan, 1967.

Emmer, E., and Millet, G., *Improving Teaching Through Experimentation: A Laboratory Approach.* Englewood Cliffs, N.J.: Prentice-Hall, 1970.

Feiman, S., "Evaluating Teacher Centers." *School Review*, 85 (1977), 395–411.

Fernandez, C., Espinosa, R., and Dornbusch, S., *Factors Perpetuating the Low Academic Status of Chicano High School Students*. Memorandum No. 138, Center for Research and Development in Teaching. Stanford University, 1975.

Findley, W., and Bryan, M., *Ability Grouping, 1970 Status: Impact and Alternatives*. Center for Educational Improvement. University of Georgia, 1971.

Flavell, J., Botkin, P., Fry, C., Wright, J., and Jarvis, P., *The Development of Role-Taking and Communication Skills in Children*. New York: Wiley, 1968.

Fleming, E., and Anttonen, R., "Teacher expectancy or My Fair Lady." *American Educational Research Journal*, 8 (1971), 214–252.

Flowers, A., and Bolmeier, E., *Law and Pupil Control*. Cincinnati: W. H. Anderson Company, 1964.

Friedlander, B., "Some remarks on 'open education'." *American Educational Research Journal*, 12 (1975), 465–468.

Fuller, F., and Manning, B., "Self-confrontation review: A conceptualization for video playback in teacher education." *Review of Educational Research*, 43 (1973), 469–528.

Gagné, R., *The Conditions of Learning*, 2d ed., New York: Holt, Rinehart and Winston, 1970.

Gallagher, J., "Expressive thought by gifted children in the classroom." *Elementary English*, 42 (1965), 559–568.

Gilhool, T., "Education: An inalienable right." *Exceptional Children*, 39 (1973), 597–610.

Glasser, W., *Schools Without Failure*. New York: Harper & Row, 1969.

Glennon, V., "Mathematics: How firm the foundations?" *Phi Delta Kappan*, 57 (1976), 302–305.

Goldberg, M., Passow, A., and Justman, J., *The Effects of Ability Grouping*. New York: Teachers College Press, 1966.

Good, T., "Which pupils do teachers call on?" *Elementary School Journal*, 70 (1970), 190–198.

Good, T. L., Biddle, B. J., and Brophy, J. E., *Teachers Make a Difference*. New York: Holt, Rinehart and Winston, 1975.

Good, T., and Brophy, J., "Behavioral expression of teacher attitudes." *Journal of Educational Psychology*, 1972, 63, 617–624.

Good, T. L., and Brophy, J. E., "Changing teacher and student behavior: An empirical investigation." *Journal of Educational Psychology*, 66 (1974), 390–405.

Good, T., and Brophy, J., *Educational Psychology: A Realistic Approach*. New York: Holt, Rinehart and Winston, 1977.

Good, T. L., and Grouws, D., *Process-Product Relationship in Fourth Grade Mathematics Classrooms*. Final report of National Institute of Education Grant (NE–G–00–3–0123). University of Missouri, October 1975.

Good, T. L., Grouws, D., and Beckerman, T., "Teaching effectiveness: A study of teachers' curriculum pacing in fourth grade mathematics." *Journal of Curriculum Studies,* 1977 (in press).

Good, T. L., and Power, C., "Designing successful classroom environments for different types of students." *Journal of Curriculum Studies,* 8 (1976), 1–16.

Good, T. L., Schmidt, L., Peck, R., and Williams, D., *Listening to Teachers.* Report Series No. 34, Research and Development Center for Teacher Education. University of Texas, 1969.

Good, T., Sikes, J., and Brophy, J. Effects of teacher sex, student sex and student achievement on classroom interaction. Technical Report No. 61, Center for Research in Social Behavior. University of Missouri, 1972.

Goodlad, J., "Classroom organization," in C. Harris, ed., *Encyclopedia of Educational Research,* 3d ed. New York: Macmillan, 1960.

Gordon, I., *Studying the Child in School.* New York: Wiley, 1966.

Grapko, M., "A comparion of open space concept classroom structures according to dependence/independence measures in children, teacher's awareness of children's personality variables and children's academic progress." Paper presented at the annual meeting of the Ontario Education Research Council, Toronto, December 1973.

Green, R., and Farquhar, W., "Negro academic motivation and scholastic achievement." *Journal of Educational Psychology.* 56 (1965), 241–243.

Greenberg, H., *Teaching with Feeling.* New York: Macmillan, 1969.

Greenspan, B., *Child Development for Adolecents: A Case Study in Curriculum Development.* Unpublished qualifying paper, Harvard University, 1972.

Greenwood, G., Good, T., and Siegel, B., *Problem Situations in Teaching.* New York: Harper & Row, 1971.

Groisser, P., *How to Use the Fine Art of Questioning.* New York: Teachers' Practical Press, 1964.

Guszak, F. "Teacher questioning and reading," *Reading Teacher,* 21 (1967), 227–234.

Haynes, H., *Relation of Teacher Inteligence, Teacher Experience and Type of School to Types of Questions.* Unpublished doctoral dissertation, Nashville, Tenn., George Peabody College for Teachers, 1935.

Heathers, G., "Grouping," in R. Ebel, ed., *Encyclopedia of Educational Research,* 4th ed. New York: Macmillan, 1969.

Henry, J., "Attitude organization in elementary school classrooms." *American Journal of Orthopsychiatry,* 27 (1957), 117–133.

Hess, R., "Social class and ethnic influences on socialization," in P. Mussen, ed., *Carmichael's Manual of Child Psychology,* 3d ed., Vol. 2. New York: Wiley, 1970.

Hess, R., Shipman, V., Brophy, J., and Bear, R., "Mother-child interaction." in I. Gordon, ed., *Readings in Research in Developmental Psychology.* Glenview, Ill.: Scott, Foresman, 1971.

Hoffman, M., "Moral development," in P. Mussen, ed., *Carmichael's Manual of Child Psychology,* 3 ed., Vol. 2. New York: Wiley, 1970.

Holt, J., *How Children Fail.* New York: Pitman, 1964.

Hoover, K., *Learning and Teaching in the Secondary School: Improved Instructional Practice.* Boston: Allyn & Bacon, 1968.

Horn, E., *Distribution of Opportunity for Participation among the Various Pupils in Classroom Recitations.* New York: Teachers College Press, 1914.

Horwitz, R., *Psychological Effects of Open Classroom Teaching on Primary School Children: A Review of the Research.* Study Group on Evaluation. University of North Dakota, 1976.

Houston, W., et al., eds., Resources for Performance-Based Education. Albany, N.Y.: State University of New York, 1973.

Hoyt, K., "A study of the effects of teacher knowledge of pupil characteristics on pupil achievement and attitudes toward classwork." *Journal of Educational Psychology,* 46 (1955), 302–310.

Hudgins, B., and Ahlbrand, W., Jr., *A Study of Classroom Interaction and Thinking.* Technical Report Series No. 8. St. Ann, Mo.: Central Midwestern Regional Educational Laboratory, 1969.

Hunt, J., "Experience and the development of motivation: some reinterpretations." *Child Development,* 31 (1960), 489–504.

Hunt, D. *Teachers' Adaptation to Students: Implicit and Explicit Matching.* Report No. 139, Center for Research and Development in Teaching. Stanford University, November 1975.

Hunt J. McV. *Intelligence and Experience.* New York: Ronald Press, 1961.

Husen, T., ed., *International Study of Achievement in Mathematics: A Comparison of Twelve Countries,* Vol. 2. New York: Wiley, 1967.

Husen T., and Svensson, N., "Pedagogic milieu and development of intellectual skills." *School Review,* 68 (1960), 36–51.

Jackson, P., *Life in Classrooms.* New York: Holt, Rinehart and Winston, 1968.

Jackson, P., and Lahaderne, H., "Inequalities of teacher-pupil contacts." *Psychology in the Schools,* 4 (1967), 204–208.

Jackson, P., Silberman, M., and Wolfson, B., "Signs of personal involvement in teachers' descriptions of their students." *Journal of Educational Psychology,* 60 (1969), 22–27.

Jackson, P., and Wolfson, B., "Varieties of constraint in a nursery school." *Young Children,* 23 (1968), 358–367.

Jersild, A., *When Teachers Face Themselves.* New York: Teachers College Press, 1955.

Jeter, J., and Davis, O., "Elementary school teachers' differential classroom interaction with children as a function of differential expectations of pupil achievement." Paper presented at the annual meeting of the American Educational Research Association, 1973.

Johnson D., *The Social Psychology of Education.* New York: Holt, Rinehart and Winston, 1970.

Johnson, D., and Johnson, R. *Learning Together and Alone: Cooperation, Competition and Individualization.* Englewood Cliffs, N.J.: Prentice-Hall, 1975.

Jones, V. *The Influence of Teacher-Student Introversion, Achievement, and Similarity on Teacher-Student Dyadic Classroom Interactions.* Unpublished doctoral dissertation, University of Texas, 1971.

Joyce, B., and Weil, M. *Models of Teaching.* Englewood Cliffs, N.J.: Prentice-Hall, 1972.

Katz, L. G., "Research on open education: Problems and issues," in D. D. Hearne et al., eds., *Current Research and Perspectives in Open Education.* Washington, D.C.: National Education Association, 1973.

Keller, F., "Goodbye, teacher!" *Journal of Applied Behavioral Analysis* (1968), 1, 79–88.

Kepler, K., "Descriptive feedback: increasing teacher awareness, adapting research techniques." Paper presented at the annual meeting of the American Educational Research Association, New York City, 1977.

Kepler, K. and Randall, J., "Individualization: the subversion of elementary schooling." *Elementary School Journal,* 77 (1977), 358–363.

Kennedy, W., Van deRiet, V., and White, J., "A normative sample of intelligence and achievement of Negro elementary school children in the southeastern United States." *Monographs of the Society for Research in Child Development,* 28 (1963), 6.

Klausmeier, H., Sorenson, J., and Ghatala, E., "Individually guided motivation: Developing self-direction and prosocial behaviors. *Elementary School Journal,* 71 (1971a), 339–350.

Klausmeier, H., Sorenson, J., and Quilling, M., "Instructional programming for the individual pupil in the multiunit elementary school." *Elementary School Journal,* 72 (1971b), 88–101.

Kleinfeld, J., "Effective teachers of Eskimo and Indian students." *School Review,* 83 (1975), 301–344.

Kohl, H., *36 Children.* New York: New American Library, 1967.

Kohler, P., "A comparison of open and traditional education: conditions that promote self-concept." Paper presented at the annual meeting of the American Educational Research Association, New Orleans, 1973.

Kounin, J., *Discipline and Group Management in Classrooms.* New York: Holt, Rinehart and Winston, 1970.

Kozol, J. *Death at an Early Age.* Boston: Houghton Mifflin, 1967.

Kranz, P., Weber, W., and Fishell, K., "The relationships between teacher perception of pupils and teacher behavior toward those pupils." Paper delivered at the annual meeting of the American Educational Research Association, 1970.

LaBenne, W. & Greene, B. *Educational Implications of Self-Concept Theory.* Pacific Palisades, Calif.: Goodyear Publishing Co., 1969.

Lahaderne, H., "Attitudinal and intellectual correlates of attention: A study of four sixth grade classrooms." *Journal of Educational Psychology,* 59 (1968), 320–324.

Lepper, M., and Greene, D., "When two rewards are worse than one: Effects of extrinsic rewards on intrinsic motivations. *Phi Delta Kappan* 56 (1975), 565–566.

Lesser, G., *Children and Television: Lessons from "Sesame Street."* New York: Random House, 1974.

Lippitt, R., and Gold, M., "Classroom social structure as a mental health problem. *Journal of Social Issues,* 15 (1959), 40–49.

Lipson, J., "IPI Math—an example of what's right and wrong with individualized modular programs. *Learning* (March 1974), 60–61.

Lortie, D., *School Teacher.* University of Chicago Press, 1975.

Loucks, S. F., "An exploration of levels of use of an innovation and the relationship to student achievement." Paper presented to the annual meeting of the American Educational Research Association, 1976.

Loughlin, R., "On questioning." *Educational Forum,* 25 (1961), 481–482.

Lucker, G., Rosenfield, D., Sikes, J., and Aronson, E., "Peformance in the interdependent classroom: A field study." *American Educational Research Journal,* 13 (1976), 115–123.

Lundgren, U., *Frame Factors and the Teaching Process.* Stockholm: Almqvist & Wiksell, 1972.

Maasdorf, F., "Effects of an individualized instruction program (IGGS) on student achievement and anxiety." Unpublished doctoral dissertation, University of Missouri–Columbia, 1976.

McCandless, B., and Evans, E., *Children and Youth: Psychosocial Development.* Hinsdale, Ill.: Dryden Press, 1973.

McDonald, F., "Report on phase II of the beginning teacher evaluation study." *Journal of Teacher Education,* 27 (1976), 39–42.

McKeachie, W., "Psychology in America's bicentennial year." *American Psychologist,* 31 (1976), 819–833.

McKeachie, W., and Kulik, K., "Effective college training," in F. Kerlinger, ed., *Review of Research in Education,* Itasca, Ill.: Peacock, 1975.

Mackler, B., "Grouping in the ghetto." *Education and Urban Society,* 2 (1969), 80–95.

McKinney, J., Mason, J., Perkerson, K., and Clifford, M., "Relationship between classroom behavior and academic achievement." *Journal of Educational Psychology,* 67 (1975), 198–203.

Macmillan, D., Jones, R., and Meyers, C., "Mainstreaming the mildly retarded: Some questions, cautions, and guidelines." *Mental Retardation,* 1976, *14,* 3–10.

McNeil, J., *Toward Accountable Teachers: Their Appraisal and Improvement.* New York: Holt, Rinehart and Winston, 1971.

Mager, R., *Preparing Instructional Objectives.* Palo Alto, Calif.: Fearon Publishers, 1962.

Martin, L., and Pavan, B., "Current research on open space, non-grading, vertical grouping and team teaching." *Phi Delta Kappan,* 57 (1976), 310–315.

Martin, M., *Equal Opportunity in the Classroom, ESEA, Title III: Session A Report.* Los Angeles: County Superintendent of Schools, Division of Compensatory and Intergroup Programs, 1973.

Medley, D., "The language of teacher behavior," in R. Burkhart, ed., *The Assessment Revolution: New Viewpoints for Teacher Evaluation.* New York State Education Department and Buffalo State University College, 1969.

Mendoza, S., Good, T., and Brophy, J., *Who Talks in Junior High Classrooms?*

Report Series No. 68, Research and Development Center for Teacher Education. University of Texas, 1972.

Meyer, W., and Thompson, G., "Sex differences in the distribution of teacher approval and disapproval among sixth-grade children." *Journal of Educational Psychology,* 47 (1956), 385–396.

Mischel, W., *Introduction to Personality,* 2d ed. New York: Holt, Rinehart and Winston, 1976.

Montessori, M., *The Montessori Method.* New York: Schocken Books, 1964.

Moore, J., and Schaut, J., "An evaluation of the effects of conceptually appropriate feedback on teacher and student behavior." Paper presented at the Association for Teacher Education Conference, New Orleans, 1975.

Moore, O., and Anderson, A., "Some principles for design of clarifying educational environments," in D. Goslin, ed., *Handbook of Socialization Theory and Research.* Chicago: University of Chicago Press, 1969.

Nash, R., *Classrooms Observed: The Teacher's Perception and the Pupil's Performance.* Boston: Routledge & Kegan Paul, 1973.

Niedermeyer, F., "Effects of training on the instructional behavior of student tutors." *Journal of Educational Research,* 64 (1970), 119–123.

Palardy, J., "What teachers believe—what children achieve." *Elementary School Journal,* 69 (1969), 370–374.

Pambookian, H., "Discrepancy between instructor and student evaluation of instruction: Effect on instruction." *Instructional Science,* 5 (1976), 63–75.

Paolitto, D., "The effect of cross-age tutoring on adolescence: An inquiry into theoretical assumptions." *Review of Educational Research,* 46 (1976), 215–238.

Pavan, B. N., "Good news: Research on the nongraded elementary school." *Elementary School Journal,* 19 (1973), 333–342.

Peck, R., "Promoting self-disciplined learning: A researchable revolution," in B. Smith, ed., *Research in Teacher Education.* Englewood Cliffs, N.J.: Prentice-Hall, 1971.

Perkins, H., *Human Development and Learning.* Belmont, Calif.: Wadsworth, 1969.

Piaget, J., *The Origins of Intelligence in Children.* New York: International Universities Press, 1952.

Piaget, J., "Piaget's theory," in P. Mussen (Ed.). *Carmichael's Manual of Child Psychology.* New York: John Wiley & Sons, Inc., 1970.

Popham, W., and Baker, E., *Establishing Instructional Goals.* Englewood Cliffs, N.J.: Prentice-Hall, ;1970(a).

_____ *Planning an Instructional Sequence.* Englewood Cliffs, N.J.: Prentice-Hall, 1970(b).

_____ *Systematic Instruction.* Englewood Cliffs, N.J.: Prentice-Hall, 1970(c).

Power, C., *A Multivariate Model for Studying Person-Environment Interactions in the Classroom.* Technical Report No. 99, Center for Research in Social Behavior. University of Missouri, 1974.

Premack, D., "Reinforcement theory." in D. Levine, ed., *Nebraska Sympo-*

*sium on Motivation,* Volume 13. Lincoln: University of Nebraska, 1965.

Price, D., *The Effects of Individually Guided Education (IGE) Processes on Achievement and Attitudes of Elementary School Students.* Unpublished doctoral dissertation, University of Missouri, 1977.

Quirk, T., "The student in Project PLAN: A functioning program of individualized education." *Elementary School Journal,* 71 (1971), 42–54.

Rist, R., "Student social class and teacher expectations: The self-fulfilling prophecy in ghetto education." *Harvard Educational Review,* 40 (1970), 411–451.

Rist, Ray C., *The Urban School: A Factory for Failure; A Study of Education in American Society.* Cambridge, Mass.: MIT Press, 1973.

Robin, A., "Behavioral instruction in the college classroom." *Review of Educational Research,* 46 (1976), 313–354.

Rogers, C., *Freedom to Learn.* Columbus, Ohio: Merrill, 1969.

Rosenshine, B., "Objectively measured behavioral predictors of effectiveness in explaining," in N. Gage, M. Belgard, D. Dell, J. Hiller, B. Rosenshine, and W. Unruh, *Explorations of the Teacher's Effectiveness in Explaining.* Technical Report No. 4, Research and Development Center in Teaching. Stanford University, 1968.

―――― "Enthusiastic teaching: A research review." *School Review,* 78 (1970), 499–514.

―――― "Classroom instruction," in N. Gage, ed., *The Psychology of Teaching Methods.* Seventy-seventh Yearbook, National Society for the Study of Education 1976.

Rosenshine, B., and Furst, N., "Current and future research on teacher performance criteria," in B. Smith, ed., *Research on Teacher Education: A Symposium.* Englewood Cliffs, N.J.: Prentice-Hall, 1971.

―――― "The use of direct observation to study teaching," in R. Travers, ed., *Second Handbook of Research on Teaching.* Skokie, Ill.: Rand McNally, 1973.

Rosenthal, R. "On the social psychology of the self-fulfilling prophecy: Further evidence for Pygmalion effects and their mediating mechanisms." New York: M.S.S. Modular Publications, 1974.

Rosenthal, R., and Jacobson, L. *Pygmalion in the Classroom: Teacher Expectation and Pupils' Intellectual Development.* New York: Holt, Rinehart & Winston, 1968.

Rotter, J., "Generalized expectancies for internal versus external control of reinforcement." *Psychological Monographs,* 80, No. 1, 1966.

Rowe, M., "Science, silence, and sanctions." *Science and Children,* 6 (1969), 11–13.

Rubovits, P., and Maehr, M., "Pygmalion analyzed: toward an explanation of the Rosenthal-Jacobson findings." *Journal of Personality and Social Psychology* 19 (1971), 197–203.

Samuels, S., and Turnure, J., "Attention and reading achievement in first-grade boys and girls." *Journal of Educational Psychology,* 66 (1974), 29–32.

Sanders, N., *Classroom Questions: What Kinds?* New York: Harper & Row, 1966.

Schachter, S., "The interaction of cognitive and physiological determinants of emotional state," in L. Berkowitz, ed., *Advances in Experimental Social Psychology*, Vol. 1. New York: Academic Press, 1964.

Schmieder, A., and Yarger, S., "Teacher/teaching centering in America." *Journal of Teacher Education*, 25 (1974), 5–12.

Schrank, W., "A further study of the labeling effect of ability grouping." *The Journal of Educational Research*, 63 (1970), 358–360.

———— "The labeling effect of ability grouping." *Journal of Educational Research*, 62 (1968), 51–52.

Schultz, K.M., *Implementation Guide: /I/D/E/A/ Change Program for Individually Guided Education, Ages 5–12*. Dayton, Ohio: /I/D/E/A/, 1974.

Sears, P., "Level of aspiration in academically successful and unsuccessful children." *Journal of Abnormal and Social Psychology*, 35 (1940), 498–536.

Shaffer, L., and Shoben, E., Jr., *The Psychology of Adjustment: A Dynamic and Experimental Approach to Personality and Mental Hygiene.* Boston: Houghton Mifflin, 1956.

Shimron, J., "Learning activities in individually prescribed instruction." Paper read at the annual meeting of the American Educational Research Association, 1973.

Shutes, R., *Verbal Behaviors and Instructional Effectiveness.* Unpublished doctoral dissertation, Stanford University, 1969.

Silberman, C., *Crisis in the Clasroom: The Remaking of American Education.* New York: Random House, 1970.

Silberman, M., "Behavioral expression of teachers' attitudes toward elementary school students." *Journal of Educational Psychology*, 60 (1969), 402–407.

———— "Teachers' attitudes and actions toward their students," in M. Silberman, ed., *The Experience of Schooling.* New York: Holt, Rinehart and Winston, 1971.

Skinner, B., *Science and Human Behavior.* New York: Macmillan, 1953.

Smith, B., *Teachers for the Real World.* Washington, D.C.: The American Association of Colleges for Teacher Education, 1969.

Snapp, M., "A study of the effects of tutoring by fifth and sixth graders on the reading achievement scores of first, second, and third graders." Unpublished doctoral dissertation, University of Texas, 1970.

Snow, R., "Unfinished Pygmalion." *Contemporary Psychology*, 14 (1969), 197–199.

Soar, R., *Follow-through Classroom Process Measurement and Pupil Growth.* Final report, College of Education, University of Florida, 1973.

Solomon, O., and Kendall, A., "Individual characteristics and children's performance in "open" and "traditional" classroom settings." *Journal of Educational Psychology*, 68 (1976), 613–625.

Stallings, J., and Kaskowitz, D., *Follow-through Classroom Observation Evaluation.* Menlo Park, Calif.: Stanford Research Institute, 1974.

Stein, A., Pohly, S., and Mueller, E., "The influence of masculine, feminine, and neutral tasks on children's achievement behavior, expectancies of success, and attainment values." *Child Development,* 42 (1971), 195–207.

Stevens, R., "The question as a measure of efficiency in instruction." *Teachers College Contributions to Education,* No. 48. New York: Teachers College Press, 1912.

Sullivan, H., *The Interpersonal Theory of Psychiatry.* New York: Norton, 1953.

Taylor, C., "The expectations of Pygmalion's creators." *Educational Leadership,* 28 (1970), 161–164.

Thomas, J., "Tutoring strategies and effectiveness: a comparison of elementary age tutors and college tutors." Unpublished doctoral dissertation, University of Texas at Austin, 1970.

Thompson, D., "Evaluation of an individualized instructional program." *Elementary School Journal,* 73 (1973), 213–221.

Tillman, R., and Hull, J., "Is ability grouping taking schools in the wrong direction? *Nation's Schools,* 73 (1964), 70–71, 128–129.

Traub, R., Weiss, J., Fisher, C., and Musella, D., "Closure on openness in education." A symposium presented at the annual meeting of the American Educational Research Association, 1973.

Trump, J., "Secondary education tomorrow: Four imperatives for improvment." *Bulletin of the National Association of Secondary School Principals,* 50 (1966), 87–95.

Tuckman, B., and Bierman, M., "Beyond Pygmalion: Galatea in the schools." Paper presented at the annual meeting of the American Educational Research Association, 1971.

Tuckman, B., and Oliver, W., "Effectiveness of feedback to teachers as a function of source." *Journal of Educational Psychology,* 59 (1968), 297–301.

Vargas, J. *Writing Worthwhile Behavioral Objectives.* New York: Harper & Row, 1972.

Vaughn, R., "Community, courts, and conditions of special education today: Why?" *Mental Retardation,* 11 (1973), 43–46.

Walker, D., and Schaffarzick, J., "Comparing curricula." *Review of Educational Research,* 44 (1974), 83–111.

Wang, M., "Maximizing the effective use of school time by teachers and students." A paper presented at the annual meeting of the American Educational Research Association, 1976.

Wegmann, R., "White flight and school resegregation: Some hypotheses." *Phi Delta Kappan,* 58 (1977), 389–393.

Weinstein, R., "Reading group membership in first grade: Teacher behaviors and pupil experience over time." *Journal of Educational Psychology,* 68 (1976), 103–116.

Weiss, J., "Openness and student outcomes: Some results." Paper presented at the annual meeting of the American Educational Research Association, 1973.

Willis, S., "Formation of teachers' expectations of students' academic performance." Unpublished doctoral dissertation, The University of Texas at Austin, 1972.

Wolfson, B., and Nash, S., "Perceptions of decision-making in elementary school classrooms." *Elementary School Journal*, 69 (1968), 89–93.

Wragg, E., ed., *Teaching Mixed Ability Groups*. London: David and Charles Limited, 1976.

Wright, C., and Nuthall, G., "The relationships between teacher behaviors and pupil achievement in three experimental elementary science lessons." *American Educational Research Journal*, 7 (1970), 477–492.

Wright, R. S., "The affective and cognitive consequences of an open education elementary school." *American Educational Research Journal*, 12 (1975), 449–468.

# Index

79 80 9 8 7 6 5 4